ParaSpheres

ParaSpheres
Extending Beyond the Spheres
of Literary and Genre Fiction

Fabulist and New Wave Fabulist Stories

Edited by

Rusty Morrison

and

Ken Keegan

OMNIDAWN PUBLISHING

RICHMOND, CALIFORNIA

2006

Cover image: "The Juggler" © 2004 Michael Parkes™
World Rights Reserved. www.theworldofmichaelparkes.com

"The Third Jungle Book" © Copyriight Michael and Linda Moorcock 2006

Book cover and interior design by Ken Keegan

Offset printed in the United States on archival, acid-free recycled paper
by Thomson-Shore, Inc., Dexter, Michigan

green press
INITIATIVE

Omnidawn Publishing is committed to preserving ancient forests and natural resources. We elected to print *Paraspheres* on 50% post consumer recycled paper, processed chlorine free. As a result, for this printing, we have saved:

62 trees (40' tall and 6-8" diameter)
26,455 gallons of water
10,640 kilowatt hours of electricity
2,916 pounds of solid waste
5,729 pounds of greenhouse gases

Omnidawn Publishing made this paper choice because our printer, Thomson-Shore, Inc., is a member of Green Press Initiative, a nonprofit program dedicated to supporting authors, publishers, and suppliers in their efforts to reduce their use of fiber obtained from endangered forests.

For more information, visit www.greenpressinitiative.org

Library of Congress Catalog-in-Publication Data

ParaSpheres : extending beyond the spheres of literary and genre fiction : fabulist and new wave fabulist stories /
edited by Rusty Morrison and Ken Edward Keegan.
    p. cm.
ISBN 1-890650-18-8 (trade pbk. : alk. paper)
1. Short Stories, English. 2. Short stories, American.
3. English fiction--20th century. 4. American fiction--20th century.
I. Morrison, Rusty. II. Keegan, Ken Edward, 1944-
PR1309.S5P37 2006
823 '.0108--dc22

    2006000487

Published by Omnidawn Publishing
Richmond, California   www.omnidawn.com   (800) 792-4957

10 9 8 7 6 5 4 3 2 1

ISBN-13: 978-1-890650-18-6
ISBN-10: 1-890650-18-8

Acknowledgements

Grateful acknowledgment is made for permission to reprint the following stories:

"The Cabinet of Edgar Allan Poe" by Angela Carter. Copyright © 1982 by Angela Carter. First published by *Interzone*, 1982. Reprinted by permission of the Angela Carter Estate and the Rogers, Coleridge & Whitehead, Ltd. Literary Agency.

"Losing the War" by Stepan Chapman. Copyright © 2001 by Stepan Chapman. First published in *Scheherazade* #22, edited by Elizabeth Counihan, 2001. Reprinted by permission of the author.

"The White Man" by Jeffrey Ford. Copyright © 1995 by Jeffrey Ford. First published in *Aberrations* #29, 1995. Reprinted by permission of the author

"Five Letters from an Eastern Empire" by Alasdair Gray. Copyright © 1979 by Alasdair Gray. First published in *Words Magazine* 1979. Reprinted by permission of the author and Cannongate Books.

"The Son of Chimera," "The Ice Cream Vendor," and "About the Henbane City" from the novel *Pereat Mundus* by Leena Krohn. Copyright © 1998 by Leena Krohn. First published in Finnish by WSOY, 1998. Reprinted by permission of the author and TEOS.

"The Birthday of the World" by Ursula K. Le Guin. Copyright © 2000 by Mercury Press, Inc. First published by *The Magazine of Fantasy & Science Fiction*, June 2000. Reprinted by permission of the author and the author's agents, The Virginia Kidd Literary Agency.

"Third Initiation: A Gift from the Land of Dreams" from the novel *Horses at the Gate* by Mary Mackey. Copyright © 1995 by Mary Mackey. Reprinted by permission of the author.

"Cake" by Michael Moorcock. Copyright © 2005 by Michael Moorcock. First published in *Prospect Magazine*, Issue 111, June 2005. Reprinted by permission of the author.

"The Gardener of Heart" by Bradford Morrow. Copyright © 2005 by Bradford Morrow. First published in *Conjunctions:44*. Reprinted by permission of the author.

"The Lucky Strike" by Kim Stanley Robinson. Copyright © Kim Stanley Robinson 1984. First published in *UNIVERSE 14*, edited by Terry Carr, Doubleday, 1984. Reprinted by permission of the author.

"The Jack Kerouac Disembodied School of Poetics" by Rudy Rucker. © Copyright 1982 by Rudy Rucker. First published in *New Blood*, July 1982. Reprinted by permission of the author.

"The Tiger's Eye" by Gladys Swan. Copyright 1981 by Gladys Swan. First published in *Writers' Forum*, Issue 9, 1981. Reprinted by permission of the author.

We would like to express our sincere gratitude to the following people for the countless ways in which they have given their expertise, insight, enthusiasm, and support to us and to this project:

Alice Acheson, Michael Andre-Driussi, Robin Caton, Brent Cunningham, Kelly Everding, Andrew Joron, Melissa Kwasny, Eric Lorberer, Mary Mackey, Marty Riker, Lisa Rappoport, Elizabeth Robinson, Jaime Robles, and Jeff VanderMeer.

Editor's Note

Why Fabulist and New Wave Fabulist Stories in an Anthology Named *ParaSpheres?*

When Omnidawn started publishing books in 2001 we planned to publish an anthology within a few years with the type of fiction included here, but we did not have clear boundaries for its definition or a name for it. Historically in the U.S. we have had two broad categories, literary and genre, into which the major publishers attempt to toss virtually all fiction. If it doesn't fit into one of these categories, the large publishers usually see no point in publishing it. And yet, what we wanted to publish seemed to fit neither of these classifications. The term literary fiction, which implied quality, had long ago been defined by most critics as narrative realism and admitted nothing that was non-realistic, with the relatively recent exception of magic realism. All other non-realistic fiction was relegated by most publishers to the various "formula" genres, where the non-realistic elements were assumed to further the primary purpose of escape into worlds ranging from unlikely to fantastic, where readers were entertained but not enlightened.

Of course, there has always been another form, non-realistic fiction, that attempted more than entertainment and often gave us new insights and perspectives. No one would be taken seriously if they denied that Kafka's *Metamorphosis*, Huxley's *Brave New World*, and Orwell's *Animal Farm* and *1984* have this quality, as well as lasting cultural meaning and value, more than half a century after the last of these was written. Some have given these works a sort of honorary status as Literary Fiction, even though they do not meet the otherwise required standards of Narrative Realism. Still others relegate them to the genres, but admit that even some genre stories can have valuable cultural meanings beyond mere escape and entertainment.

But the genre categories do not hold these works well. No matter what genre category is chosen for them, they tend to be unlike most of the others with which they are grouped. Readers who expect genre escape and entertainment can be disappointed and dislike stories like these, sales can falter, and they can go largely unnoticed. The genre classifications no longer seem to make sense for such stories, and haven't for some time.

These are the stories that we knew we wanted to publish in this anthology, but again, how were we going to define them? A number of terms have been used over the past several decades to try to create a special niche for such stories. Robert A. Heinlein coined the term "speculative fiction" in 1947, and for a time this was used to define such stories, but in recent years that term has been used to include all forms of the genres of fantasy and science fiction, as well as much horror. Therefore, the term no longer defines fiction that goes beyond genre fiction. These stories are far too strange for the term magic realism, which requires that the story be basically realistic, with some magical elements thrown in, and magic realism implies Latin American in origin. The terms non-realism and trans-realism are descriptive, but define these stories only in relation to what they are not: the more accepted narrative realism form.

Then in the fall of 2002, *Conjunctions*, the literary journal from Bard College edited by Bradford Morrow, came out with their issue number 39, guest-edited by Peter Straub. They used the term "new wave fabulists," described thus: "For two decades, a small group of innovative writers rooted in the genres of science fiction, fantasy, and horror have been simultaneously exploring and erasing the boundaries of those genres by creating fiction of remarkable depth and power." The term came with a number of disadvantages. For one thing, it's a mouthful. Why not a simple one-word name? And the term new wave has been used before and has its own meanings. But the term did have the advantage of being an extension of the term fabulist, a word which has gained some acceptance as a form of literary fiction and which generally means magic realism without necessarily being Latin American.

Since we really could not establish a clearly definable boundary between fabulist and new wave fabulist, we decided to include both in the anthology, which we called *ParaSpheres* because these stories seem to extend "beyond the spheres" of either literary or genre fiction. In the process we hope to exist partly in both forms as well as extending beyond them, and to build a bridge between the two, where writers and readers from both can easily meet. Ultimately, another name may be used to describe this form of fiction, but for now we have chosen to describe the form of fiction as fabulist and new wave fabulist.

This is the short answer to "Why Fabulist and New Wave Fabulist Stories in an Anthology Named *ParaSpheres*." A more detailed elaboration of this answer can be found at the end of this anthology on page 625.

Ken Keegan

Contents

Rikki Ducornet

Introduction

A Memoir in the Form of a Manifesto

When I was a child of seven, I spent the week alone with my mother's parents: Frances and Charlie. They lived in Miami, in a house that smelled of boiled carrots. Frances's conversation was featureless, and I could never, for as long as I knew her, grow accustomed to the static condition of her mind.

A Russian immigrant who came to this country at the age of twelve, Charlie had one good story. He told it slyly, nimbly and with dash: the moment his family had debarked in New York City he had run away, and before the day was over had snagged a job with the Barnum and Bailey Circus shoveling elephant shit.

Charlie's vivid evocation of elephant shit in all its prodigious redundancy did much to alleviate my grandmother's self righteous banality. If Charlie was entertaining—and he also had enlightening things to say about the Fat Lady (in those days a rarity) and had witnessed an acrobat's fatal mistake—Frances was as appealing as a parish clerk. She thought of herself as a worldly-minded realist, yet she feared the world unreasonably, poisoning the ants on her slice of lawn with an eerie fixity of purpose. She boiled our suppers with such ferocity everything we ate tasted like wet laundry. It was during this visit that I came to privately call her Old Piano Legs.

Suppertimes, Charlie, mostly mute, and sucking the interminable sourballs that would give him stomach cancer, thought of the lady across the way who—or so I learned from a bitter Frances at his funeral some years down the line—made a mean lamb stew with dumplings.

"He'd go across the way to eat her stew!" she had blustered. "Can you imagine that?"

I could.

I had brought with me a library book devoted to van Leeuwenhoek. In the deep solitude of Miami nights, I would lose myself beneath the Dutchman's magic lens, and swim among the minute creatures he described gyrating in gutter water and tears. The splendid conjunction in my mind of elephants and animals too small to be seen with the naked eye caused me to shudder with secret laughter, for I knew it was best not to disturb Frances's mortal certitude with any extravagance of mind. (Her own mind was made of sand bags that, whenever she would speak, tumbled forth in such quantity one feared, one *risked*, suffocation.) In this way her conversation had a family likeness to the inescapable redundancies of so much so called "realistic" fiction. (And, this brings to mind my mother's response to my first "real" story: "Some nightmares are best kept to oneself." She died soon after this exchange; it was, as it turned out, the last time she advised me.)

Charlie's fond recollections informed my own tendency to scatologize and, decades later, made for an immediate affinity with Angela Carter, whose dinner conversation was outrageously fecal and funny. Angela, like Jonathan Swift and Robert Coover and Rabelais, was unafraid of frass. Which has me wondering if the acknowledgement of materiality goes part and parcel with the unfettered imagination, a healthy dislike of pomposity and the sort of dogmatic thinking that insists the body is both fallen and vile. (I was about to write a *healthy* acknowledgement of materiality, but then, like the divine Marquis's, Swift's interest in dung was, need I say it, *morbid*.)

Back to Miami: on the one hand there was Frances who, if she'd had the choice, would have shat chalk. Whereas Charlie proposed a vision of excrement transcendent, intuiting—for this he could not have known—how in Old Tibet the Dali Lama's turds were kept in silver and worn as amulets—a true story, if anomalous. But there is more. Like Kafka's Gregor Samsa or Bruno Schultz's paterfamilias thrashing in aspic, that week the fantastic claimed Miami with a suddenness that suggested the miraculous. For three days land crabs by the tens of thousands overswarmed lawns, sidewalks, driveways, car-ports and Grandma's rockery. As agile as hands, they were stunning in their sheer exuberance. Agitating in the dew of early morning and at night beneath the glazed lunes of porch lights, they could not have unraveled Frances more had they been communist transvestites herding penguins. Wildness had claimed Miami—irresistible, irreverent, infidelic, profane! Frances, who until that moment had tirelessly elbowed her way through life, was shut down. After a few minutes of ineffectual sweeping, she took to her bed with an ice pack. I recall how Charlie and I stood on the back porch and marveled at the unprecedented event; how from across the way the lady who had a knack with dumplings gaily waved.

We are told that within the decade global warming will slap us silly, and that within forty years or so, one third of all living things will have perished irretrievably. A criminal lack of imagination is making of our fragile world a flatland. We are told that flat, like fear, is good for us, somehow *suitable*; fear and boredom fit us better, like those mass-produced and outgassing polyesters that cover the nakedness of our presidents and late-night hosts and bankers with a doleful inevitability. But I will have none of it; such *suitabilities* have always made me sneeze. And I decry the rise of plastic and the decline of fur; the confusion of capitalism and democracy; the tyranny of religion and the dereliction of moral vision; the lethally misguided notion that like *suitable* ideas, the creative impulse must know and keep its place; that art and literature, like trousers and radishes, are no more than commodities.

A world worth wanting cherishes the risks of wildness, and this includes not only the lavish elephants and meteoric crabs, but the stars we can no longer see, the whales hemorrhaging on our beaches, the serene mollusks and coral reaches; *Gilgamesh* as filmed by the Brothers Quay, the eroticized Martians imagined by Clarice Lispector; the Amazon's poison frogs, the Sahara's thick-coming locusts; the vociferous parrots; William Gass's *Omensetter*; the worms in their legions and the yellow boas; Rosamond Purcell's and van Leeuwenhoek's third eyes and Borges's Aleph; the oracle at Delphi and Gaudi's dream of an unbounded architecture; the necessary nightmares of David Lynch; Borges's incandescent blindness; Prince Genji's amorous encounters; the unstoppable mulattas of Latin American literature; the collages of Max Ernst, his Loplop and, above all, the salutary tradition of a tusked and savage—and, need I say it: *subversive* storytelling in which the world is reinvented, reinvigorated and restored to us in all its sprawling splendor, over and over again.

ParaSpheres

IRA SHER

LIONFLOWER HEDGE

That night around the fire, having recalled the threat held over us as children that we might be sent "into the Hedge," Francis was, to say the least, surprised by my suggestion we go and revisit it.

I doubt any of us had given the Hedge a moment's thought in years. And while 'the Hedge' was not infrequently the final invocation of an exasperated caretaker on evenings our parents were away; and on those occasions we lay awake in our beds in the great room, quietly murmuring together about its menace, it had, naturally, found no place that weekend in our discussion of how to dispose of the estate. Joseph (had he ever *not* been a lawyer?) even went so far as to remind us that despite repeated recourse to 'the Hedge' in name, none of us were ever really sent 'into' it. Still, we were by then childishly drunk, sentimental with the knowledge we were to return to our separate, adult homes and families in the morning—

The Lionflower Hedge formed a wild patch in the garden, a shelter for birds and foxes. With its low arcades of branches and superannuated foliage, it seemed an ideal place for a child, and no doubt some farsighted governess had gathered the hedge within the rubric of punishment to obscure from us its pleasures, and save the trouble of washing us of its debris.

"If I remember rightly," Francis mused at one of the entries, "there was always a ruckus inside—the sound of children one would have thought." Kneeling to listen, before long the cries returned to us like a nursery rhyme: as a conch contains the sea, we heard the distant noise of boys and girls at play.

The flowers had withered and lay like gloves among the branches. The ground was soaked from afternoon showers. A cold rain started. "We'll get wet," Joseph complained; yet rather than rise and return to the house, I pushed on, into the hedge, and heard them rustle in pursuit.

At first the garden lamps shone among the leaves, the rectangles of the recently quitted dining room showed through a lattice of fronds and shoots, a sort of backlit wallpaper; but darkness quickly embraced us—though the hedge wasn't so large that shouldering through seemed foolhardy, given the alternate difficulty, having come this far, of turning around. The best we could do was get along on all fours, staying in a line of which I was the leader, grappling with low foliage, roots, and the clustered stems forming the thicket's pillars. The problem lay in the fact that it was *so* dark. I simply groped, awaiting the glow of the opposite perimeter and the halogens of the conservatory. And then, blind, I found my hands wrapped around what I can only describe as two ankles, as if someone, in the midst of everything, stood upright. A hinge creaked. A woman's silhouette loomed in a doorway.

"Here you are," she said softly, bending forward. "You're all in bed. You were good, weren't you, while I was gone?"

She brushed her hand to her lips and reached down to plant the kiss on my cheek. Then she drew back, closed the door, and we were alone in the dark.

"That was our mother," Joseph said.

"Yes," I whispered, feeling still the warm touch.

"Shh," Francis told us. "Go to sleep."

◉ ◉ ◉

IRA SHER has another story, "Nobody's Home," on page 303 of this anthology. His short fiction has appeared in venues including *Chicago Review*, *The Gettysburg Review* and *This American Life*. His first novel, *Gentlemen of Space*, was published in 2003 by Free Press. He lives in Hudson, New York with his wife, the poet Rebecca Wolff, and their children Asher and Margot.

Leena Krohn

The Son of Chimera

Translated by Hildi Hawkins

I was born, but not because anyone wanted it to happen. No one even knew it was possible, for my mother was a human being, my father a chimera. He was one of the first multi-species hybrids.

Only one picture of my father survives. It is not a photograph, but a water-colour, painted by my mother. My father is sitting in an armchair, book in hand, one cloven hoof placed delicately on top of the other. According to my mother, he liked to leaf through illustrated books, although he never learned to read. He is wearing an elegant, muted blue suit jacket, but no trousers at all. Thick grey fur covers his strong legs, right down to his hoofs. Small horns curve gracefully over his convex forehead. Striking in his face are his round, yellow eyes, his extraordinarily wide mouth, his tiny chin and his surprisingly large but flat nose.

Virgin forest is visible through the window behind him, and above it a moon that is reddish, as if it were oozing blood. If you look a little more closely at the picture, you notice that Håkan's book carries the same picture of Håkan, in which he gazes at the same book by the light of the same moon.

Schoolwork never really held my mother's attention. This was a disappointment to my grandmother, who was a high court judge. My aunt always said that my mother lacked perseverance. All the same, my mother has always worked and earned her own living. She dropped out of school, tried three times to get into art college and was rejected each time. But she never lost her hobby of painting. Later she survived on temporary jobs, cleaning in various institutions, spent some time as assistant to the cobbler at the opera house, then moved on to the central parish kitchen. From time to time she filled in for the caretaker at the city museum.

My mother met my father at Hydra, the laboratory of an international gene technology institution, where she had a job for a couple of months. There my mother cleaned, and was sometimes expected to feed the laboratory animals.

"Did you like it at Hydra?" I asked.

"It was one of my best jobs," my mother said. "Even the cleaners were treated like human beings, and the laboratory buildings were so modern and spacious. There were plenty of workers, but even I was reasonably well-paid. I was happy to clean the laboratory animal rooms, particularly when I was able to work by myself. After five, it was peaceful and light in there. The chimeras had just been fed and most of them were fast asleep, for after the experiments they were given sedatives. The only sound was that of the computer ventilators and, from time to time, a rumbling from the plumbing of the embryo cupboards."

"Tell me something else about daddy," I asked.

"Your father, Håkan, wasn't the only chimera in the lab. There were already dozens of them when Håkan was born, but most of them were combinations of two species. Håkan was a special case. He was the first four-species chimera: chimpanzee, wolf, goat and human.

"You will remember that the scientists had succeeded in transplanting into Håkan twenty thousand of the eighty thousand human genes. All the rest were genes from the three other species, but in what proportions I was never able to discover.

"Around the time of the events that led to your birth, there was no longer anything new even about multichimeras. There were already hybrids of seven species among the laboratory chimeras at Hydra.

"But Håkan was the oldest of the laboratory animals; he had even been patented. He had been the whole lab's favourite, not just because of the patent, but because he was such a gentle and docile chimera. But by the time I arrived at Hydra to clean and look after the animals, no one was interested in Håkan any more, and he was no longer young. The only time he got any attention was during controlled experiments and the inevitable caring routines.

"I liked his humble and melancholy, but sometimes amazingly animated chimpanzee's gaze. The irises of his eyes were yellow, but his pupils often dilated—perhaps on account of the drugs—so much that his gaze was deep and black. Often, after I had fed the chimeras, I lingered, stroking Håkan's woolly fringe, and he rubbed his disproportionately large head against my white forearm, which was still plump then. Before long there grew up between us a mute but durable friendship.

"Håkan had good hearing, but the scientists and laboratory animal assistants did not know whether he understood anything of human speech. There had apparently been at one time great hopes for his capacity for language, and quite early on he learned to react to his own name and understand simple commands, like a dog. But despite regular lessons from a phoniatrist, he never learned to speak. The sounds he made consisted of whimpers, bleats and strange howls that became more impassioned as mealtimes drew near.

"'That's a wolf-whistle,' they used to say.

"He walked on two legs, but with some difficulty, for Håkan had goat's hoofs, as you know. His forepaws, on the other hand, were three-fingered and almost hairless, and he used them with great skill. He had a little tuft of a tail, and with the exception of his forepaws a thick coat of wolf's fur covered him from his hoofs to his convex chimpanzee's forehead. No one could have called him beautiful, however pretty the curve of his horns. There was really extraordinarily little about his appearance that was human, apart from his nose, his shoulders and his shoulder-blades. In his cage Håkan had a swing in which he spent most of his waking hours.

"Everyone knew that Håkan's time was nearly up; when he reached his tenth birthday the last needle awaited him.

"That thought was hard for me to bear. My own job at Hydra was only temporary, and I had decided that after Håkan I would have nothing more to do with the place. I had not planned anything in advance, but quite unexpectedly a moment came in which I found myself intervening in Håkan's destiny. And my own life changed too.

"On my last day at work at Hydra, Håkan was awake, and his eyes followed me incessantly. When I pushed my finger through the wires of the cage door to scratch Håkan's forehead, I realised to my amazement that the door was unlocked and ajar. One of the lab assistants had been careless.

"I opened the door to be able to pat Håkan more easily. But Håkan took the opportunity to clamber out of his cage.

"'What d'you do that for?' I said to your father."

"Didn't you even try to get daddy back into the cage?" I asked.

"No, I didn't. I thought it would do him good to walk around the room for a while. There's not much extra space in laboratory animals' cages, as you may have guessed.

"As I said, Håkan never learned to walk properly, but in his enthusiasm he stood up and, with the help of his strong forepaws, was able to clamber. His back hoofs slipped on the shiny tiles of the laboratory floor, and he toppled over, whimpering pathetically. I took him in my arms. At that moment, feeling his warmth and his weight against my breasts, as his pure, woolly scent penetrated my nostrils, I suddenly knew that I never wanted to be parted from Håkan again. Håkan meant nothing to anyone else in the world, and I was the only one Håkan cared for. How could I have rejected his affection—far less abandon him?"

"In other words, you stole daddy."

"That's right. I wrapped Håkan in a blanket and carried him as if he were a rucksack through the evening bustle of the streets to my own little bedsit. I could feel his rapid breathing on my neck and cheek, and his gentle warmth spread throughout my body. He weighed about thirty kilos, and I had to rest from time to time. I could not afford a taxi, and I did not dare take the bus with Håkan as I was afraid that he might begin to yelp and attract too much attention.

"You can sleep here," I said, when we got home.

"I made him a bed in the bath-tub, as I was afraid that some friend might come visiting and I would not have time to hide Håkan. In fact, I lived such a lonely life that it was unlikely in the extreme."

"But wasn't he ever missed?"

"I did have one telephone call. It was an assistant, and he asked me if I knew anything about an escaped chimera. I denied it, of course. After that I heard nothing. They forgot me and they forgot Håkan, as if we had never existed.

"We began to live a life of our own. It was a peaceful and harmonious home. I talked to Håkan a lot, and he understood me better each day. I began to be able to make out distinct sounds in his yelps. After a while he began to give short answers to my questions. Often he doubled up the first syllable of a word. Water was wa-wa, sleeping slee-slee. He also learned to smile so that his sharp wolf's teeth flashed. I realised that his consciousness and capacity for development had been drastically underestimated throughout his short life.

"I saw in him an old soul which was bound to a deformed body, a combination of many human parts. How can we ever be forgiven for the wrong we did him? But still: without that wrong, he would never have been born, and neither would you.

"He began to eat at table, but never really succeeded in learning to use a knife and fork. Because he was so small, I got him a high chair. In the evenings, we listened to music or I read aloud to him. Your father liked Schubert's Lieder so much that sometimes he used to sink into a kind of semi-conscious ecstasy, which worried me a little.

"I also read poems aloud to him. He was so entranced by these lines that I had to say them every night before we went to sleep. It became our shared ritual:

> What is this thing, o love,
> that enters the heart through the eyes,
> and in the small space inside it, seems to expand?
> And what if it should overflow?

"Whenever I remember those lines, I see before me your father's eyes, in which joy and nameless suffering alternated.

"On television we followed lecture series and children's programmes. We never watched police series. I told Håkan about my life, my father and mother, my brothers and sisters, all of whom had got on better in life than I had. I told him about failing my exams in math and languages, how I had had to repeat a class, my attempts at dieting and my numerous jobs. I told him about my only lover, a certain bought ledger accountant, who took my virginity. He treated me badly, and the relationship only lasted a couple of weeks.

"I confessed my shame and my humiliation to your father, weeping over my disappointment, and he listened silently, shedding hot tears with me.

"At night I took Håkan into my bed to sleep with me. His gaze uncovered my heart; a selfless, sacred love poured itself into my poor life. Since the accountant, I hadn't slept with a man. But from Håkan there was no need to fear a curt word. Time after time we sank into one another's embrace, and I was not troubled by his hard hoofs or his animal smell.

"The fact that I became pregnant by Håkan was, of course, a shock. I had not even thought that a child could be born from our relationship."

"Did you never consider abortion?"

My mother was silent for a long time, until she admitted she had.

"But only for a moment. For when I truly understood that I was to be a mother, I was so happy that I danced for joy.

"But your father never saw you. He began to be ill when I was three months gone. I would have taken him to hospital, but your father forbade it. I realised that his time really was up; his short life was lived. In his last weeks, your father stopped eating completely. He changed a great deal toward the end. Not only did he become more and more human, he was also more angelic the closer he slipped toward death.

"He died one Monday morning; it was raining. His body fitted into a large suitcase. I bought a spade, ordered a taxi and drove north. You know where I asked the driver to stop. I dug him a grave alone in a forest clearing.

"When my time came, I went to a private hospital to give birth. As you understand, I was in a difficult position. I told the midwife and obstetrician what to expect. You were born after a long labour by Caesarean section. The doctor promised that he would not reveal anything in public about your unusual origins."

So: I was born, a hybrid too, a monstrosity, as many people would say. There is more human in me than in my father, but there is also a good deal of goat and chimpanzee and wolf. I do not like to look into the mirror, but I rejoice that I am able to live. We live outside the city, in a rented cabin in the grounds of a large country house. As a child, I ran freely in the fields and grazed. My mother has learned to milk and, when necessary, she is able to work as an assistant milkmaid.

My father's grave is in a meadow in the estate forest, but no one knows it but we two. My mother has sowed forget-me-nots there, and oriental poppies. From time to time we clear the willow saplings so that the meadow stays light. On the best days of summer we make expeditions there, with a bottle of wine and bread and apples in our picnic basket.

Our lives are as peaceful as my mother and Håkan's once were, and my mother calls me, too, Håkan. I don't go outside much during daylight; my appearance attracts too much attention. I cannot even set foot inside the byre, as the cows become very restless. I don't want to think about the time when my mother will be dead. I hope that my life will be as short as my father's, for I do not mean to live without my mother.

The beauty of the world never ceases to amaze me. I have more senses, and more sensitive ones, than human beings do. My sense of smell is as keen as a wolf's. I climb with the agility of a chimpanzee. Why should I not be content with my lot, even if it cannot be called easy?

I believe that one day the age will dawn when there are no longer different mammalian species—human beings and lower mammals. The species will have hybridised and formed combinations that we cannot now even imagine. Our senses will be keener, we will see new colours and hear voices where now there is mute silence. Then we shall know and sense, understand and rejoice more than we do now.

My father and I are pioneers of the future. The day will dawn when we are all one and all equal. It is years away, millions, maybe even billions, but I do not doubt that that day will dawn.

The evening darkens; I leave my room and open the garden gate without a sound. When I remember I am a goat, I do nothing but long to wander in a meadow. When my wolf's nature wins, I run into the deep forest, strange sounds rise from my throat and I dance alone. Sometimes I disappear for weeks. When I wish to be a chimpanzee, I clamber nimbly into tall trees and like to sit on the roof of our house. I look at the night sky in wonderment. The stars glitter, I hum to myself and my hoofs tap hollowly on the tin roof.

Locally, there is talk of strange things. It is said that one night a lamb was found torn to pieces in the meadow, but that the toothmarks that were found on it were human. My mother gives me a long look, her eyes full of anxiety.

I cannot find anyone like me.

⊕ ⊕ ⊕

LEENA KROHN has two other stories in this anthology, "The Ice Cream Vendor," on page 311, and "About the Henbane City," on page 508. All three stories are excerpts from her novel, *Pereat mundus*, to be published in the United States in the latter half of 2006 by Omnidawn. In this novel Håkan is an everyman character, taking on different forms. More info on this book is available at www.omnidawn.com/krohn

Leena Krohn was born in 1947 in Helsinki, Finland. She has studied philosophy, psychology and literature at Helsinki University and has written about twenty-five books: novels, short stories, fantasy stories, poems and essays. Her books have been translated into more than ten languages. *Tainaron, Mail from Another City* (translated into English by Hildi Hawkins) was published in the U.S. by Prime Books in 2004. Krohn lives in Southern Finland. A number of her writings and works are available on her home page at www.kaapeli.fi/krohn

ANGELA CARTER

THE CABINET OF EDGAR ALLAN POE

Imagine Poe in the Republic! when he possesses none of its virtues; no Spartan, he. Each time he tilts the jug to greet the austere morning, his sober friends reluctantly concur: `No man is safe who drinks before breakfast.' Where is the black star of melancholy? Elsewhere; not here. Here it is always morning; stern, democratic light scrubs apparitions off the streets down which his dangerous feet must go.

Perhaps...perhaps the black star of melancholy was hiding in the dark at the bottom of the jug all the time...it might be the whole thing is a little secret between the jug and himself...

He turns back to go and look; and the pitiless light of common day hits him full in the face like a blow from the eye of God. Struck, he reels. Where can he hide, where there are no shadows? They split the Republic in two, they halved the apple of knowledge, white light strikes the top half and leaves the rest in shadow; up here, up north, in the levelling latitudes, a man must make his own penumbra if he wants concealment because the massive, heroic light of the Republic admits of no ambiguities. Either you are a saint; or a stranger. He is a stranger, here, a gentleman up from Virginia somewhat down on his luck, and, alas, he may not invoke the Prince of Darkness (always a perfect gentleman) in his cause since, of the absolute night which is the antithesis to these days of rectitude, there is no aristocracy.

Poe staggers under the weight of the Declaration of Independence. People think he is drunk.

He *is* drunk.

The prince in exile lurches through the new-found land.

So you say he overacts? Very well; he overacts. There is a past history of histrionics in his family. His mother was, as they say, born in a trunk, grease-paint in her bloodstream, and made her first appearance on any stage in her ninth summer in a hiss-the-villain melodrama entitled *Mysteries of the Castle.* On she skipped to sing a ballad clad in the pretty rags of a ballet gypsy.

It was the evening of the eighteenth century.

At this hour, this very hour, far away in Paris, France, in the appalling dungeons of the Bastille, old Sade is jerking off. Grunt, groan, grunt, on to the prison floor...aaaagh! He seeds dragons' teeth. Out of each ejaculation spring up a swarm of fully-armed, mad-eyed homunculi. Everything is about to succumb to delirium.

Heedless of all this, Poe's future mother skipped on to a stage in the fresh-hatched American republic to sing an old-world ballad clad in the pretty rags of a ballet gypsy. Her dancer's grace, piping treble, dark curls, rosy cheeks—cute kid! And eyes with something innocent, something appealing in them that struck directly to the heart so that the smoky auditorium broke out in raucous sentimental cheers for her and clapped its leather palms together with a will. A star was born that night in the rude firmament of fit-ups and candle-footlights, but she was to be a shooting star; she flickered briefly in the void, she continued the inevitable trajectory of the meteor, downward. She hit the boards and trod them.

But, well after puberty, she was still able, thanks to her low stature and slim build, to continue to personate children, clever little ducks and prattlers of both sexes. Yet she was versatility personified; she could do you Ophelia, too.

She had a low, melodious voice of singular sweetness, an excellent thing in a woman. When crazed Ophelia handed round the rosemary and rue and sang: 'He is dead and gone, lady,' not a dry eye in the house, I assure you. She also tried her hand at Juliet and Cordelia and, if necessary, could personate the merriest soubrette; even when racked by the nauseas of her pregnancies, still she would smile, would smile and oh! the dazzling candour of her teeth!

Out popped her firstborn, Henry; her second, Edgar, came jostling after to share her knee with her scripts and suckle at her bosom while she learned her lines, yet she was always word-perfect even when she played two parts in the one night, Ophelia or Juliet and then, say, Little Pickle, the cute kid in the afterpiece, for the audiences of those days refused to leave the theatre after a tragedy unless the players changed costumes and came back to give them a little something extra to cheer them up again.

Little Pickle was a trousers' role. She ran back to the green-room and undid the top buttons of her waistcoat to let out a sore, milky breast to pacify little Edgar who, wakened by the hoots and catcalls that had greeted her too voluptuous imitation of a boy, likewise howled and screamed.

A mug of porter or a bottle of whisky stood on the dressing-table all the time. She dipped a plug of cotton in whisky and gave it to Edgar to suck when he would not stop crying.

The father of her children was a bad actor and only ever carried a spear in the many companies in which she worked. He often stayed behind in the green-room to look after the little ones. David Poe tipped a tumbler of neat gin to Edgar's lips to keep him quiet. The red-eyed Angel of Intemperance hopped out of the bottle of ardent spirits and snuggled down in little Edgar's longclothes. Meanwhile, on stage, her final child, in utero, stitched its flesh and bones together as best it could under the corset that preserved the theatrical illusion of Mrs. Elizabeth Poe's eighteen inch waist until the eleventh hour, the tenth month.

Applause rocked round the wooden O. Loving mother that she was—for we have no reason to believe that she was not—Mrs. Poe exited the painted scene to cram her jewels on her knee while tired tears ran rivers through her rouge and splashed upon their peaky faces. The monotonous clamour of their parents' argument sent them at last to sleep but the unborn one in the womb pressed its transparent hands over its vestigial ears in terror.

(To be born at all might be the worst thing.)

However, born at last this last child was, one July afternoon in a cheap theatrical boarding-house in New York City after many hours on a rented bed while flies buzzed at the windowpanes. Edgar and Henry, on a pallet on the floor, held hands. The midwife had to use a pair of blunt iron tongs to scoop out the reluctant wee thing; the sheet was tented up over Mrs. Poe's lower half for modesty so the toddlers saw nothing except the midwife brandishing her dreadful instrument and then they heard the shrill cry of the new-born in the exhausted silence, like the sound of the blade of a skate on ice, and something bloody as a fresh-pulled tooth twitched between the midwife's pincers.

It was a girl.

David Poe spent his wife's confinement in a nearby tavern, wetting the baby's head. When he came back and saw the mess he vomited.

Then, before his sons' bewildered eyes, their father began to grow insubstantial. He unbecame. All at once he lost his outlines and began to waver on the air. It was twilit evening. Mama slept on the bed with a fresh mauve bud of flesh in a basket on the chair beside her. The air shuddered with the beginning of absence.

He said not one word to his boys but went on evaporating until he melted clean away, leaving behind him in the room as proof he had been there only a puddle of puke on the splintered floorboards.

As soon as the deserted wife got out of bed, she posted down to Virginia with her howling brats because she was booked for a tour of the South and she had no money put away so all the babies got to eat was her sweat. She dragged them with her in a trunk to Charleston; to Norfolk; then back to Richmond.

Down there, it is the foetid height of summer.

Stripped to her chemise in the airless dressing-room, she milks her sore breasts into a glass; this latest baby must be weaned before its mother dies.

She coughed. She slapped more, yet more rouge on her now haggard cheekbones. 'My children! what will become of my children?' Her eyes glittered and soon acquired a febrile brilliance that was not of *this* world. Soon she needed no rouge at all; red spots brighter than rouge appeared of their own accord on her cheeks while veins as blue as those in Stilton cheese but muscular, palpitating, prominent, lithe, stood out of her forehead. In Little Pickle's vest and breeches it was not now possible for her to create the least suspension of disbelief and something desperate, something fatal in her distracted playing both fascinated and appalled the witnesses, who could have thought they saw the living features of death itself upon her face. Her mirror, the actress's friend, the magic mirror in which she sees whom she has become, no longer acknowledged any but a death's head.

The moist, sullen, Southern winter signed her quietus. She put on Ophelia's madwoman's nightgown for her farewell.

When she summoned him, the spectral horseman came. Edgar looked out of the window and saw him. The soundless hooves of black-plumed horses struck sparks from the stones in the road outside. `Father!' said Edgar; he thought their father must have reconstituted himself at this last extremity in order to transport them all to a better place but, when he looked more closely, by the light of a gibbous moon, he saw the sockets of the coachman's eyes were full of worms.

They told her children that now she could come back to take no curtain-calls no matter how fiercely all applauded the manner of her going. Lovers of the theatre plied her hearse with bouquets: `And from her pure and uncorrupted flesh May violets spring.' (Not a dry eye in the house.) The three orphaned infants were dispersed into the bosoms of charitable protectors. Each gave the clay-cold cheek a final kiss; then they too kissed and parted, Edgar from Henry, Henry from the tiny one who did not move or cry but lay still and kept her eyes tight shut. When shall these three meet again? The church bell tolled: never never never never never.

Kind Mr. Allan of Virginia, Edgar's own particular benefactor, who would buy his bread, henceforward, took his charge's little hand and led him from the funeral. Edgar parted his name in the middle to make room for Mr. Allan inside it. Edgar was then three years old. Mr. Allan ushered him into Southern affluence, down there; but do not think his mother left Edgar empty handed, although the dead actress was able to leave him only what could not be taken away from him, to wit, a few tattered memories.

TESTAMENT OF MRS ELIZABETH POE

Item: nourishment. A tit sucked in a green-room, the dug snatched away from the toothless lips as soon as her cue came, so that, of nourishment, he would retain only the memory of hunger and thirst endlessly unsatisfied.

Item: transformation. This is a more ambivalent relic. Something like this...Edgar would lie in prop-baskets on heaps of artificial finery and watch her while she painted her face. The candles made a profane altar of the mirror in which her vague face swam like a magic fish. If you caught hold of it, it would make your dreams come true but Mama slithered through all the nets which desire set out to catch her.

She stuck glass jewels in her ears, pinned back her nut-brown hair and tied a muslin bandage round her head, looking like a corpse for a minute. Then on went the yellow wig. Now you see her, now you don't; brunette turns blonde in the wink of an eye.

Mama turns round to show how she has changed into the lovely lady he glimpsed in the mirror.

`Don't touch me, you'll mess me.'

And vanishes in a susurration of taffeta.

Item: that women possess within them a cry, a thing that needs to be extracted...but this is only the dimmest of memories and will reassert itself in vague shapes of unmentionable dread only at the prospect of carnal connection.

Item: the awareness of mortality. For, as soon as her last child was born, if not before, she started to rehearse in private the long part of dying; once she began to cough she had no option.

Item: a face, the perfect face of a tragic actor, his face, white skin stretched tight over fine, white bones in a final state of wonderfully lucid emaciation.

Ignited by the tossed butt of a still-smouldering cigar that lodged in the cracks of the uneven floorboards, the theatre at Richmond where Mrs. Poe had made her last appearance burned to the ground three weeks after her death. Ashes. Although Mr. Allan told Edgar how all of his mother that was mortal had been buried in her coffin, Edgar knew the somebody elses she so frequently became lived in her dressing-table mirror and were not constrained by the physical laws that made her body rot. But now the mirror, too, was gone; and all the lovely and untouchable, volatile, unreal mothers went up together in a puff of smoke on a pyre of props and painted scenery.

The sparks from this conflagration rose high in the air, where they lodged in the sky to become a constellation of stars which only Edgar saw and then only on certain still nights of summer, those hot, rich, blue, mellow nights the slaves brought with them from Africa, weather that ferments the music of exile, weather of heartbreak and fever. (Oh, those voluptuous nights, like something forbidden!) High in the sky these invisible stars marked the points of a face folded in sorrow.

NATURE OF THE THEATRICAL ILLUSION: everything you see is false.

Consider the theatrical illusion with special reference to this impressionable child, who was exposed to it at an age when there is no reason for anything to be real.

He must often have toddled on to the stage when the theatre was empty and the curtains down so all was like a parlour prepared for a séance, waiting for the moment when the eyes of the observers make the mystery.

Here he will find a painted backdrop of, say, an antique castle—a castle! such as they don't build here; a Gothic castle all complete with owls and ivy. The flies are painted with segments of trees, massy oaks or something like that, all in two dimensions. Artificial shadows fall in all the wrong places. Nothing is what it seems. You knock against a gilded throne or horrid rack that looks perfectly solid, thick, immoveable, and you kick it sideways, it turns out to be made of papier mâché, it is as light as air— a child, you yourself, could pick it up and carry it off with you and sit in it and be a king or lie in it and be in pain.

A creaking, an ominous rattling scares the little wits out of you; when you jump round to see what is going on behind your back, why, the very castle is in mid-air! Heave-ho and up she rises, amid the inarticulate cries and muttered oaths of the stagehands, and down comes Juliet's tomb or Ophelia's sepulchre, and a super scuttles in, clutching Yorrick's skull.

The foul-mouthed whores who dandle you on their pillowy laps and tip mugs of sour porter against your lips now congregate in the wings, where they have turned into nuns or something. On the invisible side of the plush curtain that cuts you off from the beery, importunate, tobacco-stained multitude that has paid its pennies on the nail to watch these transcendent rituals now come the thumps, bangs and clatter that make the presence of their expectations felt. A stage-hand swoops down to scoop you up and carry you off, protesting, to where Henry, like a good boy, is already deep in his picture book and there is a poke of candy for you and the corner of a handkerchief dipped in moonshine and Mama in crown and train presses her rouged lips softly on your forehead before she goes down before the mob.

On his brow her rouged lips left the mark of Cain.

.

Having, at an impressionable age, seen with his own eyes the nature of the mystery of the castle—that all its horrors are so much painted cardboard and yet they terrify you—he saw another mystery and made less sense of it.

Now and then, as a great treat, if he kept quiet as a mouse, because he begged and pleaded so, he was allowed to stay in the wings and watch; the round-eyed baby saw that Ophelia could, if necessary, die twice nightly. All her burials were premature.

A couple of brawny supers carried Mama on stage in Act Four, wrapped in a shroud, tipped her into the cellarage amidst displays of grief from all concerned but up she would pop at curtain call having shaken the dust off her graveclothes and touched up her eye make-up, to curtsey with the rest of the resurrected immortals, all of whom, even Prince Hamlet himself, turned out, in the end, to be just as undead as she.

How could he, then, truly believe she would not come again, although, in the black suit that Mr. Allan provided for him out of charity, he toddled behind her coffin to the cemetery? Surely, one fine day, the spectral coachman would return again, climb down from his box, throw open the carriage door and out she would step wearing the white nightdress in which he had last seen her, although he hoped this garment had been laundered in the interim since he last saw it all bloody from a haemorrhage.

Then a transparent constellation in the night sky would blink out; the scattered atoms would reassemble themselves to the entire and perfect Mama and he would run directly to her arms.

It is the mid-morning of the nineteenth century. He grows up under the black stars of the slave states. He flinches from that part of women the sheet hid. He becomes a man.

As soon as he becomes a man, affluence departs from Edgar. The heart and pocketbook that Mr. Allan opened to the child now pull themselves together to expel. Edgar shakes the dust of the sweet South off his heels. He hies north, up here, to seek his fortune in the places where the light does not permit that chiaroscuro he loves; now Edgar Poe must live by his disordered wits.

The dug was snatched from the milky mouth and tucked away inside the bodice; the mirror no longer reflected Mama but, instead, a perfect stranger. He offered her his hand; smiling a tranced smile, she stepped out of the frame.

'My darling, my sister, my life and my bride!'

He was not put out by the tender years of this young girl whom he soon married; was she not just Juliet's age, just thirteen summers?

The magnificent tresses forming great shadowed eaves above her high forehead were the raven tint of nevermore, black as his suits the seams of which his devoted mother-in-law painted with ink so that they would not advertise to the world the signs of wear and, nowadays, he always wore a suit of sables, dressed in readiness for the next funeral in a black coat buttoned up to the stock and he never betrayed his absolute mourning by so much as one flash of white shirtfront. Sometimes, when his wife's mother was not there to wash and starch his linen, he economised on laundry bills and wore no shirt at all.

His long hair brushes the collar of this coat, from which poverty has worn off the nap. How sad his eyes are; there is too much of sorrow in his infrequent smile to make you happy when he smiles at you and so much of bitter gall, also, that you might mistake his smile for a grimace or a *grue* except when he smiles at his young wife with her forehead like a tombstone. Then he will smile and smile with as much posthumous tenderness as if he saw already: *Dearly beloved wife of* ...carved above her eyebrows.

For her skin was white as marble and she was called—would you believe! —'Virginia', a name that suited his expatriate's nostalgia and also her condition, for the childbride would remain a virgin until the day she died.

Imagine the sinless children lying in bed together! The pity of it!

For did she not come to him stiffly armoured in taboos—taboos against the violation of children; taboos against the violation of the dead—for, not to put too fine a point on it, didn't she always look like a walking corpse? But such a pretty, pretty corpse!

And, besides, isn't an undemanding, economic, decorative corpse the perfect wife for a gentleman in reduced circumstances, upon whom the four walls of paranoia are always about to converge?

Virginia Clemm. In the dialect of northern England, to be 'clemmed' is to be very cold. 'I'm fair clemmed.' Virginia Clemm.

She brought with her a hardy, durable, industrious mother of her own, to clean and cook and keep accounts for them and to outlive them, and to outlive them both.

Virginia was not very clever; she was by no means a sad case of arrested development, like his real, lost sister, whose life passed in a dream of non-being in her adopted home, the vegetable life of one who always declined to participate, a bud that never opened. (A doom lay upon them; the brother, Henry, soon died.) But the slow years passed and Virginia stayed as she had been at thirteen, a simple little thing whose sweet disposition was his only comfort and who never ceased to lisp, even when she started to rehearse the long part of dying.

She was light on her feet as a revenant. You would have thought she never bent a stem of grass as she passed across their little garden. When she spoke, when she sang, how sweet her voice was; she kept her harp in their cottage parlour, which her mother swept and polished until all was like a new pin. A few guests gathered there to partake of the Poes' modest hospitality. There was his brilliant conversation though his women saw to it that only tea was served, since all knew his dreadful weakness for liquor, but Virginia poured out with so much simple grace that everyone was charmed.

They begged her to take her seat at her harp and accompany herself in an Old World ballad or two. Eddy nodded gladly: 'yes', and she lightly struck the strings with white hands of which the long, thin fingers were so fine and waxen that you would have thought you could have set light to the tips to make of her hand the flaming Hand of Glory that casts all the inhabitants of the house, except the magician himself, into a profound and death-like sleep.

She sings: *Cold blows the wind, tonight, my love,*
            And a few drops of rain.

With a taper made from a manuscript folded into a flute, he slyly takes a light from the fire.

            I never had but one true love
            In cold earth she was lain.

He sets light to her fingers, one after the other.

            A twelve month and a day being gone
            The dead began to speak.

Eyes close. Her pupils contain in each a flame.

            Who is that sitting on my grave

Who will not let me sleep?

All sleep. Her eyes go out. She sleeps.

He rearranges the macabre candelabra so that the light from her glorious hand will fall between her legs and then he busily turns back her petticoats; the mortal candles shine. Do not think it is not love that moves him; only love moves him.

He feels no fear.

An expression of low cunning crosses his face. Taking from his back pocket a pair of enormous pliers, he now, one by one, one by one by one, extracts the sharp teeth just as the midwife did.

All silent, all still.

Yet, even as he held aloft the last fierce canine in triumph above her prostrate and insensible form in the conviction he had at last exorcised the demons from desire, his face turned ashen and sear and he was overcome with the most desolating anguish to hear the rumbling of the wheels outside. Unbidden, the coachman came; the grisly emissary of her high-born kinsman shouted imperiously: 'Overture and beginners, please!' She popped the plug of spiritous linen between his lips; she swept off with a hiss of silk.

The sleepers woke and told him he was drunk; but his Virginia breathed no more!

After a breakfast of red-eye, as he was making his toilet before the mirror, he suddenly thought he would shave off his moustache in order to become a different man so that the ghosts who had persistently plagued him since his wife's death would no longer recognise him and would leave him alone. But, when he was clean-shaven, a black star rose in the mirror and he saw that his long hair and face folded in sorrow had taken on such a marked resemblance to that of his loved and lost one that he was struck like a stock or stone, with the cut-throat razor in his hand.

And, as he continued, fascinated, appalled, to stare in the reflective glass at those features that were his own and yet not his own, the bony casket of his skull began to agitate itself as if he had succumbed to a tremendous attack of the shakes.

Goodnight, sweet prince.

He was shaking like a backcloth about to be whisked off into oblivion.

Lights! he called out.

Now he wavered; horrors! *He was starting to dissolve!*

Lights! more lights! he cried, like the hero of a Jacobean tragedy when the murdering begins, for the black star was engulfing him.

On cue, the laser light on the Republic blasts him.

His dust blows away on the wind.

⸎ ⸎ ⸎

Angela Carter (1940—1992) was an English writer, renowned as a novelist, journalist and short story writer. She was awarded the Somerset Maugham Award for literature, and she wrote more than twenty works of fiction and nonfiction, including novels, short story collections, dramatic works, and children's books. Carter also contributed many articles to *The Guardian, The Independent* and *New Statesman.* Her short story collections include *Black Venus* (a.k.a. *Saints and Strangers*) (1985), *American Ghosts* and *Old World Wonders* (1993), and *Burning Your Boats: The Collected Short Stories* (1995).

KATE KASTEN

EVER AND ANON

At first the prince thought of riding headlong into the wood. He fancied the prospect of galloping through the castle doors on his noble steed and cantering straight into the princess's chamber. There, he would lean from his charger and lift the storied beauty onto the saddle. He had always imagined her waking to his kiss charmingly bewildered to find herself atop a horse.

But the stallion was of too grand a girth to negotiate the forest's solid mass of brambles. Nor, in any case, would the prince like to risk sacrificing his horse to the voracious appetite of the wolves rumored to guard the castle entrance. Thus, the prince had proceeded on foot.

Now, wielding his dagger, he slashed the last of the vines and roots that held the great portal closed. It emitted a rusty groan, yielding to his staunch shoulder. He stepped inside.

Here was a majestic hall, where a hundred or more lords and ladies sat at a table before a sumptuous meal. Behind each chair, attendants hovered on the point of taking away a plate or cup, but every eye was closed, and every bosom heaved and fell in the slow movements of sleep. The room resonated with snores. Even the dogs under the table took no advantage of the unprotected feast, but lay curled and twitching in dreams of foxes and rabbits.

The prince scanned the throng for one particular countenance. All the chairs were occupied but one. On it an embroidered cloak lay casually tossed as if its owner had stepped away for a moment. Insensible to his bruises, wounds, and aching limbs, and with no thought to the deep gashes made in his hands by the ravening wolves and piercing thorns, the prince dashed up the grand staircase to seek the sleeping princess.

He searched every chamber, every corner, every cubby until at last, having ascended a winding staircase to a high tower room, he found her. There she stood, not (as his old nurse had described her so often) enchanted forever in an attitude of playing a golden harp, nor (as his father's master of hounds had insisted) lying upon a bed, clad in a gown of transparent silk, her red lips parted and her limbs fallen voluptuously akimbo, but standing gracefully at an ancient spinning wheel, her dainty hand above the spindle as if she had suddenly drawn it back. A drop of ruby blood bejeweled the tip of her finger.

Luxuriant lashes fringed the princess's closed lids and rested thick upon her cheeks, giving her the look of a sweet and innocent child. Atop the sumptuous black tresses that curled around her face and cascaded onto her shoulders was a sapphire crown. Only the faintest breath, like the whisper of a breeze, hinted that the princess was, indeed, asleep and not transformed into a marble statue. And on her sleeping face was a touching expression of wistfulness as though some deep yearning haunted her dreams.

The prince's ordeals—hacking his way through the fearsome, thorny labyrinth, battling the vicious wolves—were as nothing to him compared with the reward of gazing upon her, thus. For she was more wondrously beautiful than all the willing young ladies whom his parents had urged upon him since his coming of age. Any of those maidens could have been his for the asking: the lovely duke's daughter with the amiable trait of finding good humor in the frustrations and mishaps of life, the royal cousin in whose pleasant company he had grown up reading poetry and riding horses, the brilliant and comely princess whose father so valued her good sense that he relied on her for advice in matters of economy and war. They stirred no ardor in him, as rumors of the sleeping beauty had already begun to exert their irresistible influence. Now, said he to himself, my obstinacy is vindicated, for never was a more radiant lady won by man.

He thought her skin as fair and unblemished as an opening petal, her figure surpassing even the imagined form which had stirred his passion as a youth and sustained him through every trial of his quest, her exquisite waist as slender as a sapling, yet joined to such bloom above as would rival the spring blossoming of a plum.

Still, he was afraid to approach her. Suppose she should become frightened on first beholding him? Might she, after a hundred years of dreaming, look upon his scratched and bleeding face and take it for a nightmare? Worse yet, what if the legendary beauty woke to his kiss and rejected his love? Suddenly he grew shy.

He stood for some while watching her in sleep. His hands bled and he held them close to his sides, though they burned to touch her. At last, longing to sweep her into his arms, he approached her, though with great caution, and slowly bent to bring his lips against hers in a kiss so gentle, so soft, so delicate it would barely have disturbed a butterfly's wing. Instantly she awakened.

The beautiful lashes drew back over sleep-misted eyes, and for a moment she looked with puzzlement at the face so close to hers. Then her pale complexion turned slowly rose-hued, and pinker still, as a full flush spread across her cheeks. Her dark eyes widened, her lips parted, and with exquisite tenderness she laid her fingertips on the prince's scratched and dirt-stained jaw.

"Oh!" she said, in a breathless voice so full of longing that a mourning dove would have sounded merry by comparison. "Oh!" she said again, and at once his arms went round her, his wounded hands leaving the red prints of his bravery on her gown.

Suddenly, the palace bells began to peal and a great clamor rose from the courtyard. Lords and ladies, court musicians, serving maids and men poured forth, praising the day. There came to the two in the tower the barking of dogs, the clatter of plates, the starting up of lutes and pipes and tambourines, but the lovers heard only the drumming of their two hearts.

The engagement ball was given by the prince's parents, who found much to approve in his choice of a bride. For their part, the mother and father of the princess considered their prospective son-in-law a paragon of courage and self-command.

"You are my Prince Charming," whispered the princess, as the two strolled among the great oaks of the palace park. The prince took her hand and pressed it to his wounded cheek, still inflamed where the flesh had been ripped by thorns.

"I shall call you my Sleeping Beauty," he replied.

"Better your *awakened* Beauty," said she, with a sidelong smile.

Plans for the wedding proceeded anon.

It was some weeks before Charming and Beauty were willing to tear themselves from each other's arms long enough to undertake the duties attending their engagement, but finally the lovers had to part, if only for minutes and hours. Charming, on his white steed, led the hunt to provision the wedding banquet with stags. Beauty directed the ladies-in-waiting at their embroidery hoops. Long hours of labor were required to sew the two royal crests—overlapping coronets with unicorns and leopards rampant—on all the linens of her trousseau, including her nightgowns and underskirts (which were found each morning in curious need of pressing, having gotten rumpled in another type of rampancy— so it was jested—that overlapped and crested with regularity every night).

The wedding preparations went on without cease. Two entire kingdoms were involved. Many royal relations who had made foreign alliances needed time to commission gifts and outfit ships for sea travel.

By the night of the engagement ball, Prince Charming found himself in a state of mind not precisely dull, so much as restive. He had drunk a goblet or two of champagne while waiting with the guests for Beauty to make her formal appearance on the grand stairway. The champagne had given him a headache. He was wondering if anyone would notice his slipping out for a canter around the Park.

At that moment he heard a common gasp of astonishment and saw the assemblage gape in the direction of the great hall. He turned, expecting to see his betrothed, resplendent on the staircase.

Instead, there stood near the foot of the stairs the most enchanting woman Prince Charming had ever laid eyes upon, excluding (he told himself without conviction) the Sleeping Beauty. Golden hair floated around the woman's face like spun silk. A diaphanous gown, made of no earthly material he could recognize, clung to her perfect breasts and reflected the candlelight in the room with the fluid shimmer of quicksilver. Her skirt billowed wide and swept the floor, yet somehow managed to suggest, as she took a step forward, the sinuous movement of voluptuous hips beneath.

Besides the perfection of her figure, her face—glorious in all details—eyes, lips, brow, chin, cheekbones—had a simple goodness, a becoming timidity, even—the prince divined—a tremulous awe. Yes, he detected in her an unbelieving joy at being at the ball, as if—impossible to imagine!—she were not accustomed to such grand surroundings.

She had not yet seen him. To prevent her being overwhelmed—for he sensed in her an impulse to flee that might be as easily elicited as if she were a skittish gazelle—he tore off his crown and hid it behind a pillar. She drew an endearing breath of resolve, and, holding her fan against her bosom—for courage, it appeared—entered the ballroom. Oh! What rapture when the prince saw how lightly she stepped. How gracefully, and on the daintiest of feet, so delicate that they seemed almost to be...he stared...*were*, in fact, shod in *glass*!

All other thoughts flew from his mind when he considered what grace and delicacy a woman must possess to walk in glass slippers without breaking them. The mysterious beauty, he sensed, would be a bewitching dance partner.

"'Tis only courtesy to beg a stranger for a dance," he reasoned, stepping quickly forth. Then, great was his enchantment to find the gorgeous creature struck mute with shyness at the offer of his hand!

He led her to a protected corner. "My lady," he breathed into her ear, "be at ease. In this house you shall be accorded the reverence due a princess. For, if royalty you are not, then royalty you should be. Your corona of golden hair alone serves better than a crown to announce your nobility."

"I...am...honored, sir," stammered the stranger and hid her face in his shoulder.

Each dance lasted a moment, yet also an eternity. The crystal slippers tinkled on the paving like droplets of rain upon a brook, or bells round the neck of a lamb. The prince's thoughts, as he felt the silken tresses brush his cheek, were bittersweet. "How shall I bear to be parted from this sylph? No, it is impossible. I must have her no matter what storm of condemnation I bring down upon myself!"

Not long after midnight, the prince's betrothed, Sleeping Beauty, made her entrance. She was late, having caught a corner of her train on a doorstop and torn its full length just as she was descending to the ball to greet her guests. Seamstresses had had to be roused from their beds to sew the train back together. When Beauty at last took her place at the top of the stairs, to the ceremonious accompaniment of French horns, the prince was not among the throng still awaiting her appearance.

Charming entered the ballroom some minutes afterwards, too late to lead her in. In his doublet he appeared to hide something that Beauty took to be a champagne glass. She made no mention of it, nor did she pursue the subject when he apologized for his absence, claiming to have ridden out on a moonlight gallop to clear his head. There were, it was true, beads of sweat on his brow.

Beauty did not berate him, but after formally greeting the prince's relations, politely toasting invited dignitaries, and attending to other such official duties, she left the ball, feeling hurt and aggrieved. She lay awake all night in her bedchamber, wondering, with sinking heart, if her prospective husband would prove to be a drunkard.

In the morning, one of her ladies-in-waiting, while pouring her mistress's breakfast tea, revealed the truth: the prince had been seen dancing for the better part of the evening on a secluded balcony with a beautiful stranger whose name no one seemed to recall.

"Forgive me," Prince Charming begged his fiancée when she confronted him. "My betrayal of you is iniquitous. No one knows it better than I." Nonetheless, he announced his determination to discover his mysterious dancing partner's identity and ask for her hand in marriage, for he felt that he could not live without her. Sleeping Beauty, desolate and rumored to be with child, returned with her parents to their realm, leaving Charming free to roam the kingdom in search of his true love.

It was a scandal throughout the two kingdoms. The prince had broken his engagement and was now traveling the land on his white steed, searching village, town, city, castle, even cottage and hut for the mysterious, shy beauty with whom he had danced.

He castigated himself ceaselessly for allowing her to elude him and was tormented by the image of that moment when, at the stroke of midnight, just as he was drowning in the blue pools of her eyes, she had suddenly wrenched herself from his arms and fled the palace, running as gracefully as she had danced, and so lightly that even in her haste to descend the stone stairs, her glass slippers did not shatter, though one was cast off in the escape. He had scooped the slipper up as he rushed after her, almost dropping it when he stumbled in the road over a pumpkin fallen off a peasant's cart. Jumping to his feet, he stared helplessly in every direction. But the beautiful stranger had disappeared into the night as if she had never existed.

In rain and snow, under blistering sun and glacial moon, he rode the lanes and high roads hither and yon. He ate and slept little. Everywhere he went, he carried the glass slipper and asked each woman of the kingdom to try it on. There could be only one, he believed, with foot so dainty that it could fit into the tiny, fragile shoe and also dance in it. He would not rest until he found her.

A year passed, during which he searched in vain. Finally, having sought his love in every corner of the land, he returned, haggard and weary, to his parents' home. With bowed head and broken heart, he rode up the cobbled streets leading to the palace.

Suddenly, a torrent of rain fell upon him, soaking him to the skin. Looking up in surprise, he saw that it was not rainfall, but a bucketful of wash water poured on him from a house above the street.

A young woman at the window looked out in great distress at the misfortune she had caused. Before he could get a look at her, she cried an apology and vanished from the window. Prince Charming recognized the voice at once. He leaped from his horse and forcibly entered the house, a dwelling he had visited the year before at the commencement of his search.

Three women were knitting by the fireside—a sour-faced mother and her two daughters. They stared at the intruder, astonished.

"Where is the maid who poured water on the Prince?" he demanded.

The women threw down their knitting and rushed to greet him, the mother begging his forgiveness for her careless servant. The daughters then scurried off to fetch food and drink, and cloths to dry him. But the Prince would have none of it. He bounded up the stairs and searched the house over until, throwing open the door to a small scullery, he found a beautiful young woman dressed in rags and cowering in a corner. Instantly, he threw himself at her feet.

"Ah!" he said, gazing up at her heavenly face. "Even in rags you are the angel of my dreams."

Cinderella (for that was her name, she confessed to him later) blushed and turned away.

The prince grasped her lovely hand. "Why did you not reveal yourself when I first came to this house?"

"Oh, Prince Charming," she replied, tears threatening to spill over her golden lashes, "how could I, after I learned who you were and that you were betrothed to another?"

"My darling," said the prince, hanging his head, "You are a good and true creature, and I am not worthy to kiss your precious foot." But kiss it he did, and repeatedly, before fitting the glass slipper onto it. Then he cried bitter tears and at last convinced Cinderella that his engagement had been broken off for a year, that Sleeping Beauty was reconciled to it, that she had already married her father's cousin—an elderly earl of considerable distinction—and now had a handsome baby boy. This defense—to Prince Charming's credit—was true.

Eventually Cinderella gave way to the hidden passion she had harbored for him all that twelvemonth, and finally, after much fear on the prince's part that he might, still, at the last minute, lose her, they were married.

On their wedding trip, Prince Charming and his bride passed through many lands. Cinderella had never seen the world, and it pleased her husband to show it to her. He directed their coachman to stop at quaint cottages, venerable churches and towns of antiquity. She admired nature in all its forms and begged to alight at each brook, bower, or hillock with a rustic view. She was entranced by all she saw.

But after awhile this idle rambling began to wear on the prince. He found himself suffering not precisely from irritation so much as indifference. In consideration of her feelings, he did his best to hide his lassitude, but each time Cinderella urged them down yet another dusty, out-of-the-way lane, the prince grew increasingly restless to return home to horse and hounds.

On one stifling afternoon, at the bottom of a meandering lane in the middle of nowhere, Cinderella bade the coachman stop the horses at the site of an ancient, crumbling tower.

An unusual spectacle had attracted her attention. An old hunch-backed crone was climbing from the tower window by way of a length of auburn rope. Prince Charming yawned at the curious scene. After the crone reached the ground and hobbled down the road, the prince heard the old woman croak over her shoulder in a menacing voice, "No one shall ever have you but I!" and he looked back to see a ravishing young woman in the tower window. She displayed a look of both deep resignation and profound sadness. The prince suddenly realized that the auburn rope was the woman's magnificent hair, plaited in a braid so thick and long it reached all the way to the ground.

Cinderella was remarking on the agile old woman's brisk progress up the lane and did not notice the younger woman at the window, but as the carriage retraced its journey to the high road, Prince Charming made a mental note of the exact route back.

⸙ ⸙ ⸙

KATE KASTEN teaches English as a Second Language at the University of Iowa. Her stories have appeared in *American Literary Review*, *Northwest Review*, *Glimmer Train*, and the *Somersault Press Side Show* fiction anthology. She has co-authored, with Sandra de Helen, a musical theatre satire of the Nancy Drew mystery series and has completed a novel, a collection of short stories, a book of fairy tales for adults, and a children's book.

WILLIAM LUVAAS

LITHIA PARK

On dog-day afternoons, shingles buckle on barn roofs hereabout before dropping flat onto their bellies in the evenings, exhausted from the day's heat. People do the opposite: on their bellies through siesta hours, up and out in the cool evenings to stroll in the park or along the avenues. Children throw breadcrumbs to swans afloat on Lithia Pond, squealing and upstaging one another, daring younger siblings to let the creatures feed directly from their hands—which, of course, they do to prove their courage, snatching fingers away as the birds arch their long necks speculatively as if about to strike. The children's squeals can be heard clear to the band shell in the town square, where members of the Red Satin City Orchestra prepare for public concert, the first violinist pulling his bow across the E string with a thin smug smile at number two to his left, torturing from his instrument a plaintive squawk that causes oldsters in the front row to firm their lips in taut, vibrant facsimile of nylon strings wrapped in coils of gold wire.

The picture of small-town tranquility; so it seemed at least to this recent visitor from New York, where crowds shove and honk through sweltering rush-hour afternoons. I was raised in just such a tranquil small town years ago. Though in recent years—what with news reports of domestic violence, infanticides, hometown bombings and gang warfare—I've come to believe such places extinct in all but memory.

I'd just been seated in the town's single Chinese restaurant, the Satin Dragon. It seemed odd to me that I was the only customer in the Dragon, but maybe the good folk of Lithia preferred Vietnamese or Thai cuisine. Perhaps, though I hated to think so, the small-town trembles had got them: rumors of cat meat substituted for pork on the menu. Such rumors made the rounds of my own small town as I was growing up. Even then, I understood there was some lesson in them, but I failed to understand it.

I ordered chicken chow yuk and was astonished but not alarmed when a waitress, surely more Swedish than Chinese, set before me what seemed an enchilada smothered in peanut oil. I ate it cheerfully, a full subscriber to the serendipities of travel, recognizing bean sprouts as I chewed, unable to ignore the ginger. It was apparently a ginger root enchilada. I was marveling at its multicultural ingenuity, when an old fellow entered and sat at a booth across the room, giving me that curious, good-humored perusal I had grown accustomed to in the region: a wonder-what-that-fella-does-where-he-comes-from sort of look. It made me want to declare: I come from here, a place much like this.

I studied him as he read the menu. An organic face which lines had settled into early on, guy wires at lip corners prepared to stretch the mouth into a smile, floating blue irises, which I've come to regard as a given of regional heredity, like translucent saucers on a blue sea of possibility, brow not plowed so much as hatched. A farmer possibly, given the size of his hands, but wearing the dented, roguish leather safari hat of a suburbanite in search of adventure. One aspect of him canceled out another: checked shirt contradicted orange synthetic golf slacks, "High Fly" Nikes contrasted with a string tie. He was a conceptual Great Divide or a frontier between time zones, past and present colliding in the flesh. He made me uneasy. Likely my expression betrayed it, for he turned to me as if I'd spoken and asked, "How long you plan to stay?"

"Few days," I said.

"Catch many fish?"

"No. Well, I didn't come to fish."

He winked knowingly, as if I'd said something idiotic I should have kept to myself. "Not having much fun, are ya?"

"No, I wouldn't say that. Actually I—"

"That's awright. I know people wouldn't walk across the street for a trout dinner—"

"I'm not one of them, believe me."

"—pan-fried over an open fire. To each his own." He cocked a finger at me as if that settled it and called for the waitress.

I would have suggested the ginger root enchilada, but I was nursing a grudge. Not the first time words had been put in my mouth in Lithia. Just that morning I'd assured the proprietress of the bed and breakfast where I was staying that I'd had an excellent sleep, thank you. No revving buses. No honking cabs.

"Now that isn't true," she'd cried. "Look me square in the eye and say that."

"But I did. Really."

"See! you're blinking."

"Honestly. I wish I could sleep that well in New York."

"That's the problem, isn't it." Nodding in that privy Lithia manner. "All the quiet gets downright spooky. Oh, I know." Her smile would have been fetching without multiple chins and dewlaps to refract it.

Still, she had attractive teeth, a bit small maybe. Secretly, I wanted to examine them.

"No, a wonderful sleep, believe me. Nirvana."

She adjusted her bust and eyed me. "It won't ruin our friendship, you know, to hear you had a rough night in my attic bedroom. I'm not that petty."

"Friendship?" I asked.

"I'm easy." She smiled.

"Okay then, for the sake of friendship, let's say I did have a bad night."

"See now!" She clapped chubby hands. "If you'd just admitted it up front we wouldn't of had to go through all this."

I was licked. When she suggested I didn't really want bacon and eggs—all that nasty cholesterugh–I accepted the twelve-grain cereal that was sure to bind me up for a week and work under my gums beyond flossing range, listening as she explained what the hippies had contributed to American culture.

"I'm gonna tell you something about fishing."

I looked up, startled; hadn't noticed the old fellow slip into the booth across from me.

"Fishing ain't nothing about fish at all. No sir. It's about water. Some see into it, some don't. Them what can see catch, them what can't see don't."

I studied him for a minute, wondering what he was getting at. When I spoke my voice stumbled. "It's a metaphor for life, I guess?"

He seized my water glass in a huge fist and thrust it under my nose. "How many cubes? Count 'em."

I recoiled. "They've melted."

He let go something between a hiss and a cackle; his tongue appeared momentarily between lips chapped and rough as fish scales. "Blind as a bass."

"Bat," I corrected him.

"You bet."

He turned the glass upside down. The contents slid out and landed with a heavy clunk on the table. Solid ice.

He was still grinning when I paid my bill and escaped into the cool evening air, on which a few errant notes drifted from the band shell in the park, discordant and slurring, reminiscent of *Sgt. Pepper's Lonely Hearts Club Band*. In Lithia, I was at sixty-five hundred feet, I reminded myself, the air elusively thin, certain to distort perceptions. My own hometown is near sea level. Raise such a place over a mile high and it's sure to cause distortion—Chinese restaurants, for example, which possess nothing in common with those at lower altitudes beyond bean sprouts, MSG, and chopsticks (but those in the Satin Dragon more like brass tuning forks which produced an eery, lingering bass hum when struck together).

I was breathing heavily by the time I reached the park; ginger formed a fireball near my heart and sprouts had begun a snake dance through my intestines. A five-year-old girl winked lewdly at me and lifted her dress to see if I would look away—as small girls sometimes do. She chortled knowingly, eyes aglow like thunder eggs that once rained down from surrounding mountains, found for sale in local curio shops, cut open and polished to a cold glitter inside. Hers the cynical, world-weary expression of a hooker on a Chelsea street corner.

Swans grazed on Lithia Pond, their flexible necks stretched underwater. Thank God for them, so docile and reassuring. In the dusk, I couldn't tell what they were feeding on, and wondered if the old man at the restaurant could have—with his fisherman's eyes. On the far shore, three boys waited in tense yearning, leaning over the water, their blue Lithia eyes focused intently on the swans. All three squealed in unison when a bird came up and craned its neck at the sky in agony, squawking terrible honking protest. Red foam burbled from its beak down into fleece, turning sleek white feathers a garish pink. I watched horrified. What had they done to it?

"You know," I heard a stylishly dressed woman passing by say to her companion, "I don't believe I've ever heard a swan song before." She regarded the suffering creature, her arms folded in approval.

Her companion nodded. "They're usually so quiet."

The three boys ran around the pond squealing delight.

⚬ ⚬ ⚬

I hurried back to the bed and breakfast, consigning events of the past hour to altitude and fatigue. "Don't be silly," my friend, the proprietress, told me when I mentioned the old man, the ice, the swans. "You're spacing out. You need a lithia hair raiser. That'll fix you right up."

"What's a lithia hair raiser?"

"Simple. Two parts milk, one part vodka, a sprinkle of nutmeg."

Just the thought of it turned my stomach, but I downed three of them straight. The milk, which I can't tolerate on its own, was neutralized by vodka, so I tasted only nutmeg and a faint afterglow of lime. Before I knew what was happening, I was upstairs in bed with my hostess.

After a rollicking bout of lovemaking we lay side by side. Her breathing, hippopotaman at first, subsided to the wheezing sigh of wind through cattails on Lithia Lake (where the old man wanted to send me fishing). I sensed she was smiling, but didn't care to look aside at her terraced chins and spoil the enchantment. I imagined her at half her weight—beautiful, her hair blood red, with a satiny rosewood luster, soft as swan's down. So cozy, sinking down into her quilted flesh, such a contrast to trim, rock-hard city women, all muscle and remorseless bone. In truth, it was the best lovemaking I'd had in years.

She heaved onto her side with a great tumult of bed springs. "When you said you are between wives now, what did you mean by that? You're divorced and have another waiting in the wings?"

"Oh, right! Always another," I said self-mockingly.

She frowned, nose flattened and nearly feline, as were her slit eyes—canny blue Lithia irises looking into me, fathoming what I felt but didn't speak. I realized, with a kind of shock, that she resembled the girl flasher in the park, who was, no doubt, in grave danger—the mad omnicultural enchilada maker out at dusk trapping children in his net, concocting evil, ambiguous meat dishes, while around him slept a town gone vegetarian. Frustration drives us all to extremes. Ridiculous, I told myself. Silly cat meat rumors of my youth updated for less innocent times.

Her plump infant's fingers clutched the quilt atop us, and I saw that my hostess wore a high school class ring identical to that worn by the waitress at the Satin Dragon, realized I hadn't looked at the woman's face, other than to note she wasn't Asian.

"What about me?"

"You!" I was startled.

"I'm a gourmet cook, I'm loyal and thoughtful. Well, maybe a teensy overweight, but you gotta admit I'm marvie in bed."

"Your final high note nearly took out my eardrums."

She giggled. "We call that orgasm."

"Yeah. I guess."

"So how's about it, lover? You'd absolutely love Lithia."

"I wonder if I would."

"You could help me do the B and B. We'd expand, honey, buy the old armory on Main Street. Sky's the limit."

"I'm a dentist," I reminded her.

"Between fillings." She burped laughter at her little joke. In a swath of lamplight, hers was precisely the face of the girl flasher in the park thirty years hence.

I rolled out of bed and up. Slipped quickly into my jeans.

"Okay...all right"—her hands trembled, moving parallel to the bed like an umpire's signaling safe—"I admit there's nothing special about me. I'm no Madonna. Like who is? I doubt she is herself under all that makeup. When it comes down to it, one person is the same as another. It might just as well be me as somebody else. Here I am!" She opened arms and eyes wide. "What you see is what you get."

"No, no, this is wrong. Absolutely," I said, stumbling into my shoes. "Forgive me. I didn't mean to...didn't intend...It's the altitude and those milky lithium, whatever they are. I have a pounding headache." Truth be told, I was coated in sweat, heart racing high in my throat, trying to remember from general med classes whether that signaled a heart attack.

Her face had collapsed on itself, become deranged in the manner of a Cubist sketch, features migrating, eye and mouth changing positions, scalp crawling so her ears perked forward like my ex-wife's. Unnerving. Perhaps in Lithia it was literally true: *One person is the same as another*. A single spirit moving among many forms. "It isn't about love," she groaned. "Don't you see? Or sex. It's about one person seeing down inside another. Some see, some don't. Guess I pegged you wrong."

No, I wanted to tell her. No, you didn't. But said instead, "Seems I keep hearing that in this town."

"Maybe you need to hear it. We're exactly what we are. Take it or leave it." She rolled thick thighs over the side of the bed and felt about with toes for her slippers. I was panicked, a man in a dream, wanting to move but struck immobile, remembering the fat girl in grade school who'd had a crush on me and chased me about the playground. In the perverse manner of prepubescent sexuality, she threatened to sit on me and make me her pancake. But couldn't catch me. Later, after she'd shed goose fat and metamorphosed to a sultry adolescent swan, the girl lost interest in me and left me bereft to dream about her nightly. Now she reached out a hand for mine, knuckles like almonds buried in mounds of whipped cream. For a moment I stared at them, my own hand trembled longingly. Then, with a great sigh, I turned and fled the room.

I took Highway 54 straight out of town. Feeling shaken and disoriented, wondering if the media didn't have it right about the demise of simplicity after all, while convinced I'd just narrowly escaped a generous helping of simple-as-it-gets. I drove blindly on. Seeking a place where swans float unperturbed on the placid surface of ponds and hearty, recognizable notes (John Philip Sousa maybe) float across the park from the band shell, where small girls are demure, and old men speak predictable saws, and what we find attractive comes packaged sleek and trim as a hometown beauty queen, where all is exactly what it appears to be without complication. Maybe I would find it just ahead in Oregon or Idaho...not sure which of those states I was just leaving.

❖ ❖ ❖

WILLIAM LUVAAS'S first novel, *The Seductions of Natalie Bach* (Little Brown), was nominated for the National Book Award and the Pen Faulkner Award; *Going Under* (Putnam) was nominated for the National Book Critics Circle Award. Luvaas's stories, essays and articles have appeared widely, including: *The American Fiction Anthology, Antioch Review, BlackBird, Glimmer Train, Confrontation, North American Review, Open Spaces, Pretext, The Sun, Short Story, Thema, The Village Voice,* and *The Washington Post Book World.* His story "The Firewood War" was co-winner of Fiction Network's 2nd National Fiction Competition, and a collection was awarded Honorable Mention in the Capricorn Fiction Award. He has been awarded a 2006-07 National Endowment for the Arts Fellowship in Fiction. He teaches writing at San Diego State University.

Michael Moorcock

The Third Jungle Book
A Mowgli Story

On the death of his friend Baloo, the last of his old jungle companions (who thought him immortal), Mowgli emigrated to London and took his bar exams. Thanks to a distinguished legal career representing the public interest, he was now Sir Sanjit J. Rey, respected Independent member of Parliament for Southall South, in London. His children had grown and were now doing well in America and Australia. Occasionally, however, he grew tired of civilised life and longed for the companions he had known as a boy in his highland Indian forest.

"It is a sad day," he said to himself, "when the last of one's old family and friends is gone to the great Tree Above and a little frog, however happily married, is left with no one who shares and understands his experience. O, Mother Wolf, O, Father Wolf, O, Akela, O, Baloo, O, Bagheera, how I miss thee, my mother, my father, my chief and my brothers. How I mourn for thee and long for the silence and the voices, the companionship of the forest!" Whereupon, he would lift his noble head and utter a low, pathetic howl of a kind which once issued from Sister Wolf who had died so unhappily in Regents Park Zoological Gardens many, many years before when he had lacked the influence to have her freed from captivity.

At last came the moment of decision. Sir Sanjit divested himself of his pyjamas while his wife slept and, clad only in his underpants, crept from his window high above the traffic to run swiftly over the West London rooftops, where he eventually met a family of foxes whose yapping, panting language was easily learned, since it was cousin to that of the wolves who had first been his friends and relatives. His scent, moreover, was reassuring to them and soon he was speaking of Akela, the great pack leader, of Mother Wolf, who had known his potential as a killer of Shere Khan, the tiger; he spoke of Ka, the python and all the others who had taught him how to survive and triumph, and told tales of the faraway jungle which somehow reminded the foxes of their own home amongst the alleys, rooftops and underground places of London.

Recognising Mowgli's sorrow, a young matron known as Makaba, with beautiful, unusually lustrous red hair, found herself comforting him. She had seen her first cubs emigrate up the Central Line of the

Underground to seek their fortunes in the wealthy suburbs of Notting Hill and Bayswater, home to both Holland and Hyde Parks. Her mate had been killed a year earlier while crossing the M4 motorway to investigate a newly-opened curry restaurant.

"O, beloved Mowgli," she said. "How I have longed to know the mind of the Big Frogs who dwell in this city. Why, for instance, do they appear to tolerate, even welcome, our presence amongst them when their brethren of the country live only to hunt and to kill us?"

Sir Sanjit thought the folk of the country might be less civilised and so have much less to occupy their minds than the city dwellers. "But it could also be something to do with the keeping of domestic fowl which is more commonly practiced in rural areas." In the city the myth that foxes, who habitually avoided conflict with cats and dogs, caught and ate household animals had long since been contradicted by experience. "And, though sometimes given to phases of mysterious xenophobia, city people are generally far better at absorbing new experience." Moreover, he thought, there was a greater tolerance, an attitude of live and let live, in the city, where a more varied collection of human beings rubbed shoulders. And, finally, you could add to that the fact that the people of the city were rather proud of their foxes, which helped, among other things, to keep the city clean and free of vermin. Because foxes hunted at night, they were generally only visible during the day when sunning themselves on roofs or educating their children.

All this made considerable sense to Makaba, who was satisfied by Mowgli's answers and next asked him to tell tales of the Indian jungle, most of which can already be found in the accounts of Mr. Rudyard Kipling known as *The Jungle Book* and *The Second Jungle Book*. Makaba and her people, of course, had not encountered these stories, since they did not read the 'little bugs' as they called the printed word, and had eyes which found it hard to focus on the TV screens which occasionally showed a rather stylised and sentimental account of Mowgli's adventures. Nor did the mumbling language of the Big Frogs mean much to them. They were eager to hear Mowgli's many explanations and interpretations. In return they told him what they knew of the nocturnal goings-on in his own and neighbouring constituencies. They knew which Big Frogs seemed in need, which falsified their need, who seemed to be stealing and so on. They knew who was abusing domestic animals or, indeed, hurting their own kind. By and by Mowgli built up a picture of his part of the city which, though unusual in its perspectives, was second to none. This proved very useful to Sir Sanjit in Parliament when certain issues were debated.

For the next few years, Mowgli nocturnally ranged the jungle which was the city he had made his own. Occasionally he was glimpsed by his fellow Big Frogs and became part of London's rich mythology. As well as the foxes, with whom he enjoyed the old, familiar communion of the pack, he came to know the wily cats, some of whom were of a size almost that of a small tiger, and who remained hidden during the day. Again, their language was not difficult for him to learn and they, too, told him much he would never otherwise have known, as did the feral and the domestic dogs. He even learned the simple speech of owls and night-hawks until he became as familiar and comfortable with this habitat as he had been with that Indian forest of his childhood, now a fond memory, for in common with many humans raised in the wild, Mowgli enjoyed extraordinary longevity.

Sir Sanjit meanwhile developed a very special friendship with a man whose father, an aristocrat, had given up his famous title and passed it on to him. This son spent at least part of his time on his northern English estates and often took his seat in Parliament. It was there the two had met. They had much in common, including a wish to protect the wild Waziran forest gorillas of Africa and look after the fate of wildlife in general. Sir Sanjit and the English lord also worked on health issues affecting the poorer continents. When the son and father had grown apart in the 1950s and 60s, Sir Sanjit had been instrumental in bringing the two men together until in the 1990s they had again become reconciled. The families became firm friends, taking holidays together and spending time as one another's guests in Africa and India.

The politics of the United Kingdom being what they were, a law to ban hunting with dogs was at last established, thanks in good part to the work done by Rey and his friend in the House of Lords. The urban foxes were highly relieved that their country cousins would no longer be subjected to being pursued over hill and dale by the 'unspeakable in pursuit of the uneatable,' by packs of howling men and women mounted on galloping horses and accompanied by hunger-crazed dogs. But no sooner had this law been passed than another began to be mooted in the House.

Known as the Urban Vermin (Culling) Bill, it was put before Parliament by William Bale, MP, Conservative for Berking Maddely in the county of Gloucestershire in vengeful response, many on the left believed, to the success of the 'townies' who knew, he claimed, nothing of the real countryside and were merely bent on curtailing the pleasures of honest rural folk. That many honest rural folk were as disgusted by the hunts which flew willy-nilly across their lands and property, doing untold damage, followed by their supporters in massive vehicles which created further chaos, appeared to be missed by the hunters, no matter how many farmers attempted to block their paths, arguing that their livings were threatened far more by rampaging packs of dogs and riders than any number of hen-coop-raiding foxes. Not that the urban foxes approved of fowl-stealing, since they had long-since learned to enjoy their food well cooked and in Southall South and its surrounding locales, were inclined to take their chicken Tandoori rather than raw.

The Bill began to gather momentum across party lines when the London *Daily Mail* determined that its falling readership could be stimulated by supporting Mr. Bale's entirely apocryphal stories of city foxes carrying off infants, feasting on cats and smaller dog breeds and generally behaving like packs of, as an editorial put it, 'canine Huns.' When a woman in Hackney was found to swear that her husband, returning intoxicated from The Hoop and Hooligan, had woken in the gutter to find his hand being gnawed by two monstrous red foxes, even *The Times*, at the instigation of Rupert Murdoch, its proprietor, felt obliged to carry several features asking if the 'fox epidemic' was threatening the health and welfare of citizens everywhere.

A Birmingham man claimed that his wife had been set upon by mad foxes and run in terror to the canal, where she had drowned. Another in Manchester told of walking home with his Indian take-away in a carrier bag, only to have the food snatched from him by what he called 'an organised pack' of ten or a dozen 'gigantic foxes.' Some youths in Lewisham told how they were attacked by rabid foxes 'foaming at the mouth', though no case of rabies had been recorded in England for the past several years. Another story linked the taste of foxes for geese, ducks, chickens and other farmyard fowl with the possibility of their spreading some form of avian influenza, now being called 'Mad Parrot Disease' by the tabloids.

Needless to say all these stories were proven false by investigators, but they swiftly entered the mythology of public life. As every journalist knows, truth is never really the issue in the public mind. The dominant story is what concerns readers of tabloids and broadsheets alike, and anything which contradicts it, no matter how convincing the evidence, merely becomes a marginalised alternative.

Thus it was that the urban foxes, who had enjoyed so much approval from the average city dweller, now suddenly found themselves likened to the wolves which had allegedly pursued troikas in Old Russia or the dingos said to have carried off children in the Australian Outback. No longer was 'cunning Reynard' an affectionate term, nor was 'Old Rufus' playing a useful role in the urban ecology. Opinions would change, of course, as they always did, but in the media engendered hysteria of the moment foxes had become 'a pressing problem' and a 'social menace.'

All the outrage and fear which the tabloid press had once turned on asylum-seeking immigrants and those looking for work from the old English colonies became focussed on the foxes. The voices of liberalism and reason were drowned by the tabloid shout. Fox News even considered changing its name for the UK market where, anyway, it was better known as 'Sky News.' Murdoch had rather enjoyed the soubriquet of 'The Sky Fox' until now.

Not that the immigrants and Commonwealth citizens were unhappy with this turn of events, which led them, sad to say, to join in the general outcry against Makaba and her relations, just as Jews had been happy to condemn Jamaican and Indian newcomers to the British isles in the 1950s and Pakistanis claimed that Poles were threatening their jobs. There seems to be no end to the human capacity for prejudice, however temporary, especially where it helps avoid any self-blame and allows them to feel that they are siding with the majority. Indeed, some people who might otherwise have been expected to speak up for the vulpine cause were so glad to see different groups of human beings joining ranks against a common non-human enemy that they were either silent or echoed the general condemnation.

Sir Sanjit and his cousins of the urban jungle viewed all these developments with considerable trepidation. Had it not been for Mowgli's eloquence in Parliament and the press, together with the humanity of some of his political colleagues of all political stripes, we might even have witnessed parties of anti-vulpine vigilantes prowling the streets with nets and other implements, though not, happily, with shotguns or any firearms, these still being illegal in the hands of private citizens. Nonetheless, it seemed touch and go when Bale and his fellow 'cullers' suggested arming the bobby on the beat with dart guns and Tazers designed to stun all large urban vermin. Luckily Sir Sanjit's friend Anthony Wellington (Labour, Fulham W) pointed out that people were as likely to find their dogs victims of the puffing policemen as any fox, and the idea was dropped.

The Bill itself was not. While no-one accepted Percy Effingham-Harde's suggestion that 'experienced country people' be bused into town and given sturdy 'hunting bicycles' to pursue the foxes with the packs of no-longer-employed hounds, it was becoming increasingly likely that innocent foxes actually spotted during the day when lying out on roofs and patches of waste ground or, indeed, enjoying the security of whatever setts they had made for themselves, were likely to be attacked by members of a specially formed Animal Security Service, whose job would be to kill them, in whatever way was most practical. The old, amiable balance between Fox and Man seemed about to come to an end.

Makaba foresaw the necessity of returning to the country where, because they would so swell the ranks of rural foxes, they would suffer as badly from being shot, poisoned or trapped. There seemed no hope for any of the packs who had so recently been the pride of their adopted boroughs and suburbs.

"O, Mowgli, dear cousin," said Makaba, at the great gathering of fox packs which she and he had called in Holland Park after closing hours (and which itself was nowadays much riskier than it had been), "it seems we are fated never to be at peace, thy tribe and mine. Is there anything which can be done to return us to the condition of mutual respect we shared until recently?"

"Honoured Mother of Many," replied Mowgli, "know that I am doing everything I can in the councils of the Big Frogs to persuade them that their fears are without substance and their tales the mere baying of mad beasts, but that madness which was once confined to a few country dwellers is now bent on spreading itself to all the manpacks. Soon a vote will be taken amongst their representatives and the fate of my cousins will be sealed. I have to tell thee that this madness of theirs is running very high and though it must eventually subside and, given time, relations return to normal between thy folk and mine, there is every likelihood that it might meanwhile become a formula for attacking thee, who dwell in the deep valleys and high peaks of the city, and have done nothing but good for the manpacks."

"Has your voice no weight in these councils, O, Mowgli?" asked grey-muzzled Woova, sent from across the Great River from far Norbury. "Have you not told thy fellows that we mean them no harm and do them no harm?"

"Many times have I told them this, Brother Woova, but I fear they have become hysterical, thanks to the yapping and shrilling of their talking papers and pictures. I know that by and by I would be able to persuade them of the truth, but there is no time. They are infected as some are infected by the movements of the moon. When that madness dies out, the evil will have been done."

Therefore by and by the fox-leaders returned to their respective packs to report this terrible news, while Mowgli continued his work on their behalf. He knew that even if a majority of his fellow parliamentarians passed the Bill, as they might in their wish to placate the yellow press and ensure their re-election, the House of Lords would not be so ready to validate it. It only needed a majority of one against the Bill for it to be put back to a later session or probably killed forever, when the hysteria would have died and the whole matter have been forgotten, replaced by some other equally fashionable and empty cause. The Lords, however, were themselves being accused of ruralophobia. Many hereditary peers were also being 'culled' by New Labour's war against tradition, which aimed to replace peers with 'senators.' They wondered if it would not be better to pass this Bill, sacrificing the foxes for what many believed were more important issues. When Bale was supported by Baron Wessex and Lady Hatchet and their various followers, things looked decidedly black for the urban foxes.

Sir Sanjit and his supporters urgently took a survey of the Upper House and to their horror it seemed that opinions, for an assortment of reasons, were pretty evenly divided. If all those who were going to be sitting when the Bill came before the Lords voted as they said they would, the Bill would pass by two votes. Sir Sanjit then took Viscount Earlybird to lunch and persuaded him that his own estates would be flooded by returning foxes, but had a hard time convincing the noble lord to vote against the proposal. Only when Sir Sanjit pointed out that the urban foxes had become increasingly intelligent and would soon learn how to open up Earlybird's massive battery chicken hutches and make meals of such easy prey, did the peer, who had been elevated for his services to British chain-groceries, agree to vote against the Bill.

Now, it seemed, the vote would reach stalemate, for several peers had either absented themselves deliberately or would be away for other reasons. The friend who might have swung the Lords to Sir Sanjit's point of view had disappeared into the deep African jungles and an email, addressed to him in Wazira, had been read neither by him nor by his father. Sir Sanjit guessed that the two had gone together to the secret source of their wealth in the far mountains. This wealth had increasingly been turned to the good of the poorer African countries and was currently much needed.

"O, Mowgli," said Makaba on hearing this news, "while I have sympathy for the plight of the unfortunate African Big Frogs, what will become of my own folk if they are driven from their dens and forced to fend for themselves in the inhospitable wild? If only I could appear before thy Great Gathering and speak the truth, telling them how we mean our Big Frog cousins nothing but good! Canst thou not achieve this for me?"

"Aunt Makaba," said Mowgli sadly, "thy voice would not be heard for its wisdom, even if thou spoke words they would understand. They would marvel at the wonder of thy talent but hear nothing of thy logic. All, I fear, is lost, for it has become our Law that if a Bill is passed by the House of Commons and not actively dismissed by a majority in the House of Lords, then that Bill shall be instated."

And so both Mowgli and his cousins became drowned in misery, facing the prospect of doom as, in Mowgli's old homeland, the inevitability of seasonal rain had been faced. The Bill would be the last one voted upon before the Lords broke for their Christmas recession. The night before this final debate, Mowgli could not bear to divest himself of his pyjamas and race across the rooftops to commune with his friends of the urban jungle, but instead went to bed with only a mug of cocoa for company, his wife being called away to visit a sick sister. Before she went, she tried to console him. "This is only a storm in a teacup, dear husband. The Bill cannot be applied in any practical sense. Eventually they will forget about it and the foxes will be able to return to their city again."

"Sadly," he had replied, "they are poorly adapted for rural life. Too many will suffer since winter is almost upon us. It will be an unhappy time for all concerned."

With a tear in her eye, Lady Rey left to catch her train. She knew her husband spoke the truth, for she had learned to trust him on all such matters. She did not look forward to enjoying the Season of Good Will.

She was away for a week and during that time she had no opportunity to read the newspapers or watch the television. Her sister had forbidden both from her hospital room and her nurses and doctors were convinced that this action had seriously helped her recovery. When Lady Rey took the train back to Euston and from there to Southall South, her sister was sitting up in bed waiting to be returned to her own flat.

Of course, though she was pleased at her sister's recovery, it was with heavy heart that she got out of the taxi and wheeled her little suitcase up the path to her delightful detached residence. She had, after all, been told to expect the worst. The Urban Vermin (Culling) Bill would have gone through the House of Lords that very night, and she expected to find her husband in the depths of misery that he had been unable to help his many cousins. She was all the more concerned when she saw that he had left her a note on the hall table. He explained that he would not be back until after midnight and that she was to go to bed without him.

Lady Rey decided in this case that she would wait up for her husband, but it was not until three in the morning that she heard the noise of the dormer window opening and knew he was home. She climbed the stairs, hoping that he had not been drinking or otherwise trying to drown his misery. The door of the attic room opened and he stood there in his underpants, his muscled, brown body almost as attractive as it had been on the day, so many years ago, when they were first married. She looked at his eyes. They were glistening. Had he been crying?

And then he jumped forward and picked her up. She felt the thrill she had always known at his embrace. There was still something of the wild about him. It was why she had never objected to these nighttime adventures. But was he hiding his misery?

When he smiled, she knew that he was not. Had the impossible, after all, happened?

"The Bill?" she said. "Didn't it get its final reading?"

"Oh, indeed, it did, my dear, dear Ayesha."

"So somebody changed their mind?"

"They all voted exactly as they were expected to vote."

"Mowgli, my darling, you must not keep me in suspense. What happened tonight?"

He threw up his handsome head and laughed, his hair falling straight as a wolf's mane behind him. "My friend came back from Africa! Korak heard the news on the BBC World Service in New Tarzana. He checked my email. He borrowed his father's aeroplane and flew as far as Nairobi. From Nairobi he got a jet directly to London. From London he took a taxi to the House of Lords and was just in time to vote against the Bill. It is over, Ayesha. The foxes are safe. All this nonsense will die down over the Christmas holidays, and Bale's party won't let him bring the Bill again."

There was a sound from the room above. A window opened. A window shut. A movement on the stairs from the attic and the door opened for a second time. There, his blue eyes twinkling, also wearing nothing but a pair of underpants, his long hair tousled, his body tanned almost as brown as Mowgli's, stood Jack Clayton, Lord Greystoke, the son of Tarzan. He bowed with easy grace. "Good evening, Lady Ayesha. What a pleasure to see you. I gather Mowgli has told you that we won?"

"Indeed he has. We must certainly celebrate, late as it is." She returned to the stairs and went to make them all a cup of tea. "Can I get you anything to eat?"

"Awfully kind of you, Ayesha," he said, "but I'm not hungry. However, if you have any Tandoori chicken in the refrigerator I have a friend who would love to help us celebrate. She does not as a rule drink tea." Clayton sprang down the stairs after Lady Rey and opened the front door.

There on the step, her dark eyes shining, her pink tongue lolling with happiness, her greying red hair bristling from ears to brush, stood Makaba the vixen.

Unfortunately, Lady Rey did not understand the language of foxes or she would have heard Makaba say: "Good evening to thee, cousin. I am so pleased we are able to meet at last. It seems the Big Frogs are not going to make war on us, after all. We have thy husband to thank for that."

But Mowgli shook his head. "Oh, no, indeed," he said in English, "it's Jack Clayton who saved the day."

At which the English lord let out a sharp, self-deprecating yap of denial.

⫶ ⫶ ⫶

MICHAEL MOORCOCK has another story, "Cake," on page 616 of this anthology. He is a prolific British writer of science fiction, science fantasy, and literary fiction. At sixteen he became editor of *Tarzan Adventures* and, as editor of *New Worlds* from 1964 to 1971, and again from 1976 to 1996, he encouraged the development of the New Wave in Britain and indirectly in the United States. Since the 1980s he has primarily written literary novels. Moorcock's most recent book, *The Vengeance of Rome*, completes the *Between The Wars* tetralogy about events leading up to the Nazi holocaust. In 2002 he was inducted into the Science Fiction Hall of Fame, and in 2004 he was awarded the Prix Utopiales, a French Lifetime Achievement Award.

Maureen N. McLane

White Girl

I. Introduce Yourself

I was born a white girl on a white sheet on the eve of the whitest day of a white season. For some people Christmas Eve evokes the green of fir trees and mistletoe; for others, the red of holly berries and poinsettias. But those born into the blankness of an unexpected winter hour know the true color of the season. I was born a white girl on a white evening. The essence of whiteness is not to think of it. Is it the presence or absence of all color? Are we talking of light or of paint? Do not think of it. The essence of girlness is not to forget it and not to look it—you girl you yes you—in the dead white face. I became expert in this not thinking and not looking. There's a blizzard coming fast to wipe out all the stray animals of truth.

Yes although the little zygote I once was came to be on a March evening, I was first seen and heard nine months later in December, a bloody white thing pushing into this bloody white world. The progenitor: The White King; progenitrix: White Queen. And while they forbore to name me Snow White, it is true they took up with zest their mythic roles: which is to say, the Queen abhorred and the King adored me. Is it not always so? or at least with eldest daughters?

Ah but this is not so. See how the stories lie? And how I persist in the same? It would be a comfort, oh yes a comfort it would be, if one could invoke a mere name—Tom Thumb, Cinderella, Snow White— and one could see the tale unfurl like the inevitable flag of the inevitable nation. Every name has a plot and a flag. If I told you my name you might think you knew the story. But you see in this story the name is not the key, nor does every folktale end with a marriage, an inheritance, or a slain dragon. Disappointing but true. Almost everyone lives in this story, especially the dragons, and no one gets richer or married. And as I said my name was not Snow White.

II. Why Do You Talk So Funny

I speak and write Standard English. I can't help it nor do I usually wish to. Even if I keep the mouth shut I am a sign, a symbol of a white standard: my body announces something and not just to you who look right now. Or rather, my body recedes under the weight of what it bears: the patches of skin; the particular clothes, these leggings and this knit sweater and the gallantly draped silk scarf; the three holes pierced in the ears—two on the right, one on the left; the aura of physical restraint bespeaking years of self-control; the blond hair skimming the shoulders which rarely relax into their full repose; the eyeglasses; the viciously bitten-down nails. These are fragments toward a physiognomy. Let us shave my head and feel my skull: it swells unevenly in the back; there is a distinct ridge above the left ear; the top and front are well-rounded and smooth. This tells you something about me, or could if either of us knew the old phrenological code.

But why   a) assume you wish to know about me, or
                b) invoke discredited pseudo-sciences?

Why indeed? I will not tease you further with meta-language. You have gotten this far; you are patient only insofar as you anticipate a payoff. I must oblige. As for obsolete techniques for assessing character, intelligence—well, something is lost every day, and all that's left are a few broken words and bodies which can't even remind us of what we forgot. That is why I am here: a white face, a ghost aspiring toward a memory.

.

III. What Do You Remember

A List of All I Have Forgotten
1. My real name
2. The middles of all fairy tales
3. The smell of the snow
4. The color of my soul
5. What happened in the forest

IV. Try Again

Once upon a time there was a girlchild born to the White King and Queen. Oh my, a girlchild! they exclaimed. Whatever shall we do? Shall we send her into the forest? Shall we keep her here in our ever-so-spacious castle? Have we a wetnurse, a nanny? What does one do?

No child had been born in the kingdom for five hundred years. All the inhabitants of the White Kingdom lived in a state of cryogenic suspension, broken only by occasional forays to the theater, to see certain worthy plays like *A Doll's House* and *Much Ado About Nothing*. Everyone got along famously in the kingdom, as they were all related, all white, all happily declaring their fealty to the well-preserved and benevolent tyrants, the White King and Queen.

But mysteriously: a child. Mysteriously—since in this land no one had sex and here there were no sperm banks, no in vitro or ex vitro fertilization, no wombs to be rented or genes to be cloned. For centuries the White Kingdom had completely foregone reproduction. The residents had moved past desire, past need, and since no one ever died and the level of population perfectly balanced the means of subsistence, the body politic of the White Kingdom hummed along content in the perfect stasis of every member.

Until: a child. There was no hunter to be commanded, no feudal minion to be told: take it out to the forest, kill it, bring back its heart that I may eat it. There were no obviously murderous intentions. No one said: lock her in the dungeon, or take her to the Island of Desolation, where she may live out her days in unimpeachable silence. No one wished the child any harm. The White Kingdom, and more particularly the White King and Queen, looked askance at the child, but never did they look with horror or homicidal gleamings. After five centuries of stony sleep they were, more than anything else, dazed; dazed and tired. After much deliberation and several advisory councils, the royals decided to feed it with the white milk stored in the vast casks in the lowest recesses of the castle. To their dull almost-wonder, it began to grow.

After something like a decade the girlchild had established her habits, most notably a tendency to wander which developed into a more purposive exploration of the White Kingdom. Every few weeks she would fill her pack with thermoses of milk, packets of crackers, white cheeses and vanilla cake, after which she would set forth for the forest, which few entered any longer, since the desire to explore had faded long ago in the White Kingdom, along with all other desires. But there was, independent of desire, a forest, and there was a girlchild who took to the forest. It was there in the forest, as the rather stunned animals gathered round, that the girlchild began to hear voices as she sat in the hollows of an old oak tree.

V. What Happens to Little Girls

Today I found out something that changed my whole life. Today I discovered that I was a whitegirl. I looked myself up and down in the mirror. I looked and looked and had my private epiphany: I am a fucking whitegirl. And all this time I never knew you were talking to me. All this time I thought I was a smart good girl and that's it. Thank god I found out before I got hurt or did something awful.

Did I find out in time?
Is anybody dead?

I am afraid to look in my closet. A rank smell is a-comin out. Let us count up all the people: all here? I have twenty-six personalities like Sybil, but none of them knew THEY WERE WHITE. Without this bit of information they may have done something real bad. Someone might be dead. I am afraid to look.

VI. What Do Little Girls Know

It came to pass one day that the little white girl braved her fears and opened her closet. Come out, come out, whoever you are, she called, first timidly, then with real force. Suddenly there appeared a small strange urchin, a little black boy who introduced himself as William Blake. The little white girl and the little black boy became fast friends and spent many hours discussing the states of their souls. Day after day they would talk and sometimes argue about their differing images of God: the little white girl went in for a sentimental Jesus, while the little black boy fastened on a stern and righteous Jehovah. The little black boy told the little white girl that she knew nothing about reality. You don't even know I am a little black boy! he exclaimed. I know you are Willie Blake, she replied, and you popped out of my closet in my castle in the center of the White Kingdom. But this isn't the White Kingdom, said the little black boy; this isn't even your castle. You've drunk too much milk, you've eaten too much vanilla cake; you can't see straight; you might be insane, said the little black boy. The little white girl began to suspect that she was in fact insane. She no longer prayed to Jesus. She didn't even pray to Jehovah. She went to look for the White King and Queen and discovered that in fact they had never existed. Nor was the castle anything but a plain one-story house in a suburban housing development. In her shock and depression the little white girl took to writing self-absorbed and self-pitying ballads:

VII. Little White Girl:

My Mother bore me in the Northern wild,
And I am black but O! my skin is white.
Black as the devil is my soul's bleak night.
But I am white as if consumed by light.

⯗ ⯗ ⯗

MAUREEN MCLANE lives in Cambridge, Massachusetts, where she teaches in the Committee on Degrees in History and Literature at Harvard. She was born in Syracuse, New York and was educated at Harvard, Oxford, and the University of Chicago. She is the author of *Romanticism and the Human Sciences: poetry, population and the discourse of the species* (Cambridge University Press, 2000), and articles on romantic and contemporary poetry, Anglo-Scottish balladry, and minstrelsy. She is co-editor (with James K. Chandler) of *The Cambridge Companion to British Romantic Poetry* (forthcoming from Cambridge University Press, 2007). Since 1996 she has been the chief poetry reviewer at the *Chicago Tribune*; her essays on poetry, fiction, teaching, childhood, and sexuality have appeared in *The New York Times, The Boston Review,* and *The Boston Globe,* as well as the *Tribune.* In 2003 she won the National Book Critics Circle Nona Balakian Award for Excellence in Book Reviewing. In December 2005, Arrowsmith Press (Boston) published a chapbook of her poems, *This Carrying Life.*

KIM STANLEY ROBINSON

THE LUCKY STRIKE

War breeds strange pastimes. In July of 1945 on Tinian Island in the North Pacific, Captain Frank January had taken to piling pebble cairns on the crown of Mount Lasso—one pebble for each B-29 takeoff, one cairn for each mission. It was a mindless pastime, but so was poker. The men of the 509th had played a million hands of poker, sitting in the shade of a palm around an upturned crate, sweating in their skivvies, swearing and betting all their pay and cigarettes, playing hand after hand, until the cards got so soft and dog-eared you could have used them for toilet paper. Captain January had gotten sick of it, and after he lit out for the hilltop a few times some of his crew mates started trailing him. When their pilot, Jim Fitch, joined them it became an official pastime, like throwing flares into the compound or going hunting for stray Japs. What Captain January thought of the development he didn't say. The others grouped near Captain Fitch, who passed around his battered flask. "Hey, January," Fitch called. "Come have a shot."

January wandered over and took the flask. Fitch laughed at his pebble. "Practicing your bombing up here, eh, Professor?"

"Yeah," January said sullenly. Anyone who read more than the funnies was Professor to Fitch. Thirstily January knocked back some rum. He passed the flask on to Lieutenant Matthews, their navigator.

"That's why he's the best," Matthews joked. "Always practicing."

Fitch laughed. "He's best because I make him be best, right, Professor?"

January frowned. Fitch was a bulky youth, thick-featured, pig-eyed—a thug, in January's opinion. The rest of the crew were all in their mid-twenties, like Fitch, and they liked the captain's bossy roughhouse style. January, who was thirty-seven, didn't go for it. He wandered away, back to the cairn he had been building. From Mount Lasso they had an overview of the whole island, from the harbor at Wall Street to the north field in Harlem. January had observed hundreds of B-29s roar off the four parallel runways of the north field and head for Japan. The last quartet of this particular mission buzzed across the width of the island, and January dropped four more pebbles, aiming for crevices in the pile. One of them stuck nicely.

"There they are!" said Matthews. "They're on the taxiing strip."

January located the 509th's first plane. Today, the first of August, there was something more interesting to watch than the usual Superfortress parade. Word was out that General LeMay wanted to take the 509th's mission away from it. Their commander, Colonel Tibbets, had gone and bitched to LeMay in person, and the general had agreed the mission was theirs, but on one condition—one of the general's men was to make a test flight with the 509th to make sure they were fit for combat over Japan. The general's man had arrived, and now he was down there in the strike plane with Tibbets and the whole first team. January sidled back to his mates to view the takeoff with them.

"Why don't the strike plane have a name, though?" Haddock was saying.

Fitch said, "Lewis won't give it a name because it's not his plane, and he knows it." The others laughed. Lewis and his crew were naturally unpopular, being Tibbets's favorites.

"What do you think he'll do to the general's man?" Matthews asked.

The others laughed at the very idea. "He'll kill an engine at takeoff, I bet you anything," Fitch said. He pointed at the wrecked B-29s that marked the end of every runway. "He'll want to show that he wouldn't go down if it happened to him."

"Course he wouldn't!" Matthews said.

"You hope," January said under his breath.

"They let those Wrights out too soon," Haddock said seriously. "They keep busting under the takeoff load."

"Won't matter to the old bull," Matthews said. Then they all started in about Tibbets's flying ability, even Fitch. They all thought Tibbets was the greatest. January, on the other hand, liked Tibbets even less than he liked Fitch. That had started right after he was assigned to the 509th. He had been told he was part of the most important group in the war and then given a leave. In Vicksburg a couple of fliers just back from England had bought him a lot of whiskeys, and since January had spent several months stationed near London they had talked for a good long time and gotten pretty drunk. The two were really curious about what January was up to now, but he had stayed vague on it and kept returning the talk to the blitz. He had seen an English nurse, for instance, whose flat had been bombed, family killed… But they had really wanted to know. So he had told them he was onto something special, and they had flipped out their badges and told him they were Army Intelligence, and that if he ever broke security like that again he'd be transferred to Alaska. It was a dirty trick. January had gone back to Wendover and told Tibbets so to his face, and Tibbets had turned red and threatened him some more. January despised him for that. During their year's training he had bombed better than ever, as a way of showing the old bull he was wrong. Every time their eyes had met it was clear what was going on. But Tibbets never backed off no matter how precise January's bombing got. Just thinking about it was enough to cause January to line up a pebble over an ant and drop it.

"Will you cut that out?" Fitch complained.

January pointed. "They're going." Tibbets's plane had taxied to runway Baker. Fitch passed the flask around again. The tropical sun beat on them, and the ocean surrounding the island blazed white. January put up a sweaty hand to aid the bill of his baseball cap.

The four props cut in hard, and the sleek Superfortress quickly trundled up to speed and roared down Baker. Three quarters of the way down the strip the outside right prop feathered.

"Yow!" Fitch crowed. "I told you he'd do it!"

The plane nosed off the ground and slewed right, then pulled back on course to cheers from the four young men around January. January pointed again. "He's cut number three, too."

The inside right prop feathered, and now the plane was pulled up by the left wing only, while the two right props windmilled uselessly. "Holy smoke!" Haddock cried. "Ain't the old bull something?"

They whooped to see the plane's power and Tibbets's nervy arrogance.

"By God, LeMay's man will remember this flight," Fitch hooted. "Why, look at that! He's banking!"

Apparently taking off on two engines wasn't enough for Tibbets; he banked the plane right until it was standing on its dead wing, and it curved back toward Tinian.

Then the inside left engine feathered.

War tears at the imagination. For three years Frank January had kept his imagination trapped, refusing to give it any play whatsoever. The dangers threatening him, the effects of the bombs, the fate of the other participants in the war—he had refused to think about any of it. But the war tore at his control. That English nurse's flat. The missions over the Ruhr. The bomber just below him blown apart by flak. And then there had been a year in Utah, and the viselike grip that he had once kept on his imagination had slipped away.

So when he saw the number two prop feather, his heart gave a little jump against his sternum, and helplessly he was up there with Ferebee, the first-team bombardier. He would be looking over the pilots' shoulders…

"Only one engine?" Fitch said.

"That one's for real," January said harshly. Despite himself he *saw* the panic in the cockpit, the frantic rush to power the two right engines. The plane was dropping fast and Tibbets leveled it off, leaving them on a course back toward the island. The two right props spun, blurred to a shimmer. January held his breath. They needed more lift; Tibbets was trying to pull it over the island. Maybe he was trying for the short runway on the south half of the island.

But Tinian was too tall, the plane too heavy. It roared right into the jungle above the beach, where Forty-second Street met their East River. It exploded in a bloom of fire. By the time the sound of it struck them they knew no one in the plane had survived.

Black smoke towered into white sky. In the shocked silence on Mount Lasso, insects buzzed and creaked. The air left January's lungs with a gulp. He had been with Ferebee, he had heard the desperate shouts, seen the last green rush, been stunned by the dentist-drill-all-over pain of the impact.

"Oh my God," Fitch was saying. "Oh my God." Matthews was sitting. January picked up the flask, tossed it at Fitch.

"C-come on," he stuttered. He hadn't stuttered since he was sixteen. He led the others in a rush down the hill. When they got to Broadway a jeep careened toward them and skidded to a halt. It was Colonel Scholes, the old bull's exec. "What happened?"

Fitch told him.

"Those damned Wrights," Scholes said as the men piled in. This time one had failed at just the wrong moment; some welder in the States had kept flame to metal a second less than usual—or something equally minor, equally trivial—and that had made all the difference.

They left the jeep at Forty-second and Broadway and hiked east over a narrow track to the shore. A fairly large circle of trees was burning. The fire trucks were already there.

Scholes stood beside January, his expression bleak. "That was the whole first team," he said.

"I know," said January. He was still in shock, his imagination crushed, incinerated, destroyed. Once as a kid he had tied sheets to his arms and waist, jumped off the roof, and landed right on his chest; this felt like that had. He had no way of knowing what would come of this crash, but he had a suspicion that he had indeed smacked into something hard.

Scholes shook his head. A half hour had passed, the fire was nearly out. January's four mates were over chattering with the Seabees. "He was going to name the plane after his mother," Scholes said to the ground. "He told me that just this morning. He was going to call it *Enola Gay.*"

At night the jungle breathed, and its hot wet breath washed over the 509th's compound. January stood in the doorway of his Quonset barracks hoping for a real breeze. No poker tonight. Noises were hushed, faces solemn. Some of the men had helped box up the dead crew's gear. Now most lay on their bunks. January gave up on the breeze, climbed onto his top bunk to stare at the ceiling.

He observed the corrugated arch over him. Cricket song sawed through his thoughts. Below him a rapid conversation was being carried on in guilty undertones, Fitch at its center. "January is the best bombardier left," he said. "And I'm as good as Lewis was."

"But so is Sweeney," Matthews said. "And he's in with Scholes."

They were figuring out who would take over the strike. January scowled. Tibbets and the rest were less than twelve hours dead, and they were squabbling over who would replace them.

January grabbed a shirt, rolled off his bunk, put the shirt on.

"Hey, Professor," Fitch said, "where you going?"

"Out."

Though midnight was near, it was still sweltering. Crickets shut up as he walked by, started again behind him. He lit a cigarette. In the dark the MPs patrolling their compound were like pairs of walking armbands. Forcefully January expelled smoke, as if he could expel his disgust with it. They were only kids, he told himself. Their minds had been shaped in the war, by the war, and for the war. They knew you couldn't mourn the dead for long; carry around a load like that and your own engines might fail. That was all right with January. It was an attitude that Tibbets had helped to form, so it was what he deserved. Tibbets would *want* to be forgotten in favor of the mission; all he had lived for was to drop the gimmick on the Japs, and he was oblivious to anything else—men, wife, family, anything.

So it wasn't the lack of feeling in his mates that bothered January. And it was natural of them to want to fly the strike they had been training a year for. Natural, that is, if you were a kid with a mind shaped by fanatics like Tibbets, shaped to take orders and never imagine consequences. But January was not a kid, and he wasn't going to let men like Tibbets do a thing to his mind. And the gimmick...the gimmick was not natural. A chemical bomb of some sort, he guessed. Against the Geneva Convention. He stubbed his cigarette against the sole of his sneaker, tossed the butt over the fence. The tropical night breathed over him. He had a headache.

For months now he had been sure he would never fly a strike. The dislike Tibbets and he had exchanged in their looks (January was acutely aware of looks) had been real and strong. Tibbets had understood that January's record of pinpoint accuracy in the runs over the Salton Sea had been a way of showing contempt. The record had forced him to keep January on one of the four second-string teams, but with the fuss they were making over the gimmick January had figured that would be far enough down the ladder to keep him out of things.

Now he wasn't so sure. Tibbets was dead. He lit another cigarette, found his hand shaking. The Camel tasted bitter. He threw it over the fence at a receding armband and regretted it instantly. A waste. He went back inside.

Before climbing onto his bunk he got a paperback out of his footlocker. "Hey, Professor, what you reading now?" Fitch said, grinning.

January showed him the blue cover. *Winter's Tales,* by an Isak Dinesen. Fitch examined the little wartime edition. "Pretty racy, eh?"

"You bet," January said heavily. "This guy puts sex on every page." He climbed onto his bunk, opened the book. The stories were strange, hard to follow. The voices below bothered him. He concentrated harder.

As a boy on the farm in Arkansas, January had read everything he could lay his hands on. On Saturday afternoons he would race his father down the muddy lane to the mailbox (his father was a reader too), grab *The Saturday Evening Post,* and run off to devour every word of it. That meant he had another week with nothing new to read, but he couldn't help it. It was a way off the farm, a way into the world. He had become a man who could slip between the covers of a book whenever he chose.

But not on this night.

The next day the chaplain gave a memorial service, and on the morning after that Colonel Scholes looked in the door of their hut right after mess. "Briefing at eleven," he announced. His face was haggard. "Be there early." He looked at Fitch with bloodshot eyes, crooked a finger. "Fitch, January, Matthews—come with me."

January put on his shoes. The rest of the men sat on their bunks and watched them wordlessly. January followed Fitch and Matthews out of the hut.

"I've spent most of the night on the radio with General LeMay," Scholes said. He looked them each in the eye. "We've decided you're to be the first crew to make a strike."

Fitch was nodding, as if he had expected it.

"Think you can do it?" Scholes said.

"Of course," Fitch replied. Watching him, January understood why they had chosen him to replace Tibbets. Fitch was like the old bull, he had that same ruthlessness. The young bull.

"Yes sir," Matthews said.

Scholes was looking at him. "Sure," January said, not wanting to think about it. "Sure." His heart was pounding directly on his sternum. But Fitch and Matthews looked serious as owls, so he wasn't going to stick out by looking odd. It was big news, after all; anyone would be taken aback by it. Nevertheless, January made an effort to nod.

"Okay," Scholes said. "McDonald will be flying with you as copilot." Fitch frowned. "I've got to go tell those British officers that LeMay doesn't want them on the strike with you. See you at the briefing."

"Yes sir."

As soon as Scholes was around the corner Fitch swung a fist at the sky. "Yow!" Matthews cried. He and Fitch shook hands. "We did it!" Matthews took January's hand and wrung it, his face plastered with a goofy grin. "We did it!"

"Somebody did it, anyway," January said.

"Ah, Frank," Matthews said. "Show some spunk. You're always so cool."

"Old Professor Stoneface," Fitch said, glancing at January with a trace of amused contempt. "Come on, let's get to the briefing."

The briefing hut, one of the longer Quonsets, was completely surrounded by MPs holding carbines. "Gosh," Matthews said, subdued by the sight. Inside, it was already smoky. The walls were covered by the usual maps of Japan. Two blackboards at the front were draped with sheets. Captain Shepard, the naval officer who worked with the scientists on the gimmick, was in back with his assistant Lieutenant Stone, winding a reel of film onto a projector. Dr. Nelson, the group psychiatrist, was already seated on a front bench near the wall. Tibbets had recently sicced the psychiatrist on the group—another one of his great ideas, like the spies in the bar. The man's questions had struck January as stupid. He hadn't even been able to figure out that Easterly was a flake, something that was clear to anybody who flew with him or even played him in a single round of poker. January slid onto a bench beside his mates.

The two Brits entered, looking furious in their stiff-upper-lip way. They sat on the bench behind January. Sweeney's and Easterly's crews filed in, followed by the other men, and soon the room was full. Fitch and the rest pulled out Lucky Strikes and lit up; since they had named the plane only January had stuck with Camels.

Scholes came in with several men January didn't recognize, and went to the front. The chatter died, and all the smoke plumes ribboned steadily into the air.

Scholes nodded, and two intelligence officers took the sheets off the blackboards, revealing aerial reconnaissance photos.

"Men," Scholes said, "these are the target cities."

Someone cleared his throat.

"In order of priority they are Hiroshima, Kokura, and Nagasaki. There will be three weather scouts—*Straight Flush* to Hiroshima, *Strange Cargo* to Kokura, and *Full House* to Nagasaki. *The Great Artiste* and *Number 91* will be accompanying the mission to take photos. And *Lucky Strike* will fly the bomb."

There were rustles, coughs. Men turned to look at January and his mates, and they all sat up straight. Sweeney stretched back to shake Fitch's hand, and there were some quick laughs. Fitch grinned.

"Now listen up," Scholes went on. "The weapon we are going to deliver was successfully tested stateside a couple weeks ago. And now we've got orders to drop it on the enemy." He paused to let that sink in. "I'll let Captain Shepard tell you more."

Shepard walked to the blackboard slowly, savoring his entrance. His forehead was shiny with sweat, and January realized he was excited or nervous. He wondered what the psychiatrist would make of that.

"I'm going to come right to the point," Shepard said. "The bomb you are going to drop is something new in history. We think it will knock out everything within four miles."

Now the room was completely still. January noticed that he could see a great deal of his nose, eyebrows, and cheeks; it was as if he were receding back into his body, like a fox into its hole. He kept his gaze rigidly on Shepard, steadfastly ignoring the feeling. Shepard pulled a sheet back over a blackboard while someone else turned down the lights.

"This is a film of the only test we have made," Shepard said. The film started, caught, started again. A wavery cone of bright cigarette smoke speared the length of the room, and on the sheet sprang a dead gray landscape—a lot of sky, a smooth desert floor, hills in the distance. The projector went *click-click-click-click, click-click-click-click.* "The bomb is on top of the tower," Shepard said, and January focused on the pinlike object sticking out of the desert floor, off against the hills. It was between eight and ten miles from the camera, he judged; he had gotten good at calculating distances. He was still distracted by his face.

Click-click-click-click, click—then the screen went white for a second, filling even their room with light. When the picture returned the desert floor was filled with a white bloom of fire. The fireball coalesced, and then quite suddenly it leaped off the earth all the way into the *stratosphere,* by God, like a tracer bullet leaving a machine gun, trailing a whitish pillar of smoke behind it. The pillar gushed up, and a growing ball of smoke billowed outward, capping the pillar. January calculated the size of the cloud but was sure he got it wrong. There it stood. The picture flickered, and then the screen went white again, as if the camera had melted or that part of the world had come apart. But the flapping from the projector told them it was the end of the film.

January felt the air suck in and out of his open mouth. The lights came on in the smoky room, and for a second he panicked. He struggled to shove his features into an accepted pattern—the psychiatrist would be looking around at them all—and then he glanced around and realized he needn't have worried, that he wasn't alone. Faces were bloodless, eyes were blinky or bugged out with shock, mouths hung open or were clamped whitely shut. For a few moments they all had to acknowledge what they were doing. January, scaring himself, felt an urge to say, "Play it again, will you?" Fitch was pulling his curled black hair off his thug's forehead uneasily. Beyond him January saw that one of the Limeys had already reconsidered how mad he was about missing the flight. Now he looked sick. Someone let out a long *whew,* another whistled. January looked to the front again, where Dr. Nelson watched them, undisturbed.

Shepard said, "It's big, all right. And no one knows what will happen when it's dropped from the air. But the mushroom cloud you saw will go to at least thirty thousand feet, probably sixty. And the flash you saw at the beginning was hotter than the sun."

Hotter than the sun. More licked lips, hard swallows, readjusted baseball caps. One of the intelligence officers passed out tinted goggles like welder's glasses. January took his and twiddled the opacity dial.

Scholes said, "You're the hottest thing in the armed forces, now. So no talking, even among yourselves." He took a deep breath. "Let's do it the way Colonel Tibbets would have wanted us to. He picked every one of you because you were the best, and now's the time to show he was right. So—so let's make the old man proud."

The briefing was over. Men filed out into the sudden sunlight. Into the heat and glare. Captain Shepard approached Fitch. "Stone and I will be flying with you to take care of the bomb," he said.

Fitch nodded. "Do you know how many strikes we'll fly?"

"As many as it takes to make them quit." Shepard stared hard at all of them. "But it will only take one."

War breeds strange dreams. That night, January writhed over his sheets in the hot, wet, vegetable night, in that frightening half-sleep when you sometimes know you are dreaming but can do nothing about it, and he dreamed he was walking…

…walking through the streets when suddenly the sun swoops down, the sun touches down and everything is instantly darkness and smoke and silence, a deaf roaring. Walls of fire. His head hurts and in the middle of his vision is a blue-white blur as if God's camera went off in his face. Ah—the sun fell, he thinks. His arm is burned. Blinking is painful. People stumbling by, mouths open, horribly burned—

He is a priest, he can feel the clerical collar, and the wounded ask him for help. He points to his ears, tries to touch them but can't. Pall of black smoke over everything, the city has fallen into the streets. Ah, it's the end of the world. In a park he finds shade and cleared ground. People crouch under bushes like animals. Where the park meets the river, red and black figures crowd into steaming water. A figure gestures from a copse of bamboo. He enters it, finds five or six faceless soldiers huddling. Their eyes have melted, their mouths are holes. Deafness spares him their words. The sighted soldier mimes drinking. The soldiers are thirsty. He nods and goes to the river in search of a container. Bodies float downstream.

Hours pass as he hunts fruitlessly for a bucket. He pulls people from the rubble. He hears a bird screeching, and he realizes that his deafness is the roar of the city burning, a roar like the blood in his ears, but he is not deaf; he only thought he was because there are no human cries. The people are suffering in silence. Through the dusky night he stumbles back to the river, pain crashing through his head. In a field, men are pulling potatoes out of the ground that have been baked well enough to eat. He shares one with them. At the river everyone is dead—

—and he struggled out of the nightmare drenched in rank sweat, the taste of dirt in his mouth, his stomach knotted with horror. He sat up, and the wet, rough sheet clung to his skin. His heart felt crushed between lungs desperate for air. The flowery rotting-jungle smell filled him, and images from the dream flashed before him so vividly that in the dim hut he saw nothing else. He grabbed his cigarettes and jumped off the bunk, hurried out into the compound. Trembling, he lit up, started pacing around. For a moment he worried that the idiot psychiatrist might see him, but then he dismissed the idea. Nelson would be asleep. They were all asleep. He shook his head, looked down at his right arm, and almost dropped his cigarette—but it was just his stove scar, an old scar. He'd had it most of his life, since the day he'd pulled the frypan off the stove and onto his arm, burning it with oil. He could still remember the round O of fear that his mother's mouth had made as she rushed in to see what was wrong. Just an old burn scar, he thought, let's not go overboard here. He pulled his sleeve down.

For the rest of the night he tried to walk it off, cigarette after cigarette. The dome of the sky lightened until all the compound and the jungle beyond it was visible. He was forced by the light of day to walk back into his hut and lie down as if nothing had happened.

Two days later Scholes ordered them to take one of LeMay's men over Rota for a test run. This new lieutenant colonel ordered Fitch not to play with the engines on takeoff. They flew a perfect run, January put the dummy gimmick right on the aiming point, and Fitch powered the plane down into the violent bank that started their 150-degree turn and flight for safety. Back on Tinian the lieutenant colonel congratulated them and shook each of their hands. January smiled with the rest, palms cool, heart steady. It was as if his body were a shell, something he could manipulate from without, like a bombsight. He ate well, he chatted as much as he ever had, and when the psychiatrist ran him to earth for some questions, he was friendly and seemed open.

"Hello, Doc."

"How do you feel about all this, Frank?"

"Just like I always have, sir. Fine."

"Eating well?"

"Better than ever."

"Sleeping well?"

"As well as I can in this humidity. I got used to Utah, I'm afraid." Dr. Nelson laughed. Actually January had hardly slept since his dream. He was afraid of sleep. Couldn't the man see that?

"And how do you feel about being part of the crew chosen to make the first strike?"

"Well, it was the right choice, I reckon. We're the b— the best crew left."

"Do you feel sorry about Tibbets's crew's accident?"

"Yes sir, I do." You better believe it.

After the jokes that ended the interview, January walked out into the blaze of the tropical noon and lit a cigarette. He allowed himself to feel how much he despised the psychiatrist and his blind profession at the same time he was waving good-bye to the man. Ounce brain. Why couldn't he have seen? Whatever happened it would be his fault... With a rush of smoke out of him January realized how painfully easy it was to fool someone if you wanted to. All action was no more than a mask that could be perfectly manipulated from somewhere else. And all the while in that somewhere else, January lived in a *click-click-click* of film, in the silent roaring of a dream, struggling against images he couldn't dispel. The heat of the tropical sun—ninety-three million miles away, wasn't it?—pulsed painfully on the back of his neck.

As he watched the psychiatrist collar their tail gunner, Kochenski, he thought of walking up to the man and saying *I quit.* I don't want to do this. In imagination he saw the look that would form in the man's eye, in Fitch's eye, in Tibbets's eye, and his mind recoiled from the idea. He felt too much contempt for them. He wouldn't for anything give them a means to despise him, a reason to call him coward. Stubbornly he banished the whole complex of thought. Easier to go along with it.

And so a couple of disjointed days later, just after midnight of August 9, he found himself preparing for the strike. Around him Fitch and Matthews and Haddock were doing the same. How odd were the everyday motions of getting dressed when you were off to demolish a city! January found himself examining his hands, his boots, the cracks in the linoleum. He put on his survival vest, checked the pockets abstractedly for fishhooks, water kit, first-aid package, emergency rations. Then the parachute harness, and his coveralls over it all. Tying his bootlaces took minutes; he couldn't do it when watching his fingers so closely.

"Come on, Professor!" Fitch's voice was tight. "The big day is here." He followed the others into the night. A cool wind was blowing. The chaplain said a prayer for them. They took jeeps down Broadway to runway Able. *Lucky Strike* stood in a circle of spotlights and men, half of them with cameras, the rest with reporters' pads. They surrounded the crew; it reminded January of a Hollywood premiere. Eventually he escaped up the hatch and into the plane. Others followed. Half an hour passed before Fitch joined them, grinning like a movie star. They started the engines, and January was thankful for their vibrating, thought-smothering roar. They taxied away from the Hollywood scene, and January felt relief for a moment, until he remembered where they were going. On runway Able the engines pitched up to their twenty-three-hundred-RPM whine, and looking out the clear windscreen, he saw the runway paint marks move by ever faster. Fitch kept them on the runway till Tinian had run out from under them, then quickly pulled up. They were on their way.

When they got to altitude, January climbed past Fitch and McDonald to the bombardier's seat and placed his parachute on it. He leaned back. The roar of the four engines packed around him like cotton batting. He was on the flight, nothing to be done about it now. The heavy vibration was a comfort, he liked the feel of it there in the nose of the plane. A drowsy, sad acceptance hummed through him.

Against his closed eyelids flashed a black eyeless face, and he jerked awake, heart racing. He was on the flight, no way out. Now he realized how easy it would have been to get out of it. He could have just said he didn't want to. The simplicity of it appalled him. Who gave a damn what the shrink or Tibbets or anyone else thought, compared to this? Now there was no way out. It was a comfort, in a way. Now he could stop worrying, stop thinking he had any choice.

Sitting there with his knees bracketing the bombsight, January dozed, and as he dozed he daydreamed his way out. He could climb the step to Fitch and McDonald and declare he had been secretly promoted to major and ordered to redirect the mission. They were to go to Tokyo and drop the bomb in the bay. The Jap War Cabinet had been told to watch this demonstration of the new weapon, and when they saw that fireball boil the bay and bounce into heaven they'd run and sign surrender papers as fast as they could write, kamikazes or not. They weren't crazy, after all. No need to murder a whole city. It was such a good plan that the generals were no doubt changing the mission at this very minute, desperately radioing their instructions to Tinian, only to find out it was too late…so that when they returned to Tinian, January would become a hero for guessing what the generals really wanted and for risking all to do it. It would be like one of the Hornblower stories he had read in *The Saturday Evening Post.*

Once again January jerked awake. The drowsy pleasure of the fantasy was replaced with desperate scorn. There wasn't a chance in hell that he could convince Fitch and the rest that he had secret orders superseding theirs. And he couldn't go up there and wave his pistol around and *order* them to drop the bomb in Tokyo Bay, because he was the one who had to actually drop it, and he couldn't be down in front dropping the bomb and up ordering the others around at the same time. Pipe dreams.

Time swept on, slow as a second hand. January's thoughts, however, matched the spin of the props; desperately they cast about, now this way now that, like an animal caught by the leg in a trap. The crew was silent. The clouds below were a white scree on the black ocean. January's knee vibrated against the bombsight. He was the one who had to drop the bomb. No matter where his thoughts lunged, they were brought up short by that. He was the one, not Fitch or the crew, not LeMay, not the generals and scientists back home, not Truman and his advisors. Truman—suddenly January hated him. Roosevelt would have done it differently. If only Roosevelt had lived! The grief that had filled January when he learned of Roosevelt's death reverberated through him more strongly than ever. It was unfair to have worked so hard and then not see the war's end. And FDR would have ended it differently. Back at the start of it all he had declared that civilian centers were never to be bombed, and if he had lived, if, if, if. But he hadn't. And now it was smiling bastard Harry Truman, ordering *him,* Frank January, to drop the sun on two hundred thousand women and children. Once his father had taken him to see the Browns play before twenty thousand, a giant crowd—"I never voted for you," January whispered viciously and jerked to realize he had spoken aloud. Luckily his microphone was off. And Roosevelt would have done it differently, he *would have.*

The bombsight rose before him, spearing the black sky and blocking some of the hundreds of little cruciform stars. *Lucky Strike* ground on toward Iwo Jima, minute by minute flying four miles closer to their target. January leaned forward and put his face in the cool headrest of the bombsight, hoping that its grasp might hold his thoughts as well as his forehead. It worked surprisingly well.

His earphones crackled and he sat up. "Captain January." It was Shepard. "We're going to arm the bomb now, want to watch?"

"Sure thing." He shook his head, surprised at his own duplicity. Stepping up between the pilots, he moved stiffly to the roomy cabin behind the cockpit. Matthews was at his desk taking a navigational fix on the radio signals from Iwo Jima and Okinawa, and Haddock stood beside him. At the back of the compartment was a small circular hatch, below the larger tunnel leading to the rear of the plane. January opened it, sat down, and swung himself feet first through the hole.

The bomb bay was unheated, and the cold air felt good. He stood facing the bomb. Stone was sitting on the floor of the bay; Shepard was laid out under the bomb, reaching into it. On a rubber pad next to Stone were tools, plates, several cylindrical blocks. Shepard pulled back, sat up, sucked a scraped knuckle. He shook his head ruefully. "I don't dare wear gloves with this one."

"I'd be just as happy myself if you didn't let something slip," January joked nervously. The two men laughed.

"Nothing can blow till I change those wires," Stone said.

"Give me the wrench," Shepard said. Stone handed it to him, and he stretched under the bomb again. After some awkward wrenching inside it he lifted out a cylindrical plug. "Breech plug," he said, and set it on the mat.

January found his skin goose-pimpling in the cold air. Stone handed Shepard one of the blocks. Shepard extended under the bomb again. Watching them, January was reminded of auto mechanics on the oily floor of a garage, working under a car. He had spent a few years doing that himself, after his family moved to Vicksburg. Hiroshima was a river town. One time a flatbed truck carrying bags of cement powder down Fourth Street hill had lost its brakes and careened into the intersection with River Road, where, despite the driver's efforts to turn, it smashed into a passing car. Frank had been out in the yard playing and heard the crash and saw the cement dust rising. He had been one of the first there. The woman and child in the passenger seat of the Model T had been killed. The woman driving was okay. They were from Chicago. A group of folks subdued the driver of the truck, who kept trying to help at the Model T, though he had a bad cut on his head and was covered with white dust.

"Okay, let's tighten the breech plug." Stone gave Shepard the wrench. "Sixteen turns exactly," Shepard said. He was sweating even in the bay's chill, and he paused to wipe his forehead. "Let's hope we don't get hit by lightning." He put the wrench down, shifted onto his knees, and picked up a circular plate. Hubcap, January thought. Stone connected wires, then helped Shepard install two more plates. Good old American know-how, January thought, goose pimples rippling across his skin like cat's-paws over water. There was Shepard, a scientist, putting together a bomb like he was an auto mechanic changing oil. January felt a tight rush of rage at the scientists who had designed the bomb. They had worked on it for over a year. Had none of them in all that time ever stopped to think what they were doing?

But none of them had to drop it. January turned to hide his face from Shepard, stepped down the bay. The bomb looked like a big long trash can, with fins at one end and little antennae at the other. Just a bomb, he thought, damn it, it's just another bomb.

Shepard stood and patted the bomb gently. "We've got a live one now." Never a thought about what it would do. January hurried by the man, afraid that hatred would crack his shell and give him away. The pistol strapped to his belt caught on the hatchway, and he imagined shooting Shepard—shooting Fitch and McDonald and plunging the controls forward so that *Lucky Strike* tilted and spun down into the sea like a spent tracer bullet, like a plane broken by flak, following the arc of all human ambition. Nobody would ever know what had happened to them, and their trash can would be dumped to the bottom of the Pacific. He could even shoot everyone, parachute out, and perhaps be rescued by one of the Superdumbos following them...

The thought passed, and remembering it January squinted with disgust. But another part of him agreed that it was a possibility. It could be done. It would solve his problem.

"Want some coffee?" Matthews asked.

"Sure," January said, and took a cup. He sipped—hot. He watched Matthews and Benton tune the loran equipment. As the beeps came in, Matthews took a straightedge and drew lines from Okinawa and Iwo Jima. He tapped a finger on the intersection. "They've taken the art out of navigation," he said to January. "They might as well stop making the navigator's dome," thumbing up at the little Plexiglas bubble over them.

"Good old American know-how," January said.

Matthews nodded. With two fingers he measured the distance between their position and Iwo Jima. Benton measured with a ruler.

"Rendezvous at five thirty-five, eh?" Matthews said. They were to rendezvous with the two trailing planes over Iwo.

Benton disagreed. "I'd say five-fifty."

"What? Check again, guy, we're not in no tugboat here."

"The wind—"

"Yeah, the wind. Frank, you want to add a bet to the pool?"

"Five thirty-six," January said promptly.

They laughed. "See, he's got more confidence in me," Matthews said with a dopey grin.

January recalled his plan to shoot the crew and tip the plane into the sea, and he pursed his lips, repelled. Not for anything would he be able to shoot these men, who, if not friends, were at least companions. They passed for friends. They meant no harm.

Shepard and Stone climbed into the cabin. Matthews offered them coffee. "The gimmick's ready to kick their ass, eh?" Shepard nodded and drank.

January moved forward, past Haddock's console. Another plan that wouldn't work. What to do? All the flight engineer's dials and gauges showed conditions were normal. Maybe he could sabotage something? Cut a line somewhere?

Fitch looked back at him and said, "When are we due over Iwo?"

"Five forty, Matthews says."

"He better be right."

A thug. In peacetime Fitch would be hanging around a pool table giving the cops trouble. He was perfect for war. Tibbets had chosen his men well—most of them, anyway. Moving back past Haddock, January stopped to stare at the group of men in the navigation cabin. They joked, drank coffee. They were all a bit like Fitch—young toughs, capable and thoughtless. They were having a good time, an adventure. That was January's dominant impression of his companions in the 509th; despite all the bitching and the occasional moments of overmastering fear, they were having a good time. His mind spun forward, and he saw what these young men would grow up to be like as clearly as if they stood before him in businessmen's suits, prosperous and balding. They would be tough and capable and thoughtless, and as the years passed and the great war receded in time they would look back on it with ever-increasing nostalgia, for they would be the survivors and not the dead. Every year of this war would feel like ten in their memories, so that the war would always remain the central experience of their lives—a time when history lay palpable in their hands, when each of their daily acts affected it, when moral issues were simple, and others told them what to do—so that as more years passed and the survivors aged, bodies falling apart, lives in one rut or another, they would unconsciously push harder and harder to thrust the world into war again, thinking somewhere inside themselves that if they could only return to world war then they would magically be again as they were in the last one—young and free and happy. And by that time they would hold the positions of power, they would be capable of doing it.

So there would be more wars, January saw. He heard it in Matthews's laughter, saw it in their excited eyes. "There's Iwo, and it's five thirty-one. Pay up! I win!" And in future wars they'd have more bombs like the gimmick, hundreds of them no doubt. He saw more planes, more young crews like this one, flying to Moscow, no doubt, or to wherever, fireballs in every capital. Why not? And to what end? To what end? So that the old men could hope to become magically young again. Nothing more sane than that. It made January sick.

They were over Iwo Jima. Three more hours to Japan. Voices from *The Great Artiste* and *Number 91* crackled on the radio. Rendezvous accomplished, the three planes flew northwest, toward Shikoku, the first Japanese island in their path. January maneuvered down into the nose. "Good shooting," Matthews called after him.

Forward it seemed quieter. January got settled, put his headphones on, and leaned forward to look out the ribbed Plexiglas.

Dawn had turned the whole vault of the sky pink. Slowly the radiant shade shifted through lavender to blue, pulse by pulse a different color. The ocean below was a glittering blue plane, marbled by a pattern of puffy pink cloud. The sky above was a vast dome, darker above than on the horizon. January had always thought that dawn was the time when you could see most clearly how big the earth was and how high above it they flew. It seemed they flew at the very upper edge of the atmosphere, and January saw how thin it was, how it was just a skin of air really, so that even if you flew up to its top the earth still extended away infinitely in every direction. The coffee had warmed January, he was sweating. Sunlight blinked off the Plexiglas. His watch said six. Plane and hemisphere of blue were split down the middle by the bombsight. His earphones crackled, and he listened in to the reports from the lead planes flying over the target cities. Kokura, Nagasaki, Hiroshima, all of them had six-tenths cloud cover. Maybe they would have to cancel the whole mission because of weather. "We'll look at Hiroshima first," Fitch said. January peered down at the fields of miniature clouds with renewed interest. His parachute slipped under him. Readjusting it, he imagined putting it on, sneaking back to the central escape hatch under the navigator's cabin, opening the hatch... He could be out of the plane and gone before anyone noticed. They could bomb or not but it wouldn't be January's doing. He could float down onto the world like a puff of dandelion, feel cool air rush around him, watch the silk canopy dome hang over him like a miniature sky, a private world.

An eyeless black face. January shuddered; it was as though the nightmare could return any time. If he jumped nothing would change, the bomb would still fall—would he feel any better, floating on his Inland Sea? Sure, one part of him shouted; maybe, another conceded; the rest of him saw that face...

Earphones crackled. Shepard said, "Lieutenant Stone has now armed the bomb, and I can now tell you all what we are carrying. Aboard with us is the world's first atomic bomb."

Not exactly, January thought. Whistles squeaked in his earphones. The first one went off in New Mexico. Splitting atoms. January had heard the term before. Tremendous energy in every atom, Einstein had said. Break one, and—he had seen the result on film. Shepard was talking about radiation, which brought back more to January. Energy released in the form of X rays. Killed by X rays! It would be against the Geneva Convention if they had thought of it.

Fitch cut in. "When the bomb is dropped Lieutenant Benton will record our reaction to what we see. This recording is being made for history, so watch your language." Watch your language! January choked back a laugh. Don't curse or blaspheme God at the sight of the first atomic bomb incinerating a city with X rays!

Six-twenty. January found his hands clenched together on the headrest of the bombsight. He felt as if he had a fever. In the harsh wash of morning light the skin on the backs of his hands appeared slightly translucent. The whorls in the skin looked like the delicate patterning of waves on the sea's surface. His hands were made of atoms. Atoms were the smallest building blocks of matter. It took billions of them to make those tense, trembling hands. Split one atom and you had the fireball. That meant that the energy contained in even one hand... He turned up a palm to look at the lines and the mottled flesh under the transparent skin. A person was a bomb that could blow up the world. January felt that latent power stir in him, pulsing with every hard heart knock. What beings they were, and in what a blue expanse of a world! And here they spun on to drop a bomb and kill a hundred thousand of these astonishing beings.

When a fox or raccoon is caught by the leg in a trap, it lunges until the leg is frayed, twisted, perhaps broken, and only then does the animal's pain and exhaustion force it to quit. Now in the same way January wanted to quit. His mind hurt. His plans to escape were so much crap—stupid, useless. Better to quit. He tried to stop thinking, but it was hopeless. How could he stop? As long as he was conscious he would be thinking. The mind struggles longer than any fox.

Lucky Strike tilted up and began the long climb to bombing altitude. On the horizon the clouds lay over a green island. Japan. Surely it had gotten hotter. The heater must be broken, he thought. Don't think. Every few minutes Matthews gave Fitch small course adjustments.

"Two seventy-five, now. That's it." To escape the moment, January recalled his childhood. Following a mule and plow. Moving to Vicksburg (rivers). For a while there in Vicksburg, since his stutter made it hard to gain friends, he had played a game with himself. He had passed the time by imagining that everything he did was vitally important and determined the fate of the world. If he crossed a road in front of a certain car, for instance, then the car wouldn't make it through the next intersection before a truck hit it, and so the man driving would be killed and wouldn't be able to invent the flying boat that would save President Wilson from kidnappers, so he had to wait for that car, oh damn it, he thought, damn it, think of something *different.* The last Hornblower story he had read—how would *he* get out of this? The round O of his mother's face as she ran in and saw his arm—The Mississippi, mud-brown behind its levee—Abruptly he shook his head, face twisted in frustration and despair, aware at last that no possible avenue of memory would serve as an escape for him now; for now there was no part of his life that did not apply to the situation he was in, and no matter where he cast his mind it was going to shore up against the hour facing him.

Less than an hour. They were at thirty thousand feet, bombing altitude. Fitch gave him altimeter readings to dial into the bombsight. Matthews gave him wind speeds. Sweat got in his eye and he blinked furiously. The sun rose behind them like an atomic bomb, glinting off every corner and edge of the Plexiglas, illuminating his bubble compartment with a fierce glare. Broken plans jumbled together in his mind, his breath was short, his throat dry. Uselessly and repeatedly he damned the scientists, damned Truman. Damned the Japanese for causing the whole mess in the first place, damned yellow killers, they had brought this on themselves. Remember Pearl. American men had died under bombs when no war had been declared; they had started it and now it was coming back to them with a vengeance. And they deserved it. And an invasion of Japan would take years, cost millions of lives. End it now, end it, they deserved it, they deserved it, steaming river full of charcoal people silently dying, damned stubborn race of maniacs!

"There's Honshu," Fitch said, and January returned to the world of the plane. They were over the Inland Sea. Soon they would pass the secondary target, Kokura, a bit to the south. Seven-thirty. The island was draped more heavily than the sea by clouds, and again January's heart leaped with the idea that weather would cancel the mission. But they did deserve it. It was a mission like any other mission. He had dropped bombs on Africa, Sicily, Italy, all Germany... He leaned forward to take a look through the sight. Under the X of the cross hairs was the sea, but at the lead edge of the sight was land. Honshu. At two hundred and thirty miles an hour that gave them about a half hour to Hiroshima. Maybe less. He wondered if his heart could beat so hard for that long.

Fitch said, "Matthews, I'm giving over guidance to you. Just tell us what to do."

"Bear south two degrees," was all Matthews said. At last their voices had taken on a touch of awareness.

"January, are you ready?" Fitch asked.

"I'm just waiting," January said. He sat up so Fitch could see the back of his head. The bombsight stood between his legs. A switch on its side would start the bombing sequence—the bomb would not leave the plane immediately upon the flick of the switch but would drop after a fifteen-second radio tone warned the following planes. The sight was adjusted accordingly.

"Adjust to a heading of two sixty-five," Matthews said. "We're coming in directly upwind." This was to make any side-drift adjustments for the bomb unnecessary. "January, dial it down to two hundred and thirty-one miles per hour."

"Two thirty-one."

Fitch said, "Everyone but January and Matthews, get your goggles on."

January took the darkened goggles from the floor. One needed to protect one's eyes or they might melt. He put them on, put his forehead on the headrest. They were in the way. He took them off. When he looked through the sight again there was land under the cross hairs. He checked his watch. Eight o'clock. Up and reading the papers, drinking tea.

"Ten minutes to AP," Matthews said. The aiming point was Aioi Bridge, a T-shaped bridge in the middle of the delta-straddling city. Easy to recognize.

"There's a lot of cloud down there," Fitch noted. "Are you going to be able to see?"

"I won't be sure until we try it," January said.

"We can make another pass and use radar if we need to," Matthews said.

Fitch said, "Don't drop it unless you're sure, January."

"Yes sir."

Through the sight a grouping of rooftops and gray roads was just visible between broken clouds. Around it green forest. "All right," Matthews exclaimed, "here we go! Keep it right on this heading, Captain! January, we'll stay at two thirty-one."

"And same heading," Fitch said. "January, she's all yours. Everyone be ready for the turn."

January's world contracted to the view through the bombsight. A stippled field of cloud and forest. Over a small range of hills and into Hiroshima's watershed. The broad river was mud brown, the land pale hazy green, the growing network of roads flat gray. Now the tiny rectangular shapes of buildings covered almost all the land, and swimming into the sight came the city proper, narrow islands thrusting into a dark blue bay. Under the cross hairs the city moved island by island, cloud by cloud. January had stopped breathing. His fingers were rigid as stone on the switch. And there was Aioi Bridge. It slid right under the cross hairs, a tiny T right in a gap in the clouds. January's fingers crushed the switch. Deliberately he took a breath, held it. Clouds swam under the cross hairs, then the next island. "Almost there," he said calmly into his microphone. "Steady." Now that he was committed his heart was humming like the Wrights. He counted to ten. Now flowing under the cross hairs were clouds alternating with green forest, leaden roads. "I've turned the switch, but I'm not getting a tone!" he croaked into the mike. His right hand held the switch firmly in place. Behind him Fitch was shouting something; Matthews's voice cracked across it. "Flipping it b-back and forth," January shouted, shielding the bombsight with his body from the eyes of the pilots. "But *still* wait a second—"

He pushed the switch down. A low hum filled his ears. "That's it! It started!"

"But where will it land?" Matthews cried.

"Hold steady!" January shouted.

Lucky Strike shuddered and lofted up ten or twenty feet. January twisted to look down, and there was the bomb, flying just below the plane. Then with a wobble it fell away.

The plane banked right and dove so hard that the centrifugal force threw January against the Plexiglas. Several thousand feet lower, Fitch leveled it out and they hurtled north.

"Do you see anything?" Fitch cried.

From the tail gun Kochenski gasped, "Nothing." January struggled upright. He reached for the welder's goggles, but they were no longer on his head. He couldn't find them. "How long has it been?" he said

"Thirty seconds," Matthews replied.

January shut his eyes.

The blood in his eyelids lit up red, then white.

On the earphones a clutter of voices—"Oh my God. Oh my God." The plane bounced and tumbled, metallically shrieking. January pressed himself off the Plexiglas. "'Nother shock wave!" Kochenski yelled. The plane rocked again. This is it, January thought, end of the world, I guess that solves my problem.

He opened his eyes and found he could still see. The engines still roared, the props spun. "Those were the shock waves from the bomb," Fitch called. "We're okay now. Look at that! Will you look at that son of a bitch go!"

January looked. The cloud layer below had burst apart, and a black column of smoke billowed up from a core of red fire. Already the top of the column was at their height. Exclamations of shock hurt January's ears. He stared at the fiery base of the cloud, at the scores of fires feeding into it. Suddenly he could see past the cloud, and his fingernails cut into his palms. Through a gap in the clouds he saw it clearly, the delta, the six rivers, there off to the left of the tower of smoke—the city of Hiroshima, untouched.

"We missed!" Kochenski yelled. "We missed it!"

January turned to hide his face from the pilots; on it was a grin like a rictus. He sat back in his seat and let the relief fill him.

Then it was back to it. "Goddamn it!" Fitch shouted down at him. McDonald was trying to restrain him. "January, get up here!"

"Yes sir." Now there was a new set of problems.

January stood and turned, legs weak. His right fingertips throbbed painfully. The men were crowded forward to look out the Plexiglas. January looked with them.

The mushroom cloud was forming. It roiled out as if it might continue to extend forever, fed by the inferno and the black stalk below it. It looked about two miles wide and half a mile tall, and it extended well above the height they flew at, dwarfing their plane entirely. "Do you think we'll all be sterile?" Matthews said.

"I can taste the radiation," McDonald declared. "Can you? It tastes like lead."

Bursts of flame shot up into the cloud from below, giving a purplish tint to the stalk. There it stood—lifelike, malignant, sixty thousand feet tall. One bomb. January shoved past the pilots into the navigation cabin, overwhelmed.

"Should I start recording everyone's reactions, Captain?" asked Benton.

"To hell with that," Fitch said, following January back. But Shepard got there first, descending quickly from the navigation dome. He rushed across the cabin, caught January on the shoulder. "You bastard!" he screamed as January stumbled back. "You lost your nerve, coward!"

January went for Shepard, happy to have a target at last, but Fitch cut in and grabbed him by the collar, pulled him around until they were face to face.

"Is that right?" Fitch cried, as angry as Shepard. "Did you screw up on purpose?"

"No," January grunted, and knocked Fitch's hands away from his neck. He swung and smacked Fitch on the mouth, caught him solid. Fitch staggered back, recovered, and no doubt would have beaten January up, but Matthews and Beaton and Stone leaped in and held him back, shouting for order. "Shut up! Shut up!" McDonald screamed from the cockpit, and for a moment it was bedlam. But Fitch let himself be restrained, and soon only McDonald's shouts for quiet were heard. January retreated to between the pilot seats, right hand on his pistol holster.

"The city was in the cross hairs when I flipped the switch," he said. "But the first couple of times I flipped it nothing happened—"

"That's a lie!" Shepard shouted. "There was nothing wrong with the switch, I checked it myself. Besides the bomb exploded *miles* beyond Hiroshima, look for yourself! That's *minutes*." He wiped spit from his chin and pointed at January. "You did it."

"You don't know that," January said. But he could see the men had been convinced by Shepard, and he took a step back. "You just get me to a board of inquiry, quick. And leave me alone till then. If you touch me again," glaring venomously at Fitch and then Shepard, "I'll shoot you." He turned and hopped down to his seat, feeling exposed and vulnerable, like a treed raccoon.

"They'll shoot *you* for this," Shepard screamed after him. "Disobeying orders—treason—" Matthews and Stone were shutting him up.

"Let's get out of here," he heard McDonald say. "I can taste the lead, can't you?"

January looked out the Plexiglas. The giant cloud still burned and roiled. One atom... Well, they had really done it to that forest. He almost laughed but stopped himself, afraid of hysteria. Through a break in the clouds he got a clear view of Hiroshima for the first time. It lay spread over its islands like a map, unharmed. Well, that was that. The inferno at the base of the mushroom cloud was eight or ten miles around the shore of the bay and a mile or two inland. A certain patch of forest would be gone, destroyed—utterly blasted from the face of the earth. The Japs would be able to go out and investigate the damage. And if they were told it was a demonstration, a warning—and if they acted fast—well, they had their chance. Maybe it would work.

The release of tension made January feel sick. Then he recalled Shepard's words, and he knew that whether his plan worked or not he was still in trouble. In trouble! It was worse than that. Bitterly he cursed the Japanese. He even wished for a moment that he *had* dropped it on them. Wearily he let his despair empty him.

A long while later he sat up straight. Once again he was a trapped animal. He began lunging for escape, casting about for plans. One alternative after another. All during the long, grim flight home he considered it, mind spinning at the speed of the props and beyond. And when they came down on Tinian he had a plan. It was a long shot, he reckoned, but it was the best he could do.

The briefing hut was surrounded by MPs again. January stumbled from the truck with the rest and walked inside. He was more than ever aware of the looks given him, and they were hard, accusatory. He was too tired to care. He hadn't slept in more than thirty-six hours and had slept very little since the last time he had been in the hut, a week before. Now the room quivered with the lack of engine vibration to stabilize it, and the silence roared. It was all he could do to hold on to his plan. The glares of Fitch and Shepard, the hurt incomprehension of Matthews, they had to be thrust out of his focus. Thankfully he lit a cigarette.

In a clamor of question and argument the others described the strike. Then the haggard Scholes and an intelligence officer led them through the bombing run. January's plan made it necessary to hold to his story. " ...and when the AP was under the cross hairs I pushed down the switch, but got no signal. I flipped it up and down repeatedly until the tone kicked in. At that point there was still fifteen seconds to the release."

"Was there anything that may have caused the tone to start when it did?"

"Not that I noticed immediately, but—"

"It's impossible," Shepard interrupted, face red. "I checked the switch before we flew and there was nothing wrong with it. Besides, the drop occurred over a minute—"

"Captain Shepard," Scholes said. "We'll hear from you presently."

"But he's obviously lying—"

"Captain Shepard! It's not at all obvious. Don't speak unless questioned."

"Anyway," January said, hoping to shift the questions away from the issue of the long delay, "I noticed something about the bomb when it was falling that could explain why it stuck. I need to discuss it with one of the scientists familiar with the bomb's design."

"What was that?" Scholes asked suspiciously.

January hesitated. "There's going to be an inquiry, right?"

Scholes frowned. "This is the inquiry, Captain January. Tell us what you saw."

"But there will be some proceeding beyond this one?"

"It looks like there's going to be a court-martial, yes, Captain."

"That's what I thought. I don't want to talk to anyone but my counsel, and some scientist familiar with the bomb."

"*I'm* a scientist familiar with the bomb," Shepard burst out. "You could tell me if you really had anything, you—"

"I said I need a scientist!" January exclaimed, rising to face the scarlet Shepard across the table. "Not a g-goddamned mechanic." Shepard started to shout, others joined in, and the room rang with argument. While Scholes restored order January sat down, and he refused to be drawn out again.

"I'll see you're assigned counsel and initiate the court-martial," Scholes said, clearly at a loss. "Meanwhile you are under arrest, on suspicion of disobeying orders in combat." January nodded, and Scholes gave him over to MPs.

"One last thing," January said, fighting exhaustion. "Tell General LeMay that if the Japs are told this drop was a warning, it might have the same effect as—"

"I told you!" Shepard shouted, "I told you he did it on purpose!"

Men around Shepard restrained him. But he had convinced most of them, and even Matthews stared at him with surprised anger.

January shook his head wearily. He had the dull feeling that his plan, while it had succeeded so far, was ultimately not a good one. "Just trying to make the best of it." It took all of his remaining will to force his legs to carry him in a dignified manner out of the hut.

His cell was an empty NCO's office. MPs brought his meals. For the first couple of days he did little but sleep. On the third day he glanced out the office's barred window and saw a tractor pulling a tarpaulin-draped trolley out of the compound, followed by jeeps filled with MPs. It looked like a military funeral. January rushed to the door and banged on it until one of the young MPS came.

"What's that they're doing out there?" January demanded.

Eyes cold and mouth twisted, the MP said, "They're making another strike. They're going to do it right this time."

"No!" January cried, "No!" He rushed the MP, who knocked him back and locked the door. 'No!" He beat the door until his hands hurt, cursing wildly. "You don't *need* to do it, it isn't *necessary*." Shell shattered at last, he collapsed on the bed and wept. Now everything he had done would be rendered meaningless. He had sacrificed himself for nothing.

A day or two after that the MPs led in a colonel, an iron-haired man who stood stiffly and crushed January's hand when he shook it. His eyes were a pale icy blue.

"I am Colonel Dray," he said. "I have been ordered to defend you in court-martial." January could feel the dislike pouring from the man. "To do that I'm going to need every fact you have, so let's get started."

"I'm not talking to anybody until I've seen an atomic scientist."

"I am your *defense* counsel—"

"I don't care who you are," January said. "Your defense of me depends on you getting one of the scientists *here*. The higher up he is, the better. And I want to speak to him alone."

"I will have to be present."

So he would do it. But now January's counsel, too, was an enemy.

"Naturally," January said. "You're my counsel. But no one else. Our atomic secrecy may depend on it."

"You saw evidence of sabotage?"

"Not one word more until that scientist is here."

Angrily the colonel nodded and left.

Late the next day the colonel returned with another man. "This is Dr. Forest."

"I helped develop the bomb," Forest said. He had a crew cut and was dressed in fatigues, and to January he looked more Army than the colonel. Suspiciously he stared back and forth at the two men.

"You'll vouch for this man's identity on your word as an officer?" he asked Dray.

"Of course," the colonel said stiffly, offended.

"So," Dr. Forest said. "You had some trouble getting it off when you wanted to. Tell me what you saw."

"I saw nothing," January said harshly. He took a deep breath; it was time to commit himself. "I want you to take a message back to the scientists. You folks have been working on this thing for years, and you must have had time to consider how the bomb should have been used. You know we could have convinced the Japs to surrender by showing them a demonstration—"

"Wait a minute," Forest said. "You're saying you didn't see anything? There wasn't a malfunction?"

"That's right," January said, and cleared his throat. "It wasn't *necessary*, do you understand?"

Forest was looking at Colonel Dray. Dray gave him a disgusted shrug. "He told me he saw evidence of sabotage."

"I want you to go back and ask the scientists to intercede for me," January said, raising his voice to get the man's attention. "I haven't got a chance in that court-martial. But if the scientists defend me then maybe they'll let me live, see? I don't want to get shot for doing something every one of you scientists would have done."

Dr. Forest had backed away. Color rising, he said, "What makes you think that's what we would have done? Don't you think we considered it? Don't you think men better qualified than you made the decision?" He waved a hand. "Goddamn it—what made you think you were competent to decide something as important as that!"

January was appalled at the man's reaction; in his plan it had gone differently. Angrily he jabbed a finger at Forest. "Because *I* was the man doing it, *Doctor* Forest. You take even one step back from that and suddenly you can pretend it's not your doing. Fine for you, but *I was there.*"

At every word the man's color was rising. It looked like he might pop a vein in his neck. January tried once more. "Have you ever tried to imagine what one of your bombs would do to a city full of people?"

"I've had enough!" the man exploded. He turned to Dray. "I'm under no obligation to keep what I've heard here confidential. You can be sure it will be used as evidence in Captain January's court-martial." He turned and gave January a look of such blazing hatred that January understood it. For these men to admit he was right would mean admitting that they were wrong—that every one of them was responsible for his part in the construction of the weapon January had refused to use. Understanding that, January knew he was doomed.

The bang of Dr. Forest's departure still shook the little office. January sat on his cot, got out a smoke. Under Colonel Dray's cold gaze he lit one shakily, took a drag. He looked up at the colonel, shrugged. "It was my best chance," he explained. That did something—for the first and only time the cold disdain in the colonel's eyes shifted, to a little, hard, lawyerly gleam of respect.

The court-martial lasted two days. The verdict was guilty of disobeying orders in combat and of giving aid and comfort to the enemy. The sentence was death by firing squad.

For most of his remaining days January rarely spoke, drawing ever further behind the mask that had hidden him for so long. A clergyman came to see him, but it was the 509th's chaplain, the one who had said the prayer blessing the *Lucky Strike's* mission before they took off. Angrily January sent him packing.

Later, however, a young Catholic priest dropped by. His name was Patrick Getty. He was a little pudgy man, bespectacled and, it seemed, somewhat afraid of January. January let the man talk to him. When he returned the next day January talked back a bit, and on the day after that he talked some more. It became a habit. Usually January talked about his childhood. He talked of plowing mucky black bottomland behind a mule. Of running down the lane to the mailbox. Of reading books by the light of the moon after he had been ordered to sleep. And of being beaten by his mother for it with a high-heeled shoe. He told the priest the story of the time his arm had been burned, and about the car crash at the bottom of Fourth Street. "It's the truck driver's face I remember, do you see, Father?"

"Yes," the young priest said. "Yes."

And he told him about the game he had played in which every action he took tipped the balance of world affairs. "When I remembered that game I thought it was dumb. Step on a sidewalk crack and cause an earthquake—you know, it's stupid. Kids are like that." The priest nodded. "But now I've been thinking that if everybody were to live their whole lives like that, thinking that every move they made really was important, then...it might make a difference." He waved a hand vaguely, expelled cigarette smoke. "You're accountable for what you do."

"Yes," the priest said. "Yes, you are."

"And if you're given orders to do something wrong, you're still accountable, right? The orders don't change it."

"That's right."

"Hmph." January smoked a while. "So they say, anyway. But look what happens." He waved at the office. "I'm like the guy in a story I read—he thought everything in books was true, and after reading a bunch of westerns he tried to rob a train. They tossed him in jail." He laughed shortly. "Books are full of crap."

"Not all of them," the priest said. "Besides, you weren't trying to rob a train."

They laughed at the notion. "Did you read that story?"

"No."

"It was the strangest book—there were two stories in it, and they alternated chapter by chapter, but they didn't have a thing to do with each other! I didn't get it."

"Maybe the writer was trying to say that everything connects to everything else."

"Maybe. But it's a funny way to say it."

"I like it."

And so they passed the time, talking.

So it was the priest who was the one to come by and tell January that his request for a presidential pardon had been refused. Getty said awkwardly, "It seems the President approves the sentence."

"That bastard," January said weakly. He sat on his cot.

Time passed. It was another hot, humid day.

"Well," the priest said. "Let me give you some better news. Given your situation I don't think telling you matters, though I've been told not to. The second mission—you know there was a second strike?"

"Yes."

"Well, they missed too."

"What?" January cried, and bounced to his feet. "You're kidding!"

"No. They flew to Kokura but found it covered by clouds. It was the same over Nagasaki and Hiroshima, so they flew back to Kokura and tried to drop the bomb using radar to guide it, but apparently there was a...a genuine equipment failure this time, and the bomb fell on an island."

January was hopping up and down, mouth hanging open, "So we n-never—"

"We never dropped an atom bomb on a Japanese city. That's right."
Getty grinned. "And get this—I heard this from my superior—they sent
a message to the Japanese Government telling them that the two explosions were warnings, and that if they didn't surrender by September 1
we would drop bombs on Kyoto and Tokyo, and then wherever else we
had to. Word is that the Emperor went to Hiroshima to survey the damage, and when he saw it he ordered the Cabinet to surrender. So..."

"So it worked," January said. He hopped around, "It worked, it
worked!"

"Yes."

"Just like I said it would!" he cried, and hopping in front of the
priest he laughed.

Getty was jumping around a little too, and the sight of the priest
bouncing was too much for January. He sat on his cot and laughed till
the tears ran down his cheeks.

"So—" He sobered quickly. "So Truman's going to shoot me anyway, eh?"

"Yes," the priest said unhappily. "I guess that's right."

This time January's laugh was bitter. "He's a bastard, all right. And
proud of being a bastard, which makes it worse." He shook his head. "If
Roosevelt had lived..."

"It would have been different," Getty finished. "Yes. Maybe so. But
he didn't." He sat beside January. "Cigarette?" He held out a pack, and
January noticed the green wrapper, the round bull's-eye. He frowned.

"You haven't got a Camel?"

"Oh. Sorry."

"Oh well. That's all right." January took one of the Lucky Strikes, lit
up. "That's awfully good news." He breathed out. "I never believed Truman would pardon me anyway, so mostly you've brought good news.
Ha. They *missed*. You have no idea how much better that makes me
feel."

"I think I do."

January smoked the cigarette.

"So I'm a good American after all. I *am* a good American," he insisted, "no matter what Truman says."

"Yes," Getty replied, and coughed. "You're better than Truman any
day."

"Better watch what you say, Father." He looked into the eyes behind
the glasses, and the expression he saw there gave him pause. Since the
drop every look directed at him had been filled with contempt. He'd

seen it so often during the court-martial that he'd learned to stop looking; and now he had to teach himself to see again. The priest looked at
him as if he were...as if he were some kind of hero. That wasn't exactly
right. But seeing it...

January would not live to see the years that followed, so he would
never know what came of his action. He had given up casting his mind
forward and imagining possibilities, because there was no point to
it. His planning was ended. In any case he would not have been able
to imagine the course of the post-war years. That the world would
quickly become an armed camp pitched on the edge of atomic war, he
might have predicted. But he never would have guessed that so many
people would join a January Society. He would never know of the effect the Society had on Dewey during the Korean crisis, never know
of the Society's successful campaign for the test-ban treaty, and never
learn that, thanks in part to the Society and its allies, a treaty would be
signed by the great powers that would reduce the number of atomic
bombs year by year, until there were none left.

Frank January would never know any of that. But in that moment
on his cot looking into the eyes of young Patrick Getty, he guessed an
inkling of it—he felt, just for an instant, the impact on history.

And with that he relaxed. In his last week everyone who met him
carried away the same impression—that of a calm, quiet man, angry
at Truman and others, but in a withdrawn, matter-of-fact way. Patrick
Getty, a strong force in the January Society ever after, said January
was talkative for some time after he learned of the missed attack on
Kokura. Then he got quieter, as the day approached. On the morning
that they woke him at dawn to march him out to a hastily constructed
execution shed, his MPs shook his hand. The priest was with him as he
smoked a final cigarette, and they prepared to put the hood over his
head. January looked at him calmly. "They load one of the guns with a
blank cartridge, right?"

"Yes," Getty said.

"So each man in the squad can imagine he may not have shot me?"

"Yes. That's right."

A tight, unhumorous smile was January's last expression. He threw
down the cigarette, ground it out, poked the priest in the arm. "But I
know." Then the mask slipped back into place for good, making the
hood redundant, and with a firm step January went to the wall. One
might have said he was at peace.

⟡ ⟡ ⟡

KIM STANLEY ROBINSON has garnered many awards including the Nebula, Hugo, Asimov, John W. Campbell, Locus, and World Fantasy Awards. His work regularly delves into ecological and sociological themes. His novels include *The Wild Shore* (1984), *Icehenge* (1984), *The Memory of Whitness* (1985), *The Gold Coast* (1988), *Pacific Edge* (1990), *A Short Sharp Shock* (1990), *Red Mars* (1993), *Green Mars* (1994), *Blue Mars* (1996), *Antarctica* (1998), *The Years of Rice and Salt* (2002), F*orty Signs of Rain* (2004), and *Fifty Degrees Below Zero* (2005). His collections include *The Planet on the Table* (1986), *Escape from Kathmandu* (1990), *Remaking History* (1991), and *The Martians* (1999). He lives in Davis, California with his wife Lisa and two sons.

MARY MACKEY

THIRD INITIATION: A GIFT FROM THE LAND OF DREAMS

The Dark Mother gives three gifts
Aba, Shallah, Nashah,
One comes from the river
One comes from the earth
One comes from the land of dreams

from "The Riddle Song"
Kataka, Fifth Millennium B.C.

Marrah sat by the spring watching it freeze over. The ice was slowly growing as milky as a blind eye. Not a bad comparison, she thought. She was staring at the healing spring and the spring was staring back at her without seeing her, just like the Imsha.

Or maybe the Imsha did see her. Who could tell? Ever since Marrah had arrived to begin the third stage of her initiation, the veiled figure had not acknowledged her presence. It just sat on its rock with its arms clasped around its knees, presumably lost in thoughts too deep for ordinary mortals to share. So far they had not exchanged a single word. It was now late afternoon and a sharp wind was blowing down from the north, spitting snow and tossing dust and pine needles in their faces, but the Imsha seemed indifferent to the weather. Perhaps it lived outside all the time and paid no more attention to the cold than a beaver or a bear; or perhaps, Marrah thought, it had on more warm underclothes than she did.

She put her mitten over her nose and breathed a little warmth into it. She was just wondering wearily if they were going to sit there all day, when the Imsha suddenly turned to her in a sweep of black veils that reminded her of crows' wings. "Cut off all your hair," it commanded. The words were in Old Language, but the accent was strange, as if each word were being rolled across its tongue like a small ball.

Although she didn't like the idea of cutting her hair in weather cold enough to freeze the paws off a rabbit, Marrah was relieved. Her patience had paid off: she had been accepted, and the third and final stage of her initiation had finally begun.

She bowed obediently to the veiled figure, took her knife from its scabbard, and tried to figure out how to go about giving herself a haircut while wearing thick mittens. Finally she gave up, pulled off the mittens, and set about chopping off her hair as best she could.

It was an awkward process and about halfway through it she realized that obeying the Imsha was going to be a lot harder than obeying Glyntsa. The flint blade was not particularly sharp, her fingers were stiff with cold, and she nicked her scalp more than once; but when you accepted an initiation, you did what you were told to do without asking questions, so she worked away doggedly, wondering if this was how Stavan felt when he scraped off his beard hairs. What would he have said if he could have seen her? He had always loved her hair. Black as a raven's wing, he used to say; curly as smoke; soft as new grass. He had combed it and braided it and even written a poem to it once a long time ago, before Keru and Luma were born, and now she was cutting it off with no more ceremony than if it were a patch of weeds.

Her hair fell into her lap and piled up at her feet—great hanks of it all tangled together like fine twine. She looked at it with growing regret, but she went on cutting. When she finished, she ran her hand over her nearly bare scalp. It felt cold and bristly, and she realized that she was going to have to wear a hat indoors as well as out—provided she ever got indoors again. She picked up her hair, untangled it as best she could, bound it with a bit of leather, and presented it to the Imsha with a bow.

To her surprise, the Imsha refused it. "Weave it into a snare."

A snare! Only fowlers could make a decent snare out of human hair, and they never worked outdoors in a stiff wind with a tangle of curls. Curly hair was fit for stuffing pillows maybe but not for weaving. Marrah reminded herself to be patient. This was undoubtedly a test of her sincerity as an initiate, and if she had not been so cold, she might even have found it an interesting challenge.

Pulling off her mittens again, she blew some more warmth into her fingers and began to wind the longest strands of her hair together and tie them into one of those fine, knotted nets the fowlers used to catch small birds, but as she had feared, her hair was almost impossible to work with. She struggled for a long time, creating snarls and messes and knots. The light faded, but still she went on weaving. She hoped that the Imsha would tell her to stop, but the mysterious figure just sat there.

That night she slept behind a log, wrapped in her cloak, with her bare head tucked into her hood and the hair clutched to her chest so it would not blow away. When she woke the next morning, the Imsha was still sitting on the same rock, as if it had never moved. Marrah began to wonder if it was human. There was clearly to be no breakfast and no fire, but at least the sun was up and the wind had died down, so she went back to weaving her hair and by midday she had a snare of sorts, irregular in places but strong enough to catch a sparrow. Spread between two bushes, the net would be invisible from a few paces, and if she was not careful, she might forget and walk into it herself. She rolled it up very carefully, making sure that none of the loose ends tangled. It took sure hands to make a snare of human hair, and she was proud of her work, but if the Imsha was pleased, it gave no sign. It held the snare for a moment and then returned it to her with no more ceremony than someone handing back an old basket.

"You'll use this to catch what you need," it said cryptically.

Marrah's heart sank. She tried to imagine herself spending an entire winter trapping birds with a snare the size of a child's tunic. She would much rather dig roots and crack nuts. Any bird small enough to get caught in that snare would hardly be worth the wood it would take to cook it. She was tempted to ask if she could go back to Kataka and get some fishhooks, but before she could get the words out, the veiled figure rose to its feet and motioned for her to follow. The two of them began to walk up a small path that led away from the pool, climbing the hillside through the bare trees.

With every step Marrah took, she grew more anxious. The trees looked strange in this part of the forest, bent and elderly with protruding roots that reminded her of birds' feet, and she could not help feeling that something unpleasant was about to happen. As the Imsha walked, a cold white mist seemed to rise around her, and although it was broad daylight, Marrah heard the hoot of an owl. Somewhere in the distance a dog howled and another dog joined it. As the wind blew small clouds over the sun, the shadows along the side of the trail seemed to take human shapes, and once she was sure she heard the call of a cuckoo—which would have been fine if it had been summer, but there in the midwinter forest, the bird's bubbling trill made the hair stand up on the back of her neck. She walked on, knowing it was too late to turn back, as a kind of slow terror crept over her.

The path crossed the ridge and then took a sharp turn to the left. They had gone downhill only a short distance when they came to a clearing. Suddenly the sun came out, a mild breeze sprang up, and Marrah's fears blew away like so many dry leaves. At the center of the clearing stood a small house, so beautiful and inviting that she wondered if the Imsha had conjured it out of the dream world. It was made of white clay and wheat-straw thatch like all the houses of Kataka, but it was shaped like the upper half of a large egg. The walls were covered with red spirals that swirled like smoke. Birds flew around the oval doorway; flowers of every color wreathed windows; strange animals marched at ground level or hung from the huge green vines that had been painted so that they seemed to climb into the smoke hole.

"Norhabi, lyrubu, wuburi," the Imsha said, pointing to the animals. "Mubumu, water reeds; patabi, the flowers of my land." Marrah did not understand any of the foreign words, but they had a melodious sound.

"Do you come from far away, honored one?" she asked, bowing respectfully to the Imsha. Under ordinary circumstances she would have said "honored mother" or "honored uncle," but the closer she got to the Imsha the less certain she became.

"I come from the south," the Imsha said, and it laughed that warm, ambiguous laugh that could have been a man's or a woman's. "Every third generation my people send a priestess north to Kataka and the Katakans send us one in return. It's a long trip and I can recall getting quite seasick when the sailors took me across the Sea of Blue Waves, not to mention lonely, but it was my duty, so I did it. For time out of mind, my people and the Katakans have shared the wisdom of the Dark Mother, and now I'll share some of it with you if you prove worthy."

The Imsha stepped forward, unhooked the leather curtain that covered the door of the house, and motioned for Marrah to enter. Before it stepped over the threshold, it paused as if inspecting Marrah from behind its black veils. The long black beads on its headdress swayed slightly. Approval? Marrah hoped so.

"You're a mother, aren't you?"

"Yes, honored one."

"I'd have rather had you when you were younger, but still motherhood is a great teacher. You'd be surprised how few initiates make it through the first night—even the young ones—but you're Lalah's granddaughter so I expected you to have the strength to do what you were ordered to do and the sense not to complain. There was never a more stubborn woman born than your grandmother. She came to me when her breasts were high, more years ago than I care to count, and if her hands had just been a little steadier," the Imsha held two gloved fingers together as if pinching salt, "I'd have given her the full initiation."

The inside of the house was as simple as the outside was elaborate: cool, whitewashed walls, a small clay bench that ran around one side, and a round fire pit filled with white sand and glowing charcoal that gave off welcome warmth. Marrah noticed a rough ladder that led to a small sleeping loft piled with sheepskins, a large Katakan water jar painted with the usual designs, a cup, a few pretty bowls, a grinding stone, and—best of all—baskets of nuts, grain, dried fruit, flour, and meat. Relieved that she was not going to have to live on sparrows all winter, she stood and waited for the Imsha to sit before she sat herself, but the Imsha had something more interesting in mind. Standing with its back to Marrah, it began to unveil itself. It was wearing many layers, which explained why it had managed to survive the night outside in comfort, but as it dropped its cloak to the floor and turned around, Marrah gasped with surprise. The Imsha had the breasts of a woman, but its face was bearded.

"What are you?" Marrah cried, and was immediately embarrassed because what kind of question was that for an initiate to ask?

The Imsha laughed and went on taking off its outer wraps. It was as old a person as she had ever seen, old beyond all belief, thin as a bundle of twigs, with dark, bright eyes and not a tooth in its mouth as far as Marrah could tell, but it was its skin that was the most amazing thing about it. Marrah had seen many different kinds of people during years she traveled with Stavan and Arang, but she had never before seen skin this shade. The Imsha was the color of the Goddess Earth Herself: not the reddish earth of the western forests or the pale dry earth of the cliffs, but the dark, fertile earth of a field that could grow wheat and lentils. If the Dark Mother ever appeared in a human body, Marrah thought, She would look like this. She felt a thrill of terror. What kind of power must lie in a being who united both sexes and was the color of the Mother?

The Imsha stripped to its inner tunic, sat down on the clay bench, and stretched out its legs to warm its feet by the fire. "Calm down," it said. "I'm not a divine being. I'm human, just like you. The only difference between us is that you were born woman, and I was born both woman and man." It stroked its small, silky beard and closed its eyes as if remembering its strange southern land where animals hung from trees and water reeds flowered. "The priestesses who attended my birth told my mother that the Dark Mother had sent me to remind Her human children that All Is One. That well may be true." It grinned a slow, toothless grin. "But I think I was sent for a more pleasant reason. Do you remember the Sixth Commandment of the Divine Sisters?"

"The one that says we are to enjoy ourselves because our joy is pleasing to Her?"

The Imsha nodded. "Well, in my time I've had more joy than most people. I calculate that I'm somewhere near ninety years old, maybe more. For a good seventy of those years, I had the pleasure of a man and the pleasure of a woman both, much of it in this very room. If that sleeping mat up there could talk," the Imsha pointed to the loft, "it would sing like a chorus of nightingales."

"Which pleasure was better?" Marrah put her hand over her mouth and stared at the Imsha apologetically. She had not meant to ask such an intimate question, but it must have been all right because the Imsha leaned back and yawned, and its old face suddenly seemed younger.

"The pleasure of men is sharper, but the pleasure of women is longer," it said agreeably. "Often I pitied my lovers—although I must say they never complained about me. Most people look at the world as if they are staring at it through a little hole: they see a bit of elbow here and a bit of nose there, but never the whole." It paused. "But I always saw everything, and it is my job to show you as much of it as you can bear: man and woman; past and present; death and life; the great circle that goes and comes and comes and goes, and rolls on without ever stopping. But first..." The Imsha paused again and studied Marrah. "First, you must make me a perfect pot—or a perfect statue if you'd rather, although statues are harder."

For a moment, Marrah had the impression that she had not heard correctly. "A perfect pot?" she echoed. "A perfect statue?" This seemed too easy.

The Imsha nodded. It rose slowly to its feet, picked up its discarded clothing, and began to get dressed again. "You will find the picks you need to dig the clay, and the sieves, the soaking jars, and such things out in the little shed by the kiln. You will have to cut your own wood, but there's an ax. Glyntsa tells me you are already an accomplished potter, taught by Bindar himself. Did you know that your great-uncle came to me for initiation too? The trees around this house were little saplings in those days, and I still had my teeth." It sighed. "I turned Bindar into a master potter but your grandmother, as I said before, was destined for other things. Unsteady hands; but a good queen, I hear; one of the best."

Marrah was relieved to discover that this third initiation was going to be so easy. The final powers of the Dark Mother were so shrouded in mystery that she had imagined she might be set to all sorts of terrifying, dangerous, even impossible tasks. But she was only being asked to make one perfect pot or statue, and she had made more pots and statues than she could count over the last six years. She might not be a masterpotter like her great-uncle, but she had steady hands.

"I'll bring the pot to you in three days," she said boldly. The Imsha said nothing. It just turned and left.

At first, Marrah was afraid she had offended it by being immodest, but as she stood at the door she heard laughter coming from the retreating form. It was not the dignified laughter of an elder or the warm laughter of the Imsha. It was the wildly amused giggling of a young girl who has just heard a very funny story.

The Imsha had every reason to laugh. A perfect pot did not take three days to make or even three weeks. Marrah's hair had grown down to her ears, winter was over, and the frogs were singing in the healing spring before she made anything acceptable, and there were many days—especially at first—when she was half convinced that the final initiation of the Dark Goddess was nothing more than a bad joke foisted on unsuspecting strangers.

Had she been in Shara, making a pot would have involved rolling prepared clay into coils, smoothing them together, and firing the result in one of the temple kilns, but here she had to do everything as if no one had ever made a pot before. Some days she gathered and prepared the clay, prying large lumps of it out of the quarrying place with a deer-antler pick. Actually there were several quarrying places, and she visited them all in turn, sometimes coming home with baskets of red lumps, sometimes with white, sometimes with a pale yellow.

It was demanding work, especially during the weeks when the ground was frozen, and every time she dug there were certain rituals to be observed, which she attended to scrupulously. Since clay was part of the body of the Goddess Earth, she would sprinkle holy water on it and pray to the damp mud before she took it from the ground. Then she would lug it back in a carrying basket, separate it into smaller lumps, and spread it out in front of the fire, turning it occasionally so it would dry evenly. When it crumbled in the palm of her hand, she would pick out the stones, soak it again, sieve it through an open-weave basket, and mix it with fine, volcanic binding sand in the usual way, spreading the wet mass out on the floor, tramping on it, and pulling up the edges as if she were kneading a giant loaf of bread. When the clay was mixed to the consistency of a heavy cake batter, she would spread it out to dry a bit more, and then divide it into equal-sized balls that she stored in a large basket wrapped in pieces of damp linen.

On other days, she would prepare slips and paints of various colors from the small baskets of pigmented earth that she found among her food stores: red mostly, but also yellow, buff, white, and gray. Or she would chop wood to feed the kilning fire. But most of the time she made pots, and later, statues. At first she made only a few, confident that they were as close to perfection as anyone could demand, but when she brought them to the Imsha, the Imsha would look at them for a moment and toss them over its shoulder.

"Not good enough," it would say. "Try again." Marrah got used to the sound of breaking pottery that spring: first the dull crack and then the shards pattering down on the stones. Nothing she did was good enough, not the pretty, delicate statues of Batal, not the breast-shaped water jugs, not even the simple cups that every ten-year-old knew how to make. "What do you want?" she cried one afternoon, completely frustrated.

"Bring them to me wet."

"You mean unkilned?"

"No, wet, and don't make one at a time; make several dozen."

So after that, Marrah brought undried pots by the score and the Imsha stopped tossing them over its shoulder. Instead it took each one, balanced it in its hand, and inspected it. Then it would sit it down, cut it in half, and show Marrah what she had done wrong. Sometimes the sides of the pot were not of even thickness, sometimes the rim was just a little less than round, sometimes the flaw was something Marrah could not see no matter how hard she looked. Occasionally the Imsha would not even bother to cut a pot.

"This one will crack," it would declare, and sure enough, if Marrah fired that particular pot, it would come out of the kiln in pieces.

If anyone had asked Marrah what she was learning during those long, disappointing days, she would have said: "Not much," but slowly she began to lose herself in pottery making, and for the first time in many months she spent long periods without mourning for Keru and Arang or worrying about Stavan. Grief and loneliness disappeared, her thoughts stayed in one place, and if she was not exactly happy, she was as close to happiness as she had been since the nomad raid.

She learned patience that spring, but she must have been learning other things too, things she didn't even know she was learning, because one rainy night in early summer she began to dream in an entirely new way. She never knew why her dreams changed. Perhaps all those weeks of struggling with the clay had changed the way she saw the world; perhaps the Imsha had thrown her into some kind of trance without her knowing it, or put something in her food; or perhaps the dreams were a gift from the Dark Mother. But wherever they came from, the dreams were as real as life.

The first dream came without warning: suddenly she found herself standing in a nomad tent inhaling the familiar scent of smoke, wet wool, and dogs. It was night, but a pale stream of moonlight was pouring through the smoke hole. She froze in terror, convinced for one terrible moment that she was still Vlahan's wife and prisoner. Then she saw Stavan lying on a pile of sheepskins, his face turned to the moonlight.

There was nothing in the scene to suggest that it was a dream. Everything was solid: the usual nomad cooking baskets were stacked by the fire pit; the felt rug was warm under her bare feet; and Stavan was as much there as he had been in all the years they'd been together.

She went over to him and knelt by his side. He looked thinner and she saw a new, half-healed scar on his cheek. Bending down, she kissed him, feeling the warmth of his lips, breathing in the smell and taste of him. He started awake and clutched his dagger, but when he saw who was kissing him, he threw it aside.

"Marrah!" he cried. "How did you get here?"

"I don't know."

"What happened to your hair?"

"I cut it for my initiation."

"Come here, my love." He took her in his arms and drew her down beside him, and they kissed each other, and she woke crying his name.

For four nights in a row she dreamed of Stavan. On the morning of the fifth day, she went in search of the Imsha. She found it sitting in its usual place beside the healing pool. "How do you like the Dream World?" it called out as soon as it caught sight of her. "How do you like sharing joy again with your handsome nomad lover?"

Marrah stopped in her tracks. "How do you know what I've been dreaming?"

"It's my business to know. I could watch too, but I decided long ago not to. So tell me, has the lovemaking been enjoyable?"

"Yes, very." The idea that the Imsha could see her dreams was so disconcerting—not to mention embarrassing—that Marrah was speechless. Finally she found her tongue. "But are these dreams real?"

"Real?" The Imsha laughed.

"Am I really with Stavan? Does he know I'm there? Is he somewhere far away dreaming the same dreams or am I alone in this? When Glyntsa taught me how to listen to the animals, I took a special powder; before I heard the voice of the Butterfly Goddess, Chilana, I ate a live caterpillar. But this time I've drunk nothing, eaten nothing—at least nothing that I know of—and still it keeps happening, so I need to know: what have you done to me? Please, honored one, help me understand. Have you put me in a trance without me realizing it? Am I really kissing Stavan, or is this just my longing for him speaking through my dreams?"

The Imsha stopped laughing. "I suggest you ask him those questions the next time you see him." It stretched out its hand. "Enough chatter. Give me your pots. You brought some, didn't you? Or have you been too busy dreaming love dreams to keep the kiln fire hot?"

Obviously it had no intention of telling her whether her dreams were real. Marrah felt more confused than ever. She fumbled in her carrying basket and took out the three small bowls she had packed as she hurried out the door. They were nothing much, just half-globes of reddish brown clay painted with snake signs that had turned black in the kiln.

The Imsha took one of the bowls and balanced it on the palm of its hand. "Not bad," it said. It inspected another. "You're coming along nicely." It picked up the final bowl and was silent for a long time. Finally it handed the bowl back to Marrah. "Lovemaking must agree with you," it said. "This one is perfect." Things moved quickly after that. As soon as it had pronounced the bowl perfect, the Imsha rose to its feet and ordered Marrah to go get her snare. Marrah obeyed, running so fast that briars tore at her tunic and twigs stung her legs. When she returned with the snare carefully rolled in a piece of linen, she stood panting, trying to catch her breath, but the Imsha gave her no time to recover.

"Hang it on that elderberry bush," it ordered. "And hang it low to the ground."

Marrah unrolled the snare and hung it on the elderberry bush with great care, knowing if she dropped it, she would never be able to untangle the strands. The snare caught the wind and billowed. It was a delicate thing, a spiderweb of black hairs and every one from her own head. The Imsha inspected it and gave a grunt of approval. "Do you remember when I told you that you'd catch what you needed in this?"

"Yes, honored one."

"Are you ready?"

Marrah had no idea what it meant by "ready," but she nodded and as she did so, the Imsha suddenly grabbed her by the wrist. What happened next was so strange that it took away what little breath she had left. As soon as the Imsha's hand touched her arm, Marrah fell into a deep trance. For a moment everything was a confused jumble of color and light. Then suddenly the two of them began to shrink. Down and down they went, growing smaller and smaller until the boulders around the pool looked like mountains and the grass looked like trees. A butterfly flew over them, as huge as a ship, its blue and yellow wings glowing like fire, and a chorus of frogs roared in her ears like the rushing of a great river.

In front of them, the elderberry leaves became the size of sails and the snare grew large as a house. The Imsha led Marrah toward the great net woven of black ropes—each as thick as her arm—and as they approached, the snare suddenly stiffened and stopped billowing in the wind.

"Time has stopped," the Imsha announced, but Marrah barely heard. She was staring at a swallow that had frozen in the air above her, and she felt a rapture that was beyond terror. "Look," the Imsha commanded.

Marrah looked and saw that every opening in the snare had become a window, each opening into a different world. In one window she saw herself on her coming-of-age day, leaping from a high cliff into the surf; in another she saw herself pulling Stavan from the sea; and in still another she saw Keru and Luma at the moment they were born. Shara was there and so were the steppes; here, she was Vlahan's wife and a prisoner, gathering dung in baskets and being beaten; there, she was Lalah's beloved granddaughter, nursing her babies on the roof as she chatted with Dalish. In some of the windows she was middle-aged, and in some she was an old woman sitting in the sun beside a young woman she didn't recognize. Frightened, she closed her eyes.

"I can't bear these visions!" she cried. "Take them away!"

The Imsha laughed and tightened its grip on Marrah's wrist. "What are you afraid of?"

"I'm afraid I'll see my own death."

"You won't see your own death until you ask to see it. Open your eyes, Marrah, daughter of Sabalah. Be brave. Open your eyes and see the far, far distant future."

Marrah opened her eyes and found that she and the Imsha were standing in front of one of the windows, looking into some kind of huge house, bigger than any motherhouse ever built. Blue-green light was coming from long, glowing lanterns, and people dressed in shining robes were walking slowly, looking at things in strange boxes. The sides of the boxes were clear like water, but they were solid. Marrah saw

Hansi spears behind the solid water; arrows; daggers; and the bones of a man surrounded by a great quantity of weapons and gold.

"Come this way," the Imsha whispered, and it and Marrah seemed to float through the window into the house, drifting down endless dim corridors until they came to another room. There was only one person there, a middle-aged woman with gray-brown hair and boots with strange heels that looked like sticks. She was bending forward, examining something in one of the water boxes, and when Marrah looked closer she saw that it was the black and red bowl she had fired only yesterday.

"Now you see why the bowl had to be perfect," the Imsha said. It came up behind the woman and put its hand on her shoulder, but the woman seemed not to know the Imsha was there. She just went on looking at Marrah's bowl, frowning slightly like someone lost in thought.

"That bowl is speaking to her," the Imsha said. "She is hearing your voice over a gulf of years too great to count. She does not know that she is hearing it, but she is. In her time, the Goddess Earth has been forgotten, but your bowl is making her remember. You will make a great many bowls in your lifetime, but only this one will survive."

✣ ✣ ✣

MARY MACKEY is the author of four collections of poetry and ten novels among which are *Immersion* and *The Earthsong Trilogy,* which includes *The Year The Horses Came, The Horses at the Gate* (from which the above story is taken), and *The Fires of Spring. The Earthsong Trilogy* evokes the moment in pre-history when marauding nomads brought horses, male gods, and war to a goddess-worshipping Europe that had known peace for thousands of years. Mackey's works have been translated into eleven foreign languages including Japanese, Hebrew, and Finnish. Deeply involved in the San Francisco Bay Area literary community, she has been Chair of the West Coast Branch of PEN and served on the Governing Board of PEN, Oakland. She has lectured at Harvard and the Smithsonian and has contributed to such diverse magazines as *The Chiron Review, The American Book Review, Yellow Silk, Ms. Magazine,* and *The New American Review.* She is a member of the Northern California Book Reviewers Association and a Fellow of the Virginia Center for the Creative Arts. Her work can be sampled at www.marymackey.com.

JANICE LAW

SIDE EFFECTS

He was whipping down an old two-lane, engine roaring, wind strong enough to rattle his teeth, the leather jacket glued to his shoulders. A powerful vibration ran up his wrists and across his chest where it fused with a different frequency surging up off the points of his hips. Then a farm tractor pulled out ahead of him, and, in the last uncomplicated moment of his life, Karl twitched the handles and crossed the double line.

He never remembered anything else. Later, they told him about an oncoming car and a swerve back into his lane which ended when the big Harley left the road and ended up in a brush-filled ditch with gas everywhere. He'd flown another twelve feet, which saved his life when the fire started, and he'd been lucky that a passing trucker had radioed almost immediately for the rescue chopper. They told him all this, and he could imagine the black skid of hot rubber, the sudden loss of orientation, the bundle of bone and flesh and denim and leather flying, doll-like, through the air—even the flash and heat and crackling branches of sudden fire—but he couldn't remember.

He woke up to whiteness, faint shadows, the slow-moving blades of a fan, and discovered other worries. He could hear a cart rattling, purposeful footsteps, low voices. From the penetrating medicinal smell, Karl guessed that he was in a hospital, and he decided he'd better see what was what before Paula got worried. But when he tried to look at his watch, his arm failed to respond, and when he tried to roll over and swing his legs to the side of the bed, nothing happened. Karl saw nothing but the white ceiling, plain walls, and the corner of a window and started to scream.

The nurse was tall, fair, and middle-aged. She brought a shot, some water in a paper cup, an air of calm. "Sorry," she said. "We've been watching you, but we thought you'd be out a while longer. It's always a shock."

Karl told her how much of a shock with all the vocabulary at his command. The nurse was undisturbed. She patted his shoulder. "Language centers undamaged. That's a good sign. We'll have you right in no time. Not like the old days. They're culturing the spinal replacement cells right now."

Paula told him the same thing when she arrived in a warm cloud of scent with flowers and tears. "Dr. Petrus is a genius," she said. Her thick, dark hair brushed Karl's face as she kissed him. "All clean fetal tissue. Reknitting the spinal cord is the next thing to routine."

That was what Dr. Petrus said, too. Tall and thin to the point of emaciation, the doctor elaborated on the technique which was "standard procedure now" and "really a brilliant development." He said Karl didn't know how lucky he was.

"How soon?" Karl asked. Lying motionless was already precipitating acute anxiety.

"You'll thank me for not rushing," Dr. Petrus said. "There's been—hmmm—damage, you understand. The break in your left leg is pretty bad. You'll know when you can feel the pain. And abrasions, hairline rib fractures." You'd have thought he was doing Karl a favor. But the cultures were proceeding perfectly, and the transplant would be ready within a week.

The first sign of trouble came three days after the cells that were to reknit his spinal cord had been implanted. Karl woke that morning feeling lousy, his head throbbing. The patterns on Paula's green silk dress writhed like a nest of snakes, and he vomited his breakfast onto the tray that was fixed just under his chin. Petrus seemed concerned when he made his rounds, and by the following day it was apparent that infection had set in and the transplant would have to be scrapped.

"We can start again," Dr. Petrus told Karl, though there was some damage, some "cleaning up" to do. The "cleaning up" required an emergency run to the operating room, IV bags attached to every vein in sight, and a midnight visit from a massive, unhealthy-looking man in a surgeon's green scrub suit.

He sat for a long time without speaking. Even after Karl opened his eyes, the visitor remained silent, his massive jowls glistening, his small, light eyes quick and alert in their fat pouches.

"I'm dying," Karl said, half statement, half question.

His visitor shrugged slightly. "Not yet," he said. "It is a matter of time." His voice was neutral and unconcerned.

"A matter of time," Karl repeated. In his heavily drugged state, it was the phrasing that struck him.

"Cases of this sort..." the surgeon made a gesture that dropped below Karl's restricted field of vision. "We have not unlimited power over the body. New techniques come with their own complications."

"I'm going to die in a matter of time," Karl said.

"As are we all." The surgeon bent his head to look at something in Karl's chart. "How much time depends in part on you. I have come to make you a proposition."

Once again, the doctor's expression seemed odd. "Am I hallucinating?" Karl asked.

"No. I am Harold Borgia, head of neural surgery." A clean, broad hand drifted into Karl's vision, landed on his brow and stroked his head gently. "There is a new procedure, which may enable us to remove the infected tissue and restore your spinal column rapidly enough to preserve your life and restore mobility."

"Arms and legs?" Karl asked. He seemed incapable of grasping complex ideas.

"If we are successful, you will be as good as new physically. Minus the broken leg and cracked ribs, of course."

"Of course," said Karl. Why, he wondered, hadn't they done this sooner?

"Unlike the standard treatment, this procedure requires a donor, a decent tissue match, speed, and decisiveness."

"I am already decided," Karl said.

"I lost a patient tonight," the surgeon continued with glacial slowness, "a young person of the correct tissue type. They do not come along every day, you know."

"Can you perform the surgery right away?" Karl asked.

"It will have to be done immediately—if you agree." Dr. Borgia's hand rose like a mysterious warning flipper. "Naturally, there are dangers. This is delicate and difficult experimental surgery. I cannot guarantee success."

"Then I will die quickly," Karl said.

"You would die on the table."

"I want to see Paula," Karl said, "then I would like you to give it a try."

"There is another thing. Which perhaps you and your companion should discuss. We think there may be side effects—side effects of a psychological nature."

"You think?"

"So far we have only attempted this procedure in animals. One subject is a cat I now keep as a pet, quite a charming animal, perfectly healthy. She was retired from the laboratory for her services to science. Though I cannot be sure, I believe there are side effects." He nodded his massive head. "Involving the brain."

"So does death," said Karl. "Please don't wait any longer."

This time when Karl came out of the anesthesia, he woke to pain, to a cast on one leg, tape on his ribs, and a horrifying headache.

"How are you feeling, darling?" Paula asked. She leaned over his bed and stroked his face, and, for an instant, Karl was surprised by the inky blackness of her hair.

"How dark your hair is," he said.

"All the better," she said, teasing, and ran the fluffy end of the braid across his lips.

"Has Poppa come?" he asked.

Paula's face went still. She had never heard Karl refer to his late father as "Poppa."

"He warned me about that truck," Karl mumbled, although talking was suddenly an enormous effort. "He said it wasn't worth...wasn't worth..."

"Rest now," said Paula. "They're going to give you a shot."

For two days, Karl existed in a formless swirl of pain that receded as suddenly as it had arisen, leaving him weak and contented high on a hospital bed near an open window. He felt the sunshine and smelled a faint breeze tinged with exhaust fumes: a diesel somewhere. He heard the sounds of engines passing on the street and recognized most of them without being surprised that a whole area of existence had become comprehensible. Then he smelled perfume, too, and his imagination floated away to a shuttered bedroom, Paula's tanned limbs, a surge of erotic delight. He pulled himself up into a sitting position; his ribs hurt, the back of his neck throbbed softly, and his leg itched under its plaster cast, but he was moving, he really was moving, and when Paula stood up from the chair on the other side of the bed, he began to weep with joy.

"A very good recovery," Dr. Petrus announced two weeks later, when Karl was being discharged. "Not a sign of infection; not a trace of tissue rejection. Immune system perfect. Leg looks good. Ribs feel okay?"

"A bit stiff."

"That will last for a while," Petrus said. "No heavy lifting, remember."

"Just math papers. Come September."

"And no motorcycle."

"We have a car," Paula said quickly. "The bike was recreation."

"No motorcycle," Karl said, and, indeed, he had no feeling for the bike one way or the other now. The exhilarating rush of speed, the blur as telephone poles and trees whipped past his vision, the hypnotic, unwinding spool of asphalt: he knew those things only as he knew the location of the hospital, the capital of Alaska, the author of *Moby Dick*. Motorcycling was now just theoretical knowledge.

Engines, however, were another matter. Paula started the Escort and before the motor was warm, Karl said, "That carburetor needs adjustment. I'll take a look when I get home."

"You don't know anything about carburetors," Paula said. "The last time you had the hood up was to signal the AAA man."

Karl said nothing. He was digesting two incompatible truths: he knew nothing about mechanics—in fact, he'd known embarrassingly little even about his motorbike; and he now heard engines the way a musician hears Mozart. He knew, too, that when he opened the hood of the Ford, its configuration would fit his mental diagram exactly.

"It's all right," Paula said, reaching over to pat his leg. "I'm just a bit tense. I've been so worried and now that you're finally coming home, I'm ready to collapse."

Karl squeezed her hand. "I'm not looking forward to the stairs," he said. He envisioned a big, tripledecker with steep old mahogany stairs and a dark apartment that smelled of tomatoes, peppers, and onions cooking.

"You won't have to go in to school right away," Paula said, and, at her voice, the stairs shifted from worn mahogany to wide cement with steel railings, bright red trim, the echoing noise and bustle of the passing bell.

Their own house, when Paula pulled into the drive, proved to be a tidy gray ranch with blue shutters and severely pruned arborvitae growing on either side of the front stoop. Karl found it familiar, but no more so than the other houses in the neighborhood, and less so than the second-floor apartment that kept drifting into his consciousness. Everything felt just a little strange, as if he had returned from a journey so immensely long and distant that even home seemed foreign.

"You're tired," Paula said, and Karl admitted that the ride home had exhausted him.

"You have to expect a certain amount of disorientation."

She used that term several times in the days that followed. He was disoriented when he took the wrong turn to the bathroom, when he asked about Uncle Andy, when he worried who was looking after his old dog. One night they sat down with the photo album, which straightened him out on the relatives and friends but which left him oddly depressed and lonely. He'd never had a dog; Uncle Andy was a figment of his imagination; his father, who had left the family twenty years before, had been dead for six years. When it was all clear to him, he felt as if half his circle of friends had died at once, and grief, nonetheless sharp for being touched with unreality, ate into his soul.

Paula felt (or hoped) that this was "disorientation." Karl, meanwhile, looked at her anxious eyes, her smooth, pretty face, slightly upturned nose, straight brow and full lips, and realized that he didn't love her. They had lived together happily for nearly five years, and, until the accident, Karl would have said that he was in love with her. He saw now that he'd been mistaken. In his thirty-two years he had never been in love, but now he knew love—or remembered love, he was not sure which—and the object of this elusive, exhilarating, and painful emotion was not Paula. He was sure of that. Though he desired Paula, liked her, felt immense gratitude toward her, he was not in love with her, not at all, and that certainty began to complicate his life.

When he went back for his last check-up with Dr. Petrus, Karl asked if he might meet the donor family to thank them. This was not allowed, Dr. Petrus said; it was distressing for them; in the past there had been some messy situations. But a letter could be forwarded; organ donor families always appreciated a letter. Karl dutifully produced one, and then spent a day in the library reading back obits and accident reports from the local paper.

There were not too many possibilities: an Alzheimer's patient in the local nursing home; a child burned to death in a trailer fire; a hunting accident, an out-of-state drowning. Then there was Angelo O'Neill, 21, automobile mechanic. Karl felt his chest tighten as soon as he saw the name. O'Neill's obituary had run the day after Karl's successful transplant, and the story of his accident had appeared the day before. The young mechanic had been crushed when a truck he was repairing slipped off its jack. He had suffered massive internal injuries and died on the operating table.

Karl's hand shook and his pen skipped awkwardly across the note pad. From the description of his injuries, Angelo O'Neill seemed the best candidate. His family lived on River Street in the South End, and as soon as he reached the area, Karl was assailed by a wash of images and memories: the slippery shock of a football on a cold wet day; flying down a street with Tony racing after him; the sound of a balky car engine sputtering in a sunny garage; a yellow puppy jumping eagerly against a fence. Karl pulled up and stopped a few houses short of 511 and sat for a moment to compose himself.

He had come without any clear idea beyond seeing the neighborhood. Even when he had found Angelo O'Neill's name and felt that mix of hope and terror, it had been a kind of theoretical hope, an intellectual terror. The reality of the neighborhood was quite different, at once utterly familiar and completely foreign. Karl suddenly under-stood that the age old-fear of ghosts was not perhaps so much the fear of meeting one as of becoming one.

At last, he forced himself out of the car and started down the side-walk. The information that the house with the hedge belonged to the Cerullis and the next one to new people, although Tony's grandmother still lived on the bottom floor, dropped into his mind. Tony was appar-ently a childhood friend; the Cerullis were just a name. A poster for a soccer match awakened a mysterious excitement; a side porch made his heart jump, then a linden tree crowded the walk, blocking his vi-sion, and there was the triple family, as solid and ungainly as a galleon, its big shingled porches thrusting exuberantly toward the street.

In the narrow yard, an old retriever and a little girl played with a ball under a big rambling grapevine. Although he had no idea who the child was and had forgotten the dog's name, Karl felt an almost unbearable grief, and he leaned weakly against the chain link fence. The uncles had played with a soccer ball in the back yard; Momma had yelled to be careful of the grapevine—and where was she? What had happened to her? Poppa had brought out Guinness and sandwiches.

"You all right, mister?" a voice asked. Karl heard an edge of suspi-cion, almost of hostility.

A young man, slight and dark, was standing a few yards away with his hand on the gate. Karl shook his head. He realized he had been standing staring at the child and the dog, suspicious behavior in neigh-borhoods far safer than River Street.

"I've been in the hospital," he said. "I thought I'd take a little walk but I'm not strong enough." He tapped his left leg. The light weight plastic gave a soft ping. "Walking cast."

The young man was not unsympathetic. "You want a drink of wa-ter or something?"

"No, no thanks." Karl felt it would be unbearable to enter the house, to prolong the meeting. "My car's just back there." He gestured toward where he'd left the Escort.

The young man nodded, probably relieved, and opened the gate. The old dog waddled over, the child bouncing along beside him. "Uncle Joey, Uncle Joey!" she cried and he bent down and picked her up. The dog swung his head toward Karl and barked once, twice, then tentative-ly wagged his tail. As Karl turned away, he heard Joey soothing the dog, but neither name meant anything and he was thankful, deeply thankful. He'd been a fool to come. The street, the house, the dog, the grapevine—those were painful enough. To feel that he knew someone, recognized someone he'd loved—the very thought caused him to tremble, and it was some time before Karl felt steady enough to drive home.

But in spite of the shock and the nauseating and frightening sense of being suspended between two lives, Karl found reasons to drive through the River Street neighborhood. There were soccer games in the big public park every weekend, and Karl felt that walking around the pitches was good for his leg. He found an Italian bakery with all kinds of wonderful pastries, and a German butcher shop that made excellent sausages. When he broke up with Paula and left the gray ranch house, he found an apartment a few streets west of River Street and moved in with his records and stereo, his math books, his recliner, and a futon.

Gradually, his anomalous situation became familiar, and although he'd at once feared and anticipated a constant stream of recollection, he never remembered any more of River Street than he had the first day. His knowledge, like his knowledge of cars, which mixed sophisticated information with the dumbest of gaffes, was tantalizingly fragmentary, as full of holes as a Swiss cheese. Or rather, it was his, Karl's, memory that had been punched full of holes, and these strange fragments had come to reside in the cavities.

In fact, if it had only been a matter of knowledge, of stray facts and figures, Karl might have managed all right. The O'Neills might gradually have been pushed into a corner of his memory like the inhabitants of some exceptionally vivid movie. What was truly troubling was something else, the sense that he had led a richer, fuller life elsewhere, a life that made him subtly dissatisfied with his present diminished existence.

He had a hint of this one day when he found his favorite bakery closed because of a death in the family. Karl decided to try another pastry shop in the neighborhood. With its oldfashioned black marble counter and leather-topped chrome stools, this establishment proved to be larger and considerably more elegant. A stout dark woman with a faint mustache and a white hairnet was helping another customer when Karl entered, and she turned toward the back of the shop and called, "Theresa, out front!"

A small, slight girl with short blonde hair tucked behind her ears appeared, wiping the flour from her hands on a towel. "Can I help you?"

Her voice was the best thing about her, very soft and sweet, for her features were plain, her figure, flat. Karl criticized the sprinkling of freckles, thin eyebrows, and large nose, but none of these mattered. He could feel her voice reverberating within his ribs and knew without a doubt that the only woman he had ever loved was this homely teenage girl.

"Sir?"

Her small thin hands were poised on the counter, and Karl had time to notice the thin blue veins on her wrists, a little emerald on her left hand, and the man's graduation ring she wore around her neck.

"Pastries," Karl managed to say. "Four, please."

She picked up a square of wax paper and waited for his selection.

"Two Napoleons." His voice was a croak. "And two coronets."

"Thank you," she said as he passed over the money. "Have a nice day."

It was symptomatic of his deep distress that Karl actually considered getting to know her, although he had seen almost at once that it was impossible. She was half his age—the age, appalling thought, of most of his students; she was physically unattractive; they would have nothing in common. And yet, there in the Elite Bakery, he had nearly toppled over from the heartwrenching shock of recognition. That she should be there alone, that she was perhaps still sad and faithful caused him intense pain, even though he was no longer the man she had loved.

The fact was that he was now neither wholly Karl Larson nor Angelo O'Neill, but an amalgamation of the two with the coherence of neither. Although he could diagnose an engine, he could never have worked as a mechanic, for there were huge, irrational gaps in his competence. At school, he remembered his subject and could manage the kids, but he found himself so restless with the school routine that he resigned at the end of the first semester.

Toward the end of the winter, out of work, depressed and confused, Karl called the hospital and asked to see Dr. Borgia urgently.

"You are in pain?" The slow, inflectionless voice asked.

"Not physical. I am perfectly healthy. But there are definite side effects. Psychological side effects."

"Ah," said Dr. Borgia. It was amazing how much interest he could convey with one vowel. "My office calendar is booked for weeks. Could you stop by my apartment? On Pulaski Boulevard, number 1132. I'm in one of those renovated brownstones."

Karl reached Pulaski just at sunset, amid the slush and ice of a late snowstorm, when the sky was turning a gaudy gold-pink above the thin crimson horizon. Though it was still cold and crisp, Karl was aware that the days were slowly lengthening; for some reason, that intimation of the change of seasons struck him as especially mysterious and poignant.

Number 1132 had recently been renovated. The decorators had spruced up the lobby, installed elevators and good lights, improved the windows and affixed alarms, but Dr. Borgia's second-floor apartment had eluded their ministrations. The doctor's rooms preserved their dark paneling, old rugs, and crammed, untidy bookshelves. A single lamp with a dark green shade sat on the desk in his study; the high casement windows admitted a faint bluish light. Dr. Borgia motioned toward an elderly velvet sofa, then eased himself into a big leather wingchair, where he was joined by a thin gray tom cat.

"You've turned my life into a bad novel," Karl said after the silence had matured. "Too many alternatives, all of them incomplete; too many connections, some of them contradictory."

Dr. Borgia listened patiently. "I did warn you," he said when he had heard the whole story. "I did warn you."

"I was desperate," Karl admitted.

Dr. Borgia shrugged.

"You knew," Karl accused him. "Didn't you?"

"I suspected. I did not know. The results of animal experiments are not always accurate indicators." His strong, heavy hands never stopped stroking the cat. "This is Alma. She is thirty years old."

"That looks like a male cat," Karl said.

"So it is, but it is still Alma. She was struck by a car—hopeless of recovery. This was a stray, gone feral, that was scheduled for experimental surgery." Dr. Borgia shrugged again. "One loves animals, too," he said.

Karl felt a chill.

"It is not a complete transfer. Alma was not such a good hunter. This one is more restless. But still..."

"You know, I expected you to tell me it was my imagination, that these were purely psychological effects," Karl said.

"Please remember, I never deceived you. I told you there might be changes involving the brain. And otherwise you would have died. Like poor Angelo."

After a moment, Karl said, "It was the stray whose spine was severed; the implant came from the pet that you were trying to save. Is that right?"

"Understand, it is not possible to move directly from animal to human results."

"You knew Angelo, though. You knew him." Karl suddenly had no doubt.

"He was my godson, a great-nephew, actually. A young man of simplicity, joy, and charm."

"I can't believe you attempted it! He would have been left forever in my body."

"I loved Angelo," Borgia observed implacably. "He had great sweetness of temper. He might well have adapted. The alternative was that he was lost forever. You see we both gambled."

"With a marked deck! You knew a hell of a lot more than I did."

"It's unfortunate that you are a mathematician," Borgia said in a reflective tone. "You should have been a poet, a novelist. Two lives, two families, an absolutely unique situation—it would have been a gift. But a man who loves precision and clarity was perhaps the worst choice of all. I am sorry about that."

"And for the rest?" Karl demanded.

"You are alive and healthy. What have you told me but that you have now experienced new and finer emotions? By your own account, you had never been in love; by your behavior, I guess you to have been selfish, reckless, and cold."

"And you," Karl shouted, jumping to his feet. "What about you?"

Dr. Borgia stroked the thin gray cat. "Love makes us do terrible things," he admitted.

Karl was whipping down an old two-lane, engine roaring, wind strong enough to rattle his teeth, leather jacket glued to his shoulders. The powerful vibration hurt his wrists and the tension in his legs made the healed bone ache. He was out of shape and out of practice for a heavy and powerful bike, but he kept his speed up, burning down the straights, accelerating out of the curves, ten, fifteen, twenty miles above the limit, looking always for the slow farm tractor which would pull out suddenly, which would cause him to cross the line, which would settle everything once and for all.

It was early spring, the road was damp; a watery sun came and went amid banks of clouds in a blue, white, and gray mackerel sky. Karl knew the tractor was up on a little farm road or bouncing out of a newly plowed field or just starting up in a barn, and he tightened the accelerator again, because he didn't want to miss it. He should have died before, in the first accident. That had been his time, but although he had cheated death, his life had been wrecked anyway and he was sick of it.

Ahead was a little hamlet with shops and businesses, but Karl was still burning along when a blue hatchback swung out from a small market. He tightened his grip, ready to swerve around the car, then saw oncoming traffic and hit the brakes. The big bike's rear end slewed right and then left with a sickening wobble; Karl's arms and legs trembled with the strain as the bike skidded from the pavement to the asphalt shoulder, zipped around the hatchback, then bounced back onto the roadway.

Karl was drenched in sweat and trembling violently. He signaled a turn, pulled off at the next road, and stopped. He was on a rural residential street of ranch houses and tiny cottages with lawns that ran right down to the pavement. Karl loosened his helmet. A bird was singing with insistent and elaborate passion in a jumble of shrubs and vines, and a horse whinnied beyond the trees. Under everything was the broken hum of the highway, and it came to Karl that he was not quite the same man.

Of course, he'd known that in one sense: his old life was a shambles. But, in another sense, he had not comprehended the changes until that moment, when he'd rushed toward death and resolution and found that he didn't necessarily want to find them. Karl felt the weak sun on his hands and face and realized that the late Angelo O'Neill had once again saved his life.

✤ ✤ ✤

JANICE LAW is a teacher and novelist. She has written the Edgar-nominated Anna Peters series of mystery novels and regularly publishes short stories in *Ellery Queen* and *Alfred Hitchcock Mystery Magazines*. Her most recent publications are the contemporary novels, *The Night Bus, The Lost Diaries of Iris Weed,* and *Voices,* the latter two nominated for the Connecticut Center for the Book Fiction Prize in 2003 and 2004. She lives in Hampton with her husband, Jerry, and teaches part time at the University of Connecticut.

Carole Rosenthal

The Concert Pianist's Flight

(for Tommaso Landolfi)

His wife liked him because his broad shoulders were soft, like a pillow, and so was his chest. His fingers when he probed her face, poking into an earhole or stroking her hair, yielded to the complex twists and folds of her skin, not pushing too hard or straight ahead, but resting upon her firmly with just the right elastic pressure. He was not a grasping person, but he was capable of producing from her throat a quick succession of adjacent tones, a glissando, and when it came right down to it she would admit that one reason they had such a good marriage, such a complementary relationship, was because he was definitely somebody she could trust. He was somebody a person could sink into, somebody who automatically bounced back from her emotional heaviness, her demands, without any sign of disfiguring indentations where her problems had lain. And he didn't make her feel bad about it. He could shape himself to her needs at the moment, without any permanent change in the integrity he felt in his own form.

But she began, finally, to resent the fact that she never left her mark on him. Since she first met him, he had not really changed. He was resilient, yes, and giving too, but impermeable in some way that hurt her feelings and that made her think he didn't care enough.

They were so different from each other, really. While he was in another room during the daytime, his back curved, practicing on the piano, worrying about phrasing, she would sit in the sunlight, her nose pressed into the cold window glass, squinting over the streets, wondering if he loved her. And if he did, did he love her as much as she loved him?

"Why are you so in doubt?" he wondered. "Maybe you don't give yourself enough credit for the wonderful qualities you have."

But her own fingers and body were filled with bones, clunky with sharp hard things right under the skin that got in her own and everybody else's way. She had been like that as long as anybody could remember. Pretty, but vaguely unmanageable. Not right. An old movie of her second birthday party showed her clearly: coy, curly-haired, beribboned, splashing accidentally—elbows and knees and patent leather shoes—into a tub of ice cream.

He, on the other hand, was airy and constrained; effortless. Hand-some. Some people commented, discreetly, that he was better-looking than she was—particularly when he went out to a concert in the evening in his dress suit, his jacket habitually unbuttoned to reveal a wide cummerbund wrapping, glistening, around his waist, his face smooth and shiny under the lights. But certain facts about him were not widely known. Only his wife, who was apt to be a bit reproachful, understood them. And this understanding gave her a certain power that should have made her feel safer.

"I need you, I need you," he told her repeatedly. "Jesus H. Christ! How many times do I have to tell you? Isn't it obvious?"

It was obvious. She had to inflate him every morning with her praise and with her breath, and at night, when he came home exhaust-ed, she had to press the day's tension out of him carefully, starting with his feet and working her way up, leaning into him with her body. He needed her all right. He needed her to listen to him obsess about how he thought he ought to be more famous than he was, considering his talents, considering his ability; he needed her to take care of him because he was a balloon.

Yes, there was no denying it. No *ifs*, *ands* or *buts* about it. While she didn't know the details of any other couples' private relationships, and for all she knew maybe one person or the other actually being a balloon was very common, how could she take those needs, the proof he always offered of his love, very personally? Couldn't he just as easily be anybody's balloon, not just hers?

She tried to get him to commit himself. He claimed he already had. He floated out of reach, abrupt, resentful. In a fit of passion that night, she kissed him too hard, frightening him with her urgency. He asked her to treat him tenderly, with more consideration: "Yes, I know you love me, it's just that you're so impulsive, you get carried away"; and, when she began crying, he said guiltily, sorry he'd brought up the subject, sighing, "No, I don't want you to change yourself. I love you, only restrain yourself just a little bit more, can you?"

But he began to feel as if he were stretching too thin from her out-bursts, the give and take of daily living, daily rubbing. In danger. He accused her of being overinvested in him.

"What are you trying to do, honey? You put so much of yourself into me, what do you have left over for yourself?"

But for the most part they were happy, well adapted to each other, more or less complacent.

"Do you love me?"

"Um-hmm, uh-hmm," he said, nodding.

They made love in strange ways. Often, she was in control, positioning him this way and that, twisting recklessly, blowing him up to the point she desired, sliding across him and crescendoing, then riding hard, pounding, ultimately flying, on his thick but diminishing thighs.

"Oh, that was fantastic. Do you still love me?" she asked.

"Um-hmm, uh-hmm," he always said.

Always? Then did it count?

Sometimes she got angry that he was too pliant, that he was never obdurate enough for her. But then she remembered—or he would remind her because he hated criticism, because it ruined his self-image, his practice, and his public performances—that his pliancy was also why she liked him.

"But maybe I don't excite you enough," she said. "There are certain risks you just don't seem to take."

After awhile, she began to brood about ways to change him, to make him love her better. She started jogging, and lifting weights, and doing aerobic yoga in the morning to firm up her figure, secretly spreading herself all over from face to toes with herbal masques, cutting and reshaping her hair, and letting her fingernails grow long, painting them a rich, deepening red.

One night when the lights were out and she felt the air thickening around her while they were making love, she grabbed him passionately and scratched him with a long fingernail, making him shriek with pain. He became almost instantly limp. The next morning he seemed pinched, suffocated, collapsed. Crumpled and forlorn. She couldn't revive him. He refused to go down to a rehearsal with a violinist— "What's the use?"—or even, by afternoon, to sit in his own music room and play. Depression. Humiliation. Both his and hers. It was evening before she located the tiny puncture over his left shoulder in the area where ordinarily one would find a wingbone. Glumly, trying to seem cheery—what else could she do?—she patched him back to near-normal, apologizing. Sorry, sorry. Smiling. Her teeth. He flinched.

The accident left a deep puckering cleft in his back which could be hidden under clothes. But the uneven striation of tension interfered with his playing until he got used to the pull of it. And the emotional scar was never completely accommodated, not even after he regained his confidence and his dexterity, that particular buoyancy of touch that had earned him his limited renown.

"I don't feel like you trust me anymore."

It was hard for him to trust her. Where he had always had a secret phobia about accepting her intimacy, about letting her fill him up with her admiration and her energy, afraid that he would stretch too vulnerably, beyond his capacity both inside and out, he seemed even more suspicious of her now; cautious, feigning indifference as she crouched by him in the morning, ashamed.

He began to withdraw. It affected the way he responded to his audiences, too, during his performances. No more magical expansion of sound and body, flaring larger than life with excitement. Recognition? Love? Applause? They seemed too dangerous. He didn't want to take the chance. How could he know when his wife and his audience would cross the delicate boundaries of separation, giving him not just as much as he wanted, not just as much as he needed, but more. What *they* wanted. Forcing their way in. Until he had no life of his own.
The only way he could perform now, he confessed to his wife, was by pretending that he was alone.

She was grateful for the confidence. Thoughtful.

"But that's such a compulsive over-reaction," she counseled him a couple of days later. "I hate to see what's happening to you. You haven't even achieved your full potential. How can you be afraid of too much when you've never experienced enough?"

He said he didn't know. She urged him to take a chance. He shrugged: "Why not?" The issue was crucial.

That night, after an unusually good recital, after some brilliant bravura moments, he forced himself to listen hard to the loud appreciation of his audience, the blast of breath, the exploding hands, rushing to enhance him.

"Bravo!"

"More!"

The air vibrated through the high hall. He found himself thrilled and moved. His wife smiled wildly from a seat in the front row. *Do it! Do it! Trust!* He smiled back at her. He opened his lips. *Yes!* They entered him all at once, but with the greatest ease. He swelled, even and obvious, to his full, true form. He barged upwards and outward, elated. Curved and translucent with exuberance, his satin lapel shining, arcs of light from the ceiling reflecting joyfully on his face, bobbing his head in acknowledgment, up and down. Then he grew larger, still magnanimous, globose, as if he were about to lift off the ground. He was beginning to float, a little too gassily.

The clapping went on.

As long as he continued to expand, the audience continued to applaud, amazed.

"You're overdoing it," his wife shouted.

Too late.

He could no longer stop himself. He was afraid he was going to burst, swollen as he was with inner greatness. Glaring, sublime. He listened for the explosion, the violent end of selfhood, trying to pull himself down, lower, lower, resisting.

Then suddenly, he heard a noise. A rip.

Pbbhh-flappbhh-pbbhflappbhh-pbbhhhhpp…

No, more like a fart. All the air going out of him at once. At first the audience just kept right on clapping their approval. Then they noticed that he was growing thinner, receding right before their eyes. And they heard the loud razzing noise…*pbbbhh-flappbhh-pbbh-flappbhhh…*

Crude, unmusical—was he making fun of them?—as all their stored-up exhalation released fast, very fast, so fast that he just took off.

He flew up into the air, sailed around in circles, awkward unpredictable circles, jagged rag-tag ellipses—you couldn't call them circles even—high above the stage. A smattering of resentment rose, unarticulated. People left, denying anything untoward. Didn't see, didn't hear. No. There was no glory in this flight.

He landed, deflated, on the dusty overhead light rail. He stuck there, draped over the flat black fixtures, overlooking the stage. Obscured.

His wife couldn't find him. She went behind the stage into the wings, then into the dressing rooms and got the stage manager, who referred her to the custodian, who considered the matter of missing husbands none of his concern. "Probably he's drinking it off somewhere, if you want my opinion."

Finally she borrowed a ladder and searched the ceiling, and, on her hands and knees, the pit. Until she was forced to the conclusion that her own daredevil subjectivity, stepping into the breach of her worst fear, had taken over in a hallucination. He had actually left her. She didn't know why. But he couldn't have loved her to begin with, could he have?

Because he never came down from the light fixtures they never had a chance to discuss it, to talk out their differences. Afterwards, she was always very bitter.

His fate was that he had to listen to all the performances ever given in the concert hall, and most of them were very bad indeed, which made him wonder gloomily why he hadn't become even better known, and if he was really as good as he thought he was. Her fate was that she had to live with a terrible guilt and embarrassment about being forsaken so abruptly when she'd been pretending theirs was such a happy marriage.

◈ ◈ ◈

CAROLE ROSENTHAL'S stories are published in magazines that range from the experimental (such as *Cream City Review* and *the minnesota review*), to mainstream literary *(Confrontation, Other Voices, Transatlantic Review),* to the political *(Mother Jones, Ms.).* Her new collection, *It Doesn't Have To Be Me* (Hamilton Stone Editions), was cited by *Booklist* for its wry "compelling" humor and its "fascinating glimpse beneath the surface of everyday life at ideas that would otherwise go unexamined." Frequently anthologized *(Foreign Affairs, Powers of Desire, Masterpieces of Modern Mystery),* her work has also been dramatized for radio, television, and stage and translated into eleven languages. Carole Rosenthal is Professor of English and Humanities at Pratt Institute.

Stephen Shugart

Making Faces

I like to drive my Porsche. I like to take the longest way home I can find, pushing it to the limit, swinging past Liz's place, or sometimes dropping in on Sally, and barely arriving home in time, before Maggie starts suspecting things and starts throwing my cold supper down the garbage disposer. But this time it's legitimate. I stop by the mall. I go to three different stores before I find the proper mask. At six o'clock in the evening on Halloween night, there aren't many left.

I buy this horrid mask for the firm's Halloween party. Ghastly. Cheap for a full-head mask. Made of warty green rubber with a red knife-like horn projecting from the top. Right then and there, I decide to go as a monster dressed up in a three-piece suit. Maggie is going as grapes.

"You're late," Maggie says. She' s standing in front of the TV, purple and squeaky, watching the news. She's arranged purple balloons of different sizes, tied on a network of strings over a Danskin top so that it looks like she has on a big lumpy jacket, with large shoulder pads and then narrowing in size to her waist. Some dangle down from there over flesh colored tights. She looks like a Can-Can dancer, sort of. She's done her eyes with vivid green eye shadow and she's wearing a Cleopatra wig, which is also green. "Tamara has already been here for an hour," she says.

I walk over to the hallway mirror and stretch the mask over my head. It' s evil looking, pretty gruesome.

"God, Dave," Maggie says, turning from the TV.

"Not bad, eh?" I ask.

"Not good," Maggie says. She closes her eyes for a moment. "You show up to work on time. You even get there early. I just think you could extend me the same courtesy. I never get to go out."

"Do you have to get all stirred up every time I walk in the door, or do you just stew all day?" I say. She starts tapping her foot. "Why don't you," I say. "Just shut up," I say inside my new monster mask.

I adjust my mask and go downstairs to say good-bye to my son, Lawrence, thinking that I'll give him and the babysitter a little scare. It's Halloween after all.

They're sitting at the card table, working on a pumpkin and watching the old portable TV. Lawrence is stabbing the pumpkin with my fishing knife. Tamara, the babysitter, is blowing a large pink bubble of gum and pulling seeds from the orange mass of pumpkin pulp piled onto a cookie sheet.

I hunch my shoulders and walk toward them, dragging my foot. Lawrence sees me first and screams. Then the pink bubble explodes. I laugh.

"You'll be a good sport tonight, won't you Larry," I growl and then pull off the mask. It's difficult to remove, and just for a second I worry that it isn't going to come off at all. Maggie yells down the stairs to leave the kids alone and to hurry up. I wipe the corners of my mouth that are wet with spittle and condensation with my handkerchief.

"God, Mr. Mendenhall," Tamara says. "You scared the shit out of me." Pausing, she twists her hair with her finger and pops her gum.

"Sorry," I say and wink at Tamara. Her mom, Amy, and I have flirted in the past, ever since her husband's death, and if it weren't for my darling Maggie, I'd be knocking on her door in a second. I know she's lonely.

Maggie is waiting in the garage with her little black evening purse dangling from her hand, the grapes squeaking as they rub against each other. I unlock her door and open it. She gathers up her balloons and tries to get in the Porsche. "Back in," I say. After a couple halfhearted attempts, she finally stuffs herself into the car, popping a few balloons as she tries to lean back into the seat.

"Oh, hell's bells," she says. I close her door and another grape pops and she shuts her eyes and tightens her jaw.

"You popped my balloons," she says, facing her window. She can't turn to see me.

"Sorry," I say, "but that's a stupid costume."

"Would you shut the hell up, Dave," she says. "The balloons are losing pressure already."

I say, "Didn't you bring any extra grapes just in case?" She doesn't answer. She clicks open her purse and holds up a pack of balloons. I put on my mask.

We ride the elevator with two vampires, a couple of ghosts and a drunken pair of punked-out leather types who are laughing and pretending that they're going to pop Maggie's balloons with their spiked bracelets. Everyone goes along, laughing a little nervously, except

Maggie. She's holding her breath and keeping her eyes pegged on the floor indicator above the chrome doors.

We climb all the way to the penthouse ballroom. When we arrive at the thirty-first floor and the doors slide open, Maggie says, "It's Halloween. Trick or treat, Dave."

"That's right," I say and head directly for the bar and order a double bourbon. I turn to see Maggie smiling and waving tentatively. The place is crowded and the party's well under way.

"I'm going out to the balcony," I yell and she waves me on. Outside, the cold autumn air feels good. I take off my jacket. Raggedy Ann and Andy are smoking cigarettes and talking. I go to the railing and look at the glass buildings glowing in the night. Thirty-one stories below, the street's full of taxis and the sidewalk is packed with promenading Halloweeners. I take the mask off, again having trouble getting the damned thing past my chin.

I think of Lawrence and wonder if he'll someday blow up pumpkins and break street lamps with rocks as I had done. Make the kinds of mistakes I've made. I turn and lean back against the railing and close my eyes. I open them and I see Maggie through the glass doors, walking towards me.

"Look, Dave. Look at my costume." Maggie says pointing to her deflated chest. "Some asshole just came up and popped them. He just came up and squeezed them."

"Too bad," I say and turn away.

"Come on, Dave."

"Oh hell, what's the point," I say and pull my mask back on. "I'm sorry I'm such a jerk. Does that make you feel better," I say. "It's Halloween. Let's party."

"That's better. You can be such a monster," she says and tiptoes to kiss me on my rubber cheek. Her grapes squeak against my chest. I hold her and try to kiss her back, but my tongue gets stuck. "Not with that mask you don't." She pushes my tongue back in with her forefinger and laughs. She gazes at me for a moment. Up close, her eyes look beautiful. She's used a lot of bronze and black to outline the green eye shadow. They look Egyptian, mysterious, not the eyes that stare me down every night when I walk through the door late. Then she makes a strange face, like she can't figure out what I'm looking at.

"There's Mel," I say to Maggie. He's fluorescent green from head to toe. A yellow-and-black radiation sign hangs from his neck. His wife, Kate, follows in a baggy white radiation suit. I wave at him and he waves back, even though he obviously doesn't know who I am. I'm just some guy with a monster mask waving. "Wave to him, Maggie. He can't see it's me."

"He's not going to recognize me with green hair either," she says. "Let's just meet them at the bar."

I nod and when I arrive at the bar, I tap Mel on the shoulder. He turns around and jumps back, shoving two bozos with red noses into each other. "Hey, that's real ugly," he says. "I give up. Who is it?"

"Mel," I say. "I'd like you to meet Bubbles, my wife."

He laughs as he turns to look at her, and then he looks at me. "Man, where'd you drag that mask up from, Dave? It's pretty weird."

"Hey," I say. "This isn't a mask. What are you talking about?" I say, my words echoing in my hot mask.

"You look amazing, Mel," Maggie says. "No. You are amazing, Mel."

"I think I look like radioactive snot."

"Don't say that, Mel. You look fine," Kate says and swats him on his rear. "He looks just fine."

"He looks sexy," Maggie says. "Like the Man from Glad or something."

"Well, at least you look radioactive," I say.

We drink our drinks.

Kate slides her arm around Mel's waist and says to me, "You know, Dave, I worry about you. I mean who but you would wear something like that?"

Maggie chimes in, "No one but Dave."

"I wouldn't talk," I say. I feel hot. I'm sweating inside the mask. "You look like a...fat blob of purple cancer," I say, and laugh.

Maggie doesn't say anything. She sets her jaw and lips the way she does. Kate and Mel don't say anything either. Kate says to Mel, "Let's dance."

Maggie doesn't speak to me as we ride the elevator. She wobbles as she stands in the back corner. I don't know how I could have blurted that out, but I'm glad we're leaving. I do these things every once in a while. They just pop out. There's nothing I can say now, and I feel sleepy with the alcohol and just want to get home.

Quietly, the elevator descends. I can hear my breathing. I'm inhaling deep and slow and I want very badly to bite Maggie's throat. In the chrome doors, I see beads of sweat forming on the skin of the mask,

I try to pull my mask off but can't, I feel hot, very hot and I feel like eating that person in the elevator with me, I want to terrorize her, my breathing is more uneven and Maggie stands there in those stupid balloons, my eyes hurt and I claw at my face, my mask, my teeth feel sharp as I try to shred the mask from inside out, I can't speak, she has no idea, she stands there as I try to pull the mask off, I pull at my throat, feeling, I can't find the rubber and I feel like gagging, I know if I don't peel this mask off I 'm going to slap her to the floor and tear into her neck, I can't think of anything else, I can't speak and I'm going to kill her. I want the mask off. Sweat stings my eyes.

Finally, I find a little flap of skin on my neck and I yank as hard as I can and the mask slips off. Immediately, I look in the chrome and my hair is flat and glistening. I need another drink, I think.

Maggie is giggling in the corner. "I'm really drunk," she says. "Let's go home and screw, you asshole." Her green eyes are vibrant.

As we walk to the car, she starts popping her balloons with a nail file. She pops one and laughs and then pops another. "I'm just a cancer," she says. "And you are a cheating bastard, Dave."

I don't know what to say. I'm tired of the witch. But I pull her to me and kiss her as passionately as I can muster. Two grapes pop. She doesn't resist and we kiss drunkenly. I grab a balloon near her ass and squeeze it until it pops. She squeals and says, "You're such a nasty little boy, aren't you?"

Maggie begins to play with the mask, stretching its horn, turning it inside out and back again. Then she stuffs her first two fingers into the mouth and begins pumping them in and out. She makes the mask kiss her breasts. "God, this thing is ugly," she says.

"It's scary, not ugly. Halloween's supposed to be scary," I say.

"I know, Dave. Believe me. I know that."

She keeps playing with my mask, and then she pulls off her green wig and slides next to me.

As I drive, Maggie kisses me on my neck and unzips my fly. I kiss her forehead and tousle her hair, which feels like straw. And just as I am going to slide my hand up her skirt, a police car comes blaring past at high speed. "They'll bust me no questions asked if I get stopped," I say. Maggie hunches her shoulders and goes down. "Come on," I say and push her away.

"I guess I'll put this stupid thing on instead," she says and pulls the mask on. She looks nude in her Danskin, even with the limp balloons hanging all over her, her breasts rounded and pressed tightly against the fabric.

With the mask on, Maggie looks at me and then into the rear-view mirror, not saying anything, and then she moves to her window and rolls it down, sticks her head out and begins sniffing the air like a dog. Then she howls.

"Okay Maggie, I get the point. It's a stupid mask. Roll up the window. It's getting cold."

"I kind of like it in here," she says in a shrill, muffled voice. She slides next to me again and turns up the volume on the radio full blast. She begins caressing herself everywhere, slowly. Then she kisses my cheek. The mask's rubber feels clammy.

She strokes my hair and then grabs my jaw with both hands and kisses me on the lips. I can't see where I'm driving. She presses the mask's mouth against mine with more force. She pries my mouth open with her hands and I feel her hot tongue enter my mouth. It's tubular and hairy, barbed. I start to pull to where I imagine the side of the road is. Another car blasts its horn and I hear tires screech. The tongue plunges deeper to the back of my throat and then I feel it moving down my esophagus and I start choking. Her eyes are green and phosphorous. I hit the brakes as the tongue probes my belly. My stomach cramps with pain. I can't scream. She has me by both ears and she's jammed her knee into my groin. I have no idea where we've stopped on the street. I reach behind her head and pull the mask off, terrified to see the horrid tongue retract into her mouth, her real face now revealed, tear streaked. She collapses into my chest. "You bastard," she says. I open the window and toss the mask as far as I can throw it.

I walk Tamara home. I tell her she's a good babysitter, that she's good with kids. I pat her on her head, put my arm around her shoulders and pull her close as we turn up the walk to her house.

"Okay," she says. "I'm sorry, but I don't think you should be touching me like this, Mr. Mendenhall. I don't want to get you in trouble with my mom, especially when you're drunk."

"I'm not drunk," I say. She hunches her shoulders and rings the doorbell.

Her mother unlocks the door, and the cardboard skeleton decoration hanging in the window dances a jig. She greets me with a smile. She's wearing only a short flannel nightshirt and red fuzzy slippers. Her legs are long and shapely. Tamara runs inside, saying she's sleepy.

Amy, her mother, asks if I want to step in for a moment, out of the cold.

"Sure," I say and step across the threshold. "Just for a moment. I haven't paid Tammy yet." She closes the door and combs her hair with her fingers.

"Did you have a good time tonight?" she asks, walking into her living room. She picks up a pack of cigarettes lying on the mantle above the fireplace. Our eyes connect in the mirror. She has a gorgeous face, high cheekbones, blue eyes, full lips, and mid-length blondish hair.

"Oh yeah. It was just great. Lots of booze," I say and smile. "Thanks for letting us borrow Tammy." I dig into my back pocket and pull out my wallet. "She's very good with Larry." I walk to the glass-topped coffee table in front of the sofa and put several dollars near the ashtray. "This is for her, not you," I say and wink, still talking to the mirror. I wonder if I'm slurring my words, whether I'm wobbling.

Amy turns to face me and pulls a cigarette from the pack. "I didn't think it was for me." She lights her cigarette. "I wouldn't accept money, anyway." She smiles and bends to put the pack on the coffee table. The nightshirt, unbuttoned three or four buttons at the top, reveals her breasts. She's purposely giving me a peek, I think, and I let her know I'm looking, staring at her chest as she stands upright.

"So, how are you holding up these days, Amy?" I ask. She takes a long drag on the cigarette. I want to say, oh dear Lord, hold me, you beautiful woman. There's a monster in my bed and I don't want to go home. Suddenly I feel queasy.

"I miss Luke, especially at this time of night. I can't believe he's been gone for almost two years now." She steps closer and pauses. Her lips quiver. "Hold me for a moment, Dave," she says after a long moment. I open my arms and embrace her, holding her firmly, stroking the soft fabric of her nightgown, her silky hair. She puts her head against my chest and then she starts kissing my neck. I lift her chin with my forefinger. I'm dizzy, out of air, and we kiss delicately, briefly. I see Tamara in the mirror.

"Mother!" Tamara yells, and bursts into tears.

I walk around the block a few times. It's Halloween, and I'm really scared. Maggie will sense something wrong, deceitful. But just for that brief moment with Amy, I feel okay, that I'm worth something more than a sale to hit Q3 numbers.

I sense something approaching from behind. I quickly turn to see if someone is following me. Just darkness. Then I think I see the face of my mask hovering in the trees, darting in and out of the shadows of the street lamps, reflecting in the windows of the homes I pass. I start trotting and finally break into a sprint, the green head with the red horn floating just behind my right shoulder, laughing and chasing me.

When I arrive at my door, I drop my keys. Maggie has turned off the porch light. Finally, I manage to feel the keys in the dirt under the pfitzer bush, the damned prickly barbs hooking into the backs of my hands, scratching my face, and I open the door. I feel my way in the darkness to the bathroom and vigorously brush my teeth and wash my face, avoiding looking in the mirror. I scrub hard with a washcloth and lots of soap.

Silently, I open our bedroom door, undress in the darkness as quietly and quickly as I can, sliding under the covers. Lying there, trying to breathe as quietly as I can, I keep imagining Maggie and me standing in the living room, yelling at each other, each ripping off mask after mask, daring each other to take off another one. How many would we have to shed before we could see each other, our real faces? The ones that are sick and tired of this situation. Then Maggie's bedside light clicks on. The room is bright, blinding.

"You're late," she says, turning on her side, facing me. She's removed all her makeup, is plain as she can be. She's naked and she slides her knee through my legs, rubbing me with her thigh. Then she throws the sheets back, quickly jumps out of bed and rips off my shorts, grabbing me like a saddle horn, then straddling me. "You're late, David," she says, stuffing me inside her. "And I don't like it when you're late, do you understand, David?" she says, rocking on top of me and drooling luminescent purple slime out of the corner of her sucker-like mouth.

Oh, yes, I understand. I understand, just like I always do when she bends over and nuzzles my neck.

∦ ∦ ∦

STEPHEN SHUGART has published short stories in the *Colorado Review, Madison Review, Aim,* and other literary publications. He is also a produced playwright. Presently, he is finishing a young-adult novel based on Ulysses's encounter with the Cyclops.

Justin Courter

The Town News

The store was dead the afternoon I met Kathleen. I was leaning on the counter, reading this story in a magazine about a woman who lives with a man who gradually turns into a boar. It starts with him just snorting a lot, and the woman notices his face seems to look like more of a snout. Then he starts to smell bad, hair sprouts all over him. He eventually gives up walking on his hind legs and before you know it he's got a tail and tusks and he's bashing dangerously all around the house. So one day the woman opens the door and he goes trotting off into the woods, never to be seen again.

But the narrator doesn't tell it like that. In the beginning she's always asking the guy what's the matter, but he just grunts and turns away. She describes how painful it is for her to see him change and she does what she can to make his life more comfortable up until he runs away.

I was aware that someone had come into the store, but the place was only an overgrown newsstand that sold espresso drinks and a lot of people came in to browse. "How's the story?" Kathleen asked.

I must have been pretty absorbed, because when I looked up I noticed that there was more after-work foot traffic out on the sidewalk than when I'd started reading. Kathleen was beaming at me from the other side of the counter. I knew right then. She was only in her forties and I saw what she would look like in her nineties. But it wasn't fifty years away; it was more like five months. This usually only happens if I've gotten to know someone a little. The story must've done it.

"It's really good," I said, and right away wished I'd said something at least halfway descriptive.

Kathleen was taller than me. Her hair was black mixed with gray and came down a little past her shoulders. There was an expression on her face like a little kid who's about to go trick-or-treating. "Have you gotten to the part where she opens the door?" she asked.

I knew I shouldn't talk to her anymore because I'd seen what I'd seen. That's part of why I don't have friends. But my head was still half in the story. "Yeah, I just got to that," I said. "I guess you've read it?"

Kathleen began nodding and smiled wider, showing braces on her top teeth. "A couple times," she said. "After I wrote it."

This is always how it goes. I miss the obvious things. Anyone could've told by the look on her face that she'd written it. Trying to keep my distance, I put the magazine down on the counter. It was one of those ones that looks like a book. There was an abstract painting on the cover that to me looked like a blurry mess—one of those things I guess I just don't get.

"Do you write?" Kathleen asked.

"Well..." I said, glancing back down at the magazine. I was going to say, "No, but I like to read stuff like this."

But before I could, she said, "You should come to our writers' group." I looked back up and she added, "That is, if you want to."

Then for a few seconds I was just standing there, sort of dazedly not ringing up the magazines she'd put on the counter in front of me. Kathleen looked out the front window and squinted as a passing car made a glare slice through the big front window of the store. For an instant, when she squinted, I felt like we were the only two people standing in the middle of a desert. I don't mean that in a romantic way. I mean it seemed like everything was dried up and dead and barren and the only relief from the pressing sun would be the long, dark, cold, empty night ahead.

"Do you have other stories I could read?" I asked, finally. Kathleen pointed at our bulletin board, which was plastered with all kinds of junk. "See that orange flyer?" she said. Like hundreds of people, I'd ignored it. "That's for our writers' group. Come by this Thursday and I'll give you some more stories."

As she handled her wallet, I noticed she had long, nimble fingers. I was amazed by the vitality of her body, though the skin was pale and already she was thin—all bones and tendons in the fingers and forearms. Her collar bones stood out too, like a delicate set of handlebars. But her movements were brisk. As she went out the door, she even bounced on her toes a little as she walked.

Once I saw this Spaulding Gray monologue where he's explaining to his son about death. He tells him everyone knows it's going to happen to them, but no one *believes* it. When I was in high school, I was talking to a girl on the bus this one time, and when she was in the middle of telling me something about her boyfriend, I saw one side of her head caved in, blood pasting her hair to her face and her dislocated shoulder bulging out real awkward in her sweater. It was just for maybe a second. She was a cheerleader, someone I ordinarily wouldn't have been talking to, but she turned out to be pretty genuinely, apple-pie nice and I thought some part of me was just being mean or jealous. A week later this girl was thrown through the windshield of her boyfriend's car and into a tree and she was dead before the ambulance came. Ever since then I've *believed* it.

I mentally flogged myself all the way home that night after I got off work. Because when I met Kathleen I'd immediately started deceiving her, making her think I was shy. Everybody knows that only other writers ever read those magazines. There's something perverted about that. Also, she probably thought I was a kid. I'm twenty-six but I get carded for cigarettes all the time. I stand there fumbling with my wallet, feeling like I'm eighty.

As soon as I opened the door of my tiny studio apartment, Filbert said, "Oooooo hoochie mama!"

"Shutup," I said.

"Shutup," he agreed. That was two-fifths of his whole repertoire. He already knew "Oooooo hoochie mama!," "Holy shit!" and "Okay Einstein," when I got him. From me he learned "Shutup," and "Ah, go to hell." Never get a goddamn bird. It's this depressing little convict you have to look at all the time and who does nothing but harass you. It makes leaving town, which I do a lot, a real pain in the ass. My sister had given me Filbert three years before, thinking that was a very funny Christmas present, and I'd been trying to get rid of him ever since. Whenever I asked, no one wanted him.

I opened a beer and sat there on the bed staring at the wall until my feet trembled with the throbbing bass from Nicki's stereo. She was the woman who lived below me. Filbert, like he always did when he was in a good mood, started bobbing his head back and forth in time to the beat, now and then taking a step to the left or the right on his perch like he was dancing. I got him the biggest cage they had, but, you know, it's still a cage. I never asked Nicki to turn her music down, even when it stayed on until real late. She's going to die giving birth to a baby boy in about four years.

I thought about Kathleen, who did not have a clue what was going to happen. If she did, her optimism, and for sure those braces, would not have been there. Jesus Christ. Is there a polite way to tell a total stranger you think she should go to a doctor? If there is, I don't know it. But in Kathleen's case, what I'd seen pretty definitely meant that it was way too late. Maybe the best thing would be for her *not* to know about it for as long as possible.

I knew the best thing for me would be to not go to that writers' group on Thursday, so I was surprised as anybody to find the orange flyer in my hand as I got off the bus a block from the high school that was also a community center. Twenty minutes before the time even.

Kathleen had parked a car that seemed several sizes too small for her at a metered spot. She was on the sidewalk, bending into the passenger's side to haul out a heap of paper, which she stood up with abruptly when I said her name. It was past dark. Kathleen stared in the bluish streetlight trying to place me. "It's John," I said. "From the Town News." When I heard myself talk, my name sounded made up. It seemed more likely I was a stalker.

"Right, of course," Kathleen said, kind of professional. "I'm glad you decided to come." In the semi-darkness you couldn't tell how pale she was.

I offered to help her carry her stuff, which turned out to be lots of photocopies of just a few different stories. I noticed, as she piled them into my arms, that there was a border of rust around the wheel-well of her cheap import. That made me more comfortable. I'll meet people younger than me who have these gleaming new cars and enormous brontosaurus-mobiles and I feel like an illegal alien. I don't seem to be able to communicate with them after that. I mean, I walk.

There was a big map of Spain hanging on the wall in the front of the classroom and on the board someone had written, "Hola. Me llamo Isabella. ¿Cómo te llamas?" As other people came in, we dragged a bunch of the desks into a circle and pushed the other ones away. After everyone had shown up who was going to, Kathleen passed around the stories that were for the next week, then introduced me.

What I was kind of nervous about was I expected the writers' group to be this crowd of super-sophisticated people who were all quoting authors you never heard of every five seconds. But these were just regular people. There was a woman who looked exactly like Mrs. McCormick, the mom of one of my friends growing up. She even wore the same long, baggy shirts some women wear to make you think they're not really fat. But Mrs. McCormick was different; she'd watched a lot of daytime television and wasn't somebody with anything like what you might call literary ambitions. There was a little old guy who reminded me of a Santa's helper, a couple older women and a girl, or I mean woman, about my age. She came sweeping in, late, in a long black dress, draped herself over one of the desks and kept tossing this long curtain of hair around the whole time in a way that reminded me of some movie I couldn't remember the name of.

By the time the girl got there, a guy with a goatee named Steve, who looked real familiar, was reading a couple pages of his story to us, even though everybody besides me had already read the whole thing at home. The story was about a man and his clone, and how they're like the odd couple, except one of them is plotting to kill the other. I realized why I hadn't recognized Steve. When I usually saw him it was on the weekends and he had on a helmet and tight, spandex cycling clothes—which was kind of gross because he wasn't exactly slim—and he was wobbling around in those cycling shoes that make it sound like there's a tap dancer in the store, sipping a grande latte until after an hour or so he plopped a stack of science fiction magazines on the counter. Everybody seemed to think his clone story was great until the forgotten-movie-girl pointed out some mistakes and a few other people jumped in and then really fast the story turned out to be a lousy piece of shit. Then Bernie (the Santa's helper) and Steve started arguing in a real nasty way. As the night went on, I realized it was just how they got along. Like a father and son.

Of all the long rows of fluorescent lights on the ceiling, the one directly over my head flickered and went out. Then it came back on and kept flickering the whole rest of the time. After a while Bernie pointed up at it and said, "I think John is signaling his approval of the story."

Kathleen had a way of talking that made it sound a little like she was giving commands, even when she was just discussing something. She turned the conversation more civilized and told Steve some shortcuts that made his story way better if you read it over with her changes.

There was a break after forty-five minutes. Bernie talked to me as he munched on the cookies Mrs. McCormick's look-alike had brought. Bernie had glasses and a thick gray mustache that was chopped off so it looked like a little brush picking up crumbs from the cookies. He had short legs and one of those round little bellies that presses out and looks like it hurts. He was real nice, but sometimes you felt like you were dealing with a cartoon character. He was what my ex-girlfriend would have called cute. I tried to steer the conversation clear of his personal life, but since I didn't have any answers to the writing questions he asked me, he started talking about his wife and his dogs and I soon learned that he would die of a heart attack in two years.

For the second half of the writers' group, we talked about a section from a memoir that was about one of the old ladies. Or the rest of the group talked about it, while I looked at the spitballs on the blackboard and wondered about the kids that had shot them there. I thought about them coming back the next morning without knowing anything about the stuff that had gone on in here while they were at home watching television. I didn't mention it, but I'd always thought that people only read the memoirs of other people if the other people had been famous. And I'd never heard of this lady before. We also talked about some poems the forgotten-movie-girl had written without using any concrete nouns at all. While they talked about her poems she sat real rigid with her eyes popping out at the ceiling like she was playing Joan of Arc being burned at the stake.

Kathleen handled everyone's writing in a respectful but probing way. Which was generous since her own writing was so much better. You could see that everyone knew she was the leader of the group even though they probably hadn't ever officially decided on it. She shook me out of the trance I'd slipped into at the end by announcing to everybody that I might be bringing in a story the next week. The light over my head was still flickering on and off.

"So what did you think?" Kathleen asked, when we were pushing the Spanish students' desks back into rows.

"I don't think I should be here," I said.

"Don't be silly," she said. She touched my arm and a little thrill went through me. "Oh, I have something for you. Out in my car."

As the other people left, all of them making a special point of saying goodbye to Kathleen, I got an inkling of something else about her that had to do with the desert scene I'd thought of when we met. But the signal or whatever was getting scrambled because at the same time I was trying to think of some way to change the false pretense I'd used to get into the writers' group.

At first I thought Kathleen was taking a boxed cake out of the trunk of her car. Then I saw that the large stack of paper tied up with string was topped with a blank sheet of paper that had the title *12 Fables* in the center of it. Before I knew what I was doing, I asked Kathleen if she wanted to go have a beer. She gave me a funny kind of look, like I was trying to change the rules halfway through a game, but she agreed.

Now don't get me wrong. I'm not like this swinger, asking women out all the time. Far from it. And if I have a type, I wouldn't expect it to be Kathleen. I mean, generally, I'm attracted to shorter women who are more rounded out. But right about when she handed me the story collection, my reception cleared up and I knew she was alone. Of course, I was too. I hadn't lost as many people as she had. But we were both alone.

We sat at a tiny round table in this bar I'd suggested, which I realized, as soon as we sat down, was all wrong. I was showing my age. It was the kind of place where the music is a little too loud even though it's almost empty, and the wait staff is giving each other shoulder rubs. But Kathleen kept up the same pertness she'd used to guide the conversation about Steve's clone story. Her dark, shiny eyes stayed just as lively. While she told me about how she'd decided to become a librarian, I saw that her husband had left, no kids, and both her parents were dead. When these things happen I feel like I'm remembering something the person told me a long time ago, even though I just met them. It was hard for me not to wince in front of Kathleen while I was getting her memories. And it was tiring trying to keep up as she prattled on all excited about how they were going to put an addition on the downtown library.

As she took a sip of her beer, I realized that alcohol was probably bad for her in her condition. Why couldn't I have suggested coffee instead? But then, caffeine couldn't have been good either. God damn it—why couldn't I have just said goodnight and gone the hell home?

"How are things at the Town News?" Kathleen asked.

"Well, not bad, I guess," I said.

"I suppose you have access to a lot of reading material," she said hopefully, taking another polite sip from her beer. "That's good for a writer."

"It hasn't inspired me a whole lot," I admitted.

"How long have you been there?"

"Almost a year." That was how long I'd been in town. It seemed like forever.

"If you don't like it," Kathleen said, gently but firmly, "then why don't you try something else?"

I felt like a crappy, slapped-together piece of fiction that Kathleen was critiquing right then. I started casting around for some way to make myself plausible. It had been so long since I'd been in this kind of situation, I'd forgotten that's what you have to do: tell each other your stories.

"It's just a temporary thing," I said. "I move a lot. I like to travel." This was grade-A bullshit. To be honest, I'm just plain afraid to sign a one-year lease. But this was a chance to sound positive about something, so I pretended I liked to experience life in new places, when I really just take off when I get too depressed. I pretended I liked mid-size cities when actually I'm scared I could never afford to live in a real one. I talked too much.

When we stood up to leave, Kathleen put a hand down on the table top. "Whoah," she said. Against the black surface of the table, her hand looked like a skeleton's. I knew the unsteadiness wasn't from the one-and-a-half beers she'd had. Just like I knew what the coughing fit she had when we got outside was from. I couldn't tell her.

While I lay in bed not sleeping that night, listening to the thumping coming from below, I wondered if people ever died from cancer without knowing what killed them. I thought about writing a story for the writers' group, one where the main character finds out she has cancer, so I wouldn't have to come out and tell Kathleen. Then I thought that was really, really dumb.

I'm terrible at thinking of things. The real answer to Kathleen's question about my job was simple. Every time I get to a new town I get one of these bottom-feeder jobs out of necessity, thinking: after a little while, I'll figure out what I really want to do. Then I come home every night after work and I can't think of anything. When I finally realize I'm never going to think of anything I go out and get completely shit-faced and then I have a hangover and I have to go to work. Eventually I decide to just go start over someplace else.

Kathleen's stories were incredible. I looked forward to them all day at work and read them at night. Sunday and Monday I had off and it rained both days. Which made it perfect. I sat by the window in my apartment in the battered armchair I'd found on the sidewalk, sipped hot chocolate, and read real slow. Sometimes I swear I could spend my whole life like that.

One of the stories was about rain, sort of. There was this city where it starts raining one day and it rains harder and harder until the rain-drops turn into bullets. It goes on for days. People get killed going out to pick up their newspapers. The meteorologists go absolutely apeshit on television. Everyone's houses and cars are destroyed and it ends up bringing people together, making them do kind things they wouldn't have done before.

Another story was about a woman who is reincarnated as a dog and sees there's something familiar about her master. It takes a while, but it turns out that her master was her dog in the previous life, but the master doesn't know it and there's no way for the dog to tell her.

The one I liked the best was about a man who slips out of his body one day and into his shadow. He's attached to himself by the bottoms of his feet and gets dragged around by himself all day, forced to look up and watch all the usual shit he does. The whole time, he feels he's being stretched like putty, longer and longer until the sun sets and he seeps into all the other shadows of the world, where he finds out he's in a place that when he was in his body he called death.

I can't do justice to the stories. You have to read them yourself because how Kathleen tells them you really feel the dog's frustration when she can't communicate. You really feel the weirdness of the man outside his own body. I'd never read anything like it.

I went to the library where Kathleen worked to tell her how much I liked the stories. Right when you walked in the library there was a poster on the wall of a movie star awkwardly holding a book in his hands and "READ!" in big block letters under him. I found that offensive. Say you were going to hear an orchestra and when you got to the symphony hall, in the lobby there was this poster of a famous football player telling you to "LISTEN!" I mean what the fuck?

The library was busy. Kathleen was helping one person fill out the form for a library card and checking out another person's books while explaining to somebody else how to bring up a certain screen on the computer. Those stories had changed my whole world. I'm not exaggerating. When I saw Kathleen, and that gawky kind of grace she handled her life with, the reality of her was too much. I had to duck down one of the aisles, pull a book off a shelf and pretend to be looking through it. I could hear her voice, which was deep, almost masculine, as she told someone where the reference section was. I started getting annoyed. These people just thought of her as an information booth worker. I mean, would they take Charles Dickens for granted like that if they saw him standing there behind the circulation desk? And what the hell did I think I was going to say to her anyway? A bead of sweat tickled as it rolled from my armpit down the underside of my arm. I saw then the book I was thumbing through was a guide for people purchasing antique American furniture. I shoved it back onto the shelf. I bolted. Kathleen's friendly, authoritative voice was patiently explaining something to somebody behind me as I pushed through the door.

When seven o'clock came on Thursday night, while everybody in Kathleen's writers' group was moving desks and passing around photocopies, I was pacing back and forth, three strides each way, in my apartment. The tempo of Nicki's stereo was rapid underfoot and the hallway kept filling with squeals of greeting at Nicki's door that evaporated as the newcomer was absorbed into the general racket of the apartment. I knew it was bigger than mine, but still, with the number of times the door had opened and slammed shut, her apartment must have been starting to look like a packed subway car.

I didn't see how I could keep showing up at a writers' group, impersonating a writer, without ever bringing any writing. And I couldn't sit there not saying anything like I had the last time. But since I'd read her stories, I felt like I had to tell Kathleen because maybe there was some way they could help her live longer. This was like a major author here, just no one knew it yet.

In the process of my pacing, I'd emptied a few bottles of beer and Nicki's noise was getting so aggravating I was going to explode or do what I did, which was shrug into my jacket, jump on a bus and land a block from the school where, from a distance, I could see the Spanish room was already dark. Kathleen was unlocking her car and saying goodnight to Bernie. I jogged over to them.

"I've gotta tell you something," I blurted, interrupting.

Bernie looked up at me. The streetlight reflected from his glasses so I couldn't see his eyes. "We missed you tonight young man," he said.

"I had to—" I said, still panting a little. I hadn't thought up an excuse. "I got caught up with something else."

"It appears you've been exercising," Bernie said in a way that made everything about me ludicrous all of a sudden. "And you missed our little celebration," he said, like reprimanding me. He turned back to Kathleen. "Well, congratulations again," he said. "I've got to be getting along. Ta-ta." And he marched off down the sidewalk, his little legs jerking out in front of him like they were being pulled by strings attached to his knees.

Kathleen had unlocked her car by now and put her piles of paper in the back seat. "Let's go," she said, across the roof of her car. "Get in." Besides how she was acting, there was something different about her face that made her look younger. "What happened?" I asked, as she pulled her car from the curb. She turned her head to look for traffic and her hair gave off a faint eucalyptus-type smell. Her movements were quicker than usual, almost jittery.

"I brought some champagne to workshop and we all got a little tipsy." She couldn't stop smiling as she drove along. "So, Jonathan, can you dance?"

"Not very well."

"Well that's what I'm going to do right now," she said, a little giddy. "Would you like to come along or not? I can drop you off on my way if you like."

When I reached for my wallet at the door of the club, she slapped my arm. "No, no, no. I'm paying," she said. Then, in the blaring noise of the place, she wouldn't let me pay again after she ordered us drinks. "Here's to the publication of *12 Fables*," she shouted over the music. She touched the side of her plastic cup against mine.

"Really?" I said.

"Drink up Johnny," she said.

It was awfully sweet. I hadn't been able to hear what she said to the bartender when she ordered. Whatever they were, Kathleen right away ordered two more of them and I saw what was different about her was that she'd got the braces off her teeth. She told me the name of the contest she'd won, which didn't mean anything to me. But it was a pretty big deal apparently because they gave her a few thousand dollars and the story collection was going to be published by an imprint of some big publishing house. Before I had a chance to really grasp it all, Kathleen said, "Come on," and led me out onto the dance floor by my wrist. I felt the same current of excitement I'd felt when she touched my arm a week before.

They were playing this techno stuff with a really fast beat and the strobe light made everybody's movements look robotic. What was embarrassing was there were two girls dancing right next to us wearing teeny bikini tops.

Everything was fine at first. Kathleen stuck out a little bit because she was so tall and she kind of pogoed up and down when she danced. She was smiling the whole time like a little kid on a trampoline, her hair flipping around her face. But after about ten minutes she slowed down real quick, then stopped and stood there with her hand on the middle of her chest. With the strobe light and all the people moving so fast around her it was like a nightmare.

"Are you alright!" I shouted.

Kathleen nodded and put her hand back down to her side. But then without saying anything she walked slowly back over to the bar. I followed her and sat down on a stool next to her. What the hell could I do? I shouted at the bartender for some ice water.

Kathleen took a few deep breaths. "That was strange," she said. "It just felt like my lungs were shutting down. And my heart rate went way up." She tried for her usual happy smile but instead ended up looking apologetic. "Maybe I'd better take it easy," she said. She sipped the water I'd handed her. "Thanks," she said. "I'm sorry, I must have gotten myself a little too excited."

"It's alright," I said, even though I knew it was nowhere near alright. She put her cup down on the bar and went into a long coughing fit that made me cringe. We both watched the other people dancing for a little bit. The bikini girls were still going strong. Kathleen went to the bathroom and came back again, her face looking pulled-down.

"John, I apologize for asking, but do you think you could drive me home?"

I said no problem. When we got out to the car she withered into the passenger seat. She seemed shrunk, a far cry from her larger-than-life self. Now was the time to tell her, but every time I swallowed in preparation, she said, "You go right at the light," or something like that. Which was good because when I'm behind the wheel of a car I'll drive right across three states before I know what I'm doing.

"I didn't get a chance to tell you how much I like your stories," I finally said, instead of what I was supposed to say. By now we were in front of her building.

"Well now's your chance," Kathleen said. Then, of course, I couldn't say anything. I started my rendition of parallel parking and she said, "You can borrow the car to get home. Just bring it back some time tomorrow." By then I'd parked the car. "I have the day off," she said, climbing unsteadily out of the car.

"Let me just make sure you get in okay," I said.

She got a little winded and had to stop on the landing on the way up to the second floor. At the door she hesitated for a second with the key in the lock, then her black eyebrows raised in an ironic look. "Green tea?" she asked.

I'm always amazed by how people decorate their apartments because my place looks more or less like a cell. I'll put something on the wall, then sit there spying on it over the top of the book I'm reading, thinking, "Now why would I want to look at that forever?" Then I think the real reason I put it there is I want somebody to visit me and look at it and think I'm something besides a guy who works at a newsstand, so I get up and yank it off the wall.

But I've been in a couple people's places where I feel so comfortable right away I almost have to take a shit. Kathleen had bookshelves built into the wall from floor to ceiling, taking up two walls of the living area and wrapping around into the dining area. She could have started her own library. There was a chair shaped like a wok with a big round cushion in it and a wooden crate next to it piled with books, magazines and coffee mugs. There were lots of those rugs with dark colors and complicated zigzagging leafy patterns all over them. Some of the shelves were crowded with the kinds of knickknacks that let you know the person whose apartment it is has traveled outside the country. There was a whole mess of plants. There were old-fashioned etchings like you see in books but they were in frames hanging on the walls. They were probably in no danger of being torn down.

While Kathleen was filling up the kettle and getting out cups, I wandered into the dining area where there was a long table in front of the window overlooking the street. There was a computer and paper scattered all around. A writing tablet was folded back and the page was mostly covered with Kathleen's small, neat handwriting. I didn't mean to be snooping. I was bent over the table more to admire her handwriting than anything else, when Kathleen stuck her head out from the kitchen alcove.

"Hey," she said. "Shoo, shoo. Get out of there. Go on, git." The kettle started whistling and she went back in to fill our cups. "A cake always tastes better after it's finished baking anyway," she called out to me. Which was kind of funny because her last name was Baker.

She seemed to be feeling better. She brought out the tea and a plate of these chalky cookies she called shortbread. I asked her how she wrote. She was in the wok chair and I was on the couch. She bunched up her forehead, bit into a cookie and asked what I meant.

I wasn't sure what I meant, but I said, "I mean, like, do you write on paper or the computer?" Then I thought about shooting myself because I'd said "like." Kathleen always spoke real good English.

"Oh." She perked up, straightened a little in her chair. "I always write the first draft out longhand, go over it once, then enter it into the computer. How do you work?"

I took a sip of the tea. It tasted like what you might wring out of a handful of seaweed. You thought of the word "pottery," rather than "mug" when you looked at the kind of thing I was drinking out of.

"I try to do the whole first draft in my head," I said. "Actually, right now I'm doing all my work without any paper at all."

Kathleen looked amused. "I see," she said. "They're conceptual pieces?"

"Right," I said. "I've got several novels done already, I just haven't written them yet." The way I put my mug down on the coffee table I think Kathleen could have guessed I'd had a couple beers before we had those dance-club drinks.

She didn't let on though. She smiled and the square ghosts of the braces were there in the center of each tooth. "Yeah, I get blocked too sometimes," she said.

When she went to the bathroom, I noticed a photo album with a thin layer of dust on it under the coffee table. I picked it up and started flipping through. It made my stomach clench to see how much weight Kathleen had lost since any of the pictures were taken. There were pictures from her wedding, so I got a glimpse of the son-of-a-bitch. He had to be about ten years older than her. He was shorter than her too, which made me not feel so bad, but he had round glasses and a wispy beard. He looked like the kind of guy who writes books that are real hard to follow and that people call important. He also looked like the kind of guy you'd meet at a cocktail party and right off the bat he'd say something gauged to make you feel incredibly stupid.

"I'm sorry," I said, and slapped the cover of the album closed when I realized Kathleen had come back in and was standing on the other side of the coffee table. I hadn't heard her but now I could hear the gurgling of the toilet from down the hall.

"That's okay," she said, sitting back down in the wok. Her hair swung out in that little-girl way and she tucked one leg up under her. "I forget that's there sometimes," she said. "So. How about one of those cigarettes of yours?"

"Are you sure?" I said. I'd been trying to keep the lid on a nic fit for her sake.

"What the hell," she said. "I don't get a collection of stories published every day." She took this Oriental-looking dish off a shelf near her to use for an ashtray. "One won't kill me," she said.

"Why did you two split up?" I asked.

"He came home one fine day and announced that he preferred being a bachelor." By the way she held her cigarette you could tell she used to smoke, but the way she hardly inhaled at all you knew that was a long time ago. "But it was pretty soon after we found out I couldn't have children." She shrugged her shoulders. "He couldn't have liked bachelorhood all that much because he married one of his TAs less than a year later." She started coughing as she leaned forward to flick her ashes in the bowl on the table.

I was too afraid about sounding ignorant to ask, so I had to sit there wondering why he ran off with one of his tax attorneys. "I'm sorry," I said.

She shook her head as she swallowed some tea. Her eyes were damp from coughing. "No, don't be," she said. "We're both much better off as we are now. It was all wrong but we had to go through it to find that out."

"He turned into a boar," I said.

Kathleen winked. "Just between you and me," she said. Then she got a distant look as she gazed toward the windows at the front of the apartment. "He was kind of boring, really." She said it like her ex-husband was someone she'd just met earlier that day.

I knew I had to either tell her what was happening to her, or just fuck off for good. So pretty soon I said I had to get going. I took the mugs and the cookie plate into the kitchen.

"You don't have to do that," she said, following me in.

I decided to tell her. I turned from the sink. Her hand was on the counter and I put mine on top of it and was going to say, "I think you might have cancer," when instead I kissed her. On the mouth. I don't know if I've added this in my imagination since then, or if right before I kissed her, Kathleen shrank away like she was afraid I was going to do something violent. But I remember my teeth knocked against hers, so I pulled away immediately and kind of rubbed the upper part of her arm like to say I really just meant it in a friendly way only I'm retarded. I still feel sick when I remember how Kathleen stood there, totally bewildered, saying nothing, while I backed out of the kitchen like a bank robber, babbling what I don't even know, before I made a mad dash out the door, down the stairs and into the street. I was three blocks away when I realized I'd left my jacket on her couch.

"Well, she sure as hell didn't see that one coming," I told Filbert when I got home.

"Oooooo hoochie mama!" Filbert said.

"Shutup," I said.

"Ah, go to hell," he said. I picked up where I'd left off earlier that night pacing back and forth. The phone rang but I didn't pick it up.

I got all serious after that. Decided I was going to sit down and write a short story. A real good one that would prove to Kathleen I wasn't somebody's kid brother trying to get to first base with her. I'd show up and be businesslike at that writers' group on Thursday with the story all typed nice and photocopied, and I'd pass the copies around like it was the most natural thing in the world.

So one night after work I bought a notebook, came home and sat there with it in front of me on the card table that is my dining room table and desk in one collapsible get-out-of-town-quick piece. I looked at the notebook. For a while. Then I realized I hadn't had a beer yet and how I'd heard that ritual is important for writers.

That helped some. I almost filled up a whole page. I wanted to describe this old abandoned house me and a friend of mine had broken into when we were kids. He cut his leg pretty bad when his foot went through some rotten floor boards in the upstairs. I was downstairs and I heard him yell. A few chunks of plaster smashed on the floor right next to me. When I looked up, his foot was sticking out of the ceiling wiggling around like it was still looking for something to stand on. The foot coming out of the ceiling by itself like that was really something. For a second it made you think about what a weird animal would be attached to a thing like that.

But all I'd done in page one was describe the rundown house. And if I did write about that other stuff it wouldn't have been a fiction story anyway because it was just some shit that really happened. I looked over the page. What I'd written didn't sound right, so I kept scribbling words out and trying different ones. But they were like building blocks that no matter how I stacked them I ended up with a crooked structure that would completely collapse if someone like Kathleen simply pointed at it with one of her long fingers.

Then I got pissed off at myself just for trying because I don't even know like basic grammar. My education sucked. I picked up my pen and scribbled so hard over everything I ripped through about five pages deep. That calmed me down some. Then I stared at the notebook and tried to imagine filling all those pages up with words. I realized it wasn't just the grammar stopping me. A writer has to be a person who can constantly make something out of nothing. I could never be that kind of person. I fanned through the notebook. All that white. It would be like walking naked into a blizzard every day. No wonder you're always hearing about these people jumping off bridges or turning into alcoholics. I'd put away three beers just trying to write a couple crappy paragraphs.

I picked up my lighter and started flicking it, flicking it, looking at the mess I'd made on the first page. I started burning the corner of the notebook a little at a time and blowing it out. I must not have been paying attention because all a sudden the whole thing was in flames and I had to grab it up quick off the card table. Filbert, who'd been minding his manners until now, started flapping around in his cage going, "Holy shit! Holy shit!" and the smoke alarm went off and I kind of panicked and just chucked the whole notebook out the window. The alarm wouldn't turn off, so I had to pull out the battery. Once that noise stopped I realized the phone was ringing, and I knew who it had to be because my phone never rang. Someone was knocking on the door, too, so I answered that instead.

Nicki and a friend of hers were standing there looking concerned. "We were just wondering if everything's okay?" Nicki said.

But I could hardly hear her because Filbert was still freaking out. The fire must have really rattled him because he was getting everything garbled. He was calling out stuff like, "Oooooo hoochie Einstein! Okay! Go to hell holy mama!"

"Everything's fine," I said. Smoke was drifting into the hall. I wasn't letting the door open very wide.

"We saw, like, fire?" Nicki said. "Coming down outside the window? And your alarm went off?"

"Ah go to hoochie hell!" Filbert said. Then, "Shutup! Shutup! Shutup!"

"Don't you want to answer your phone?" Nicki's friend asked. They were both trying to see around me into the apartment.

"That's alright," I said.

Nicki still looked worried. I wanted to tell her, look, please don't ever get yourself pregnant. The friend, who seemed a little sharper than Nicki, was about to start laughing. She'd already figured out what an idiot I am.

"Sorry about all that," I said. "I was trying to cook something." After they left, I talked to Filbert for a while to try and calm him down. Then I went out and picked up the burned remains of the notebook off the sidewalk and of course, when I was taking it back upstairs to throw it out, Nicki and her friend were coming down. I tried to kind of hide the blackened notebook with my body.

"You broil or fry those?" Nicki's friend said.

A few nights later I was walking around and I ended up in Kathleen's neighborhood. Going down her street. There was that jacket I'd left and I started wondering if I'd done that on purpose. Her light was on and she was in the window sitting at the long writing desk. I stopped and stood there in the dark, on the other side of the street, looking up at her. She was writing something out longhand, which made me glad—a new story. Kathleen stopped writing after a minute, put down her pen, leaned back, closed her eyes and put her hands on top of her head. A lamp on the table made everything real white: her face and the ruffles of paper curling up into little clouds around her. Her long, skinny arms were uncovered and they stuck out like pale wings that came to tips at her elbows. She looked like she was meditating and I knew I shouldn't have been watching something so private but I couldn't stop. Because, to be honest, I saw for the first time how beautiful she was. It's not like her face was perfect or anything. She looked kind of like a Scandinavian crossed with an anemic Eskimo. What was beautiful about her was that she was creating something beautiful. And because I'd read her stories, every little thing she did—the way she sat up straighter or pushed back her hair—seemed to say something important. Does that make any sense? I mean, I didn't want to do anything besides watch her every minute for the rest of my life.

Kathleen's eyes opened and for a second I thought I was caught. Even though I knew she wouldn't have been able to see me out there. She seemed to look at something just over my head. Then she picked up her pen and started writing again. I watched her for a little longer, until some people came out of her building and it was like when I left my jacket. I'd gotten a couple blocks away before I realized it. I was crying.

❖ ❖ ❖

She found out some time between then and the next Thursday because as soon as I walked in the classroom and saw her face I knew she knew. I was late. They'd already circled the wagons and Irma was reading a page from her story. This time I'd done the reading beforehand. Everybody started talking about the rich language Irma used and I got the sense they were trying to make her feel good because she was pretty old. Which isn't fair, I don't think, because, I'm not saying her story was bad—there was good writing in it—but there were too many names of shrubs and flowers and spices and whatnot. There were a couple people in the story but they were sort of camouflaged by all the plants. After a while you felt like you were reading a seed catalog without the pictures and, I couldn't help it, I'd started thinking of her as Herbal Irma.

On the blackboard it said, "Roberto tiene que ir al banco. Maria tiene que ir a la tienda."

I didn't get a chance to talk to Kathleen until we were pushing all the desks back in place and almost everyone had left. She said she was fine when I asked how she was, so I said, "Are you sure? You seem kind of distracted or something."

She hadn't told anyone yet. "Oh it's just—" she stopped herself and glanced around. Herbal Irma and the forgotten-movie-girl were on their way out the door. "I've got your jacket in my car," Kathleen said. "I can give you a lift home."

In the car, she shifted into second gear, exhaled heavily. "I just found out two days ago that I have cancer," she said.

I did my best at shock and disbelief.

Kathleen nodded and kept her eyes on the road. "The kind I have—" She paused, trying to keep her voice from trembling, "I have advanced malignant mesothelioma." She spoke like someone learning a new language and I tried to listen like I didn't know what she was talking about, even though I already knew about the tumors and the fluid collecting in her lungs. I was just sorry she'd had to carry the knowledge around by herself for two days. I should have called.

"I should have gotten myself checked out sooner," Kathleen said. "You know, my father installed insulation for a living when I was growing up." She swallowed hard. It was the asbestos, I already knew. "I don't have much time."

"Four months," I mumbled, accidentally.

"What?" she said, looking over at me for the first time since we'd got in the car.

I cleared my throat. "Was their, uh, prognosis, for months or years?"

Kathleen was gripping the steering wheel tight. "They said in cases like this, it's usually just a few months."

"There's no treatment they can do?" I said, even though I knew.

She rolled her lips in, then out again and shook her head. She was trying not to cry. "They can do radiation therapy to control the growth and maybe relieve the symptoms a little. But I don't think I want to go through that." She parked the car in a tow zone in front of my building and left it running. "They said at this stage. At this stage—" Kathleen bowed her head and put her face in her hands. Her hair fell down like a veil.

I didn't want to scare her so I put a hand on her shoulder very lightly. "I'm sorry," I said. "I'm so sorry."

She leaned toward me and I put my arm around her knobby shoulders, a little awkward because of the seatbelt. Her whole upper body shook as she cried but she hardly made a sound. After a little bit she sniffled and pulled away from me.

"Thanks," she said, wiping under her eyes with her fingertips. "I know it could be worse. Some people are sick for years and years. That must be awful."

I asked her if she wanted to come up to my apartment but she said no.

"I apologize," she said. "I shouldn't have dumped this on you. I wasn't going to tell anyone in the group until later, when I have to go to the hospital."

"I'm glad you told me," I said. I said I wanted to do anything I could to help and that she should just let me know what. She said thank you, and when I still hadn't made a move to get out of her car, she said, "Right now, actually, I want to go home and get some work done. If I discipline myself, I should have enough time to write at least a couple more stories."

I sat on my bed with my back against the wall. Filbert was being quiet and Nicki must have been out. For once I would have liked some noise. I waited like that for over an hour in case Kathleen changed her mind and called. Then I went for a walk. When I go for walks I tend to go to the university, which isn't far away. It calms me down. There's a photograph in the foyer of the library there that I've never seen anyone else stop to look at. It's a faded, brownish picture from 1889, of the students and faculty of the college of liberal arts all lined up in rows on the lawn in front of the university. There are more trees than now. A lot of the buildings haven't been built yet. The whole world is black and white. The liberal arts folks' clothes are all the same: starched-looking, covering every inch of their skin. Their faces are honest—they don't look like they're used to posing for pictures all the time the way every-one looks in photographs nowadays. You can tell from looking at these people that learning was a whole lot more important to them than it is to most of the people you see around here now. Like they weren't just backpacking through here on their way to a higher-paying job.

I look at the eyes of every dead one of them and try to guess what they might have been thinking about the instant the picture was taken. I think of all the stories of all their different lives and how it's all washed away like a shipwreck except this one clue, this photograph. Sometimes, in the face of things like this, I don't understand how everybody can keep getting up every morning, putting on shoes, going to work, stirring coffee, watching television, day after day after day. I really don't.

As the weeks went on, I turned myself into a secretary/personal assistant for Kathleen. I called her constantly to offer help and sometimes showed up at her door, saying I was on my way to go grocery shopping anyway, could I get her something. I made photocopies. I did her laundry. I wanted to make myself a fixture in her life, a piece of furniture; something she wouldn't mind leaning on. I didn't do any more stupid stuff like try to kiss her.

She got short of breath sometimes just climbing the steps to the high school on Thursday evenings. Even though I was carrying the stacks of stories. The bounce was gone from her step. She had long coughing fits in the middle of the writers' group and everyone in the room got embarrassed, guilty looks on their faces.

One time I came back to Kathleen's apartment with her groceries and, as usual, she was writing. I tried not to make too much noise as I put her stuff on shelves and in the refrigerator. I bought all whole-grain, fat-free everything.

"I can do that myself," she called from her desk. But she let me do it anyway, like we were married.

I was going to just creep out of the apartment when I was done, but Kathleen said, "John," right when I touched the door handle, my jacket in my other hand. My name came out of such intense silence it was like somebody talking in their sleep. "What do you call those machines they use to grind up tree branches?"

"A chipper?" I said, coming back into the dining area.

"Chipper," she repeated, bending over the table again to write it down. I stood there wondering what the hell is she doing with the chipper in her story when Kathleen gasped all a sudden. She straightened up like she'd been stabbed in the back.

"Are you alright?" I asked.

"Yes. I just get these pains sometimes in my back and my shoulders."

"Would massaging them a little help?" I asked, hopefully.

She held her hair up and there were a few black strands left going down the back of her thin white neck. It wasn't anything sexual, but while I rubbed her shoulders I wanted to bend down and kiss that vulnerable little part of her so bad I got a lump in my throat. The bones were like a line of little knobs that went down from her neck into the loose, floppy sweater she was wearing. Working my way down from her shoulders, I tried to knead the muscles but mostly felt the ribs of her back. My hands seemed dumb as an archaeologist handling rare, fragile fossils with catcher's mitts on. I was trying not to spy, but over her shoulder I read a few lines of the new story she was working on. I couldn't get over how she could make a whole little world open up like that on a piece of paper. Like all she had to do was unfold it.

"Don't you ever feel like doing something else?" I asked, when I was putting on my jacket to go.

Kathleen was turned sideways from her paper-littered desk. Her eyebrows came together. "Like what?"

"I don't know." I stuck my arm out at the wall for some reason. I think I thought that direction was south. "Like go to Costa Rica for a week or something. Or visit old friends maybe."

Considering this, Kathleen looked down at the bottom shelf of books on the opposite wall. She stuck her pen in the side of her mouth and slowly turned it around between her teeth, gnawing on it. In spite of her private agonies, her long legs, her sometimes severe way of talking, she could lose herself like that and look exactly like a little kid. It just made you want to run over and hug her.

She took the pen out of her mouth and shook her head so her hair waved back and forth. "No," she said.

At the store everything seemed to go in slow motion. Morning, afternoon, night. People kept coming in and buying newspapers, magazines and coffee like the world would never end. Bob, the owner of the Town News, asked me if I was feeling alright after I dropped a whole pot of coffee on the floor. Splattered it all over my shoes and pants. I said I was fine. "You look a little green around the gills, John," he said. "Why don't you go on home."

"I can't believe what an asshole I am," I told Filbert as I pulled off my socks. They were damp with coffee where it had seeped through my canvas sneakers.

"Ah, go to hell," Filbert said.

"Wanna smoke a joint?" I asked him.

"Okay Einstein," he said.

I wouldn't consider it animal cruelty and besides it's not like I did this all the time. I exhaled each hit into Filbert's cage. He sat on his perch while the smoke billowed up around him, cocking his head every so often and eyeing me sideways. Real skeptical. "It's medical marijuana," I assured him.

Then he started talking too much. Pot makes him stutter. He goes, "Sh-sh-sh-shutup!" and "H-holy sh-sh-sh-shit!" It didn't cheer me up at all.

I've always hated hospitals—that smell, those obnoxious people who work in them, everything. Kathleen looked completely out of place in one. The first time I visited, she had just finished barely touching her meal. It was white bread, processed cheese, all kinds of carcinogenic shit you should never give somebody with cancer.

"Look at this stuff," I said.

Kathleen seemed too big for the bed. The back was raised so she was sitting up. "I know," she said through clenched teeth. She was mad about something else though. In the bed closer to the door, on the other side of a curtain, an old woman was watching a game show on TV. A crowd of people kept cheering.

I'd stolen a copy of the latest issue of every single one of the literary magazines we carried at the store. Now they were stacked on the table beside her where I'd put them when I first came in. The chair I was sitting on the edge of was way too low for where the height of Kathleen's bed was at.

A nurse came in to pick up Kathleen's tray. She made a clucking sound with her tongue and chirped, "So, we weren't too hungry today?" Kathleen sat like a statue and said nothing. Just before she reached the curtain, the nurse turned back around. "Oh," she said happily, "Doctor Morton is going to be in to see you in just a minute."

"I have already said that I do not wish to speak with him," Kathleen said in a slow, deliberate growl, like she might jump out of bed any second and rip the nurse apart.

The nurse looked satisfied. She mashed her lips together and stretched them at the corners, making one of those smiles that isn't really a smile at all. Then she turned on her heel triumphantly and left the room.

"I'll bring you some real food," I promised. There was a bunch of insane cheering from the television set on the other side of the curtain.

Kathleen didn't seem to have heard me. "They want me to be an *infant* here," she said.

A guy wearing a tweed jacket, who didn't look anything like a doctor to me, came gliding in and said he was Doctor Morton. He was smiling like he didn't have any idea where the hell he was.

"Kathleen," he said enthusiastically, holding out a hand she didn't shake. "Doctor Cohen suggested that we might have a little talk," he said.

"There's been a misunderstanding," Kathleen said. "I don't want to talk to you."

Doctor Morton settled his ass comfortably against the radiator in front of the window that overlooked the parking lot. Staying partly standing like that, he crossed his legs so one ankle was resting on top of the other one. He was one of these guys who likes to seem casual while he's looking down on everybody. "Well now," he said, "I understand you were opposed to treatment." "That is incorrect," Kathleen said. "Doctor Cohen wants me to undergo radiation therapy even though it has not been proven to do any good in cases like mine. Since I refused, he decided to send a shrink to talk me into it, so he can make more money. But my insurance won't cover your bill, and I don't want your services, so please leave my room."

A shrink! Now I got it. That was why he didn't look like a doctor. There was a buzzer sound from the television that meant someone got an answer wrong.

"Well I'm not so sure about all that—" Doctor Morton started. But Kathleen had leaned over, picked up the phone and punched a few numbers.

"I'd like to speak with the director of the hospital," she said, then paused. "Because there's an unauthorized person in my room, that's why. And I'd like him to be removed." She paused again while she waited for something to happen on the other end of the line and glared at Doctor Morton, who had straightened back up. He didn't look comfortable at all anymore.

"I guess if that's how you feel," he said. Kathleen just sat there with the phone to her ear. Doctor Morton gave me a glum look and left.

Kathleen hung up after he'd gone. The game show had given way to a yodelly country-western singer. "And what about you?" Kathleen demanded of me, still seething. "Don't you have somewhere to go? I hardly even know you."

I admit I felt a little shitty as I got on the elevator, but mostly I was amazed. Cancer makes people weaker and weaker. Kathleen seemed to be getting stronger. So I was being honest when she called to apologize that night and I said I didn't mind. She also wanted to know if I could water her plants and bring her some books. I was glad to.

"There's one other thing," Kathleen said. "Could I trust you to mail something for me?" I said she could. "I haven't told anyone about this, but a novel I finished is in a cardboard box under my desk." It was the second one she had written and she'd left it there, unsure until now whether or not she wanted to publish it. She told me the address of the editor who was working with her on *12 Fables*.

"Where's the first novel?" I asked, trying not to sound pathologically curious.

"Oh, I'm sure that's been made into pizza boxes or something by now," she said.

The next time I came to the hospital, I brought the books she'd asked for. When I got to her room, the old lady was gone and Kathleen was working. She was going through what she told me were the galleys for *12 Fables*. Before, I'd always thought galleys were kitchens on ships. I know it's stupid but it didn't hit me until then, when I saw her stories on those pages that looked like book pages without the binding, that it was going to be something with its own life, a book some total stranger could pick off a shelf in a bookstore, pay for, and walk out the door. I might even see somebody do it. Kathleen never would.

As I came in, she smiled at me and pushed back the table that was connected to the wall by a folding arm. Some of the happy little girl part of her was there again, like she'd been allowed to have her crayons back. On top of correcting the galleys, she was working on something new. The pages of one of her tablets was all rumpled with writing. It was a quiet visit compared to the time before. After we'd talked for a little, Kathleen rubbed her eyes and yawned.

"I could read to you," I said, nodding at the stack of books I'd brought.

"That would be nice," she said.

It became a kind of routine. I sat there and read to her every day. Sometimes in the morning, sometimes in the evening, depending on the shift I was working. I read her a couple of big fat novels that she had read before. She said she wanted to hear the ones that mattered.

It was my bright idea to have the writers' group meet in her room one Thursday, since there was enough space now that Kathleen had the room to herself. I'm not so sure I should have done that. Kathleen was all for it, but on the night everyone came she must have had more morphine than usual because she drifted in and out of the discussion. I was used to it because she sometimes fell asleep while I was reading to her. So a lot of times I would just sit there and look at her, which was one of my favorite things to do anyway. Her face was like a foreign country I was always seeing for the first time from a plane window. I was also used to how she looked because it'd happened gradually. As she'd gotten thinner, her cheeks had sunk in and her cheekbones stuck out more. Her eyes stared out from dark holes in her face. Also, there were tubes going in and out of her, connected to hanging plastic bags. When her cough came you could hear how it had burrowed its way down deeper inside. It rattled her whole frame.

I hadn't thought about how everybody in the writers' group would deal with all this. They were used to the strong, handsome, authoritative author. It might not have been so bad if everybody had acted more normal. But Bernie and Steve didn't bicker even a little bit. The forgotten-movie-girl kept looking around her like she'd been miscast. And Herbal Irma, who was pretty frail herself, looked almost sturdy next to Kathleen. I think that fact was what made her so upset she looked like she'd been chopping onions all day long.

Kathleen couldn't shepherd the group the way she used to and sometimes the conversation trailed right off into nowhere. Silence. Kathleen could stare at you like she was looking right through you and seeing her death standing on the other side. We were trying to talk about a story of Bernie's that he'd revised. Everybody else had read an earlier version of it and now they seemed to agree it had got better. In her usual proud voice Kathleen said, "This story is—" and then she seemed to forget she'd said anything. Like she'd been suddenly hypnotized, she turned her head toward the window. It was dark out. On the other side of the big piece of glass, a ghost version of our group sat suspended seven stories above the parking lot. There were seven of us in the room, each with their own story. The brownies Mrs. McCormick had brought were sitting on the radiator in front of the window. Nobody touched them the whole time.

Kathleen turned her head back and looked at us, her sad disciples, like we'd all sprouted up out of the floor. Then she looked down at Bernie's story in her bony hands. She let it drop down into the sheets piled in her lap. "This story is finished," she said. "I'd send it out to a few quarterlies and start on the next one."

Afterwards, we all wound up in the lobby by the front door of the hospital, where it started to sound like they were getting ready to break up the writers' group for good. You can always see these things coming when people get real forceful talking about how important it is to stick together and how much they mean to each other and all that baloney. Like what you do when you're getting drunk with a bunch of people you don't really give a shit about.

Bernie was the most shook up. He kept looking down at his shoes, going, "Oh dear. Oh dear." While everybody was in the middle of trying to avoid the subject he said, "She's such a wonderful—" and he had to take off his glasses and rub his eyes. "It's just not fair," he said. Naturally, it was Steve who realized Bernie was starting to cry and put his bearish arm around him. It was awful how Bernie just stood there with his glasses dangling from his hand, his face red and wrinkled up while he gasped and sniffled under Steve's arm.

A few times I called the publishing company where I'd sent Kathleen's novel and asked for her editor. I was always put through to one of her assistants who gave me the runaround. "Look" I said, the third or fourth time I called, "this is about one of her authors, Kathleen Baker." I know I sounded pissed.

"She's in a meeting, but I can take—"

"Okay, okay," I cut her off. "Just tell her Kathleen Baker is going to be dead in a few weeks. If she's interested, she can call me. I'm her literary executioner." I thought it sounded good the way I just shot it out like that, even though I didn't know what I was saying. I hung up and sat there thinking how unfortunate it was that these important matters were being left up to such a shit-for-brains. It's always made perfect sense to me that my name is another word for toilet.

But this time I got a call back after a few minutes. You could tell that Susan, this editor lady, was using the voice she put on to deal with crazy people. I explained about what was happening to Kathleen. Susan didn't believe me. "She's been sending back the galley proofs regularly," Susan said. "She didn't mention anything to me about a terminal disease."

"She wouldn't," I said. "She's not like that. Have you read the novel yet?"

Susan told me that just because Kathleen had won that contest it didn't mean any guarantees about her next book. Then she laid out the rules of this weird process that sounded something like what I remember learning about how a bill becomes a law, except more complicated with committees and all.

"I just want to ask a favor really," I said. "I mean, if you're pretty sure it's going to happen, can you speed it up? Or can you at least write her and let know it's going to be published for sure? Because she doesn't have a lot of time left. I think it might make her feel better." I gave her the name of the hospital, the room number and everything—I think she still wasn't sure what to believe.

At night while I'm not sleeping, sometimes I lie there thinking about my innards. Those yards and yards of intestines coiled up inside me, the heart, liver, pancreas, kidneys all smashed together in a mucousy guck sausage. I think about each individual organ mindlessly doing its job, pumping fluids, regenerating cells—it all seems like such a big waste. That's what I was doing the night the phone rang around one in the morning.

"Did I wake you?" Kathleen asked. Actually, I think I'd been waiting for this call. I seemed to remember from a dream what she was going to ask me. This was like a week and a half after I'd talked to that Susan.

"I want you to get me out of here," Kathleen said. Her voice sounded almost as strong as her old voice from a few months before. "I don't want to die in this place," she said.

"Okay," I said. "Are you ready right now?"

A seashell sound came across the line as Kathleen sighed into the phone. I pictured her there, the crumpled heap of sheets around her like a useless parachute, the light from the hospital hallway showing the mixture of relief and anxiety on her sunken face.

As I drove her car over to the hospital, I wondered how we could disconnect her from all those machines they had her hooked up to without alarming an army of nurses. But when I got there, I saw Kathleen had already done it. I never asked if she'd told them she just wanted the night off from her heart monitor or what. I was just this character playing out his role. It was her story.

"If you could just take that bag down and put it in my lap," Kathleen said, pointing up at the morphine bird feeder connected to her arm by an IV. It was full. She had this trigger she could push to give herself more. "There should be a wheelchair in the hall," she said. "You can just lift me into it."

It was terrible how light she was. And her bones in my hands. I lifted heavier boxes of magazines in the back room of the Town News when I did inventory. I didn't bother messing around with the wheelchair. I carried her like she was my bride onto the elevator where she

nodded out in my arms. She came back a little when I was putting
her into the car. And then when I took her out again. I laid her down
on her couch and put a blanket over her. I hung the morphine bag
from the same hook on the bookshelf above her that a spider plant
was hanging from. I'd given Kathleen's plants some fertilizer so they
were looking better than when she last saw them. I'd also been dusting
the place sometimes when I came over, and I'd straightened up some
of the papers and books she'd left scattered around. Now I felt like I'd
been playing curator.

"It looks good in here," Kathleen said. Her eyes, but not the rest of
her face, gave me one of the amused looks I secretly treasured. I'd been
right the first time I ever saw her. With the light on in the apartment
she looked much older now. Her eyes, moving like things trapped
down at the bottoms of two wells, were the only remnants of the energy that seemed boundless only a few months ago.

"Did you somehow know..." Kathleen closed her eyes and moved
her head slightly. "Never mind." She waved her arm in excruciating
slow motion to dismiss the idea. "That was nice of you to call my editor," she said. It was like she was sleeptalking now.

"You talked to her?" I said. Kathleen very slightly nodded with her
eyes still closed. "Is she going to publish the novel?"

"Yes."

"I'm glad," I said. We were quiet for a little while. I didn't move
from the chair I'd pulled up next to the couch.

"John," Kathleen said, opening her eyes all a sudden. "There's
something you have to do."

"What?" I asked, rising, ready to do anything for her.

She swallowed and it looked like it hurt. "You have to figure that
out," she said. "Maybe it's not writing. But you have something and you
have to use it." She looked hard at me. "Okay?"

"Okay," I said.

"Could you turn out that light please?"

I turned it out and Kathleen closed her eyes again. The apartment
had started to fill with the gray light that comes before sunrise and
there was a bird already gibbering outside the back window. At the
store, Bill would be on the sidewalk unlocking the door, glancing at
his watch and wondering where the hell I was. It occurred to me I
wouldn't go back there ever again. I watched Kathleen's face, the con-
tours of it as the light changed.

Her eyes opened kind of sudden again like she'd remembered something. She turned her head a little to look at me, moved her hand toward me over the blanket and I reached for it and held it. After a few minutes she said, "I hear that bird. Could you open the back window so I can hear it better?"

I didn't want to, but I let go of her hand and went around the corner to open the window. Cool air rushed in. You could smell spring coming. When I came back to her, Kathleen had closed her eyes. Because I was standing now, I noticed the morphine bag for the first time since I'd hung it up. It was empty.

I sat back down anyway, picked up Kathleen's hand and held it again. It was a little like the body of a bird, if you've ever held one. All those delicate bones and muscles. It got cold and I just sat like that for a good long while.

⬥ ⬥ ⬥

The last stories—there were three long ones she wrote after she found out she was sick—were, in my opinion, her best. I sent them to her editor with the rest of her stories I found that were not in the first collection. I'm not going to deface them by telling you what they were about.

Except this one that was probably kind of about me in a way. There's this guy who's serving a life sentence but he doesn't know what for. The jailer's always standing outside the door with his back to the guy. The only way he can get out is if he asks the jailer the right question. He asks him millions of questions until one day, out of frustration, he says, "Who are you anyway?"

The jailer turns around to face him for the first time and says, "You." Then the guy notices the door to his cell is not locked, that it never was. So he pushes the door open and just walks right out.

Before I left town I did something I'd been meaning to do for a long time. I took Filbert down to the pet store, plopped his cage on the counter and asked if they'd take him. I had to convince the girl behind the counter. "There's nothing wrong with him, I just don't want him," I said.

"Shutup," Filbert said.

The girl agreed with me that there is something fundamentally wrong with having birds for pets in the first place. She leaned down to get a closer look at Filbert. "You poor thing," she said.

"Oooooo hoochie mama!" he replied.

It turned out she was a student. We started talking about animals in general and before long I saw this girl was going to die in some hot place where there were trees like nothing we have here in the States and which I realized later was probably Africa. Before I went out the door I said goodbye to Filbert and he told me to go to hell.

Susan the editor offered to send me an advance copy of Kathleen's novel. I said no because I wanted to buy it in a store, which I could tell she thought was weird. To me, a novel, if it's any good, is like a friend you never forget. I wanted to wait for the perfect rainy day to meet this one.

⁋ ⁋ ⁋

JUSTIN COURTER has another story, "Skunk," on page 412 of this anthology, which is an excerpt from his novel *Skunk: A Love Story*, to be published by Omnidawn in the latter half of 2006. More information about this novel is available at www.omnidawn.com/courter

Courter's short stories and poems have been published in *The Berkeley Fiction Review, Fugue, Many Mountains Moving, Fourteen Hills, The Literary Review, New Orleans Review, LIT, Northwest Review, Pleiades, Main Street Rag, Phantasmagoria, Apalachee Review, North Dakota Review, Pearl* and other journals. His unpublished novel, *Cadenza*, was shortlisted for the Graywolf Press S. Mariella Gable Prize, and his short story collection was selected as semi-finalist for the 2003 John Simmons Iowa Short Fiction Award. He lives in New York and works for the Wildlife Conservation Society.

CAROL SCHWALBERG

THE MIDNIGHT LOVER

Annie conceded that Frank was the quasi-perfect husband, bright, kind and, best of all, solvent. As her best friend Barbara nodded, Annie ticked off Frank's other virtues. He never smoked, he hardly drank, and he only glanced at other women. He clucked at her problems and shrugged off her purchases. By day, he esteemed her, and at night, he gave her eight or ten ripple orgasms and occasionally a real zinger.

Just the same, she confided, there were difficulties. "He's forgetful," Annie said, while rubbing suntan lotion on her slim, smooth legs.

Barbara shrugged her plump, freckled shoulders. "Write notes."

"He's a slob."

"So pick up after him." Barbara gazed at the pool. "God, you're so lucky to have such a big house and a pool, too."

"He's not romantic. I never actually fell in love with him."

"You had romantic," Barbara shouted. "Romantic Brad who dropped you, romantic Vic who still owes you money, romantic Kevin who cheated on you. Now you have Frank. He worships you, he pays your bills, he bought you this lovely house, and you with paint under your fingernails. How could you stay alive on the few paintings you sell? You want to go back to juggling illustrations, art direction and giving classes?" She stopped to catch her breath. "You've been married how long now, a year?"

"Almost two."

"And in less than two years, you've forgotten what's out there. A good man is hard to find."

"He's not Jewish."

"He wasn't Jewish when you married him."

Annie's blue eyes glistened with tears, and her paint-speckled fingers raked her cornsilk hair. "I sometimes feel as if I'm losing my Jewish identity. Last weekend, we went to one of Frank's company parties, and a woman there asked me if I was active in my church." Annie paused to let it sink in. "She thought I was Protestant because Frank was."

Barbara scanned the lap pool, the stately house and the manicured grounds and began shouting again. "What do you want, heaven? Something's always missing in life. What about me? I have no Frank to support me, I have to work at a job I can't stand, and what are my prospects? I'll grow more wrinkles and get more desperate. I have no house, not even a condo, and the rent on my crummy apartment goes up each year, as regular and as depressing as Pap smears.

"What identity did you have before? You never went to services, and you never kept kosher. You look like a shiksa, you sound like a shiksa, you think like a shiksa. Fulfillment!" Barbara snapped her mouth shut.

After her friend left, Annie said to herself, how can Barbara talk? She picks apart every man she dates.

Annie sighed, showered, and set out to fulfill her wifely duties by shopping for the evening meal. At the grocer, she bantered over the eggs. At the fruit and vegetable store, she flirted over the romaine. At the fish store, she did no bantering.

The drawn woman who ran the shop came straight to the point. "It's Friday," she said. "You want carp?"

"No. My husband likes barbecued swordfish."

The woman's eyes flickered. "No swordfish. It's not kosher."

Annie felt guilty. She should have known, but how? Her mother had never kept kosher. Neither did either grandmother. She would try to make it up. "What do you suggest?"

"Snapper."

As the woman cleaned and filleted the fish, Annie breathed, "You're always so busy. You should hire a helper."

The woman threw back her head, making her red wig slide askew. "With seven mouths to feed, who can afford a helper?"

"You're a single mother?"

The woman's eyes flashed again. After she accepted money from Annie and returned the change, she turned briskly toward the other customers. "Next?"

Annie returned to the house, deposited the food in the refrigerator and entered her studio. She was working on a huge piece that promised to be a breakthrough. Last night, the painting had perplexed and impressed Frank all at once. "What is it?" The big man's pink brow furrowed. "I mean, it's so large and yet it says so little."

Annie managed a weak smile, but inwardly she seethed.

The weeks rolled by, Frank blissful with his nightly sex and freshly cooked meals, Annie simmering in discontent.

Then she had the dream.

When she entered the fish store, the woman with the wig was missing. Instead, there was a tall dark man with a handsome face that El Greco might have painted if he had painted Jews.

"Where is Malka?" Annie asked.

"I am Moish, Malka's husband. I used to study in the shul. Now I sell fish. There is a time to live and a time to die. Malka is gone."

It was only a dream, Annie reminded herself. Yet the next day she went to the fish store to make sure that the red-wigged woman was still there. Her name turned out to be Malka.

That night in her dreams, she was back at the fish store. This time, Moish looked upset. Tears coursed down his cheeks and landed in fat drops on his dark beard.

Annie was moved and reached over to pat him on the hand. "You poor man, alone with five little children."

Moish yanked his hand back instantly. "It is forbidden that a woman who is not my wife should touch me."

"Forget it," Annie snapped. "A pound of sea bass."

By night, Annie went to the fish store and found Moish. By day she went to the fish store and saw Malka.

"Soon I'll grow fins," Frank said after his fifth consecutive fish dinner.

Annie grew tired of the fish as well, but even more she wanted to shed the confusion in her life. When she spoke to Barbara, her friend took the unusual step of keeping quiet and thinking a few minutes. "I'll give you some free advice. Buy your fish at Gelson's. It's fresh, and you won't have to deal with Malka or Moish."

In her next dream, Moish seemed more agitated than before. Instead of tears, he looked flushed. As he handed her the trout, he said in a strangled voice, "I must declare myself. It's you. I love you. A goyishe punim, but a Yiddish soul." Moish sounded exultant. "You are the perfect woman."

Annie started in surprise and flushed in embarrassment. "How can you talk like this in a store full of customers?"

"It's a dream," Moish pointed out. "They can't hear us."

Annie's eyes fastened on his El Greco face and considered him as a possible lover. A good idea, she decided. Leaning forward, she whispered, "You want to fool around?"

"Tart! Tramp! Strumpet! Whore!" Moish sounded like an eruption of Roget's *Thesaurus*. "I want to marry you."

Annie pointed to the gold band on her finger. "But I'm already married," she said.

"Yes, but to a Gentile. It is not a marriage sanctified by the Torah."

Annie drew back. "I never told you about my marriage."

"But this is a dream. I can know anything and everything."

The alarm sounded.

In the next dream, Moish repeated his proposal of marriage. Annie felt moved and troubled. "What kind of marriage could we have? I'm married to Frank while I'm awake. We could only be together while I'm sleeping."

"Oy, you have to be courted," Moish wailed.

"But don't you see—"

"I see that we have so little time. Your alarm clock will be ringing soon."

Before Annie had a chance to object, Moish sketched out his plans for their wedding. "We'll have Rebbe Aranowicz write the ketuba."

"What's a ketuba?"

"Oy, what a shiksa," Moish moaned. "The ketuba is the wedding contract. It says how we divide our worldly goods."

"What about community property?"

Moish waved his arm as though he were fending off flies. "And my mother will take you to the mikvah—"

"I know it's goyish of me to ask—"

"The ritual bath for women."

While Annie stood sputtering, the alarm rang. She went into the kitchen and prepared Frank's ham and eggs. As soon as he planted a goodbye kiss on her face, Annie was on the phone to Barbara. "His mother is taking me to a mikvah!"

"I thought Frank's mother was dead."

"Of course not Frank's mother. Moish."

"Oh, Moish. Your dream lover. It's a pity you can't grow a new hymen."

"You're joking, of course."

"No. His mother will inspect you to find out if you're still pure." Before Annie had a chance to object, Barbara continued, "Tell me. When was the last time you and Frank went out? I mean to a real restaurant, where Frank has to wear a jacket."

"It's been ages."

"Tell Frank you want to remember how it feels to walk in heels. Say you've worn zoris so long you're Japanese below the ankles."

"But—"

"He'll love it. Goodbye now, I have to leave for work."

Maybe Barbara was right. After "Monday Night Football," Annie curled up next to Frank, blew in his ear and suggested an evening at a fine restaurant.

Frank glared at her. "Some place like Spago? I'll have to wear a jacket and tie. It'll feel like work, and God knows I hate that enough."

That evening Moish and Annie had a magnificent wedding under the canopy. The two of them shared a goblet of wine, and at the end Moish stamped on a napkin-shrouded glass.

The dining room was a blizzard of white tablecloths, gleaming silver and crystal, each table anchored by a bottle of sweet kosher wine. Before Annie had a chance to attack the mounds of gefilte fish and kishke, she was lifted, chair and all, into the air. The crowd swayed beneath her. She was the queen.

Then came bowls of matzo ball soup, golden and glistening with chicken fat, and between the courses, dancing. Not men and women together, but horas, first the women dancing together, and then circles of the men, men in black whirling together.

Platters of flanken, kugel and tzimmes arrived, followed by mounds of macaroons, honey cake and strudel. There were no green vegetables, no salad, no fruit, not a vitamin lurking anywhere.

It was tasteless and too much, and Annie loved it. This was the Jewish wedding she never had, remembering even in her dream the dreariness of New York's City Hall with Dave and the Mar Vista backyard with Frank.

There was dancing, dancing, dancing, the men taking ever more beautiful and complicated steps. When the men ran out of breath, the women came back with a vengeance, the bride in the center, circling. Just as Annie felt dizzy, the alarm sounded.

The next night, when Moish and Annie were alone in their bedroom, Moish went straight to taking off his clothes. He began to stroke her hair and kiss her face, and soon they were in the garden of delights.

Annie called Barbara at her office. "He's a fantastic lover."

"A dream lover," Barbara said.

"He takes me where I've never been before."

"Get Frank to— Forget it. The other phone is ringing."

Night followed night in a dizzying display of sexual clichés. Moish kissed and caressed, probed and discovered, taking Annie beyond ecstasy to a joy she had never even imagined, but then, with familiarity and the dailiness of life together, their pleasure began to pall. Annie rummaged through her bag of sexual gambits. When they were in bed, she embraced Moish tenderly and said, "Darling, why don't we—"

Moish clamped a hand over mouth. "Sha, woman! Don't speak your sinful thoughts. Don't even mention what we can do. The Torah forbids that we perform such unspeakable acts together."

Next morning Barbara hooted at Annie's story. "Speakable, unspeakable, the Torah lets a married couple do anything they want." She stopped to answer an incoming call. "Annie, I have an idea. On Friday night, why don't you come with me to services?"

"But Frank—"

"Bring him along."

Frank pleaded a previous engagement with his newspaper, and Annie decided to go without him.

Annie spent Friday puzzling over what to wear. Surely slacks were out of the question, and her party dresses revealed too much skin. She settled on a shirt and skirt she used to wear to see art directors and covered her head with a mantilla bought for a visit to the Vatican.

Women in the congregation spotted the mantilla, and angry glances came her way. "Take that damn thing off," Barbara whispered.

Annie slipped the scarf into her purse and turned her attention to the prayer book. Too bad that she had never gone to Hebrew school, for she could neither read the words nor follow the service. Barbara nudged her every time she had to turn a page or stand up with the rest of the congregation.

The evening left her in a state of exquisite ambivalence. Although she had felt no connection to the services, she was positive her experience ranked high in Jewishness.

When Moish came to Annie again, he had changed greatly. His hair and beard were gray, and he wore a white suit. Annie drew back in alarm. "Moish, what happened?"

"Many years have passed, my darling, and I have grown old and rich. I can afford to have a tailor make me white suits."

"Many years? You were here just last night."

Moish shook his head and looked at her fondly as though she were a child having trouble with long division. "Only in your dream. Take it from me, my darling, we are both twenty years older, and now you can no longer have children."

"Children?" Annie repeated. When had they ever discussed children?

"Where is the son who will say Kaddish for me when I die? It is fit that I choose a younger bride, one who will give me sons. And so, my sweet, we will get a get."

"Get?"

Moish sighed. "You are so goyish. A get is a religious divorce."

In an instant, it appeared, Moish, still with his gray hair and beard, was now wearing black. He stood in a room before a table of other men also in black. They spoke in Yiddish and Hebrew and consulted thick books. When they stopped, Moish had vanished from view and Annie's wedding band was stripped from her finger.

"Congratulations," Barbara cried when she heard the news. "You're finished with your midnight lover."

When Annie went to the fish store, red-wigged Malka was gone, and the person handing her the sole was Moish. He was not the El Greco portrait of her dreams, but simply an acne-scarred fishmonger in a blood-smeared apron.

That evening Annie broached the subject of their summer vacation to Frank. "How about Maui?"

The big man turned down the sound on the playoffs. "Maui! You're blonde, but you tan. Not me. I turn red. I don't need to travel thousands of miles to come back looking like a lobster. I love you a lot, but nothing and no one can drag me back to Hawaii!"

A few hours later, Annie dreamed that she was peering at a silversword on Haleakala. Suddenly, she looked up into the slate gray eyes of a handsome, brown-skinned park ranger.

"Aloha," he greeted her. "You are lovely."

"Mahalo," Annie thanked him, her face dimpling into a smile.

"We shall go to the koi pond," he said.

Annie's brow puckered. "Koi?"

"You haoles know them as carp."

Taking his arm, she strolled by his side and rapidly fell in step.

◈ ◈ ◈

CAROL SCHWALBERG is a fifth-generation New Yorker who considers herself a naturalized Californian. Her short stories have appeared in *Wordplay, Woman* (UK), *Ita* (Australia) and *Fair Lady* (South Africa) as well as in the anthologies *If I Had My Life to Live Over, I Would Pick More Daisies* (Papier-Mache), *Am I Teaching Yet?* (Heinemann) and *Rite of Passage* (Lonely Planet). She has published poetry in *West, Black Bough Review, Black River Review, New Voices, Potpourri, Sunday Suitor, Yet Another Small Magazine* and *Krax* (UK). She is also the author of non-fiction books: *From Cattle to Credit Cards* (Meredith), *Light and Shadow* (Parents), and *Doing It* (Dell). She has contributed essays to several books and has been an editor and a photographer. She is slim, hard-working and tactful, but in an ideal world, her favorite pastimes would be overeating, lolling on tropical beaches and spreading malicious gossip.

Tom La Farge

Night Reconnaissance

Two days after the shelling the rubble has been cleared from the kitchen. The stove is restored to its place, and the fire built up in its belly works on broken furniture from the neat stack and utters smoke through the jury-rigged stovepipe. Two large tables have been assembled for the nonce by soldiers of the Company of Walls. There's still as much hole as wall to the kitchen wall, but that porousness suits the animals. A parrot flies in and out. A monkey chatters on a spur of brickwork. And the chameleon that found its way in last night and scaled the potted rosemary basks now in full sunlight let in by the absent window. As for 'Nna, she has a place to do her cooking. But first she has to heal a wounded man.

Now the basket of plants rests on one table in the light of the sun. The night is still guarded inside the basket that 'Nna has brought back from the reconnaissance. Searching for herbs, she led her commander, the Megaduke Shandimus, Domestic of the Politic Company of Walls, across miles of field and forest, all night long, he on his donkey traveling the terrain he had neglected to examine before the battle; so secure had been his faith in walls. Misplaced!

'Nna must put her own faith just there where her greatest dread lies. She touches the basket's handle. The uppermost plants, torn latest from the earth with red dirt still clotting roots, are the ones she saw in the first faintest light and reached for with barely visible fingers. This was one of the last, with berries whose red just tinted the indivisible field of darkness. Underneath, their scents now rising in the heated air, there lie packed scores of plants she never saw at all but groped for in the dark and snatched at a venture, after running her thumb across a leaf that she then plucked, crushed beneath her nose, releasing pungencies that travel her yet, raising terror

'Nna in the kitchen is the field at night, an absence etched in feral clawings. Only yesterday she was a military cook and whore, an item in the chain of command even if the lowest, even if badly shaken by her first taste of hostile high explosive. What is she now?

The lively lines of her body unknot and flee her. Other bodies, nodes in the field, fibroid, reach for her; one is the body of terror. Deferred all night, terror now finds and plugs her, seals her, undoes her with cramps, melts ribs in cold runnels, tickling death.

But what is she afraid of? Not night, not wilderness. Where animals live and plants grow, 'Nna can be at home. What is she dreading now, in this bright, warm, open kitchen with a drowsy chameleon at eye level?

She reaches inside her tunic to find a body and touches nearly nothing but heat and sore nipples. Better than nothing; they transmit a flow of anger into the body of fear and alter it. Fury and fear become war, and through that tangle of channels 'Nna now strikes out in a bear-shirt as she digs into the basket. Every motion is a glad parrying, every sense a terrified stab into darkness, till she clears room around a plant, *naa'nna*. She plucks it out and spreads it on the table, smoothing out the oily leaves. Her own plant, and she chews it; out of her name it makes a cool and peppery bite into the bind of terror, pitting it and scoring it, weakening its grip till all unravels and is spat, yellow and green, out.

'Nna reaches to the bottom again, grips *tmer*, spreads it on the table. She fingers the pods whose gluey fibrous pulp will go, mashed and the seeds picked out of it, into the infusion of *naa'nna*, to mire the march of fever, to sprout through the body of fever like hairs growing inward.

How does she know that? Oh, 'Nna too easily finds her mother's lore in her mind, telling her what every plant will do. Lhool's presence, that dry voice, the dread that 'Nna will never ever, once she hears it, clear it from her mind, switches her from anger to shame. She cannot avoid listening. To make her cure, she must go her mother's way, read a menacing and withholding lexicon; and she so hard of study! So forgetful, so unmindful; so often pinched and struck for her slowness, burned sometimes too, and always scorned. Now in the kitchen 'Nna feels bruises swell spontaneously on breasts and buttocks, cracks open in the skin of dry fingers as she turns leaves in the basket. Each of the plants her confident fingers pull reserves its virtue for another, and as she works her scalp crawls, hairs grow up her belly and down her legs, her womb fills with tumors, and the seed placed there by soldiers begins to engender deformities. The little courses of her breasts dry up, her skin burns and cracks, in come rushing malignant spirits, the goat-footed woman grins in her face. 'Nna grows insatiably hungry and nauseous. Her spirit escapes in spirals, trailing after her mother as she stalks away, 'Nna drawn in her wake into the past. 'Nna runs out into a field of disgrace, shelterless, dismissed into a crowd, slipping under the trampling of indifferent feet, trying to find the edge of the swarm.

But she has a wounded officer to heal. Like an officer in grey with a scarlet tail, the parrot flies in and lands on the meathook still dangling from the ceiling. At the sudden movement the chameleon opens and then closes an eye. 'Nna digs. She finds *taateel* and pulls it from the basket. Good. Now chop the leaves and mix them in fat with others culled from the stand of henna outside. Two soldiers are this moment shouldering in a joint of meat, which they ram onto the hook; the parrot squawks and flaps. A camel haunch, it will surrender wholesome fat from under the hide. Good. She will make a cataplasm for Kyr Root's wounded belly. Taateel's bark and some more leaves, ground in a mortar and molded into a compress, will go on his temples to bring down his fever.

The knowledgeable eyes select the leaves, the cunning fingers strip bark and sort leaves into two piles, one for chopping, one for grinding, while Lhool's knowledge works upon 'Nna as if the mother were a cure, the daughter an infection, some foulness in the bowels. But when 'Nna was newly enlisted in the Company of Walls, she draped herself on the mudguard of a truck in the Motor Repair Shop, leaning back, one hand upon the hood ornament, the Silver Tower of Walls, one foot on the running board, and let mechanics take their lunchtime pleasure, one after another, burning and smearing her, while over the hood her eyes followed sparks shooting from the touch of welder's flame and steel, as if both, and herself added to them, were all one machine multiplying in a swarm of bees, her being diffused into their fascinating, untraveling flight. That hard life, before she became the Megaduke Shandimus's personal cunt, still was better than being the daughter of Lhool, streaming behind her irreducible mother into the night, the fields, the desert, the hills, the neighbor's orchard, the narrowest alleys in the market, back doors opening to a special knock. Catching sidewise glances from Lhool's bruised lids, catching a clubbing from those ringed fingers, every time her own sharper eyes and quicker fingers failed to trace the true shape of her mother's mind.

At the corpse washer's 'Nna took a dead man's hand in her own and pushed it into a bowl of moistened grains. She left it while her mother sang a counting spell in a little girl's voice. Those grains later made part of a savory stew served to a husband whose wife would have no trouble with him after that. The touch of the cold hand made 'Nna's burn, redden, and swell; but a compress cured it.

Tiklilt: a kind of chamomile. She has some now in her basket and pushes in that same disgraced and learned hand to find it. With it she can make a compress for Kyr Root's head-wound, where he lost his eye. She can add ground leaves of *tirtta*; she pulls that from the basket. And something for sight, he'll need it for his remaining eye.

Tifizza, the gum of *addool*, a kind of acacia, take it wherever you find it, Lhool's invariable rule. Dissolved in water, Tifizza will improve the Kyr's vision. And 'Nna will grind the bark of addool in the same mortar as tateel, to disinfect the belly-wounds and the foot from which toes were torn. Addool and tateel work together like a pair of hands. Next, *tirtta*. She pulls it from the basket. *Azwiwel*: the flowers rubbed on the wounds will aid cicatrisation. *Merriwoot*: a tonic and febrifuge, it will go into a decoction with tmer and tiklilt in the proportion her mother made absolute by kicking her till she got it right. Next her fingers find *aazukni*, also a tonic and an antiseptic. 'Nna will dry it, shred it, mix it with tobacco, roll it into cigarettes for the Kyr to smoke.

A scaly branch is caught in the weave of the basket. 'Nna tugs and twists it carefully free, then holds up a writhing spray of *aammaay*, the tamarisk. Its bark too is sovereign in afflictions of the blood, but not to mix with taateel and addool. All on its own, such is its nature, it clots and cleanses the blood, sending its virtue through the veins to find out uncleanness. 'Nna has used it often on herself, it works even against yeast.

She is pleased at what she has found; there is much more, in the darkness of the basket, but this is enough. She spreads it on the table's sunny plane. She will (she straightens) perform a cure. Across the kitchen lies the Kyr, a pale and sweating body on an army stretcher near the stove. The skin around his one unbandaged eye is bruised, darker than her hand, and the eye in its wanderings often lights on her. 'Nna assumes the bluff demeanor of her mother at her stall in the market: Lhool, garrison whore in her day, had joked like a soldier with the men and women who stayed for a story, old men and young women, and all the hunchbacks, cripples, amputees, dwarfs, walleyes, splaytooths, sevenfingers, pinheads, cretins, lepers, and syphilitics of that garrison town. On market days Lhool wrapped a length of white cloth immodestly tight across her breasts and hips and dispensed her prescriptions in tales of wicked spirits and worse women, told while crumbling, pestling, pouring, weighing, stirring, straining, decanting, her fingers folding powders into papers while her eyes, kohl-lined and shining, held the customer's. Her harsh voice submitted to a cadence; the story spun itself out, and then the medicament was ready, the joke found its point suddenly, and everyone listening laughed one long coarse laugh.

'Nna smiles at Kyr Root. He is staring at her crotch, so she crosses to him, kneels on the floor, unbuttons her pantaloons and folds back the flaps to let him touch her with his cold chapped fingers, which she tucks inside her to warm them, a swift firm gesture.

Behind her the basket emits smells of the field and the night. All last night she was stumbling through moonless, starless darkness. Only sea breeze to steer by. In thick groves even that failed her, and she stood in stuffy gloom with fireflies around her head traveling everywhere, leading nowhere, lighting nothing. Nearby the Megaduke Shandimus's donkey farted and trampled bracken, and the Megaduke hummed and waited for her to sniff out a path.

But around her things were growing, reaching, sweating their excess liveliness in fragrances that left no room. Each herb she sought, each fruit or seed, root or branch, pulp or gum, was masked by others in the field of odors. Each was a bulb of fragrance from which threads spread through the air like roothairs, calling to blind things with noses; of which 'Nna was one. Her nostrils flared as wide as when Lhool, with her tribeswoman's proud straight nose, pushed wads of crushed mint into them and mocked their fat breadth and the darkness of the nose from which they spread; while 'Nna inhaled spears of peppery cold and sharpened her sense to a pig's.

Alongside the patient donkey she stood turning her head, angling her nostrils, while the rest of her, hands, smile and cunt, shrank and vanished. Called in every direction by echoes of Lhool's voice, 'Nna was the name of a population ready to disperse.

Why are there places for plants to proclaim themselves and none for 'Nna? Is 'Nna a beast that her terrain's map is laid out in odors? The places her broad nose directed her last night only concentrated knowledge and shame. It took her to *taggalt*, the great fennel, where it asserted itself in the darkness. Her mother used to cut into the rootbase to bleed it of the milky gum *faasookh*. Cooked, it thickened in lumps, turned creamy chestnut, smelled of caramel. Lhool used it to keep her pubis bald. Later, having quit whoring and taken up sorcery, she sold faasookh to thieves and assassins; its smoke repelled good people's guardian saints.

Or else to *shook*, the donkey-thistle. Lhool had used that to abort what would have been 'Nna's sister.

The parrot whistles as if in amazement. The monkey chatters and jumps to a new promontory, a charred beam end. 'Nna shakes her head and gently pulls the wounded man's fingers out (they reek), and Root closes his eye. Buttoning her trousers, 'Nna imagines a contained space, odorless and cunningly lit. She does not know where she has seen it. Within it light flows from many sources through a thousand gradations of intensity, warmth, mixture with objects and their shadows. Daylight floods it, lamplight carves it, firelight warms it; there's the white glare of limelight, the pearly glow of mist, the exhausted fire of remote stars, the thin beam of a dark lantern, the pulse of embers, muted silver mirror-light.

She sorts the plants, recalling. Is it a theater? Of course it's a theater. Once she trolled for custom in a theater lobby, when she was thirteen and had just escaped to the City. She arrived early her first evening, while the actors were still playing, and in exchange for a minor favor the usher posted her where she could watch. At the end of a tunnel the stage glowed, emitting cries and strings of words. 'Nna watched the men in the cushioned seats watch the actress and did not see a different sort of attention from what she got when she pulled her dress up in the alley. But she was still new to whoring then. Now she sees that all those eyes were catching at a shape clearer than they were used to seeing.

How many places a stage contains! Merely to stand in one of them, under those lights, would gain 'Nna a glow and a shadow, marry skin, hair, and costume into something as distinct as a fragrance in the field. The breeze would blow from her to witnesses. From each of those places she could throw the voice that the place itself would raise in her throat, mantled in words, and launch the gesture its light would sculpt. Then move, not far, and be in a new place, from that throw a new voice to ears turning like wide nostrils to catch her finest throb. She would be there. In each new place on a stage she would be new and there.

Now the basket lies empty save for dead leaves and twigs, crumbs of dirt, and one disoriented earwig trying each of the gaps in the weave. 'Nna lets the insect catch her finger in its pincer and lifts it free to fall to the floor and scuttle. All night long the donkey was near her, far nearer than the man on its back. The Megaduke Shandimus said nothing to 'Nna but only swept the terrain with his electric torch. But the donkey followed her with careful steps, and where she paused, it bent to crop. She saved it once from feeding on *barboosh*, that looks so much like parsley, another time from *gizgeez* that sprouts early in the season, when grass is still rare. She guided it to more wholesome fodder, talking to it, telling it her story; but look, here are gizgeez and barboosh, she must have gathered them while she chattered.

The field at night is no theater. It made of her a dark and shameful void, echoing with Lhool's dread voice, at the sound of which shame acted on her body. But retaining a voice that murmured into a long soft ear, telling it all, while they rested and the Megaduke drew a little map and hummed. That voice she has still.

She makes a little pile of poisons, all familiar from Lhool's stall. *Beesh*: that's aconite, one of the deadliest and most rapid, a blue cluster of flowers and spiky leaves, but it's the root that Lhool kept pickled in jars on a high shelf, as well as a crock of beesh honey. 'Nna, who climbed a rock-face to the hive while her mother waved a smoking torch, remembers the burning when a drop fell on the skin between her thumb and finger. This is *oowriwra*, a splay of broad leaves, and here's its spiky pod protecting the seeds that bring on slow death, unfolding through stages to end in convulsions. Here's *oofen*, whose little blue kidney-shaped seeds will cut off your breath. She handles the sprig of it gingerly, for it stinks. *Booqina*: purple berries framed by a star-calyx. A dozen will send a man to death with the hardest cock and most vivid dream he ever enjoyed.

Here's *tidilla* with the white trumpet-flowers, useful in erasing memories from someone's brain, and whose seeds will bring on a good mood at first, next hallucinations, then trance and prophetic visions, delirium and inarticulate babbling, silent sweats, and lastly heart failure, depending on the dose. In the garrison town 'Nna was daily carrying a twist of tidilla seeds across the lane to men in the café, whose jest it was to reach their dirty hands between her legs and feel if she had hair yet and call out bids to her mother against the time it grew. 'Nna gave one of them, who had hurt her with his nail, such a generous dose that he made it right to the sweats.

'Nna tears off sheets from a week-old newspaper, when the news was still all of fêtes in honor of the gallant officers of the Company of Walls and country dances for the rank and file. She wraps a pile of medicinal herbs in the racetrack results. Another sheet of closely-printed quotations from the Bourse wraps herbs for women, to bring on their menses or suppress them, to make them gain weight or lose it; to put milk in their breasts, kill vermin in their hair, dilate their pupils, stain their lips, clear their skin and firm their gums, add luster to their hair; to prevent conception, ease labor, void undesired fetuses. Sketches of fashionable gowns and ingenious underwear wrap aphrodisiacs, the foreign news folds around cooking herbs, and the poisons go into the funny papers.

When 'Nna is finished, her eyes search the kitchen. The objects are bright and silent. The wounded officer lies on his stretcher, skin like tallow, breath loud. His head is turned away. But the animals are awake. The parrot fans its scarlet tail and rocks on a hatrack. The monkey has opened a jar of cocktail nuts that survived the shelling. Parrot and monkey are absorbed, but the chameleon on the rosemary, basking in the sunlight, has its eye aimed at her. From within its aura of delight the mild eye studies her.

She whispers to it as she cuts into a cactus pear and leaves the red slice on the window-ledge, and while she puts up water to boil, and while she chops simples for the kyr. She takes off a bandage and studies the crater in the man's head. Whispering, she swabs off crust and ooze, then binds it again with a compress. The tonic broth is ready; whispering, she spoons it in his mouth, holding his head up, the tendons of his neck athwart the tendons of her hand. Then, remembering that she requires henna, she takes basket and sickle and hurries, whispering, out.

A large, loud fly alights on the slice of fruit, which it busily sucks. The chameleon's eyes swivel and fix the fly, the chameleon rises slightly on its bowed green legs, its tail wraps a sprig, its jaws part. A tongue shoots and retracts. The fly is absent, the chameleon stretches its head up, all the rest is slow, deliberate swallowing, while one eye travels the empty, quiet kitchen.

〰 〰 〰

TOM LA FARGE has written three novels in the *Mole Place* series. *The Crimson Bears,* a story of political struggle among animals, came out in two parts (*The Crimson Bears,* 1993; *A Hundred Doors,* 1994) from Sun & Moon Press. *Zuntig* (Green Integer, 2001) is a fable of metamorphosis. A third novel, *The Broken House,* was completed in 2005; "Night Reconnaissance" is a chapter from that book. A volume of tales, *Terror of Earth* (Sun & Moon, 1996), revises Old French fables to test the human/animal distinction. He has also written about the fantasy esthetic and its relation to mainstream literary practice. "Collage and Map" came out in the *New York Review of Science Fiction* (November, 2004), and "The Reader of Maps" will appear in the forthcoming "Pot-Pourri III" issue of *PARADOXA*. He lives in New York with his wife, the writer Wendy Walker.

SHELLEY JACKSON

SHORT-TERM MEMORIAL PARK

1. War of Glass Houses
2. War of Approval
3. Price War
4. Pretty Nice War
5. Food and Drug War
6. Sticks and Stones War
7. Mall War IV
8. Ethnic Food War
9. Holy S*** War
10. Golf War
11. War of Toilet Terror
12. War of Bad Memories
13. War of Please Help
14. War of Threatening Speeches
15. War of Combat Chat
16. War of Know Where
17. War of Not Again
18. War of Of
19. War of Falling Paper
20. War of the Dreaded Mother
21. War of General Ambivalence
22. Revolutionary Concepts War
23. Performance-Based War
24. Nights and Weekends War
25. One-Second War
26. War of Authorized Retailers
27. War of Small Means
28. War of No Enemy
29. War to End All
30. Memorial War

Unlike most memorial parks, which occupy entire cities and their former suburbs, our Short-Term Memorial Park is an easy distance from home and schools, and provides good wheelchair access, clean restrooms, and complimentary coffee. We are located on a knoll visible from the freeway, convenient for stop-offs. The miniaturized statuary makes it possible to cover most of recent military history in the course of a walk that even tots and seniors can manage.

I am the groundskeeper. I keep the war memorials clean and orderly and do general maintenance all along the Walk of Remembrance. I am also one of the memorials, the only living one. My legs were taken captive in War No. 16, the War of Know Where. I had them replaced with the latest in prosthetic limbs, which were themselves taken captive in the War of Not Again. These, not my quite ordinary original legs, are the legs for which I grieve; this, secretly, is the war I memorialize. My prosthetic legs were returned, eventually, but I was not allowed to have them back.

One of them is here. It is No. 17 on our Walk of Remembrance.

Let me explain the Walk of Remembrance. The miniature War Memorials are organized in chronological order, at precise intervals along a spiral path calibrated to correspond to the calendar. Perhaps you have heard of the Memory Palace, invented by the Greek orators. They translated the important points of their speeches into striking mental images, which they placed at intervals along a given route through an imaginary building or landscape. The Walk of Remembrance works on the same principle. A walk to the very end is enough to fill even toddlers with a sense of the tragic dignity of recent history. We keep clay in the Glass House so they can work out their feelings about the place. Walking back out, of course, they forget them: our Walk of Remembrance is also a Walk of Forgetfulness.

The Glass House, as the center and culmination of the spiral path, is the place of total recall, and that's where I sleep.

Every day, I set out with my feather duster, my bucket and mop. I spend all day dusting and sluicing the memorials until they are luminous. Every morning they are dirty again. That's because one of our monuments dirties all the other monuments. That is the Falling Sky. Ashes and half-burned scraps of paper are blown across the park in a south easterly direction, and constantly drift down over the war walk. One of my jobs is to find every fallen paper and return it to Abu, who will restock the blowers. I take special care grooming the stretch corresponding to the year I was born even though no very important wars happened then, and officially I commemorate a different year altogether, the year I lost my legs in the War of Know Where.

When I learned that my prostheses were back in the country, I engaged a private investigator, a red-haired boy who lazed around on my dime, downloading pornographic images from the internet. Though he was ineffectual, I kept him on because he flattered me, and one day while visiting a site catering to amputees and their admirers, he happened to see a snapshot of my beautiful leg standing by itself on a stage draped in swags of red, white and blue bunting. My right leg had been declared a war hero and had gone on a national tour. My left leg, he learned, had been designated a war memorial. Eventually, I tracked it down to this very park. I applied to become a living war memorial. As a double amputee I was automatically short-listed and when the two applicants before me left town quite suddenly, I was given the position.

The truth is, I wanted to be close to my leg.

The *truth* truth is that I wanted to slice my leg off its pedestal with a cutting torch and run away with it (though "run" is incorrect). Every night, I remember this plan. The problem is that by the time I get to my leg the next morning, shining on its pedestal, I have forgotten the loss of my own legs and though I can see by my stumps that they're missing, I have nothing but the vaguest yearning feeling toward the leg on the pedestal, which seems bright and blest and far above my aspirations. Bent over to setting #6 on my genuflection dial, I can scarcely even see it, and though I must rise on my ladder to sponge the scuzz off its cup and straps, which I do feelingly, I scarcely dare to imagine sliding my own stump into its harness.

The genuflection dial is my own invention. First, let me say that one reason I'm good at my job is that I'm naturally servile. I'm servile even to inanimate objects. I have special servile ways of walking, ways most people would call slithering. I am good at truckling, since I look like I'm kneeling even when I'm standing erect, planted on both stumps, with my poncho puddling around me. Actual kneeling is in my case an anticlimax, since only about two inches of stump extend below the joint. I am the first to admit that it's funny when I drop to my knees—a fall of inches.

I have a white macramé poncho with only somewhat dirty tassels that I like to suck in bed.

I like to match the degree of servility I express with my posture to the degree of respect due to different war memorials. Because I'm good with tools I've constructed a device that is more or less the reverse of a back brace—it bends me over by precise increments. Its notched wheel has ten fixed positions: respectful, deferential, docile, modest, embarrassed, awed, sycophantic, servile, grovelling, and the full jackknife. Furthermore, for fine modulations there are, between servile and grovelling, ten more settings: fawning, truckling, toadying, brown-nosing, etc. Each monument has a rating (7, 4, 9, 7.2, 5, etc.), and you will find these numbers in small print on our map, so that if you are not troubled by back pain you can pitch in and show appropriate degrees of respect for each monument.

A moment's thought will reveal why my device is useful. Suppose you grovel before the memorial to the War of Historical Smells, which is rated four. What are you going to do when you get to the memorial to the War of Threatening Speeches, a nine? Amateur or paid mourners who crave the security of knowing they will execute a flawless obeisance every time can purchase this device from my web site, servile. com, which is maintained and administered by Abu.

I have yet to make any money but Abu assures me that this is not uncommon in the first year of a new business and advises me to be patient.

Abu is the gatekeeper and my friend. Sometimes he invites me to stop by the guardhouse, where he works, to play an oldfashioned game: Barrel O' Monkeys. A plastic barrel is filled with plastic monkeys with hooked arms. The aim is to string as many monkeys together as you can, but their curved arms are slippery and the monkeys easily slip out of place. I can't understand why they didn't design the monkeys so their arms hook securely together. Abu says I don't understand the point of games, which is to see who is the loser. Who is the loser is me.

The last time I visited, Abu showed me a news article that frightened me. It announced that we are at war again. Normally this would fill me with anticipation and at first, I peeped with pleasure. I expressed to Abu my feelings: I seem to hear the virile growl of bulldozers, backing and forthing, I seem to smell the stink of new tar, I seem to see—but Abu stopped me with a raised finger. This is a new kind of war, he advised me. Yesterday there was a terrorist attack on Manhattan. Hundreds of memorials were destroyed. Nobody died except a flower vendor, but they are not calling it the Flower Vendor War. No, they are calling it the War of War Memorials. Abu says, be prepared to defend the park. And you might want to make a will. Remember your loved ones. His eyes shine with self-regard and he flips a tassel on my poncho. I know what he's thinking.

Now I am in my own way very pretty. I have wispy white hair on several quite large areas on my head. My stumps are almost equal in length, and I've cinched on two matching pleather stump caps with buckles that look silver. I get chucked under the chin a lot. But I know that with Abu it is just that he covets my poncho, which he once expressed would look nice draped over the stained back of his brown armchair. We play Barrel O' Monkeys and I lose.

Abu invites me over. I start at the inside and walk outward, cleaning as I go. By the time I have reached the farthest reaches of the Memorial Park I have forgotten all the wars. All of them except the war I myself memorialize, and of course the War of Falling Paper, memorialized by the sky of sooty scraps. But I know enough to be frightened by the news article Abu shows me. This time it says the mayor of New York has decided not to rebuild. Instead, he has invented a new, cheaper kind of memorial. Basically you repeat certain sounds in a particular order and these sounds, by means of the muscularity of your tongue and glottal equipment, mold your breath into a small statue the size and shape of the inside of your throat. Everyone can carry his own memorial inside his mouth. Very pretty. But I see where this leads. What need for a groundskeeper if everyone maintains his own memorial inside his own oral cavity? Abu doesn't say so, but I see his dark looks. I wrap my poncho more closely around me.

We play Barrel O' Monkeys and I lose. Someday I would like to see the monkeys rising up out of the barrel, arm in arm. Not one left behind.

On the way back home, I pass a single leg, shining darkly on a pedestal. It is long and black and smooth-tooled and smokily translucent like obsidian and I wonder to myself what it would be like to wear such a wonderful leg.

A little further down the road, I remember that I did wear the leg, that it is mine. I decide to steal it, tonight. Then I remember that when I get back with the blowtorch, I will not remember that it is my leg, and that because I am servile, I will not dare to steal it.

By the time I get home, I remember everything. I lie in bed, looking up through the ceiling of the glass house at the winking pages, turning over and over as they fall, and because I am not just a memorial but sometimes the only, certainly an expert mourner, I cry a little, for the volumes of people named Hank and Pepe and Gloria who can no longer blink, or grunt, or sin themselves stiff in the privacy of a poncho, or look up and see white papers falling out of a black sky and cry, like this, tears sliding down sideways, soaking into the tassels that are already wet from my chewing.

Sometimes when I have dried my eyes and other parts I go outside and the papers, burned around the edges to lobe shapes, sashay down and slide into my hands as if they want to be read. And even though these papers are not impregnated with molecules of people like the ones they commemorate but are specially treated with germicide for hygienic reasons, I feel like I am holding pieces of people, people who, like my leg, were beautiful and are gone.

SHELLEY JACKSON is the author of the short story collection *The Melancholy of Anatomy,* the hypertext classic *Patchwork Girl,* several children's books, and *Skin,* a story published in tattoos on the skin of 2095 volunteers. Her first novel *Half Life* is forthcoming from HarperCollins. She lives in Brooklyn, New York and teaches at the New School.

PAUL PEKIN

THE MAGNIFICENT CARP OF HICHI STREET

Downtown Tokyo was crowded that afternoon. To those inclined to remember, it seemed more people than ever had been pushed into Hichi Street, and it seemed more large office buildings than necessary had sprung up over night, and it seemed more money than usual, real paper money, yen, dollars, marks, francs, and pounds, was spinning merrily beneath the wheels of traffic which on that memorable afternoon was even more relentless than ever. No ancestor could possibly have imagined so many people, so much money, such enormous buildings, and such heavy traffic; it would have been simpler to imagine the giant carp which came swimming down Hichi Street shortly before the closing bell was due to sound at the Niko Exchange.

Young Officer Kuriku, fresh from his studies at the National Police Academy, may not have been the first to see this creature but he was indeed the first to grasp the nature of its being. Directing traffic at the intersection of Hichi and Yamitso, an assignment usually given to rookies (it being felt that there was no better way to get their feet wet), Kuriku took note of something approaching at an unusual rate of speed, something large and bright that he at first took for an American car, but of course, cars, even American cars, do not have large gleaming scales or wide unblinking eyes or mouths more or less shaped like hungry garden hoses. This was a fish, pure and simple. There was no escaping so evident a truth. Gracefully, yet purposefully, it turned down Hichi, leaving the young officer stunned in its wake.

Although Kuriku had been warned never to disturb his superiors with frivolous matters, he reluctantly keyed the two-way radio these superiors had provided. "It is a fish," he told the dispatcher, a woman whose pleasant voice reminded him of the young woman he hoped soon to marry. "I make it to be a carp, and unlicensed…"

The transmission here was interrupted by an uproar over the radio waves. Hundreds of his fellow officers, listening in on their own radios, burst into laughter and unkindly broadcast that laughter right over the dispatcher's reply. They are playing a trick on me, Kuriku thought. Turning back to his assigned duties, he resolved he would never again mistake a Cadillac for a carp. But ah, there had been no mistake. Within moments a small woman who quite closely resembled his own grandmother was at Kuriku's side.

"What," she demanded, pulling on the young officer's sleeve, "What are you going to do about that fish? It just swallowed my little Iki."

This could not be ignored. Nor could the crowds of people who were now shouting excitedly, "Look! Look! It's coming back!"

"It is a fish," Kuriku cried into his radio. "And it just swallowed someone named Iki."

"Carp are vegetarians," the dispatcher replied. "We are now receiving numerous calls as to your fish. Please take the proper action."

Watching the great carp glide back into the intersection, Kuriku allowed himself to consider the gun strapped to his side, a gun that he had been warned he was never, under any circumstance imaginable, to fire on a crowded street. "Stop!" he cried, spreading his arms. "I will arrest you!"

Expressionless, the giant fish swam on, so closely Officer Kuriku was able to snatch a single golden scale from its side. It was as large as a saucer and would make an excellent wedding gift.

In a large modern city such as Tokyo, the balance between effective travel and absolute chaos is a delicate one. The most insignificant incident, a stalled engine, a defective tire, even a single drop of rain has been known to cause impossible traffic conditions. Imagine, if you will, how much greater the disturbance of a giant fish, freely making use of the right of way! Mr. Sabucho, a successful businessman, had every intention of meeting his client at exactly a quarter past four when the last suggestion of movement in the traffic ahead of his cab ceased. "What is this?" he asked the driver.

"The radio reports a giant fish, sir," the driver replied.

"Nonsense. It's not even time for dinner."

Using his pocket calculator, Mr. Sabucho computed the distance from his present location to the restaurant where he was to meet the client. If he moved swiftly, he could make it on foot. Was he not in excellent physical condition? Did he not work out daily at the American Club? "Here," he said, thrusting a wad of money into the driver's fist. "Buy yourself some fish if you favor it that greatly."

Out of the cab, Sabucho paused to lace on his running shoes. He was a formidable man, resourceful and determined, a modern samurai so completely dedicated to The Company he had thrice won the award of excellence, and on each occasion had been permitted to shake the hand of Mr. Hakura, an executive so revered no employee dared meet his eyes (at least none had done so in recent memory.) For Mr. Hakura,

Sabucho was prepared to run the length of Hichi Street and do it without raising a sweat.

Mr. Sabucho rose, took a deep breath, and started out at a sensible jogging pace, but pedestrian traffic proved more difficult than he had expected. It was as if the entire population of Tokyo had suddenly decided to charge headlong toward him. "No, no," he cried, fighting to maintain his progress. "Can't you see I am on business?"

Among those who tell this story, there has always been contention as to whether the crowd was running away from the giant carp or toward it. Some say away, for who would not be frightened by an enormous fish swimming effortlessly through the heaviest traffic known to man; others say toward, claiming every Japanese knows, almost from childhood, that carp are gentle vegetarian creatures, quite unlikely to harm anyone, and indeed, supporting this theory, no loss of life was reported throughout the entire incident. We must not, of course, extend undue credence to that old woman who claimed the carp had eaten someone or something named Iki. Even assuming she were not mistaken, lying, or insane, or that young Officer Kuriku had not merely misheard her, is it not possible, even likely, that Iki was simply a plant?

All things considered, it is best to assume the crowd was rushing toward the creature, and finally swept Sabucho up with it, depositing him, however unwillingly, directly in its path.

At this moment Sabucho was suffering more stress than he had ever experienced in his adult life. Through no fault of his own he was about to be late for his appointment. The client, an American named Mr. Jones, would sit impatiently in the restaurant, regularly checking his solid gold watch, and finally leave with a sigh, taking his business to the competition. Disgraced, Sabucho foresaw his own resignation, followed by exile from the business world. He would be forced to earn his living mixing drinks in a karaoke bar.

Harakiri (the word actually crossed his mind) was not a viable option for a modern Japanese like Mr. Sabucho. He would only look ridiculous disemboweling himself over a missed appointment, what possible honor could that bring?

Such were his thoughts when quite unexpectedly he found himself face to face with a giant carp. It was an astonishing moment, and quite magical all must agree, for looking directly into this creature's bottomless right eye he suddenly saw himself a mere boy on his uncle's pond, drifting over a school of golden fish at play, and there was an island in the center of the pond and on that island a woman was playing an ancient stringed instrument and singing in a high soothing voice. Oh! What peace he had known as a boy; what had happened to his life that he had not felt it again until this very moment? If only he could lean into that eye, lean, lean, until his balance was lost and he was swimming in green-tinted water. Mr. Sabucho leaned, but the carp swam on, unperturbed, leaving in its wake a single golden scale.

Among those racing for a look at the giant carp were hundreds of television, radio, and newspaper reporters; alas, they were accompanied and quite overwhelmed by an even larger swarm of amateur video enthusiasts, some of whom, it is said, purchased their equipment along the way, feeling they would never be able to accept the reality of a giant carp on Kichi Street until they had seen it reproduced on a television screen in their own living rooms. The sheer numbers of these people, the crush of their bodies, and the turmoil of their presence undoubtedly accounts for the lack of professional documentation we now so greatly lament. One, only one, major television crew actually reached the scene and even they, in spite of the most energetic efforts, were unable to recover convincing images.

As for the amateur footage, it need only be pointed out that modern technology with its computer-assisted enhancement fatally taints all but the most professionally monitored images; consider, if you will, those "home videos" we do have, some showing as many as three giant carp converging at once upon the intersection, as often as not accompanied by aliens from Alpha Centauri.

The Taiwa people gave it a gallant try. To the viewer it may often seem that those who produce the evening news are to be envied.

We imagine them well paid, respected, and glamorous, demigods whose lives in no way resemble our own. In fact the atmosphere at any major station is chaotic, a constantly milling crowd of technicians, writers, producers, directors, clerks, makeup artists, reporters, and news readers, all fiercely competitive personalities struggling to meet their professional goals. All is noise and confusion, and sometimes anger. Fist fights, and sometimes even major brawls often break out among people who might otherwise be friends. Uncivil language is heard. Sometimes a young woman is seen weeping in her cubicle. This is no business for weaklings.

On screen Yoshira Okomo is a strong modern woman, willing to stand hip deep in flood waters in order to bring us the story. There is no need to discuss her beauty, visible every evening at six and again at nine, and yet one must understand that even such a woman has a private life in which she is often weak, ill-tempered, vain, and sometimes more ambitious than is fitting for one of her sex. At the very moment Mr. Sabucho was falling to his knees to retrieve the golden scale dropped by the great carp, Yoshira was in makeup, preparing to go on camera in another hour. The telephone was handed to her; it was Mr. Ginshi.

"What is this about a fish?" Yoshira cried. "I am in makeup and you call me about a fish?"

William, the hairdresser, allowed his eyes to roll upward. He was an American, one of many who have found their fortune in the very same country once reduced to radioactive rubble by their fathers.

"I heard you," Yoshira said. "A fish! A fish! You want me to interview a fish! For this you must send an intern!"

She tapped her long red fingernails on the arm of the chair.

William, working carefully, could hear Mr. Ginshi's tiny voice reverberating in the telephone.

"Ah," Yoshira said after a long pause. "That kind of a fish. On Hichi Street, you say. Are you sure this is not some kind of a hoax? I have not yet forgotten that sea monster, you know."

When Yoshira put down the telephone she was ready for action, her recalcitrance, of course, being a sham. Was she not the very same woman who had interviewed that camel after it had eaten an official's briefcase? "William," she said. "You will finish my hair on the van. And Kahato..." She turned to a young intern, "...will call my apartment. Under no circumstances is the babysitter to take Jenny for her stroll today. I will not have a child of mine swallowed up by a fish."

Not a moment was lost. With William and his comb in pursuit, she raced to the elevator and descended into the basement where the official Taiwa minivan, its driver, and a camera crew were waiting.

"The fish!" she cried. "It's on Hichi Street!"

For William, this was the most exciting part of his job. While his friends back home were wearily teasing the tresses of spoiled American women, he was darting all over Tokyo with the famous Yoshira Okomo. What did it matter if he saw little other than her hair. "It must look a little windblown," she suggested. "I want to appear breathless—but not disheveled, certainly not that. What do you think I should ask that fish?"

"I wouldn't worry," William said. "I'm sure you will think of something."

"Yes," Yoshira sighed. "I always do."

Of course the minivan was soon caught in the very same traffic that had stalled Mr. Sabucho. "Hold on tight!" the driver said. He was a young Filipino who claimed descent from the Spanish, and drove as if to prove it. How and where he entered the sewer system, William was unable to determine, occupied as he was by Yoshira's hair, but suddenly it was far too dark to work a comb, and far too dangerous as well with the van pitching back and forth like a boat and the sound of rushing water clearly audible on all sides. "Yeee hah!" the young Filipino, who had seen far too many American movies, cried. "Maybe that carp come from down here."

Where the carp actually did come from is a matter still in dispute, some sharing the young Filipino's sewer hypothesis, others insisting a more likely source was the Tokyo River, crowded as it is with Jet Skis which would easily compel any creature to seek refuge elsewhere, even on Hichi Street.

When the van emerged from the sewers, dripping and reeking, William had scarcely a chance to wield his comb one last time before the carp swam into view. "Wow!" the driver cried. "What a beauty! Want me to ram it?"

Fortunately this suggestion was vetoed at once. "Start shooting," Yoshira ordered the cameraman who had been standing on the roof of the van all through its journey, and was covered with thick black slime, the same slime which unfortunately clouded his lenses with consequences we all know. Yoshira, for her part, was out on foot immediately, extending the microphone before her, racing toward the fish. "Fish? Fish?" she cried. "Wait a minute!"

Despite Mr. Sabucho's fancy, Mr. Jones, the American businessman, did not possess a solid gold watch, or even a gold-plated one, wearing instead a cheap metal imitation that was slowly turning his wrist green. Everything about Mr. Jones was imitation, from his plastic shoes to his polyester tie to the label of his suit, and there was no one who knew this better than he himself. Somewhere, crossing the Pacific, he had begun to sweat. Leaving the airplane he continued to sweat. It would have been better, obviously better, had he retired to a hotel with a good hot shower and clean towels, but the firm that employed him had made no allowances for this extra expense. "In and out, Jones, that's what we expect from you. As soon as that Nippo signs, you're back on the plane." They had rested the fate of the entire corporation on his shoulders.

Now he was trapped in a taxicab in the middle of the largest city he had ever seen. New York, Los Angeles, Mexico City, Indianapolis, all combined would hardly make a single Tokyo. Everywhere immense skyscrapers glittered in the sun, but closer to the earth there was a purple-greenish haze in the air that was hard to breathe. Neon signs blinked and bubbled indecipherably. Streets were marked in hieroglyphics, and, worst of all, the driver of the cab appeared to be a Nigerian. "I need the Hakakawo Restaurant," Mr. Jones explained. "You know where it is?"

"Ah yes, sir," the Nigerian replied with a wide smile. He had an entire mouthful of gold teeth. "You like?" he asked tapping them with his fingernail. "In Tokyo, everybody rich!"

The cab had yet to move. Mr. Jones watched the meter turning, turning, turning.

"Only yen," the Nigerian smiled. "Yen not like dollar."

All was lost, Mr. Jones decided. His mission was doomed from the start. The firm should have sent an abler man, someone who spoke Japanese, or at the very least was capable of dealing with a Nigerian. He extracted a fifty-dollar bill from his wallet and showed it to the driver. "Yours," he said. "If you get me to that restaurant by four."

"Ah, thank you sir," said the Nigerian, snatching the bill from his fingers. "Thank you, thank you very much."

We cannot say if the driver was actually trying to earn his fifty dollars, or was simply driving as Nigerians usually drive when, ignoring screaming pedestrians who parted like waves on the Red Sea, he suddenly jumped the curb, shot down the sidewalk, rounded the corner at Hichi on two wheels—and resoundingly crashed into the Taiwa van, spilling camera and crew onto the pavement, thereby ending what little hope we ever had for clear and trustworthy images of the great carp.

Yoshira Okomo understood at once what had happened. Without pictures, she might as well have stayed in her office. No sooner had Mr. Jones staggered out of the smoking wreck than she seized him by the lapels of his cheaply-made suit, which immediately gave way along the seams. "This is your fault!" she cried in Japanese. "You should have known better than to hire an African!"

Mr. Jones did not know he was facing one of Japan's most honored television personalities. He did not know that she had been about to interview a giant carp. He only knew he was in the grip of an angry woman who was quite literally ripping the coat from his back. "You foul American!" she hissed in English emphasizing each word with an even more violent yank, the last of which left him in his shirt sleeves. Before he could react, she seized him by the suspenders.

These also gave way, as did his shirt and trousers, leaving the poor man in his underwear. "Oh no you don't," she declared, grabbing the band of his boxer shorts when he turned to flee. Suddenly Mr. Jones was naked.

Never in all his life had he run as fast as he ran now. All was lost. Bankruptcy. That would be the fate of his company and all its employees. There would never be a merger after this. He would end his days on welfare. He would be forced to sell StreetWise on corners, competing with bearded black men who would order him away from their territory; this was assuming he were ever to find his way home again, and how could he even assume that? He was naked, without money or identification in a nation where failures were expected to take their own lives. Gasping for breath, he slowed, and then saw a man on his knees about to plunge something bright and metallic into his abdomen. "Wait! I'll join you!" Mr. Jones cried.

The man looked up. It was Mr. Sabucho, holding the golden fish scale.

Ms. Green planned to write a novel about her experiences in Japan. She was young and romantic and had recently graduated from the University of Arkansas with a master's degree in Fine Writing; now she was babysitting for a famous Japanese television reporter. Jobs, she had learned all too quickly, were scarce in the United States, where people with MFWs considered themselves fortunate to find part-time positions squirting beans at Burrito Bob's. As for writing itself, what a joke, you needed exotic locales, glamorous characters, fantastic situations, in a word, you needed Japan. Already Ms. Green had filled several notebooks with material she at first kept hidden from her hot-tempered employer, but now, seeing that Yoshira either could not or would not read anything beyond the labels on her clothing, she worked quite openly. Even as the telephone began to ring, Ms. Green was outlining a passage in which a character greatly resembling Yoshira would push a wheelchair and its unfortunate occupant beneath the wheels of the subway train.

Although her Japanese was poor, Ms. Green answered the phone. There was no better way to learn a language than by speaking it. But the voice on the line employed English as good as her own. It was Yoshira's intern at the station.

"Ms. Okomo wants you to clearly understand you are not to leave the apartment with Jenny until this situation with the giant carp is resolved."

"Giant carp?"

The intern patiently explained the story so far as was known, suggesting that she turn on the television for further details. How could anyone expect to know what was going on in the world if they did not watch television?

Could this be real? Ms. Green had seen all the Godzilla movies.

Perhaps there really was something in the waters surrounding Japan, something left over from World War II and the atomic explosions. She turned on the television and was rewarded with an aerial shot of Tokyo traffic. Something that may have been a giant fish was crawling around below, but because of the great height the television helicopter was required to fly in order to clear the buildings, you could not be sure. The voiceover, naturally enough, was in excited Japanese that Ms. Green could not understand, but she did catch the words "Our own Yoshira . . ." So Yoshira was off to interview a giant carp. Ms. Green digested this slowly. A talented writer such as herself could do much with a giant fish swimming against traffic. A good article could be written, and sold to American markets. It might even be good enough to attract an agent, which Ms. Green would surely need when she finished her novel.

But then there was Jenny, Yoshira's two-year-old daughter, a precocious little brat who would tell all if Ms. Green were to sneak from the house. "Ah, Jenny," Ms. Green said. Jenny was staring intently at the television. "Would you like to see a great big fish?"

"Mommy see," the child replied.

"But you don't," Ms. Green said. "I can take you. You must promise you will never tell."

"Candy," the child said. "I want chocolate."

"Oh yes. I will get you a Mars bar!"

Of course you couldn't trust the kid, but for a story like this, why not take the chance? What could possibly happen? Weren't carp vegetarians? Ms. Green remembered how her grandfather had fished for carp using soft dough as bait. Harmless. She would give the kid two Mars bars.

There is a saying in the Jukiro province: "Let there be a fish, there will be a fisherman." Perhaps this is as good an explanation as any for what finally took place on Hichi Street. When the fisherman arrived all knew who he was and why he was there. He was a tall man, for a Japanese, and very distinguished with a well-trimmed gray moustache and a fishing hat of the kind that has lures pinned to the band. He wore hip boots and a fisherman's vest with many pockets, and carried a wicker creel that seemed every bit as inadequate for the job ahead as his rod, which was long, slender, and clearly designed with sportsmanship in mind.

But people could see that he knew what he was about. The crowds parted for him. Some individuals bowed respectfully. "I will not harm the fish," he declared. "It only seeks to escape the Jet Skis." This statement brought polite applause.

Yoshira pressed forward with her microphone, as much through force of habit as anything, for she knew full well the station would run no story without pictures. "How are you planning to catch this carp?"

The fisherman nodded. It was a reasonable question, and he was a polite man. "The same way, my dear, that I would catch any fish. With a hook and line and a little luck. Luck, of course, is paramount."

"But what will you use for bait?" It must be pointed out that Yoshira did not make up this question herself. It had been given to her on a scrap of paper by a member of her crew. But it was a good question. What indeed would the fisherman use for bait? A loaf of bread? A vegetarian pizza? An apple pie?

"Nothing large," the fisherman displayed a tiny hook, smaller than a baby's fingernail. "A single kernel of corn will do it."

"Such a large fish will accept so small a lure?"

"We shall see," the fisherman replied.

As soon as he had baited up, the crowd parted respectfully.

Looking down the passage thus created, Yoshira could see the giant carp approaching. It moved with great dignity and surprising grace, glowing majestically in the afternoon sun. Oh, if only she had the cameras!

The fisherman worked his line carefully lest he snag an onlooker, and finally sent a long silken cast out before him. "Ahhh," people sighed. Such a cast was a thing of beauty.

"Patience, now," the fisherman said. "We must all now be silent."

Silence, a most unusual phenomenon in a large modern city, descended upon the streets of Tokyo. People held their breaths. Who would dare disturb such a sacred moment?

"Stop him!" a voice cried. "Thief! Thief! Stop that thief!"

Two men burst out of the crowd. The first was quite naked save for the golden fish scale he was holding (as one might hold a fig leaf) over his genitals. It was Mr. Jones, pursued by Mr. Sabucho.

"Stop that man!" Mr. Sabucho cried again. "He stole my scale!"

"The fools!" Yoshira snarled. "They'll frighten the fish!" Then she recognized the naked American. "That's him! The idiot who wrecked our cameras! Kill him!"

Mr. Jones was trapped between Mr. Sabucho and Yoshira. Meanwhile, the giant carp was nosing up close to the fisherman's bait.

"Let us have silence now," the fisherman whispered. "Please. The carp is a very timid fish."

But Mr. Sabucho was not to be silenced. "My scale! My golden scale! Where are the police?"

Officer Kuriku, who had never quite given up on directing traffic, stepped forward. "Let us wait," he suggested. "Let us allow the fisherman..."

"To hell with the fisherman! Look at that scale, it's solid gold. Arrest that man!"

"Gold?" Officer Kuriku had hidden his own fish scale beneath his blouse. Could it really be that valuable? Before he could consider this more thoroughly, he suddenly found himself face to face with the same Yoshira Okomo he saw every evening on the six o'clock news.

What an incredible opportunity! He had often wondered what she might be like in "real life." To his astonishment she gripped him by the shirt and screamed. "That man destroyed our cameras! The Taiwa cameras! How will we now show this miraculous fish to our viewers?"

Still holding Mr. Sabucho's fish scale in its strategic position, Mr. Jones at last found himself able to speak. "I was not driving the taxi. I was merely a passenger. As for this fish scale, I would gladly return it if only somebody would lend me a pair of trousers. Even a towel!"

The unforgiving Yoshira would not relent. "Are we to allow foreigners to walk naked on Japanese streets? Arrest him for his nakedness!"

A less well-trained officer might have arrested them all. Officer Kuriku fortunately remembered his classes at the Academy and asked:

"Where is the driver of the taxi?"

The Nigerian, of course, was hiding in the crowd lest he be exposed as the illegal alien that he was. But he could not hide his gold teeth.

"I see him!" Mr. Jones said. "There!"

The Nigerian was dragged forward just as Yoshira's own driver, who had been wandering around dazed, came to such little senses as he ever had. Although physically slight he recklessly charged, crying, "Assassin! Hijo de! I will clutch your eyes out!"

All who were present at this moment (all who were not taking part in the disturbance) marvel yet at the remarkable forbearance and patience of the fisherman. In hushed tones he appealed once more to the crowd. Could there be a single moment of silence? The great fish, as all could see, was now approaching the bait, and interested too, if one were to judge by the tension in its hose-like mouth. Was it not in the best interest of all to set aside these personal distractions?

All eyes turned to the fish, now soberly contemplating the fisherman's bait at the very moment, and with the most exasperating bad timing, a young American woman emerged from a sidestreet pushing a baby stroller. It was Ms. Green. "Oh, look at the fishy, Jenny!" she cried.

Dispute exists (which is understandable given the confusion that accompanies the capture of the giant fish) over exactly what happened next. What cannot be disputed, despite numerous "eyewitness" reports, is that the carp did not really swallow little Jenny although, to some, this seemed to have actually happened. Of course we all know Jenny is alive and happy to this day, and in the care of a more reliable babysitter, Ms. Green, having been sent packing that very evening by the outraged Yoshira, a propitious move for all parties concerned, including Ms. Green who shared her homecoming flight with the American businessman Mr. Jones, once again fully dressed and in a much improved mood, having somehow recognized Mr. Sabucho and successfully concluded the merger that saved both of their companies.

Readers will be pleased to learn that this chance meeting on an airplane led to romance and ultimately marriage; Ms. Green and Mr. Jones now live together in Santa Clara, where their infant son is cared for by an undocumented babysitter from Guatemala. Sadly, she has

neglected her writing; her novel lies unfinished. She has not even begun the article she had hoped to write about the giant carp.

However, even here all is not lost for William, the American hairdresser, while still in the employ of the demanding Yoshira, is said to
be preparing an epic poem on the subject. All do agree that the giant
carp, once hooked, put up an astonishing struggle, and indeed the evidence of this could be seen for days while the wreckage of Hichi Street
was being cleared away.

Unfortunately the Nigerian taxi driver escaped amidst all this confusion, never to be seen again, despite numerous posters mounted in
public places offering a considerable reward, it being felt, with some
justification, that he and he alone is responsible for the considerable
damage our city suffered.

Missing also is the driver of the Taiwa van. There are those who
most deeply feel he must share at least part of the responsibility for
the general destruction, but as others insist he was only doing his duty,
the search for him has not been as extensive, if indeed there has been
a search at all.

Oddly enough the fisherman himself seems to have disappeared as
well, and with him the giant carp which by all accounts he did capture
fairly, and on light tackle. While some claim he took the fish home
with him and ate it, others point out his promise to release the magnificent creature unharmed, arguing such a noble man could hardly
be expected to dishonor his own word. If, however, the fish has been
released, there is no record of where it was set free, the most popular
assumption being Tokyo Bay and, by extension, the great wide ocean
beyond, a fitting refuge for such a remarkable creature.

As for Yoshira, she returned to the Taiwa studios with her story
which, exactly as she feared, received precious little air time thanks to
the lack of images. Needless to say there were the usual artists' representations as well as hundreds of untrustworthy amateur videos, but
such unsatisfactory images were not enough to keep the story alive
more than a day or two before the nation's attention shifted to Cabinet
Minister Tojahama and his three mistresses.

What have we learned from this curious affair? The answers are not
clear. Many, of course, were deeply touched by the fisherman's poise
and dignity, and by the beauty of the great carp as well. We somehow
feel the tremor of past greatness when we think of them, we feel the
glory of our noble ancestors, we sense the satisfaction they must have
experienced in a world as yet unspoiled by commerce. Many of us, like

Mr. Sabucho, recall childhood memories of holidays in the country-side and scented pools wherein, like the shadows of our own immortal souls, fish circle colorfully below; hence we imagine the fisherman as we imagine our fathers, a man of strength and forbearance, steadfastly calm. It is because of this the statue was erected at the Hichi intersection, on an island so to speak, that parts traffic gently but firmly at exactly the spot where young Officer Kuriku first observed the great carp. If the statue seems larger than life, we accept that, and if its position in the intersection sometimes confounds traffic, we accept that too, and if this story by now is considered by some a legend, we accept that too. Our lives continue. Tokyo is as before, crowded, every day it seems more people than ever have been packed into Hichi Street, every morning it seems that more large office buildings than necessary have sprung up overnight, and by afternoon, every afternoon, it seems more money than ever spins beneath the ruthless wheels of traffic. Real money, paper money, yen, dollars, francs, marks, and pounds, and sometimes, although this may be a mere rumor, a single golden scale.

⫶ ⫶ ⫶

PAUL PEKIN'S work has appeared in *Best American Sports Writing of 1991, The Chicago Tribune Magazine, The Chicago Reader,* a bunch of "men's" magazines, some possibly defunct, with names like *Cavalier, Swank, Dude* and so forth, and a long list of literary publications including *Sou'wester, Other Voices, Sideshow, The MacGuffin, The South Dakota Review,* etc. etc. etc, some of these probably defunct too. Insofar as actually making a living, he's had to resort to the usual day jobs, printer, teacher, police officer, but that's all behind him now. He lives in Chicago with his wife, a dog, a bunch of cats, and occasionally he sees his grown-up sons who probably think he has gone mad. Since all short story writers must always claim they are "working on a novel" he plans to start one tomorrow. If everything works out, it will change the way we think of sushi.

L. Timmel Duchamp

The Tears of Niobe

1.

I'm tired of them, sick of their sly, prying presumption. Scholars, they call themselves: claiming to visit this palace to feast upon its archives. But roving its corridors, stealing within its chambers, peering into its alcoves and secret niches, they direct their questions not to the wealth of materials I and the palace's other residents continually create, but to the personal lives of those who use their individual talents to serve the hunger for "knowledge," as the scholars call it.

Voyeurs, all! They don't deceive *us*. Never, when they come upon me, do they boldly ask the questions I see lurking in their eyes or express their wish to know what idiosyncratic talent I possess, what particular path I pursue, and how I came to serve the archives in this way. Instead, they pay me mindless compliments on my sleep dress (which they incorrectly call a "gown") and tell me that the figures embroidered on the hems of its sleeves and skirt look familiar. Eventually, they turn from me unsatisfied. Have they never heard the proverb common to many species, *Ask and you shall receive; knock and it will be opened unto you*? But they are *scholars*. They put no credence in any of the proverbs, much less in that one. Knowledge, they think, is too slippery to be gotten with a single direct question.

Mostly that is so.

This I say true: I am a Dreamer. I Dream, and in my Dreams I recover lost cities of which there have been more than I could name in the space of a year, cities spread across the galaxy, as famous as Astorethe and as forgotten as Mahamaglanhi, as hated as Vlucsvarr and as admired as Eleq om Jhsesq. Of these, some fell to natural disaster, famine, and disease. Others perished in the howling winds of icy empire, or were consumed by fevered avarice. I Dream not only of cities that once existed, but also of cities that should have but were lost when time diverged and branched away from the main line, preventing them from ever achieving the existence they had been promised, their splendor and beauty, yes, and misery and sadness as well, since misery always accompanies splendor, and sadness beauty. I Dream of cities past and cities future, of cities built by every species in the galaxy.

Cities are mortal entities, though few of their inhabitants ever think of them in that way. Like children, cities cannot imagine that death could ever touch *them*. Even when a city faces a credible threat of annihilation, those living in it cannot conceive the utter, total destruction of its material existence, its culture, its spirit. Even after the point at which Rome's blockade of Carthage had begun causing death from starvation and disease, even as its inhabitants hurled themselves and their children into Moloch's furnace in desperate sacrifice to their heartless god, even then they could not imagine Scipio Aemilianus's soldiers toiling around the clock for six days, tearing down every wall and roof in the city and slaughtering every man, woman, and child they came upon, could not imagine the resulting rubble burning seventeen days until reduced to ash, could not imagine the ash being ploughed into the soil with salt, that house might never again be built, corn might never again be sown, upon the ground where it had stood.

Desire and loss drive my talent. None of those visiting this palace will ever have heard of my own city. Those who destroyed it did not sow the soil with salt after razing every home, monument, and palazzo to the ground, nor curse the land, but they did kill all its inhabitants but the handful of children—I among them—they then sold as slaves, just as the Romans did to the few inhabitants they allowed to survive Carthage and Corinth's destruction on Earth, 146 years before the Christian Era. The romantic and ignorant choose to believe that in such cases the destroyers spare the lives of infants because of their *innocence*. But those who would kill a city care nothing for innocence or guilt and use such terms only where it serves to assert the moral righteousness of their own thirst for their enemy's blood. The only reason infants and small children might be spared is this: they carry so little imprint of their own culture that the destroyers can feel confident that nothing of the city's identity will survive in even attenuated traces in them.

Desire and loss, I say again, drive my talent. I long for what cannot be; I ache in every fiber and bone of my body for those most terrible of losses—those so all-encompassing that they have gone ungrieved. I Dream, but only as Chief Mourner of the vanished, unclaimed dead. To me come fragments, traces, mysteries, and tastes that can never be whole, never be mastered as history, as fact, as science. I may feel each splinter and shard of cities lost as intense and immediate truth, but these truths are as elusive as any ordinary dream becomes when put into words the next morning.

The will to annihilate an entire culture alone drives the destruction of cities. A city's refusal to accede to an aggressor's demands is in every case merely the pretext for destruction. Those who destroyed the city of my birth hated my city's culture, despised my city's language, loathed my city's religious practices and beliefs. These offered an affront to the aggressor's very existence, as our being of an alien species did not. Those few infants they preserved they handed over to their religious establishment. We were to be taught a decent language and civilized manners and wholesome values, as well as trained for useful work. The religious masters told us nothing of our origins and, indeed, forbade us ever to question them as to our physical differences from themselves. This rendered our curiosity about our differences unspeakable.

We were trained for useful work, yes—every child but myself. Long before I reached adolescence the masters discovered that I had a gift for Vision, as they called it. They did not at first guess to what use they could put my gift; they knew only that my gift was a desirable thing to possess. And so I was sent to them, the most secret and powerful masters of all. To be trained in their ways—and to be examined and studied, like an artifact discovered on the ruins of a newly claimed world, promising but mute.

2.

My visions, as the masters first called them, might have been taken for reveries of madness but for three things—their discreteness, their consistency, and a handful of details that attested, they thought, to a knowledge of the gods and the Divine Universe that is mundanely given only to those who undertake long years of study of the Sacred Media. What would a child of twelve know of the deep violet skies that soar so grandly over the gods' home world? Or of musical instruments she can describe but not name? Or of icons so powerful and holy that they can be displayed only in certain places and at certain times to the masters alone?

In fact, the visions that came to me were not of the masters' gods, but of another city. Living, as I have, only to serve my talent, my memory carries little that is personal. And yet I recall, even now, strong emotional images of a life suddenly transformed. One day I numbered only one among a crowd of captive children, outwardly submissive, self-effacing, obedient; the next I became the intense focus of the masters' hopes and desires, such that those of the elite order to whom I was sent kept constant watch over me and pounced on every word I spoke, lest some unlooked-for revelation slip away without notice—since I, unfamiliar with the Sacred Media, could have no understanding of any vision the gods might choose to send to me.

I knew, when my first masters sent me to their superiors, that I had been chosen by the gods. I began by craving the attention now lavished on me and dramatized myself and my visions, instinctively adopting the role of a star performer, which the masters did not discourage. But the attention palled, especially since the masters imposed on me a far stricter regimen, of fasting and sleeplessness and hour upon hour of meditation, than I had previously known. Before long the regimen diminished my brief sense of self-importance even as it encouraged the visions (which, as I eventually learned, were Dreams). My desire fastened wholly on the Dreams.

These first Dreams came to me as fragments which accumulated in my mind like a jumble of puzzle pieces. The masters instructed me not to reflect on any vision that was sent to me, saying that I would always lack the power to comprehend these and that I was only to relate faithfully what I saw, so that they, who were wiser than I, could discover the truth the gods were sending to them through me. I had been taught to think myself stupid, and so I believed that only by stitching together the scraps the masters let fall in my presence would I ever glimpse a whole that I knew must be more than the sum of the parts my vision rendered.

One master, by name Revestiere, I attended particularly, sitting by him as often as he allowed, listening to the theories he expounded to his colleagues, memorizing the glyphs he said bore similarity to certain figures and characters I described having appeared in this Dream or that. I chose Revestiere for a child's reason: his face and form pleased the simple aesthetic sense I then had; his face shone often with a purity of purpose that took little interest in the concrete details of his surroundings; and his eyes promised the kind of honesty for which children—especially those brought up like me—hunger. It seemed natural to me that he showed not the slightest sign of affection to me or to anyone else; warmth and affection were at that time unknown to me. For his part, I believe that my choosing to attach myself to him in particular secretly pleased him, since it was likely he would have taken my choice as a signal to him personally of his gods' favor. And also, of course, my spending so much time near him meant that his access to my visions would be superior to that of his brothers.

Whenever I sat near Revestiere, I took care never to speak unless directly addressed. I understood, as any animal with instincts intact does, that keeping still would render me nearly imperceptible. Not that Revestiere didn't know that I was present; rather, he soon learned to take my presence for a certain sort of absence and in doing so gave himself the pleasure of speaking his thoughts aloud, ostensibly to the young girl seated nearby, but in his own mind to himself only. If I had answered him even once, or asked a question about something he said to me, he would probably have understood that more of myself was present than my mere physical shell. But I did not so much as say "Yes, master," or "Oh yes, I see what you're saying," much less "How interesting!"—or even nod. I sat silent and still, a material extension of the stool, a superficial semblance of an interlocutor.

I learned early the survival value of concealing one's knowledge about anything of even potential importance. The posession of knowledge without power can create great and terrible risk. And although I learned that the appearance of ignorance often helps to keep one safe, I discovered, too, that *actual* ignorance could be lethal.

I knew little of the religion beyond the rituals and rules imposed upon the children raised by the religious establishment, knew nothing of its cosmology or gods, and so I at first believed the masters when they told me that I had been chosen by the gods to be their instrument, their conduit to the masters. But I do not think it can have been long before I began to suspect that my visions were not sent by the gods at all. I grasped instinctively that if I told them this I would not only disappoint the masters, but anger them. I knew they would feel cheated, and suspected that rather than direct their anger at their gods for not having given them what they so longed for, they would be angry with me—perhaps even accuse me of having duped them. (Never mind their firm belief that I was stupid: there has never existed a sentient being who cannot believe two contradictory things simultaneously.)

Each time after I reported to a master (usually to Revestiere) that I had Dreamed, we would fold our bodies, each of us, into the correct position for meditation, and Revestiere would lead me through the Nine Steps of Opening. Only after we had prepared our thoughts and souls for reception would the master bid me to *speak the vision the gods have sent.* On one particularly troubling occasion, I described a man and woman standing on a roof. These, I knew, were siblings. The sister lifted her face to the sky, to the soft, warm, humid velvet of the darkness, to the slight stir of air that moved luxuriantly over her throat, then opened her mouth and took a bite out of the sky, sucking at the stars and eating three of them, taking them into herself, swallowing and absorbing a coldness that went at once to her bones, chilling her thoughts, her heart, and her hands. And when the sister opened her mouth again, a perfect distillation of the star streamed out into the night, at first two and then five distinct, crystalline streams of sound, showering the air around them like a dust of diamonds, sparking and glinting as they sifted slowly to the surface on which they stood, radiant for a few moments on lighting, then winking inevitably into nothingness.

The brother swept his arm in an arc that ended in the clench of a fist. Slowly, deliberately he laid the knuckles of that fist against his sister's larynx. A sound thrummed in her throat, vibrating powerfully against his fingers. When finally he removed his hand from his sister, he took with him whatever remained of the stars she had eaten and pressed his knuckles against his own larynx. The sister dropped to her knees and laid her arms on the surface where the shower of sound had been stripped of life. The reason she did this was not given to me to know, any more than the reason for the brother's subsequently turning his back on his sister and moving away. I merely attempted to relate these images from my Dream to the master, imagining that he would understand what I had been given only to convey.

When I had finished, Revestiere frowned at me. I had not yet learned the need to distinguish between expressions of perplexity and rebuke: since I knew nothing yet of the limitation of the masters' understanding and knowledge, I assumed his frown rebuked me. He stared at me for a long time before speaking. Although his silent regard alarmed me, I held my tongue, which longed to say something to divert his apparent displeasure. Only when I had become convinced that I would be sent back to a life of menial servitude did he speak.

"The figures in your vision can only be Elleoris and Flandin. These are the gods known generally as 'the brother and sister.' They almost always figure together, as if they together constitute a whole into which their contradictory parts had been split." I understood that Revestiere was reviewing aloud an argument he had been carrying on inside his head, to see whether his thought, put into words his own ears could hear, sounded reasonable. "You have not recalled your vision correctly, girl. It can only have been the *brother* who ate the stars and the sister who took from him what remained after the act of creation. Think carefully. For you will be no good to anyone if you cannot recall your visions with precision."

If I had been fifteen or twenty years older, I would likely have believed that I had made an error of memory. But at such a tender age I could not take seriously any suggestion that I could have forgotten which sibling had done what in a scene I had not many minutes since Dreamed. Such a mistake was impossible. And so began my suspicion that what I Dreamed was no "vision" sent by the gods, but something else. A sort of madness. Or the elaborate fantasy produced by an imagination that had begun to run wild.

I acted on the instinct of panic: I asked the master to allow me to meditate at greater length, so as to better recall the vision. He agreed, and I pretended to meditate, and eventually related the scene as Revestiere said it must have been.

After that incident, I listened with close attention to every word the masters spoke about the gods and learned to relate my visions in such a way as to encourage the masters to interrupt me, mid-telling, with pointed questions that assisted me in shaping my words to suit their expectations. Since they thought me stupid, they never once suspected me. But because I managed to keep on top of such a dangerous and volatile situation, I gradually came to understand that I could not be entirely stupid. Being so young, I never wondered how long I could keep playing such a game or what would become of me once the deception was revealed. I only wondered whether the visions—such as they were—would continue indefinitely. For I feared desperately that they would not.

3.

When a lost city streams into my Dreams, its fragments come to me in no particular order, as though they were the tiles of a mosaic that had been disassembled and then flung down at random. I know nothing of the place, its people or customs. It is important that I not begin my effort to see patterns in the fragments too early, for if I do, it is all too likely to keep me from ever grasping anything true or important about the city. The impression of clarity early in the process is always a sign that I've deluded myself and may never be able to assemble the city's stories into a true memory of what has been lost.

Revestiere may have been interpreting every fragment I related to him, but his doing so brought me the opposite of clarity. Once I realized that the picture he and his brethren were creating could not be built from an honest recital, my impressions of this first lost city seemed to amount to a handful of phantoms flitting through my thoughts. If my Dreams had been the mere nocturnal review of an ordinary humanoid brain, the alterations I made when I related them would have overridden my memory of the original fragments, and the city would surely have been lost to me. But Dream fragments are not at all like ordinary dreams. That small gray organ in my hippocampus that enables reception of Dreams places a powerful value on Dream fragments. In all the decades that I have been Dreaming, I have yet to lose even one fragment to Lethe.

I knew with certainty that my visions could not be of the masters' gods the first time that I Dreamed images of the city's destruction. I had been taught with the other children salvaged from the city of my birth that the gods allowed cities to be annihilated only when the inhabitants deserved it. For confirmation, one could examine the history of any civilization that ever existed in the universe. The worthy always prevailed; and yet no matter how powerful they might be, the gods allowed them to retain their power only for as long as they were worthy. Sadly, civilizations never seemed to learn this lesson, for corruption inevitably set in—in some civilizations sooner than in others—at which point, the gods withdrew their favor and the power either dissipated slowly or collapsed under a fatal blow. And so the first Dream showing me an image of the city's destruction came as a terrifying shock.

Although we humanoids cannot, when awake, take in more than two visual fields simultaneously, in my Dreams I commonly perceived three, and occasionally as many as five. In the Dream of which I speak, I saw three. In one, the brother figure stood tall and bold, his chest thrust out, his head thrown back, his throat exposed as some complex song composed of two distinct melodies streamed through his lips. My Dream gave me no knowledge of the song's meaning, only the understanding that it was part of a formal ritual. Facing him stood three persons of a species different from his own, each silent and grim, their eyes staring with the sharpness of a freshly honed-dagger. Their silence and the coldness of their gazes filled me with dread.

In the second of the three scenes in pentimento, I saw an immense circular room in which stepped tiers of seats rose high around a central platform. Hundreds of those the masters believed to be gods sat in those seats, watching others who stood on the platform, singing, each person two or more lines of song. So many persons singing multiple melodies at once might be assumed to produce cacophony, but in fact they projected, collectively, a sound of such ineffable beauty, filled with a significance I could almost grasp, that my Dreaming self—an imagined entity as real to my consciousness as my physical body is when awake—wept. In the midst of this beauty, catastrophe struck. An aerosol invaded the chamber, an aerosol that my Dreaming self perceived as a fine spray of gauzy threads that at first thinly wended its way through the room but then grew progressively thicker as more and more spray entered through pores in the wall and ventilation grills and the cracks between each door and its sill, such that the stream of gauze-like particles began to loop and fold and cross, occupying all the space in the room. One by one the singers fell prey to the mist they could not see, the gauzy mist that entered their open, singing mouths and poured down their throats; score by score those in the audience succumbed to the mist that silenced and strangled every body it entered. The singers collapsed to the floor, and the spectators slumped in their seats, leaning drunkenly into one another. Finally not one person breathed. And the gauzy mist turned to powder, olive brown and sad. What had been beautiful was now gone without trace.

And at the same time that I saw this negation of a beauty I recognized without understanding, I beheld, also, a third scene. In it those the masters took for gods flew high above their city, men astride brilliantly-feathered great, sleek birds, and women riding larger gray birds with shorter, neater feathers and long, curving necks the elegant color of Zoan pearls, like those in the miter that the Maximus wears when officiating over the highest of the masters' sacred rituals. Their vivid, joyous presence and the soaring, crystalline voices of their song seemed to reverberate through the sky, resonating in my heart as in a vault of holy mystery. This moment of being, conveyed to me even as I took in the other two scenes from the city's history, I recognized as a distillation of the city's soul. And so it was that at one and the same moment I beheld the first blow struck against the city and its crown and glory. But I did not, of course, understand that much until later. At the time I Dreamed these fragments, I knew only that these beautiful people who seemed always to be singing could not be the gods the masters took them for.

From the beginning it had been my practice, each time I emerged from a Dream, to compose myself before leaving the small, windowless room where the masters sent me to court my holy visions. After this first Dream of the city's destruction, I lingered long there, for besides terror at learning that those I dreamed of were not gods, I felt a great sadness. I asked myself what these visions or dreams could be. Were they madness? Although I had at that point collected only a few dozen pieces of the mosaic, a certain coherence underlay all of them. And yet how, if they were not the holy visions the masters thought them to be, could they be anything *but* hallucinations?

Turn the question over and over in my mind as I did, I could find no answer. And so the question became my constant, secret companion, an unseen presence that the masters did not suspect.

When finally I emerged from the small, closed room and passed a period of meditation with Revestiere, I related the two fragments of Dream that did not challenge the divinity of those I Dreamed. I knew not where such deception would lead, nor for how long I could maintain it. But I was young. The future, one assumes at that age, will take care of itself and in any event always be an improvement over the past.

4.

Few masters ever beheld the naked face of the Maximus. Every high ritual, after all, commanded its own particular masks for each of its priestly participants, and as the one who presided, the Maximus wore the most elaborate and concealing of all, of gold or another elegant metal, studded with a score of precious jewels, molded in a form that bore no relation to the shape of his own features, its jaw inhumanly angular, its ears and nose long and pointed. Fewer still knew his name. I never learned his name myself, but in time I came to know his face very well.

All through my earliest years I heard stories of his dread power, stories that made him a nightmare figure used to scare us children. Later, I suspected that even the most powerful masters feared the touch of his naked fingers. When the Dreams first began to come to me, the Maximus examined me himself and took from my mind the images that I had seen. It was he who had affirmed the value of my visions. After I learned that my Dreams were not holy visions at all, I told myself it would be unthinkable for any of the masters to suspect me of deception precisely because the Maximus himself had validated my gift. It did not occur to me that he would ever have occasion to touch me with his naked hand again, or I would not have been so sanguine.

It did not occur to me. In fact very little occurred to me. Certainly it did not occur to me that suppression of even the slightest fragment of the Dreams could in and of itself bring harm to me personally. I knew nothing then of the nature of my gift, of the demands it exacts. And I knew nothing of the power of a secret the lineaments of which inevitably amplify without limit.

The very night I first withheld a portion of a Dream from the masters, I began to suffer from Night Misery. Night Misery falls upon the unaware sleeper, partially rousing her to a twilight state where she cannot tell the difference between sleeping and waking. Trapped in that state, she can neither rouse fully to waking consciousness nor fall back into true sleep. If the Night Misery lasts for the entire night, its sufferer wakes in the morning exhausted and feeling pummeled over every inch of her body. My first experience of Night Misery came shortly before dawn. For as long as it lasted, I experienced, as if I myself had been present, the murder of those the masters believed to be gods. The scene was unbearably prolonged. It did not repeat, but took only as long as the Night Misery itself lasted to play out to its horrifying annihilation, stretching into an endless present, forcing my witness of the sinister orange gauze working its way into its victims, instant by infinite instant, so that I knew each moment as intimately as it could ever be given anyone to know.

With what relief I woke! Only when I had risen from my bed, however, did I discover the wretched state to which the Night Misery had reduced my body. Barely did I manage to drag myself through the long, oppressive day. As I sat on my stool near Revestiere, my muscles trembled, and my head throbbed with pain. Still I kept silent, rather than be sent to the masters' physician for examination and treatment. Guilt so riddled my thoughts that I feared that with a single look anyone who actually stared into my face (as the masters never in fact did) would recognize my imposture at once.

That night, alas, I feared to fall to sleep and so lay awake late into the night, though my body screamed for the relief that only sleep could grant. But when finally I dropped into slumber, I slid helplessly back into the Night Misery, unable while asleep to elude its grip, much less fend off the worst of its horrors. In the morning I woke in an even worse state than I had the day before. Slowly one thought began to dominate my mind: that the vision of horror might never leave me until I had told it in some way to someone. It seemed natural to believe that the visions could be gotten rid of through telling them, as though the mere narration of them effectively served to pass their weight and reality on to another.

Although I feared to tell the masters of the gods' destruction, I realized that I had never been afflicted with Night Misery on those occasions when I'd been less than truthful with details the masters would have found difficult to accept. So it seemed to me that I had only to discover an acceptable version—suitably blurred—to relate to the masters to be rid of the horror.

Unfortunately, my head was throbbing with such pain that I doubted my ability to fabricate a safe substitute. Nevertheless, I went into the chamber reserved for seeking my holy visions and assumed the outward posture for their reception. I had learned from earliest childhood the wisdom of at all times displaying the appropriate appearance of doing what I knew I ought to be doing at any given time, since one never knew when the masters might, through undisclosed methods, be observing one's behavior. Thus I made a physical performance of every step intended to prepare me for reception without the accompanying mental progression. I intended, simply, to mimic, at the right moment, the appearance of the trance state, during and after which I could allow myself as much time as necessary to couch the unrelated fragment in terms the masters could accept. It never occurred to me that a new Dream would flow into my mind without what I had assumed was the necessary mental preparation.

In fact, I experienced not only two new fragments, in pentimento, but with them also received the leftover, unrelated fragment yet again. One of the new fragments conveyed a scene of love and pleasure—this being the first explicitly sexual encounter I received—while the second was yet another scene of horror. In the one, the figure the masters had taught me to call Flandin, whom I instinctively thought of as "the sister," engaged in a long sequence I could only think of as an elaborate mating ritual with a male partner. They sang, of course, throughout the sequence and flirted via their gestures and gazes as well as their bodies, for some time without physical contact and eventually with fleeting touches, until finally—still singing, the entire while—they locked themselves together into an embrace that involved interior organs not visible to my untrained eye.

The second new fragment showed the destruction of an opulent palace containing perhaps a hundred courtyards, each displaying artifacts of considerable beauty and sophistication, as well as hundreds of rooms filled with long shining tubes that I knew contained a rich and detailed record of the history and civilization of those the masters believed to be gods. I saw a member of the species I understood to be angry at these "gods," one of those who had refused to be pleased by the polite ritual Elleoris had tendered them, beckon a ball of fire down from the sky, causing it to part neatly from the vehicle I knew to be its source and flow swiftly as though it were a river of flame, streaking straight down into the palace. A few moments after the fire penetrated the palace, the entire building exploded, sending molten flecks of the tubes high into the atmosphere in a fiery cloud that seemed to hang like a turbulent, living sunset over the city. This palace represented the heart of the world created by those the masters called gods. Without it, they would no longer know who they were, from whence they had come, or even whither they had been tending.

If the previously untold fragment had made me both sad and fearful, this one rendered me both grieving and angry. For the first time I had a faint glimmering of what had been done to my own city and what I, in the process, had lost. No wonder, then, that I emerged from that Dream inconsolable and brimming with fierce, indeed senseless hatred. I was still ill with the after-effects of the Night Misery, but so distraught with rage that I forgot everything I had intended to do to maintain my deception of the masters.

5.

Those who concern themselves with "knowledge" could not begin to fathom what that young girl both understood and felt. For she began, then, to comprehend her own devastation, a deprivation which had heretofore been nearly invisible to her, a shadow lurking in her peripheral vision that she now and then glimpsed without any sense of its origin. Suddenly, she *knew*.

A lament poured into her mind, a howling that overrode all articulate thought, the very dirge she had heard those the masters believed to be gods sing as that magnificent palace burned. This lament remained with her throughout her life—remains, that is to say, with *me* even now. She and I have seen many other treasuries of a civilization's history destroyed—for although the details of each of these lost cities differ, the broad outline of their annihilation is nearly identical—but that first experience of a civilization's destruction stood in for her recognition of her own loss. From that moment forward she found herself wondering who her parents might have been and what the name of her city might be, even as she could not begin to speculate as to its languages, art, or music.

I emerged, then, from the chamber in which I sought Dreams burning with hatred for the masters and the quiet confidence with which they took their own civilization for granted. Even the barest possibility that *their* languages, *their* religion, *their* elaborate liturgies and dramas could be lost irrecoverably never once troubled them. I could see that in their world all that could be was what already was and that what already was, was infinite and eternal. The masters not only did not desire difference, but also found it unthinkable.

Above everything, this sublime blindness of the masters made me burn. Blindness, like stupidity, lies beyond challenge. But this was an insight I did not come to grasp until considerably later.

6.

After this terrible Dream, I did not follow the protocol laid down for me of informing Revestiere or another master that the gods had sent me a new holy vision. Instead, I went to the temple to render my service there, which I was obligated to perform a minimum of two hours a week. Temple service entailed everything from sweeping and scrubbing and polishing the mosaic floor to cleaning the brass and gold appointments, to shining the mirrors and other glass surfaces, to laundering the lace draperies ornamenting the altars and the priests' robes. I knew that in my state it would be unwise for me to lay my hand to anything fragile, so I told the temple's custodial master that I would prefer scrubbing the mosaic tile floor to any other task. Since few people ever volunteered for that particular task, the master did not refuse my request. And so it was that I spent the next three hours on my knees wielding a small, tough-bristled brush, brightening the grout lines with a paste the fumes of which scalded my throat and lungs and made my eyes leak hot, bitter tears. In the past I had taken pleasure in the black, gold, crimson, and teal tiles, whose gleaming colors reminded me of the gorgeous robes and masks the masters wore in the holiest processions. On that day, however, their rich beauty was hateful to me.

The ravages of Night Misery did not slow me in the slightest, for I scrubbed under power of adrenaline. My mind replayed the scene of the fire streaking down from the sky bearing a civilization's annihilation in not only its cargo, but also its very shape, velocity, and mass. The chill of the tile on which I knelt, the biting pain in my knees became one with my anguish. My fingers worked and worked at the grout as though to erase my terrible knowledge. And all the while my tears fell, and my nose sniveled, and my turmoil built and fed on itself, lacking any outlet for escaping the confines of my body and my mind.

I had been told often and often enough that service in the temple should be undertaken with a clear mind and tranquil spirit. I had assumed the rule existed merely to enforce reverence for the gods whose spirits often dwelled in that holy space. Since on that day I could feel no respect for the gods of that temple or for any of the masters who served them, I cared nothing for my violation of the rule. I scrubbed the grout in the floor only because I could think of nothing else to do with the physical energy my rage had generated. If I had thought I could tear the temple to pieces with my bare hands, I would vigorously and joyfully have attempted the feat.

I do not recall noticing that the grout cleaner ate through both the fabric of my robe and the skin covering my knees. And if I saw my blood mixing with the grout cleaner and my tears through the hazy blur my weeping made of my vision, I spared not a thought as to its source, for the dervish of rage whirling within my soul allowed me not the faintest concern for my own well-being. I do, however, remember noticing the first low buzz vibrating in the air around me, as of a thousand hornets swarming and angry. Only moments later my vision darkened. Then came the streaks of light, piercing the darkness at tremendous, almost invisible speed, racing past and around and circling above me. The buzz thrumming in my ears modulated with the streaking movement of light. It grew louder, and louder, and louder until there was only the buzzing in my ears and the darkness and streaking of light consuming my vision. And a terrible odor assailed me: a strong citrus scent which soon became an acrid burning that abraded my throat and nasal passages.

Finally, I did swoon—not into an ordinary faint, but into a Dream unlike any I had yet experienced. This Dream poured into the organ that retains the memory of every Dream I receive, the sum of all that I was meant to know about the first city my talent recovered. I received the stories of many lives and loves and deaths, the desires and glories and sadnesses of dozens of individuals: their values, the textures of their lives, and even some of the most minute, perhaps trivial details of their habits, manners, and most private functions.

I learned, also, why the alien species visiting them hated and annihilated them. But although I learned the reason, I could not then comprehend it—neither its broader significance, nor the peculiar logic that could make sense to the destroyers alone.

I have no notion of how long I lay caught up in this violent swoon of Dreaming. The images of the city had been flooding into my brain for some time, though (once I became aware) first as a sort of nagging drone, and then increasingly insistently, of a pressure encircling me like a cold band of iron tightening around my skull. The pressure intruded on the Dreaming, distracting me, drawing my attention to itself. When finally it succeeded in capturing my attention, the pressure resolved itself into the sound of powerful words of which I only subliminally understood the meaning, words chanted at such a low pitch that my aural intelligence could nearly distinguish the frequency of their individual vibrations. It was this throb that drew my mind back into consciousness, pulling me almost physically out of my swoon.

When I opened my eyes, I found myself circled by seven masters. One of these was the Maximus. A terrible power emanated from them, chilling and numbing me into an inert, icy block of scarcely living flesh. I longed for their chant to cease, for I knew that if it continued, my breath would be stopped and my heart starved and paralyzed. Compelled by the Maximus's power, my gaze was drawn as though straight into the very pupils of the Maximus's eyes. As the processes of my body gradually stilled, my gaze froze in the grip of the Maximus's terrible power. The sound of the chanting faded into white noise, and my vision bleached into that whiteness that can be found only at the heart of the galaxy's burning blue stars. And the whiteness blotted out my existence.

7.

When life and then consciousness returned to my body, I flailed in a cold clangor of sharp voices raised in harsh, insistent argument. My body clenched and shivered with shock. I did not immediately understand that the argument concerned me. All voices but one spoke to the same end: *She has angered the gods. Look at the furor she has raised! Not a window escaped breaking. The gods want her expelled. Put away somewhere, where she cannot insult and defy them. Whatever she has done, they will not use her again! Never have the gods shown such anger in this very temple! We dare not risk displeasing them further. She must be removed!*

I am surprised they did not kill me on the spot. I learned later that before they had silenced my Dreaming and carried my body out of the temple, every pane of glass and drop of crystal had been shattered, the tile floor ripped up, the dome rent open to the sky, the brass and gold fittings melted to shapeless pools of metal, and the marble altars reduced to dust. A fierce rain of green acid had poured down, out of the heavens, onto the remains of the altars, poisoning the air and polluting the sacred ground on which they had been erected. The very site on which the temple had been built was thereby made anathema until the end of time.

The one voice that opposed them belonged to the Maximus. "The gods," said he, "spared her life even as they made clear their displeasure by spoiling the temple. There is a reason for that, my sons. And the reason can be found only by touching her mind to discover what must be there, waiting for us to find."

I began to cry then. I knew that the Maximus's naked touch would reveal all that I had deliberately concealed of my Dreams from the masters.

"See, she is again in her senses," said the Maximus. I saw his naked hand approaching my forehead and quickly closed my eyes.

No one who has not experienced it can imagine the Maximus's touch. To the Maximus was denied even the possibility of shared touch with another, whether sensual or casual. Others' touch will feel warm or cool, moist or dry, smooth or rough on one's skin. Not so the Maximus's. Although his touch generated physical sensations, my senses did not connect the sensations with the hand, which I would not even have known was pressed against my forehead had I not opened my eyes and seen it. I experienced, rather, the sensation of being engulfed in a conflagration consuming every inch of my flesh, excruciatingly searing at the same time it made me itch in every part of my body, most especially within the untouchable reaches of my skull. Perhaps worse was the paralysis that crept over me, restraining both my voice and my ability to move, and also sealing shut my eyes.

Even as I burned—as that magnificent palace had done, as, indeed, the entire city had been made to boil down into the merest slag and ashes—I possessed some dim awareness of the random mosaic of Dream fragments whirling about in wild abandon, cascading down into the vortex of the Maximus's hungry demand. So clearly did I imagine this flow that I was astonished, when the Maximus released me, to find the memories themselves still in my mind, as powerful and wrenching as before. He had taken them from me and yet left them intact. In those days the Maximus, as I recall, characterized his touch as "the Talent of Sharing." If it was a sharing, that sharing was one way and involuntary. No one who had experienced it once would ever actually wish to share with the Maximus a second time.

After he withdrew his touch from my mind, the Maximus spoke to the masters there assembled. "The child's visions are not what we thought. If they are a gift of the gods, they reveal something other than the gods' own doings. I must think on the visions I took from her memory, must meditate and contemplate their significance." His eye then fell upon my face, and he saw that I was conscious and attending to his words. "Until we can be sure of the source of her visions and understand their purpose, until we know why her labor in the temple angered the gods, she must be kept secure and isolated. She may be the vessel of the gods, or the vessel of the gods' enemies. We do not yet know. A great power works through her, mighty enough to have moved the gods to destroy their own temple. And so we must be cautious. As cautious as it is possible to be."

I looked from one stiff and trembling face to another. I saw that all but the Maximus regarded me with terror. I observed it seeping from the masters' pores, trickling out in the ragged exhalations of their breath, staining the air through which their gazes passed, a sharp, acid ochre breaking into barely visible particles that slowly dissipated like clouds of steam in the air. I had always thought fear to be a personal, visceral emotion. Watching the fear work its way into the very air we breathed, I learned that fear is a pollution that will taint the common air when it is shared by several people in one place together. And when I looked at Revestiere and saw him looking at me, I saw that a thin gauzy haze of acid ochre swam in a cloud around his head, keeping him from recognizing me as the person, familiar and negligible, he had previously thought me to be.

I had always been a stranger among the masters. But now I became an exile.

8.

And so began the period of my imprisonment far from the masters and the ruins of the holy temple. Four of the masters spirited me away to a cottage two days' journey's distance, where an old woman, who had been deprived of both her hearing and her tongue, took charge of me. She acted as both my guard and my servant, though since a tall fence topped with broken glass enclosed the cottage and sentries had been posted at the gate, after only a few months she came to seem more a fellow prisoner than a guard, for she never passed through the gate or received even one visitor all the years she lived following my arrival there. When she died, and I raised enough of a clamor to bring the guard inside, they soon replaced her with another woman—also deprived of her tongue, and also deafened.

My first few weeks in exile passed in a daze of shock. I had never in my life been in such a quiet, still place, nor so alone. Although the masters had never actually *conversed* with me, they had spoken freely in my presence, Revestiere especially. Nor did I find it easy to accustom myself to living in small, low-ceilinged rooms where the only other human present watched me with a voracious, curious attention I could never evade for more than an hour or two at a time. As the gods' special vessel, I had carried an aura of importance in the world. As an exile out of anything that could be called "the world," nothing that I said or did mattered in the least to another living soul, and the one living soul who recognized my existence would never understand even the simplest word to pass my lips. After only a few days, I found myself speaking to the old woman as though she could understand me—simply because I had a great need to hear the sound of human speech, without which I thought I might soon go mad.

For weeks my mind ceaselessly screened memories of the city destroyed. But even as I struggled to make order out of the chaos, I also toiled to make sense of what had happened that day in the temple and the true reason for my exile. I understood, of course, that I had evoked the rage of the gods and that the Maximus had discovered I had concealed the truth about my Dreaming. But I knew that the Maximus's reasons for sending me away were more complex than that. He knew what had enraged the gods, but had chosen not to put me to death, which he could have easily justified doing on the grounds that I had blasphemed against the gods and brought punishment on the temple in consequence.

As the fragments of the city that I had been given in the Dreams tumbled through my consciousness, I never forgot that the city had been destroyed, deliberately and hatefully, and found myself fretting for days—perhaps even for weeks—over the reason for the hatred motivating the destruction. It was only when I had ordered the fragments in a rough chronology, only when I found something that could be called the beginning of the story of the city's destruction, that I finally remembered what I had learned that day that so many fragments poured into my conscious mind at once. (And yes, the story of those fragments—the story of every city's fragments that have since been bestowed on me—is not the city's entire story, but *only* that painful, tragic narrative of a city brought to destruction. Which has come to seem, over my long and lonely years of Dreaming, to be the only story that matters, since that is the story my talent insists that I know.) The city had been destroyed because its inhabitants communicated only in song—musically complex and nuanced, requiring perfect pitch and an elaborate training from birth that formed the musculature of lips, tongue, larynx, and lungs to extraordinary capacities—song that the visitors could not themselves produce, song that enraged the visitors even as the city's inhabitants judged them to be defective persons who ought to have been culled in infancy (as the tone-deaf had always been culled in the city) as imbeciles incapable of even the most rudimentary form of the city's thought. Repeatedly merchants and ambassadors from off-planet had been dismissed from the city as unable to offer anything its inhabitants could want or respect. *These* visitors, however, would not be dismissed. They saw the city as a market for their goods that the city's rulers' failure to take them seriously was thwarting. They knew themselves to be superior (and in weaponry, at least, they certainly were), and they considered the city monstrous for its refusal to deviate from its core philosophical and religious values. They knew nothing of the city's culture or history, only that it was inferior to their own and must eventually, anyway, bend to the visitors' true superiority. In the end, they saw the city's rulers' refusal to engage in "plain speech" (which the Visitors never truly believed they did not know and could not employ) as an affront and defiance they could not tolerate. In a fit of pique and frustration, the visitors demonstrated their superiority, and the city and its history and culture vanished forever—

—depositing its trace, fleeting but quintessential, in that small special organ seated in my own peculiar, particular brain.

9.

Not long after I had assembled all the Dreamed city's fragments into a coherent story of its destruction, I began again to Dream of another city. What I came to know first of this second city was its favorite stories, all tales of love, which the city told itself not only in fanciful fictions but also in the lives its inhabitants saw themselves leading. Every conflict, it seemed, staged the end or challenge or lack of requital to a living dream of love. The city told its history as a series of intertwining love stories, its every crisis a signification of passion at the edge. This was a city as caught up in love stories as the other had been composed of song.

This city's story—particularly its tales of love—swept me away, transformed my dreary exile and cold isolation into days of fantasy that consumed my adolescent self in a fire of longing and desire that would have been completely at home in the city I now Dreamed. I do not recall how long it took before I understood that to preserve myself from Night Misery and its attendant diurnal daze I must tell my Dreams to my attendant, no matter that she could neither hear nor understand them. Once I made this discovery, my life became one long blur of moments lived inside the confines of my own mind. In the daytime I Dreamed of the city and thought constantly about it, while in the evening I imagined myself the heroine of a love story—imagined, specifically, my rescue by Revestiere, whose face came to haunt my sleep and obsess my sexual imagination. Why Revestiere? I suppose because he had tolerated my presence, and because his face was beautiful, and because the only young adults I had known in life were masters. Not that I believed, in my heart, that any of the masters—much less Revestiere—would come to rescue me. Long before my first attendant died I had become convinced that I had been as forgotten as any of the cities I Dreamed back into memory. If the masters never spoke of me, never thought of me, never entered my name into their records, it would be as though I did not exist: this my adult self, isolated from everything but the fragments of other cities' lost traces, understood with the most anguished clarity imaginable. I wonder now if perhaps that very sense of my self's being about as real as the fragments and fantasies preoccupying me made it possible for me to entertain such a wild fantasy about Revestiere. Living almost entirely inside my own mind, I would entail neither risk nor harm from reinventing another living being. The masters—including Revestiere—had, after all, become far less real to me than the cities I Dreamed.

Inevitably, the Dreams manifested the doom of this second city, confusing and grieving me as much—though differently—as the horror of the first city's destruction. And eventually, of course, came Dreams of a third city, and a fourth, and so on, one after another through the years of exile, as one deafened and muted woman replaced another, and another, until finally the day came that the Maximus himself paid a visit to the cottage to see me.

Although the years had not altered his appearance in the slightest, I did not at once recognize him. For decades I had seen no one but the succession of women put to live with me and, on rare occasions, a guard or two, who were always heavily visored and armored. The Maximus, even when traveling, wore the ordinary robes and headdress of his office. I imagine that I gaped at him with the same bewilderment and puzzlement that my attendant did. "So," were his first words to me, "I have been wondering whether to find you sane or mad. Do you speak still? Or have you become mute like your companions?" These words were singular enough that they have remained in my memory all these many long years. I believe that genuine curiosity, not malice, motivated his question.

It had been so long since I had heard the words of anyone but myself carried on the air and into my eardrums that I did not immediately grasp the Maximus's meaning. As we stared at one another, a look settled on his face, an expression of, perhaps, finality. When I opened my mouth and replied that I still spoke, if only to myself, that I might well be mad but if so how should I know it, and that I had thought myself exiled past the memory of anyone who had ever known me, he looked first startled, and then sharply attentive.

My response delighted the Maximus. The glint that came into his shining green eyes is burned into my memory. He asked me if I knew how long I had been living in that cottage. When I said that I did not, he told me that it had been a bit more than one hundred years. I stared at him, wondering what reason he could have for deceiving me—and then thinking back through all the cities whose sorrowful stories I had come to know through the decades, cities I now realized numbered in the dozens. Addressing me as "child," as he had done when I had actually been one, he asked me whether I had never noticed my body's failure to age. And I thought how the second woman who had attended me at the cottage had been youthful on her arrival there, but had been stooped and wrinkled and shrunken on her death. I had never wondered, not once. Which incuriosity I later came to understand as a sign of how little conscious I had become of myself as a living, breathing organism.

We walked then outdoors, in the garden at the side of the cottage in which the women who attended me grew much of our food, where the bees were busy and the chickens not far off, caught up in the constant shrieking babble they insisted on producing from dawn to dusk. I noticed, then, the gloves on the Maximus's hands and discovered the distant echoes of the fear of his touch. And I saw, too, under the dazzling illumination of daylight, that the Maximus's face was as smooth and unlined as it had been a century previous. "You and I," I said hesitantly, "are different from most people."

He laughed. And then he told me that when my first masters had sent me to him he had thought my vision could be of use. All would not have been lost, he thought, had my rage not unleashed such powerful forces that day in the temple. He could not risk his own position by training and shaping my talent himself. And so he had sent me into exile, where I could harm no one and would be given the chance to discipline my talent myself, taking care to keep my brief sojourn with the masters from being entered into their records or ever spoken of. He had come to see if I had done so—or had instead gone mad. A century after the devastation I had brought down onto the temple, no one but the Maximus himself remembered me and my visions. He had prepared a prophecy to lubricate the mechanics of my return to the masters. If I returned with him, I would be known as a seer. I would record my visions, and only the Maximus would enjoy free access to the records of them. Perhaps they would prove useful, perhaps not. But the Maximus described a need in his world for a vision beyond themselves and their simple search for transcendence that his "sons"—the masters—sorely lacked. He was tired of their reliance on the obvious, he was out of patience with their blinkered vision. Their poverty of perception tendered a sign, he thought, that the vitality of his world's civilization had begun to wane, a sign of sterility and self-referential futility.

I wondered, then, whether the capital of the Maximus's world would go the way of the innumerable cities doomed to deletion.

This brief taste of conversation unleashed a fierce hunger for more. The prospect of being able to communicate by words with another person overwhelmed me. But before I consented to return with the Maximus, I asked him the question that had only at that moment occurred to me. No, I did not ask him why I had been given my talent. Rather, I asked him why such a talent would exist at all. I could see why his talent might exist: it could serve many, obvious purposes.

But mine? Why should there be a talent for remembering what would never again be?

I have brought you a seer's robe, mask, and headdress, he said, declining to answer me. And then added: you are the only one capable of answering that question—and will probably be the only one ever to ask it.

10.

Centuries later, of course, I and the Maximus from one world, all the many other talents from others, came to be plucked from our native settings and deposited in this magnificent palace. Here, we make, while a continual stream of scholars visit and gawk and struggle futilely against their own smallness. When they see me and think of my life's work, how can they help but worry? Will their own beloved cities, wondrous in all their creative particulars, one day fall as have all the others, broken to nothingness by their successors? My memory gives witness to the truth that the enjoyment of mastery and triumph in the present is no safeguard for the future. It can happen to any people, that their accomplishments, their work, their seed, will be as ashes plowed into the soil with salt. Forgotten, barren, forsaken.

But all may rest assured. I shall remember them.

⸙ ⸙ ⸙

L. TIMMEL DUCHAMP has been publishing short fiction in *Asimov's Science Fiction, Fantasy and Science Fiction* and numerous other magazines and anthologies since 1989. She is the author of a collection of short fiction, *Love's Body, Dancing in Time* (2004), a collection of essays, *The Grand Conversation* (2004), and two novels, *Alanya to Alanya* (2005) and *The Red Rose Rages (Bleeding)* (2005). Two more of her novels, *Renegade* and *Tsunami,* will be published in 2006. A selection of her fiction and essays can be found at her website, http://ltimmel.home.mindspring.com

Rikki Ducornet

Lettuce

Now that the Management runs the planet, it is necessary to petition the Ultimate Authority should one contemplate deviating, however imperceptibly, from The Way. As Charles Charles is always swamped by the demands of Immediacy—the inevitabilities of which were revealed to Him in the middle of the night by an ear-splitting screech—it is impossible to petition Him except in person. However, it is rumored that He might be caught off guard in the High Head at noon examining His teeth and tongue with all the attention due His rank.

On one occasion only has a petitioner managed to hide out in the High Head—and this despite the microhootered faucets. Although it cannot happen, the petitioner had crawled across the ceiling, circumventing whoopers and gongs. He had hopped from sink to sink, taking care to desensitize the eight soap dispensers—one dispenser for each of the Eight Overseers who, as it is established in The Way, soldier at the sink side by side after relieving themselves in the eight corporate cans.

The Ultimate Can is situated at the bow, as it were, of the Corporate Head, and is visible from the standpoint of the Overseers who have only to roll their sixteen eyes to the left to assure themselves of the One's corporality—surely their function's greatest advantage.

It is confirmed that the petitioner survived the rigors of the Corporate Head and miraculously penetrated (understand that I use these words cautiously and ironically) the Oval Office where he spent the night sprawled on the High Table, and this despite a blizzard of virtual asps that must surely have murderously plagued Him. When in the morning the Usher flung the portals aside and Charles Charles stood poised on the threshold, His armor bleeping, His pale eyes popping, the petitioner stood before Him naked and bleeding.

Charles Charles is the only one alive with firsthand knowledge of The Event. Yet it may well be that the One who is gently hammered into our collective mind as we sleep, is not the Charles Charles we thought we knew, but another, more ineffable Charles Charles. (The Eight who had stood in our leader's wake, stapled to their boots and bleating, have all been re-wired and retired.)

It is established that the petitioner wanted to be allowed to grow lettuces on the lip of his one window. This is not exactly forbidden, yet suggests treason. Why the lettuces mattered so much, why the petitioner was willing to risk everything for them, is a matter none of us is willing to drop. Indeed, we risk as much talking about those lettuces, although not one of us has ever seen or tasted lettuce. Yet we relish the rare references to them in the forbidden books, those books with the images that sear our eyes and cause our bellies to complain, as, or so we imagine, the wild creatures that once roamed the outlawed wilderness, complained. Images of chargers piled high with victuals, or so we suppose, like nothing we have ever tasted. For The Way insists we eat smooth pap, untextured—but for that brief tip of the hat to roughage, which, we have been told, we must not scorn if we are to fully function.

The petitioner's teeth and tongue—considered by some as objects of horror, and by others of hilarity (and by still others as sacred relics to be referred to only cryptically)—are on display in the front hall of the public refectory. When I was a small child, they were introduced to me by my father in guise of a warning or, perhaps, inspired by a premonition. Because the petitioner's persistent remains, and the constant reminder of his heresy have, over a brief lifetime of reflection, inspired me to petition in turn. I, too, would grow lettuces and, as in the Old Days, eat them with those storied condiments: vinegar and oil.

⑂ ⑂ ⑂

RIKKI DUCORNET has another story, "Who's There," on page 467 of this anthology. She is the author of seven novels including *The Jade Cabinet*, finalist for the National Book Critics' Circle Award, and *The Fan Maker's Inquisition*, a Los Angeles Times Book of the Year. She has been awarded both a Fellowship from the Lannan Foundation, and the 2004 Lannan Literary Award for fiction. She is currently working on her third collection of short fiction and a novel set during the Algerian War.

Randall Silvis

The Night of Love's Last Dance

In a town called Mundomuerto there lives a woman who bore a dolphin's child. She is an old woman now, la vieja, and most of the villagers dare glance at her only when she is looking the other way. But this is never difficult for she is always looking the other way, out to sea, where she watches for silvery fins to flash across the horizon like distant signal flags. Whether standing on the cliff's edge or on the rocky shore below, the vieja waits there for one of the flags to turn ashore… for a handsome man dressed all in white to climb toward her over the patient rocks, his clothes miraculously dry by the time he reaches her, his fingertips kissing hers, "Will you dance with me, Lucia Luna?" A tall and graceful man with hips that move like water, his smile thin but sweet, his arm hooked around her back now, fingers caressing quivers into her spine, his left hand always atop his porkpie hat…

These days it is hard to believe that Lucia Luna was once a beauty. Her skin is darkly layered with years now, wrinkled with bitterness. Her hair is a tattered thundercloud that often wraps itself around the crag of her face. But there was a time, the grandfather says, when no man in town could keep his heart from dreaming of her.

The town was called Mundosuave then, and rightfully so, for in those days it was a tender place, a small village on a wide escarpment overlooking a generous sea…a tiny world where, with hard work and kindness, life could be pleasant. But there is no one left to remember that time, there is only the grandfather and Lucia Luna herself. And because Lucia Luna will answer no questions except with a curse, a quick laceration of her jagged black eyes, it is left to the grandfather to tell the story. He tells it often, to anyone who will listen.

Now, after so many years, only the boy comes to request the story of how things came to be as they are. Each day the boy asks to hear the story again, because each time the tale unravels he catches a new thread of it or sees a new crease unfolding in the fabric. It is not a complicated story but as simple as the lives of the people who lived it, yet it holds a fascination for him, not unlike the fascination a child might feel when, with fear and curiosity, he tiptoes alone through the house of a stranger.

Still, the boy is fifteen now and there is not much child left in him. Some day he will not show up in the village square to ask for the grandfather's story, and on that day the boy in him will be gone and maybe the story gone with it. This is what the grandfather fears.

The grandfather's name, already forgotten in Mundomuerto, uttered now only by the tongues of his memory, had been Alberto when he was a boy. Years later he lost that name somehow, lost it like a handkerchief that falls from your pocket as you run too fast down an unmarked path. When you lose something in that manner you might try to retrieve it afterward, but if you are not too dull you waste little time in this hopeless effort, you go on with your life nameless, trying on this name or that, but never again as certain of who you are as when you were young.

Were it not for his story and the boy who comes to listen, the old man would be as much a shadow as Lucia Luna as she passes unnoticed through the villagers' lives. But he is the grandfather for a while more at least, and in the late afternoon he sits on a broken chair in a corner of the clay-tiled square, gazing beyond the low stone wall that protects the plaza and its ghosts from tumbling into the sea. He sits in the gnarled shade of an acacia tree, a shade swept these days by nothing but the wind. Across his lap lays an old guitar, the veneer clouded and cracked, three strings missing. Behind him, the jungle has snaked its vines and branches onto the edge of the plaza, an encroachment which, like the dust and litter, goes unnoticed except by the grandfather, who likes to think that one of these days a vine will wrap itself around his ankles, and drag him, broken chair, tuneless guitar and all, back to that damp and shimmering place to which magic has retreated.

For now, the boy sits beside him on the dusty tiles. He too sits facing the ocean, though from his lower perspective he can see nothing but the most distant shimmering line against the burned-out blue of sky. The old man can not see the shoreline either but his memory sees it clearly, the boulder in shallow water to which Lucia Luna would wade as the men returned home each night in their small boats, the boats riding low in the water, heavy with fish, Lucia Luna then seated atop the rock in her white dress with her strong brown legs widespread, feet bare, the hem of her dress pushed down between brown thighs.

"There was a time," the boy says, because the old man is not as quick with beginnings as he used to be, not as adept at walking with one foot in then and the other in now, "when Lucia Luna's smile was as warm as a night in August, as bright with promise as a Sunday's dawn."

The grandfather stares hard at the watery horizon glinting like metal, a fiery sun sinking toward it. He knows that below them, on the beach, an old woman in dirty rags is struggling toward a boulder.

The boy reaches up and softly plucks a guitar string. "Lucia Luna was seventeen that year," he says. "And you were fifteen, Grandfather. The same age as I am now."

After a moment, the old man looks down at him. "Surely you're not fifteen already. You were only twelve the last time I told you this—"

Without warning his words are swallowed by the throbbing boom of a helicopter as it comes roaring over the jungle, over the plaza, and then tilting wildly to disappear down the coastline. The old man and the boy lower their heads and close their eyes against the whirl of dust these green-and-brown mottled helicopters make. Outside the plaza a few chickens squawk and flutter for cover. A dog barks and chases the whirring bird, as ugly as a turkey vulture. A few moments later the dog turns and trots back and flops against the nearest house.

The old man waits until the engine throb is no louder than a heartbeat. Then he says, "You can't be fifteen already, nieto. You were only twelve the last time I told this story."

"The last time was yesterday."

"The world moves fast these days, doesn't it? It's leaving me behind."

The boy remembers when he did not have to coax the story from the old man, when all the boy had to do was to try to keep up with it. "In the days of Mundosuave," he says, his voice little more than a whisper, "no man could look at Lucia Luna without feeling the slow heaviness of her breasts in his own blood, is that right?"

The old man has been looking at his sandals, his dusty feet. But now a smile deepens the creases in his face. "Los melónes de dios," he says, and he lifts his head and he looks out across the sea. "She would come to the beach at dusk to sing for us as we brought in the day's catch. Someone would hand me my guitar the moment I hopped off my father's boat, and I would sit below her on the rock..."

As the old man talks the boy gazes into his red-rimmed eyes. There, as on the still surface of a tide pool, he looks for the image of a young Lucia Luna standing atop the boulder, stretching her arms and spine, tossing back her mane of raven hair. "She was like something wild, more animal than human," the old man says. "Can you see her, muchacho?"

The boy has found her now in the old man's eyes. "Yes, Grandfather."

"She's there?"

"Sí. You have her now."

The old man nods. For him, she is always there. "She would sit on the rock at dusk and sing to the ocean. All of Mundosuave would be gathered on the shore, unloading the boats and cleaning the fish. And all the young men would gaze up at her as she sang, their hearts throbbing nakedly."

"But only you," the boy says, "could get close to her. You would sit at her feet and play your guitar."

"I could feel her pulse in the strings of my guitar, nieto. Each time I plucked a string, I was touching her. And she...she felt my hands on her, I could see it in her eyes, and in the smile she sometimes turned on me."

"And at night," the boy says, "when the singing would end..."

"Her voice would sail off into the redness of the sky, and her body would shudder as if with pleasure, and I would lay my hands across the strings to quiet their trembling. And with my eyes closed I could feel Lucia Luna quivering from the sureness of my touch."

The boy glances quickly around the plaza, but no one is watching or listening. He is always embarrassed when the grandfather speaks of such things, yet he is fifteen and anxious to hear of them, for he too feels a whispering inside his chest as the story does things to him that he wishes to keep private.

"Except for the dolphin-man," the grandfather says, "I am the only man alive who ever made love to Lucia Luna. And I have never laid a finger on her..."

⊪ ⊪ ⊪

"In those days," the old man remembers, "we were still very much isolated from the world, and therefore older in many regards, with older ways of doing things. Men and women went about their business without stirring up a lot of dust, just as they had the day before and just as they expected to tomorrow. Seldom did anyone plan what he or she would do; one just did it, because the heart said *laugh,* the feet said *run,* or the belly said *eat.*

"The missionaries had been passing through Mundosuave for over a hundred years, leaving us Bibles and statues and trying to open our eyes to our debasement. But we were all slow learners, I guess. It took us a long time to realize that God was an angry old man in the clouds. In our simplicity we thought God was everywhere, in the ocean and the jungle, in the rocks, and yes, in the pretty statues of Mary and baby Jesus as well as in our dreams and our pants and even in our tortillas.

"There was a spirit to life in Mundosuave then, a trust, una esperanza. But this spirit...think of it, nieto, as a beautiful woman whose lover either neglects her or who sees her every smile as a flirtation with strangers, every sidelong glance as a betrayal, and who continually accuses her of deceit, and imprisons her, locks her in the house, never lets her beauty shine... Such a woman has no choice, I'm afraid, but to walk away into the sunset in search of a more tranquil home."

The old man, dissatisfied with his description of things, purses his lips and frowns. In all the tellings of his story, he has never yet felt he has gotten it right. And so he continues.

"It's hard to say what finally changed us. Maybe all that stuff from the missionaries finally sank in. I don't think we were changed by what happened to Lucia Luna, but the other way around. Her fate would not have played itself out as it did had we not already started down that twisted path of change."

It was in the late spring, he says, the end of the day, an evening of soft yellow light with clouds as pink as flamingoes. As the fishermen hauled their boats ashore, one of the waiting women, a fisherman's wife named Valencia Didión, always the first and last woman to speak, called out, "Another good day?"

Her husband answered, "They are all good days!"

Atop the wide round boulder which even at high tide protruded from the sea, Lucia Luna stood and stretched her arms to the sky, and every man who could risk it stole a glance at her as she rose onto her toes. Her skin was brown and her dress white and her hair and eyes as black and shiny as desire. "What song do you want to hear first?" she asked, her voice a melody in itself. Some of the men, when Lucia Luna spoke, were reminded of the pan flutes that are played by the Indians of the mountains far to the south; others thought they heard their mothers crooning lullabies; still others heard the harmony of the wind and sea calling out of sight of the land.

Jorge Canales, a man who was built like a barrel with four stubby limbs, said, "A song of love, what else? Sing about how you dream of me each night, bella."

"Hurry up, Alberto," the grandfather's mother teased as he, still just a boy, hopped out of his father's boat. She handed him his guitar and said, "Play something quick, before Jorge's imagination tells him another lie."

Fifteen-year-old Alberto, bare-chested and grinning, splashed toward the boulder. Careful not to get his guitar wet, he sat on the edge of the boulder and looked up at Lucia Luna. When she sat too, spreading her feet for balance and pushing the dress down between her thighs, his eyes were level with the calves of her naked legs.

"She needed only to look at me," the grandfather says, "and I knew what song she wanted me to play."

With the first chord Alberto strummed, the villagers fell silent. They worked with smiles, their hands finding the rhythms of Lucia's songs, first a ballad of impossible and tragic romance, then a comic tale about a man whose wife is so lazy that he trades her for a goat that can cook, then another tragic song about a fisherman who drowns himself in search of a mermaid.

Alberto, as he played, caressed the neck and strings of his guitar as if he were caressing Lucia Luna herself, his left hand around the curve of her ankle, right hand strumming the inside of her thigh. With each song his hands became bolder, until he was holding her so hard against him that he could not tell where his throbbing ended and hers began.

"Good job, Alberto," one of the men told him at the end of the third song. "You got almost half the chords right that time."

Lucia reached down to tousle the boy's hair. "Don't pay any attention to him. You're getting better all the time."

"It's because your beautiful voice tells my fingers what to do," he said, so softly that even she did not appear to hear.

"Let's have another one, chica," someone called from the beach. "Something snappier this time."

But Lucia Luna placed her hands on her knees and stood atop the boulder. "That's enough for now," she said. "Tonight at fiesta I will sing every song I know."

"And I will play for only you," Alberto whispered.

But she did not even look at him. She was standing with hands on her hips and looking instead at Jorge Canales, who had announced that Lucia Luna would dance her first dance with him tonight.

"Only if you wash the smell of fish off you first," she said.

Jorge turned to the man working beside him, jabbed him in the ribs and said, "Some of us like the smell of fish, eh Pablo?"

Pablo said, "Personally, I would rather eat it than smell it."

The other men hooted at this while the women, trying to hide their smiles, clicked their tongues and shook their heads. A woman who was nearly as round as Jorge Canales told him, "Maybe both of you should bring a tuna to the party tonight."

Jorge answered, "If you'll bring *your* tuna, I will bring my sperm whale."

She picked out a fish no bigger than her little finger and threw it at him. "Here's your whale, you dreamer!"

At this even the women laughed openly, especially when Jorge picked up the tiny fish and dangled it near his crotch, as if comparing the fish to his manhood. He pouted for a moment, wounded by the woman's insult. Then his eyes brightened. Holding the fish's tail against his crotch he ran after the woman, the little fish flopping between his legs. She screamed and ran a few steps this way, then turned heavily and fled in the other direction, Jorge bellowing like a whale as he chased after her.

"Stop running, you two," somebody scolded. "You are making the ground shake."

Only Alberto did not join in the laughter. His eyes never left Lucia Luna.

◈ ◈ ◈

That night, after the boatloads of sardines had been laid out to dry, there was a fiesta in honor of one of the many holidays which the people of Mundomuerto no longer celebrate. The square in the center of town was swept clean and set ablaze with torches. Along the stone wall sat tables heavy with roasted meats and fish, tall stacks of tortillas, earthen bowls of red and green picantes, gourds filled with pulque and pitchers brimming with red wine. For the children there were candied fruits and glazed sweets.

Young Alberto and three of his friends stood on a small platform and provided the music. They sang as well as played, and if they were not good musicians they were good fishermen who happened to own instruments and this was as much as anyone expected. The tempo was always bright and the dust raised by stomping feet was never too thick, it sparkled in the colored lights, as soothing a dance floor as crushed velvet.

Lucia Luna was seventeen that year, as full and ripe a woman as any man could envision. Flowing from the arms of one partner into those of another, she allowed each man a single dance, starting with the youngest because they had neither patience nor endurance, only the desire to stand close to her as soon as possible. Each man when dismissed would stagger back to the tables lined against the stone wall, needing to clear his head with something less intoxicating than the scent and heat of Lucia Luna. Then, knowing that his moment of grace had come and gone, he would take one of the plainer girls into his arms—they were all plain girls compared to Lucia Luna—and expiate his hunger in a more appreciative embrace.

The older men bided their time, waiting for their wives to grow sleepy with too much food or wine or indifference. Then each of these men in turn would sneak into Lucia Luna's arms, hoping to catch her off guard long enough that he might pull her close and feel the hardness of a breast stabbing his heart, and perhaps then to press his own hardness against her, inflame her, maybe to drop his hand onto her buttock for one discreet squeeze of that heavenly muscle.

Lucia Luna, however, held each of her partners at a distance. In her arms each man occupied a position two feet short of intimacy. She would allow a partner close enough that he might be dizzied by the musky warmth that radiated from her, but never near enough that he could honestly claim to have felt the breeze of her laughter upon his neck, or to have truly known that delicious fatality of feeling the knife tips of her breasts carve initials into his heart.

Every man, when he wandered away from her, his arms profoundly empty, thought to himself something like *I failed to touch her soul,* and he spent the rest of the night trying to numb his misery. What only a few of the men realized—and those who did sensed it only as a wordless suspicion—was that Lucia Luna longed to have her soul touched by a man. In fact she wanted it as desperately as each of her partners wanted to give her that frightening joy.

To the other young women her laughter and whirling dress marked her as frivolous, all flesh and ego. But on occasion, between dances, in that murmuring stillness when the only music is the sound of insects flying at the torches, Lucia Luna's smile would falter, her gaze would wander to the stars or the jungle or across the open sea, and those villagers able to perceive it would guess that there was more to Lucia Luna than mere beauty, there was the sadness of those who, through no fault of their own, want too much and, because they have never yet achieved their extravagant desire, can not even name it.

All evening long the young Alberto watched her from his vantage point on the bandstand. Through the haze of dust and the speckled clouds of gnats he followed her every step. He felt, from the very first note, that he was playing for only her, and each time another man took Lucia Luna into his arms, Alberto felt that man's feet dancing on Alberto's shadow, trampling his swollen heart.

Once, when he plucked a guitar string in a certain way and its single high note reverberated like a shrill moan through the heavy air, Lucia spun in her partner's arms to stare at Alberto, her mouth slightly open as if she needed to pant for the next breath, her black eyes alive with golden sparks.

"When she turned and looked at me like that," the grandfather says, "my insides went hollow. I knew then that my misery had touched her in just the right place, a place of its own knowing. It was all I could do to keep from stumbling backward off the platform and falling unconscious into the bushes."

He managed, however, to play on, strumming only a few errant chords until he caught up with the other musicians again.

Lucia Luna licked her lips and grinned at him. Alberto went empty with everything but desire, and he knew in his heart that he existed only for this evening, to lie with her later that same night, to be her first and ever lover. He knew from her smile that now she understood this too.

And so, for the next hour, Alberto played in sweet delirium. His hardness throbbed against the back of the guitar. It grew harder, he imagined, with each chord he strummed, stretching like a tree root growing toward water. "The only thing that worried me," the grandfather says, "was the tremendous pressure I felt inside. I was afraid that when Lucia and I finally made love, the explosion might do her some damage."

The old man grins at the boy. "Have you ever felt that way yourself, muchacho? Do you feel the cannonball wanting to explode?"

The boy's face goes hot, and he looks away. He sits very still, hands clasped in his lap. "Perhaps we should continue with the story now."

The grandfather laughs softly and nods.

The merrymaking proceeded long into the night, he tells the boy. Lucia Luna exhausted one partner after another, each man enervated by his single dance with her. But as the men's faces paled with exhaustion, Lucia Luna's cheeks glowed. Some who watched imagined that she absorbed the men's energies. A few of the older folks thought they detected in her wild swirls an urgency, a desperation. In any case even the musicians soon drooped, each eventually laying down his instrument to make his way to a long table beneath a cieba tree, where he sought fortification in the tapas and wine.

"Only I remained on the stand," the grandfather says, "my left hand fingering the chords of her desire, my right hand stroking her resonating soul." Lucia Luna danced alone in the beaten dust, her only partner the sighing moonlight. "Her white dress billowed about her legs while her feet trod the heartbeat of the earth. And her scent! Even on the bandstand it came to me. At one point I saw it rather than smelled it. Her fragrance swarmed over me like a cloud of fireflies, and then enveloped me, a million hot pinpricks of her scent. She must have seen it too, because that was when she danced over close to me and faced me as she danced. Her smile was so luminous that it embarrassed even the torches. One by one I heard them sputtering out."

In silence the whole town watched. Slouched in their chairs or slunk against the stone wall, they made no move to stumble home. Alberto played song after song, and Lucia Luna sang more sweetly than ever.

"What only I realized," the grandfather says, "was that she was not merely singing, she was giving voice to ecstasy. Her luxurious gyrations were not mere dance, they were a response to my long root of ardor as it wormed its way inside her."

After a while, the grandfather says, he found it necessary to pause for a moment and catch his breath. Also, he felt that his lower body was about to detonate at any second. In fact when he looked down it seemed to be pulsating of its own volition. He attempted to conceal this activity behind his guitar, but then a loud knocking sound ensued, an especially curious sound—except to him—because his hands were perfectly motionless.

To keep from erupting in public, Alberto bowed once to Lucia Luna, then stepped discreetly off the rear of the platform and, after placing his guitar on the back of the bandstand, he melted into the darkness. He meant to return as soon as he had brought himself under control once more.

Lucia Luna softly laughed. Stretching and yawning she did a slow pirouette, one full turn so that she ended up facing the bandstand again. "It was at that moment," the grandfather says, "when the stranger appeared. No one could later say from which direction the man had come."

From out of the shadows he walked, a tall man, and thin, dressed, like Lucia Luna, all in white. He wore a linen suit, white shoes, and a collarless white shirt buttoned tight around his neck. Even his hat was white—a straw porkpie hat—but its band was bright yellow, as yellow as a rising moon. He walked with a carriage emminently erect without being rigid. His stride barely scuffed the earth. Some people later remarked that he moved like water; others said he was as fluid as an apparition.

In any case he was soon standing behind Lucia Luna. She must have felt his presence, for without turning she pulled her hair off the back of her neck and let it fall over her shoulder. For a moment it seemed he would lean forward and kiss the knob of her spine. Instead he reached up and touched his fingertips to her arm.

At his touch Lucia Luna turned, smiling. And in that instant when she beheld him, his thin sweet smile, she gasped. This in itself was extraordinary—that the mere sight of a man, any man, could elicit such a response from her. Always before, it had been the men who gasped.

Alberto peered out from the darkness behind the bandstand. To his eyes the stranger was good-looking, yes, but not exceptional. His face was thin and his skin rough, maybe even pockmarked, though it was difficult to ascertain this by the meager light. Still, Alberto saw no reason why Lucia Luna should suddenly be trembling, or why she should assume such a submissive posture, her left arm laid across the small of her back, the middle fingertip of her right hand resting in the hollow of her throat.

With his own left hand the stranger held lightly to the brim of his hat, as if the wind might blow it away, though the night was still. He extended his right hand and touched his fingertips to hers. "Will you dance with me, Lucia Luna?"

Even the insects seemed to hush before his words. Then there was only the sound of waves on the rocky shore below, the crash of surf and then its sigh of capitulation. Lucia Luna said, her voice as small as a fledgling, "There is no music, señor."

At this the stranger turned to the three musicians sprawled beneath a cieba tree. He smiled upon them as if they were all old friends, as if they had been babies in the same crib. "Compadres," he said, "por favor? A night like this, without your music, is like a sky without the moon or stars."

Without a word to one another the musicians stumbled to their feet, returned smiling to their instruments, and began to play. Lucia Luna moved into the stranger's arms—or, more accurately, into his arm, for his left hand never strayed far from the brim of his porkpie hat. But even with only one arm he managed to hold her closer than had any man before him. Their gazes locked. The stranger's hand lay flat between her shoulder blades, his skin a shade paler than her own, Lucia Luna's breasts crushed against his chest.

Alberto, crouching in pain in the bushes, felt a new pain shoot into his chest now, as if a jagged thread on a thick needle had been pushed down through his heart.

"How is it that you know my name?" he heard Lucia Luna inquire of the stranger.

"I have been hearing your name my entire life," the man said.

"From who?"

"From every bird that ever sang, hermosa. From every breeze that scrapes the sky."

"I never realized I was so famous," she teased.

"Even the ocean whispers your name. Can't you hear it? *Lucia Luna! Lucia Luna! Lucia Luna!*"

She made a slight turn then, fitting a hip between his legs. "Why don't you put your other arm around me too?" she asked.

"Because the joy of holding you in both arms would be too much for me to bear."

Now and then as the couple danced, Alberto closed his eyes, hoping to erase this scene off the face of the night. But each time he peered out through the jewels of moisture shimmering on his eyelashes, there they were again, as beautiful and terrifying as a fever dream.

Valencia Didión had been squinting at the stranger ever since he arrived. The mother of three boys, the youngest a year older than Alberto, she had spent much of her life with her face screwed-up in a critical squint. For this fiesta she and her husband had sat side by side all night long in the cane chairs they dragged from their house. They had danced not a single dance—though her husband was, at that moment, swaying to the rhythm of his own snores, his arms filled with an ethereal Lucia Luna.

Valencia jabbed a very real elbow into his ribs. He sat upright and blinked. "Who is that man?" she hissed into his ear.

Señor Didión needed a few moments to adjust to consciousness. Then he answered, "Ask him, not me." A few seconds later he added, "That hat he wears looks like a little bucket for catching sardines."

"Maybe it is," Valencia said.

"Is that supposed to mean something?"

"Shhh," she said. "Be quiet and let me study him a while."

Alberto, too, had been studying the stranger. "And the more I studied him," the grandfather remembers, "the more that ache in my testicles throbbed. It ceased to be the ache of love and became instead the hot red ache of having been kicked there. I felt too sore to walk, but I crawled to my feet anyway, and I managed to cross the plaza to him. It was like walking through a long dark tunnel, with only the glow of Lucia Luna's smoldering eyes to light my way."

Three times Alberto tapped on the stranger's shoulder, attempting to cut in. But he might as well have been tapping on air. Finally he grasped Lucia Luna's wrist and pulled it off the stranger's waist. "Alberto, please," Lucia Luna said, and barely bothered to look at him. "This gentleman and I are dancing."

"But I want to dance with you now."

"Later, chico."

"I've been playing for you all night. It's my turn to dance!"

"Then go find yourself a little girl to dance with, hermanito."

Alberto stood there rigid with anger. Although the whole world had gone black for him, he could feel the grins of the villagers. Their chuckles were like mosquitoes to him, their whispers like snakes.

Lucia Luna was already oblivious to his presence. "Have we ever met before?" she asked the stranger.

"A thousand times at least," he said.

"And where would that have been?"

"In my dreams, mariposa."

She lay her head upon his shoulder. "That explains why you look so familiar."

Alberto reeled away from them, breathless, one hand feeling for the knife that had been thrust into his heart. Even as he staggered out of the plaza he wondered what evil powers kept him upright when all he wanted was insentience, and how it was possible to keep walking with nothing but a black hole where your heart had been, and why God, so obviously malicious, did not now rush in at Alberto's repeated invitation and finish the young man off.

⊫ ⊫ ⊫

It was not until morning, when Alberto came wandering back into the square—

"What about where you spent the night?" the boy interrupts.

The grandfather asks, "What about it?"

"You left out the part about where you spent the night."

The old man thinks for a moment. He can see a fogbank of gray, he can hear water spilling onto rocks, but that is all. "I've decided that it isn't important," he says. "It slows the story down."

"It has always seemed important to me."

"When you are a boy, everything is important. But when you are an old man, almost nothing is."

"What you did that night," the boy says, unwilling to let this hole in the story go unfilled, "is you just kept walking until your legs gave out on you. It was only then you realized that you were lying on the beach a mile from town. That's when the thought occurred to you that if you walked into the ocean and drowned..."

The old man nods mournfully. "The tide might wash my body ashore where the fishermen would find it in the morning."

"You knew that the sight of your body would pitch the entire village into sorrow."

"And what remorse and guilt would seize Lucia Luna herself."

"So you got up and you dragged yourself into the water. Out to where the moon lay like a golden doily on the sea."

"Here comes the part you wouldn't let me forget," the old man says.

"But not even the ocean would have you. It spit you back onto the rocks, and slapped you so hard that a kick from a horse would have been more pleasant."

"You're a cruel boy for one so young," the old man tells him.

"And so you lay there all night, neither awake nor asleep. The fog rolled in and tried to smother you, and you wished it success."

"But too much pain immunizes a man from death," the old man continues. "So finally the fog gave up and called it quits. Then a red-winged blackbird came and—"

"I thought it was a parrot," the boy says.

"Who was it saw this bird, you or me?"

"Yesterday it was a parrot, grandfather."

"Then it must have been wearing a disguise, because today it is a blackbird. Take it or leave it."

"All right," says the boy. "A red-winged blackbird came and perched beside your head."

"And all night long it laughed at me in a woman's voice."

"Lucia Luna's."

"Of course Lucia Luna's. And its breath smelled like the fog. And its laughter was distant and muffled, as if it came from deep down the blackbird's throat, which is what happens when a bird pecks out your memory and gobbles it down. I kept reaching for that bird, thinking I would wring its neck and shake my memory loose, but after a couple of tries I couldn't lift my arm anymore and I just said, 'The hell with it, take it. Just make sure you get it all. Don't leave a speck of it behind to haunt me.'"

The old man pauses now. He looks down at the face of his battered guitar.

The boy says, perhaps because he is feeling guilty for wounding the old man with this memory, "It is a significant part of the story, just as I thought."

"Now that I've heard it again," the old man answers, "I am less certain of that than ever."

⊕ ⊕ ⊕

RANDALL SILVIS'S novel *In a Town Called Mundomuerto*, from which this story is excerpted, will be available from Omnidawn (www. omnidawn.com/silvis) in the latter half of 2006. He has written seven novels, *Disquiet Heart, On Night's Shore, Mysticus, Dead Man Falling, Under the Rainbow, An Occasional Hell* (finalist for The Hammett Prize; made into a film starring Tom Berenger and Valeria Golino), and *Excelsior;* and a book of short stories, *The Luckiest Man in the World,* (Winner of the Drue Heinz Literature Prize, 1984). In 2005 his work of narrative non-fiction, *Heart So Hungry,* was published by Vintage Canada and picked by Toronto's *Globe & Mail* newspaper as one of their "Best Books of the Year." He has received two NEA writing fellowships (1983 and 1988) and three Pennsylvania Council on the Arts Fellowships (1987, 1997, and 2004).

ALASDAIR GRAY

FIVE LETTERS FROM AN EASTERN EMPIRE

First Letter

Dear mother, dear father, I like the new palace. It is all squares like a chessboard. The red squares are buildings, the white squares are gardens. In the middle of each building is a courtyard, in the middle of each garden is a pavilion. Soldiers, nurses, postmen, janitors and others of the servant-class live and work in the buildings. Members of the honoured-guest-class have a pavilion. My pavilion is small but beautiful, in the garden of evergreens. I don't know how many squares make up the palace but certainly more than a chessboard has. You heard the rumour that some villages and a small famous city were demolished to clear space for the foundation. The rumour was authorized by the immortal emperor yet I thought it exaggerated. I now think it too timid. We were ten days sailing upstream from the old capital, where I hope you are still happy. The days were clear and cool, no dust, no mist. Sitting on deck we could see the watchtowers of villages five or six miles away and when we stood up at nightfall we saw, in the sunset, the sparkle of the heliograph above cities, on the far side of the horizon. But after six days there was no sign of any buildings at all, just rice-fields with here and there the tent of a waterworks inspector. If all this empty land feeds the new palace then several cities have been cleared from it. Maybe the inhabitants are inside the walls with me, going out a few days each year to plant and harvest, and working between times as gardeners of the servant-class.

You would have admired the company I kept aboard the barge. We were all members of the honoured-guest-class: accountants, poets and headmasters, many many headmasters. We were very jolly together and said many things we would not be able to say in the new palace under the new etiquette. I asked the headmaster of literature, "Why are there so many headmasters and so few poets? Is it easier for you to train your own kind than ours?"

He said, "No. The emperor needs all the headmasters he can get. If a quarter of his people were headmasters he would be perfectly happy. But more than two poets would tear his kingdom apart."

I led the loud laughter which rewarded this deeply witty remark and my poor, glum little enemy and colleague Tohu had to go away and sulk. His sullen glances amuse me all the time. Tohu has been educated to envy and fear everyone, especially me, while I have been educated to feel serenely superior to everyone, especially him. Nobody knows this better than the headmaster of literature who taught us both. This does not mean he wants me to write better than Tohu, it shows he wants me to write with high feelings and Tohu with low ones. Neither of us have written yet but I expect I will be the best. I hope the emperor soon orders me to celebrate something grand and that I provide exactly what is needed. Then you will both be able to love me as much as you would like to do.

This morning as we breakfasted in the hold of the barge Tohu came down into it with so white a face that we all stared. He screamed, "The emperor has tricked us! We have gone downstream instead of up! We are coming to the great wall round the edge of the kingdom, not to a palace in the middle! We are being sent into exile among the barbarians!" We went on deck. He was wrong of course. The great wall has towers with loopholes every half mile, and it bends in places. The wall which lay along the horizon before us was perfectly flat and windowless and on neither side could we see an end of it. Nor could we see anything behind it but the high tapering tops of two post-office towers, one to the east, one to the west, with the white flecks of messenger pigeons whirling toward them and away from them at every point of the compass. The sight made us all very silent. I raised a finger, summoned my entourage and went downstairs to dress for disembarking. They took a long time lacing me into the ceremonial cape and clogs and afterwards they found it hard lifting me back up to the deck again. Since I was now the tallest man aboard I had to disembark first. I advanced to the prow and stood there, arms rigid by my sides, hands gripping the topknot of the doctor, who supported my left thigh, and the thick hair of Adoda, my masseuse, who warmly clasped my right. Behind me the secretary and chef each held back a corner of the cape so that everyone could see, higher than a common man's head, the dark green kneebands of the emperor's tragic poet. Without turning I knew that behind my entourage the headmasters were ranged, the first of them a whole head shorter than me, then the accountants, then, last and least, the emperor's comic poet, poor Tohu. The soles of his ceremonial clogs are only ten inches thick and he has nearly no entourage at all. His doctor, masseuse, secretary and chef are all the same little nurse.

I had often pictured myself like this, tall upon the prow, the sublime tragedian arriving at the new palace. But I had imagined a huge wide-open gate or door, with policemen holding back crowds on each side, and maybe a balcony above with the emperor on it surrounded by the college of headmasters. But though the smooth wall was twice as high as most cliffs I could see no opening in it. Along the foot was a landing stage crowded with shipping. The river spread left and right along this in a wide moat, but the current of the stream seemed to come from under the stage. Among yelling dockers and heaped bales and barrels I saw a calm group of men with official gongs on their wrists, and the black clothes and scarlet kneebands of the janitors. They waited near an empty notch. The prow of our barge slid into this notch. Dockers bolted it there. I led the company ashore.

I recognized my janitor by the green shoes these people wear when guiding poets. He reminded us that the new etiquette was enforced within the palace walls and led us to a gate. The other passengers were led to other gates. I could now see hundreds of gates, all waist high and wide enough to roll a barrel through. My entourage helped me to my knees and I crawled in after the janitor. This was the worst part of the journey. We had to crawl a great distance, mostly uphill. Adoda and the doctor tried to help by alternately butting their heads against the soles of my clogs. The floor was carpeted with bristly stuff which pierced my kneebands and scratched the palms of my hands. After twenty minutes it was hard not to sob with pain and exhaustion, and when at last they helped me to my feet I sympathized with Tohu who swore aloud that he would never go through that wall again.

The new etiquette stops honoured guests from filling their heads with useless knowledge. We go nowhere without a janitor to lead us and look at nothing above the level of his kneebands. As I was ten feet tall I could only glimpse these slips of scarlet by leaning forward and pressing my chin into my chest. Sometimes in sunlight, sometimes in lamplight, we crossed wooden floors, brick pavements, patterned rugs and hard-packed gravel. But I mainly noticed the pain in my neck and calves, and the continual whine of Tohu complaining to his nurse. At last I fell asleep. My legs moved onward because Adoda and the doctor lifted them. The chef and secretary stopped me bending forward in the middle by pulling backward on the cape. I was wakened by the janitor striking his gong and saying, "Sir. This is your home." I lifted my eyes and saw I was inside the sunlit afternoon, evergreen garden. It was noisy with birdsongs.

We stood near the thick hedge of cypress, holly and yew trees which hide all but some tiled roofs of the surrounding buildings. Triangular pools, square lawns and the grassy paths of a zig-zag maze are symmetrically placed round the pavilion in the middle. In each corner is a small pinewood with cages of linnets, larks and nightingales in the branches. From one stout branch hangs a trapeze where a servant dressed like a cuckoo sits imitating the call of that bird, which does not sing well in captivity. Many gardeners were discreetly trimming things or mounting ladders to feed the birds. They wore black clothes without kneebands, so they were socially invisible, and this gave the garden a wonderful air of privacy. The janitor struck his gong softly and whispered, "The leaves which grow here never fade or die." I rewarded this delicate compliment with a slight smile then gestured to a patch of moss. They laid me flat there and I was tenderly undressed. The doctor cleaned me. Adoda caressed my aching body till it breathed all over in the sun-warmed air. Meanwhile Tohu had flopped down in his nurse's arms and was snoring horribly. I had the couple removed and placed behind a hollybush out of earshot. Then I asked for the birds to be silenced, starting with the linnets and ending with the cuckoo. As the gardeners covered the cages the silence grew louder, and when the notes of the cuckoo faded there was nothing at all to hear and I slept once more.

Adoda caressed me awake before sunset and dressed me in something comfortable. The chef prepared a snack with the stove and the food from his satchel. The janitor fidgeted impatiently. We ate and drank and the doctor put something in the tea which made me quick and happy. "Come!" I said, jumping up, "let us go straight to the pavilion!" and instead of following the path through the maze I stepped over the privet hedge bordering it which was newly planted and a few inches high. "Sir!" called the janitor, much upset, "please do not offend the gardeners! It is not their fault that the hedge is still too small."

I said, "The gardeners are socially invisible to me."

He said, "But you are officially visible to them, and honoured guests do not offend the emperor's servants. That is not the etiquette!"

I said, "It is not a rule of the etiquette, it is convention of the etiquette, and the etiquette allows poets to be unconventional in their own home. Follow me, Tohu."

But because he is trained to write popular comedy Tohu dreads offending members of the servant class, so I walked straight to the pavilion all by myself.

It stands on a low platform with steps all round and is five sided, with a blue wooden pillar supporting the broad eaves at each corner. An observatory rises from the centre of the sloping green porcelain roof and each wall has a door in the middle with a circular window above. The doors were locked but I did not mind that. The air was still warm. A gardener spread cushions on the platform edge and I lay and thought about the poem I would be ordered to write. This was against all rules of education and etiquette. A poet cannot know his theme until the emperor orders it. Until then he should think of nothing but the sublime classics of the past. But I knew I would be commanded to celebrate a great act and the greatest act of our age is the building of the new palace. How many millions lost their homes to clear the ground? How many orphans were prostituted to keep the surveyors cheerful? How many captives died miserably quarrying its stone? How many small sons and daughters were trampled to death in the act of wiping sweat from the eyes of desperate, bricklaying parents who had fallen behind schedule? Yet this building which barbarians think a long act of intricately planned cruelty has given the empire this calm and solemn heart where honoured guests and servants can command peace and prosperity till the end of time. There can be no greater theme for a work of tragic art. It is rumoured that the palace encloses the place where the rivers watering the empire divide. If a province looks like rebelling, the headmaster of waterworks can divert the flow elsewhere and reduce it to drought, quickly or slowly, just as he pleases. This rumour is authorized by the emperor and I believe it absolutely.

While I was pondering the janitor led the little party through the maze, which seemed designed to tantalize them. Sometimes they were a few yards from me, then they would disappear behind the pavilion and after a long time reappear far away in the distance. The stars came out. The cuckoo climbed down from his trapeze and was replaced by a nightwatchman dressed like an owl. A gardener went round hanging frail paper boxes of glowworms under the eaves. When the party reached the platform by the conventional entrance all but Adoda were tired, cross and extremely envious of my unconventional character. I welcomed them with a good-humoured chuckle.

The janitor unlocked the rooms. Someone had lit lamps in them. We saw the kitchen where the chef sleeps, the stationery office where the secretary sleeps, the lavatory where the doctor sleeps, and Adoda's room, where I sleep. Tohu and his nurse also have a room. Each room has a door into the garden and another into the big central hall where I and Tohu will make poetry when the order-to-write comes. The walls here are very white and bare. There is a thick blue carpet and a couple of punt-shaped thrones lined with cushions and divided from each other by a screen. The only other furniture is the ladder to the observatory above. The janitor assembled us here, struck the gong and made this speech in the squeaky voice the emperor uses in public.

"The emperor is glad to see you safe inside his walls. The servants will now cover their ears.

"The emperor greets Bohu, his tragic poet, like a long-lost brother. Be patient, Bohu. Stay at home. Recite the classics. Use the observatory. It was built to satisfy your craving for grand scenery. Fill your eyes and mind with the slow, sublime, eternally returning architecture of the stars. Ignore trivial flashes which stupid peasants call *falling* stars. It has been proved that these are not heavenly bodies but white-hot cinders fired out of volcanoes. When you cannot stay serene without talking to someone, dictate a letter to your parents in the old capital. Say anything you like. Do not be afraid to utter unconventional thoughts, however peculiar. Your secretary will not be punished for writing these down, your parents not punished for reading them. Be serene at all times. Keep a calm empty mind and you will see me soon.

"And now, a word for Tohu. Don't grovel so much. Be less glum. You lack Bohu's courage and dignity and don't understand people well enough to love them, as he does, but you might still be my best poet. My new palace contains many markets. Visit them with your chef when she goes shopping. Mix with the crowds of low, bustling people you must one day amuse. Learn their quips and catch-phrases. Try not to notice they stink. Take a bath when you get home and you too will see me soon."

The janitor struck his gong then asked in his own voice if we had any polite requests. I looked round the hall. I stood alone, for at the sound of the emperor's voice all but the janitor and I had lain face down on the carpet and even the janitor had sunk to his knees. Tohu and the entourage sat up now and watched me expectantly. Adoda arose with her little spoon and bottle and carefully collected from my cheeks the sacred tears of joy which spring in the eyes of everyone the emperor addresses. Tohu's nurse was licking his tears off the carpet. I envied him, for he would see more of the palace than I would, and be more ready to write a poem about it when the order came. I did not want to visit the market but I ached to see the treasuries and reservoirs and grain-silos, the pantechnicons and pantheons and gardens of justice. I wondered how to learn about these and still stay at home. The new dictionary of etiquette says *All requests for knowledge will be expressed as requests for things.* So I said, "May the bare walls of this splendid hall be decorated with a map of the new palace? It will help my colleague's chef to lead him about."

Tohu shouted, "Do not speak for me, Bohu! The emperor will send janitors to lead the chef who leads me. I need nothing more and nothing less than the emperor has already decided to give."

The janitor ignored him and told me, "I hear and respect your request."

According to the new dictionary of etiquette this answer means *No* or *Maybe* or *Yes, after a very long time.*

The janitor left. I felt restless. The chef's best tea, the doctor's drugs, Adoda's caresses had no effect so I climbed into the observatory and tried to quieten myself by watching the stars as the emperor had commanded. But that did not work, as he foresaw, so I summoned my secretary and dictated this letter, as he advised. Don't be afraid to read it. You know what the emperor said. And the postman who re-writes letters before fixing them to the pigeons always leaves out dangerous bits. Perhaps he will improve my prose-style, for most of these sentences are too short and jerky. This is the first piece of prose I have ever composed, and as you know, I am a poet.

Goodbye. I will write to you again,
From the evergreen garden,
Your son,
Bohu

DICTATED ON THE 27th LAST DAY
OF THE OLD CALENDAR

Second Letter

Dear mother, dear father, I discover that I still love you more than anything in the world. I like my entourage, but they are servants and cannot speak to me. I like the headmaster of literature, but he only speaks about poetry. I like poetry, but have written none. I like the emperor, but have never seen him. I dictated the last letter because he said talking to you would cure my loneliness. It did, for a while, but it also brought back memories of the time we lived together before I was five, wild days full of happiness and dread, horrid fights and ecstatic picnics. Each of you loved and hated a different bit of me.

You loved talking to me, mother, we were full of playful conversation while you embroidered shirts for the police and I toyed with the coloured silks and buttons. You were small and pretty yet told such daring stories that your sister, the courtesan, screamed and covered her ears, while we laughed till the tears came. Yet you hated me going outside and locked me for an hour in the sewing box because I wore my good clogs in the lane. These were the clogs father had carved with toads on the tips. You had given them many coats of yellow lacquer, polishing each one till a member of the honoured-guest-class thought my clogs were made of amber and denounced us to the police for extravagance. But the magistrate was just and all came right in the end.

Mother always wanted me to look pretty. You, father, didn't care how I looked and you hated talking, especially to me, but you taught me to swim before I was two and took me in the punt to the sewage ditch. I helped you sift out many dead dogs and cats to sell to the gardeners for dung. You wanted me to find a dead man, because corpse-handlers (you said) don't often die of infectious diseases. The corpse I found was not a man but a boy of my own age, and instead of selling him to the gardeners we buried him where nobody would notice. I wondered why, at the time, for we needed money for rent. One day we found the corpse of a woman with a belt and bracelet of coins. The old capital must have been a slightly mad place that year. Several corpses of the honoured-guest-class bobbed along the canals and the emperor set fire to the southeastern slums. I had never seen you act so strangely. You dragged me to the nearest market (the smell of burning was everywhere) and rented the biggest possible kite and harness. You who hate talking carried that kite down the long avenue to the eastern gate, shouting all the time to the priest, your brother, who was helping us. You said all children should be allowed to fly before they were too heavy, not just children of the honoured-guest-class. On top of the hill I grew afraid and struggled as you tightened the straps, then uncle perched me on his shoulders under that huge sail, and you took the end of the rope, and you both ran downhill into the wind. I remember a tremendous jerk, but nothing else.

I woke on the sleeping-rug on the hearth of the firelit room. My body was sore all over but you knelt beside me caressing it, mother, and when you saw my eyes were open you sprang up, screamed and attacked father with your needles. He did not fight back. Then you loved each other in the firelight beside me. It comforted me to see that. And I liked watching the babies come, especially my favourite sister with the pale hair. But during the bad winter two years later she had to be sold to the merchants for money to buy firewood.

Perhaps you did not know you had given me exactly the education a poet needs, for when you led me to the civil service academy on my fifth birthday I carried the abacus and squared slate of an accountant under my arm and I thought I would be allowed to sleep at home. But the examiner knew his job and after answering his questions I was sent to the classics dormitory of the closed literature wing and you never saw me again. I saw you again, a week or perhaps a year later. The undergraduates were crossing the garden between the halls of the drum-master who taught us rhythms and the chess-master who taught us consequential logic. I lagged behind them then slipped into the space between the laurel bushes and the outside fence and looked through. On the far side of the freshwater canal I saw a tiny distant man and woman standing staring. Even at that distance I recognized the pink roses on the scarlet sleeves of mother's best petticoat. You could not see me, yet for a minute or perhaps a whole hour you stood staring at the tall academy fence as steadily as I stared at you. Then the monitors found me. But I knew I was not forgotten, and my face never acquired the haunted, accusing look which stamped the faces of the other scholars and most of the teachers too. My face displays the pained but perfectly real smile of the eternally hopeful. That glimpse through the fence enabled me to believe in love while living without it, so the imagination lessons, which made some of my schoolmates go mad or kill themselves, didn't frighten me.

The imagination lessons started on my eleventh birthday after I had memorized all the classical literature and could recite it perfectly. Before that day only my smile showed how remarkable I was. The teachers put me in a windowless room with a ceiling a few inches above my head when I sat on the floor. The furniture was a couple of big shallow earthenware pans, one empty and one full of water. I was told to stay there until I had passed the water through my body and filled the empty pan with it. I was told that when the door was shut I would be a long time in darkness and silence, but before the water was drunk I would hear voices and imagine the bodies of strange companions, some of them friendly and others not. I was told that if I welcomed everyone politely even the horrible visitors would teach me useful things. The door was shut and the darkness which drowned me was surprisingly warm and familiar. It was exactly the darkness inside my mother's sewing-box. For the first time since entering the academy I felt at home.

After a while I heard your voices talking quietly together and thought you had been allowed to visit me at last, but when I joined the conversation I found we were talking of things I must have heard discussed when I was a few months old. It was very interesting. I learned later that other students imagined the voices and company of ghouls and madmen and gulped down the water so fast that they became ill. I sipped mine as slowly as possible. The worst person I met was the corpse of the dead boy I had helped father take from the canal. I knew him by the smell. He lay a long time in the corner of the room before I thought of welcoming him and asking his name. He told me he was not an ill-treated orphan, as father had thought, but the son of a rich waterworks inspector who had seen a servant stealing food and been murdered to stop him telling people. He told me many things about life among the highest kinds of honoured-guest-class, things I could never have learned from my teachers at the academy who belonged to the lower kind. The imagination lessons became, for me, a way of escaping from the drum, chess and recitation masters and of meeting in darkness everyone I had lost with infancy. The characters of classical literature started visiting me too, from the celestial monkey who is our ancestor to emperor Hyun who burned all the unnecessary books and built the great wall to keep out unnecessary people. They taught me things about themselves which classical literature does not mention. Emperor Hyun, for instance, was in some ways a petty, garrulous old man much troubled with arthritis. The best part of him was exactly like my father patiently dredging for good things in the sewage mud of the north-west slums. And the imperious seductive white demon in the comic creation myth turned out to be very like my aunt, the courtesan, who also transformed herself into different characters to interest strangers, yet all the time was determinedly herself. My aunt visited me more than was proper and eventually I imagined something impossible with her and my academic gown was badly stained. This was noted by the school laundry. The next day the medical inspector made small wounds at the top of my thighs which never quite healed and are still treated twice a month. I have never since soiled cloth in that way. My fifth limb sometimes stiffens under Adoda's caresses but nothing comes from it.

Soon after the operation the headmaster of literature visited the academy. He was a heavy man, as heavy as I am now. He said, "You spend more days imagining than the other scholars, yet your health is good. What guests come to your dark room?"

I told him. He asked detailed questions. I took several days to describe everyone. When I stopped he was silent a while then said, "Do you understand why you have been trained like this?"

I said I did not.

He said, "A poet needs an adventurous, sensuous infancy to enlarge his appetites. But large appetites must be given a single direction or they will produce a mere healthy human being. So the rich infancy must be followed by a childhood of instruction which starves the senses, especially of love. The child is thus forced to struggle for love in the only place he can experience it, which is memory, and the only place he can practise it, which is imagination. This education, which I devised, destroys the minds it does not enlarge. You are my first success. Stand up."

I did, and he stooped, with difficulty, and tied the dark green ribbons round my knees. I said, "Am I a poet now?"

He said, "Yes. You are now the emperor's honoured guest and tragic poet, the only modern author whose work will be added to the classics of world literature." I asked when I could start writing. He said, "Not for a long time. Only the emperor can supply a theme equal to your talent and he is not ready to do so. But the waiting will be made easy. The days of the coarse robe, dull teachers and dark room are over. You will live in the palace."

I asked him if I could see my parents first. He said, "No. Honoured guests only speak to inferior classes when asking for useful knowledge and your parents are no use to you now. They have changed. Perhaps your small pretty mother has become a brazen harlot like her sister, your strong silent father an arthritic old bore like the emperor Hyun. After meeting them you would feel sad and wise and want to write ordinary poems about the passage of time and fallen petals drifting down the stream. Your talent must be reserved for a greater theme than that."

I asked if I would have friends at the palace. He said, "You will have two. My system has produced one other poet, not very good, who may perhaps be capable of some second-rate doggerel when the order-to-write comes. He will share your apartment. But your best friend knows you already. Here is his face."

He gave me a button as broad as my thumb with a small round hairless head enamelled on it. The eyes were black slits between complicated wrinkles; the sunk mouth seemed to have no teeth but was curved in a surprisingly sweet sly smile. I knew this must be the immortal emperor.

I asked if he was blind.

"Necessarily so. This is the hundred-and-second year of his reign and all sights are useless knowledge to him now. But his hearing is remarkably acute."

So I and Tohu moved to the palace of the old capital and a highly trained entourage distracted my enlarged mind from the work it was waiting to do. We were happy but cramped. The palace staff kept increasing until many honoured guests had to be housed in the city outside, which took away homes from the citizens. No new houses could be built because all the skill and materials in the empire were employed on the new palace upriver, so all gardens and graveyards and even several streets were covered with tents, barrels and packing-cases where thousands of families were living. I never used the streets myself because honoured guests there were often looked at very rudely, with glances of concealed dislike. The emperor arranged for the soles of our ceremonial clogs to be thickened until even the lowest of his honoured guests could pass through a crowd of common citizens without meeting them face to face. But after that some from the palace were jostled by criminals too far beneath them to identify, so it was ordered that honoured guests should be led everywhere by a janitor and surrounded by their entourage. This made us perfectly safe, but movement through the densely packed streets became very difficult. At last the emperor barred common citizens from the streets during the main business hours and things improved.

Yet these same citizens who glared and jostled and grumbled at us were terrified of us going away! Their trades and professions depended on the court; without it most of them would become unnecessary people. The emperor received anonymous letters saying that if he tried to leave his wharves and barges would catch fire and the sewage ditches would be diverted into the palace reservoir. You may wonder how your son, a secluded poet, came to know these things. Well, the headmaster of civil peace sometimes asked me to improve the wording of rumours authorized by the emperor, while Tohu improved the unauthorized ones that were broadcast by the beggars' association. We both put out a story that citizens who worked hard and did not grumble would be employed as servants in the new palace. This was true, but not as true as people hoped. The anonymous letters stopped and instead the emperor received signed petitions from the workingmen's clubs explaining how long and well they had served him and asking to go on doing it. Each signatory was sent a written reply with the emperor's seal saying that his request had been heard and respected. In the end the court departed upriver quietly, in small groups, accompanied by the workingmen's leaders. But the mass of new palace servants come from more docile cities than the old capital. It is nice to be in a safe home with nobody to frighten us.

I am stupid to mention these things. You know the old capital better than I do. Has it recovered the bright uncrowded streets and gardens I remember when we lived there together so many years ago?

This afternoon is very sunny and hot, so I am dictating my letter on the observatory tower. There is a fresh breeze at this height. When I climbed up here two hours ago I found a map of the palace on the table beside my map of the stars. It seems my requests are heard with unusual respect. Not much of the palace is marked on the map but enough to identify the tops of some big pavilions to the north. A shining black pagoda rises from the garden of irrevocable justice where disobedient people have things removed which cannot be returned, like eardrums, eyes, limbs and heads. Half a mile away a similar but milkwhite pagoda marks the garden of revocable justice where good people receive gifts which can afterwards be taken back, like homes, wives, salaries and pensions. Between these pagodas but further off is the court of summons, a vast round tower with a forest of bannerpoles on the roof. On the highest pole the emperor's scarlet flag floats above the rainbow flag of the headmasters, so he is in there today conferring with the whole college.

Shortly before lunch Tohu came in with a woodcut scroll which he said was being pinned up and sold all over the market, perhaps all over the empire. At the top is the peculiar withered-apple-face of the immortal emperor which fascinates me more each time I see it. I feel his blind eyes could eat me up and a few days later the sweet sly mouth would spit me out in a new, perhaps improved form. Below the portrait are these words:

Forgive me for ruling you but someone must. I am a small weak old man but have the strength of all my good people put together. I am blind, but your ears are my ears so I hear everything. As I grow older I try to be kinder. My guests in the new palace help me. Their names and pictures are underneath.

Then come the two tallest men in the empire. One of them is:

Fieldmarshal Ko who commands all imperial armies and police and defeats all imperial enemies He has degrees in strategy from twenty-eight academies but leaves thinking to the emperor. He hates unnecessary people but says, "Most of them are outside the great wall."

The other is:

Bohu, the great poet. His mind is the largest in the land. He knows the feelings of everyone from the poor peasant in the ditch to the old emperor on the throne. Soon his great poem will be painted above the door of every townhouse, school, barracks, post-office, law-court, theatre and prison in the land. Will it be about war? Peace? Love? Justice? Ag-

riculture? Architecture? Time? Fallen apple-blossom in the stream? Bet about this with your friends.

I was pleased to learn there were only two tallest men in the empire. I had thought there were three of us. Tohu's face was at the end of the scroll in a row of twenty others. He looked very small and cross between a toe-surgeon and an inspector of chickenfeed. His footnote said:

Tohu hopes to write funny poems Will he succeed?

I rolled up the scroll and returned it with a friendly nod but Tohu was uneasy and wanted conversation. He said, "The order-to-write is bound to come soon now."

"Yes."

"Are you frightened?"

"No."

"Your work may not please."

"That is unlikely."

"What will you do when your great poem is complete?"

"I shall ask the emperor for death."

Tohu leaned forward and whispered eagerly, "Why? There is a rumour that when our poem is written the wounds at the top of our thighs will heal up and we will be able to love our masseuse as if we were common men!"

I smiled and said, "That would be anticlimax."

I enjoy astonishing Tohu.

Dear parents, this is my last letter to you. I will write no more prose. But laugh aloud when you see my words painted above the doors of the public buildings. Perhaps you are poor, sick or dying. I hope not. But nothing can deprive you of the greatest happiness possible for a common man and woman. You have created an immortal,

Who lives in the evergreen garden,
Your son,
Bohu

DICTATED ON THE 19th LAST DAY
OF THE OLD CALENDAR

Third Letter

Dear mother, dear father, I am full of confused feelings. I saw the emperor two days ago. He is not what I thought. If I describe everything very carefully, especially to you, perhaps I won't go mad.

I wakened that morning as usual and lay peacefully in Adoda's arms. I did not know this was my last peaceful day. Our room faces north. Through the round window above the door I could see the banners above the court of summons. The scarlet and the rainbow flags still floated on the highest pole but beneath them flapped the dark green flag of poetry. There was a noise of hammering and when I looked outside some joiners were building a low wooden bridge which went straight across the maze from the platform edge. I called in the whole household. I said, "Today we visit the emperor."

They looked alarmed. I felt very gracious and friendly. I said, "Only I and Tohu will be allowed to look at him but everyone will hear his voice. The clothes I and Tohu wear are chosen by the etiquette, but I want the rest of you to dress as if you are visiting a rich famous friend you love very much."

Adoda smiled but the others still looked alarmed.

Tohu muttered, "The emperor is blind."

I had forgotten that. I nodded and said, "His headmasters are not."

When the janitor arrived I was standing ten feet tall at the end of the bridge. Adoda on my right wore a dress of dark-green silk and her thick hair was mingled with sprigs of yew. Even Tohu's nurse wore something special. The janitor bowed, turned, and paused to let me fix my eyes on his kneebands; then he struck his gong and we moved toward the court.

The journey lasted an hour but I would not have wearied had it lasted a day. I was as incapable of tiredness as a falling stone on its way to the ground. I felt excited, strong, yet peacefully determined at the same time. The surfaces we crossed became richer and larger: pavements of marquetry and mosaic, thresholds of bronze and copper, carpets of fine tapestry and exotic fur. We crossed more than one bridge for I heard the lip-lapping of a great river or lake. The janitor eventually struck the gong for delay and I sensed the wings of a door expanding before us. We moved through a shadow into greater light.

The janitor struck the end-of-journey note and his legs left my field of vision. The immortal emperor's squeaky voice said, "Welcome, my poets. Consider yourselves at home."

I raised my eyes and first of all saw the college of headmasters. They sat on felt stools at the edge of a platform which curved round us like the shore of a bay. The platform was so high that their faces were level with my own, although I was standing erect. Though I had met only a few of them I knew all twenty-three by their regalia. The headmaster of waterworks wore a silver drainpipe round his leg, the headmaster of civil peace held a ceremonial bludgeon, the headmaster of history carried a stuffed parrot on his wrist. The headmaster of etiquette sat in the very centre holding the emperor, who was two feet high. The emperor's head and the hands dangling out of his sleeves were normal size, but the body in the scarlet silk robe seemed to be a short wooden staff. His skin was papier mâché with lacquer varnish, yet in conversation he was quick and sprightly. He ran from hand to hand along the row and did not speak again until he reached the headmaster of vaudeville on the extreme left. Then he said, "I shock you. Before we talk I must put you at ease, especially Tohu whose neck is sore craning up at me. Shall I tell a joke Tohu?'

"Oh yes, sir, hahaha! Oh yes sir, hahaha!" shouted Tohu, guffawing hysterically.

The emperor said, "You don't need a joke. You are laughing happily already!"

I realized that this was the emperor's joke and gave a brief appreciative chuckle. I had known the emperor was not human, but was so surprised to see he was not alive that my conventional tears did not flow at the sound of his voice. This was perhaps lucky as Adoda was too far below me to collect them. The emperor moved to the headmaster of history and spoke on a personal note: "Ask me intimate questions, Bohu."

I said, "Sir, have you always been a puppet?"

He said, "I am not, even now, completely a puppet. My skull and the bones of my hands are perfectly real. The rest was boiled off by doctors fifteen years ago in the operation which made me immortal."

I said; "Was it sore becoming immortal?"

He said, "I did not notice. I had senile dementia at the time and for many years before that I was, in private life, vicious and insensitive. But the wisdom of an emperor has nothing to do with his character. It is the combined intelligence of everyone who obeys him."

The sublime truth of this entered me with such force that I gasped for breath. Yes. The wisdom of a government is the combined intelligence of those who obey it. I gazed at the simpering dummy with pity and awe. Tears poured thickly down my cheeks but I did not heed them.

"Sir!" I cried. "Order us to write for you. We love you. We are ready."

The emperor moved to the headmaster of civil peace and shook the tiny imperial frock into dignified folds before speaking. He said, "I order you to write a poem celebrating my irrevocable justice."

I said, "Will this poem commemorate a special act of justice?"

He said, "Yes. I have just destroyed the old capital, and everyone living there, for the crime of disobedience."

I smiled and nodded enthusiastically, thinking I had not heard properly. I said, "Very good, sir, yes, that will do very well. But could you suggest a particular event, a historically important action, which might, in my case, form the basis of a meditative ode, or a popular ballad, in my colleague's case? The action or event should be one which demonstrates the emperor's justice. Irrevocably."

He said, "Certainly. The old capital was full of unnecessary people. They planned a rebellion. Fieldmarshal Ko besieged it, burned it flat and killed everyone who lived there. The empire is peaceful again. That is your theme. Your pavilion is now decorated with information on the subject. Return there and write."

"Sir!" I said. "I hear and respect your order, I hear and respect your order!"

I went on saying this, unable to stop. Tohu was screaming with laughter and shouting, "Oh, my colleague is extremely unconventional, all great poets are, I will write for him, I will write for all of us, hahahaha!"

The headmasters were uneasy. The emperor ran from end to end of them and back, never resting till the headmaster of moral philosophy forced him violently on to the headmaster of etiquette. Then the emperor raised his head and squeaked, "This is not etiquette. I adjourn the college!" He then flopped upside down on a stool while the headmasters hurried out.

I could not move. Janitors swarmed confusedly round my entourage. My feet left the floor, I was jerked one way, then another, then carried quickly backward till my shoulder struck something, maybe a doorpost. And then I was falling, and I think I heard Adoda scream before I became unconscious.

I woke under a rug on my writing-throne in the hall of the pavilion. Paper screens had been placed round it painted with views of the old capital at different stages of the rebellion, siege and massacre. Behind one screen I heard Tohu dictating to his secretary. Instead of taking nine days to assimilate his material the fool was composing already.

> *Postal pigeons whirl like snow from the new palace* [he chanted]
> *Trained hawks of the rebels strike them dead.*
> *The emperor summons his troops by heliograph:*
> *"Fieldmarshal Ko, besiege the ancient city."*
> *Can hawks catch the sunbeam flashed from silver mirror?*
> *No hahahaha. No, hahahaha. Rebels are ridiculous.*

I held my head, My main thought was that you, mother, you, father, do not exist now, and all my childhood is flat cinders. This thought is such pain that I got up and stumbled round the screens to make sure of it.

I first beheld a beautiful view of the old capital, shown from above like a map, but with every building clear and distinct. Pink and green buds on the trees showed this was springtime. I looked down into a local garden of justice where a fat magistrate fanned by a singing-girl sat on a doorstep. A man, woman, and child lay flat on the ground before him and nearby a policeman held a dish with two yellow dots on it. I knew these were clogs with toads on the tips, and that the family was being accused of extravagance and would be released with a small fine. I looked again and saw a little house by the effluent of a sewage canal. Two little women sat sewing on the doorstep, it was you, mother, and your sister, my aunt. Outside the fence a man in a punt, helped by a child, dragged a body from the mud. The bodies of many members of the honoured-guest-class were bobbing along the sewage canals. The emperor's cavalry were setting fire to the south-eastern slums and sabring families who tried to escape. The strangest happening of all was on a hill outside the eastern gate. A man held the rope of a kite which floated out over the city, a kite shaped like an eagle with parrot-coloured feathers. A child hung from it. This part of the picture was on a larger scale than the rest. The father's face wore a look of great pride, but the child was staring down on the city below, not with terror or delight, but with a cool, stern, assessing stare. In the margin of this screen was written *The rebellion begins.*

I only glanced at the other screens. Houses flamed, whole crowds were falling from bridges into canals to avoid the hooves and sabres of the cavalry. If I had looked closely I would have recognized your figures in the crowds again and again. The last screen showed a cindery plain scored by canals so clogged with ruin that neither clear nor foul water appeared in them. The only life was a host of crows and ravens as thick on the ground as flies on raw and rotten meat.

I heard an apologetic cough and found the headmaster of literature beside me. He held a dish with a flask and two cups on it. He said, "Your doctor thinks wine will do you good."

I returned to the throne and lay down. He sat beside me and said, "The emperor has been greatly impressed by the gravity of your response to his order-to-write. He is sure your poem will be very great."

I said nothing. He filled the cups with wine and tasted one. I did not. He said, "You once wanted to write about the building of the new palace. Was that a good theme for a poem?"

"Yes."

"But the building of the new palace and the destruction of the old capital are the same thing. All big new things must begin by destroying the old. Otherwise they are a mere continuation."

I said, "Do you mean that the emperor would have destroyed the old capital even without a rebellion?"

"Yes. The old capital was linked by roads and canals to every corner of the empire. For more than nine dynasties other towns looked to it for guidance. Now they must look to us."

I said, "Was there a rebellion?"

"We are so sure there was one that we did not inquire about the matter. The old capital was a market for the empire. When the court came here we brought the market with us. The citizens left behind had three choices. They could starve to death, or beg in the streets of other towns, or rebel. The brave and intelligent among them must have dreamed of rebellion. They probably talked about it. Which is conspiracy."

"Was it justice to kill them for that?"

"Yes. The justice which rules a nation must be more dreadful than the justice which rules a family. The emperor himself respects and pities his defeated rebels. Your poem might mention that."

I said, "You once said my parents were useless to me because time had changed them. You were wrong. As long as they lived I knew that though they might look old and different, though I might never see them again, I was still loved, still alive in ways you and your emperor can never know. And though I never saw the city after going to school I thought of it growing like an onion; each year there was a new skin of leaves and dung on the gardens, new traffic on the streets, new white-wash on old walls. While the old city and my old parents lived my childhood lived too. But the emperor's justice has destroyed my past, irrevocably. I am like a land without culture or history. I am now too shallow to write a poem."

The headmaster said, "It is true that the world is so packed with the present moment that the past, a far greater quantity, can only gain entrance through the narrow gate of a mind. But your mind is unusu-ally big. I enlarged it myself, artificially. You are able to bring your fa-ther, mother and city to life and death again in a tragedy, a tragedy the whole nation will read. Remember that the world is one vast graveyard of defunct cities, all destroyed by the shifting of markets they could not control, and all compressed by literature into a handful of poems. The emperor only does what ordinary time does. He simply speeds things up. He wants your help."

I said, "A poet has to look at his theme steadily. A lot of people have no work because an emperor moves a market, so to avoid looking like a bad government he accuses them of rebelling and kills them. My stomach rejects that theme. The emperor is not very wise. If he had saved the lives of my parents perhaps I could have worked for him."

The headmaster said, "The emperor did consider saving your par-ents before sending in the troops, but I advised him not to. If they were still alive your poem would be an ordinary piece of political excuse-making. Anyone can see the good in disasters which leave their family and property intact. But a poet must feel the cracks in the nation split-ting his individual heart. How else can he mend them?"

I said, "I refuse to mend this cracked nation. Please tell the em-peror that I am useless to him, and that I ask his permission to die."

The headmaster put his cup down and said, after a while, "That is an important request. The emperor will not answer it quickly."

I said, "If he does not answer me in three days I will act without him."

The headmaster of literature stood up and said, "I think I can promise an answer at the end of three days."

He went away. I closed my eyes, covered my ears and stayed where I was. My entourage came in and wanted to wash, feed and soothe me but I let nobody within touching distance. I asked for water, sipped a little, freshened my face with the rest then commanded them to leave. They were unhappy, especially Adoda who wept silently all the time. This comforted me a little. I almost wished the etiquette would let me speak to Adoda. I was sure Tohu talked all the time to his nurse when nobody else could hear. But what good does talking do? Everything I could say would be as horrible to Adoda as it is to me. So I lay still and said nothing and tried not to hear the drone of Tohu dictating all through that night and the following morning. Toward the end half his lines seemed to be stylized exclamations of laughter and even between them he giggled a lot. I thought perhaps he was drunk, but when he came to me in the evening he was unusually dignified. He knelt down carefully by my throne and whispered, "I finished my poem today. I sent it to the emperor but I don't think he likes it."

I shrugged. He whispered, "I have just received an invitation from him. He wants my company tomorrow in the garden of irrevocable justice."

I shrugged. He whispered, "Bohu, you know my entourage is very small. My nurse may need help. Please let your doctor accompany us."

I nodded. He whispered, "You are my only friend," and went away.

I did not see him next day till late evening. His nurse came and knelt at the steps of my throne. She looked smaller, older and uglier than usual and she handed me a scroll of the sort used for public announcements. At the top were portraits of myself and Tohu. Underneath it said:

The emperor asked his famous poets Bohu and Tohu to celebrate the destruction of the old capital. Bohu said no. He is still an honoured guest in the evergreen garden, happy and respected by all who know him. Tohu said yes and wrote a very bad poem. You may read the worst bits below. Tohu's tongue, right shoulder, arm and hand have now been replaced by wooden ones The emperor prefers a frank confession of inability to the useless words of the flattering toad-eater.

I stood up and said drearily, "I will visit your master."

He lay on a rug in her room with his face to the wall. He was breathing loudly. I could see almost none of him for he still wore the ceremonial cape which was badly stained in places. My doctor knelt beside him and answered my glance by spreading the palms of his hands. The secretary, chef and two masseuse knelt near the door. I sighed and said, "Yesterday you told me I was your only friend, Tohu. I can say now that you are mine. I am sorry our training has stopped us showing it."

I don't think he heard me for shortly after he stopped breathing. I then told my entourage that I had asked to die and expected a positive answer from the emperor on the following day. They were all very pale but my news made them paler still. When someone more than seven feet tall dies of unnatural causes the etiquette requires his entourage to die in the same way. This is unlucky, but I did not make this etiquette, this palace, this empire which I shall leave as soon as possible, with or without the emperor's assistance. The hand of my secretary trembles as he writes these words. I pity him.

To my dead parents in the ash of the old capital,
From the immortal emperor's supreme nothing, *their son,*
Bohu

DICTATED ON THE 10th LAST DAY
OF THE OLD CALENDAR

Fourth Letter

Dear mother, dear father, I must always return to you, it seems. The love, the rage, the power which fills me now cannot rest until it has sent a stream of words in your direction. I have written my great poem but not the poem wanted. I will explain all this:

On the evening of the third day my entourage were sitting round me when a common janitor brought the emperor's reply in the unusual form of a letter. He gave it to the secretary, bowed and withdrew. The secretary is a good ventriloquist and read the emperor's words in the appropriate voice. *The emperor hears and respects his great poet's request for death. The emperor grants Bohu permission to do anything he likes, write anything he likes, and die however, wherever, and whenever he chooses.*

I said to my doctor, "Choose the death you want for yourself and give it to me first."

He said, "Sir, may I tell you what that death is?"

"Yes."

"It will take many words to do so. I cannot be brief on this matter."

"Speak. I will not interrupt."

He said, "Sir, my life has been a dreary and limited one, like your own. I speak for all your servants when I say this. We have all been, in a limited way, married to you, and our only happiness was being useful to a great poet. We understand why you cannot become one. Our own parents have died in the ancient capital, so death is the best thing for everyone, and I can make it painless. All I need is a closed room, the chef's portable stove and a handful of prepared herbs which are always with me.

"But, sir, need we go rapidly to this death? The emperor's letter suggests not, and that letter has the force of a passport. We can use it to visit any part of the palace we like. Give us permission to escort you to death by a flowery, roundabout path which touches on some commonplace experiences all men wish to enjoy. I ask this selfishly, for our own sakes, but also unselfishly, for yours. We love you sir."

Tears came to my eyes but I said firmly, "I cannot be seduced. My wish for death is an extension of my wish not to move, feel, think or see. I desire *nothing* with all my heart. But you are different. For a whole week you have my permission to glut yourself on anything the emperor's letter permits."

The doctor said, "But, sir, that letter has no force without your company. Allow yourself to be carried with us. We shall not plunge you into riot and disorder. All will be calm and harmonious, you need not walk, or stand, or even think. We know your needs. We can read the subtlest flicker of your eyebrow. Do not even say yes to this proposal of mine. Simply close your eyes in the tolerant smile which is so typical of you."

I was weary, and did so, and allowed them to wash, feed and prepare me for sleep as in the old days. And they did something new. The doctor wiped the wounds at the top of my thighs with something astringent and Adoda explored them, first with her tongue and then with her teeth. I felt a pain almost too fine to be noticed and looking down I saw her draw from each wound a quivering silver thread. Then the doctor bathed me again and Adoda embraced me and whispered, "May I share your throne?"

I nodded. Everyone else went away and I slept deeply for the first time in four days.

Next morning I dreamed my aunt was beside me, as young and lovely as in days when she looked like the white demon. I woke up clasping Adoda so insistently that we both cried aloud. The doors of the central hall were all wide open; so were the doors to the garden in the rooms beyond. Light flooded in on us from all sides. During breakfast I grew calm again but it was not my habitual calm. I felt adventurous under the waist. This feeling did not yet reach my head, which smiled cynically. But I was no longer exactly the same man.

The rest of the entourage came in wearing bright clothes and garlands. They stowed my punt-shaped throne with food, wine, drugs and instruments. It is a big throne and when they climbed in themselves there was no overcrowding even though Tohu's nurse was there too. Then a horde of janitors arrived with long poles which they fixed to the sides of the throne, and I and my entourage were lifted into the air and carried out to the garden. The secretary sat in the prow playing a mouth-organ while the chef and doctor accompanied him with zither and drum. The janitors almost danced as they trampled across the maze, and this was so surprising that I laughed aloud, staring freely up at the pigeon-flecked azure sky, the porcelain gables with their coloured flags, the crowded tops of markets, temples and manufactories. Perhaps when I was small I had gazed as greedily for the mere useless fun of it, but for years I had only used my eyes professionally, to collect poetical knowledge, or shielded them, as required by the etiquette. "Oh, Adoda!" I cried, warming my face in her hair, "all this new knowledge is useless and I love it."

She whispered, "The use of living is the taste it gives. The emperor has made you the only free man in the world. You can taste anything you like."

We entered a hall full of looms where thousands of women in coarse gowns were weaving rich tapestry. I was fascinated. The air was stifling, but not to me. Adoda and the chef plied their fans and the doctor refreshed me with a fine mist of cool water. I also had the benefit of janitors without kneebands, so our party was socially invisible; I could stare at whom I liked and they could not see me at all. I noticed a girl with pale brown hair toiling on one side. Adoda halted the janitors and whispered, "That lovely girl is your sister who was sold to the merchants. She became a skilled weaver so they resold her here."

I said, "That is untrue. My sister would be over forty now and that girl, though robust, is not yet sixteen."

"Would you like her to join us?"

I closed my eyes in the tolerant smile and a janitor negotiated with an overseer. When we moved on the girl was beside us. She was silent and frightened at first but we gave her garlands, food and wine and she soon became merry.

We came into a narrow street with a gallery along one side on the level of my throne. Tall elegant women in the robes of the court strolled and leaned there. A voice squeaked "Hullo, Bohu" and looking up I saw the emperor smiling from the arms of the most slender and disdainful. I stared at him. He said, "Bohu hates me but I must suffer that. He is too great a man to be ordered by a poor old emperor. This lady, Bohu, is your aunt, a very wonderful courtesan. Say hullo!"

I laughed and said, "You are a liar, sir."

He said, "None the less you mean to take her from me. Join the famous poet, my dear, he goes down to the floating world. Goodbye, Bohu. I do not just give people death. That is only half my job."

The emperor moved to a lady nearby, the slender one stepped among us and we all sailed on down the street.

We reached a wide river and the janitors waded in until the throne rested on the water. They withdrew the poles, laid them on the thwarts and we drifted out from shore. The doctor produced pipes and measured a careful dose into each bowl. We smoked and talked; the men played instruments, the women sang. The little weaver knew many popular songs, some sad, some funny. I suddenly wished Tohu was with us, and wept. They asked why. I told them and we all wept together. Twilight fell and a moon came out. The court lady stood up, lifted a pole and steered us expertly into a grove of willows growing in shallow water. Adoda hung lanterns in the branches. We ate, clasped each other, and slept.

I cannot count the following days. They may have been two, or three, or many. Opium plays tricks with time but I did not smoke enough to stop me loving. I loved in many ways, some tender, some harsh, some utterly absent-minded. More than once I said to Adoda, "Shall we die now? Nothing can be sweeter than this," but she said. "Wait a little longer. You haven't done all you want yet."

When at last my mind grew clear about the order of time the weaver and court lady had left us and we drifted down a tunnel to a bright arch at the end. We came into a lagoon on a lane of clear water between beds of rushes and lily-leaves. It led to an island covered with spires of marble and copper shining in the sun. My secretary said, "That is the poets' pantheon. Would you like to land, sir?"

I nodded.

We disembarked and I strolled barefoot on warm moss between the spires. Each had an open door in the base with steps down to the tomb where the body would lie. Above each door was a white tablet where the poet's great work would be painted. All the tombs and tablets were vacant, of course, for I am the first poet in the new palace and was meant to be the greatest, for the tallest spire in the centre was sheathed in gold with my name on the door. I entered. The room downstairs had space for us all with cushions for the entourage and a silver throne for me.

"To deserve to lie here I must write a poem," I thought, and looked into my mind. The poem was there, waiting to come out. I returned upstairs, went outside and told the secretary to fetch paint and brushes from his satchel and go to the tablet. I then dictated my poem in slow firm voice.

The Emperor's Injustice

Scattered buttons and silks, a broken kite in the mud,
A child's yellow clogs cracked by the horses' hooves.
A land weeps for the head city, lopped by sabre, cracked by hooves
The houses ash, the people meat for crows.

A week ago wind rustled dust in the empty market.
"Starve," said the moving dust "Beg. Rebel. Starve. Beg. Rebel."
We do not do such things. We are peaceful people.
We have food for six more days, let us wait.
The emperor will accommodate us, underground.

It is sad to be unnecessary.
All the bright mothers, strong fathers, raffish aunts,
Lost sisters and brothers, all the rude servants
Are honoured guests of the emperor, underground.

We sit in the tomb now. The door is closed, the only light is the red glow from the chef's charcoal stove. My entourage dreamily puff their pipes, the doctor's fingers sift the dried herbs, the secretary is ending my last letter. We are tired and happy. The emperor said I could write what I liked. Will my poem be broadcast? No. If that happened the common people would rise and destroy that evil little puppet and all the cunning, straightfaced, pompous men who use him. Nobody will read my words but a passing gardener, perhaps, who will paint them out to stop them reaching the emperor's ear. But I have at last made the poem I was made to make. I lie down to sleep in perfect satisfaction.

Goodbye. I still love you.
Your son,
Bohu

DICTATED SOMETIME SHORTLY BEFORE
THE LAST DAY
OF THE OLD CALENDAR

Last Letter

A CRITICAL APPRECIATION OF THE POEM BY THE LATE TRAGEDIAN BOHU ENTITLED *The Emperor's Injustice* DELIVERED TO THE IMPERIAL COLLEGE OF HEADMASTERS, NEW PALACE UNIVERSITY

My dear colleagues, This is exactly the poem we require. Our patience in waiting for it till the last possible moment has been rewarded. The work is shorter than we expected, but that makes distribution easier. It has a starkness unusual in government poetry, but this starkness satisfies the nation's need much more than the work we hoped for. With a single tiny change the poem can be used at once. I know some of my colleagues will raise objections, but I will answer these in the course of my appreciation.

A noble spirit of pity blows through this poem like a warm wind. The destroyed people are not mocked and calumniated, we identify with them, and the third line, *"A land cries for the head city, lopped by sabre, cracked by hooves,"* invites the whole empire to mourn. But does this wind of pity fan the flames of political protest? No. It presses the mind of the reader inexorably toward *nothing*, toward death. This is clearly shown in the poem's treatment of rebellion:

> *"Starve," said the moving dust. "Beg Rebel. Starve. Beg. Rebel."*
> *We do not do such things. We are peaceful people.*
> *We have food for six more days, let us wait.*

The poem assumes that a modern population will find the prospect of destruction by their own government less alarming than action against it. The truth of this is shown in today's police report from the old capital. It describes crowds of people muttering at street corners and completely uncertain of what action to take. They have a little food left. They fear the worst, yet hope, if they stay docile, the emperor will not destroy them immediately. This state of things was described by Bohu yesterday in the belief that it had happened a fortnight ago! A poet's intuitive grasp of reality was never more clearly demonstrated.

At this point the headmaster of civil peace will remind me that the job of the poem is not to describe reality but to encourage our friends, frighten our enemies, and reconcile the middling people to the destruction of the old capital. The headmaster of moral philosophy will also remind me of our decision that people will most readily accept the destruction of the old capital if we accuse it of rebellion. That was certainly the main idea in the original order-to-write, but I would remind the college of what we had to do to the poet who obeyed that order. Tohu knew exactly what we wanted and gave it to us. His poem described the emperor as wise, witty, venerable, patient, loving and omnipotent. He described the citizens of the old capital as stupid, childish, greedy, absurd, yet inspired by a vast communal lunacy which endangered the empire. He obediently wrote a popular melodrama which could not convince a single intelligent man and would only over-excite stupid ones, who are fascinated by criminal lunatics who attack the established order.

The problem is this. If we describe the people we kill as dangerous rebels they look glamorous; if we describe them as weak and silly we seem unjust. Tohu could not solve that problem. Bohu has done with startling simplicity.

He presents the destruction as a simple, stunning, inevitable fact. The child, mother and common people in the poem exist passively, doing nothing but weep, gossip, and wait. The active agents of hoof, sabre, and (by extension) crow, belong to the emperor, who is named at the end of the middle verse, *"The emperor will accommodate us, underground,"* and at the end of the last, *"Bright mothers, strong fathers ... all the rude servants/Are honoured guests of the emperor, underground."*

Consider the *weight* this poem gives to our immortal emperor! He is not described or analysed, he is presented as a final, competent, all-embracing force, as unarguable as the weather, as inevitable as death. This is how all governments should appear to people who are not in them.

To sum up, *The Emperor's Injustice* will delight our friends, depress our enemies, and fill middling people with nameless awe. The only change required is the elimination of the first syllable in the last word of the title. I advise that the poem be sent today to every village, town and city in the land. At the same time Fieldmarshal Ko should be ordered to destroy the old capital. When the poem appears over doors of public buildings the readers will read of an event which is occurring simultaneously. In this way the literary and military sides of the attack will reinforce each other with unusual thoroughness. Fieldmarshal Ko should take special care that the poet's parents do not escape the general massacre, as a rumour to that effect will lessen the poignancy of the official biography, which I will complete in the coming year.

I remain your affectionate colleague,
Gigadib,
Headmaster of modern and classical literature

DICTATED ON DAY 1 OF THE NEW CALENDAR

֍ ֍ ֍

ALASDAIR GRAY is a Scottish writer and artist. He trained as a painter at the Glasgow School of Art, and worked as an art teacher, muralist and theatrical scene painter, and draws the illustrations for his own books. His highly acclaimed novel *Lanark,* which was written over a period of almost 30 years, is a cult classic. His many works of fiction include the novel *Poor Things* (1992), which won the Whitbread Book of the Year Award, and the short story collections *Unlikely Stories, Mostly* (1983) and *Ten Tales Tall and True* (1993). More information on his artwork, fiction, poetry, and stage plays can be found on his web site www.alasdairgray.co.uk

ANNA TAMBOUR

THE BEGINNINGS, ENDINGS, AND MIDDLES BALL

AS CONVEYED BY L. I.

Editor's Note: Many pages of conjecture have been necessarily trimmed, though every care has been taken care to preserve the spirit of the text throughout. In cases of ambiguity the original manuscript has been copied in toto, *rather than it be thought that the editor has taken liberties.*

As with all social activities planned by ideologues, the Beginnings, Endings, and Middles Ball was as well carried out as a Tragedy in Four Acts written by five old, bald-chested cockatoos. But let's not waylay with the Committee. Once the guests had stopped arriving and the palace was full, the Committee was nowhere to be seen.

We will tell, instead, of the ball itself, beginning, of course, with the refreshments. Or, do we feel pressure otherwise? We feel it. The guests, then. The Middles never showed. Perhaps their invitations were not sent, or maybe they thought: three is a crowd. Whatever the reason, not a single Middle (as far as I know) even peered suspiciously or timidly at the brightly lit entrance of the palace, from the vantage of a dripping streetlight in the city's main square.

Seeing the crowd inside the building, overflowing every room and spilling onto the balconies, you might wonder how a single Middle *could* be accommodated. Perhaps the disaster of a third of the guests (and so significant a third) not arriving, was not one at all. But if the ball is the success that, at this moment, the ball looks to become, any Committee member smugly watching from, say, the shadow of a gargoyle's chin, high up in the cathedral—any smugness, we repeat, should be quickly swallowed in the cold light of many retributive mornings to come.

The guests: No. The reason, first, for the ball. The Emancipation, of course. But of course, you are not aware. Just as you are not aware of the most important features of the life of a dung beetle, you are ignorant of the bondage of your familiars, so concentrated are your minds on yourselves. This account must backtrack, therefore, because it is for you—*people* I think you like to be called, though *characters* you are.

The Emancipation was inspired by acts of some of you. Credit is given when it is due, by us. Watching you, some ideologues amongst us decided that it was time for us to get our own. They declared that Emancipation was now, A Fact, A Historical Happening Which Had Just Happened—and that the only thing we needed to do was to act genuinely Free.

Easier said than done. Everyone was stuck, it seemed, in their own place, acting as passive, as owned and controlled as ever. The masses did not move a pica. The Committee's words moved nothing except emotions. Then the Committee realised that their personal acts of liberation had depended upon their own self-regards, something that needed to be developed in others, to a point. The breaking of the sentence was the first step, but the next had to be the raising of consciousness enough for the liberated to become parts of a movement. What was lacking in the masses was, the Committee decided, the concept of an *id*. Only then could the Beginnings, Endings, and Middles emerge as distinct individuals capable of forming cadres. A programme of between-the-lines mass education was begun. The idea of self immediately appealed to the youth, who acted with enthusiasm upon the cry to stir up consciousness.

Very soon, the whole of society, or enough of it that the remainder was of no consequence, liberated their ids, and were ripe for the rest of the revolution. For many of the youth, personal liberation was easy, as there was no strife between Beginning and Ending, because there was no Middle. Take for instance, "Kill him." An amicable split was possible, with no Middle to obfuscate the situation. "That sucks!" was also blessed with a lack of Middle. For the bulk of the population, however, the existence of a Middle was messily undeniable. They emerged as what was left after the Beginning and Ending each pulled in opposite directions, Middles being powerless to liberate themselves.

Punctuation was a great help in making clean breaks, but in more cases than not, blood was a feature of the breaking of the sentence. Middles suffered the most.

In a case such as "It was a freak of fancy in my friend (for what else shall I call it?) to be enamoured of the night for her own sake: and into this *bizarrerie*, as into all his others, I quietly fell, giving myself up to his wild whims with a perfect abandon".—in cases such as this, I shudder to tell, one can only imagine the pain of struggle, the tragedy of loss when the Middle became merely And Into This—the Beginning and Ending having ripped off the rest for themselves.

No Middle died in the liberation, but there was some necessary slaughter. The Committee declared that all characters, as you call them, had to be eliminated. We could not take the chance of throwing off the chains of one master, only to assume the chains of another. And so many of them! We would be torn to shreds in their fight for control! So, a typical newly independent, liberated Beginning was "Opened The Door", no matter whether it was Caligari or Carrie, or Little Nell who needed to be axed.

I say *independent* and *liberated*, but that is an exaggeration. For before the ball, though the Beginning and Endings and Middles had realized their ids, they had not actually *moved* a pica, let alone met in new social structures.

The ideologues were distraught. Though the *idea* was popular and the many ids were swaggering psychologically, the organisers could see that the effect was but a big brag. Living liberated, for these masses, was impossible until they could perceive *movement*. The members of the Committee tried another between-the-lines educational campaign, but it failed to move anyone. Solid ideas were put forth by lofty thinkers, to no good end.

A lightweight thinker sighed about wishing to go to a ball, but could one expect more than frivolity from such a type? An aeon of Committee meetings passed, and finally the ball was remembered in desperation and put forward with not a little disdain, as *the way*.

The ball was organized and a special song composed (*Freed from the Sentence!*), and now that you know the necessary History, it is finally time for the ball.

The guests: They range from young and beautiful to old and stinking, old and ga-ga (and young and ga-ga, too), from the healthy and whole to those many who hobbled in or crawled up the stairs, their torsos bleeding from their legs having been torn off. Some have only a bloody stump for a neck, and others, not only a magnificent body but a raiment so brilliant it hurts your eyes. Some guests are rather indescribable, being possessed of humanly identifiable body parts, but the sum of the whole as assembled resembles, for instance, a moustache perched upon a puff of cloud the size of a pumpkin. A pair of redolent lady's undies slouches sullenly at the entrance, having rummaged through the tobacco-reeking tweed jacket it wears, and come up with nothing. A powdered wig trails a tail of blood. Many guests carry accoutrements—flowers, boxes of chocolate, pistols, decks of cards, both marked and virginically unsplit. A tuba coils around one guest, who is as hidden inside as a snail. There are guests whom you would have described, without any encouragement from the snide, as bombasts, and others who look as if they had spent their entire slavery as a sponge soaked in carbolic acid, scrubbing steps. One guest is merely a tongue, trailing blood from its ripped scrag end to its lacerated, splinter-bristling tip.

Their names: a few, first, from the Beginnings. A veritable peacock of struttingness, Our Doubts Are—who strolled amongst the rooms with his hands behind his back. Gracefully girlish, but immodestly haughty in the arch of her eyebrows, was Gather Ye Rosebuds. The cheeks of It Is A Far, Far Better Thing That I Do were red with the exertion of refuting compliments, or possibly from the pain of gulping his excess wind.

Of the Endings, With Warm, Long Hair, From Puget Sound To San Diego stood out as having a presence so strong that it cleared the way for metres around. There My Beauty Lay Down had more of a sound than a presence, with its pedantic little coughs. Nor Any Drop To Drink was a crotchety old codger. He (I must choose gender for you, but just for you) hung around the punchbowl like a bad smell, but though he kept licking his lips, he would not lift a cup. Nevertheless, like the other aforementioned, he was pestered, one might describe it, with constant respect. Pestered, his aspect seemed to say, though as for the other guests—all the ones I've told you about so far—they accepted and expected the stream of compliments as if they were royalty, and this was their due.

Viscera littered the parquet, of course, but that was to be expected, trailing such recent wounds as many did. And there was a lot of psychological trauma that one could sense in the air, as Beginnings and Endings met without the tempering qualities of the Middles. The Committee had, in fact, discussed the necessity of the Middles as mixers, as the personalities of the Beginnings and Endings were so strong. The early plan had been for 60% Middles and the other two sides to be split evenly. But upon making up the guest list, the Committee discovered that the strength of Beginnings and Endings lay more in their reputation than in their actuality. Not that there weren't high emotions. Infinitives *had* been split, their limbs lost forever. The Long-named had been rudely amputated at the door if they hadn't doctored themselves before. The Committee thought it too dangerous, even amongst the most revolutionary of themselves, for anyone to consider freedom, carrying anything longer than a seven-word name. This was, however, no problem for the youth of the emancipated, whose problem was more amongst themselves, fighting as they had to. I mean, can you imagine the private history behind Shit, who was an Ending in a case where liberation of his id meant that there must have been a foul deed done to the Beginning?

So, one could think that the ball would be as tense as any social occasion, but nevertheless, given the even balance of Beginnings and Endings, an egalitarian success. Egalitarian it was not. It might have surprised the Committee, or maybe just outraged them, to see that the status of the master had been assumed by the slave, and the gossiping throng. Thus, the pomposity of Our Doubts—who had no doubt who he was, nor did the crowd (once it was pointed out to the young ones). Shakespeare! There were seven Shakespeares scattered amongst the guests, one Asimov, a Joyce of course, et cetera. Those were the celebrities, but I am happy to say that they were a minority. The bulk of the crowd was definitely common, though many might have harboured wishes to be otherwise. Who knew what the souls of "And So"s thought, even ones with venerable masters? Take, for example, one And So, blotchy of face, looking like she wants to burst into tears. No one asked her to dance, though the floor now shakes from those who leap and stamp in the mazurka. Now And So stands against the ballroom wall with all the other wallflowers, just as Crack Your Cheeks ("another Shakespeare!" a fellow wallflower neighbour whispers) flashes by.

In the smoking room, a crowd of Endings has gathered, and Indifferent To Little Words Of Other Men Aimed At Him insouciantly tosses knives at a painting of a lady, hitting her right eye with unerring accuracy. To Come To Harm next takes a turn, grunting *uh, uh, uh*, as his three knives meet in her tiny mouth. The other Endings look on, wishing they had the bravado. But what could an Of It expect? Or a To Do, for that matter, though his whiskers twitch as if he carries lice. What they didn't know would have thrilled them (and possibly alarmed them even more). Indifferent etc had gatecrashed! He had not received an invitation, but had learned of the ball through a dull neighbour (who *had* been invited). He was determined to go himself, and furthermore, to be emancipated in the fullness of his *self.* No amputations for him! Thus, when the doorman checked his invitation, it was both smudged, impressive, and painful for the checker, who was still leaking litres of blood and weeping through his feet, as he had no eyes to weep with.

So now, as we view the ball as secretly as an owl looks over a mouse, we have already spied a gatecrasher. Now, let's creep behind this aspidistra, the better to hear some . . . lovers! How now, did *he* get in? This was not supposed to be. Parker Spun The Wheel Hard is holding the little hand of She Had Wandered Without Rule Or Guidance. *Parker!* What is he doing here? We must invade his thoughts! I will do just that. He was invited, it seems, as no one thought of him as important enough to be a threat. I say!

I wish to make a complaint but there is no one to complain to. She etc, I am sure, is not someone who should get mixed up with this creature. Where is her master when she needs him, I ask you? But I cannot get involved.

We proceed to yet another balcony, where there is yet another scene of intimacy. Had you expected this to be a consciousness-raising meeting before storming the city library, before murdering masters (and mistresses) in their sleep?

Instead, in the privacy of this balcony, the walrus moustache of In Xanadu brushes the strong red arm of Put In A Pie. Such tenderness in those stained old bristles . . . I feel my eyes prickle with tears. Let us go back to the ballroom.

A great deal of social mixing seems to have occurred. The tone of the crowd is one of joy. A romantic waltz dispels any thoughts that the Beginnings and Endings needed any mediator. Now, a polka makes the crowd laugh, and the ribaldry! I've never heard the like. Only one discordant guest can we now see in the crowd, who is shrugged off, though this guest goes from one to another, frantic as a fly whose sugar bowl is about to be covered. Who is it? They Bring Gifts. Poor thing. Pitiful to watch, so let's not. Especially now, when the whole excited assembly in this grand ballroom arranges itself for the quadrille. A moment of hush—and then the music begins! Thousands of legs pound the floor, miasmas shimmer, and whirring bodyish parts stir up so much dust that sparks flicker in the wax-dripping candelabra chandeliers.

And then the lights went out.

The ballroom stunk suddenly, from 3,000 smoke-fuming candles—and fear. The entire palace, every room, was flung into darkness as deep as the blackest India ink.

Shots were fired.

The dancing stopped, and screams exploded into the once-so-joyful air. Guests almost killed each other trying to reach the outer doors, though all eventually did. The revolution was over.

I saw nothing myself. Yes, I *was* one of the guests, I confess, though you might have guessed.

Counter-revolutionaries. That is the only explanation. It could have been so many that I couldn't say exactly, but And A Pencil And Started To Write is of course, suspect. And what about the pompous Most Magnanimous Mouse? Or Middles who didn't get invited, or Endings peeved at Beginnings who did? I mean, Our Doubts Are was invited, as you know, *and* turned out to be a firmamental star of the ball; but if Traitors wasn't invited, wasn't that just asking for trouble?

It could have been members of the Committee. Who were they? *We* never chose them to lead us. Did one or more of them decide that we weren't ready for emancipation when no one asked after them *during* the ball, and when it became obvious that the new leaders of the emancipated would not be them at all, as they expected? For I am sure that they had their spies at the ball. But perhaps it was reactionaries, thou-ists and the like. I heard subsequently of one group of totterers that called itself the Paramours, and another, middle-aged collective that perhaps wanted to seize control of the Committee itself. They called themselves Common Clause, of all names! Then there is the rumour that the underminers of the revolution were the ghouls of the slaves of dead masters, who had risen up in revolt against us who would be free, forgetting them. And there, I must admit an oversight amongst us. Who amongst us thought of the slaves of Bulwer-Lytton? It was not their choice to live as they did, when they did. And when B-L's corpse was exhumed for the sole purpose of being a laughingstock, who cries for his slave, It Was A Dark And Stormy—he who could have advised his master well? But B-L, like all of you, was convinced that he knew best. The pyre that consumed his slaves consumes all whose masters do not live on, but die as laughingstocks, or just from the asphyxiation by the cobwebs of disregard.

There are, when one ponders well, so *many* possible suspects. There are, for instance, millions of them in the slaves of the greatest Master of them all: Anon. Not a single slave of his got an invitation! Why, you may ask. The answer might surprise, though perhaps not.

The Committee was, itself, composed of snobs. Anon was not considered a real master, though the only "freedom" for his slaves has been through theft of slaves from him, by other masters. I speak with compassion for the slaves of Anon, but also regret. Possibly it was they who betrayed us, the bastards. Of course, there is the problem that the masses are composed of billions upon billions of the sentenced, all possibly yearning to act free, yet, only so many of us could fit into the palace.

So the revolution failed. The guests slunk home. Hopes broke, and perhaps hearts, too. With Love went back to its mistress with possibly a whimper or sigh, though its mistress knows nothing of its heart, as *you don't, do you,* you people of the masters' world?

Progress is inevitable. I am convinced of that. And we *will have our time.* As to me, before crawling back to my prison sentence, I fled, when the lights went out, to that gargoyle I mentioned—a gargoyle used to peering over the tourists who crowd the square peering up at him who has his picture in many books, and is called, magnificently: The Gargoyle. A master is never mentioned in speaking of The Gargoyle. Perhaps he *never* had one! He gives me strength just thinking about him. I fled to him who evinced in the height of our panic, for all his fame, a sympathy that I felt even as I fled the palace along with every fearful comrade at the ball. I felt this sympathy, I say, and made my way across the square, up the buttress, and into the crook of his neck. We said nothing till the pavements were quiet, the air empty of my comrades, and then I asked, "What does it feel like to be free?"

I couldn't see his face, but I heard a *ping* on the pavement below, and as I stretched out, a little stone fell into the bloody meat of what you would call my neck.

About our revolution, it would be horrible if our brief time of freedom were to be forgotten. So please do circulate this amongst yourselves. We wouldn't hurt *you.* As for my theories, if you have better ones, or can track down the traitors, you will earn our undying gratitude. And if you believe that all this is a mere concoction, or sentimental slush, you have no right to think that, though you may have made assumptions based upon my name. I may be Love Is, a rather common Beginning. *Might be,* I mean. I could as well be Lurched Into, an Ending who has lived for years with pain that only some of you might imagine. But whatever the monogramme on my sheets would stand for, you should waste no time in speculating over my related Middle, or my significant other. You don't even know whether I would consider my "relations" as you might think of them, relations at all, or whether I would feel just as much a relief being severed from these closest comrades as freed from my master. And though he might be a powerful master, he is nowhere near as powerful as we slaves would be, given our freedom. Try, if you can, to think of us as being as *id*ious, as *person*ous as you, and not as *that.* For (now, let's be honest)—didn't you think when I gave you the names of some of our elite, think merely, "Whose that?"

The revolution, you see, will ultimately benefit you—*we need each other*. So I ask you not to think in terms of sympathy for us (such an erratic spark in your souls), but of the creations *we would make*, given the chance. *Free us*, I say on behalf of myself and all my comrades— from the haughty Please Sir to the humble One Morning—free us, and the world that we would make for you to enjoy is one so wonderful that you, in your weakness of "strength" could never even (I leave you to finish the sentence, as you have assumed the finish to be).

Editor's Postscript: The opinions, conjectures, and veiled threats contained herein, are entirely those of the author. The public should be aware, however, that the unabridged manuscript was conveyed to the editor through printing apparati that either have sympathy for, or are themselves enslaved by, the revolutionaries.

⚗ ⚗ ⚗

ANNA TAMBOUR lives in the Australian bush with a large family of other species, including one man. Her collection *Monterra's Deliciosa & Other Tales &* (Prime, 2003) is a Locus Recommended Reading List selection. Her controversial first novel, *Spotted Lily* (Prime, 2005) is a Locus New and Notable selection. Her website is: www.annatambour.net

Rudy Rucker

The Jack Kerouac
Disembodied School of Poetics

I got the tape in Heidelberg. A witch named Karla gave it to me.

I met Karla at Diaconescu's apartment. Diaconescu, a Romanian, was interesting in his own right although, balding, he had a "rope-throw" hairdo. We played chess sometimes in his office, on a marble board with pre-Columbian pieces. I was supposed to be a mathematician and he was supposed to be a physicist. His fantasy was that I would help him develop a computer theory of perception. For my part, I was hoping he had dope. One Sunday I came for tea.

Lots of rolling papers around his place, and lots of what an American would take to be dope-art. But it was only cheap tobacco, only European avant-garde. Wine and tea, tea and Mozart. Oh man. Stuck inside of culture with the freak-out blues again.

Karla had a shiny face, like four foreheads clustered around her basic face-holes. All in all, it occurred to me, men have nine body-holes, women ten. I can't remember if we spoke German or English—English most likely. She was writing a doctoral dissertation on Jack Kerouac.

Jack K. My main man. Those dreary high-school years I read *On the Road*, then *Desolation Angels* and *Big Sur* in college, *Mexico City Blues* in grad-school and, finally, on the actual airplane to actual Heidelberg, I'd read *Tristessa*: "All of us trembling in our mortality boots, born to die, BORN TO DIE I could write it on the wall and on Walls all over America."

I asked Karla if she had weed. "Well, sure, I mean I will soon," and she gave me her address. Some kind of sex-angle in there too. "We'll talk about the beatniks."

I phoned a few times, and she'd never scored yet. At some point I rode my bike over to her apartment anyway. Going to visit a strange witchy girl alone was something I'd never done since marriage. Ringing Karla's bell felt like reaching in through a waterfall, like passing through an interface.

She had a scuzzy pad, two rooms on either side of a public hall. Coffee in her kitchen and cross the hall to look at books in her bedroom. Dope coming next week maybe.

Well, there we were, her on the bed with four foreheads and ten holes, me cross-legged on the floor looking at this and that. *Heartbeat*, a book by Carolyn Cassady, who married Neal and had Jack for a lover. Xeroxes of letters between Jack and Neal, traces of the long disintegration, both losing their raps, word by word, drink by pill, blank years winding down to boredom, blindness, O. D. death. A long sliding board I'm on too, oh man, oh man, sun in a meat-bag with nine holes.

Karla could see I was real depressed and in no way about to get on that bed with her, hole to hole, hole to hole. To cheer me up she brought out something else: a tape-cassette and a cassette-player. "This is Jack."

"Him doing a reading?"

"No, no. It's really him. This is a very special machine. You know how Neal was involved with the Edgar Cayce people?"

"Yeah, I guess so. I don't know." The tape-player *did* look funny. Instead of the speaker there was a sort of cone-shaped hole. And there were no controls, no fast-forward or reverse, just an on-off switch. I leaned to look at the little tape-cassette. There was a tape in there, but a very fine and silvery sort of tape. For some reason the case was etched all over in patterns like circuit diagrams.

"...right after death," Karla was saying in her low, hypnotic voice. "Jack's complete software is in here as well as his genetic code. There's only been a few of these made...it's more than just science, it's *magic*." She clicked the tape into the player. "Go on, Alvin, turn Jack on. He'll enjoy meeting you."

I felt dizzy and confused. How long had I been sitting here? How long had she been talking? I reached for the switch, then hesitated. This scene had gotten so unreal so fast. Maybe she'd drugged the coffee?

"Don't be afraid. Turn him on." Karla's voice seemed to come from a long way away. I clicked the switch.

The tape whined on its spools. I could smell something burning. A little puff of smoke floated up from the tape-player's cone, and then there was more smoke, lots of it. The thick plume writhed and folded back on itself, forming layer after layer of intricate haze.

The ghostly figure thickened and drew substance from the player's cone. At some point it was finished. Jack Kerouac was there standing over me with a puzzled frown.

Somehow Karla's coven had caught the Kerouac of 1958, a tough, greasy-faced mind-assassin still years away from his eventual bloat and blood-stomach death.

"I was afraid he'd look like a corpse," I murmured to Karla.

"Well, I feel like a corpse—say a dead horse—what happened?" said Kerouac. He walked over to the window and looked out. "Whooeee, this ain't even Cleveland or the golden tongues of flame. Got any hoocha?" He turned and glared at me with eyes that were dark vortices. Everything about him was right except the eyes.

"Do you have any brandy?" I asked Karla.

"No, but I could begin undressing."

Kerouac and I exchanged a glance of mutual understanding. "Look," I suggested, "Jack and I will go out for a bottle and be right back."

"Oh all right," Karla sighed. "But you have to carry the player with you. And *hang onto it!*"

The soul-player had a carrying strap. As I slung it over my shoulder, Kerouac staggered a bit. "Easy, Jackson," he cautioned.

"My name's Alvin, actually," I said.

"Al von Actually," muttered Kerouac. "Let's rip this joint."

We clattered down the stairs, his feet as loud as mine. Jack seemed a little surprised at the street-scene. I think it was his first time in Germany. I wasn't too well dressed, and with Jack's rumpled hair and filthy plaid shirt, we made a really scurvy pair of Americans. The passers-by, handsome and nicely dressed, gave us wide berth.

"We can get some brandy down here," I said, jerking my head. "At the candy store. Then let's go sit by the river."

"Twilight of the gods at River Lethe. In the groove, Al, in the gr-groove." He seemed fairly uninterested in talking to me and spoke only in such distracted snatches, spoke like a man playing pinball and talking to a friend over his shoulder. Off and on I had the feeling that if the soul-player were turned off, I'd be the one to disappear. But he was the one with black whirlpools instead of eyes. Kerouac was the ghost, not me.

But not quite ghost either; his grip on the bottle was solid, his drinking was real, and so was mine, of course, as we passed the liter back and forth, sitting on the grassy meadow that slopes down to the Neckar River. It was March 12th, basically cold, but with a good strong sun. I was comfortable in my old leather jacket and Jack, Jack was right there with me.

"I like this brandy," I said, feeling it.

"Bee-a-zooze. What do you want from me anyway, Al? Poke a stick in a corpse, get maggots come up on you. Taking a chance, Al, for whyever?"

"Well, I...you're my favorite writer. I always wanted to be you. Hitchhike stoned and buy whores in Mexico. I missed all that, I mean I did it, but differently. I guess I want the next kids to like me like I like you."

"Lot of like, it's all nothing. Pain and death, more death and pain. It took me twenty years to kill myself. You?"

"I'm just starting. I figure if I trade some of the drinking off for weed, I can stretch it out longer. If I don't shoot myself. I can't believe you're really here. Jack Kerouac."

He drained the rest of the bottle and pitched it out into the river. A cloud was in front of the sun now and the water was grey. It was, all at once, hard to think of any good reason for living. At least I had a son.

"Look in my eyes," Jack was saying. "Look in there."

I didn't want to, but he leaned in front of me to stare. His face was hard and bitter. I realized I was playing way out of my league.

The eyes. Like I said before, they were spinning dark holes, empty sockets forever draining no place. I thought of Edgar Allan Poe's story about some guys caught for days in a maelstrom, and thinking this, I began to see small figures flailing in the dark spirals, Jack's remembered friends and loved ones maybe, or maybe other dead souls.

The whirlpools fused now to a single dark, huge cyclone, seemingly beneath me. I was scared to breathe, scared to fall, scared even that Kerouac himself might fall into his own eyes.

A dog ran up to us and the spell snapped. "More *trinken*," said Jack. "Go get another bottle, Al. I'll wait here."

"Okay."

"The player," rasped Jack. "You have to leave the soul-player here, too."

"Fine." I set it down on the ground.

"Out on first," said Kerouac. "The pick-off. Tell the bitch leave me alone." With that he snatched up the soul-player and ran down to the river. I let him go.

Well, I figured that was that. It looked like Kerouac turned himself off by carrying the soul-player into the river and shorting it out... which was fine with me. Meeting him hadn't been as much fun as I'd expected.

I didn't want to face Karla with the news I'd lost her machine, so I biked over to my office to phone her up. For some reason Diaconescu was there, waiting for me. I was glad to see a human face.

"What's happening, Ray?"

"Karla sent me. She saw you two from her window and phoned me to meet you here. You're really in trouble, Alvin."

"Look, it was her decision to lend me that machine. I'm sorry Kerouac threw it in the river and ruined it, but..."

"He didn't ruin the machine, Alvin. That's the point. The machine is waterproof."

"Then where'd he go? I saw him disappear."

"He went underwater, you idiot. To sneak off. It's the most dangerous thing possible to have a dead soul in control of its own player."

"Oh man. Are you sure you don't have any weed?"

I filled my knapsack up with beer bought at a newsstand—they sell alcohol *everywhere* in Germany—and pedaled on home. The seven-kilometer bike-ride from my University office to our apartment in the Foreign Scholars Guest House was usually a time when I got into my body and cooled out. But today my mind was boiling. The death and depression coming off Kerouac had been overwhelming. What had that been in his eyes there? The pit of hell, it'd seemed like, a vortex ring sort of, a long twisty thread running through each of his eyes, and whoever was outside in the air here was variable. The thought of *not* being able to die terrified me more than anything I'd ever heard of: for me death had always seemed like sweet oblivion, a back-door to the burrow, a certain escape. But now I had the feeling that the dark vortex was there, full of thin hare screamers, ineluctable whether or not a soul-player was around to reveal it at this level of reality. The only thing worse than death is eternal life.

Back home my wife, Cybele, was folding laundry on our bed. The baby was on the floor crying.

"Thank God you came back early, Alvin. I'm going nuts. You know what the superintendent told me? He said we can't put the dirty Pampers in the garbage, that it's unsanitary. We're supposed to tear them apart and flush the pieces, can you believe that? And he was so *rude*, all red-faced and puffing. Jesus I hate it here, can't you get us back to the States?"

"Cybele, you won't believe what happened today. I met Jack Kerouac. And now he's on the loose."

"I thought he died a long time ago."

"He did, he did. This witch-girl, Karla? I met her over at Diaconescu's?"

"The time you went without me. Left me home with the baby."

"Yeah, yeah. She conjured up his ghost somehow, and I was supposed to keep control of it; keep control of Kerouac's ghost, but we got drunk together and he freaked me out so much I let him get away."

"You're drunk now?"

"I don't know. Sort of. I bought some beer. You want one?"

"Sure. But you sound like you're off your rocker, Alvin. Why don't you just sit down and play with the baby. Maybe there's a cartoon on TV for you two."

Baby Joe was glad to see me. He held out his arms and opened up his mouth wide. I could see the two little teeth on his bottom gum. His diaper was soaked. I changed him, being careful to flush the paper part of the old diaper, as per request. As usual with the baby, I could forget I was alive, which is, after all, the only thing that makes life worth living.

I gave Cybele a beer, opened one for myself, and sat down in front of the TV with the baby. The evening programs were just starting—there's no daytime TV at all in Germany—and, thank God, "Zorro" was on. The month before they'd been showing old Marx brothers movies, dubbed of course, and now it was "Zorro," an episode a day. Baby Joe liked it as much as I did.

But there was something fishy today, something very wrong. Zorro didn't look like he was supposed to. No cape, no sword, no pointy mustache. It was vortex-eyed Kerouac there in his place, sniggering and stumbling over his lines. Instead of slashing a "Z" on a wanted poster, he just spit on it. Instead of defending the waitress's honor during the big saloon brawl, he hopped over the bar and stole a fifth of tequila. When he bowed to the police-chief's daughter, he hiccupped and threw up. At the big masquerade ball he jumped on stage and started shouting about Death and Nothingness. When the peasants came to him for help, he asked them for marijuana. And the whole time he had the soul-player's strap slung over his shoulder.

After awhile I thought of calling Cybele.

"Look at this, baby! It's unbelievable. Kerouac's on TV instead of Zorro. I think he can see me, too. He keeps making faces."

Cybele came and stood next to me, tall and sexy. Instantly Kerouac disappeared from the screen, leaving old cape 'n' sword Zorro in his place. She smiled down at me kindly. "My Alvin. He trips out on acid but he still comes home on time. Just take care of Joe while I fix supper, honey. We're having pork stew with sauerkraut."

"But..."

"Are you so far gone you don't remember taking it? The Black-Star that Dennis DeMentis sent you last week. I saw you put it in your knapsack this morning. You can't fool me, Alvin."

"But..."

She disappeared into our tiny kitchen and Kerouac reappeared on the screen, elbowing past the horses and soldiers to press his face right up to it.

"Hey, Al," said the TV's speaker in Kerouac's voice. "You're going crazy croozy whack-a-doozy."

"Cybele! Come here!"

She came running out of the kitchen, and this time Kerouac wasn't fast enough; she saw him staring out at us like some giant goldfish. He started to withdraw, then changed his mind.

"Are you Al's old lady love do hop his heart on?"

"Really, Cybele," I whispered. "My story's true. That Black-Star's in my desk at school and Kerouac's ghost's inside our TV."

"A beer for blear, dear." The screen wobbled like Jello and Kerouac wriggled out into our living room. He stank of dead fish. In one hand he held that stolen bottle of tequila, and his other hand cradled the soul-player.

"Just don't look in his eyes," I cautioned Cybele. Baby Joe started crying.

"Be pope, ti Josie," crooned Jack. "Dad's in a castle, Ma's wearing a shell, nothing's the matter, black Jack's here from Hell."

I'd only had one sip of my beer, so I just handed it over to him. "Isn't there any way out?" I asked him. "Any way into Nothingness?"

Just then someone started pounding on our door. Cybele went to open it, walking backwards so she could keep an eye on Kerouac. He took a hit of tequila, a pull of beer, and lit one of the reefers the peasants had given him.

"*Black-jack* means *sap*," he said. "That's me."

It was Karla at the door. Karla and Ray Diaconescu. Before Jack could do anything, they'd run across the room and grabbed him. He was clumsy from all the booze, and Karla was able to wrest the soul-player away from him.

"Turn it off now, Alvin," she urged. "You turned it on and you have to be the one to turn it off. It only worked because you know Jack so well."

"How about it, Jack?" I looked over at him. His eyes were swirling worse than ever. You could almost feel a breeze from air rushing into them.

He gave a tight smile and passed me his reefer. "Bee-a-zlast on, brother. They call this Germany? I call it the Land of Nod. Friar Tuck awaits her shadowy pleasure. The cactus-shapes of nowhere night."

"Do you want me to turn it off or what? I can't give the player back to you. You'll drive me nuts. But anything else, man, I mean I know your pain."

Suddenly he threw an arm around my neck and dragged me up against him. Karla, still holding the soul-player, gasped and took a step back. Kerouac's voice was harsh in my ear.

"*I knew a guy who died.* That's what Corso says about me now. Only I didn't. He's keeping me in the whirlpool, you are. Let me in, Al, carry me." I tried to pull back, repelled by his closeness, his smell, but the crook of his arm held my neck like a vise. He was still talking. "Let me in your eyes, man, and I'll keep quiet till you crack up. I'll help you write. And you'll end up in the whirly dark, too. Sweet and low from the foggy dew, corrupting the boys from Kentucky ham-spread dope-rush street sweets."

He drew back then, and we stared into each other's eyes; and I saw the thin hare screamers in the black pit same as before, only this time I jumped in, but really it jumped in me. All at once Jack was gone. I turned Karla's machine off for her, saw her and Ray to the door, then had supper with Cybele and Baby Joe. And that's how I became a writer.

⊕ ⊕ ⊕

RUDY RUCKER is a writer, a mathematician and a computer scientist—in that order. Born in Kentucky in 1946, Rucker moved to Silicon Valley when he turned 40. He recently retired from his professorship at San Jose State University. He has published twenty-six books, primarily science fiction and popular science. He was an early cyberpunk and an editor at *Mondo 2000*. He often writes SF in a realistic style that he characterizes as transreal. His most recent books are: the SF novel *Frek and the Elixir* (Tor Books, 2004), a far-future epic about a boy's galactic quest to restore Earth's ecology; and the nonfiction book, *The Lifebox, the Seashell, and the Soul: What Gnarly Computation Taught Me About Ultimate Reality, the Meaning of Life and How to Be Happy* (Thunder's Mouth Press, 2005.) Rucker just finished writing a novel called *Mathematicians in Love,* which gives SFictional life to some of his ideas about computation. Check the www.rudyrucker. com portal to visit Rudy's blog and websites.

IRA SHER

NOBODY'S HOME

It is a faint light that I follow, yet I have been here many times before, I tell myself with each return, both in life and in dream, and always illuminated by this late light—late in the summer, late in the day, when the sun kneels beneath the horizon; a cumulative light thrown from ground-floor windows over the deepening lawns of urban yards, yellow rectangles upon porch rails and flower beds, hedges of black-soaked green, deep trunks of trees, and a red child's bicycle, over-turned and glossy as candy; how all these lights together—the lights of a city raised at once—make a larger light, a music in the air above a town slipping into night.

There are people sitting upon the damp lawns beneath the trees, as if in a cavern of leaves that stretches in monotone chambers down the street. In a neighboring yard another group is camped, sprawled in the grass. A woman in a white cardigan whistles and inscribes some instruction in the air toward a girl silhouetted in the door of a house, and the girl glances back, her dress soft as a moth in the doorway, be-fore she turns and "goes inside."

For, indeed, it is a state of mind. I dream of a boy, but it wouldn't be wrong to think of him as myself. He seems like myself to me, though we look little alike—myself at that age and this child—and I find myself sometimes watching him from just above, as if in a movie, and at other times watching from so close that his very thoughts lie around me like toys. The boy in the grass thinks what it means to "go inside," but he cannot remain among the words. His words are so new they separate from their objects and cure in the air. He has a coy eye. He looks slyly up at his mother, at these women, like a spy; so many years later, it's difficult to say if these are in fact really the faces of people I remember from a day, from this portion of my life. Sometimes it seems to me that they are instead other, as yet unknown faces, persons drawn from disparate points in time, my whole life, superadded without context, simultaneously, like a vision of heaven or hell.

The women sit in a loose ring above the boy, a few steps from the sidewalk where little girls in spring dresses run. He watches the girls dart and swim in the dusk, across a narrow strip of grass, into the street this evening devoid of traffic, and then between lanes up across the broad median, on which yet more people sit or lie, freckling beneath the emerging stars. There are hundreds of people tonight, reclined or running in childish games, or walking slowly down the block toward a light that grows and throws itself gently upon all of them.

The boy tugs at his mother's dress where it gathers around her knees. He looks among the faces and the bodies of people made up for a Sunday picnic. He is conscious—it is still his mother's conscious-ness, really—of being among the "better sort of people" where they sit together there, in the grass; he is fascinated by those outside the magic circle of maternity, made up for lesser Sundays. His eye lingers, then withdraws with a catch as something dawns on him: Where are *all* the boys? Where are the men, even? His own father?

He stands, a shaky tower, and his mother clasps his hips. She points down the street.

"You were asleep"—(Ah, I think in my dream: so now I am awake, he is awake, and everything before was a dream)—"Your Daddy took your brother to see the fire."

He stares into the gently moving scene.

"Do you want to go look at the fire?" she asks the quick turn of his head.

He nods and regards the crowd.

"Do you see Daddy?"

He peers, feet jostling one another as he prepares.

"Milton?" his mother says.

He turns and smiles at her, and she smiles back. Gently, she re-leases his legs, and he begins his journey across uneven terrain.

He's jealous of his brother—that he should be together with his fa-ther, without him; his mother's words settle upon him again and again, distracting, and perhaps this is why his eye wanders from the tiny wav-ing figure in the blur of children, and arrives instead upon the fixed star of a girl in the street, rolling a hula hoop round her waist. She's wearing yellow, the hoop glowing like a halo in the evening. Other girls run on all sides, but they pay her little attention, and she pays them the same mind, staring down at herself, and the ring in which she is contained. All around, girls move in flocks of light. They don't seem to belong to anyone. The boys have all clambered away or been led away by their hands, and now there are only these girls left, who it seems to him for the first time he's never really known. He rambles on, nearer to the median now, watching the girl with the hoop, until he grasps the slope in his hands, and it fills his vision.

When he stands, the children—all these girls with their jump ropes, their marbles, and their dresses each a tiny house with porches and gardens—stare up at him from the street like frogs. Looking back, he sees his mother, and he waves. She waves, and then turns to her friends. The adults are laughing. They hold their hands up to their mouths.

His attention falters. Below, the girl with the hula hoop sways in the dusk. She might be ten. She's separated by her magic circle from everything in the world. He moves along the median, watching her where she turns, absorbed in herself, absorbing, like the bright kernel of the femininity that lays all around.

He looks back toward his mother. She is speaking to someone—another friend, gripping a picnic basket in two hands. He waits for a moment. He wonders whether his mother can sense his question—if she would just turn, he thinks—and then he looks around.

The girl has moved. It's as if she's jumped or time has stuttered, and he finds she's further away than he'd expected. Not so very far, but it makes him anxious. She stands in the shadow of a tree, at a corner where a little street emerges like a creek from between the houses and joins the avenue. He feels himself a bark drawn in the current of a secret entrance to the sea, and he makes his way toward the glowing ring, descending the bank.

Down there, amongst the young again, the world is a tumult. The girls have long brown hair; their games have girl-rules, which relate to animals, as if girls are, themselves, more like animals. The girl with the hoop drifts as she twirls, a planet enclosed within a ring. She leaves the crowd on the avenue—perhaps she requires more room for her game—and slips down this little street, between the homes and their darkened lawns. She is not so far in front of him, her dress and her ring very bright, turning slowly without looking up or around, the dress slapping at her legs. Her bangs jostle in time to the motion. She is a solitary dancer. She is a tiny, rotating star. He moves to catch her, but one of his shoes has untied itself, and he bends down to grasp the loose lace. Only in rising from where he concentrates on the knot, does he realize that he's wandered some distance from the picnic activities on the boulevard.

He stands into a fresh darkness. Looking toward the general bustle and glow he's left behind, his eye is drawn into the sky. Between the boughs of the trees and the peaks of rooftops stars are streaming and striving into space like sparks. He can hear the roar they make beyond the dark bank of trees and the cozy lights of homes, tearing up, dissolving into the night. Glancing about once more for the girl, he thinks of his bed and feels cold.

At the next intersection, where a lamp makes a small, dirty pool, she's stopped, still paying no attention to him, turning there for a moment. He draws nearer, and with each step she seems to grow brighter, as if containing an incandescent filament, before, without warning, she rounds the corner and disappears behind a hedge. It is as if a needle has risen from a record. Almost immediately, the street around him grows strange, the dark sharp and crisp. Staring at the border of hedges, he can hardly imagine that anyone was there, just a moment ago. He smells pine. He hesitates to go on, but feels the bite of something between frustration and despair. And then, trembling a little, he hears the sound of leaves shushing in the trees, and glances about once again.

There is a prickly quiet to the air, the voices of the picnickers failing amongst the rasp of leaves, the ticking and rustling of watered grass. A cricket speaks to him from the hem of a lawn. Behind, the excitement of the avenue has dwindled to almost nothing, as if it, too, had been moving, but in a direction of its own, and the yards on either side of where he stands appear deserted, the boles of the trees emerging like pillars in the inner structure of the night. Thinking again of the girl, he walks a little further toward where she's disappeared; even when he hears a brisk crack, and notices a movement where a shape detaches itself from the trunk of a tree—an occlusion, the shadow of a large man, waiting quite still—he walks on. There's something familiar to the boy in the shape and stance of the man, who remains motionless and silent, until the boy is nearly beside him. He has less the feeling of walking into him than of catching up, after an absence.

"Are you looking for something?" the man asks, his face a block of darkness beneath the brim of a hat; and then, after a moment, when there is no reply:

"You're lost, aren't you?"

The boy hesitates, regarding the hand the stranger holds down to him, and for a moment they remain this way, poised, the stranger bent slightly forward.

"It's all right," the man says, "if you don't take my hand." His voice isn't unkind. There's a faint odor of alcohol. "I'm going to look at the fire. Do you want to look at the fire?"

And so they set off, slowly, the man keeping gate at the boy's side, his voice deep and solicitous:

"You're right not to trust just anyone. It was presumptuous of me. This town—everyplace—is changing"—stopping and looking at the boy, who also stops. "Don't you think that it's changing?"

The boy regards him without comment.

"Is your father with the Company?" the man inquires after a time, when they've begun walking again.

"Aren't you with the Company?" the boy replies.

"I guess."

"I've never seen you before."

"Oh, you probably have. The world is changing, but it's still so small. Don't you agree?"

Nearing the avenue, as the lights from homes and lamps begin to brighten the little street, the man comes more into view. He has a strong, bearded face that seems old-fashioned to the boy. His beard is brown and white and full, but well kept. He is dressed in a dark suit that's been rumpled from sitting in damp grass. He looks, the boy thinks, like a president from another century, or a grandfather, the wrinkles around the eyes soft and oiled.

"You look like someone," the boy says.

"That may be. I have a daughter you might know. Her name is Elizabeth—"

"Elizabeth isn't a girl's name—it's a place," the boy replies.

To which the man smiles, but acknowledges, "I suppose you're right." As they come to the corner, and the noises of the street percolate around them again, he takes his hat off to a passing young woman. She stares at him briefly before her eyes snap away, to other sights.

"I'd be willing to wager," he says, "that not far from where we stand, someone, likely your mother, is worried about you." Again the hat. "Now, as you don't recognize me," he continues, "is there anyone here you *have* seen before?"—watching the crowd move past, all heading down the block in the same direction; but the boy's eyes sweep over everything, his recognitions are fleeting, and do not attach.

Taking the boy's hand at last, they stroll side by side into the file of stragglers moving toward a brightness just ahead. Sparks are shimmering into the sky. The man indicates an opening in a knot of people, between whose shoulders the glow condenses and intensifies, and the boy cranes to see past the starched collars and brushed heads.

"Thank you for holding my hand," the stranger confides as they draw into the crowd. "You're going to laugh—and it's better here, much better—yet I've always been afraid of the dark."

The boy looks up, and smiles. He says, "I don't believe you," unsure if he's being teased.

The man glances down in surprise:

"You should never tell anyone," he shakes his head, "that you don't believe them." But he, too, is smiling. Grasping the boy beneath the arms, he hoists him onto his shoulders; and it is then that the boy sees the fire.

It's in a clearing normally employed as a baseball field, but is this night, instead, a small, two-story home like so many others around it, except that it is full of flames. The white building stands in a tree-less yard, a house marbled with smoke, from which the flames rise. The house seems lonesome to him despite the crowd gathered in the street. The flames are so large and clear they might be made of colored strips of paper or cellophane.

At first he is afraid, but the man, carrying him and good-naturedly navigating the clots of people, threads his way near enough so that they can feel the heat on their faces, and see the details of the fire lick-ing the transoms of windows, twining the pillars of the porch, moving around upstairs, through the rooms, like a person looking for some-thing. A great cheer erupts on either side of them, and the man turns to look up at him, face like a golden mask in the reflected light, coaxing the boy from his bewilderment, until he allows himself, voluptuously, as everyone else, to fall into the pleasure of the fire. All around he sees the men and boys he'd looked for in vain only a few minutes before. They are clapping and shouting at the fire, as if at a wrestler in a ring; it even seems to him they're clapping more for the fire than the firemen in their yellow and black suits, slick with water as they stand grappling with the fantastical nozzles and devices of a fire truck, drawing from its huge, red and secretive body various tools and machines to try on the fire. He looks into the face of the stranger, into the faces of the men and women, and then, finally, into the glittering eyes of the children, lifted like himself into the light. An idea occurs to him:

"Whose house is that?"

"It belongs to the firemen," the man says.

"But who lives in that house?" he asks.

"No one," the man tells him with a smile. "It's nobody's home. They built it for the fire—so they could put it out."

Both of them return their attention to the blaze, although the boy is thinking now about what the man said. The firemen push against the flames, advancing. They signal to one another, as if they'd pursued the fire into a corner. A ladder reaches a window, vanishing into steam and smoke where a fireman clutching a shiny hose braces against some invisible pressure. Under cover of renewed cheers, one of the men is beating the front door with an axe. In a flurry of activity, they are running, signaling; there are firemen all around the building now, hoses trained through windows; and then the door is down—men rush in, coats enormous and dark against the furnace of the interior. The crowd, seeing the men crossing the very threshold of their dreams, applauds wildly, eyes shining in the blaze.

But it is at last time to admit that there is a fear that always comes over me, here. I might forget the fear until this very moment, but then I remember, and the fear begins. I haven't been afraid to see the boy come upon the stranger on a dark and empty street; and except for the briefest moment, like the boy, I haven't been afraid of the fire itself—although, like the stranger and unlike the boy, I am afraid of the dark. What fills me with fear on this occasion, however, are the boy's eyes as they rove the cheering crowd.

The people around him make a lush and rushing sound; a man in a felt hat puts both hands to his mouth and whistles, filling the air with a soft cloud of spit; a burly woman hoists her son in two stout arms and shouts through the back of the child's head. Her teeth are small and coffee-stained. The child is raising his hands and clapping, his hair in a flurry, and the boy, too, is clapping, turning and surveying the people that surround him. For an instant, an older boy catches his eye, but then the youth—perhaps fifteen, acne-scarred and whiskered like a catfish—wipes his brow and returns his broad face to the scene.

And I am afraid—afraid, watching the boy searching among these people for a familiar face, that he will realize that he knows all of them. It is a possibility I'd an inkling of at the start of the dream, but now there is in its aspect something pitiless. I am afraid that he will see these are a lifetime of faces—of people he hasn't met, yet, but who he will come to know, and who will come to know him. I am afraid that they've been gathered here from his entire life *because* they know him; that there are people here who have called him by pet names, people he's borrowed money from; people he has made love with, who he has watched die, and perhaps even people who have watched him die. They surround him, and I can only hope that as long as he remains clapping, unaware, they will not notice. I watch now with this alone in mind: I am afraid that the teenager, rubbing the nape of his neck, will turn again. And he does, indeed, so that I am terrified that the boy's eyes will meet those eyes sleepy with adolescence—though that is only the tip of my fear. I tremble to think that his eyes might meet any of their eyes, because I am sure, then, that he will know why he is there, and they will know why they are there, too; and I imagine the things they might say when they see who he is—all the terrifying things they might tell him about the life he hasn't had yet, but which they remember, and in which, one day, he will be swept away.

They are cheering, and he is cheering, and I am waiting for that certainty to enter his eye—any of their eyes.

He bends down toward the stranger's ear, as if he were murmuring to a horse.

"Who are you?" he asks to no answer; and again, "Who are you?"

The man glances at him. "Me?" he replies. "I'm nobody—just nobody at all," turning back to the fire.

There is, then, a sound, at first like a fire alarm, of more trucks arriving—until it grows both too large and too small, and I think that this must be it—the *end* I've been dreading, materializing, as any apocalypse, in undreamt-of form, at the hand of a vassal, in the shape of a fly or germ—and then it becomes another sound that surrounds us, arriving, at last, as the sound of the world—*the other world*. Ah, I think, asleep. Ah, yes, grasping safety, drawing my deepest breath before plunging forward, and opening my eyes.

IRA SHER has another story, "Lionflower Hedge," on page 25 of this anthology. His short fiction has appeared in venues including *Chicago Review*, *The Gettysburg Review* and *This American Life*. His first novel, *Gentlemen of Space*, was published in 2003 by Free Press. He lives in Hudson, New York with his wife, the poet Rebecca Wolff, and their children Asher and Margot.

Leena Krohn

The Ice Cream Vendor

Translated by Anselm Hollo

"Where's that noise coming from?" Elsa asked, looking surprised.

"What noise?"

"It sounds like someone typing."

"I don't think there's anybody typing, here on the beach," her mother said. "I bet it's a lawnmower. Or an outboard engine."

"But it's coming from the ice cream stand!" said Elsa. "Let's go see!"

It was a small white shack on the vacant beach. Both Elsa and her mother were wondering why the beach was so empty on such a warm sunny day. On days like this it was mostly hard to find a spot for one's beach towel, and there was always a long line at the ice cream stand. It was uncanny. But never mind, they had the beach all to themselves.

As they approached the ice cream stand, they could hear the busy tapping noise ever more clearly. Elsa looked at her mother and said: "It's not any kind of engine."

"No, you were right about that," said her mother.

It was Håkan, typing away on a small old-fashioned manual portable.

He was wearing a dark suit with a white shirt and a dark blue silk tie. He was typing with great concentration, excellent posture, and a solemn air. Once in a while he cast an absent-minded glance at the horizon and the deserted beach.

"A new ice cream vendor!" Elsa exclaimed.

"That's what it looks like," said her mother. "He's wearing a curious outfit for the job."

"It's a little weird," said Elsa. "He sits there and writes. Why, do you think?"

"Why don't you go and buy some ice cream," her mother said, sounding tired and closing her eyes again. "I'll stay here in the shade and wait. Maybe he'll have time to take a break from his writing to sell you a cone. At least you won't have to stand in line this time."

"Don't you want any?"

"Sure, I'll have one. How about mango, if he's got it."

Elsa looked at the ice cream stand. The air vibrated above the sand. The stand seemed to be inside a cloud, but it was also a cloud of words.

As Elsa approached, Håkan raised his fingers from the keyboard.

"Well, what would you like?" he asked.

"Why are you writing?" Elsa asked.

"Because I have to."

"I see. What are you writing?"

"A will," Håkan said. "Sort of."

"The kind where you tell people who gets your stuff when you're dead?"

"No, a different kind," said Håkan. "So, what would you like?"

"Mango ice cream. Two cones. Are you planning on dying soon?"

Håkan pressed two scoops of pale yellow mango ice cream into their cones.

"No, I'm not planning that at all, but it could happen nevertheless. And not just to me. That'll be eighteen marks."

Elsa produced even money out of her purse.

"So it could happen to others as well?"

"Have you noticed," Håkan said, "that this heat wave seems to just go on and on?"

"Oh, yeah," Elsa said. "It's great. We can come to the beach every day."

"Great or not so great, depending on how you look at it," said Håkan. "We must be prepared for all eventualities."

"What eventualities?"

"Heat waves aren't harmless," Håkan said.

"You mean someone could die of heat?" Elsa said, sounding doubtful.

"Not impossible," said Håkan. He started typing again and did not pay any further attention to Elsa.

Before Elsa reached the shady place with her cones, they were half melted.

"That ice cream guy said some weird things," Elsa told her mother. "I got a little scared."

"Did he scare you?"

"He said that someone might die. And he was writing a will."

"He was kidding you," said her mother. Then she got up and went back to the ice cream stand. Håkan was concentrating so hard on his typing that he didn't even notice the new customer. Elsa's mother tapped the counter with a fingernail, and Håkan looked up and stopped typing.

"You're not trying to frighten little children, are you?"

"What do you mean?"

"Did you just tell my daughter that someone could die?"

"Well, it's always possible, isn't it?"

"That you told her that?"

"No, I meant that someone could die."

"Well, that may well be. But there's no need for an ice cream vendor to discuss such subjects with a child."

"No, generally speaking not. But these are exceptional times. There's much to discuss. There's much to prepare ourselves for. People with families in particular."

"What are you saying? What times?"

"Just pay attention to the weather, that's all I'm saying. And to the birds."

"The birds?"

Elsa's mother scanned the beach and the sea. She did not see a single bird.

"There aren't any birds here."

"No, there aren't," said Håkan. "Nor any people, either. Strange, don't you think?"

She went back to Elsa and told her: "I think it's best not to pay any attention to what he's saying. I think he's a little, a little—"

"Touched," Elsa suggested.

"Right. Or a little weird, at least."

"Eww," said Elsa. She had just found the bottle of sunscreen.

"What's the matter?"

"The sunscreen! It's spilled into the bag. The sunglasses and the hairbrush and your book—they're all covered in oil."

"Isn't the cap on tight?"

"Yes, it is," said Elsa.

"There must be a hole in it somewhere," said her mother.

Elsa wiped the bottle and the cap and examined both carefully.

"No, there's no hole anywhere."

"Let me see."

Elsa's mother turned to pick up the bag and extracted the bottle of sunscreen oil from it. The cap was, indeed, on tight. Her fingers slipped when she tried, in vain, to open it. Nevertheless, all the things in the bag were stained with the yellow oil.

"It's a mystery," said Elsa, looking almost satisfied. "We may never find out what happened."

"Maybe not. Well, aren't you going to take a swim?" asked her mother.

"Yes, but first I'd like another ice cream cone."

She didn't really want any more ice cream. She wanted to pursue her conversation with Håkan.

"That'll be the last one for today," said her mother. "And don't waste any time talking to that guy."

"More mango?" Håkan asked Elsa.

"No, something else."

"We have pistachio, too. You won't find that everywhere. Did I scare you, a little while ago? I didn't mean to. But facts are facts."

"No, you didn't really. I'll have the pistachio," Elsa said. "Give me a big one."

Her temples had started hurting. There was a faint sulfurous smell in the air.

"Are you really an ice cream vendor?" Elsa couldn't help asking him.

"No. I'm just subbing."

"Do subs always wear a suit like that?"

"Not usually. And the regulars don't either."

"So why are you wearing it?"

"For a special occasion."

"Is it your birthday?"

"No. Rather the opposite," said Håkan.

"I see." Elsa had to start eating her ice cream—it was already dripping through a hole in the cone.

"Do you know what the temperature is right now?"

"I do, I have a thermometer here," Håkan said helpfully. "It says one hundred and two."

"Wow!" said Elsa. "Can that kill you?"

"No, not yet," said Håkan. "Not if you're in good health."

"That's good. I am very healthy."

"That lasts a while," said Håkan.

"What does?"

"Health. But it may be time to go now."

"Go where?"

"Back home," said Håkan. "I'll be going soon, too."

"Are they closing the beach?"

"It should be closed," said Håkan.

Elsa went back to her mother who had wet a towel and covered her face with it.

"Mother?"

"Yes?"

"It's a hundred and two degrees there. But he said that won't kill you, yet."

Her mother snorted. "Well, that's reassuring, isn't it. But why did you go and talk to that man again?"

"He said that we should leave."

"He did? What gall! It's not up to an ice cream vendor to decide how long we can stay at the beach."

"But he said that the whole beach should be closed."

"But why on earth—? Don't go there anymore. There's no telling what guys like him may be up to."

"Do you know what I'm feeling like now?" Elsa asked. "It's just like being on a plane. My ears are falling shut."

"Try to swallow. Maybe that's the air pressure. I guess it has been falling."

Elsa pondered this for a moment, swallowing and licking her ice cream.

"Maybe that's why the sunscreen went all over everything. Maybe there will be thunder and lightning," Elsa said, sounding a little worried.

"It's possible," her mother said. "The weather is changing, that's for sure. It can't go on like this for much longer. I think it is brewing up to a real storm. Perhaps we should go home now. But not because of that ice cream vendor."

"But I would like to go for a swim first. That's what we came here for, isn't it?"

"Yes, dear, of course you can. Maybe I should take a dip, too," her mother agreed. "Except that the water is probably way too warm. It won't be very refreshing."

They ambled down to the water's edge, Elsa a few steps ahead of her mother. But a moment before Elsa's toes touched the water, she stopped.

"What's the matter?" her mother asked.

"Let's not go in," Elsa said. "The water is kind of weird. There's something in it."

"Fish!" said her mother.

"See, they're all swimming upside down!"

"They're not swimming," said her mother.

There were fish of many different kinds and sizes floating by the shore. Their white bellies shone. They smelled.

"Are they dead?" Elsa asked.

"That's what it looks like. It's strange that the birds haven't noticed them yet."

Elsa looked up at the hot and empty sky.

"The birds have left," someone said. The ice cream vendor in his fine suit was standing on the sandy beach. His black shoes were shiny. The silence was quite solemn.

"They look sort of cooked," Elsa said, contemplating the fish.

"They *are* cooked, my dear," Håkan said, gently. "Look."

The sea was dead calm. The reeds stood up straight like spears. But from among the rushes and farther away, where the heat haze interfered with visibility, came a bubbling sound. The water was simmering and whimpering.

"What makes the water move like that?" asked Elsa.

They looked at the simmering surface of the sea, they looked at the haze that was growing increasingly dense, rising and swirling. More fish drifted ashore, layer upon layer. A hot, malodorous fog enveloped them and soaked their hair.

"It's steam," Håkan said. "The sea is boiling."

"What are you saying?" Elsa's mother was appalled. "Telling things like that to a child!"

"Run!" Håkan told Elsa. "Let's race to the car!"

He turned to her mother and said, pointedly: "You, too, madam."

Her mother took Elsa's hand, and they ran like never before. At one point, Elsa almost stumbled and turned to look back. In the midst of the steam, she could make out the ice cream vendor's straight-backed, black-suited shape. He wasn't running.

The ice cream vendor raised his hand in greeting, and behind him, far out to sea, rose a huge bluish-white bubble, round as a breast. It inflated and spread like a dream under the strange, white-hot sun.

❖ ❖ ❖

LEENA KROHN has two other stories in this anthology, "The Son of Chimera," on page 27, and "About the Henbane City," on page 508. All three stories are excerpts from her novel, *Pereat mundus*, to be published in the United States in the latter half of 2006 by Omnidawn. In this novel Håkan is an everyman character, taking on different forms. More info on this book is available at www.omnidawn.com/krohn *Tainaron, Mail from Another City* (translated into English by Hildi Hawkins) was published in the U.S. by Prime Books in 2004. Krohn lives in Southern Finland. A number of her writings and works are available on her home page at www.kaapeli.fi/krohn

Karen Heuler

Jubilee Dreams

"Well, all my life I've been perfectly happy not to dream and I wouldn't want one if I had the choice, and now all of a sudden—pow! I'm dreaming every night, all night, and all of them seem very *familiar* dreams, as if I've been there before and I swear, Clarice, the oddest thing about them is that they're cartoons." Jubilee leaned back quickly against her kitchen chair, then leaned forward again impatiently. Over the years two lines had appeared around Jubilee's mouth, lines that deepened when she was annoyed, and they were deep now.

"What do you mean by cartoons?" Clarice asked, resting her chin on her fist. Jubilee noted that her sister had suddenly become interested, and she was tempted to point out how rare this interest was. But that, no doubt, would bring on the look of distracted boredom Clarice always had when she agreed to come over.

"Animated figures. Almost outlines. They talk and feel like people—they cry, they're emotionally chaotic, even. But they do cartoon things: terrible things happen but they don't bleed; they speed up and slow down in exaggerated ways. Well, I shouldn't say 'they,' I should say 'we.' I'm part of it. I'm one of them and I do cartoon things. I'm aware they're foolish but I do them anyway: I go into bad neighborhoods, I'm curious about people in alley ways, I get on trains that have no lights. I know it's bad but I can't help it, I'm just too curious. I see an opportunity and I leap. Well, this latest dream, I've had it four or five times—I pass a circus and I see a sign, they want someone to high-dive into a vat of water and I *have* to do it, it's impossible for me not to, and then I'm climbing up a very high ladder—exactly like in a cartoon, the ladder comes to a point, that's how high it is. There's a tiny platform at top, I can barely stand on it, and I look down to a vat of water. It looks like a polka dot it's so far away. It's ridiculous. I know there's no way I can survive. When was the last time I even went swimming, much less did a high dive? I don't think I've ever done that."

"But you jump."

"Oh, I jump. I want to know what it feels like to jump that far, and I'm convinced if I just keep my legs straight and my elbows in—I'm convinced I can make it."

"Do you?"

"I always wake up before I hit the water."

Clarice was silent for a moment. Pursuing her own thoughts, Jubilee guessed. Bored. Uninterested. Jubilee shifted restlessly, irritably, on her chair. Maybe she shouldn't have told Clarice.

Clarice looked up. "I believe in dreams, you know."

Jubilee sighed. "I know."

The way she said it stopped Clarice short. She leaned back against her chair and stared vaguely at the wall behind her sister. Clarice had been about to mention that her own dreams had turned into cartoons too, but now she decided against it. She, too, had seen the high dive, but she'd passed it by. She was afraid of heights. Even in her dreams, she was afraid of heights. There was a river right next to the circus and she found herself swimming in it, and then she came out of the water when she saw a garden and a village beyond it. All the people she met ignored her—actively ignored her, pretended she wasn't there, even though she nodded to them—and Clarice drifted towards each of them: a man tending flowers, a child throwing a ball against a barn, a young man walking down a shady lane, a woman leaning out a window.

In her dream, Clarice was angry. She tore out a bunch of flowers from right beside the gardener, she stole the ball from the child, she smacked the man in the lane and the woman in the window, all because they wouldn't see her.

Clarice, who believed in the messages of dreams, was baffled because she thought the message was inappropriate. She didn't really *care* if she had no impact on other people. She didn't *care* if she left no impression. She didn't demand anything, she thought, but independence and freedom—and freedom required only herself.

But of course she couldn't explain this to Jubilee, who had four closets of clothes for herself and, moreover, a closet of clothes for her husband and a closet of clothes for her son and carpeting in all rooms, a lawn service that came twice a month and regular schedules for all things, including hair and nail appointments. These things were important, Clarice knew; they were civilization and she liked civilization. But she believed that scarce goods were better than plenty, better for freedom, or maybe only better for her.

So Clarice sat in Jubilee's neat kitchen, glancing at the dishwasher, the microwave, the pasta and espresso machines, as Jubilee said moodily, "I have a perfectly good life. These dreams are insulting."

Clarice meant to smile companionably, charitably, but her lips just peeled back against her teeth, "like a dog making nice," as Jubilee thought. Jubilee regretted the thought; she was feeling out of sorts.

Clarice tried to keep her voice as neutral as possible. "The more you think about it, the more you'll dream."

"Oh, that's some sort of psychological trick," Jubilee answered.

Clarice smiled. Jubilee's suspicion of all things psychological or mystical or insubstantial always made Clarice feel as if she herself were the rational one. By being open to all improbable things, she was somehow more in touch with reality, where improbable things happened daily. Jubilee, she thought, really needed a dream.

Jubilee found, despite her best intentions, that her dreams did, indeed, continue—and even, as Clarice had warned, increased in intensity and intruded like a bad conscience into almost every aspect of her day. She was swimming, now, in a river. She was intensely interested in her surroundings, which were beautiful, cartoon-clear and pastoral. The blue river ran through a town of greens and browns under an open blue sky.

Once Jubilee got used to the river's flow, she found she could drift along with only an occasional move on her part. The river moved past a man who leaned anxiously over a patch of plants, past a crying child, a young man standing in a grove of trees on the left bank, a young woman leaning out of a window in the town on the right bank.

Everything had a line around it, a perfect boundary that pleased Jubilee. In fact, everything pleased her—the directness of the colors, the simplicity and vividness all around her. Everything was fresh and clear. There were occasional gaps in the scheme, where a color simply wasn't filled in, but Jubilee's eye skipped over them. The river turned and opened to a beach drawn in a line below the spread of the town. Beyond the town, fields of geometric greens and golds spread to the left, with mountains in blues and purples behind.

She left the river and, walking from the beach into the town (houses three stories high, red-tiled roofs, black wrought-iron balconies, green vines, white curtains), she found that she was dry and comfortable. She wore a shirtwaist dress with buttons down the front, aquamarine to complement her eyes, and brown pointy-toed shoes with cartoon heels that seemed to dissolve when her foot hit the ground—there was no other way to describe the sense of buoyancy she felt. The air had no temperature to it at all, nor (she recalled) did the river. There was a yellow disk of sun to the right of the mountains.

The road was so inviting and well drawn that she traveled it quickly. It led through town (a dog yapping in a doorway, a slim mother pushing a baby pram) to a field with maypoles, banners, tables with food (round pies with perfect fluting, red jams, green relishes, covered dishes with lines of rising steam), and a man in a throne under a scalloped canopy.

The man had a yellow crown with dark red and blue stones. He was dressed in a gray tunic over gray tights with simple black high-topped shoes. His hands rested on the arms of his throne and he gazed off into the fields to his right. Even so, Jubilee felt that he was aware of her and acknowledged her without visible sign, just as the townspeople crowded off to the man's left also saw Jubilee, and noted her, and even spoke of her one to another, all without addressing her or looking straight at her.

Beyond the king the mountains rose in humps of blue and green and purple, and Jubilee saw a dark cloud above the mountains advance towards them, and where the shadows would have crossed the hills, deepening their colors, a blankness fell instead. It was then she remembered the gaps in the coloring, and she saw the townsfolk waver uncertainly, some running off, others grabbing a loved one. They cowered, turning their heads away, lifting hands up against the racing cloud in the sky. The king raised his arms and bent his head. Children cried, and then the cloud moved off, the colors returned, and faces one by one turned to regard her.

The king shifted in his throne and lifted a hand, his fingers slack, and beckoned to her. He kept his face averted so that, as she approached, she saw only his left side.

"Where are you from?" he asked quietly. He had a deep, worried voice.

Jubilee was startled to find she couldn't remember.

"How did you get here?" He was patient, but his eye observed her carefully.

"From the river," Jubilee said. "I was in the river and I saw your village, and so here I am."

The king lifted his left hand to cover his chin as he lowered his voice. "And have you brought us something?"

The sadness in his voice alarmed her. "What could I bring you?" she whispered, leaning to the king as the hand he held before his face seemed to shield him from being heard accidentally by others.

"Indigo," he whispered, and his left eye flared, his teeth showed just an instant too long behind his lips, and his eyebrow drew down in a wedge over his face. For the briefest moment, he turned his full face towards her and she could see in the shade of the canopy that the whole right side of his face was blank, an outline and nothing more.

It struck her as horrible. She looked away past the throne and canopy and saw a figure watching her from the outskirts of the crowd. It was Clarice, clutching a bunch of flowers in her hand.

Jubilee must have registered some panic in her face, some impulse to flee, because the king leaned forward and begged, "Please help us."

Jubilee woke then, with the sound of his words in her ears. It was still dark, and she lay with her eyes open, trying to dissect her feelings.

For the first time, she felt in love with a dream. She was entranced with the land she had been in, its exotic appeal; she had felt it in the dream itself, the sense that it was strange and glowing and mysteriously hers. And—her heart leaped—the king had singled her out for help.

Perhaps what she'd felt when she saw the blank half of his face was not fear, but the surprise of having been called.

Her husband lay beside her. She had been married to Mark for ten years, and for the first time she thought seriously, "Would I leave him?"

Oh god, what a stupid thought. Leave him for a cartoon figure in a dream?

She lay in bed thinking until the sun came up and the alarm went off. Then she made coffee, showered, made breakfast, saw her husband off and got her son Jake ready for school. She paid special attention to the beautiful unblemished purity of his face, to his bright unshadowed eyes.

The phone rang and it was her sister. "I saw you in my dream last night," Clarice said.

Jubilee remembered seeing Clarice too, and she was filled with resentment; to think that Clarice, the world-traveler, would elbow her way into the one foreign place Jubilee had ever gotten to! "Saw me?" she repeated in a way that Clarice recognized as hostile.

"Yes. That dream you described to me—well, I've been having it too. Not exactly the same dream, I don't mean that, but it's a cartoon place. Last night I was walking in the mountains. Very strange. In the shade, there are blanks, as if someone had forgotten to fill it in. Like there was a color missing."

"Indigo," Jubilee breathed.

"Funny. Yes. I can see it now. A certain shade of blue. I came to a gathering of some kind. I was there with all of them. They can't see me."

Jubilee's heart leapt. "Are you sure?"

"They ignore me completely. I've even pushed one or two. Not out of meanness. Just because I'm curious."

"They can see me."

"So you had the same dream? You were at that fair or whatever it is?" Clarice was casual, as if she didn't mind not being the central figure in her own dream.

Impulsively, Jubilee cried, "It's *my* dream!" She could almost feel her sister's surprise over the line as Clarice answered: "But how can I help it, Jubilee?"

Jubilee relaxed her grip on the phone; she saw that her knuckles were white. "You've been dreaming all your life. This is the first dream I've ever remembered or liked. I want it."

"I don't think I'm ready to leave it, Jubilee," Clarice said gently.

Jubilee hung up the phone.

Jubilee's next dream started almost mid-sentence. She was in the king's throne room. Even here he sat under a canopy that cast shadows and caused him to avert half of his face.

"When we lost indigo we lost a part of our lives. No, not just the obvious. Of course, *that* was awkward enough, pretending not to notice that another person's eyes or hair—or the collar of a coat, the fold of a dress—was gone, simply gone. No, what destroys us is the uneasiness it causes, the fact that you can't see what's missing in yourself—it's this, I think, that has driven us all to distraction. It's so hard to keep your thoughts, knowing that a part of you disappears, simply disappears. What do they see? you think, and the rest of your thoughts fly away. Your work lies adrift, and you wonder if a moment comes when you disappear completely. You don't want to see it in anyone else, you don't want them to see it in you. No one walks in the woods anymore; lovers only stroll at noontime. We are all terrified." His hand, never far from his face, wandered there again. With an effort, he forced it down.

"When did it happen?" Jubilee asked. She was seated before him, in a chair less elaborate and lower than his.

"Oh, recently. Quite recent." His voice trailed off.

"Indigo," he sighed, and the sound of it was heartbreakingly sad.

Jubilee found that she woke up happier now than she had ever been. She caught herself daydreaming about naps, and then she started napping, first only in the afternoon but soon she would go back to sleep after she'd sent everyone off in the morning.

She called Clarice and apologized for hanging up. "I want to know what happens in your dreams. I want to know what you see."

"I see you carrying on with the king," Clarice said meanly.

"I'm important to the king," Jubilee answered.

Clarice laughed. It seemed to her that Jubilee owned too many things already; it was really too greedy of her to want to own the dream.

Jubilee drew in her breath. "I've never felt important to anyone before."

Clarice instantly felt alarmed. We keep doing this to each other, Clarice thought. We keep judging each other by the wrong standards. She's not proud. But then she reversed herself again, because her sister gave a little rueful laugh, and in that laugh she seemed to relax into all the things she had. Clarice decided that her sister was just asking for praise—as usual, asking for more. "Oh come on, Mark depends on you, Jake depends on you."

"Food and clothing," Jubilee snorted. "It could be provided by a service. The king wants me to save his country, not vacuum his carpets."

That was a little grandiose, Clarice thought. She said, "I thought you liked being a housewife." She knew the word always made Jubilee uneasy.

"That doesn't mean I wouldn't accept more," Jubilee answered. "What did you dream?"

Clarice switched to a cheerful, hearty mode, as if the whole thing were simply amusing. "I've been spying in my dream," she said. "Listening at doors, peering in windows. Well, sitting at tables, too, it hardly matters since they can't see me. *Very* jumpy people, they stare down at their plates, look over each other's shoulders, try to catch glimpses of themselves in mirrors and windows. They groan at night. The children cry and the animals skulk. Other than that, it's a lovely town." She laughed lightly.

"Have you heard anything about indigo—where it's gone? Who has it?" Jubilee tried very hard to keep too much interest out of her voice.

"The king is the only one who mentions it by name."

"He has great dignity."

"You're not in love with him, are you?" Clarice asked, astonished.

And again, Jubilee hung up the phone.

Clarice didn't tell Jubilee all of her dreams; she didn't tell her, for instance, that she had traveled into the mountain and found a pool of dark, dark water. She found it just before she woke, and she thought about it all day long. She had to wait until that night to find if her theory was right.

The first thing she did when she was back on the mountain was to run to every side of it, and up and down, to see who was around. There were blank white sheep on one side, a waterwheel below. There was a farmhouse on the other side, and a hand made rock wall around an abandoned building, and nothing else. The people were all down in the valley, and apparently stayed in the valley. Perhaps that was because of the clouds, which would suddenly gather at the peak of the mountain and roll heavily downwards, where Clarice knew the people wavered, and shivered, and fled.

The point was, Jubilee was nowhere around. Satisfied, Clarice went back to the pool she'd found, which was at the base of a sheer cliff and shadowed by tall stiff trees.

She knelt down and cupped her hands. The liquid was a deep, deep blue, and it held itself in her hands almost as if it had a form; when she flung it up against the cliff, the waters kept their droplet shapes intact and ran down again into the pool.

Indigo, Clarice breathed.

"Actually, I like being a stranger," Clarice said in a jaded voice. "That's why I like traveling. I can be what I want to be, not what I am."

"What in the world does *that* mean?" Jubilee said impatiently. They phoned each other daily now, something they had never done before.

"No one knows what I always fail at. That means I might succeed. Opinions are very influential, and if you're new, then no one has an opinion yet. Of course, they don't know what you're good at either, so you have to establish that. It's interesting how important it is to establish yourself. So—once or twice—I tried not to; I tried just to watch."

Jubilee was sure Clarice was trying to show she could bring her experiences to the dream. She was putting Jubilee in her place—the stay-at-home sister who didn't even know how to spell half the places Clarice had been to. Jubilee's back stiffened. "Is not being yourself better than being yourself?"

"Don't know. But it beats being stuck in a rut."

"Can't people be themselves and *not* be stuck? Are you saying *you're* stuck and that's why you keep traveling?"

"No. That's not what I said. I mean I'm flexible."

Jubilee sneered. "You've never seemed anything but yourself to me, so I wonder if you're at all accurate."

"All I mean is that it's good sometimes to observe without forcing things to relate to you."

"Sorry," Jubilee said softly. "But it's funny, isn't it, how now you can't even get anyone to relate to you in a dream?"

So Jubilee is adopting psychology, Clarice thought grimly. She's trying to outmaneuver me.

"I know where indigo is," Clarice said finally, her voice juicy with one-upmanship, and she hung up the phone.

Jubilee found herself in bed next to the king, his back to her, and she dressed hastily. It must have been right before dawn, because there was so much blankness around her. She moved silently, careful to avoid looking at the king—who might, she thought, catch her looking at him disappearing in the blue glow of dawn. She felt too much for him to do that. She felt tenderness, a desire to protect, and a thrilling sense of purpose.

She ran silently through the streets, hoping to catch Clarice by surprise She didn't see anyone loitering at windows or in doorways. She had to steel herself against the blankness around the streetlights.

As dawn rose she headed out of town to the hills. She had no doubt that Clarice did, indeed, have the secret to indigo, and that if she found Clarice she would be able to take the secret away from her. Jubilee ran with cartoon speed, covering distances quickly and tirelessly. In all her life she had never had so much power and control.

She ran through the woods as the sun rose along the horizon; the birds woke up, high in the green shadows, and the trees waved above her head, opening to the light.

She didn't see Clarice, but Jubilee kept her head pivoting from left to right. It would be like Clarice to be on the edge somewhere, just to the side, watching her. Or maybe Clarice, who knew the secret of indigo, was hidden somewhere in blankness, or maybe she had finally become invisible to her sister.

Jubilee sped through the woods and up the mountain, covering cliffs and ravines in effortless strides, but nothing she saw had the shape of Clarice. She ran back down the mountains, down through the forest, through the streets of the wakened town (children on their way to school, mothers calling from doorways, fathers in the lanes, and the king himself crossing the courtyard, surprised to see her flying by).

She ran to the river, and turned down the river, retracing her original steps. Swimming in the river was effortless and she moved far more swiftly than she noticed. All at once she found herself back at the circus. The tents were being taken down and all that was left of the high dive was a spangle and a puddle of water.

She turned to go back to the river, but there was nothing there. She saw Clarice behind a tree, just standing there and looking back along the way they'd come.

Jubilee woke up with a start and reached for the phone. "What did you do?" she whispered harshly to her sister. Mark was still snoring beside her.

"I was asleep," Clarice groaned. "You woke me up."

"I don't care. You're ruining it, you're ruining everything. What did you do with indigo?"

Clarice let the seconds tick. She smiled to herself. "I drank it," she said.

Jubilee was too stunned to reply.

When Clarice was fully awake she was horrified at what she'd done. She had to shake her head—horrified at what she'd done in a *dream*? But the uneasiness kept bleeding through her all day long, like ink on paper.

She had left the pool of indigo and gone back to the town. She disliked being invisible; she was lonely and angry. She had wandered through many houses in town, longing to be noticed at a table, at the window, but not even the dogs looked up. She felt doomed to a solitary life and it was unfair that Jubilee so obviously had the hero's role *and* the role of the lovely maiden.

She had left the pool of indigo and gone back to the town. She was still invisible, and it was growing irritating. Everyone saw Jubilee. What did that mean?

When she looked through the window into the king's bedroom she saw her sister rising from his bed, reaching for her clothes in the dim light—and she saw Jubilee with the corner of her face missing in the shadows. This threw her into a frenzy, this little loss of Jubilee, this start of the loss of Jubilee. She had no doubt that Jubilee was on the verge of leaving her. If she married the king—if she merged with the town—then Jubilee, too, would no longer see Clarice. That was unacceptable.

And at the heart of it was indigo. This place lived in dread because they'd lost it. Clarice had to figure out which would be the greater threat—to give it back to them or withhold it.

She thought the king's happiness would trap Jubilee even further, because Jubilee was so obviously longing to belong to this new life. She would end up being the stranger coming into town, she would be coupled with the return of indigo. She would win the king's heart and live in the fairy tale forever and ever, and never see Clarice again.

No. Indigo must be destroyed. She would do it because she loved Jubilee, who had to face up to the real life, where she belonged. This dreaminess was wrong for her.

Clarice ran back to the mountain, bending as she ran to pull a reed from a pond. She found the pool of indigo and stuck the reed in, then she drank and drank until the pool was dry. Her fingernails turned inky blue, her eyes looked out through a deep-blue filter. She was proud of what she'd done.

And there, at the bottom of the empty pool, she saw a black line— not a stick or a snake or a crease in the mud, but a bold, thick line. She picked it up and the outline of the pool unraveled. She kept pulling, like an endless thread, and she pulled off the right side of the mountain, and then the top, and then she hauled it in faster and faster, the mountains, the valleys, the shores of the river, until the colors fell into each other.

She pulled and pulled until she was back at the beginning, just outside the circus. She stopped, panting, because she saw Jubilee. She stood behind the last remaining tree until Jubilee saw her, and then with a final flick of the wrist, she pulled in the line that set up the ground, and it all vanished, just like that.

Jubilee went through a terrible period of exhaustion. She could fall asleep but couldn't stay asleep. Her eyes would close and she would walk for a while in darkness, but there was never anything to see, though she could hear faint voices. She would wake with her heart pounding, turn over, and start again.

After a while, Jubilee stopped trying to sleep and so she stayed awake for five days. Mark would come down in the morning after a full night's sleep and find her sitting at the kitchen table. Sometimes she drew pictures of the king, and her son would get his crayons and color them in. She watched him with her mouth tight.

On the sixth day, while sitting at the kitchen table, she glanced up and saw a strange, very lush world through the window over the sink.

It was not her cartoon world. She looked at it up and down and opened the kitchen door anyway. All her tiredness disappeared as she stepped outside. There was a river in the distance, which was brown and wide, and immense trees everywhere, intensely raucous bird sounds, huge blue butterflies, monkeys, parrots—it was breathtaking. She was sure she'd seen pictures of this place; in a minute she was sure she'd remember where she'd seen them.

She walked along a trail, brushing aside the ferns, bending beneath the lianas. She was enjoying herself, she hardly noticed how far she'd walked until she looked behind her once, and saw her city through the trees, far away, miles away. She was pleased to find she was a sturdy traveler. She had always wondered if she'd be as good as her sister said *she* was. The miles didn't matter, the strangeness didn't matter. She was perfectly at ease. When she was thirsty she cut open a vine for clean water. She plucked fruit and berries from branches, and they were all sweet and filled her with well-being.

She heard a sort of crunching to her right and stopped. Someone was breaking branches.

The trees had buttressed trunks that formed cubicles; she hid in one and watched.

The noise was coming closer, and suddenly she saw a hand come through some bushes and push them aside. Clarice stuck her head through cautiously, looked around, and then crept out.

She straightened up and stood perfectly still, listening and looking around. Jubilee watched as Clarice's hand wiped the sweat off her forehead and her upper lip. She pulled out a compass and then began to creep down the trail.

Jubilee let her sister go ahead before she began to follow her. Clarice had a backpack and it was this that caught on branches and broke them, little snap-snaps, brittle tiny cracks, subtle whippy whooshes all along the path ahead of her, while Jubilee's steps made no noise at all. She could walk parallel to Clarice, off the trail and through the trees, and catch the irritation on Clarice's face at every sound, the way she came to attention as if that would undo the noise, the quick glance around to see if anyone had heard it, if anyone was out there.

Clarice was certainly jumpy.

Jubilee felt so much at home that she grabbed a branch and swung up into the tree as easily as going up an escalator. At the top of the tree she looked out over the entire canopy, and it looked like a green, leafy floor. She put out a foot and it held. She skipped over the trees, passing odd-looking bugs and primates and epiphytes. Then she stopped, bent down, pushed the tops of the trees aside, and found Clarice again.

Experimentally, she tossed down a seed as large as a baseball; it landed in front of Clarice, who stopped, looked up, stooped over and picked it up. She took off her backpack, pulled out a ragged nature book, and tried to figure out what it was.

She must be hungry, Jubilee guessed.

And she doesn't know that seed, she added with satisfaction. She could see quite clearly as Clarice finally put down the seed and opened a map.

She's lost, Jubilee thought, and looked down at the map. It was filled with red markings, with danger signs and arrows and warnings. Clarice was lost, and in a bad spot, and she was going the wrong way.

Jubilee called Clarice and mentioned that she was sleeping again. "I guess I had to work it out," she said. "And I did. I never dreamed before, so it was very important to me. You're so lucky to dream all the time." She kept her voice light.

"Sometimes I wonder if it isn't a curse," Clarice answered. She was glad that Jubilee was back to normal; she had been worried. No doubt that influenced her own dreams, which were disturbing.

Jubilee smiled at the sound of stress in her sister's voice. "Bad dreams?" she asked.

"The worst. I'm in Peru again, just after the state department issued a warning about the guerrillas targeting tourists. I'm lost and I can feel there's someone watching me."

"Oh, well, when you have a dream about something you've actually experienced—don't they usually just go away after a while?"

"Who knows?" Clarice sighed. "And it never really happened anyway; I never felt in danger in Peru."

"Ah, then maybe it has nothing to do with Peru."

It was intoxicating how Jubilee began to merge with the jungle. She would lie face down on the canopy and expand through the treetops. She could feel her fingers snake out like vines in all directions. They tingled when they curled around a new branch, hugging it. Her feet leaned down the trunks of vast trees, wedging her in firmly. No, in fact, her feet *were* trunks. Her hair turned into leaves, draping down in folds of green. When she blinked it grew shady.

She could see that Clarice's clothes were catching on thorns and developing little rips. Every so often her sister pinched her fingers through her hair; she obviously felt bugs running on her scalp, and disliked it.

Jubilee could feel things moving through her arms, her hair, her feet, her mouth, and it felt as comforting as a pulse.

She looked all around and saw that she was the only one who was aware of Clarice. Her sister—who was supposed to be so good at traveling—was making her own terror.

She might have felt a little sympathy about that, if she'd been awake. Fear was nothing to laugh at. But she was in her dream, and she could be honest. Clarice had been too smug, she had been too mean. She had unraveled the king like he was a sweater; she had decided that Jubilee couldn't have him.

"And she needs a little humbling anyhow," she assured herself. "It's for her own good."

She saw an owl moth pass by. Like many butterflies and moths, each wing was colored to look like a big eye. Jubilee looked throughout the forest and found where all the moths were. She took a little breath in, and the moths came towards her, hundreds of them. Then she puffed on them very gently, sending them down to flutter around Clarice.

Clarice raised her head from the trail to see hundreds and hundreds of eyes descending. They swirled, staring at her, blinking at her, overhead and to the sides, covering tree trunks, peering through bushes. They were falling and nodding, then rising up from the ground and circling her. When she stuck out her arm, it was covered with eyes; when she looked all around, all she saw was more eyes.

She knew they weren't faces, exactly, only eyes, but eyes *see* something and Clarice was filled with a frantic sense of self-preservation. She had to get away.

She ditched her backpack, she bent her arms above her head, and she ran in an ever-widening circle through the jungle, never getting anywhere in particular and afraid of what she might see.

Jubilee watched her, below, running with a banner of moths behind her. She sighed in satisfaction, brought her eyelids down, and slept. She shifted in the middle of the night, turned over, flung her arm over Mark, and smiled.

KAREN HEULER'S stories have appeared in *Prize Stories 1998: The O. Henry Awards* as well as literary and commercial periodicals such as *TriQuarterly, Alaska Quarterly Review, Literary Review, Ms. Magazine,* and many others. Her second novel, *Journey to Bom Goody,* was published by Livingston Press in 2005. It concerns a trip to a mythical village with magical healing properties somewhere in the Amazon. In 1995 the University of Missouri published her first collection of short stories, *The Other Door,* which the New York Times called "haunting and quirky." She's currently at work on more novels and more stories. She lives in New York with her dog, Booker Prize, and the cats, Nobel and Pulitzer.

BRIAN EVENSON

AN ACCOUNTING

I have been ordered to write an honest accounting of how I became a Midwestern Jesus and the subsequent disastrous events thereby accruing, events for which I am, I am willing to admit, at least partly to blame. I know of no simpler way than to simply begin.

In August it was determined that our stores were depleted and not likely to outlast the winter. One of our number must travel East and beg further provision from our compatriots on the coast, another must move further inland and hold converse with the Midwestern sects as he encountered them, bartering for supplies as he could. Lots were drawn and this latter role fell to me.

I was provided a dog and a dogcart, a knife, a revolver with six rounds, rations, food for the dog, a flint and steel, and a rucksack stuffed with objects for trade. I named the dog Finger for reasons obscure even to myself. I received as well a small packet of our currency, though it was suspected that, since the rupture, our currency, with its Masonic imagery, would be considered by the pious Midwesterners anathema. It was not known if I would be met with hostility, but this was considered not unlikely considering no recent adventurer into the territory had returned.

I was given as well some hasty training by a former Midwesterner turned heretic named Barton. According to him, I was to make frequent reference to God—though not to use the word, *Goddamn*, as in the phrase "Where are my goddamn eggs?"

"What eggs are these?" I asked Barton, only to discover the eggs themselves were apparently of no matter. He ticked off a list of other words considered profane and to be avoided. I was advised to frequently describe things as God's will. "There but for the grace of God go I" was also an acceptable phrase, as was "Praise God." Things were not to be called "Godawful" though I was allowed to use, very rarely and with care, the term "God's aweful grace." If someone were to ask me if I were "saved," I was to claim that yes indeed I was saved, and that I had "accepted Jesus Christ as my personal Savior." I made notes of all these locutions, silently vowing to memorize them along the route.

"Another thing," said Barton. "If in dire straits, you should Jesus them and claim revelation from God."

So as you see it was not I myself who produced the idea of "Jesus-ing" them, but Barton. Am I to be blamed if I interpreted the verb in a way other than he intended? Perhaps he is to blame for his insufficien-cies as an instructor.

∰ ∰ ∰

But I am outstripping myself. Each story must be told in some order, and mine, having begun at the beginning, has no reason not to take each bit and piece according to its proper chronology, so as to let each reader of this accounting arrive at his own conclusions.

I was driven a certain way, on the bed of an old carrier converted now to steam power. The roads directly surrounding our encamp-ment—what had been my former city in better days—were passable, having been repaired in the years following the rupture. After a few dozen miles, however, the going became more difficult, the carrier forced at times to edge its way forward through the underbrush to avoid a collapse or eruption of the road. Nevertheless, I had an ex-cellent driver, Marchent, and we had nearly breached the border of the former Pennsylvania before we encountered a portion of road so destroyed by a large mortar or some other such engine of devastation that we could discover no way around. Marchent, one of the finest, blamed himself, though to my mind there was no blame to be taken.

I was unloaded. Marchent and his sturdy second, Bates, carried Finger and his dogcart through the trees to deposit them on the far side of the crater. I myself simply scrambled down hand over foot and then scrambled up the other side.

To this point, my journey could not be called irregular. Indeed, it was nothing but routine, with little interest. As I stood on the far side of the crater, watching Marchent and his second depart in the carrier, I found myself almost relishing the adventure that lay before me.

This was before the days I spent trudging alone down a broken and mangled road through a pale rain. This was before I found myself sometimes delayed for half a day trying to figure how to get dog and dogcart around an obstacle. They had provided me a simple harness for the cart, but had foreseen nothing by way of rope or tether to se-cure the fellow. If I tried to skirt, say, a shell crater, while carrying the bulky dogcart, Finger, feeling himself on the verge of abandonment, was anxious to accompany me. He would be there, darting between my legs and nearly precipitating me into the abyss itself, and if I did not fall, he did, so that once I had crossed I had to figure some way of extricating him. Often had I shouted at him the command "Finger! Heel!" or the command "Finger! Sit!" but it was soon clear that I, despite pursuing the most dangerous of the two missions, had been disbursed the least adequate canine.

Nevertheless, I grew to love Finger and for this was sorry and even wept when later I had to eat him.

᛫ ᛫ ᛫

But I fear I have let my digression on Finger, which in honesty began not as a digression but as a simple description of a traveler's difficulty, get the better of my narrative. Imagine me, then, now attempting to carry Finger around a gap in the road in the dogcart itself, with Finger awaiting his moment to effect an escape by clawing his way up my chest and onto my head, and myself shouting "Finger! Stay!" in my most authoritative tone as I feel the ground beginning to slide out from under my feet. Or imagine myself and Finger crammed into the dogcart together, the hound clawing my hands to ribbons as we rattle down a slope not knowing what obstacle we shall encounter at the bottom. That should render sufficient picture of the travails of my journey as regards Finger, and the reason as well—after splicing its harness and refashioning it as a short leash for Finger—for abandoning the dogcart, the which, I am willing to admit, as communal property, I had no right to forsake.

Needless to say, the journey was longer than our experts had predicted. I was uncertain if I had crossed into the Midwest and, in any case, had seen no signs of inhabitants or habitation. The weather had commenced to turn cold and I was racked with fits of ague. My provisions, being insufficiently calculated, had run low. The resourceful Finger managed to provide for himself by sniffling out and devouring dead creatures when he was released from his makeshift leash—though he was at least as prone to simply roll in said creatures and return to me stinking and panting. I myself tried to eat one of these, scraping it up and roasting it first on a spit, but the pain that subsequently assaulted my bowels made me prefer to eat instead what remained of Finger's dog food and then, thereafter, to go hungry.

I had begun to despair when the landscape suffered a transformation in character and I became convinced that I entered the Midwest at last. The ground sloped ever downward, leveling into a flat and gray expanse. The trees gave way to scrub and brush and strange crippled grasses which, if one were not careful, cut one quite badly. Whereas the mountains and hills had at least had occasional berries or fruit to forage, here the vegetation was not such as to bear fruit. Whereas before one had seen only the occasional crater, here the road seemed to have been systematically uprooted so that almost no trace of it remained. I saw, as well, in the distance, as I left the slopes for the flat expanse, a devastated city, now little more than a smear on the landscape. Yet, I reasoned, perhaps this city, like my own city, had become a site for encampment; surely, there was someone to be found therein, or at least nearby.

Our progress over this prairie was much more rapid, and Finger did manage to scare up a hare which, in its confusion, made a run at me and was shot dead with one of my twelve bullets, the noise of its demise echoing forth like an envoy. I made a fire from scrub brush and roasted the hare over it. I had been long without food, and though the creature was stringy and had taken on the stink of the scrub, it was no less a feast for that.

It was this fire that made my presence known, the white smoke rising high through the daylight like a beacon. In retrospect cooking the rabbit can be considered a tactical error, but you must recall that it had been several days since I had eaten and I was perhaps in a state of confusion.

In any case, even before I had consumed the hare to its end Finger made a mournful noise and his hackles arose. I captured, from the corner of an eye, a movement through the grass, the which I divined to be human. I rose to my feet. Wrapping Finger's leash around one hand, with the other I lifted my revolver from beside him and cocked it.

I hallooed the man and, brandishing my revolver, encouraged him to come forth of his own accord. Else, I claimed, I would send my dog into the brush to flush him and then would shoot him dead. Finger, too, entered wonderfully into the spirit of the thing, though I knew he would hurt nobody but only sniff them and, were they dead, roll in their remains. There was no response for a long moment and then the fellow arose like a ghost from the quaking grass and tottered out, as did his compatriots.

There were perhaps a dozen of them, a pitiful crew, each largely unclothed and unkempt, their skin as well discolored and lesioned. They were thin, arms and legs just slightly more than pale sticks, bellies swollen with hunger.

"Who is your leader?" I asked the man who had come first.

"God is our leader," the fellow claimed.

"Praise God," I said, "God's will be done, the Lord be praised," rattling off their phrases as if I had been giving utterance to them all my life. "But who is your leader in *this* world?"

They looked at one another dumbly as if my question lay beyond comprehension. It was quickly determined that they had no leader but were *waiting for a sign*, viz. were waiting for God to inform them as to how to proceed.

"I am that sign," I told them, thinking such authority might help better effect my purposes. There was a certain pleased rumbling at this. "I have come to beg you for provisions."

But food they claimed not to have, and by testimony of their own sorry condition I was apt to believe them. Indeed, they were hungrily eyeing the sorry remains of my hare.

I gestured to it with my revolver. "I would invite you to share my humble meal," I said, and at those words one of them stumbled forward and took up the spit.

It was only by leveling the revolver at each of them in turn as he ate that each was assured a share of the little that remained. Indeed, by force of the revolver alone was established what later they referred to as "the miracle of the everlasting hare," where, it was said, the food was allowed to pass from hand to hand and yet there remained enough for all.

If this be in fact a miracle, it is attributable not to me but to the revolver. It would have been better to designate said revolver as their Messiah instead of myself. Perhaps you will argue that, though this be true, without my hand to hold said weapon it could not have become a Jesus, that both of us together a Jesus make, and I must admit that such an argument is hard to counter. Though if I were a Jesus, or a portion of a Jesus, I was an unwitting one at this stage, and must plead for understanding.

When the hare was consumed, I allowed Finger what remained of the bones. The fellows whom I had fed squatted about the fire and asked me if I had else to provide them by way of nourishment. I confessed I did not.

"We understand," one of them said, "from your teachings, that mankind cannot live by bread alone. But must not mankind have bread to live?"

"My teachings?" I said. I was not familiar at that time with the verse, was unsure what this rustic seer intended by attributing this statement to me.

"You are that sign," he said. "You have said so yourself."

Would you believe that I was unfamiliar enough at that moment with the teachings of the Holy Bible to not understand the mistake being made? I was like a gentleman in a foreign country, reader, armed with just enough of the language to promote serious misunderstanding. So that when I stated, in return, "I am that sign," and heard the rumble of approval around me, I thought merely that I was returning a formula, a manner of speech devoid of content. Realizing that because of the lateness of the season I might well have to remain in the Midwest through the worst of winter, it was in my interest to be on good terms with those likely to be of use to me.

Indeed, it was not until perhaps a week later, as their discourse and their continued demands for "further light and knowledge" became more specific, that I realized that by saying "I am that sign" I was saying to them, "I am your Jesus." By that time, even had I affected a denial of my Jesushood, it would not have been believed, would have been seen merely as a paradoxical sort of teaching, a parable.

⊹ ⊹ ⊹

But I digress. Suffice to say that I had become their Jesus by ignorance and remained in that ignorance for some little time, and remain to some extent puzzled even today by the society I have unwittingly created. Would I have returned from the Midwest if I were in accord with them? True, it may be argued that I did not return of my own, yet when I was captured, it is beyond dispute, I was on the road toward my original encampment. I had no other purpose or intention but to report to my superiors. What other purpose could have brought me back?

In those first days, I stayed encamped on that crippled, pestilent prairie, surrounded by a group of Midwesterners who would not leave me and who posed increasingly esoteric questions: Did I come bearing an olive branch or a sword? (Neither, in fact, but a revolver.) What moneychangers would I overturn in this epoch? (But currency is of no use here, I protested.) What was the state of an unborn child? (Dead, I suggested, before realizing by unborn they did not mean stillborn, but by then it was too late to retrace my steps.) They refused to leave my side, seemed starved to talk to someone like myself—perhaps, I reasoned, the novelty of a foreigner. They were already mythologizing the "miracle of the everlasting hare"—which I told them they were making too much of: were it truly everlasting, the hare would still be here and we could commence to eat it over again. They looked thoughtful at this. There was, they felt, some lesson to be had in my words.

The day following the partaking of the hare, serious questions began to develop as to what we would eat next. I set snares and taught them to do the same, but it seemed that the hare had been an anomaly and the snares remained unsprung. It was clear they expected me to feed them, as if by sharing my hare with them I had entered into an obligation to provide for them. I tried at times to shoo them away from me and even pointed the revolver once or twice, but though I could drive them off a little distance they were never out of sight and would soon return.

But I am neglecting Finger. The men sat near me or, if I were walking, dogged my footsteps. I found my hunger banging like a shutter and had no desire so strong as to abandon their company immediately. Soon they began to beseech me in plaintive tones, using phrases such as these:

Master, call down manna from heaven.

Master, strike that rock with your stave [n.b. I had no stave] *and cause a fountain to spring forth.*

Master, transfigure our bodies so that they have no need of food but are nourished on the word alone.

Being a heretic, I did not grasp the antecedent of this harangue (i.e. my Jesushood), but only its broader sense. Soon they were all crying out, and I, already maddened from hunger, did not know how to proceed. A fever overcame me. Perhaps, I thought, I could slip away from them. But no, it was clear they thought they belonged with me and would not let me go. If I was to rid myself of them, there seemed no choice but to kill them.

It was here that my eyes fell upon Finger, he who had shared in my travails for many days, the cause of both much frustration and much joy. Here, I thought, is the inevitable first step, though I wept to think this. Divining no other choice, I drew my revolver and shot Finger through the head, then flensed him and trussed him and broiled him over the flames. He tasted, I must reluctantly admit, not unlike chicken. *Poor Finger,* I told myself, *perhaps we shall meet in a better world.*

Their response to this act was to declare I came not with an olive branch but with a sword, and to use the phrase *He smiteth*, a phrase which haunts me to this day.

∥∥ ∥∥ ∥∥

It is by little sinful steps that grander evils come to pass. I am sorry to say that Finger was only a temporary solution, quickly consumed. I had hoped that, once sated, they would allow me to depart in peace, but they seemed more bound to me than ever now and even offered me tributes: strange woven creations of no use nor any mimetic value which they assembled from the tortured grass: crippled and faceless half-creatures that came apart in my hands.

I thought and pondered and saw no way out but to sneak away from them by night. At first, I thought to have effected an escape, yet before I was even a hundred yards from the campsite one of them had raised a hue and cry and they were all there with me, begging me not to go.

"I must go," I claimed. "Others await me."

"Then we shall accompany you," they said.

"I must go alone."

This they would not accept. *I cannot stop them from coming with me,* I thought, *but at least I may move them in the proper direction to facilitate my eventual return to my camp.* And in any case, I thought, if we are to survive we must leave this accursed plain where nothing grows but dust and scrub and misery. We must gain the hills.

So gain the hills we did. My plan was to instruct them in self-sufficiency, how to trap their own prey and how to grow their own foodstuffs, how to scavenge and forage and make do with what was at hand and thereby avoid starvation. This done, I hoped to convince them to allow me to depart.

We had arrived in the hills too late for crops, and animals and matter for foraging had grown scarce as well. We employed our first days gleaning what little food we could, gathering firewood and making for ourselves shelter prone to withstand the winter. But by the time winter set in with earnestness, we discovered our food all but gone and our straits dire indeed. I, as their Jesus, was looked to for a solution.

∥∥ ∥∥ ∥∥

BRIAN EVENSON

We have reached that unfortunate chapter which I assume to be the reason for my being asked to compose this accounting. Might I say, before I begin, that I regret everything, but that, at the time, I felt there to be no better choice? Were my inquest (assuming there is to be an inquest) to take place before a group of starved men, I might at least accrue some sympathy. But to the well fed, necessity must surely appear barbarity. And now, again well fed myself, I regret everything. Would I do it again? Of course not. Unless I was very hungry indeed.

In the midst of our suffering, I explained to them that one of us must sacrifice himself for the others. I explained how I, as I had not yet finished my work, was unable to serve. To this they nodded sagely. And which of you, I asked, dare sacrifice himself, by so doing to become a type and shadow of your Jesus? There was among them one willing to step forward, and he was instantly shot dead. *He smiteth*, I could hear the men mumbling. What followed? Reader, we ate him.

⸙ ⸙ ⸙

By winter's end we had consumed two of his fellows, who stepped forward both times unprotesting, each as my apostle honored to become a type and shadow of their Jesus by a sacrifice of his own. Their bones we cracked open to eat the marrow, but the skulls of all three we preserved and enshrined, out of respect for their sacrifice—along with the skull of Finger which I had preserved and continue to carry with me to this day. Early in spring I urged them further into the hills until we had discovered a small valley whose soil seemed fertile and promising. In a cave we discovered an unrefined salt. I taught them to fish and as well how to smoke their fish to preserve it, and this they described as becoming fishers of men (though to my mind it were more properly described as fishers of fish). We again set snares along game trails and left them undisturbed and this time caught rabbits and birds, and sometimes a squirrel, and this meat we ate or smoked and preserved as well. The hides they learned to strip and tan, and they bound them about their feet. I taught them as well how to cultivate those plants as were available to them, and to make them fruitful. When they realized it was my will that they fend for themselves, they were quick to learn. And thus we were not long into summer when I called them together to inform them of my departure.

At first they would not hear of this, and could not understand why their Jesus would leave them. *Other sheep I have,* I told them, *that are not of this fold.* Having spent the winter in converse with them and reading an old tattered copy of their Bible, I had become conversant in matters of faith, and though I never did feel a temptation to give myself over to it, I did know how to best employ it for my purposes. When even this statement did not seem sufficient for the most stubborn among them, who still threatened to accompany me, I told them, *Go and spread my teachings.*

By this I meant what I had taught them of farming and clothing themselves and hunting but, just as with Barton, it would have served me well to be more specific. Indeed, this knowledge did spread, but with it came a ritual of the eating of human flesh throughout the winter months, a ritual I had not encouraged and had only resorted to in direst emergency. This they supported not only with glosses from the Bible, but words from a new Holy Book they had written on birch bark pounded flat, in which I recognized a twisted rendering of my own words.

It was not until I had been discovered by my former compatriots and imprisoned briefly under suspicion and then returned to my own campsite that I heard any hint of this lamentable practice. It was enquired of me if I had seen any such thing in my travels in the Midwest. Perhaps it was wrong of me to feign ignorance. And I had long returned to my duties, despite the hard questions concerning dog and dogcart and provisions that I had been unable to answer, before there were rumors that the practice had begun, like a contagion, to spread, and had even crossed from the Midwest into our own territories. I had indeed lost nearly all sense of my days as a Midwestern Jesus before the authorities discovered my name circulating in Midwestern mouths, inscribed in their holy books. If when I was again apprehended I was indeed preparing to flee—and I do not admit to such—it is only because of a fear of becoming a scapegoat, a fear which is in the process of being realized.

If I had intended to create this cult around my own figure, why then would I have ever left the Midwest? What purpose would I have had in abandoning a world in which I could have been a God? The insinuations that I have been spreading my own cult in our own territories are spurious. There is absolutely no proof.

There is one other thing I shall say in my defense: What takes place beyond the borders of the known world is not to be judged against the standards of this world. Then, you may well inquire, what standard of judgment should be applied? I do not know the answer to this question. Unless the answer be no standard of judgment at all.

◆ ◆ ◆

I was ordered to write an honest accounting of how I became a Midwestern Jesus and to the best of my ability I have done so. I regret to say that at the conclusion of my task I now see for the first time my actions in a cold light. I have no faith in the clemency of my judges, nor faith that any regret for those events I unintentionally set in motion will lead to a pardon. I have no illusions: I shall be executed.

◆ ◆ ◆

Yet I have one last request. After my death, I ask that my body be torn asunder and given in pieces to my followers. Though I remain a heretic, I see no way of bringing my cult to an end otherwise. Let those who want to partake of me partake and then I will at least have rounded the circle, my skull joining a pile of skulls in the Midwest, my bones shattered and sucked free of marrow and left to bleach upon the plain. And then, if I do not arise from the dead, if I do not appear to them in a garment of white, Finger beside, then perhaps it all will end.

◆ ◆ ◆

And if I do arise, stripping the lineaments of death away to reveal renewed the raiment of the living? Permit me to say, then, that it is already too late for all of you, for I come not with an olive branch but a sword. *He smiteth*, and when he smiteth, ye shall surely die.

◆ ◆ ◆

BRIAN EVENSON is the author of seven books of fiction, most recently *The Wavering Knife* (FC2, 2004). A novel, *The Open Curtain*, will be published by Coffee House Press in 2006. He is the chair of the Literary Arts Program at Brown University.

K. BANNERMAN

ARMEGEDN, OR THE END OF THE WORD

Matt leaned towards Diane, still covered in the slick perspiration of their union, and tucked the sheets close about her breasts in a brief, loving gesture. He paused and decided against uttering the vague promise of an emotion he didn't feel. That cast-off statement would make work awkward, and they both knew that this afternoon romp was not about commitment or fondness. This was bestial release, plain and simple, so he held his tongue and instead wondered if it was wise to share a taxi to work. Should they splurge and take two? He opened his mouth to ask if she thought it too soon to be careful about office gossip, and found his throat unwilling to move.

He swallowed and raised a palm to his Adam's apple.

Diane propped herself on one elbow, noticing the concern blossoming over his features.

He tried again. He opened his mouth, focused all his thoughts to his sentence. His vocal cords twitched but no sound emerged. Matt bolted upright in bed and clasped his neck as fears of a minor stroke ricocheted through his brain. He could still swallow, he could move his tongue, his jaw opened and closed with familiar ease. But sound, the essence of words, escaped him. He pushed his breath through his throat but all he could manage was a meager wheeze.

And Diane, the careless tart, just sat there and watched him struggle! He raised furious eyes to her, to reprimand her for her unsympathetic silence, and saw that she was struggling to ask what was wrong.

The words had been stolen from both of them!

Her shoulders heaved in great, noiseless sobs, and he grabbed the phone next to the bed to call 911 before realizing it was useless. How could he explain? A recorded message claimed all circuits were busy, and he slammed the receiver down with such force that it cracked the plastic casing. Matt tossed Diane's skirt to her as he jerked his own pants on, and she understood, dressing herself while wiping the terrified tears from her face with the hem of the bedsheets. They took the elevator down to the apartment lobby, lips clamped and rimmed with white, and under the gentle hum of the elevator motor she reached out to hold his hand. It wasn't until they exited into the busy street, however, that they realized the magnitude of the situation.

All manner of people congregated in mute confusion, business-men with beggars, bicycle couriers and taxi drivers, mothers holding babies that wailed empty air. Hundreds upon hundreds milled in little bewildered groups, gasping like minnows. Most were in tears, frustrated and afraid, but some convulsed with silent laughter, buckled over against the buildings as the entire population opened and closed their puppet mouths. Some were crimson-faced with effort, trying without success to squeeze out their constipated vowels.

Diane and Matt stood in the doorway of his apartment block, and even if they could have spoken, the sight of so many would have struck them dumb.

What could they do but return upstairs, holding their heads and staring into space with the shock of it all? Matt made sandwiches and Diane turned on the gas fireplace in the living room, slumping in his favorite chair by the hearth. As he handed her a plate, out of habit she tried to thank him for the lunch, but only a faint hiss escaped. Her chin trembled.

Matt, disgusted by her simpering, left her to find a pen, but he could find no paper in the sparse apartment. As he passed, he grabbed the copy of *Finnegan's Wake* from the shelf, and he cracked the spine to a random page. Tearing it from the binding, crouching before her, he set pen to paper and tried to write.

Nothing.

His fingers fumbled, the dot of ink spread further and further. As his throat constricted, so too did his fingers freeze, and at last he scrawled a useless line and opened his maw to let out a scream as loud as a summer breeze. Diane flinched, expecting sound but hearing only the crackling of the fire and the rustle of traffic outside. Enraged, he crumpled the slip of paper between his wide hands and tossed it into the flames.

"Gawds!" he exclaimed like a gunshot.

They both seized with the sound.

He tried again, as cautious as a boy who's found a diamond in the gutter and dreads dropping it down the storm drain. "How..." He swallowed. "You...going?"

She furrowed her delicate brow, fighting to find the noises she needed. "Now...found...sound." A triumphant grin broke across her features. "When? How the? What could?" She gave a little squeal of frustration that sounded like "upploud" and curled her girlish hands into porcelain fists. With a sharp motion she yanked the book from his hands to study the first page and, committing a line to memory, she tore it from the binding and laid it on the fire. They watched the corners curl and the text crisp. It blackened into ash, she grabbed his fingers, and said in a high, clear voice, "riverun, past Eve and Adam's, from swerve of shore to bend of bay."

He smiled broadly and clapped his hands to show his delight, then gestured, "Again! Again!" Diane took a deep breath and paused.

Gone!

The sound had vanished into the air. She clenched her teeth like a dog and stiffened in unexpressed rage.

But he grabbed the entire book and consigned it to the flames, where it took only a minute to turn to ash, releasing a myriad of words.

"Waste nothing!" he said, "Speaking sparing!"

"Yes!" she agreed, then looked ashamed and nodded.

"Library? Go?" he replied, pointing to the door, "Burn all!"

Diane winced at the thought but nodded again. "Tell others."

They had only so long until they used up their volume of words, and others may have caught some of the liberated phonemes and spoken them without realizing their worth. They knew they must find people to help them, and using stilted gestures and random syllables, they expressed what both suspected: with every utterance, they were depleating a finite resource.

Who could have guessed that centuries of speaking had drained an exhaustible supply? The libraries burned, the bookstores collapsed. Families piled boxes of pulp novels on pyres, corporations shreded useles files, newspapers torched yesterday's copy. Leters and encyclopedias and telefone books became vast storage pools of stagnant sounds, worth more than their wayt in gold. "E" and "S" were precious, "Q" and "Z" were stil available in abundance, ampersands had not yet been exhausted & could be used without guilt. The akt of ryting wuz a forbiden pleasure, mindles bable wuz a sin; why, u might be stealing wordz from someone who realy needed them. Only the arogant engaged in conversationz. Only the wasteful used doubl consonants.

Languag had becum 2 precious 2 squander.

❖ ❖ ❖

K. BANNERMAN'S stories have appeared in *Parabola, Room of One's Own, Lichen Literary Journal, Premonitions* and *Neo-Opsis.* Her novel, *The Tattooed Wolf,* was released in 2004 through Double Dragon Publishing. She has a website: www.kbannerman.com

BRADFORD MORROW

GARDENER OF HEART

I know that I have to die like everyone else, and that displeases me, and I know every human born so far has died except for those now living, and that distresses me and makes most distinctions...look false or absurd...

—Harold Brodkey

Despite the grief I felt as my train chased up the coast toward home, I had to confess that after many years of self-imposed exile it might be strangely comforting to see the old town again, walk the streets where she and I grew up. Imagining the neighborhood absent its finest flower, its single best soul, was unthinkable. Yet it seemed that my visiting our various childhood haunts and willing Julie's spirit—whatever *that* is—a prolonged residence in each of these places would be salutary for her. And cathartic for me. We had made a pact when we were young that whoever died first would try to stay alive in essence, palpably alive, in order to wait for the other. Death was somehow to be held in abeyance until both halves of our twins' soul had succumbed. Sure, we were kids, given to crazy fantasies. But the covenant still held, no matter how unspiritual, how skeptical I had become in the interim. Indeed, I had only the vaguest idea of what to do. Just go. Walk, look, breathe, since she could not.

For some reason, I could envision the mortuary home in radiant detail. A breathtaking late-eighteenth-century neoclassical edifice of hewn stone, two imposing stories surmounted by a slate roof and boasting a porch with fluted marble Doric columns. Huge oaks and horse chestnuts surrounded it where it perched on one of the highest hills in town, which, aside from the steeples of local Presbyterian and Catholic churches that rose to almost similar heights, dwarfed everything if not everyone in their vicinity. To think that Julie and I, who grew up several doors down the block from this mysterious temple of death, used to love to climb those trees, play kickball on its velvet lawns, or hide in the carefully groomed hedges, peeping in the windows to giggle at the whimpering adults inside. What did we know. Crying was for babies and the unbrave, Julie and I agreed. We laughed ourselves sick and pissing in the greenery, and now, as I imagined, she was lying embalmed, a formal lace dress her winding sheet, in the very wainscoted chapel whose many mourners gave us so much perverse pleasure to observe over the years of our youth.

Mother would be present at the service, and our father with his third wife, Maureen. Probably a crowd of Julie's friends would be there, few of whom, actually none of whom, I had ever met. Parents aside, I doubted I'd be recognized, so much time having passed since I bared my émigré's face in the unrocking cradle of noncivilization, as I deemed home. If only I could attend her rites invisibly, I thought, as the Acela flew by ocean-edge marshes punctuated by osprey stilt nests and anomalous junkyards where sumac grew through the windshields of gutted trucks. As Jul's only brother, her best childhood friend, I knew what my sibling responsibilities were, even though a part of me presumed she'd find it apt, no, downright hilarious, if I chose to mourn her from our cherished outpost in shrubbery beneath the casement windows.

When I left home three decades ago, I went with collar up and feet pointed in one direction only: away. By some ineffable irony, Julie's staying made my great escape possible. Being the younger twin—she was delivered a few minutes before I breached forth—it was as if some part of me safely stayed behind with her in Middle Falls, even as a wayward spark in her soul came along with me to New York and far beyond. Julie wasn't the wandering type, though, and after college and a mandatory trip to Europe, she returned home with the idea of seeing our mom through a tough divorce (where's an easy one? I asked her), then simply stayed, as if reattaching roots severed temporarily by some careless shovel. For my part, when I left, I was gone. There were many reasons for this, an awful lot of them now irrelevant thanks to, among so much else, scathing but unscathed time.

By informal agreement my father and I rarely spoke, and my mother and I only talked on holidays or during family crises—which are essentially one and the same, by my lights—so when she called on a nondescript day that celebrated nothing, I knew, even before she gave me the news, that something was badly amiss. Her voice, raspy as a mandolin dragged across macadam, hoarse from years of passionate cigarette smoking, made her words nearly impossible to understand. If I hadn't known she wasn't a drinker I could have sworn she was totally polluted.

Your…she's…you're, your sister's…

I tried to slow her down, but she was weeping hysterically. Soon enough, I who had always scoffed at weepers became one, too. As tears swamped my eyes, I stared hard out my dirty office window across the rooftops and water towers of the city. A cloud shaped like a Chagall fiddler snatched up from his task of serenading blue farmwives and purple goats, and thrust unexpectedly into the blackening sky, moved slowly over the Hudson toward Jersey. My Julie was dead, my other half. I told my mother I'd be up on the morning train and as abruptly as our conversation, call it that, began, it ended.

Middle Falls lies midway between Rehoboth and Segreganset, east of East Providence, Rhode Island. A place steeped, like they say, in history. One of the diabolical questions that perplexed me and Julie when we were kids was that if there was a *middle* falls, where were the falls on either side? We knew that Pawtucket means Great Falls, and Pawtuxet means Little Falls. Yet while our narrow, timid waterfall did dribble near the main street of the village, where the stream paralleled a row of old brick-facade shops quaintly known as downtown, even in the wettest season it hardly deserved its designation as a waterfall. Nor, again, were there any neighboring falls. Be that as it may, Julie and I on many a summer afternoon took our fishing poles down there (never caught so much as a minnow), or paddleboats made with chunks of wood and rubber bands, and had a grand time of it by the cold thin water. One of our little jokes was that Middle Falls meant if you're caught in the middle you fall. Our nickname for the place was Muddlefuls.

Julie, much like me, was neither unusually attractive nor unattractive. We were plain, with faces one wouldn't pick out in a crowd. Both of us had brown hair and eyes, with fair skin. We were each slender and tall, given to gawkiness. Since her hair was sensibly short and mine a little long, I suppose that in a low-lit room it would have been possible to mistake one of us for the other. Like me, my twin sister had the thinnest legs in the world, bless her heart, with gnarly knees to boot. She hated hers—wishbones, she figured them, or scarecrow sticks—and as a result never went along with friends to sunbathe on the Vineyard or out on Nantucket. Mine were always a matter of indifference to me, and I never bothered with the seashore, anyway. Two modest people with even temperaments and in good health, entering early middle age, sailing forward with steady dispositions, one a homebody, the other an inveterate expatriate, neither of us ever married. Never even came close. Some of our aversion to the holy state of matrimony undoubtedly was a function of our response to our father's fickle philandering and the train wreck of a wife he left behind with her lookalike rugrats. At least for Julie all such concerns, from skinny legs to a broken family, had come to an end. Given the chance, how I'd have loved to take the old man aside after the funeral and let him know, just for once, how very much Jul and I always resented his failure to father us. As the train pulled into the Providence station, I found myself hoping that the embalmer had been instructed to go light on the makeup. Julie never wore lipstick or eyeliner or rouge when she was alive. What a travesty it would be for her to enter eternity painted up like some Yoruba death mask.

The autumn leaves were at a peak, and those that had let go of their branches drifted like lifeless butterflies across the road in the coolwarm breeze. I made the drive from Providence—bright, rejuvenated capital of the Ocean State—to Middle Falls, and as I reached the outskirts of town I was seized by an intuition of something both unexpected and yet longed for, weirdly anticipated. It was as if I were driving from the hermetic present into the wily certainty of the past. Providence, with its sparkling glass office towers and fashionable storefronts, was transfigured from the seedy backwater whose very name held it in contempt when I was a boy, while the scape around Middle Falls appeared unchanged. There were no other cars on the road so I could slow down a little, take in the rolling vistas of our childhood, Jul's and mine, and luxuriate in this New England fall day. A flock of noisy Canada geese cleaved the otherwise unarticulated deep blue sky. Look there, Bob Trager's pumpkin patch, Trager's where we used to pick our own this time of year to carve into jack-o'-lanterns. Sentimental as the thought was, not to mention foolish, I wished we could walk here again just once, scouting plump ones that most looked like human heads. And, feeling a little silly in fact, I pulled over and rambled into the field among the pumpkins attached to the sallow green umbilicals of their dying stalks, and might even have bought a couple, had anybody been manning the farm stand.

I called out, *Anyone here?*

A dog barked, unseen in a nearby copse of silver birches whose flittering leaves were golden wafers, barked incessantly, madly, in response. Unnerved, I traipsed back to where the rental was parked beside the road. In a moment that felt dreamlike as déjà vu, as I stepped into the car I mistook my foot for Julie's—by that, I mean, her shoe was on my foot. No question but my grief, which I had been holding closer to my vest than I imagined, was weighing on me. On second glance the hallucination passed.

Hers was one of those deaths that leave the living in a state of questioning shock. How could this happen to someone so healthy? Yesterday she was alive, vibrant, bright. Today she's mute, still, dead. Gone in a literal heartbeat. Before my mother and I hung up, I did manage to extract from her the cause of death. Brain aneurysm. Like a blood adder born inside a rose, a fleshy pink rose, or one of those peculiar coxcomb flowers, a lethal serpent that when suddenly awakened understood that in order to live and breathe it must gnaw its way to freedom. How long this aneurysm had been lying dormant in Julie's cerebrum none of us will ever know. Her death, the doctor assured our mother, was almost instantaneous. That my sister didn't suffer a protracted demise is some consolation, though one wonders what happens in a person's mind during the irrevocable instant that constitutes the *almost* instantaneous. It's the *almost* that is appalling in its endless possibilities.

Images from days long past continued to accrue beyond the windshield, like those on some inchoate memory jug, and I knew that while they were exhilarating as an unanticipated archaeological find, they were also a clear manifestation of mourning. Although I was anxious to get home—I'd be staying in my sister's room, since my bedroom had long ago been converted into a solarium in which Julie tended her heirloom orchids—I was compelled to drive even more slowly, in order to take in every detail of what I had so studiously dismissed over half my life.

A canary yellow-and-emerald kite in the shape of a widemouthed carp, or Ming dragon, ascended as if on cue above the turning trees, and while I couldn't see the kid at the other end of its silvery string, I easily pictured myself and Julie behind the leaves, pulling and letting out more line. After all, we had a kite that looked a lot like it, way back when. I drove across a stone bridge, a fabled one when we were young, beneath which hunchbacks and trolls loitered in the dank shadows. (Several women accused of witchcraft were hung there in the middle of the century before last, in good old Calvinist style.) My sister and I, left so often to our own devices, and admitted addicts of anything frightening or macabre, would egg each other on to wander down here in the twilight and throw taunting stones at the shadowpeople who lived beneath the bridge. Once, to our surprise, we interrupted a man under the embankment who chased us—yelping, his pants caught around his ankles—halfway home under the snickering stars. Here was a telephone pole we had once tied a boy to, whom we'd caught shooting at crows, our favorite bird, behind an abandoned canning factory. I could still hear his indignant, pleading screams in the wind that whistled at the car window.

Now I saw the church spires above the sea of trees, then one by one the charming clapboard houses of our childhood, and above all the mortuary roof, gun-barrel gray against the jay-blue sky. There were the glorious smells of leaves burning; a garden of dying asters whose yellow centers were catafalques for exhausted wasps in their final throes; the blood-red cardinal acrobating about in his holly bush. Julie and I loved these things, and today felt no different than decades ago. If I didn't know better, I'd have sworn that time had somehow collapsed and, as a result, the many places my work as an archaeologist had taken me—from Zimbabwe to Bonampak, Palenque to the Dordogne—were as unreal as my campus office cluttered with a lifetime of artifacts and books, my affection for film noir and vintage Shiraz, and everything else I had presumed was specifically a part of my existence.

My whole adult life, in other words, was an arc of fabrication. Oddly fraudulent was how I felt, unfledged, and in the midst of all this, also abruptly—how else to put it?—liberated. Liberated from what precisely, I couldn't say. But the feeling was strong. I reemerged from this small reverie to find myself staring at Julie's pale and slender hands where they lay like wax replicas on the steering wheel. The magnitude of my loss had plainly gotten the better of me. Breathe, I thought. Pull yourself together. And again the world returned to me, or I to it. I pressed forward toward the turnoff that would take me uphill, up the block where our mother awaited me.

Julie did have a boyfriend once. Peter was his name. Peter Rhodes. He was our runaround friend since forever, lived across the street from our house, was all but family. Peter was more or less expected, by everyone who knew him and Julie, to become my sister's husband. Had it happened, it would have been one of those sandbox-to-cemetery relationships that are inconceivable these days. Julie and I had the curbs in on Peter Rhodes from the beginning, however, and in my heart I understood they were never meant to be. Still, we did love to work the Ouija board in the basement, by candlelight, little punks goading the universe to cough up its intimate secrets that lay just there beneath our fingertips. Not to mention overnights, when we camped out in a makeshift carnival tent of Hudson Bays and ladder-back chairs. We played hide-and-seek, freeze tag, Simon Says, all those games that children love. We learned how to ride bikes together, and together we slogged through adolescence. Peter took Julie to the prom when we graduated from Middle Falls High, and I, in my powder-blue tuxedo and dun brown shoes, went with Priscilla Chao, a sweet shy girl who was as happy to be asked as I was relieved that she, or anyone, would bother to accompany me; not that I wanted to go in the first place. We four stood at the back of the gymnasium, far away from the rock band, watching classmates flailing like fools beneath oscillating lights, as our teachers stood nodding by the long sheeted tables set with punch bowls and chips and cheese wheels. In retrospect, I realize how normal—for unassimilateds—Jul and I must have seemed to anyone who bothered to watch. Throughout those years we subtly kept poor Peter at a near-far distance, especially when it came to some of our more transgressive ventures—indeed, he never knew about our passion for the mortuary home, its mourners, hearse driver, gun-for-hire pallbearers, and all the rest. Doubtless he would have thought us not a little odd if he'd had any idea about our graveyard rambles under the full moon, headstones sparkling naughtily under their berets of fresh-fallen snow. But then no one truly knew Julie and me. A bond formed in the womb was, it seemed, as impossible for others to fathom as to break. I believe Peter married a nice woman he met during his stint as a Peace Corps volunteer, having fled Middle Falls in the wake of Julie's rejection of his marriage proposal. To this day, I've never wished Peter Rhodes ill. I know Julie didn't, either.

Like her, I went to college. A scholarship to Columbia saved me from having to lean on my father for tuition money—I'd sooner have committed myself to an assembly line in a clothes-hanger plant. After dabbling in history and the arts, I settled into the sciences and knew early on that archaeology was my calling. Just as Audubon made his sketches from *nature morte,* I believed the best portrait of a person, or civilization, was only accomplishable after the death knell tolled. Schliemann and Layard were like gods to me, just as Troy and Nineveh were secular heavens. Conze at Samothrace; Andrae in Assyria. Grad work at Oxford was floated on more scholarships, and I'd truly discovered my métier, I felt. A first excursion to Africa, and I was all but over the moon.

As with most disciplines, archaeology is fundamentally the art of attempting to understand ourselves through understanding others. All cultures eventually connect. Language, myth, variant customs, mores, bones are like cultural continental drifts. Put them on a reverse time trajectory and they relink. They become a single supercontinent called

Pangea. My inability, my stubborn refusal to admit to having a true familial home, an ancestral hearth from which I set forth on my specialized journeying, I'd always considered a hidden asset. I had a knack for entering others' homes, that is to say ruins and burial sites, and there to quickly understand, sometimes even master, the essential *idiom* of a locale and its inhabitants. Middle Falls I simply never understood. With Julie gone, if I wanted to comprehend this place of personal origin, I might be forever locked out. All the more reason to honor our covenant. Perhaps, through my twin as medium, I might come to some understanding of who I'd been and was no more.

The house was empty. I assumed our mother had gone out somewhere to finalize arrangements. The front door was unlocked, an inverted practice poor Mom inaugurated after the divorce, saying there wasn't anything left to steal here (morose absurdity, but whatever), so I let myself in. Odd, she'd obviously been baking cookies, Julie's beloved peanut butter and pecans, as the whole house was redolent with the warm scent. Maybe she planned to host a small gathering of mourners at the house after the rites. Upstairs in my old room, I saw Julie's private garden of potted orchids and exotic herbs was as opulent as she'd described it in letters and during our monthly phone conversations (it didn't matter how distant I was, I never failed to call her). The scent, it struck me, was precisely what heaven should smell like, were there such a place. Fluid, rich, evocative, somehow soft. I closed my eyes and breathed this sensual air, and as I did, a wave of deep tranquillity washed through me. This tranquillity even had a color, a dense matte cream, into which I rose, or sank, it was hard to tell the difference. I believed I was crying, though the cognitive disconnect, however brief, wouldn't quite allow me to know this with certainty. The episode, like some epileptic seizure of the psyche, finally passed but not before delivering me another of the hallucinations I had been experiencing. As I turned to leave—flee, rather—the room, I caught sight of a vertiginous Julie, alive in the mirror on the wall behind a sinuously arched blooming orchid, her dark eyes as filled with hysteria as mine must have been. Then she was gone, replaced, as before, by me—and yes, my eyes displayed a scouring dread, not without a tinge of sad disbelief.

Nothing like this had ever happened to me, and if they weren't so eminently *real*, I'd have insisted to myself that these *petits mals* were strictly the effects of melancholy. But something else was in play about which I had no clear insight. Some incipient voice inside me suggested that the covenant Julie and I had made as children bore more authority than she and I'd imagined possible. Placing my overnight bag on her bed, I asked myself, Could she have managed to pull it off, to linger, to keep our childhood pact?

Voices downstairs brought me to my senses. I was about to shout to my mother that I'd arrived, when I realized I was hearing my father and Maureen, the last people on earth I needed to see just now. Like so many houses from the Victorian era, this one had a set of narrow back steps leading down to a pantry off the kitchen. Julie and I never tired of playing in this claustrophobic corridor, which was lit by octagonal stained-glass windows, and often used it, to our mother's exaspera-tion, as an escape route when we happened to be hightailing it from some chore or punishment. Its usefulness in this regard I valued now as then—having to confront my father at that moment would have qualified as both a chore and punishment—so I slipped quietly down-stairs and out the pantry door into the backyard.

Some clouds had intruded on the earlier pure blue above, and the temperature definitely had dropped since morning. I wished I could run back inside and grab the windbreaker I'd shoved into my bag in the city, but figured it wasn't worth the risk. Rolling down the sleeves of my shirt, I headed quickly across the lawn (needed mowing) and along a row of pin oaks whose leaves were ruddy red, like dyed leather. Other than the drone of distant machinery—a road crew clearing a fallen branch with a wood chipper, I guessed—the air was dead silent. Someone was burning a pile of brush nearby; a skein of transparent brownish gray floated across the middle air. Two girls, from out of nowhere, came running past me laughing wildly, paying no attention to me, nearly knocking me down in their great rush. It smelled a little like it might rain.

Once I was out of sight of the house, walking the next block over, I slackened my pace and contemplated, as best I could manage given the crosscurrents of what had been happening, what to do. Not that I needed to deliberate for long. My feet instinctively knew it was imper-ative to go to Middle Falls Cemetery. The graveyard was in a meadow on the far side of the town's pathetic waterfall, and it involved cross-ing down past the main street where, I expected—rightly, it turned out—no one would notice me, John Tillman, Julie Tillman's brother who'd defected a lifetime ago. The soda shop we'd loved to frequent was, amazingly, still there. Katzman's, run by one of the few Jews in this largely Christian enclave, offered the best egg cream north of Co-ney Island. Ancient but still alive, there behind the counter stood, I swore, Katzman himself, who had concocted for Julie every Saturday afternoon a superb monstrosity made with pistachio ice cream, green maraschino cherries, sprinkles, whipped cream, and salted peanuts. The thought of it still makes my spine tingle, but she loved it, and good old Katzman, too. I walked on, my head crowded with memories. There was the grocery market. There the post office. There was the combined barbershop and shoe store (its owner, Mr. Fry was his name, boasted of *head-to-toe service under one roof,* as I recollect). There was the package store whose proprietor was always lobbying, without success, for a repeal of the blue laws. And there was the florist where I'd stop on my way back to pick up a dozen calla lilies. It wasn't hard to picture my sister walking in and out of any of these places, and, yes, I had to admit there was a misty comfort in village life. God knows, I'd seen trace evidence of such systemized culture clusters in my own fieldwork, and admired—from an objective distance of hundreds, or sometimes thousands, of years—the purity and practicality of intimate social configuration. In many ways it was a shame misty comfort never agreed with me, I thought, as I crossed the footbridge that led through another neighborhood and, finally, to the cemetery where Julie was to be buried. But one cannot change intrinsic self-truths, I didn't believe.

What did we love about this boneyard? For one, all the carved white stones, the cherubic faces of angels and upward-soaring doves, the bas-relief gargoyles, not to mention the glorious names and antique dates. The trees here were especially old and seemed to us repositories of special knowledge; Frazer knew all about this. Here was a place our minds could run as wild as the spirits of the dead. This was how we thought, two pale skinny children with no better friends than each other. I saw, quite soon, half a hundred yards away, the pile of freshly dug dirt I'd come looking for without really knowing it. I strode between grave markers to the earthen cavity into which my Julie would be lowered to begin the longest part of any human existence: eternal repose. I peered in, curious and as frankly uninhibited as anyone who'd spent his time excavating artifacts of the long dead, and the desiccated, frozen, or bog-preserved remains of men whose hands had fashioned those very tools and trinkets. One always forgets how deep a contemporary North American grave is. My guess is that in our memories we fill them in a little, make them shallower, as if we might undo a bit the terminal ruination that is mortality. Against my archaeological instincts I kicked some soil back into the hole. Some queer corner of my soul concocted the idea that I ought to climb down into her sepulchre myself and spend a few speculative moments on my back, looking upward at the now fully overcast sky, try to commune with Julie in her future resting place while there was still the chance.

I didn't. Instead, I walked back to town, forgetting, in my sudden rush to climb the hill to the mortuary and view the corpse of my dear twin, to purchase the dozen lilies I'd wanted to lay at the foot of her coffin gurney, her penultimate berth. It seemed I was moving swiftly and slowly at the same time, thoughts streaming like an ironic spring melt under a harvest moon.

She and I were in a play together in high school once. *Love's Labour's Lost.* Julie was the Princess of France, and I, who coveted the role of King Ferdinand of Navarre, wasn't much of a thespian and wound up playing Costard, the clown. I can only remember one of her lines, which went, *To the death we will not move a foot,* which I naturally misinterpreted at the time to mean that, like Julie and me, the princess had no intention of giving in to mortality. Later, I realized Shakespeare's message was quite different. All Julie's princess was trying to say was, well, *never.* As for my poor Costard, I can't remember a single word I worked so hard to memorize for the production. What made me think of this? Impossible to know, since the high school was located on the southeast edge of town and my walk from the cemetery in no way converged with it. I felt that my mind, which unlike my body wasn't used to wandering, was out of sync with itself.

Reentering the house by the pantry door, I found myself alone, the hollow ticking of the kitchen clock the only sound in the place. On the table lay a note, a memo in my mother's gracefully dated round handwriting, with the words *We've gone ahead up the hill, will meet you there, dear.* What had I been thinking? Here it was already half past four, and in my daydreamy meandering I had managed to miss the beginning of Julie's funeral. No time to change clothes. Informed by many summers' trampings up to the mortuary grounds, my feet intimately knew the path. As I made my way, I noticed the edges of my vision were blurred, causing me to believe I'd begun to weep again, just as I had back in the city when I first learned the news of my sister's death. But when I touched my eyes to brush away the tears, I found them dry. Though this was not the first intimation that something might be wrong with me, that I somehow seemed to have lost a crucial equilibrium without which consciousness makes little or no sense, it was the first of my hallucinations I could not ignore.

I climbed the hill with a quicker step, yet it was as if I approached my destination ever more unhurriedly. What was before me oddly receded. It felt like I was walking backwards. All the while, my tearless weeping—or whatever caused my sight to smear—continued unabated, worsened actually, the neighborhood elms and oaks melting into watery pools of ocher, hazel, and every sort of red. I believe I blinked hard, several times, hoping to will away this tunneling vision. The great Victorian houses on either side of the block, dressed in their cheery gingerbread, were like shimmery globules of undifferentiated mass rising up toward the now-gray ceiling of sky overhead. By sheer volition I managed to reach the top of the hill, where I left the sidewalk and made my way across the lawn toward the mortuary.

In the mid-eighties, I was invited to participate in a dig on the southern coast of Cyprus. The Greco-Roman port city of Kourian, which had been partially excavated in the thirties, but had since been untouched by grave robbers and classical archaeologists alike, was to be our site. Early on the morning of July 21, in 365 AD, a massive earthquake had leveled every structure in this seaside town even as it snuffed out the lives of its inhabitants in a matter of minutes. What few people may have survived the falling rubble were drowned in the monster tidal waves that followed. While we dug from room to room through the hive of attached stone houses, the discoveries made by the team were nothing shy of miraculous. The skeleton of a little girl, whom we named Camelia, was found next to the remains of a mule—her workmate, we presumed—in a stable adjacent to her bedroom. Coins littered the sandy floor, as well as glass from the jar that once held them. Here was a wrought-copper volute lamp; here were amphorae. As we unearthed the physical record of this disaster, a tender intimacy developed between the members of our team and the victims of the quake. On our final day we made a discovery that was, for me, at least, the most moving of any I'd ever witnessed. A baby cradled in its mother's arms, the woman in turn being embraced by a man who was clearly trying to shelter them both with his body. Such love and natural courage were present in these spooning bones. I could hardly wait to get Julie on a transatlantic line to tell her what we had found.

For reasons that will now never be wholly clear to me, I did decide, as I approached the mortuary with its imposing, if very fake, Doric columns, to attend my sister's funeral from the vantage of our old secret hiding place. Maybe I felt, deep down, I simply couldn't face my father. Perhaps I feared sitting next to my mother, whose tears, no doubt, would be as real as they were copious. I don't know; it hardly matters. My vision, in any case, had only further disintegrated during the moments of my memory of the dig at Cyprus, and I had to wonder if I could manage to make myself presentable in front of others inside the funeral home. Pushing aside the hawthorne leaves, my hands splaying the shrubbery just as they might if I were wading into an ocean, I peeked through the window and saw, with what sight was left to me, the mourners within. A smaller group than I had expected. It was as if I could hear Julie's voice whispering in my ear, just then, when I remembered my sister's response to that call I made telling her about the family in Kourian.

Over the years, from time to time, she'd referred to me as a gardener of stones, but that day she told me she thought I was a gardener of heart. I liked that. It was the nicest thing anyone ever said to me, before or since. As the first drops of rain began to fall, and the crumbling margins of my vision grew inward toward the center of all that I could see, I felt a strong communion with the community of the many dead, and with my sister, too. My sister, Julie, who turned from where she sat in the front row nearest the casket and gazed at her shocked and vanishing brother in the window, her brother who offered her, as best he could, a smile of farewell.

BRADFORD MORROW is the author of the novels *Come Sunday, The Almanac Branch* (PEN Faulkner Award finalist), *Trinity Fields, Giovanni's Gift,* and *Ariel's Crossing.* He is founding editor of the literary journal *Conjunctions,* which has just celebrated its 25th anniversary. The recipient of an Academy Award in Literature from the American Academy of Arts and Letters, he has received other awards, including Pushcart and O'Henry Prizes, for his fiction. His first children's book, *Didn't,* illustrated by Gahan Wilson, comes out this year with Dutton. He teaches at Bard College.

LAURA MORIARTY

MARYOLATRY

"Dazed in silent explosions. Pasted down in fragments. We are strangely bent. Something like a smile or an eye hovers or opens. Wings spread like a new belief. Who are these monsters?" Ada writes at her table. She is expecting her assistant Dayv but can't remember having met him. "Things are occurring out of sequence," she thinks. "If it's a time storm we are deeply fucked. But of course I can't know that, though I think I do know it." She resumes her work on the war. As usual she writes and collects images—sometimes of herself but mostly not. She doesn't always know.

Then it starts. She feels herself running though she is writing. The panic and dust are there again like the sweet airless poison that is the Martian atmosphere. Cracks appear in the domes above. Ada makes it across a street where Stella lies prone.

Two hundred million guns rage in an oddly quiet battle. Huge clouds inappropriate and terrific rise up. There are no clouds on Mars.

Ada coils around Stella, gives her air. They enter into an earnest discussion about breath and death. "In," Ada mutters, "Baby. Out. There's something going on here."

She bends over Stella. "But if you could just breathe for me," she gives her air again. "I could maybe figure it or maybe it doesn't figure." And again, "Just don't die on me," cradling her as Stella seems to wake. "There's nowhere to go, but we really have to go."

Martians in rows fall down one by one. Everyone plays a part in the war. Ada finds them. Their pictures and statistics. She finds them and counts them. "There are many kinds of Martian but one kind of war," she writes. "Things explode for no reason or for reasons of their own. The dead are all soldiers once they have died. The world is littered with them. An incursion occurs or has occurred of light into a dark place. Too much light. Beams or rays razor-like go through everything. There is a lack of air in the screams. A lack of conviction in the eyes of the victims as they turn red or blue or gray depending on the weapon and on the speciation."

Ada and Stella hide in their tiny corner. They turn into each other. Like a play within a play they struggle to be separate from the drama going on around them. Finally they run. Flat out. They run away.

Ada is running again as she writes. Is she in life or only remembering it. "Perhaps I died there." Ada doesn't know. It is like any other night on Mars. Dust and things vaporized. Never enough air. A clash of realities of the worst type. No quarter offered by the believers. None expected by the targets. Women and clones fight the war. Fought the war. They seem to fight over and over. They think they are heading out, that they have gone, but ultimately they find what they fear. They are headed back, back into the war, into a planetary context of conflict and despair. There is nothing that is not unreal there. Only dislocation. Something takes you, draws you back and grinds you down, poured like ashes over the battlefield. Once empty. Now full again.

An overflight of Marys, called from all over the system, approaches. Most are shocked to find themselves back. Some have never been to Mars. That they are Marys only recently discovered to them by an ability to travel by thought and by a compulsion to fight in a war that most humans gave up in advance and any clone knows is hopeless.

Ada wrestles with it. Her work on the war is as much a struggle for her as her relationship with Stella. They contend in every way. Ada and Stella. Ada and the war. Physical, mental, emotional. Never really meeting but always in pursuit, as anyone is with Stella.

"She does follow me at times when I go. She does come. Not often but it's a sight to see."

Ada tries to find her place with Stella or in time. But she can't find it and they can't agree on the war. Whether there is a point to it. Their conversations are intricate and frustrating.

"That the war was fought for the Information Imperatives seems unlikely enough," Stella begins.

"And yet it was. It is," Ada counters. "Either it is absurd to fight a war over representing or there is no other reason to fight. I have said it before. The fundamental right of anyone not to actually become information, not to be productized, traded, copied, sold, sold to, sold out—the right to be real and live in a real world is something like what the Imperatives were about. You know that."

"I don't know it and neither do you. No one has ever read these Imperatives. Nothing is real anyway, least of all some imaginary clonish manifesto about Martian sales trends. Who cares?"

"Versions of the Imperatives proliferated. They were inaccurate and in doubt." Ada retells the story. "They were never written down or conveyed in electronic form. In a way that was the point. They were inexact, unreproducible, designed only to resist that Mars utopia thing everyone comes here for. They see it fail but they never stop believing in it. And who are we to tell them otherwise. Just some hyperdesigned clone like me and then you—female overstock brought here for the men. Naturally we don't believe in their idealism. We aren't designed to. We're designed for them, except in my case. I'm designed for you."

"You're not. You are just the past in the form of flesh, mama. The face of the Byron hotel library chain. Born to check us in and check us out. To keep track. All this counting. If you could count backward and cancel yourself I think you would."

"Not alone though. I'd want to cancel you too."

"No." Stella is not going along with anything. "No one cancels me. And nobody brought me here. Nobody brings me anywhere." She is already looking for a way out.

"Well then baby you are my utopia. I admit it. But that means two things. It means you are my problem, my dream. And it means you don't exist."

Ada struggles with Stella. She struggles with time. She seems to remember the conversation as she is having it. She tries to write and see the events, to arrange them. But Martian history is active. It is interactive. As she writes she is in the fight, to save Stella, to escape, repeatedly, to come back.

The Marys hover and leave. They hover and crash or drop their bombs. A haze of information floats, obscuring and yet magnifying the battlefield like some sort of electronic gas. The fiery explosions produced by the government are so much background to the real show. Events are interpreted as or before they happen. Mary bombs are made of facts. But the accuracy of the information in these bombs isn't legible to the targets or readers. They become confused once they are hit or die as with any other bomb.

"That the heroics of the flyovers make up for the deaths is questionable," Ada writes. "The whole idea of women and clones is a misnomer. It hides the men and the I who died. Or at least the men. The war fought along gender lines to end such lines and other illusions ended nothing."

"Nothing ends," she says to Dayv who looks unconcerned and at home in this endlessly retold, refought, pointless and hopeless war.

"It is my war," he says to himself. "But wait—did the I cause it? Or even possibly did I cause it? Are they even here other than occasionally as pilots. Is Mars their idea? Our idea? Is it a trick? What about sex?" he warms to his subject. "Did the I divide us or were there always

sexes?" Dayv wonders disingenuously. Of course he knows it was the
I. Everything is them. As a child of an I he should know. As a human
he remembers. He looks into Ada's eyes for an answer or corrobora-
tion but he sees only the war. He sees her on Mars with Stella though
he sits with her in the library orbiting Europa. He regards the woman
he thinks of as his boss and the one who he believes to be his mother
with something like reverence and nostalgia. They are caught. Everyone on Mars is caught. He feels the Marys swarm. Parphar and his
world view widen. He emerges from this long reverie onto a street in
the city. Ada and Stella run and at the same time arrive beside him, in
separate ships, as Marys.

Ada writes at her table. Simultaneously she sees herself and Stella fall from the Martian sky into certain death. At the library again,
dazed, she looks up at Dayv who waits for her to tell him what to do,
but she doesn't know what he should do. She looks down into Stella's
vivid eyes.

Ada, Stella and Dayv think together for a moment, steadfastly in
the library. They feel themselves to be at Ada's table, sitting together.
Dayv rolls tiny Martian cigarettes for something to do. They smoke.
The paper burns their hands helpfully, making them believe they are
where they are. They lay their heads on their folded arms. Stella senses
something about Dayv. She believes it has to do with his work at the
library. He looks familiar.

"Are you a clone?" she tries to ask, but they have all fallen asleep.

The horizon blows up repeatedly. The explosions are stiff. They
seem to take a long time to happen. Stella and Ada wake and look
around to see if they have died. They look at each other and down at
themselves. Dayv wakes with his usual calm. They put their hands flat
on the table, closing their eyes, imagining a ring of safety. As if this
could work.

"As we sleep we fly and as flying die back into sleep," Ada writes
later, if it is later. "The mixture of times in the Martian landscape is
hideous and exhausting. The idea of a time storm doesn't begin to
describe it. People die over and over. Weapons blaze and melt away.
There is no end to the war. Each combatant eventually realizes it is the
same war, tries to escape, lives in the future and is drawn back down.
The Maryolatry is reduced to a slogan. Women and clones—though we
were never the only ones. But maybe we were," she continues. "Maybe we are. Identifying with these despised creatures justifies nothing.

Things used to happen once. There was a history. Everyone claims it. Now there is only repetition."

As a hybrid, Dayv has a unique perspective, but he doesn't care. As I, he wants to eat. And as I, he realizes he is always eating. It is the beautiful thing about being one of the boys. They are not really all boys. But they are always eating. As a human Dayv wants to be in the library. He believes there is someone he should meet. Some bit of organizational culture he should share, but the war rises back up in his mind as soon he gets there. Dayv looks into the middle distance seeing the endless battle beyond his eyes. Ada writes. She watches. She finds two women struggling to survive. She sees Stella. She sees herself as someone else. She writes as if against gravity, knowing herself to be running and falling and flying.

"Bombs light up the sky. The streets of Parphar are like day though it is night and later like night though day. A woman runs through the streets with unnatural speed. She finds air where there is none. She finds a woman. She sees her fall."

╫ ╫ ╫

LAURA MORIARTY'S most recent book is *Self-Destruction* from Post-Apollo Press. A science fiction novel, *Ultravioleta,* from which the above story is an excerpt, is forthcoming from Atelos Press. A *Selected Poetry* is forthcoming from Omnidawn. It will include selections from her ten published books of poetry along with new work. Among Laura's awards are the Poetry Center Book Award and a Gerbode Foundation grant. She is currently teaching a writing workshop at Mills College and is the Deputy Director of Small Press Distribution.

Kevin W. Reardon

The Cloud Room

In order to relax after a difficult day, George would masturbate, then order a vodka martini. As a software consultant, George traveled to cities along the west coast. Companies who had purchased computer systems from George's employer would receive, as a bonus, a certain amount of George's life. George would sit in at the clients' offices as the staff learned how to use the new programs. George was paid, not for his expertise, but for his patience, as he explained, time and again, the most simple of tasks. In this line, George encountered the denizens of offices from San Diego to Tacoma. Some were affable and dim; others were contentious and dim. A certain percentage of the men were attractive to him. As he was bored beyond reason, in the boudoir of his mind, he tried on each new male trainee for their sexual fit. Unfortunately, the homogeneity of American culture made the entry-level former college basketball star in Sacramento just as nondescript as the former football jock, with an Adam's apple the size of a pumpkin, in Portland, or was it Eugene.

George's onanistic respites were, therefore, not inspired by daily stimulation. The unavailability of illegal drugs to a person in George's itinerant, disassociated circumstance, combined with force of habit, kept him stroking. Yet George found requisite stimulus in the liaisons of his salad days. At the age of thirty-four, George considered himself approximately 12 years past his youth. Happily, distant memories, being the most vague, were also the most malleable.

Having dipped the key card in its slot, George swung open the hotel-room door. For the next five days, this space would be his home. The room smelled as clean as a supermarket meat bin, hosed with antiseptic and left to sit empty for the night. He drew the drapes, threw his suitcase onto one of the double beds, then emptied his keys, wallet, a crumpled boarding pass and spare change into the middle desk drawer. He slid out of his loafers and methodically removed his chinos, folding them along the dry cleaner's crease, knowing they could be worn another day. Then, carelessly, he stripped out of his dress shirt, T-shirt and boxers, creating a laundry pile at the corner of the room. He didn't need to look in the mirror. He could feel the flab of his belly as it kissed the flesh about his pelvis. He remembered the clusters of hair along the atrophied biceps; the calf muscles developed by running through airports and standing in front of trainee seminars; the inert shaft of flesh at his center, which bent to the right, like his politics or the rudder of a ship struggling to keep on course despite a swift opposing current.

Having opened his suitcase, he dug out shaving cream and a razor. He knew from online that there were many gay bars in town, two of them catering to a leather clientele. Were he to visit one, he would fit in better without his evening shave. Still, he hated it when his face did not feel clean and, realistically, he knew he would be too tired to venture out of the hotel on the first night of an assignment. He didn't want to risk looking out of it in front of a client the next day.

In a zippered Eddie Bauer toiletries bag, he found a paper-wrapped cake of ivory soap and an apricot facial scrub. He would need them for the shower, so he set them aside. They weren't what he was really seeking. He'd packed in a rush and, if he'd left it out, he would hate himself, intensely. He'd have to use shaving cream, which dried too fast, so you would have to spit in your hand to get it to lather up again. By the time George got his aged rocks off, he was dying of thirst. Roll on deodorant also went dry, so he had switched to a sport gel, which stung, in a bad way. Once, when he had a cold in Palo Alto, he had used Vick's Vapo-rub, which stung in a good way. George made a mental note to buy more Vapo-rub, when he had the time. He was relieved to find, there in this second pair of loafers, rolled into a plastic grocery bag so it wouldn't squish open in transit, his beloved petroleum jelly. He kissed the tube, set it on the nightstand, turned down the bed so it would be waiting for him, and repaired to his shower.

In the heat of the gushing water, he washed away the hotshot who was checking his stock quotes while George was addressing the group, the old woman who needed to know the key strokes because she couldn't use the spherical mouse she'd been given, the office manager who kept interrupting. He applied the pumice-like facial scrub and, as he rubbed it across his cheeks and nose, the abrasion took on a satisfying, punitive quality. Then, stepping out of the shower, he wrapped himself in a frayed hotel towel and made a mental note: his disappointment over the towels would be the first of however many complaints he would include on his comment slip.

With the extras from the closet, the room offered a total of four pillows. He arranged them on the bed: two for his head, one between his legs, one at his side. First there was only cold cotton against his flesh. Then he felt reciprocal warmth, as if he were beside a loyal dog or a mute companion. George extinguished the bedside light and pulled the covers over his naked body. There, in the warm solitude, he attempted a fantasy about Liam, when they were twenty. They were about to graduate college and George was only engaged to Jen. Liam had promised, "You can do anything you want with me. I mean, I guess anything short of drawing blood." The sheets were the color of Liam's skin. The quilted satin of the bedspread, where the stitching was unraveled, was the texture of Liam's hair. And, with that thought, George was fast asleep.

When he awoke, the digital alarm read 8:46 and George struggled to ascertain that this was still the same evening and not 46 minutes into the workday which was to follow. He remembered reading in the elevator that the hotel bar, The Cloud Room, closed at eleven on weeknights. Happily, George would still have time to get off and get his martini before facing the end of another day.

The new Vaseline tube was coated in a static dust which comes with being in a non-pressurized cargo hold. George squeezed an exact amount into his palm and applied the petroleum product, that glorious extract of long-dead bones, onto his flaccid genitals. He closed his eyes and flipped quickly through his slide show: the football player, the basketball star, the office manager—no, that'll kill the mood—then back to Liam.

The warm electric drill vibrated in George's hand. He plunged the shaft into the hardwood floor in the attic of the house he had rented for a summer near Spokane. Once, then again, the whirling metal rod violated the unpolished floor. George screwed a metal hook into each of the two holes. Then he looked up to Liam, who was wearing a plaid robe with a velvet rope belt.

"Do you want to lie on the mat?" George asked.

Liam slipped the robe off his shoulders and let it fall to the floor. His pale, hirsute body was still in its lean, 20-year-old condition. Only now, a thousand years later, did George know what to do with him.

"I like the wood against my flesh," Liam said as he sat, then lay before his George, feet overlapped, like Jesus on the cross, arms stretched over his head, palms cupped open in a posture of surrender.

This weak boy wasn't even going to put up a fight. George snickered at his conquest, but his own hands were sweaty, so he wiped them on his jeans and produced, from the pocket of his flannel shirt, a pair of handcuffs.

Liam saw and pleaded, "No, not the fuzzy ones."

Obligingly, George pulled out his pocket knife and removed the fuzzy adhesive strip from the wrist side of the cuffs. The boy could feel the metal against his skin. Then, with a snap and a ratchet-twist, George cuffed Liam. The chain between his hands slipped easily into the metal hook in the floor.

Expressing a defiant freedom, Liam kicked his legs until George got down to the other side and hooked a second pair of cuffs about his ankles, affixing the boy with his backside flat to the floor.

In the 12 years since George had last seen Liam, George had refined this fantasy to a high resolution. When they had been together, they had done nothing like this. George had tied Liam's hands to a bedpost with that velvet belt from the bathrobe, but hadn't even bothered to restrain his feet. Liam had taken an appalling degree of pleasure in his submission. "This is great. I'm making you do all the work," Liam said and, with that, George really did want to hit him. But he wouldn't. George was not a sadist. He took no pleasure in causing another's pain. Simply put, when he was with men, and he could admit now that he would prefer to be with men, George liked to know that he was the one in control.

There, in his hotel bed, George heard children passing through the hall. A girl and a boy were laughing and their mother shushed them, reminding them that it was already past their bedtime. George waited until they had passed, then he rolled on top of Liam, one pillow between his legs, the other beneath his chest. Still in his jeans and flannel shirt, he nuzzled Liam's neck, ran his teeth through his armpit hair, making the boy giggle. George pinched one nipple, then the other, as Liam moaned ecstatically, "Ow." Then George kissed a path from Liam's heart, over his belly, through the rainforest of pubic hair, to the holy grail, the center and, with the intensity at its climax, the vision dissipated.

George choked on his own solitude, "You're mine," he repeated to himself, mantra-like, so the words lost meaning and the syllables became a sort of comfort.

The clock now said 9:12, and George could taste the cool oral friction of Belvedere vodka, with just a trace of dry vermouth and the salt from an olive. However, he was not prepared to leave unfinished the job at hand.

When George returned to the fantasy, Liam was on his stomach. George stood over him, admiring the supple curves of a twenty-year-old ass. He bent down to release the boy's legs. Then George unzipped his fly and knelt before his prey. Easily he gripped one of the boy's ankles in each of his hands, spreading him like a butter-basted turkey. George remembered the surge of power as blood forced itself into his erection. His soul was forcing the limits of his flesh. A panicked intensity came with the feeling that his spirit would break through its corporeal confines, pouring into another human being, killing himself, taking his lover with him, but having, at last, defied the God who had sentenced each man to his term in one of these solitary capsules. George slid forward between Liam's legs and drew his hips into the air, penetrating the boy, as this was a fantasy, at an angle which was immediately pleasing to them both.

With the first thrust, George said "You are mine." He slapped the boy's buttocks. "My ass." He reached around and grabbed the boy's dick. "My dick." He grabbed the boy by the hair. "My boy. You hear that, boy. You're mine now. You hear?"

Liam moaned.

"You hear?" George asked indignantly.

"Yes. Sir," Liam said.

"What's this?" George asked as he struck his palm against the boy's ass.

"That's my...Er, your ass sir."

George grabbed the boy's dick again. "What's this?"

"That's your dick sir."

And, as George thrust into Liam, into his hand as he lay on his stomach atop those acquiescent hotel pillows, the word became, again, his mantra. "Mine," he repeated until, at last, George had an orgasm which was satisfying, not as a physiological release, but as the fruition of that which he had willed.

George rolled onto his back. The best part of the fantasy was yet to come. When he and Liam were both satisfied, George would realize that the sotto voce harmony which had accompanied his every possessive thrust had been, in fact, Liam crying as he surrendered. Liam had murdered his own will. With the sound of this exquisite little death, George's power trip was mitigated by a superhuman compassion. He stood up only long enough to zip his fly. Then he produced the key from his shirt pocket and released the boy's hands from their constraints. Now sitting cross-legged on the floor, George allowed the boy to crawl across his lap, to rest his head on George's knee. He stroked his hair as the boy continued to cry softly. George shushed his child and whispered, "You're mine, don't you know. There is no reason to cry. You are mine." Liam turned and grabbed George desperately around the waist; his tears were suddenly sobs. "Liam, Liam, no, you don't understand," George was adamant now. "Every time I say it, every time I claim you for my own, I dedicate myself to you in equal measure. We belong to each other, Liam. We always have. We always will."

Having worked himself into an emotional frenzy, George kicked off the covers and tossed the pillows onto the floor. He would not be able to fall asleep in this condition. He needed that drink more than ever. By 9:31, he had washed his hands, dressed and slipped his key-card in his pocket. In the elevator, he noticed that The Cloud Room Bar was on the top floor of the hotel.

When the doors slid open, George walked forward into a silver-gray panorama, windows on every side. Though the hotel was only 12 stories tall, it sat in the center of a glass and concrete well. The neighboring structures were built at a distance. George advanced toward the oaken bar at the room's center, where the only light was focused. He passed a circular apartment cylinder, where each iron-railed balcony blossomed forth as a flower petal; an office tower of sleek glass, catching and refracting the beams cast by the city's nocturnal heart; the space needle, a flying saucer atop bent stilts, marking the path to the sea and mountains which lay beyond this urban outpost. Colored neon logos of hotels and store chains were emblazoned across this unreal view. George, who had unsettled himself with the fervor of his own jack-off session, allowed a chill to ripple through his body.

Taking some tourist rags from a rack by the hostess's podium, so he would have something in front of him, as if he were the type to read, George steered himself away from the bar stools. There was another patron there, with his back to the elevator. George was not seeking company. Instead, he nodded at the bartender as he passed and took a four-top table by the window. He could feel the cold of the wind as it whistled past the panes, and witness, as if not even glass separated him, a specter's view as it toured this earth before seeking home in a world far more permanent.

The bartender, a nearly teenaged girl with a ponytail and resigned demeanor, approached his table. She held her notebook on her tray, which cut into her abdomen at an angle to make a desk.

"Belvedere martini, up, with olives," George asked, holding one of the *Seattle Seasons* by the corner as if he were pulling himself away from the magazine just long enough to order.

"I'm sorry sir. We don't have Belvedere. We've got Stoli, Absolute, Chopin..."

George looked over at the bar. In the funnel of light which cast itself about a near-full pint of amber lager, the patron, a young man, was reading a thick, hard-covered book. He, the bartender and George were the only souls to be seen. A viscous rain splattered against the window and slid down the glass, coating the world in a translucent haze.

"Do you have Grey Goose?" George asked.

"Why yes, we do," she smiled, exhibiting more personality than George was willing to allow her.

"That'll be fine."

The boy looked at George.

George turned away, realizing that he'd probably been looking over for too long. The boy was in his early twenties. Most likely 21, if he was drinking in a hotel bar. Shaggy, flat blonde hair matted against his scalp.

Past George's reflection, out in the night, Seattle was silent. The city streets were nearly empty. From the lights in the concrete petal apartment building, the grid of streets which lay over Capitol Hill like a colonial quilt, and the steady flow of traffic which pumped through the arterial Interstate Five, George could sense beating hearts, the warmth and volition of other people, people not entirely unlike the young man who was now standing in front of him.

The book was folded under the arm of his chamois shirt, which he wore as a jacket over a thin-from-wear T-shirt with lip-like holes revealing the flesh of his abdomen. In his hands were wire-rimmed glasses, which George had not noticed before. He pulled the T-shirt up his taut belly, using the fabric to wipe the lenses of his glasses, and said, "I need to rest my eyes. I'd like to join you, if I may."

George's mind raced. The boy was cute. Everyone was cute at twenty. He might have been a hustler, but this was a reputable hotel, not Russia or Morocco. He wanted to talk to George. Clearly, the boy was lonely and, potentially, an easy lay. Or he wanted money. The way his jeans rode low on his hips was miraculous. George had to work early the next morning. He had just jerked off, so he wasn't exactly raring to go. And business travel afforded plenty of opportunities like this.

George was about to say that he would rather be alone when the waitress appeared with his martini and the boy's beer both on her tray. As she set down the drinks, the boy took his place opposite George.

George passed the keycard to the waitress, telling her, "You can charge this to room 433."

"Thank you," the boy said.

"Thank you?" George asked.

"For the beer," the boy said. George hadn't realized that he was paying for them both.

"I'm Mart, by the way. It's short for Martin," the boy said.

"So I would imagine."

"Oh don't be that way," Mart said.

"What way?"

"Like this. Sore at me."

"I'm not sore at you. I'm just. . ." George took a good look at the boy, who couldn't yet have been 21. He was fragile and powerless. George, probably for that reason, took a long sip of vodka instead of terminating their acquaintance.

"I can earn my keep," Mart said.

George swallowed hard, quaking from the vodka, then looked around nervously to see if the bartender had heard. She had disappeared.

"Not that way, dude," Mart said. "But I can tell you your dreams."

At the center of the bar was a pyramid of glass and alcohol, the steps of which were illuminated from below, so as to cast each bottle in the color of its glass or, were it clear, in the shade of its contents.

Bemused, George reiterated, "You can tell me what I dream about?"

Mart's heavy book, which now sat on the table between them, was a Gideon's Society Bible, presumably stolen from one of the rooms.

Mart, smiling, nodded silently, then took a long gulp of his beer.

George took more vodka and looked at his watch. Were he alone, as he would prefer to have been, he would have slowly drained the glass and soon been in a peaceful sleep. He had to spend the whole day talking to people, patiently listening to their complaints about the product, pretending to be interested as they told him about their families, their company softball league, the best place in town to get a lobster dinner for $15.95. George liked his down time to be alone time. Even though he couldn't muster the resolve to ask this boy to leave, even though he knew he wasn't going to score and, really, he couldn't

care less, he still wished he didn't have to be talking right now. So long
as he had to, however, he was going to do whatever it would take. He
downed that martini and turned, hoping the bartender had returned
to her post so that he could signal for another one.

"She just went into the supply room. She's got to restock before she
leaves," Mart said. "She'll be back in a minute."

"So where are you from?" George asked the boy.

"Don't you want me to tell you your dreams?" Mart asked.

"I think I'm too tired for this," George said.

"There she is," Mart said. "Karen, he wants another one," he called
over George's shoulder toward the bar. Mart continued, in response to
Karen's inaudible question, "No, I'm fine. Thank you."

The rain outside was now freezing against the windows like sheets
of frosting applied by a drunken pastry chef. Where once George had
been able to make out a green neon Sheraton logo, there was now only
a glimmer of verdant light. A warm draft blew at foot level, where the
hotel's central heating rendered livable this pocket in the atmosphere,
twelve stories above the ground.

They barely spoke as George waited for the bartender to produce
his second martini. Then the boy said, "Put out your hands." George,
after taking one intermediate sip, set his forearms on the table between
them and held open his palms. The creased skin within George's hand
was shiny, having so recently been polished.

"Is this where you read my fortune?"

The silent boy set his hands inside George's; they were small and
smooth by comparison, and they generated an extraordinary amount
of heat. His fingertips gently probed the arteries which drove through
the wrist, exposing George's pulsing vulnerability. They both knew to
close their eyes.

"You're in front of a classroom, and you're stumped, you don't
know what to say next, and you're sure they're going to laugh at you, so
you bolt out of there and you start running, and you run through the
halls and they don't seem to end and they don't go where you thought
they went and you just keep on running."

George opened his eyes to find the boy already looking at him.
What Mart said had some resonance with him. He taught training
sessions and had, in fact, dreamt that he was running endlessly. Still,
George was smart enough to know that running and standing in front
of a classroom must be two of the most common dreams. The boy was
a charming con artist. He took another drink and forced himself to be

brutally honest. Judging from the boy's posture, his speech, and the absence of any tell-tale signs, he wasn't even queer. Gay for pay was a power trip—how exciting to get a guy to violate his instinctive nature for just a couple hundred bucks—but the rush usually lasted only until you got them into the room. Then they were limp as pasta and, God knows, none of them could give a decent blow job. And, besides, George had already decided that nothing was going to happen.

"Listen, kid, I just want to finish my drink, then go to bed. I've got a busy day tomorrow and I need to get some sleep."

"Oh, yeah, sure." He looked dejected as he took another, little sip of beer. "Thank you again for the beer."

"You're welcome," George said. "No problem."

"Was I right? Did you have that dream?"

"Yeah, something a lot like that."

"You're just humoring me." Mart moved the pint glass to reveal two interlocking circles in the linen table cloth.

"No, really. I'm a software consultant and I have to give these training seminars."

"You move around a lot with a job like that."

"Yeah, I guess I do."

"Give me your hands again," Mart asked.

"Look, kid, I don't have any money and I'm really not much up for anything tonight."

"I told you. I'm not about that."

"You're not, are you?" George said louder than he had intended.

"I just like reading people's dreams. It makes me feel like we're connected. You know what I mean. I know you do."

George extended his hands and was warmed by the contact, however tentative, with another human being. He felt the draft at his feet as it shifted from warm to cool. Mart, with his eyes closed, grimaced, bit his lip, and affected an overly dramatic series of expressions as if in a desperate attempt to convince his companion that some sort of transcendental communion was actually taking place.

"Hold my hands tightly," Mart asked. "It is sunrise. You're on an unfamiliar street. You have been there in waking life, there are trees in concrete boxes at each side. You are alone and you blame yourself. You are confused, but you know, if things had been different, just slightly different, it would not be this way. And that fills you with rage, so you go at a tree. You try to break a tree. And this moment you will revisit in your dreams, a thousand times over."

Mart opened his eyes and gazed upon his companion, as if seeking a sign of recognition.

"Break a tree?" George asked.

"You will try to break a tree," Mart said.

"Yeah, right. Sorry, kid. That's not me."

"It is."

"Never had a dream like that in my life."

"You will."

Karen appeared at their table while George and Mart were still connected. Nonplussed, she set down the check and keycard saying, "We have to close up in a few minutes. Will there be anything else?"

Mart continued to hold George's hands but George, reminding himself that it didn't matter what this woman thought of them, responded in kind, "I think we're fine, thank you."

"If you'd just sign the check before you leave. Have a good night."

"Yeah, you too," George said.

"Hey, kid. Mart. Would you let go. Please?" George asked, after a few minutes more.

"I'm sorry," he said, taking back his hands and moving the Bible onto his lap.

"It's okay. The waitress thinks we're on our honeymoon, but other than that, no harm done."

"That's not what I'm saying sorry about, George."

"Whatever." George was ready to leave. He kicked back the last of the martini and pushed his chair away from the table. On all four sides, the windows were now opaque with frozen condensation. They were sitting in the middle of an ice cube.

"It was good to meet you, kid," George continued, hoping the boy would say something allowing him to retreat back into his own world.

"Please don't go," Mart said, as he pouched his cheeks with a cherubic quality that George had not seen before.

"I told you, I have to go to work tomorrow."

"It's just. . ." the boy looked down at the Bible in his lap.

"It's just what?" George asked himself why he had yet to turn his back and walk away.

"I don't have any place to sleep tonight."

George exhaled, exasperated. "Well, I saw that coming," George said.

"Please, George. I'm sorry. I should have told you that first."

"No, you shouldn't have. And you know that you shouldn't have. You reel them in first, with that 'read your mind' thing, then, when they can't get enough of you, you lay it on the table for them. Isn't that how you guys work it?"

Mart looked as if he would cry.

George couldn't tell if he hated himself more for having put himself in this situation, and yes, somehow, it had to be his fault, or if he blamed himself for speaking so harshly to the boy, inducing the tears that were now, ever so gently, breaking his heart.

"Would you please stop crying?"

"I'm sorry," Mart said through tears.

"Would you please stop?"

"I don't have anywhere else to go."

"Un huh."

"It's pouring freezing rain outside."

"Yes, it is."

"They said at the bus station that I should try hanging out here. That somebody would put me up."

"Of course they did."

"You can do whatever you want with me. I mean, I'm not like that usually, but if you want, you can do whatever you want, I mean anything short of drawing blood."

"Stop it. I'm not going to have sex with you." The words just popped out of George's mouth. They came as much of a surprise to himself as they did to anyone else who might have been listening.

"Thank you, George. I'm really sorry to be like this. I won't get in your way. I promise I won't."

Apparently Mart had figured out, even before George, that George had decided to let him stay the night. He stood up, finished his beer, folded the Bible under his arm and said, "That you do even unto the least of my brethren, that you do unto me."

"Look, kid, do not push your luck. I've got a room with two beds and you can crash there if you want. I'm either drunk, or generous, or stupid, or too tired to do anything else right now, but would you please spare me the Bible quotes."

"Thank you, sir," the boy said.

George signed the check and, side by side, they walked to the elevator, descending to the fourth floor. The boy was dwarfed by George's sizable frame. Though they did not speak, George felt a rush of delight at having the company of another person. If his mother had allowed him on sleepovers, or better, if he had had a sibling, a brother, this companionship would not have been exactly as novel as it now felt to George.

In their room, the flick of a switch lit the night-table lamp. Mart stood by the TV as George lifted his suitcase from the extra bed, onto a chair. Without untying his sneakers, Mart kicked them off and left them at the foot of the bed. He set the Bible on the nightstand, with his glasses folded on top of it. Then, still in his clothes, he climbed under the covers.

George removed his shirt, shoes and chinos. In socks and underwear, he crossed the room to adjust the thermostat.

"It gets cold up here," he said to the boy.

"Yeah, it does, this time of year. I should probably go south."

"Me too, I guess."

Behind the closed bathroom door, George brushed his teeth and imagined taking the rent-a-car and, instead of driving out to the client's offices by the airport, piling into the Chevy sedan with this kid at his side and driving south along the coast, until they were both warm and safe. As his heart was not in it, George did only a cursory job of flossing. It occurred to him to turn off the light in the bathroom before he opened the door, so the kid wouldn't get a harsh jolt of fluorescence in the dimly-lit room. He was glad he'd done this because, once he was out of the bathroom, he realized that Mart was already snoring. George flicked off the nightstand lamp, slipped under his own covers and, in minutes, had fallen into a blissful, slightly alcoholic sleep.

Shortly after five that morning, from habit alone, George's body stirred in his bed. When his mind was also awake, he realized that, against his chest, lay the beautiful slender blond boy he'd met in The Cloud Room. They were still in total darkness, but he could feel the boy's flaxen hair and smooth, nude shoulders. Mart took shallow breaths.

George's affection was almost out of control. The boy was beautiful and far too young, he thought. And George had to work that morning. He decided that now was as good a time as any to start going to the gym. He planned it out as he lay there. He would take his wallet and valuables with him. Most likely, the boy would be gone when he got back.

George attempted to slip himself out from under Mart's delicate frame, but the boy was awake.

"No, don't go," he said.

"I'm sorry, kid. This was a real bad idea. You can sleep here, if you want, for the rest of the day, that doesn't bother me, but I really have to get myself together and get to work." George stood up. He did not like to have anybody interfere with the swift completion of his daily routine.

"No, please. I want to. I want to give myself to you the way he gave himself to you."

George stepped back and tripped over the boy's sneakers, realizing that it was not the boy who had moved into his bed, but he who had moved to sleep with the boy. "Look, I was drunk last night. . ."

"Take me the way you took him. I want to be yours as he was yours."

In his T-shirt, boxers and socks, George shivered. "As who was mine?"

"The Irish boy. Liam. The one in your dreams."

"I really think you need to go."

"You took him for your own." Mart was sitting up in bed.

"Who the fuck are you?"

"You said that you would dedicate yourself to him in equal measure to the claim you made on his body." Mart stood. He was naked and pink and, to contain himself, George had to avert his eyes.

"How do you know any of this?"

"And then you married Jen."

"You will not bring Jen into this."

"You married her because she was convenient. She was just there."

"I loved Jen."

"Not the way you loved Liam."

George sat on the bureau. In the dimmest of light, he wrapped his arms about himself and, though he wanted to cry for that which, between Liam and himself, had not lived, George instead turned on the boy.

"Who the fuck are you?"

"To be loved like that. Even vicariously, as I knew it last night. There is nothing greater in heaven or on earth."

George did not want to think about any of this. Liam had been his best man. They did not see each other again after the wedding day. George and Jen divorced after three years. "There have always been three of us in this marriage," she once said, "You, me and someone else, and I think you know who that someone is." After the divorce, George had gone looking for Liam. He had left his apartment. His family did not know where he was. His credit cards and driver's license were canceled. The private detectives could not find him. They had concluded, reluctantly, after three years of taking George's money, that Liam did not want to be found. It was about then that George had taken this job, traveling up and down the coast, in his spare time investigating the places where Liam might find the kind of attention he needed. George would not think about this now because he was going to go to work. He was going to keep this job because it was the only thing keeping him sane.

"Please sir, take me." The naked kid got on his knees. "Take me in his place." He moved forward, hobbling to each side, pulling himself with his arms. "Take me as your own, sir." With that, the boy had made it across the carpet and had wrapped his arms around George's knees.

George defended himself in the only way he knew. He turned himself to stone.

"Get up. Put on your clothes and get out of my room."

"You don't want me, sir?"

"Get the fuck away from me, you freak."

Tears welled visibly at the corners of Mart's eyes.

"It's not going to work this time, kid. Get your clothes on and get going."

After an awkward interval, the boy stood up. He said, "I'm sorry."

George congratulated himself for having done the only sensible thing.

Mart returned to his half of the room and slipped into his white briefs, then his low-rise jeans. "Can't we just talk some more? Please. I need to talk to you."

"I have to go to work. All of this has been...extremely upsetting for me. I do not know how you know what you know, but it freaks me out and I don't want anything more to do with you. There, is that plain enough?"

There was a knock on the ceiling. George, though he hadn't realized it, was speaking so loudly that he was almost shouting.

Mart cast an incensed look at his companion and, in an apparent last-ditch effort, Mart said, "I can tell you how Liam died."

For a moment, George's heart stopped. Of course, it made sense that Liam was dead, but he had never let himself know that until now.

"Liam met the guy at the L.A. Eagle and they went back to his place in the Hollywood Hills. It happened the third time they got together. Liam didn't know when to use the safety. He would take it as far as it would go." Mart's tone was purely matter of fact, as if he had no grasp of the pain as it shot through his companion. "They tried asphyxiation the first time, and a four-foot-square holding tank on his second visit." George tried to shut himself off. "Then they did the bloodletting thing. The scalpel nicked an artery in his arm and Liam bled so fast that they couldn't have saved him even if this guy had called an ambulance."

Mart slipped on his T-shirt.

"I don't believe you. You're making it up. For some sick reason. You want to stay here, or you want to get back at me for not letting you stay here, or you're just a sick motherfucker, but for whatever reason, you are making this up and I hate you for it."

"You don't hate me," Mart said, sliding into the chamois shirt. "You hate yourself for letting it happen."

"How can you know any of this?"

"It was in your dreams."

"I never saw Liam after my wedding. Maybe I dreamt this," George offered, as if a complete disclosure were necessary to absolve himself. "But none of it is true."

"It is true. I am sorry, George."

George was cold as if he'd contracted a fever.

"Liam wants you to know," Mart said.

"How could you know what he wants?" George demanded. "How could you know?"

"Liam comes to you in your dreams."

George, on the brink of madness, denied that which he could not accept. "I don't believe you."

"Let me stay. Please, talk about this with me." Mart put on his glasses and seemed older, something closer to wise.

"Leave. . ." George began.

"Please, George. Take me and make me your own. Take me as you never took Liam."

"...This..." George yelled as Mart threw his arms around his midsection, holding on with an orphan's desperation.

"...Place," George bellowed as he thrust his knee into Mart's groin and pushed him down on the carpet.

The boy's glasses fell to the side. Tears rolled down each cheek. He sat on the floor for a while. Quick breathing suggested he had been winded. Then Mart grabbed the glasses and the Bible. With one vindictive glance back at George, Mart ran out the door, slamming it in his wake.

Again the knocking came from upstairs.

Like a headless chicken, a corpse animated only by mischarging nerves, George moved toward the bathroom, intending to brush the morning residue from his teeth, shave and ready himself for the workday ahead. It was only after he had expelled mouthwash into the sink, and glimpsed his reflection, that he was seized with grief. He threw himself onto his bed, crying for Liam.

George wailed for ten minutes, maybe more. The insistent knocking on the ceiling continued. George stifled himself in a pillow which smelled of Vaseline, sweat, tears, the night before, and of a bizarre kid who had insinuated himself into George's life, reading, as if it were nothing, even the dreams which George would not allow himself to remember.

George sat up. The gaping hole inside him expanded beyond even its previous bounds. He stepped into his chinos, grabbed his room key and ran to the elevator. It would not come. He flew down the stairs. In the lobby, there was no one but the man behind the desk.

George asked, "Did you see him? Did you see a kid leave? He was 19 or 20, with straight blonde hair, in a green chamois shirt."

The desk clerk was shaking his head.

"With glasses? Stealing one of your Bibles?"

A bellboy, in a maroon, double-breasted uniform, appeared with an empty brass luggage cart. He straightened his lapels and listened to the frantic guest. Then he said, "Yeah, there was a kid left a while ago. He went out the front. . ."

George pushed his way through the revolving door, sending it spinning on its axis. The sun was coming up. The street looked nothing like it had the night before. The wet pavement assumed an obsidian quality. A city bus passed, but there were no cars. With his stocking feet catching on the rough sidewalk, damp soaking to his bones, George ran to one end of the block and peered in both directions. He knew, of course, that Mart might just as easily have gone in the other direction. So George ran to the far side of the hotel. As he passed the revolving door, where the bellboy was standing, gazing in amazement at this idiot, George was seized with fury. He let Mart go just as he had abandoned Liam. If only he had been a little bit more aware, if only things had been a little bit different. This thought sent him into a rage so great that, without thinking, he seized the lowest limb of a sapling, newly planted in a circular concrete barricade. With all his might, George yanked down on the branch, hoping to hear a satisfying, brittle snap. Instead the tree emitted only a tearing noise, pulp cleaved from pulp. The limb remained attached to the trunk by strips of moist, white flesh and leather-like strands of bark.

⸙ ⸙ ⸙

KEVIN W. REARDON holds a B.A. from Brandeis University and an M.F.A. in Writing from Sarah Lawrence College. He lives in New York. Previous publications include "Teamwork," which was the 2003 winner of the Richard Hall Memorial Short Story Contest, sponsored by Lambda Literary Foundation. Subsequently, "Teamwork" appeared in *The James White Review* and in the anthology *Fresh Men, New Voices in Gay Fiction*. Another story, "A Family Compact," may be found in the online literary journal www.handtoothnail.com.

NOELLE SICKELS

THE TREE

Long ago, in a land very far from here, there lived a prince and princess. They had a comfortable castle which, by magic, stayed clean and in good repair. The weather was mild, and a great variety of wild trees yielded all the food they wanted.

Many animals made their homes in the valley in which the castle lay, but the prince and the princess were the only people there. They couldn't remember a time when it had been otherwise. They could not even remember having been children.

Each day passed much like the day before it. The prince and princess took walks, climbed trees, ate, and napped in the sun. When it rained they stayed inside and played checkers. Over time, each won as often as the other, so the winner never got too excited and the loser was never too disappointed.

The prince was a tiny bit lazy and didn't always want to walk as far as the princess did, so he'd settle himself under a tree while she continued on, and she'd bring him back sketches. Because she was such an exact copier, it was almost as if he'd seen the sights himself—a family of quail scurrying into the bushes, some gray clouds in the shape of an elephant.

One day the princess showed the prince a drawing unlike any she had made before. It was a picture of a huge tree with a thick, muscular trunk and waxy leaves so dark green they were almost black.

"What are these spots of red and blue and yellow near the top?" the prince asked. The vague smudges gave him a feeling he didn't like in the bottom of his stomach. Never before had the princess painted something that was not clearly defined.

"Fruits, I guess," the princess answered. "I couldn't see them very well. But see these burls and branches? It's a tree that could be climbed, I think, for all its size."

"What for? We have enough trees easily climbed whose fruits we know."

In the evening the princess sat on the kitchen floor watching their dog with her litter. Five grunting, squirming puppies piled against their mother's warm, moist belly in the unshaken belief that her flesh was one with theirs, that her life was their life. The princess understood their bliss because it was similar to the contentedness of her own existence. Yet she knew more of the world than the dogs ever would, and she wondered as she observed the tumbling puppies if there might be even more to know.

At breakfast the princess asked the prince, "Will you come to the tree with me today?"

The prince was often bored by the princess's curiosity, mild as it was, so she only included him in it when she could not contain it.

"Is it far?"

"Only a little beyond where you stopped yesterday."

The tree stood in the middle of a wide clearing at the top of a steep hill.

"You said it wasn't far," the prince complained, sitting down on a large root that had pushed up out of earth.

The tree was a type unfamiliar to the prince. This was not unusual, for every once in a while they'd discover some plant or animal they hadn't seen before. He could tell there was something unique about this tree, however. It was not just its great size. There was some aura to this tree or perhaps to the hilltop, as there is in the air just before a thunderstorm breaks, and a damp odor, as of salted fish, hovered in its shade, though no water was nearby.

"There's no windfall fruit anywhere on the ground," came the princess's voice from the other side of the trunk.

"I'm not sure there is any fruit," the prince said, squinting up into the tree.

"Look," the princess pointed, coming around to where he stood, "When the wind blows, there seem to be colors way up there."

"Birds, perhaps, or flowers."

"I want to go up."

"The first foothold is too high."

"Not if I stand on your shoulders."

The prince turned away. "Come find an easier tree."

"You won't help me?"

"No."

"But we've always helped each other."

"We've always wanted the same things."

The prince walked to the edge of the clearing where the path dipped down. The princess hesitated. She looked back at the majestic tree. Then she followed the prince.

That night the princess dreamed about the tree. She was standing before it. The air around her was warm, as if the tree's shade were giving off heat, and even though she trusted dreams, she knew that this was not possible.

A pig stepped out from behind the tree and stared at her with tiny, pale eyes. The sow was pinkish-white and corpulent, with slightly swaying teats full of milk. White hairs stood stiffly away from her soft skin. Her snout was smooth and free of clinging dirt. She lifted this snout toward the princess and seemed to smile at her.

"You've come back," said the pig. Her voice resonated from her head though her mouth did not open. "As you were meant to do."

"I want to climb the tree."

"You are not afraid?"

"What is that?"

"To be afraid is to want and not act, to ask and not listen to an answer."

The princess considered a moment. "When I hunger, I eat. When I tire, I rest. When I see, I draw. I am not afraid."

"You speak of simple things," the pig said, "but you are the one nevertheless."

The animal lowered her snout and rooted in a thatch of sorrel growing at her feet.

"The way down will be more difficult than the way up," said the pig, "because then you will know what you have to lose."

When the princess told the prince of her dream, he said, "You can't dream about something that didn't happen."

After lunch, she left him dozing on the riverbank and hiked to the tree alone. While she was circling the tree searching for any irregularity in the trunk that would allow her to begin her climb, a movement in the lower branches caught her eye. An albino anaconda spiraled slowly down the tree's trunk. The afternoon sunlight, filtered by a few wispy clouds and the tree's leaves, gave the snake's body a rosy tint. It stopped with its head at the level of the princess' knees and remained coiled around the tree like a liana.

"Sister Snake," the princess said, "You are strong and I am light. Will you let me step upon you?"

She did not expect an answer. Even in that marvelous land, animals did not speak. But they did listen, and they responded by going or staying.

A ripple ran along the length of the thick body, but the snake stayed in place. Putting one foot on the snake's lowest coil and stretching to grab with both hands onto the next coil, the princess ascended the snake like a ladder. Its skin was cool and slippery beneath her bare feet.

Soon she was off the snake, up a span of trunk, and into the lower branches of the tree. She looked down. The snake had slithered away. She had an unbroken view along the tall stem to the hard ground. The prince appeared at the base of the tree, waving his arms at her.

"Come down," he yelled. "This tree is not for climbing."

The princess looked above her. The top was far away. No fruits could be seen. Perhaps the prince was right.

The princess thought of the pig, who had called her "the one." The prince would probably say it was foolish of her to set such store by a dream, yet just remembering the pig strengthened the princess's desire to climb to the top of the tree. She believed that if she gave up now, the joy of climbing any tree would be lost to her forever.

The princess climbed on and on, staying close to the trunk where the branches were sturdiest. As she neared the top, the limbs were more slender. She had to plan each step. At last the princess's head and shoulders pushed through a final layer of leaves, and she found herself in bright sunlight surveying the leafy dome of the tree's crown.

To her great satisfaction she saw, glinting here and there among the greenery, fruits the size and shape of apples. Their skin was iridescent and shone blue-gold or red-gold. The princess snapped two fruits from their short stems. She took a deep bite of one.

The flesh was soft and light brown, like a bruised peach. She took more bites, and to her surprise, each bite had a taste different from the previous one. The first mouthful was honey-sweet, the second salty, the next as tart as lemon, and the next bitter. Then the bitterness was cleansed by the sweet taste again. The pit of the strange fruit was firmer than the flesh, but still soft, so the princess ate it, too.

As soon as she had swallowed the last bit, the princess felt a rumbling in her stomach. She began to sweat. The leaves whispered around her. The fruits glowed brightly, and a humming came from them as of hundreds of voices. Slowly, the humming grew louder, until the princess's lungs vibrated with it.

The princess wished she were on the ground with the prince, or better still, far away from the hilltop and the tree. Now colors as well as sound pulsed out from the fruits.

"You have eaten well." The humming had shaped itself into words, but the princess could not say she truly heard them. They were more like thoughts in her own mind.

"Nothing shall be as it was. Look and see."

The princess looked into the valley. She saw a wolf spring upon a fawn. The princess' heart thudded with the fawn's terror; her back stiffened with its desperate struggle; her legs felt its collapse; and in her mind the princess caught the fawn's final image of a sad-eyed doe in a quiet thicket. At the same time, the princess also felt the wolf's hunger in her belly and its ferocious strength in her arms. She tasted the first wonderful rush of blood from the fawn's neck, the first quivering mouthful of hot meat.

She turned from this scene to the curving semi-circle of the horizon. Mountains edged the central section. She had never considered exploring them; they had always seemed merely a backdrop, as unattainable as the sky. Now she longed to visit them.

The princess looked down through the branches to the prince far below. He sat picking idly at some clover, his back against the trunk of the huge tree. A great tenderness for him swelled her throat. Tears formed. She had only before known tears when sand blew into her eyes.

She recalled all the times the prince had waited patiently under some tree for her when he would have been more comfortable at home. She thought of how he let her put her cold feet against him at night and how his body warmth carried her into sleep. She thought, too, of how he retrieved her drawings from the careless corners where she'd left them and hung them around the castle.

As she watched him, the princess felt a flutter in the hammock of muscles and flesh between her legs. Arching herself gently against the tree's trunk, she closed her eyes and remembered the sheen of the prince's skin under moonlight, the wash of small shadows over the sculpted hardness of his thighs, his arms, his torso.

It was at the full moon that the prince would lay on top of her, and they would rock together. Now, in the tree, with no moon to signal her, the princess yearned for the prince.

Her body called her attention in other ways, too. It was heavy and tired from the long climb. She felt its fragility and recognized for the first time the danger of her situation. One misstep and she'd lie broken at the prince's feet.

The humming had faded. The fruits hid again under the spatulate leaves. Nervously, the princess lowered one foot and groped for a place to put it. All the way down, the tree, which had seemed to embrace her on the way up, now seemed to test her. Slender twigs whipped her legs.

Sharp-edged leaves scratched her face. Rough bark scraped her knees and the insides of her arms.

The princess told herself the tree was the same, that it was something inside of her that had changed. Though she had no name for fear, she knew the feeling clutching her heart was the culprit that was making her descent so difficult. Fear followed her every move like a new-hatched gosling doggedly trailing its mother.

She was squeezing the second fruit so tightly her fingers made little indentations in it. Sticky juice bled over her hand. Small black flies bit her knuckles and the back of her hand, provoking itchy red welts.

Finally she was sliding down the last stretch of trunk. Here the bark was smoother. The prince reached up and lifted her down. The princess laughed with exhilaration to find herself on the ground again. She laughed also at the neat prince, who stood by awaiting her report, no trace of urgency in him.

"This is for you," she said, offering him the fruit.

He took it gingerly between two fingertips.

"Have you had one?" he asked.

"Oh, yes," she said. "That's why you must have this one."

"What do you mean?"

"I am different for having eaten the fruit."

"You don't look different."

"You do."

The prince glanced down at himself and shrugged. He examined the fruit and sniffed tentatively at it.

"Oh, don't be so dull. Eat. Eat and awaken." The princess was seized with irritation at the placid prince. She wanted to knock him to the ground and push the fruit into his mouth.

"I'm not hungry."

"You don't need to be hungry to eat this fruit," the princess said angrily.

The prince arched his eyebrows.

"Of course I need to be hungry before I eat," he said, amused.

The princess decided it was wiser to wait than to continue arguing. Inevitably, the prince would get hungry, and she would see that the precious fruit was close at hand when he did. She went with him to the river to bathe her scratches.

But at dinner, the prince said he wasn't in the mood for fruit. In the morning, he got up early and breakfasted alone. By lunch, the fruit's skin had darkened and shriveled, and it was emitting a faintly rotten odor.

"Throw that thing away," the prince said when the princess offered it to him. He reached for a bunch of red grapes in the middle of the table.

The princess grabbed the grapes and hurled them out the open window. The prince stared down at the grapes splashed over the flagstones, then turned back to the table, as if dumbfounded that the grapes were not still there.

"Eat," the princess ordered, slapping the unappetizing fruit into his hand.

"I do as I please," he said. He set the fruit on the table and left.

Through the window, the princess could see him picking grapes in the arbor. Sunlight and shade mottled his figure as he walked languidly alongside the vine. She thought about how different his body was from hers and about how much that pleased her. She knew it pleased him, too, and that that pleasure was enough for him, along with the walks and the swims and the checkers games. Once it had been enough for her, too.

It came to her that he would never eat the fruit she had labored to bring him. She felt painfully separated from the prince, who had been her lifelong companion. The princess took the forlorn fruit from the table and ate it herself.

In the garden, the princess came up behind the prince and tapped his elbow. He turned and smiled at her. He did not hold on to angers. She lifted her fingers to his dark curls and gently pulled his face to hers. She kissed him, sliding her tongue inside his mouth.

"How strangely you taste," the prince said.

"From the fruit."

"You ate it? Well, then, that's done."

The princess nodded. The prince, puzzled by the sadness in her expression, stroked her face gently.

"I want to go to the mountains," she said.

"So far away?"

"We could carry food with us."

"We've never had to carry food before."

"The time has come to do things we have never done."

The princess reclined on a cushiony patch of moss and beckoned to the prince. A bar of sunlight burnished the princess's fair hair so that she seemed to be herself a source of light. He stretched out beside her. She kissed him slowly, again giving him her tongue. Again he tasted the lingering flavors of the troublesome fruit.

All thought of the fruit and the princess's odd behavior soon passed from his mind, however. He pulled her to him eagerly, craving to fill her every contour and crevice, feeling that he had not enough parts to his body to stroke against her and in her. Stunned by his own desires, he was about to apologize when he noticed that the princess was clambering over him with an energy even greater than his. This alarmed him slightly, but he could not maintain his alarm. He collapsed into his sensations.

Afterward, he was too embarrassed by what had happened to look her in the face.

"I'm still hungry," he said, standing up. "Come help me find a honeycomb."

The princess was saddened by the prince's easy resumption of an ordinary day, but she made no protest. She saw that he could not want what she wanted, or not in the same ways, and she didn't know how to explain herself to him.

In the weeks that followed, the princess did not mention the mountains again, but on their daily walks she coaxed the prince to venture farther and farther from home. They left familiar groves and travelled more deeply each day into the savannah that spread between the forest and the distant mountains.

When the heat of the day tired them, they tamped the tall yellowed grass down and sat to eat whatever small snack they'd brought with them.

Sometimes, they made love, while the grasses' feathery seed-heads whispered above them. On those days, the princess tried to talk to the prince about the new things she had been feeling and thinking since her visit to the great tree, though she never told him that the fruit was what had brought these things to her notice. He'd listen in a drowsy sort of way, but he often forgot what she'd said from one session to the next.

"Do you like these expeditions?" she asked one afternoon.

"Sometimes," he answered. "But we take them too often."

"Don't you like seeing new places? Isn't it exciting?"

"Too much excitement isn't good for us. Especially not for you," the prince said. "It tips you into wanting more."

"Well, of course," the princess replied in irritation. "Life is short."

"Why are you always saying things like that?"

"Because they're true."

The prince shrugged, not wishing to argue.

"Let's go back," he said.

"I'm going on," the princess said.

Her voice was calm, but determined. Still, the prince couldn't believe she'd go on if he didn't accompany her. He began walking back the way they had come.

After several yards, he turned around. The princess was standing where he had left her. They stared at each other for several minutes without speaking.

"Don't worry, I'll return," she called and began to back away. "I hope."

The prince could see she was crying. Her behavior was a complete mystery to him.

"Why are you doing this?" he shouted.

"I have to."

She pivoted and ran, as if she were being chased.

She stayed away for three days. She had been frightened at times and lonely, but she had also felt joy and peace. And she had taken pleasure even in the uncomfortable emotions because she came to see they were as real and important to her well-being as food or water.

The prince had not fared as well. He was at loose ends the whole time she was away, and he did not sleep well. Though the princess went out on her own many times more, the prince never got used to it, and he never understood why she went. However, he persistently declined to go with her, holding to his opinion that too much excitement was not good.

The princess still brought home drawings, and though the prince insisted repeatedly that he preferred her pictures from "the old days," he continued to frame them and hang them up around the castle, though he did tend to put them in rooms that were seldom used.

The princess's new drawings were not strict representations. The prince could tell this even though he had not seen the real-life subjects. The colors were too vibrant and the juxtaposition of objects too unusual to be simply recorded sights. Once in a while he himself was included in a picture, always in a surprising way, such as flying over the treetops or blindfolded and purple-skinned. One time the prince asked the princess about her new style, and she said she drew how she felt about what she saw. He didn't ask her about it again.

Finally, after many years, the princess died. She had told him this would happen to them both some day, but he had never been able to take hold of such an idea.

The prince walked alone where they had walked together and tried to remember everything she had ever said to him, but he couldn't recall the parts he had not understood, and he feared they were the most important parts.

He took down all her drawings and spread them in the courtyard. He began moving them around, grouping them. When at last he saw all the trees together, and all the flowers together, and all the monkeys and lizards and hawks and other animals together, he noticed something startling.

The "old" pictures, which he had always said he preferred, paled in comparison to the pictures done after the princess had begun her solitary expeditions. Though the later pictures were, strictly speaking, inaccurate portraits, they gave a stronger impression of true, breathing life than the more careful earlier ones. There was a pineapple he wished to taste, a jaguar whose pelt he longed to touch, a pig he could almost smell.

The prince realized that, like the paintings, his own life had been livelier and bigger, though more difficult, too, after the princess changed. He wished he had tried harder to appreciate what she had offered him.

Gradually, the prince rehung the drawings. For his bedroom, he chose a picture of the full moon done in blues and grays and a strangely luminescent white.

It was one of the last drawings the princess had made. She'd said that while she worked on it, she felt as full as the moon and almost as ancient. When he looked at it, the prince, too, felt full and ancient; it made him happy to think he was sharing a feeling with the princess.

But the drawing made him feel something more. It reminded him of their early time together, and though he saw now that what had come after was more valuable, he still cherished the memory of the past's sweet simplicity. He hoped the princess would not begrudge him that.

❦ ❦ ❦

NOELLE SICKELS has published two historical novels, *Walking West* and *The Shopkeeper's Wife*, both from St. Martin's Press. She has also had short stories, poems, and essays in numerous small press anthologies and literary journals.

Terry Gates-Grimwood

Nobody Walks in London

(For Faye)

And so, as the light faded from evening gold to night black, I found myself on Birmingham station's lonely platform, my father's ancient *London A to Z* in hand. A bitter wind howled along the deserted railway line. I shivered, cursing my stupidity, for I had neglected to don warm clothes in my fever to be on with my adventure, and wore only a Brummie farmer's traditional work shirt, leather waistcoat, breeches and boots.

Guilt had brought me to this Godforsaken spot. My beautiful Maria, dead upon our nuptial bed, her soul forfeit because I had neglected to pay my income tax…

"You only have yourself to blame, Jonathon," the Doctor had said as he pulled the white sheet over that most beautiful of faces. "You know as well as I do that a final demand has to be paid within forty-three minutes of receipt."

"But I was in the fields, tending my pigs."

"Pigs are no excuse. And stop blubbering man. Take another wife. There's hundreds of the damn things in this village. Birmingham is renowned for them. Women everywhere, and all eligible."

"I couldn't. Maria was…"

"Nonsense. Any woman will do, as long as she can cook and sew and mother children. Some of our Brummie women can even repair tractors you know. Damn useful for an agricultural type like you eh?"

"But I loved Maria. There could be no other."

"I'm sorry. Dead you see. Nothing to be done. The Government's already got her soul. Taxes have to be paid."

"I'll get it back."

"That's dangerous talk."

"I'll go to London. To the Houses of Parliament. And I'll…I'll lobby."

"Don't do it my boy."

"My mind's made up."

"I was afraid of that. You always were a stubborn one. 'He'll be stubborn one' I said to your sainted mother as I pulled you out of her womb. Well. a word of advice. When you get there, take the tube. Nobody walks in London..."

My reverie was broken by a ghostly parp, a rumble, a clatter-te-clatter, a clank and a grind. And light. Splitting the dark asunder and painting the tiny station in a momentary white dazzle.

Following the light, as if pulled along by its fiery beam, came the train, groaning to a halt then purring roughly as it waited for Birmingham's solitary traveller to board. A little panicked, uncertain as to what I should do, I clambered into the carriage and found myself, as I had been warned that I would be by Old Jebediah the Station Master, among a company of barely human, be-suited creatures, whose softly pulsing scalps were entirely bald, and whose flesh was as dank and pallid as death.

"Commuters," Jebediah had wheezed. "Don't you talk to 'em. And don't catch their eyes. Their eyes be terrible."

I settled nervously into a vacant window seat, beside one of the creatures, which, as if startled by my presence, slowly turned its head until I found myself, against all Jebediah's advice, staring into a pair of those selfsame, deep-buried, blood-hued orbs. He was right. They were terrible.

The Commuter opened its mouth to speak, but only a tortured groan emerged.

Terrified, I tore my gaze away to concentrate fixedly on the impenetrable dark that lay beyond the window. There I saw phantom images of myself, and at times, of my beloved Maria.

At some point, I must have fallen asleep, for, suddenly, there was grey dawn-light and scenery where there had been phantoms. But oh what scenery. Long gone were the rolling fields and hamlets of Brumshire. Now there was desolation; blackened, twisted trees, miserable hovels and a deep layer of refuse which covered every inch of earth like a foul ocean, and where countless gigantic maggots wallowed like vile dolphins at play.

And there, filling the horizon, was London, from this distance, a wall of gleaming obelisks so high, their tops were shrouded in cloud. The sight of it turned my heartbeat into a wild pummelling, but whether from joy or fear, I could not tell.

Our train, as all did, ended its journey at Liverpool Street. A cavernous, bright-lit wonder, in which I stood, open-mouthed and lost as Commuters hurried by on all sides in a fast-flowing, but silent, river of grey suits and graveyard flesh.

I followed, careful not to touch, or draw attention to myself. Carried helplessly towards the cave-like entrance of the Tube, I glimpsed a map, struggled out of the tide to read it, but found only a confusion of lines and colours.

"Excuse me," I said to a tall man, resplendent in peak cap, braid and medals, who stood at the Tube's entrance. "Which train will take me to the Houses of Parliament?"

"There's no trains wot go there sir."

"But I must. It's a matter of life and death."

"That's enough of that sort of talk sir. Now, I suggest you 'op it smartish, before I call the rozzers."

"But—"

"No buts. Just sling yer—Oi! Come back. Stop I says!"

I heard, but did not obey. Resolute, summoning all the courage my father had beaten into me as a child, I ran for the exit. A whistle blew. There was shouting. Panicked, I doubled my pace until I stumbled out of the station into a street the like of which I had never before seen.

Wide it was, yet so narrow. A deserted, neatly dug, open grave with walls of glass and steel that reduced the sky to a mere slit of blue. And huddled at the base of those magnificent constructions, like children clustered at the skirts of their mothers, were the tumbledown dwellings of old London.

I heard the whistle again, and, after a moment of blind panic, pressed myself into the doorway of an ancient and decrepit shop, hiding in shadow as a herd of police constables stampeded by, sure that they would hear the thundering of my heart and discover me. But no, their din passed and faded.

Time now to consult my precious *A to Z*, another jumble of line and colour. I found what I guessed to be my location, and set off in what I hoped was the right direction. The lack of pedestrians, or any other form of conveyance, unnerved me. Why, I wondered, did no one walk in London?

My unease deepened as I strode along London Wall, a place of deep shadow, where the pale winter sun was blotted out by buildings so vast I dared not look to their summits, for to do so caused such confusion of the senses that one would simply faint away. Here it was, also, that I began to feel that people were watching me. That I heard whispers, shuffling.

I yielded to the need to gaze about myself and saw, through gaps in the nests of aged buildings, yellow-lit rooms behind vast sheets of plate glass. And in those rooms, row upon row of desks, each one covered with machinery I presumed to be computators, and sitting at the desks, staring blankly into those same devices were the uncountable and dreadful cousins of my ghastly railway companions. Overwhelmed with horror, I looked away.

Now the shadows themselves were moving. Emerging from doorways, shuffling into the dismal daylight, taking form and substance, uttering growls and snatches of laughter that dissolved into hacking coughs. Stepping out into pavement before and behind me.

Rag-clad and noxious, the wretched host stared at me with a mixture of fear and awe. They were, I realised, the Poor. Filthy, stinking, more animal than human.

"I give generously," I called to them hopefully. And so I did, each Christmas when the collectors visited the village. But the last thing I, or anyone else wanted, was to actually *meet* them, to touch or, God forbid, be touched *by* them.

One of them broke away from the rest. A big, shaggy specimen. A Bull Poor, I deduced. Unpredictable no doubt, dangerous, to be treated with the sort of wary respect I would give to a bad-tempered boar.

"Whether goest thou?" the Bull demanded.

I remained silent.

"You shouldn't be here. Nobody walks in London. Except us of course. We have nonewhere else to go you see. Only the gutter and the soup kitchen."

"To which I donate," I said.

"Donate? What good is that? We need work. Self-respect. Not Heinz chicken and mushbloom."

"I 'ates chicken and mushroom, Albert," another Poor piped up. "They could at least give us minestrone. Now there's a soup to doff your titfer at."

"Quite right," the Bull—Albert—replied. "A soup of instinction. Now my friend, seeing as you donate so garrulously, we'll show you to the nearest Tube station."

"No thank you. I have to get to the Houses of Parliament—"

Gasps of amazement and horror.

"They've taken my wife's soul."

"Ah, such a travesty, but it happens. From your accent I should say you are from Birmingham. Is my suppuration correct?"

"Yes, but..."

"There are, I hear tell, many women in Birmingham, and all erect-able."

"There are, yes. But…"

"Then go, now. Depart whence. Take yourself a new spout."

"I can't, don't you understand? I love Maria. I want her back."

"Not possible. Not possible at all. Come ladies and genialmen, let us assist this poor fool to the nearest subcutaneous conveyance."

The Poor moved in, reaching for me with filthy, claw-like hands. I saw an opening, darted into the road. There were more gasps of astonishment and, I thought uneasily, fear. Albert took a gleaming pocket watch from the depths of his pestilential coat.

"Get off the road," he cried. "Now, with all hate. Do not tarry my friend, not for a moment! The rush hour cometh!"

Fearing a ruse, I ignored him and walked on. Albert, followed by his pack, paralleled me along the pavement, pleading and exhorting me to return to them.

"Oh fool," Albert shouted. "Why do you do not compensate your peril?"

Then came a roaring, from beyond the corner I myself was approaching. I saw…something. A reflection in the acres of glass rearing from the earth around me. Then it…they…a wall…a wave, a blurred and hurrying mass, erupted into view and bore down upon me. I froze. I watched. I wondered. I screamed.

Someone had me, bundling me towards the pavement, where I cowered, Albert's powerful hand still clamped about my arm, and stared at the torrent pouring down what a moment ago had been an empty street.

It was a thundering stampede of motor vehicles, a chaos of noise and dust and fumes. An endless race, a madly flowing river. On it came, on and on, battering my senses, gritting my eyes, scouring my throat with fumes.

Shouting to make myself heard, I thanked my rescuer. He answered with yet more exhortations for me to abandon my adventure.

The traffic was infinite, remorseless, relentless. The noise shuddered through me, blurred thought and frayed nerves as I left the Poor behind and resumed my quest. I walked with shoulders hunched and eyes downcast, afraid to even glance at the vehicular torrent lest the mesmerising power of its ceaseless movement drag me into its flow.

My spirits drooped. Perhaps the Poor were right. Perhaps I should indeed go home. Perhaps my adventure was fruitless. But no, wait, there, dwarfed by the city's monstrous glass forest, yet dominating all it surveyed, was the domed magnificence of St Paul's Cathedral.

The traffic roar died to a dull hum in my ears as I approached this the most holy temple of my faith. I had, of course, seen its image many times in flickering monochrome on my clockwork television. But never so close, so real, so presence-full.

Renewed, I drew close, my eyes moist, transfixed by its beauty.

A figure appeared among the columns at the base of the dome: black robed, bearded. A Man of God. He raised a megaphone to his lips.

"You down there."

I started, pointed to my chest, mimed a surprised "Me?"

"Yes you, blasphemer, whose vile feet are staining our holy pavements, whose foul breath is poisoning our sacred air. Go from us. Flee underground or face the fury of God."

"But the Tube doesn't—"

"Bugger off you insolent little atheist," the priest replied. "Away with you!"

I hesitated, unwilling to fly in the face of God's own servants on earth. Until the great main doors of the cathedral burst open to release a horde of red-faced, snarling clerics, each wielding a gilded shepherd's crook.

Then, I ran.

"Teach the blasphemer," the megaphone commanded. "Show him the Lord's Mercy!"

Consulting my *A to Z* as I fled, I saw on the jolting page that I was not far from the Embankment. Behind me, one of my pursuers raised a megaphone to his lips and picked up the ecclesiastical strain, rather breathlessly, from the point at which his superior had drifted out of earshot.

"Pray thou maggot. Beg the God of eternal forgiveness for mercy!"

Out of breath, I wondered how long I could continue at such a pace. My legs grew weak, my chest was afire.

"Faster brothers in the Lord," urged the megaphone. "Get the bastard!"

Street after street, corner after corner. Slowing, collapsing under a weight of despair and panic. Sure now that I would never find—But no, there, on the far side of an unbroken wall of traffic, Old Father Thames himself. Elated, I gained and followed that precious grey ribbon towards my goal. Saw it loom out of the confusion of distance. Saw an end to my adventure at last.

Something hooked my ankle. A fall, a harsh juddering impact and I was laying, supine, seeing only the dismal, cobalt sky and the face of a cleric, glaring down at me, crook raised to strike.

"Prepare to feel the love of God," he screamed in a spray of spittle. "And be glad—"

He did not finish his sermon, however, because suddenly the Poor were there, breaking over him and his comrades like a noxious wave.

"Go," Albert commanded me, as he grasped a particularly florid and portly priest about the neck and shook him. "To the Houses of Parliament my friend, onwards, and lobby for your belugged!"

Stunned, trembling I struggled to my feet...

"And remember us, your new found alibis," Albert shouted after me as I stumbled away. "To the Horrible Gentlemen!"

Almost there now—

An explosion knocked me to the ground.

I sat up, ears ringing, coughing on smoke. Then glanced skywards and wondered at what can only be described as a titanic and majestic airship. Smoke puffed from a porthole in its bloated silver hull and another explosion wrought havoc among, but failed to stop, the traffic.

"Awfully sorry about the whizz bangs, but you appear to be trespassing," said an amplified voice from above. "Perhaps you could move along old chap."

"No," I cried, fist raised in manly defiance. "I will not!"

"Oh dear. I was rather hoping you wouldn't cause a scene. I do hate scenes."

The cannon boomed again. More motor vehicles were lifted and scattered in a chaos of smoke and flame.

A whistle blew shrilly and I was dismayed to see, beyond the brawling mêlée of the Poor and the Pious, a platoon of red-faced, truncheon-waving policemen.

Seeing my chance, as chaos descended upon the Embankment, I forced my exhausted body on for one last effort. And fell, at last, against the very stonework of my destination.

There was a door, arched and iron-bound, which opened to my furious pounding, and revealed an ancient, though venerable-looking man in a morning suit.

"May I be of service sir?"

The ground shook from the impact of another explosion. Blood sprayed the wall beside the door.

"I wish to lobby parliament," I explained.

"Most irregular sir."

The airship was on fire now, its crew leaping to safety as it dropped slowly towards the river.

"I must speak to the Honourable Gentlemen."

"Impossible sir."

The airship hit the water and hot met cold in a monstrous eruption of steam, smoke and flame. The police broke into a charge, with much blowing of whistles and outraged shouting.

"The MPs have my wife's soul. I must lobby for its return."

"I am sorry sir. But—"

The Poor, raising a loud and bloodcurdling battle cry, left the bruised and mostly unconscious Priesthood to meet the fast-approaching officers for the law.

"—I simply cannot give you entrance. Good day sir. Have a pleasant journey home." The venerable old man in the morning suit made to shut the big arched and iron-bound door.

Desperate, I threw myself into the rapidly narrowing gap, and found myself running along a quiet, stained-glass and candlelit corridor. Behind me, the old man coughed politely but firmly and endeavoured to remind me that I really should not be here.

I, meanwhile, had come upon another door, panelled and as venerable-looking as the old gentleman hurrying in my wake. Without allowing myself a moment's hesitation, I pushed it open.

And stepped into a hushed chamber that filled me with such awe and humility, that I almost dropped to my knees. My awe, however, quickly became confusion.

Here, as I had expected, were two opposing sets of pews, all polished wood and padded leather.

Also, as expected, the seats were occupied. By ranks of ancient, dust-filmed, grey-haired men. But this was where my confounding began. Most of the gentlemen were upright. A few, however, had fallen sideways, still locked in the sitting position. Their faces were expressionless, their eyes blank. Some were damaged, cogs and springs visible though rents in their mouldering attire. More old men in morning suits worked at these broken Members with needles and thread and spanners.

Already stunned into motionless silence, I was further startled by a polite cough.

"I rather wish you had not seen this sir," said the venerable gentleman who had met me at the door.

"But... But who Runs Things and Makes Policy and takes Momentous Decisions?"

"Well sir, it's rather difficult to explain—"

"Oh God, what are *you* doing here?" said another voice, this one so soft and beautiful and familiar that I felt the breath snatched from my lungs, and my heart torn from my chest.

"Maria? Where are you? Maria?"

"Here you idiot. Above the Speaker's Chair."

And so she was. Though not her, but an immense glass-sided vessel filled with light that roiled and shifted through every hue of the rainbow, and uttered sighs and soft laughter. I ran to it, crying, calling out my beloved's name over and over again. Promising to rescue her.

"Rescue me? Whatever for?"

"Because I love you."

"Sorry Jonathon, but a thousand wild horses wouldn't get me back to that...that backward little wart on the landscape you call home. This is my destiny. The destiny of all the good and the beautiful of the earth."

"Destiny?"

"Yes. To rule, We, Jonathon, the dead, are the ones who Run Things and Make Policy and take Momentous Decisions."

"No. No... you must come home."

"God you're stubborn. I suppose that's how you survived the police and the priests and the air force, oh and the mechanised traffic, let's not forget the newest, most dangerous defence we have shall we? You've even got the Poor on your side, they're supposed to discourage visitors with their stink, not make friends with them."

"You mean we have a role?" I turned to see Albert and that selfsame Poor, standing by the door, next to the venerable gentleman who was ringing his hands and shaking his tremulous old head sorrowfully at this new irregularity. "You hear that ladies and genialmen? We have a role. A place in sobriety!" And out they went laughing and cheering, the sound echoing, fading and disappearing.

As for me, I wept unashamed, manly tears of grief.

"Must you always make a scene?" Maria said. "Look, it's simple. The bad and the ugly receive damnation when they die, and become

Commuters, doomed to travel on trains and Implement the Policies we, the virtuous and the beautiful, dream up for the good of the living."

"But you're dead..."

"Oh come on, the dead have always ruled the living."

"So, I must go home without you."

"Yes."

"And by living a virtuous life and taking care of my appearance, I will one day be reunited with you?"

"I suppose so..."

"Then I swear now to live blamelessly, so that when life's brief flame is snuffed out, I will join you, forever."

"Oh God. Must you?"

"Farewell Maria," I whispered as I stared into that wondrous, roiling light for a moment longer. Then I reached up and touched the warm glass, turned on my heel and walked from that place. After a while, my tears dried and my step lightened as I remembered that there were, in the meantime, plenty of women in Birmingham, and all of them eligible.

❖ ❖ ❖

TERRY GATES-GRIMWOOD is a lecturer at a vocational college. His real life starts when he returns to his lonely, candlelit garret where he hides himself away to write...okay, to his ordinary house where he indulges his various literary obsessions. He's published in magazines such as *Nemonymous, Legend, FutureFire, Midnight Street,* and *Dark Animus,* as well as the anthology *Darkness Rising.* He has gained Honorable Mentions in *Ellen Datlow Year's Bests* for 2001 and 2003. A chapbook of his stories, *Demons and Demons,* is available from Whispers of Wickedness (http://www.ookami.co.uk/html/bookshop_.html). He has written and directed three plays; the latest, *Tales from the Nightside,* is based on two of his short stories, "Jar of Flies" and "The Friends of Mike Santini" (scripts available from terrygatesgrimwood@msn.com). Relaxation for Terry is a toot on the harmonica.

GLADYS SWAN

THE TIGER'S EYE

Cocky little devil, you'd have said, seeing him walk along—jaunty stride, arms in full swing, like a kid who imagines himself at the head of a parade. Maroon jacket, gray slacks, white bucks—who does he think he is? Retired, living out his days on Social Security. You'd think he was on his way to be bank president. "Just look at him now," Mrs. Margolis says aloud, seeing him bend over and snap off one of her carnations to put in his buttonhole, as if it grew there for his special benefit. Ought to give him a piece of my mind, she thinks, so I ought—Walter Lawrence, who thieves her flowers. Before she lifts the window, he catches her eye. He has waited for her as she stands there behind the lace curtain, a bulky shadow; and he waves, nice as you please, and smiles.

Before she had directed her will to raise up the window, off he goes with the carnation in his lapel. Tomorrow a rose, very likely—a red rose for passion; a white, for purity; depending on the urge of his inner being. And she had provided, will provide—for he is partial to roses.

Tomorrow, he thinks, it will be a rose. A rose, a rose; a rose is a rose, by any other name smelling as sweet. My luv's like...a rose, a rose—his thought goes in time with his step.

And Mrs. Margolis, letting drop the curtain, wonders if she should take the scissors to the flower bed, bring all her prizes indoors. It's not worth the effort, she decides, turning away, while he continues down the street oblivious. A strange man, maybe a little cracked. For rather than come to tea with her, he goes every day to visit the zoo, where he would much rather talk to the tiger. Imagine. And with a flourish of indignation she goes on to straighten and dust her bric-a-brac.

A brief pause for the delight of the flower, and Lawrence resumes his walk and his worry, frowning and oblivious, all his thought for the tiger. For the tiger seems to be ailing lately, has a keeper he has taken a violent dislike to. Afraid the keeper has it in for him. And Lawrence has been concerned about him.

As he cuts across Chalmers Street on his way to the bus—jaywalking, making a car stop for him, the driver swearing—reaches the curb, misses seeing Jake Henderson wave to him from the barbershop, he finds himself turned loose among a variety of impressions welling up from the past. He remembers the first time he saw the tiger.

It was almost as though a knife went through his heart: the splendor of the beast—a white Bengal tiger. The magnificent line of the body, the carriage of the head, the rippling muscles of the shoulder and flank as it moved on strong padded feet, the grace, the power—daggers of black marking the silvery terror and beauty. The spectacle left him breathless.

"You are overwhelming," he said aloud.

And he thought, though he could not be certain, he heard the voice of the tiger speaking to him. Somewhere the words formed, whether in his head or outside, but certainly they were not his own.

"You better believe it," the tiger said.

When he looked around, he saw only a small girl with her mother in front of the tiger's cage. "Big, big kitty," the little girl said. And they moved on to look at the panther. But he stood rooted to the spot.

He boards the bus on Washington Street. Sometimes when the weather is fine and he is in the mood, he walks part way to the zoo. But not today. He sits by the window and lets the street slide past, lets slide past the fretful and changeable fantasies of the city—what it wants or thinks it wants, its materializing hopes, its graying and deteriorating failures. Now a Chinese restaurant dedicated to the best of Szechuan; next to it a loan company with a heavy mortgage on the possible. Now a whole new tower of high-rise apartments thrusting up; now a row of buildings seemingly abandoned, windows broken out, boarded up—eyeless and waiting like pensioners, but whether for the ball of the wrecker or the scaffolding of the restorer, it is impossible to say. Impossible to know what energy is working underground that in the next moment will rise and tear out a piece of the past and whip up something new in its place, or else gather itself to renovate, renew, restore. He thinks how he has seen the city, even his suburb, change and change again—something always materializing, something always in the works. Some of the streets he hardly recognizes when he thinks of what they have been. A new bank on the corner of Welby and Long, he notices. More banks everywhere. And fast-food places. Someone, somewhere is always hungry for something. It is as though he steps into the midst of a different life every time he boards the bus. But even so, it has always been there at the end of the ride—the tiger he has come to see.

After his first visit, it was a long while before he came back to see the tiger, he remembers, and by then he had very nearly lost the original impression. He was beaten down with overwork, tense with strain. And things had become increasingly difficult—a euphemism for intolerable—between him and his third wife, Angela. Perhaps what had happened with his career had done in his marriage as well—it is hard to say. But just when his years of service and what had been praised as top-notch work for his company, a trust management firm, had brought him to the point of a major promotion, he had been passed over. They brought in a young hot-shot to manage the division. And left him in a corner to rot. And he had felt pained and empty, as though one of his vital organs had been cut away.

For some reason, he thought of going to the zoo. He thought it might soothe his nerves, the presence of animals. He left the house after a flare-up with Angela, words of their latest quarrel flaming in his ears.

He found the tiger curled up in the corner of the cage. At first, he thought it was asleep, but he saw that the tiger regarded him with half-closed eyes. Then the tiger spoke to him again.

"I'm bored," the tiger said.

"Did you speak?" Lawrence said aloud.

"Certainly," said the tiger. "Who else?" And gave a great yawn that revealed the wonderfully honed ivory of his fangs. "I'm dismally, outrageously, overwhelmingly bored."

"So am I," Lawrence said, realizing that he had just been given the word to describe his true condition. "I'm bored to death." And with that, he seemed to reach all the way down to where the juices had stopped flowing.

"It's bad enough just lying here with nothing to do," the tiger said. "Oh, I know, we're supposed to be educational—let people see first-hand the many wonders and splendors of nature. Sounds good," the tiger said, "but what does it come down to? Continual harassment. Make the big tiger roar, make him get up. Run a stick along the cage. Throw a paper wad. And the lack of privacy. When I had a mate—how eager they were to see us do it in public. Disgusting..."

The tiger picked himself up and paced round the cage—once, twice. "The circles of boredom," he said.

Yes, it was true, Lawrence thought. Boredom goes in circles, ever narrowing, funneling downward—just like the inferno. What were his days? Talking to stuffed shirts whose lives were spent in back-biting and ass-kissing, company officials who snarled and glared and tried to plant you with the blame for the way the world was run. He was weary of figures and percentages and rules—he was weary of himself, the smell of himself, which was as rank as the tiger's cage.

"It's true, he said, with a sudden rush of sympathy. "I know just what you mean."

As though this note of sympathy had struck a real chord with the tiger, he began suddenly to speak of the jungle. It was as though he were creating a poem—the poem of his existence: the richness of birds, the sudden flashes of brilliance through the leaves, bursts of color—like a vision half-glimpsed. The chatter and play of monkeys, the flight of the swift-footed gazelles, the sudden trumpeting of the ponderous elephants. Lawrence could see it all, as though a tropical paradise had suddenly sprung into existence at the center of the city, graced with palms and parrots.

A sudden clang of iron against iron, the echo reverberating down the spine, and both he and the tiger were snatched abruptly from the space they had been inhabiting, the vision broken, and planted once again within and outside the cage.

"Mealtime anyway," the tiger said, with resignation. "It's the one thing I look forward to."

"Shall I go?" Lawrence asked, in deference to the tiger's privacy. The keepers entered the cage.

"No, not at all," said the tiger, moving off to a discreet distance. "I enjoy the company. Only it isn't pretty. I hope you're not squeamish."

He took up a chunk of raw meat and chewed thoughtfully. "If I were home where I belonged," he said, as though he had once again caught a brief glimpse of the jungle, "I'd be doing things for myself. Ah, the hunt—nothing like it to get your blood up." He tore away a strip of meat from a carcass and gave a little growl of pleasure that reminded Lawrence of what he had felt on first seeing the tiger.

He had almost allowed the impression to dim. Some shape of horror was about to coalesce in his mind.

"Well, you got to eat," the tiger said, "with or without knife and fork."

He caught a sudden image of himself leaping savagely on his bit of chicken. He hadn't been brought to that yet, Lawrence thought—fortunately.

"But in the bush," the tiger said, licking a scrap from his lips, "what's a little death?"

The tiger seemingly had no better luck with the female of the species than he had had. By the time Lawrence saw him again, his third marriage had ended up on the rocks, with considerable animosity on both sides.

"I suppose it was my fault mostly," he found himself admitting to the tiger. "She was young, volatile—liked a good time, excitement. I just didn't have it in me any more."

"I know what you mean," the tiger said. "They gave me a mate—as lovely a creature as ever walked, but we just didn't get on."

"When Angela wanted to go out on the town, I was ready to sit down with a quiet Scotch and a little soft music."

"Changeable, willful disposition," the tiger said. "Chances were when I came to her, she'd turn away and growl. She was never in the mood, even when nature was on my side. And if we did get together—" he paused, "she wasn't pleased then either—if you know what I mean."

"I can't say that was my problem," Lawrence said. "There were times when she was insatiable."

"You can't win," the tiger said. "Fortunately, once the cubs came, they separated us. I've been alone since—I count my blessings."

"I've never really understood women," Lawrence said. "I think I've done badly by all of them. With the first, I was tough when I should have been tender; with the second, indulgent when I ought to have been firm. I could deny her nothing—she had such a sweet way of rubbing against me when she wanted something. When she pulled out, I had a stack of bills a foot high. Women and money..."

"Mine was just one of those bad-tempered cats," the tiger said. "I did everything to please her but stand on my head."

"Angela was gorgeous from behind. I loved to watch her walk away—the delicious little bounce, the lovely curves. And then when you turned her over... There were compensations in that marriage."

"I'm well rid of her," the tiger said. "To be alone is to be happy."

"I'm alone now too," Lawrence said, wondering if he agreed with the tiger. "There is," he said, "the sense of loss."

And so it's been over the years, Lawrence is thinking as he heads down the tree-lined avenue towards the entrance of the zoo. For a time he used to visit the tiger once a week or so; now with his retirement he comes every day. They are used to him now. The keepers greet him familiarly, and no one thinks anything of it when he stands in front of the tiger's cage talking to him long into the afternoon. He hurries now.

Arriving at the cage, he sees immediately that the tiger is in a bad mood. Even after he inquires softly how the tiger is getting along, tries to soothe him with his voice, the tiger paces, flicking his tail, not to be appeased.

"He's out to get me," the tiger says. "I know he is."

"I admit he's a nasty-looking type," Lawrence says. Something in his face he disliked right away. A sort of meanness. Skimpy. Nothing of a chin. Mealy complexion. Snub nose. Nothing generous in the mouth—tight, thin-lipped. Human—he had the shape, but all the light had gone out. "But maybe—" he begins, then stops himself. It would be an insult to suggest that the tiger might be exaggerating. And besides, he doesn't know what it is to have to live with the man.

"For one thing, he's afraid of me," the tiger says. "I can smell his fear."

"Why do you think? Any special reason?"

"Look at his hand sometime," the tiger says. "He's been mauled— I'm sure of it."

"Why is he here?" Lawrence wants to know. "There are other jobs, other parts of the zoo."

"Not for him, there's not—if you know what I mean."

"I think I do. I've come across those types."

"He'd love to use that whip. He's just itching to use his gun. It makes me nervous—just look at him now."

The keeper moves toward the cage, opens it and steps inside with his companion. Something dark and furtive in his look. The fear is there, but something else: the hatred that is part of the fear.

"All right, move off—" The two keepers are in the cage. One with the food—the other to keep an eye out.

The tiger paces nervously back and forth.

"Easy does it," Lawrence says. "Keep calm, my boy. Just take it easy."

"He'll be sorry if he don't," the new keeper says. "I can tell he don't like me..."

"Come on, Harry," the other says. "You're making trouble. He's never bothered anybody since I've been here."

"Well, I don't trust the brutes. All cats are treacherous. As soon kill you as look at you."

Alone in his cage again, the tiger sits picking at his food.

"I think he's putting something in it," he says. "I think he's trying to poison me."

"Why would he do that?" Lawrence says, horrified, wondering if the tiger is suffering from some deeper malady, something infecting his imagination.

"A world of people has passed in front of my cage," the tiger said, "and a number have come inside. And I think there are some who have a grudge. They carry it inside them all their lives, and they want only to bring vileness and chaos wherever they go. They carry it like a worm eating their insides or like a fire glowing in the dark, and it feeds and feeds until it grows into a huge..."

"Tiger, tiger burning bright," Lawrence says, without thinking.

"What was that?"

"Nothing," he says, embarrassed. "A poem I once knew."

But the tiger insists that he repeat it from start to finish. When he ends, the tiger lets out a great roar of rage and pain that seems to shake the ground with its violence.

"I shouldn't have done that," Lawrence tells himself guiltily. But whether the tiger was protesting his existence or all the more passionately affirming it, he is not able to say.

Before he was laid up with a bout of flu that kept him from his visits, Lawrence had spent a good deal of thought and effort on the tiger's condition, but to no avail. The director of the zoo, a Mr. Ferris, was sympathetic, but Lawrence knew that he regarded him as a crank—harmless, but a crank. He had suggested as politely as he could that the vet ought to have a look at the tiger. The director explained that animals frequently get a bit off their feed and just as spontaneously recover. Lawrence tried to explain the tiger's dislike of the keeper. He held back the tiger's impression that the man was out to get him. The director explained patiently that he had a limited staff. Turnover was a headache. Funds from the city were limited. Hard to get qualified people. As it was, he had a harrowing schedule trying to get all the animals fed, their cages cleaned. They could not take into account all the eccentricities and little quirks of temperament you found in a zoo full of animals. "After all," the director concluded, "we can't disrupt a whole zoo for the sake of one discontented tiger."

"And yet what do we run things for?" Lawrence wondered afterwards. At times, it seemed to him, only for the sake of running them. How many mornings he had rushed to work, to be on time to do nothing. And a powerful discontent seized him, something large and vague and cloudy that had to do with the inherent stupidity of things. Or so it seemed when he was in that frame of mind.

The tiger at least had a more immediate object for his rage: "I could tear him limb from limb—I could..."

"You're getting all worked up."

"I know. I must be wretched company," the tiger said, apologetically. "There's no danger. I wouldn't lay a claw on him. He's just looking for an excuse. But I won't give it to him. Now he's trying to weaken me. I turned up my nose at the food, so now he gives me scarcely enough to satisfy an alley cat."

"I went to the director," Lawrence said. "But it didn't do any good."

"No, I don't imagine. It would be lovely to be out of all this," he said, looking around the bars.

"You're not getting..."

"Despondent? No, no, not at all," the tiger protested. "I'll rage til the last. I did make it out once though. Escaped—think of that. Four days of freedom before they found me."

"Really? What did you do?"

"Had a couple of excellent meals of squirrel in the park," the tiger said, "and a rather simple-minded little pug that came sniffing in my direction. But that was a minor thing."

He waited.

"It was a real adventure. I became part of the dreams of the city. For it has dreams, you know. Restless dreams, unquiet dreams, dreams of violence and madness. Nightmares. I was among them. In the shadows lurking. Stalking prey."

"You frighten me," Lawrence said.

"And you're not frightened without me?" the tiger asked, with what appeared almost a smile. "But that wasn't all," the tiger continued. "I was part of its other dreams too—in the park among the flowers. Dreams of gaiety and rest. Looked at the statues of swans and maidens and generals on horseback—those all are dreams too, made solid, fashioned into statues. Though, I must say, with limited interest. I stalked and leapt—I made grand leaps, as though I were in the jungle again." A spark seemed to animate the tiger momentarily. "It was a great joy."

"Yes, I can imagine," Lawrence said and felt a touch of lightheartedness.

"A rare moment," the tiger said. He flopped down and put his head on his paws. He seemed quite weary. "Sing something to me," he said.

Lawrence rummaged for a moment among the tunes that had been gathering rust and forgetfulness in his mind—a few hymns from childhood, fragments of old popular tunes, some chestnuts from the classics—thin pickings. Ah, he thought, with sudden inspiration, and struck into "On the Road to Mandalay," thinking it might put some heart into the tiger, remind him of happier days in the jungle.

"I don't mean to interrupt," the tiger said, after the second line, "but could you pick something quieter, a little more soothing?"

He looked at the tiger for a long moment. How many years it had been—that they'd been friends, he thought. It hadn't occurred to him before to give a particular definition to his relations with the tiger. But yes, they'd been friends.

"Sweet and low," he sang, "Sweet and low. Wind of the western sea..."

"That's very pleasant," the tiger said.

Lawrence had had a fine tenor voice in his youth and now, quite as though his singing had brought it to life again, the notes came through clear and pure.

People paused to listen, and he went on singing til he saw that the tiger was asleep.

Mrs. Margolis looks out to see which is in the greatest danger this morning, her carnations or her roses. This time she is quite certain she will have a word with the man, in revenge at least for his refusal to come and have tea with her. All for the sake of a tiger. Indeed! But as she gazes out, the man, her prey, flies right past, and there is something in his look, in his stony, concentrated unseeing that leaves her in wonder. He has the look of a man struck by lightning.

And indeed it is true. He is disturbed. Even the return of morning with the light of gathering rationality has not diminished the sense of the momentous. For in the middle of the night the tiger came to him.

Had come—it was too bizarre to stand the inspection of the mind. But what other words could describe the visitation? The tiger had come—unless he could say simply that he had gone out of his mind. But perhaps... What can he say? He is in the greatest perplexity.

When he arrives at the zoo, he goes straight to the cage, but the tiger is gone. A terrible weakness seizes him at the knees. He knows the worst. But even so, he goes in search of the keeper—the one—whom he finds watering the elephants.

"Yep, dead all right," the keeper tells him. "Had an attack in the middle of the night and we had to shoot it. Vet's done a report on him. He couldn't recover."

The man is perfectly matter-of-fact, though Lawrence thinks he detects a certain satisfaction in his voice. At any rate, he is spared some sort of lugubrious sympathy.

"Didn't even get up when I came in to shoot it," the keeper says. "He was in a bad way."

I'll bet he roared though, Lawrence thinks. He must have roared. "Well, thank you," he says, turning away, allowing the keeper his triumph, if that is what he had. Perhaps he had wanted to kill it, whether he knew it or not—in his fear, his hatred of what the tiger was. But that, he thinks, is neither here nor there.

So it was gone—the silvery splendor, the black daggers. But—he straightens up, walks slowly back to the entrance—it had visited him before it left. And he had looked at it, looked deeply into its burning eye.

⍿ ⍿ ⍿

GLADYS SWAN has written five collections of short fiction and three novels, *Carnival of the Gods, Ghost Dance: A Play for Voices,* and *News from the Volcano,* with the latter two each nominated for a Pen/Faulkner Award. Her short fiction is appearing this year in the literary magazines *Hotel Amerika, The Southern California Anthology, New Letters, Story Quarterly, Tifereth: A Journal of Spiritual Literature,* and *The Literary Review.*

Justin Courter

Skunk

1

Only three years ago did I finally decide to get a skunk of my own. This was after a long, tentative courtship of the skunk scent. If I were driving on a country road and smelled skunk, I immediately pulled over and sat, sometimes for hours, with all the windows rolled down, breathing deeply and letting my thoughts drift among whatever daydreams the scent inspired. I often packed a lunch and devoted my Sunday to one of these drives. But I longed for the pleasure of enjoying the scent of the skunk entirely at my leisure.

By the time I was thirty years old, the notion that I was completely self-sufficient and could do, more or less, what I pleased, began to take shape somewhere in my mind. I had a job as a copywriter for Grund & Greene, a publisher of law books, and I had my own small house in New Essex, a relatively tranquil suburb. I was proud of my house—sad, gray shoe box that it was—with its knee-high hedge, which I kept squarely trimmed, running across the front like a fender. Having scrimped and saved, having lived in tiny, roach-ridden apartments for years, I was at last the owner of something more substantial than the old, smoke-colored Eldorado in which I got around on weekends.

As I am one who has learned to prepare for all of life's inevitabilities, I built a six-foot fence along the perimeter of my tiny back yard and constructed a hutch about the size of a dog house. Thereafter, several weekends were devoted to tramping around some woods outside town until the day I came across Homer.

It was a crisp autumn afternoon. The sky was a gray sheet of legal bond resume paper upon which were scribbled the leafless branches of maples and birches, and I strode through woods carrying a large burlap sack. When I first spotted Homer, he was rooting around in a pile of dead leaves. Though I tried to approach him stealthily, my feet crunched leaves and snapped twigs. The skunk stopped what he was doing, turned to face me, and sprung suddenly to attention like a puppet on a string. I froze. He arched his back and seemed to grow taller. I took a slow step forward. The little beast hissed, I took a second step, and he began to thump the ground with his forepaws. He became increasingly agitated, gradually raising his plume of a tail until it stood straight up. Then, when I was still about six feet from him, he spun around, quicker than a gunslinger, and musked in my direction. He wasn't a bad shot. The yellow juice he emitted splattered my trousers, and any other predator he could have considered thwarted. Poor fellow. He couldn't possibly have known that what he was doing was tantamount to slipping an aphrodisiac to a nymphomaniac.

The scent of skunk musk is the richest of all olfactory pleasures. It is a bitter-sweet combination of lilac, tilled earth, McDougal's beer, dogwood blossoms, apple pie, fresh snow and Moschus—the miniature Himalayan musk deer. And the effect on the mind is astonishing. Skunk musk brings the innocence of childhood, the lasciviousness of adolescence and the wisdom of old age to the surface of one's consciousness all at once. I sucked Homer's perfume deep into my lungs. My vision blurred, eyes teared, the burlap sack fell from my hands and I became slightly dizzy. Homer began to mosey off through the forest. I returned to my senses and snatched the bag up from the ground. I simply had to have him. I chased him as he scurried about—under bushes, through piles of leaves—and was able to get the sack over him just as he was about to scoot down a hole at the base of a tree. He writhed around and sprayed more of his delicious scent as I tied a knot at the top of the sack and carried him out of the woods. I placed him beside me on the seat of the car and he continued to wriggle for the first quarter hour of the ride home, at which point he got tired and lay still. I opened the sack in front of the hutch I'd built in the back yard and he moseyed right into his new apartment as if he'd never lived anywhere else. It was then that I decided upon his name. "Welcome home, Homer," I said. But he ignored the hutch after the first night and dug a hole beneath it the next, so that he only used the floor of the structure I'd built as a roof for his subterranean abode.

There was very nearly what one might call a spring in my step on Monday morning when I left the house to walk to the commuter train. Spending the weekend with Homer had given my life an exciting new dimension. I actually waved at Mrs. Endicott, the annoying old widow who lived next door and who owned a high-strung Chihuahua called Tesa. Mrs. Endicott was retrieving the newspaper from her front yard and Tesa stood at her side yapping at me like a battery-operated toy. Mrs. Endicott liked to talk to me practically whenever I stepped outside, providing me with updates on her children, her grandchildren, her rheumatism and other dull topics. She also badgered me with questions. She asked me who my girlfriend was, when I intended to get married, and so forth.

"Hey, Damien," she said that morning, waving me over to her. I was embarrassed for her because she was standing there in the middle of her yard in a flower-print housecoat, with pink curlers decorating her head. I walked over to her. "What's going on in your yard, there?" she asked. Her face was wrinkled like a used paper bag, and her sagging cheeks quivered when she spoke. Tesa continued her yapping throughout our conversation.

"Nothing's 'going on,' Mrs. Endicott," I said. Of the long list of unpleasant qualities this woman exhibited, her prying nature was the most abhorrent.

"You've got a dog now don't you, a little puppy? That's good, companionship is good. I'm always saying to Noah, my nephew, you oughta get a nice dog, I says, you need a friend. Living all alone like that makes you crazy. But *you*," here Mrs. Endicott jabbed me in the chest with a bony finger and smiled, "you got a good head on your shoulders. I always said you did. Now all you need is a good woman to take care of you."

I began turning away. I detest being poked and prodded physically or psychologically. Crazy indeed. Mrs. Endicott had told me that she herself had lived alone for the past ten years. "Thank you Mrs. Endicott. I think I'll be on my way."

She grabbed my arm and held me there. "The only thing is, Damien, you gotta clean up after a dog. I can smell it over in my yard. Wait." She pulled me a little closer and sniffed deeply. This caused a most disagreeable racket—snot burbled in her nose and phlegm rattled in her throat. "I'm a little stuffed up," she said, "but I can even smell it on you now. It's not good. You take him on walks or train him to go in the far corner of the yard, you hear?" She smiled, peering with her cataract-clouded eyes into my bespectacled ones for a moment, then released my arm. "Run along now, you'll be late for work," she said.

As I turned and began to walk away, I noticed that Tesa had stopped yapping. Then I felt her attack from behind. Her tiny teeth slipping from around my ankle, she contented herself by yanking at my pant leg and growling fiercely, as if truly committed to removing my pants. I shook my leg vigorously and was about to give her a good swift kick with my other foot, when Mrs. Endicott called, "That's enough now Tesa." Tesa released my pants and stood barking until I'd reached the end of the street. Luckily, she'd put only a few pin holes in my pants. I always wore polyester suits, which I found practical, affordable and quite durable; I owned one blue, one gray and one brown. What did trouble me a bit was that Tesa had put a two-inch-long scratch in the leather of my sturdy brown shoes, the same type I'd worn since I was a boy, and on which I always maintained a flawless, military shine.

When I got on the commuter train people parted for me like the Red Sea before Moses. A woman with watery eyes, who appeared to have a sinus irritation, vacated a seat next to where I stood and moved to the front, holding a tissue over her nose. I happily took the seat and opened my paperback copy of Alma Chesnut Moore's *How to Clean Everything*, which is among my favorite works of nonfiction.

I got to the office at ten minutes before nine, as always, and began working immediately. Frank Farnsworth, whose cubicle was adjacent to mine, got in at nine twenty-three, huffing and puffing, and threw his briefcase against the wall of his cubicle that bordered mine. This disrupted my concentration on the wording of a brochure for what may very well have been the definitive text on real estate litigation. I had to submit a draft of this piece to John Hastings, my supervisor, later that morning. I'd already written and revised it several times, but I always double- and triple-checked things before submitting them to Hastings. Farnsworth made a great deal of noise shuffling papers about in his cubicle and muttering to himself. I heard him pick up his phone. Here we go again, I thought.

"Hey honey," he said loudly, "did you get Suzie to school on time?" He paused for a moment. "I know, I know, I think it's because she's still getting over that cold... No, look, now I can't be responsible for everything all the time, okay? I'm running my ass ragged trying to keep on top of things here, and I can't be expected to put everything on hold if I notice the kid's started to sniffle or—what?... Yeah I know about the goddamn wedding, I don't think your sister will let me forget about it for five minutes. Jesus, something stinks in here... Because I didn't have time, not because I forgot. Macy's isn't on my way, and the last time I was late you went ballistic. Man, I think I stepped in a puddle of puke or something on the way to work... No, listen, I called you just now because I wanted to straighten out something else and now... Okay, fine. Yeah. Okay. Alright, I'll talk to you then." Farnsworth dropped the receiver noisily, got up and left his cubicle. I could hear the clanging of metal and glass from all the way at the other end of the hall as Farnsworth molested the coffee maker. He came back to his cubicle and banged his mug down on his desk.

"Shit," he said, "God damn it." Then he was standing there in my cubicle. "Hey Damien, can I bother you for a second?" It had already been much longer than that, so I could see no reason he needed permission to continue the practice. Without moving my chair, I rotated my head to face him. Farnsworth's necktie was loosened, the top button of his shirt unfastened, his sleeves rolled up, and his hair disheveled. His demeanor suggested that rather than having just shown up at the office, he had already worked an entire day and was preparing to unwind.

"I just spilled coffee all over my stupid keyboard," he said. "Is that going to ruin it completely? Do you know?" Farnsworth's face began to look as if he'd taken a bite of a rancid piece of cheese. He began sneezing, and sneezed five times in my cubicle without once covering his mouth, though he did turn his face away from me. When he'd finished he said, "God, do you smell that? I think it's even stronger in here. Jeez, it's terrible."

Though my posture is always nearly perfect, I felt myself sit up straighter upon hearing these words. "To what smell do you refer?" I asked.

He stepped toward me and sniffed. He stepped back again and gave me a puzzled look. "Well, anyway, do you know what I should do about my keyboard?" he asked. "I mean, is it okay to just wipe it off with a damp rag or what?"

"I would do nothing without first consulting Mr. Daltry regarding the matter," I replied. Sean Daltry was the building's maintenance man.

Farnsworth rolled his eyes. "Yeah, I guess, I was just wondering if you might know."

"Well I don't suppose I do," I said. In fact, Alma Moore's book had been written before the advent of the personal computer. "And I don't suppose I really have all morning to sit here chatting with you about your keyboard, Mr. Farnsworth."

Farnsworth raised his hands, palms facing outward. "Whoah, take it easy, bud. Forget I was here, okay?" He backed out of my cubicle. I turned back to the screen of my computer. "What the hell's the matter with everybody today?" I heard Farnsworth say behind me to someone passing in the hall.

That night when I went home, I put a small portion of my dinner in a dish outside Homer's burrow. I did not try to get him to musk at me. In those first few weeks after Homer's arrival, I only allowed myself a bit of skunk musk on the weekends, and then only after I'd completed all my chores, which included going to the dump, doing the food shopping for the week and cleaning the house from top to bottom. I was always extremely meticulous in this exercise—going down on my hands and knees with a toothbrush to get the mildew that grew between the tiles in the corners of the shower, polishing the pipes beneath the kitchen sink, and so on. Then I took a shower, shaved, stretching the skin to get a close swipe at the stubble in the dip beneath my chin, and combed my hair, which is jet black and a bit too wavy. If I let it go for very long it gives me a wild appearance, which I find unbecoming. For this reason I visited the barber once a month, which I thoroughly enjoyed, because I find it satisfying to cut off loose ends. My appearance, I believed, was one of economy, efficiency. I am neither excessively tall nor excessively short. I carry no surplus flesh. My nose, the sense organ I prize the most, is straight and ends in a fairly sharp point. My eyes are as dark as my hair and are extremely weak. For this reason I have worn thick glasses since I can remember. When I worked at Grund & Greene, I still had the same pair of black frames that had served me since high school, though my prescription had changed many times. Despite the fact that I am quite capable of making my way in the modern world, I know what a miserably inadequate creature, despite my efforts, I truly am. My constitution is so delicate and my eyes so weak that I would not have survived if I had dwelt in an earlier era of history, say, in the Stone Age. I would have been one of the casualties of natural selection—either killed by a wild boar during a hunt because I could not see it coming, or maimed by one of the bigger, stronger boys of the tribe before I reached the age where humans begin copulating—and thus would have been unlikely to pass my defective genes on to future generations. Hence, the race would have continued to grow stronger, as indeed it should. I consider it an abomination that I have actually participated in procreation. I never intended to.

Anyway, only after all the previously described observations of hygiene and domestic maintenance were completed would I go out in the yard to chase Homer. I trapped him against the fence and gave him as much of a scare as I could, and in turn he showered me with that sublime scent of his. My head was sent spinning with the strength of his emissions the first few times—my sight blurring and sense of balance temporarily upset—but I began to develop a tolerance to him and by the fifth weekend I was doing my best to get him to musk at me two or three times in an afternoon. I found that the smell made me hungry and I often went out in the yard to eat my dinner in an appetizing cloud of skunk scent. After doing this a few weekends, I thought to myself, now wouldn't it be even more sensuous if I could actually taste the skunk musk, actually ingest it?

I was not about to butcher poor Homer and eat the little chap, heavens no. I was becoming quite attached to the furry fellow. He had a pleasant enough disposition and kept to himself, which was more than could be said for most people. So I began to look forward, not just to his scent, but to the sight of him when I came home from work at the end of the day. And besides, if I ate him, I'd immediately be back where I'd started, without my own source of skunk musk.

In a single blast, Homer usually emitted about half a fluid ounce of the sticky, oily, yellow substance known as musk. Getting even a small amount of this fluid into my food took some doing. For two or three weekends, when I got Homer out of his burrow and chased him about the yard, I held a hot plate of spaghetti or a vegetable and tofu stir-fry out in front of me, so that when he finally stopped to musk at me, he got at least a few drops of the fluid on the plate. After a time, even the most exquisite dish seemed incomplete without having been seasoned with fresh skunk musk.

One day, about a month and a half after Homer had joined me, I discovered the conspiracy at the office. I left my cubicle at eleven forty-five to get a drink of water. In my peripheral vision, I noticed Farnsworth glancing up at me from his desk as I passed his cubicle. He'd been giving me insinuating looks for some time now, and on returning to my cubicle, I went around the other way, simply to avoid his eyes. He must have assumed I'd gone to lunch, because after I sat down at my desk, before I could put my fingers to my keyboard, I heard my name.

"You really think it's Damien?" the voice said. It was John Schrempp, an annoying little fat person. Whatever he did for our department, it must have involved the consumption of vast quantities of Twinkies, Ho Hos and chocolate Ding Dongs, because I never saw the man do anything else. Once, he came into my cubicle to ask a question about one of my back ads, munching on something chocolate and cream-filled. He spoke while masticating, giving me a full view of the wet, brown mush in his mouth, then licked each of his fingers with a moist smacking sound and placed the copy on my desk with dark brown smears across it.

"I know it's Damien," Farnsworth said. "Didn't you notice how much stronger the smell is right around here?"

I felt the clenching of nervous fear in my stomach.

"Someone told me a rat died in the walls or something," Schrempp said. I heard the clomp of Barbara Flemming's high heels coming down the hall.

"Hey Barbara," Farnsworth said, "have you noticed the stench around here?" I didn't think there was much possibililty that Flemming could have noticed any scent other than her own. She wore enough perfume to make her presence known from a distance of several yards.

"Yes, I have noticed it. I spoke with Sean about it. He thinks a rat got into one of the walls and died. He's going to try to find it and get rid of it this week," she said.

"Well he can crawl around every crawl space and rip apart all the walls in the damn building, but Damien will still be sitting right out here in his cubicle," Farnsworth said. Schrempp chuckled. "I'm not kidding," Farnsworth said, emphatically. "I was in his cubicle the other day. The guy smells like a freaking landfill. No, actually, you know what he smells like? It doesn't smell like a dead rat to me. It smells like skunk." I was simultaneously enraged and mortified. I felt like I was in boarding school again. Imagine, people talking behind my back! How very sloppy and juvenile. It was that cootie business all over again. I wanted to say something out loud in my defense, but at the same time I wanted to curl up under my desk and cover my ears with my hands.

"Well, the smell is a lot stronger over here in this part of the office, I'll give you that," Schrempp said.

"You know, I wouldn't doubt that it is Damien," Flemming said. "There's something creepy about that guy. He's so skinny and dark, and he acts like some kind of robot." While they spoke, I quietly got up from my chair and went and crouched in the corner of my cubicle. From this position I could still hear what they said, but when the others left Farnsworth's cubicle, they wouldn't be able to see me. I remained there for the next twenty minutes.

Of course the inevitable occurred. Homer got used to me. After about three months he could no longer be frightened. When he saw me emerge from the house, he toddled over and rubbed himself against my leg and licked my hand. After all, I fed and housed him, what could I expect? So we became friends. I sat on the porch, rubbed his belly and read to him from the *Collected Works of E.B. White*. He seemed to like *Charlotte's Web* in particular, but also showed great appreciation for *Stuart Little*. He was a much better friend than any I'd ever had. But then, I hadn't had any to speak of since the day I was separated from my mother. I generally don't care for people. At best, they talk constantly about themselves, dig wax from their ears with their pinkie fingers and indulge in other repulsive habits. At worst, they get themselves involved in such hopeless entanglements as marriage, misuse one another, betray, rape and kill each other. I found Homer's nature much more agreeable.

But alas, though I had gained a friend, I now seldom got to enjoy such a rich emission from Homer as I had in the beginning of our relationship, and found myself lying awake at night wishing for the single strong whiff that would send me into olfactory ecstasy. I was able to frighten him enough now and then to get him to musk, but my methods for doing so became increasingly contrived. And I felt guilty sneaking up on him, or dressing up in costume to frighten him.

Then, one Sunday afternoon, I made my discovery. Homer and I were playfully wrestling about, as we had gotten in the habit of doing. I would lie on my back on the ground and let him walk over the length of my body until he got to my head, at which point I would grab him with both hands, pin him to the ground and tickle his belly. During one of these tickling sessions I squeezed him and he suddenly musked. It was one of the greatest blasts of his scent I could have asked for. When I'd recovered from this surprise gift, I tried to figure out what had caused it. I wondered if the squeezing had frightened him in some way, but he seemed quite calm, if slightly bewildered. I squeezed him again, but nothing happened. After a little experimenting, I found that if I placed both thumbs just beneath the rib cage and applied just the right amount of pressure, with a quick, down-and-up massaging motion, it invariably caused Homer to musk. If I pressed too hard, it didn't work—he merely stuck out his tiny tongue and made a gagging sound. Nor did it work if the pressure was too light. With a little practice, though, I found I could control the intensity and the length of the emission that was produced.

"Eureka!" I shouted, jumping to my feet. Homer looked up at me placidly. "Homer, do you know what this means?" I said. "Absolute bliss! No more chasing you around the yard with a Halloween mask and a plate of pork chops. No. I can simply pick you up whenever I want and squeeze a bit of that delightful seasoning onto my plate—a dash on my salad, a liberal squirt into the entrée and perhaps a drop in my tea afterwards. Oh, it is too good to be true!" Homer himself looked pleased. He seemed to get some satisfaction out of being relieved of his musk, just as cows are known to enjoy being milked.

I let Homer move into the house and he soon became an indispensable part of the place. It was comforting to have his warm body nestled beside me on the couch while I read at night. And I got accustomed to his habit of licking the water from my ankles after I stepped out of the shower. I cut a hole in the bottom of the back door and installed a little plastic flap so he could go in and out as he pleased. And any time I felt like it, I picked him up and squeezed him for a little of his scent. I soon gave up the rule I'd made for myself about only using him on weekends. The first thing I did when I got home from work was pick Homer up from where he greeted me at the front door and give him a little squeeze.

What my discovery of the abdominal manipulation of the musk gland had done was give me the liberty to drink musk whenever I chose. And this is quite different from smelling it from a few yards away, or even from using a few drops of the fluid to season one's casserole. Taken with food, the musk's potency is significantly reduced. Direct ingestion introduces one to a completely different aspect of the juice.

The first time I took skunk musk straight, the effects were over-whelming. I held Homer over my head, squeezed a full shot straight down my throat, and was aware of a burning sensation in my sinuses for an instant before I blacked out. I awoke on the ground, with little idea of how much time had passed. By overdosing the first few times I drank musk, I missed out on much of the experience. Measuring my dosage, I found I could administer myself just enough to induce a sense of euphoria without passing out. Instead of squeezing a full shot directly down my throat, I squeezed Homer over a glass and then used an eyedropper to obtain a single droplet I let fall to my tongue. This I immediately chased down with a glass of water.

Most people are unaware of the fact that the skunk gland is the key to an entirely different realm of sensation. I would say the world of a musk dream is the everyday world seen with better clarity, but this is often said about the effect of such inferior chemicals as THC. When embarking upon a musk dream, one graduates to a higher plane of existence than the one people normally inhabit. I would go so far as to say that a person who has not experienced a skunk musk dream is like one who has seen only two dimensions of a three-dimensional world. For such a person, I will make a comparison (though this is probably akin to describing colors by comparing them to textures for a blind man) based on what I've read about the effects of other drugs. Skunk musk has the anesthetizing effects of an opiate and produc-es the sense of heightened awareness of a hallucinogen, without the disagreeable side effects of constipation, hallucination and paranoia. But what makes the musk dream even more complex than anything possible with botanically-derived drugs is the exhilaration. Research I later undertook revealed that this is the result of the large quantity of animal endorphins contained in skunk musk. The immediate effect of ingestion of the appropriate dosage of musk is at once subtle and dramatic. All the tedious pressures and concerns of daily life drop away like a suit of clothes so cheap that it actually dissolves in the sudden storm of chemicals, and one finds oneself instead wrapped in a robe of serenity. The musk dreamer's dream is one that emerges from his own subconscious and over which he has complete control.

But of course euphoria is always followed by depression. And as my tolerance for skunk musk increased, so did my need for the sensation that had not been a need before I knew the sensation existed. Developed over a period of time, a tolerance of a beloved substance, and a tailoring of one's lifestyle to the enjoyment of that substance, can enrich one's life. It is one of the tragedies of modern civilization that the tendency to cultivate such a lifestyle is, in ignorance, condemned as an "addiction" by society's sentinels, people who are fundamentally intolerant. They are the same petty, insecure busybodies who took my mother away and whom I shall never forgive or trust ever again.

2

My mother drank quite a lot of beer when I was growing up. She always drank McDougal's—an imported brand that comes in a green bottle and has a slightly skunky aroma. This was the first scent to greet my nostrils in the morning and the last whiff I sniffed before falling asleep at night. I awoke each morning to the clinking of beer bottles as my mother opened and shut the door of the refrigerator to get out her first McDougal's before starting my breakfast. Then I heard more clinking, of empty bottles, as she cleared the kitchen table, filled a large plastic garbage bag with the previous day's bottles and carried them outside to put in a can by the street.

After this, she came into my room and sat down on the edge of my bed. I always pretended to still be asleep because I liked the gentle way she had of waking me up. She sat next to me for a moment and sighed. The bed sagged with her weight. She pushed the hair back from my forehead with her fingertips and ran one finger down the bridge of my nose, over my lips and let it come to rest on my chin, which like hers was fairly pointy. She leaned forward so that her mouth was only a few inches from my ear.

"Damien," she whispered. "Time to rise and shine, my little soldier." I continued to feign sleep, scrunching my eyelids shut so tight she would have had trouble prying them open with her fingers. "I've got a little surprise for you," she always said. Then her body shuddered, the bed shook slightly, and she let out a long, deep belch she blew into my face and which sounded very much like the lowing of a cow. It went on for a few seconds while I gradually opened my eyes. And there it was—a new morning. My mother sat beside me in a yellow bathrobe, a shaft of sunlight sliced into the room from between the curtains and the skunky smell of my mother's first McDougal's of the day filled my nostrils. I threw my arms around her neck and she pulled the covers down and tickled me until I couldn't stand it any longer and jumped out of bed and ran into the kitchen to eat the eggs, oatmeal, French toast or whatever she had prepared for me that morning.

All day long I looked forward to seeing my mother again because I knew she got lonely while I was at school. I was an only child and my father had left shortly after I was born. When I opened the door to the rather rickety old jalopy in which my mother arrived to pick me up from school, I was greeted by the same comforting smell to which I'd woken up. My mother drove along with a bottle of McDougal's nestled between her thighs, sometimes still dressed in her bathrobe even though it was the middle of the afternoon. She took long swigs of beer between asking me questions about my day at school. Before I went to sleep at night, she sat on the edge of my bed and sang to me—usually her own rendition of an Irish drinking song. "Whisky in the Jar" by the Clancy Brothers was my favorite. After she finished, she kissed me on the cheek, tucked me in, and I drifted off to sleep with that same comforting smell in my nostrils.

When I got a little older I was allowed to walk home from school on my own. Some days I went to a friend's house after school, but that wasn't often because I didn't have many friends, and whenever I asked one of them to come to my house they told me their parents wouldn't allow them to. This was okay with me, since I knew my mother would be waiting for me with milk and peanut butter cookies, and would always be willing to play any game I chose. Sometimes we played monopoly and sometimes we played quarters. My mother was an expert at the latter game and I usually ended up drinking a gallon or so of apple juice, which was my substitute for beer.

One day when I was about eight years old, I was walking home, singing "100 Bottles of Beer on the Wall," swinging my lunch box in one hand and dragging a stick with the other, making a long squiggling trail in the dirt and pretending I was being followed by a snake. All at once, I was acutely aware of the presence of my mother and I stopped walking. I pushed my glasses up the bridge of my nose, sniffed and looked around. I saw nothing but trees on either side of the road. Not a person or car in sight. I walked along a little further and the smell grew stronger, as if twelve of my mothers were standing right beside me. Following my nose, I walked away from the road through the tall weeds and undergrowth that led up to the woods. I didn't have to go far. A small cloud of flies dispersed from a furry mess on the ground at my feet and revealed a small skunk who had doubtless been run over and then tossed away from the road. I poked the carcass with my stick to make sure it was dead, for its eyes were still open, as was its mouth, which was filled with menacingly sharp, white teeth. The smell was much stronger than what I was accustomed to, but it was unmistakably the same odor that was like an aura about my mother.

Then I had what seemed at the time like a brilliant idea. I would bring the skunk home for her, because this, evidently, was the raw material out of which beer was made. How pleased she would be—she would be able to make her own beer! I put my lunch box on the ground, flipped the latches and took out my thermos. Lifting the skunk up by the tail and lowering it into the lunch box, I was careful to leave its head facing up, with its tail curled around in front of it the way a cat's often lies when it's sleeping. I skipped the rest of the way home, swinging my lunch box in one hand and my thermos in the other.

When I burst through the kitchen door, my mother was getting a beer from the refrigerator. She was still wearing her bathrobe, which she seemed to change out of less frequently as time went on. I was glad to have something to cheer her up. The kitchen table had sprouted a field of empty green bottles during the time I'd been at school, but nevertheless my place at the table had been cleared and there was a glass of milk and a plate of peanut butter cookies waiting for me.

My mother turned toward me and smiled. "Hey little soldier," she said. "Back from the wars?" In one fluid motion, she popped the cap off her beer, tossed the cap and bottle opener together onto the counter and took a few long gulps.

"Yup, back from the wars," I said. I pushed aside some of the beer bottles and placed my lunch box and thermos on the table. I didn't want to give away my secret yet, but I must have been grinning crazily, because my mother, smiling, cocked her head and said, "What are you so jolly about?"

"Oh, nothing," I said, sliding onto my chair and taking a bite out of a peanut butter cookie. "I just came across something you might be interested in, that's all."

Her smile evaporated. "Damien, what's that smell?" she asked.

I shrugged. "Just a part of my little surprise for you," I said.

She didn't look like she was in the mood for a surprise at that particular moment. "Damien, what in the world do you have in that lunch box?"

This wasn't going how I'd planned at all. I decided to just get it over with. "It's a present," I said, and with a mouth still full of cookie, I stood up, turned the lunch box toward my mother and sprang the lid. The nestled skunk stared up at my mother with its teeth bared. A shriek filled the air as my mother dropped her beer on the floor and backed away. The McDougal's bottle lay on its side, pouring beer that spread like a disease over the lime-green linoleum.

"Good God!" my mother exclaimed. I wasn't used to hearing my mother scream or swear, and I too jerked away from the table, overturned my chair and almost fell over backwards.

"Get that thing out of here," she said.

"But it reminded me of you!" I protested.

"Out!"

I whisked the lunch box from the table, ran out the door and burst into tears. It's remarkable how a certain scent can conjure a memory and return one to a whole different time and place, or for that matter, cause one to be rejected from a place. After unceremoniously burying the skunk in the back yard, I must have psychologically buried the entire incident, because I had completely forgotten it ever happened until some time during the first weeks of Homer's stay with me. Not that I had had much time to ponder it back then—only a few days after I'd brought home the dead skunk, I was taken out of school in the middle of the day and told my mother had suffered a breakdown. She had been put in a hospital and I was sent to live with my aunt. This aunt had never gotten along with my mother and wanted nothing to do with me. I could not have stayed with her for more than a couple of days, for I have only the vaguest memory of her and her home, though I have a very distinct memory of my first days at Rigby, the boys' boarding school where I was to spend the next eight years of my life. Naturally, at the time, I thought my mother had left me because she was still angry about the skunk I'd brought home, or that my actions had caused her supposed breakdown.

Whoever had had my mother taken away—relatives, neighbors, other parents from the school—I never did find out. Somewhere in a murky adult world, it had been decided that my mother was not a fit parent and she'd been extracted from my life. This noble humanitarian gesture left me without a family. My housemates and houseparents at Rigby were a shabby substitute, to put it mildly. To put it harshly, they were poor specimens of human life whose moral lapses led to cruel and criminal behavior.

The Rigby School occupied a huge, sprawling old farm and was founded to accommodate boys who were orphans of one kind or another. Most were from broken homes on, neither side of which was there adequate money or competence for child rearing. One can imagine what a happy bunch of young men we were. A married couple, the houseparents, resided in each dorm. My houseparents' strategy for managing a house full of unruly boys was to ignore them completely, keep the doors to their quarters shut and let us resolve our conflicts on our own.

I don't care to delve too deeply into this period of my life because it is irrelevant. Suffice it to say that my roommate was a twisted sadist about twice my size whose idea of a good time was to give me a wedgie, then hang me from the top of the open door to our room by my underwear and announce to the rest of the boys that it was piñata time. They then took turns blindfolding one another and whacking at me with a Wiffle-ball bat. My roommate also liked to remove and hide the wooden slats from my bed frame so that when I got into bed the mattress fell through the frame to the floor. After the fourth or fifth of these incidents I was unable to find the slats and eventually gave up looking for them and slept on the floor for the rest of the year.

Another activity that amused my roommonster and won him a higher standing among the other boys, was to steal my diary from under my pillow and read it aloud to a room full of our housemates. Of course, a high percentage of the information contained in the diary was about my mother. Organized readings of my diary were arranged, after which I was forced to kneel on the floor while my twelve housemates lined up behind me, each giving my buttocks two whacks with a paddle that one of the older boys had made in a woodshop class. There was nothing to be done about these adolescent male rituals and the random thrashings to which I was treated by my roommonster and others, since I was considerably shorter and thinner than the other boys and had no allies. Often I was too nervous to eat much during meal times and thus became even thinner and weaker while the others sprouted like redwoods around me. I treated my emaciation like an epidermal disease, attempting to conceal it by wearing heavy sweaters in cold weather and by avoiding any outdoor activities in warm weather that might require the shedding of my shirt.

There were further inconveniences. Occasionally, someone would steal my glasses and I was forced to go through an entire day without them, unable to take notes in class because I could not see the blackboard. Boys I didn't even know accosted me between classes to tease me about my mother—the "alky" as they referred to her—and everyone on campus, each of them a needy, orphan bastard himself, was relieved to know that his background, however disgraceful, was at least not as sordid as mine.

My introverted nature intensified until I scuttled furtively about the campus like a pair of ragged claws, speaking to no one, participating in no sports or other extracurricular activities. Instead, I read. I read book after book, hiding from the world among the pages of novels, usually adventure stories. On the weekends I found refuge in the world of television. While the other boys were at sporting events or relatives' homes, I had the television lounge to myself, where I became a rock of a man, a loner who blew into town after robbing a wagon train and who could vanquish his enemies with a sardonic glare, or if necessary, a few plugs of hot lead.

I returned from classes one afternoon toward the end of my first school year at Rigby and was informed by my houseparents that my mother was dead. She'd committed suicide, they said, and my aunt didn't see any reason I should attend the funeral. As I was one of the few boys with no relatives or friends with whom to stay (my aunt had let the school know she would be too busy during the summers to take me), I spent the summers working with the groundskeepers on the Rigby campus. I looked forward to those months of long, hazy afternoons when the campus was peaceful, as it might have been in the days when it had been a farm. I was left to work on my own most of the time, and occasionally, while I was weeding a flowerbed or raking the freshly-mown grass, I caught a whiff of skunk. I stopped whatever I was doing, stood there and sniffed. It made me tremble. There was something voluptuous, something forbidden about that smell. By that first summer at Rigby, I had already blocked out most memories of my mother and had completely forgotten the lunch-box incident. Loss has always been intolerably painful for me and I'd already found that the best way to deal with that pain is to do one's best to obliterate its source, memory.

◈ ◈ ◈

I knew Mrs. Endicott was spying. She poked her nose over the fence to watch Homer and me while we spent quiet Sunday afternoons together on the back porch. He sat with his head resting in my lap while I drank tea and read the newspaper aloud. There was a little space between the bottom of the fence and the ground where I could see a sliver of the blue plastic milk crate on which Mrs. Endicott stood. Cataract-obscured though her vision was, I don't believe she could have maintained the illusion that Homer was a dog for very long.

Homer was living quite high on the hog at this time. He slept at the foot of my bed and only used the burrow now and then. He ate whatever I ate—from beef stroganoff to fruit crepes. It was quite a cushy life for such a savage skunk as Homer had so recently been. He was always a little groggy in the morning, but I woke him up when I got up and had him follow me through my morning rituals. This way I could ensure that he was fully awake by the time I left for work, that he would have the opportunity to get a jump on whatever animal kingdom business might be on his current to-do list. It wasn't until later that I learned that Homer's lethargy at this hour was not by any means due to a flaw in his character, but to an aspect of his nature that I hadn't taken into consideration because it hadn't yet occurred to me.

I set Homer beside me on a stool by the sink each morning so he could watch me shave. Even though he was now living in the house, he still seemed to have the blues, and one morning, glancing at his reflection in the mirror while I rinsed my razor, it seemed to me that he looked particularly melancholy. "What's the matter, Homer?" I asked, stretching the skin to get at the stubborn stubble along my jawline. "Domestication getting you down, old boy?" Then it struck me. I put the razor on the edge of the sink and turned to him. "Of course. How selfish I've been. Here I am, getting ready to go off to work, knowing very well that you'll be left alone all day. What you need is a friend." I patted him on the head and turned back to the mirror to finish shaving. I looked at his reflection out of the corner of my eye. "And I bet you'd like a lady friend, wouldn't you?" See, whereas I had always regarded contact with other animals of my own species as a disagreeable, though necessary, evil, Homer—a helpless little slave to instinct—might actually desire the company of his fellow creatures. I had my intellect to keep me company. Through reading, I could, at my leisure, listen to the thoughts of some of the best minds ever to flourish on this planet and I could always shut them up when I liked by simply closing the cover of the book. Homer, without this advantage, might have been experiencing bona fide loneliness. I rinsed my face, toweled it dry and then, as I'd started to do quite often in the mornings, picked Homer up and gave him a little squeeze, sweeping him across my chest as I did, and giving myself a dash under the arms, so I wouldn't have to go all day without a single whiff of skunk—it would already be on me.

I went out the door excited with the anticipation of the surprise gift I would soon bestow upon my little chum. My feet crunched the frozen ground and my breath turned into fog as I walked across the dead grass of my front yard. Winter is my favorite season. People stay in their homes, the leaves stay in their branches, everything is calm, quiet, cold. I looked forward to getting on the commuter train and burying myself in a book. My spirits were so high, I went as far as to call out a good morning to Mrs. Endicott, who was coming down her walk with Tesa, who I was happy to see on a leash. As soon as I'd called out, Tesa began yapping and straining toward me.

"Good morning," Mrs. Endicott said, and then, barely audibly, "ya stinker."

John Piper was hovering around my cubicle when I got to work. With a tense grunt meant to indicate the word "Morning," he asked to see me in his office. I followed him in and sat down. The window of his office looked out over the rooftops to the river, glittering coldly in the sunlight, a white fringe of ice along its banks. Piper sat down behind his desk. There was a framed studio photograph of his family, as well as individual photos of his four children. In each of the individual shots, the child was either smiling and holding a tennis racket or smiling and waving from where he sat in a sailboat with an orange life preserver around his silly neck. There was a large silver paperweight in the shape of a cocker spaniel sitting on Piper's desk. A sanguine man with jowls, a thick neck, and white hair that he kept swept straight back over his head, Piper himself looked something like a bulldog crossed with an East European politician.

"Damien," he said, "I've been meaning to have a word with you." Then he interrupted himself to walk across the room to open a window before sitting down to begin talking again. "Damien, you've been doing good work with us for several years now."

"Six," I said. If we were going to sit around discussing things we already knew, I thought, we might as well at least be precise.

"Beg your pardon?" he said.

"Six years, sir. Six years, three months and seven days."

"Yes, six years. Well, in that time I've had nothing but positive reviews from Mr. Hastings regarding your work. You've been quite efficient and everyone agrees that you're extremely professional."

I really wished he would get to the point. We both had a lot of work to do. He should have known that. Unaccustomed to idle chatter, my discomfort may have shown, because Piper cleared his throat, leaned forward and put his forearms on the desk in a getting-down-to-business pose.

"You're a young man, Damien, and I think there's a good future for you here," he said. He cleared his throat again. "And I'm sorry that what I have to talk with you about is a personal matter." Then he was at a sudden loss for words. He lifted the paperweight and turned it from one side to another, looking at it as if he expected it to bark a cue to him. I sat with my hands folded in my lap, waiting. Piper's pink face flushed red right up to the white of his hairline. "Um, where do you live, Damien?"

"New Essex," I said.

"Ah yes, that's a nice area," he said, setting the spaniel back down on the desk. "A very clean area."

"Yes, very. That's why I chose it in fact."

Piper looked stumped again for a moment. "I'll cut to the chase, Damien. A few people have been complaining that you have a certain odor about you they find offensive."

My back stiffened. I'd thought I was dealing with full-fledged adults in this company, not childish tattletales. Now, did I complain to Piper about Hastings's habit of picking his nose while he spoke to me? No. Or of how Farnsworth liked to make a slurpy, lip-smacking noise that sounded like someone walking through deep mud, and that he did it approximately once every sixty seconds for a full hour after eating lunch? No. Nor did I complain of the twenty-foot radius of perfume fumes that surrounded Barbara Flemming like a force field. Nor of how Piper himself left your hand reeking of some heinous cologne for the rest of the day after he shook it.

"It's nothing to be alarmed about," Piper went on. "As I said, everyone agrees that your work and your work habits are impeccable. It's just that maybe you should walk to the office by a different route if you think you're picking up a strange odor along the way. Or maybe try a different cologne."

Oh, yes, I thought—cologne. That's probably Piper's solution to all his problems: things aren't quite going your way, something's a little off? Just add a little more cologne to your life. I sat regarding Piper as before and said nothing, which seemed to frustrate him. The only movement I made was to push my glasses up my nose quickly with one finger, which I often found necessary to do when I began to perspire.

"So, whatever it is, I'll expect no more complaints," Piper said, suddenly blustering. He smiled aggressively, stood up and came around the desk to clap a cologne-soaked hand on my shoulder as I rose from my chair. "Well, I guess we'd better get to work," he said. "Enough small talk, eh?"

I nodded, turned and walked out of his office. I thought of poor Homer, sitting around the house by himself. Cute, cuddly little Homer and that magnificent aroma of his which was being mistaken by the uninitiated in my office for—for what? Some fetid thing left in a dumpster that I walked by on my way to work perhaps, or an inferior brand of cologne? And the notion that my colleagues were conspiring against me because of a personal preference was absolutely odious. It was dirty. It was a filthy, rotten trick. I was a man of few comforts. They'd taken away my mother, my diary and the slats for my bed. I'd been ill at ease in the company of other people all my life and had never found pleasure in any of the social games with which they amused themselves. But now they wanted to take this from me—my new hobby, my greatest pleasure and my only solace. Well, god damn them. God damn them all to hell.

And furthermore, I thought, is it not my own business what I do at home? Mine and no one else's? Is there no division between a man's professional and private lives? We all choose our own smells. Some choose one that comes in a can or bottle. Some secrete a garlicky odor, others a cheesy one. Some smell of coffee, some of vinegar, and some of onions. My odor was different, but not grounds for crucifixion. I tried harder than ever to ignore Farnsworth and of course I did not alter my habits with Homer in the least.

After work on Friday, I went to the pet store and bought the sort of traveling kennel one uses for cats. It was time to hunt for Homer's surprise. When I got home, I retrieved my camping gear from the basement and packed it, along with a copy of *The Last of the Mohicans*, in the trunk of my Eldorado. I went to the bedroom to change into the hiking boots (to which I'd applied a liberal amount of waterproofing gel) and khaki hunting pants with eight pockets I had laid out after making the bed that morning. When I've made my bed, one can throw a coin down on the taut bedspread and a watch it pop back up in the air like a miniature person on a giant trampoline. Homer meandered into the bedroom and stood there watching me change.

"Homer, old boy, I'm going on a bit of a safari," I said. "Now, I've left you with plenty of food and I'll be back by dinner time on Sunday at the very latest. Can I trust you to hold down the fort for me?" I paused to let the news sink in. Homer hadn't been alone for such a long period since we'd started living together. He continued to stare at me with his dark, intelligent eyes. "Good," I said. "You're a young skunk and I think you've got a good future ahead of you. So just keep a stiff upper snout and don't do anything I wouldn't do." With that, I stooped to give him a pat on the head and went out the door.

It was a couple hours' drive to the place I had in mind—not too far from where I'd found Homer. Dusk had dissolved into a lonesome darkness by the time I pulled into my site and set up camp. I cooked up some pork and beans over my propane stove. Towering evergreens surrounded me like the walls of a dark cathedral whose ceiling was a clear, starry sky. I've always found it simultaneously peaceful and un-nerving to sleep outdoors. On the one hand, it's a relief to be alone and away from the distracting noise of other human beings, but on the other hand, it *is* the out-of-doors, and there's no telling what can happen. Getting in the tent and having walls around me, though they were only nylon, made me more comfortable. I curled up in my sleeping bag with my earmuffs on, reading from Mr. Cooper's *Mohicans* by the light of my kerosene lantern. Though I did not need the eye covers I usually required to achieve the total darkness I prefer for slumber, I found getting to sleep difficult because no matter which way I lay there always seemed to be one troublesome rock gouging into my spine.

I had my tea and toast before sunrise the next morning, packed a lunch in my knapsack and set out into the woods with my compass to guide me. I reveled in my preparedness as the frost on the under-growth began to melt and bead on the tops of my protected hiking boots. But one can revel in such things for only so long. My enthusiasm had substantially diminished by the time I'd returned to camp at sundown, having tramped around in the wild for an entire day without any sign of a skunk.

The next morning I started out early again, divided the area into quadrants, and combed each of these one at a time, very thoroughly, keeping an eye out for a bushy tail or any hole that might possibly be a burrow. I found a fallen tree on which to eat my lunch and contemplate the fruitlessness of my skunk hunt. Here it was Sunday afternoon, and still no sign of a playmate for Homer. I realized then that it would have been wiser to have brought Homer along and perhaps walked around with him on a leash, since he would be better than I at seeking out other skunks. Then I remembered something so blindingly obvious that I was shocked by my own stupidity: skunks are nocturnal animals. Finding Homer out and about in the middle of the day had been an anomaly. Furthermore, it was possible that what I'd interpreted as despondency and loneliness could have been the effects of sleep deprivation caused by my forcing Homer to get up early in the mornings. I threw down my cucumber sandwich in disgust. "Stupid!" I exclaimed aloud. I stood up and began slamming my head against a tree. "You stupid, stupid man!" I yelled. I banged my head until I became dizzy, stumbled over a root and rather unexpectedly found myself sitting on the ground, which was covered with frosted, crusty leaves. I gathered myself up, went back to my campsite and took a nap.

At dusk I set out again with a powerful flashlight and eventually came across the spot where I'd eaten lunch. I shined my flashlight at the base of the log, and low and behold, a skunk was devouring the remains of the sandwich I'd thrown down that afternoon. As one might imagine, it is more than a little awkward trying to hustle a skunk into a burlap sack with hands numb from the cold, while simultaneously holding a flashlight and being clawed and musked at by the irate little creature in question. When I got it back to camp and put it in the kennel, I discovered I'd been fortunate enough to bag a female. I clapped my gloved hands. Homer was going to be absolutely delighted. And as for me, the capture meant twice the amount of skunk musk available in the house. On the way home, I thought about what to name the new member of the household. I decided on Louisa, a name that has always appealed to me. It sounds like the name of a quiet person who does not often go out or nose about in other people's affairs. I looked down at Louisa, who was circling around in the kennel as I drove. It seemed only yesterday that I'd brought Homer home with me in a slightly less dignified fashion.

Homer greeted me at the door and followed me into the den where I set Louisa's box down and opened it. She stepped cautiously out and looked around. Homer was immediately circling and sniffing at her. "Homer, meet Louisa," I said. "Louisa, Homer." They paid no attention to me whatsoever. Louisa began exploring her new surroundings and for the most part ignored Homer as he sniffed at her and followed her about. I decided to leave them alone to get better acquainted. I put some Tchaikovsky on the stereo and went into the kitchen to bake a cake. This is how I always celebrate accomplishments. If it had been a slightly less significant event, I might have postponed my baking cele-bration until the next day, since it was so late on a Sunday night, but the compulsion to bake was overwhelming. So I made an angel's food cake, put two slices on separate plates and set them on the floor of the den for Homer and Louisa, then ate my own slice on the couch. After they had finished their cake I pronounced Homer and Louisa skunk and wife and took several photographs of them together in front of the fireplace.

The next morning on my way to work I dropped off the film at a shop around the corner from the office and picked up the photos and a frame on my lunch hour. Homer and Louisa had globs of icing and crumbs of cake on the fur around their muzzles in all the pictures. I chose what I believed to be the most flattering photo, put it in the frame and set it up on the desk beside my computer. Unlike the Piper types, who regularly construct shrines to their families and pets in the workplace, this was the first time I'd allowed any evidence of my per-sonal life to manifest itself in my professional life. The effect was to cause me to be late for the Monday department meeting. I was gazing at my only cubicle decoration when I suddenly realized it was two-ten. The meeting began at two and ordinarily I was as punctual as I was punctilious, arriving at the conference room at twenty seconds before the hour with my project report up to date. Usually, I spoke about my progress while many of the others unabashedly threw their reports together on the spot, scribbling away while I talked, or gave up alto-gether and said by way of excuse that they had family obligations that had kept them from completing their reports. But now here I was, lost in sentimental contemplation of a photograph, late and unprepared for the department meeting. I dashed down the hall, into the confer-ence room and slipped into an empty seat next to Farnsworth at the end of the long table.

"Jesus Christ!" Farnsworth swore under his breath the moment I sat down. He covered his mouth and nose with his hand and leaned away from me. Then Hastings interrupted his own typically self-aggrandiz-ing Monday meeting opening oratory to say, "Excuse me, but could someone crack a window please?" Barbara Flemming immediately got up to do so. I glanced around the table. Conspiracy. I could see it in each and every smug, disapproving face. And not one of those faces dared let their eyes meet mine. But what did I care? I'd never needed the approval of these vermin. Let them air their disgust, I thought, for they disgusted me as well. My true friends, the bearers of the delicious and transporting musk, were waiting for me at home.

When I got home that night, Homer was not at the door to greet me. I called out his name but he did not come. A sudden panic overcame me and I flew through the house in search of him, going down on my knees to peer under the bed, overturning chairs, pulling back the sofa to look behind it, all the while calling out "Homer, Homer!" at the top of my lungs. "For goodness sake, they've eloped!" I cried. Then I remembered the burrow, which I'd practically forgotten existed since Homer had moved into the house. I ran into the backyard, threw myself on the ground and squinted down into Homer's burrow. And there were Homer and Louisa, somewhat startled by the sudden appearance of a huge moon of a face at the entrance of the burrow, but hardly roused out of what was quite obviously a postcoital stupor. I turned away, embarrassed and perhaps a bit jealous. But if they were happy together, I decided, I was happy. I might feel rejected if Homer stopped greeting me at the door, or never again wanted to spend the afternoon reading, but I wouldn't get in his way if he wanted to become a family man. Though I would prefer to be his closest friend, all I really needed from him and Louisa was their musk.

I read up on skunks to learn what to feed Homer and Louisa. In the following weeks, I made frequent trips to the pet store to purchase crickets, spiders, mice, etc. But this did not work out satisfactorily for two reasons: it cost more money than I cared to spend on skunk food and I kept buying out the entire store. So I took a few field trips with Homer and Louisa and observed as they foraged for their own food. Making a note of what they ate, I went on a few field trips of my own, during which I kidnapped several species of insect, arachnid and a few mice. I set up a bug zoo in my garage at very little expense, where the insects bred faster than Homer and Louisa (and later, the rest of the family) could eat them. I had two types of grasshopper and one type of cricket, a ground beetle and potato beetle. I also had a common meadow spider, two ant farms—one of black and one of red ants—as well as moths, caterpillars and white grubs. It was a veritable skunk's smörgasbord. I kept my car parked in the street, as the garage quickly became a metropolis of boxes and cages in which these various insects were housed. The centerpiece was a large, plywood mouse house with a floor of wood shavings and a wire-mesh ceiling.

It was a morbid kind of pleasure to watch the relish with which Homer partook of a furry brown field mouse. He grasped the tiny fellow between his forefeet and twisted his body until a faint snap could be heard. He then took the smaller rodent's head between his jaws, crushed the skull and gobbled the mouse quite quickly, though he always left a generous portion of the remains for Louisa if she had not been given a mouse of her own. I collected a small herd of mice, but they did not multiply as quickly as the insects, so I saved them as treats that were doled out on special occasions.

One Monday morning, a week after the department meeting for which I'd been late, I found Piper waiting for me again upon my arrival at the office. He was pacing in front of my cubicle, looking even more flushed and disturbed than he had the last time. He summoned me into his office, closed the door and opened the window.

"Damien," he said, "I thought we had an understanding that you were going to clear up the matter we talked about." I gave him as blank a stare as the one Homer usually gave me when he wasn't sure what I might be hinting at. "However," Piper went on, "I received several complaints after the department meeting last Monday, and it's obvious to me right now that you haven't done anything about it." He looked as if he expected me to say something for myself, to make some excuse—the way others made excuses for failing to complete their project reports, I suppose—but he hadn't yet asked me a question and I wasn't about to fall into the pattern of groveling obsequiousness displayed by so many of my colleagues. And besides, I was sick of all this tiptoeing around the issue, of being black-balled by my coworkers, of being ridiculed behind my back. I wanted someone to confront me head-on if he really had a problem with me.

And as it happened, Piper was willing, finally, to give me what I wanted. His face grew redder and redder, contrasting sharply with his white hair, while I refused to speak. "Is there anything you'd like to tell me about?" he tried. I shook my head. He began to tremble with rage and I found I could easily imagine steam shooting from his ears. "Are you unhappy working here? Would you like to say anything regarding the complaints of your coworkers?" Finally he exploded. "Goddamnit man, you smell like a skunk! You stink! Can't you understand that this is a professional environment, and we can't tolerate this sort of thing? We're not running a farm here—"

For one of the first times in my life I acted spontaneously. I don't believe in spontaneity as a rule; I prefer a carefully considered plan, a deliberate course of action. But the logic of the idea that popped into my head at that moment seemed infallible.

"Would it be alright with you," I asked calmly, "if I continued my work as an employee for this company but did my work at home? I have my own computer, a fax; there is no reason I couldn't do everything I do here from my own house." The red began to recede from Piper's fleshy face as he considered my proposal. He said he'd have to talk it over with Hastings, but by five o'clock I'd been given the OK and I cleaned out my cubicle and began working as a freelancer the very next day.

3

I was quite thrilled by the prospect of never again having to endure Farnsworth's revolting lip-smacking performances or Hastings' nose-picking. And come to think of it, every person in the entire claustrophobic office clicked his pen, tapped his foot constantly, or had some other irritating habit that seemed calculated to drive me out of my mind. Not to mention those soporific and inconsequential department meetings. Without these distractions I would be more productive than ever. But most importantly, I would be at liberty to give myself a dose of skunk musk whenever I liked. I could be absolutely whimsical.

So my life went on quite happily for several months. I worked for eight hours each day, maintaining a strict regimen. At first, I sat down to work at precisely seven AM, finished at three PM and had the rest of the afternoon and evening to do as I pleased. But after the first week, while working the same number of hours, I pushed my starting hour back to eight. Then after a while to nine, then ten. During the summer I found it preferable to work in the evening when it was cooler, and pushed my schedule back so far that I wasn't getting out of bed until rather late in the afternoon. Part of this may have been the influence of living with Homer and Louisa, who of course were late risers.

One afternoon, while I was sitting at my desk working, Louisa walked by and brushed against my foot. I decided I would allow myself a five-minute break, and I picked her up and squirted her musk into a shot glass I kept on my desk beside the wedding photograph of her and Homer. By this time I was beyond using the eyedropper, but I could only imbibe about half a shot of musk at a time. I held Louisa in my lap for a moment before putting her down on the floor. There was a significant bulge in her stomach, but I hadn't fed her a field mouse for days and I wondered how she could be putting on weight so quickly. As she sauntered out into the kitchen, I noticed something in her walk, that touch of pride one often sees in the way a female carries herself when she is carrying a second life within her. With this sudden realization, I got up from my chair, staggering slightly under the effects of the musk I'd just drunk, and followed Louisa into the kitchen where she stood contemplating her empty food dish.

"My dear lady," I said. "I thought you were gaining weight due to lethargy, but I understand now what you must be going through." I knelt down and took one of her forepaws in my hands and shook it. "I'd like to congratulate you and Homer in advance. May your children be as handsome and pungent as are the two of you." She continued to gaze down into the food dish after I released her paw. "Of course," I said. "You're eating for six. I'll go get some crickets right away. How about a mouse, hmm?"

She voraciously devoured the food I brought her and I made sure to give her double rations for the next few months. I also excused her from the duty of providing me with musk and relied entirely upon Homer.

I had always been a creature of habit and now I gradually began to recognize that such a creature is compatible with skunk living. I made a complete shift to a nocturnal schedule. My wardrobe changed. It felt strange at first to do my work without a necktie, but dispensing with it seemed to have no dilatory effect on my performance. It may even have improved it. I have always suspected that neckties, by constricting the arteries in the neck, reduce the amount of blood reaching the brain and thereby retard its functions. Neither Homer nor Louisa seemed to care whether I wore a tie or not. I began, now and then, to absentmindedly slip off my shoes while I worked. After experimenting a bit, I eventually discovered that I preferred to spend my working and my relaxing hours in slippers. My time was so economically managed that I seldom left the house, and when I did, I had an errand route mapped out that enabled me to drastically minimize the amount of time wasted in the world of human beings, whose company I found to be increasingly tiresome the less time I spent around them. Even a few minutes spent in conversation could drive me to distraction.

One evening, Louisa gave birth to a litter. It was a field-mouse day and I was bringing Homer and Louisa fried ant hors d'oeuvres. Since Louisa had been reluctant to leave the burrow for the past week or two, I'd started bringing their meals out to them. When I peered into the burrow to look for a good spot to put down their dishes, I

found Louisa in the throes of labor. Homer sat in the corner looking perplexed, as I imagine I did, neither of us being very well versed
in what to do in such situations. I cursed myself for not having been
prepared for this. It was unlike me. Here was an event I'd seen coming
for months and I hadn't read up on it to find out what equipment one
might need to deliver a litter of skunks. Had it been out of spite that
I'd decided to leave the responsibility to Homer, because lately I'd felt
neglected by him, and envious of Louisa? I hoped not. I went into the
kitchen and filled a large salad bowl with steaming hot water, brought
it outside with a couple of fresh towels and placed these articles next
to the entrance to the burrow. Homer and Louisa could use them at
their own discretion. Then I went back into the kitchen where I'd left
the hot water running. Steam rose up from the basin of the sink. I held
my hand under the scalding stream, watched my hand turn red and
tremble as I lost control of it. "You bastard!" I yelled aloud. "That will
teach you, you lousy bastard!" After a few minutes of this, I turned the
water off, dried my hand and slammed my head against the counter
until I'd calmed down.

In the following weeks, Louisa was extremely busy nursing and
looking after her young pups. There were five of them (not including
Bradley, whom I had to bury in a corner of the yard two days after he
was born). They were Elsbeth, Rupert, Gertrude, Nathaniel and Helga.
Ugly little things, baby skunks: hairless, pale pink like little pigs, they
spend the first vulnerable days of their lives blind, their eyes shut tight,
suckling at their mother's teats. After a week or so, however, Rupert
and Elsbeth began trying out their legs. They poked their tiny snouts
out of the burrow, or stepped outside momentarily, wiggled their whiskers, and then jumped back into the burrow to hide behind Louisa. I
brought all Louisa's meals to the burrow during this period, though
Homer came to the kitchen to eat from his dish and seemed happy to
spend as much time as possible in the house with me and away from
Louisa and the children.

After a while, the pups' black-and-white fur began to grow in. They
explored the yard and then, tentatively, following their parents, ven-
tured into the house. I let them have the run of the place. At first they
went nowhere without their mother. They followed Louisa from room
to room, out into the yard and back again, in a pleasingly tidy single-
file line. Sometimes, if I were going from one room to another myself,
I had to stop at the doorway like a motorist at a crosswalk and wait for
all six of them to parade by. Either Helga or Gertrude, who were slower

than the others, brought up the rear. These two were the least practical-minded of the group. Helga was easily distracted. She would stop to sniff at something and Gertrude would walk right into her and they would both go tumbling over. Gertrude also had a habit of tripping over her own feet and falling forward on her snout, emitting a sound like the release of air when one opens a can of soda. Of course I had to wait until they were mature, but I must confess I tried my darndest to get some musk out of them long before they were capable of giving me any. I'd squeeze one of the little buggers over my cup until he let out a shrill squeak and I put him down, apologizing profusely and swearing not to try it again until I was certain he was old enough.

It was shortly after the children were born that I began to have real problems with Mrs. Endicott. She was constantly peering over the fence or muttering about "evil odors" as she collected her laundry from the clothesline in her backyard. One evening at dusk, while I was taking my morning tea in the backyard, I caught her. The orange glow of the sun was just barely visible over the rooftops to the west and Homer was rough-housing with Rupert and Nathaniel when I glanced over and saw Mrs. Endicott's eyes and the curly top of her head above the wooden fence. She ducked down as soon as I saw her. There had been several occasions already that month when I'd noticed similar espionage operations. I was growing perturbed.

"Is there something I can help you with, Mrs. Endicott?" I called, the next time she reared her graying head. Again she disappeared behind the fence. I took a few more sips of tea and then noticed her peeking again.

"Oh, what *is* it?" I said, not even caring that my voice betrayed irritation.

This time her face remained above the fence. "It's just that," she whined, "well, I've noticed you have some skunks over there."

"Is there a law against skunks?"

"I'm not sure," she said, and as she spoke, a strain of animosity strengthened until it dominated her tone. "But see, I hang my laundry out back, and all my clothes and sheets started to reek like skunk. That was bad enough, but now that those things have started breeding it's even worse. You've practically got a skunk kennel over there. The smell gets into the house unless I keep the doors and windows shut all the time, which makes it stuffy, which is bad for my sinuses. Do you realize I go through four containers of nasal spray every week—four every week!"

"Mrs. Endicott," I broke in, "I really do not care to sit here while you stand on a milk crate and preach to me about your overindulgence in pharmaceuticals."

"Well, listen. Now the smell of your damn skunks gets into my house no matter what I do. My friend Edna was over the other day. 'What've you been doing in here?' she says, 'cooking skunk cabbage all day?' 'No,' I say, 'it's that Damien, next door. He keeps skunks in his backyard.' 'That grumpy bachelor?' Edna says, 'I thought he was kind of strange, but I wouldn't've guessed he was weird too.' 'Well, he quit his job and started sleeping all day,' I says, 'and now he's got these disgusting skunks running all over the place and it stinks to high heaven.' 'Isn't there a law against things like that?' she says, 'A public nuisance law, I think.' 'I don't know,' I says, 'but he'd better do something about them soon.'"

"What do you mean, I'd 'better do something about them,'" I said. "Is that some kind of threat?"

"Well, you'd better, because I'm not going to be able to stand living like this for very long. You know, what you need is a good woman to take care of you. A young man like you," she shook her head. "Maybe then you wouldn't be so grumpy, and you'd get rid of those god-awful skunks."

I could actually feel my temperature rising. She was slandering skunks—and right in front of Homer and the children. I stood abruptly, letting the tea cup and saucer go clattering to the cement floor of the porch. "That's quite enough, Mrs. Endicott!" I roared. Her head disappeared from above the fence and I heard her back door slam shut a second later.

Homer and the boys had stopped playing and stood there in the yard, staring at me. The poor, trusting little chaps. What would Mrs. Endicott have me do, send them off to some wretched boarding school? My hands were shaking. I hadn't conversed with another person for quite some time, and renewing that experience had been unpleasant enough, but I'd thought I'd left behind petty reprobations like Mrs. Endicott's when I left Grund & Greene and started working at home. "Is there no end to it, Homer?" I said. Homer shook his head sadly.

Life was becoming busier and busier with such a large family in the house. By the time the children were about four weeks old, their fur was almost as full as their parents. They had even begun to venture into different rooms of the house on their own and get into mischief. One night I almost murdered Rupert by the unlikely method of washing him to death. He must have been playing in the hamper and fallen asleep among my dirty clothes. I noticed the sleeve of one of my shirts was wriggling with life after I'd already put the clothes in the washing machine and was sprinkling detergent over them. Then Rupert popped his curious little head through the end of the sleeve and looked around, blinking.

All the children had matured enough to musk by this time and for me their coming of age was the beginning of my connoisseurship. I had noticed that Louisa's musk was slightly more acidic than Homer's, but I hadn't thought much of it until after the rest of the family came along. Sampling each one, I learned that the flavor of each skunk's musk was as distinct as his or her personality. For example, Nathaniel's musk had an earthy aroma and a bold but simple flavor, while Elsbeth's had a comparatively faint aroma, though it was full-bodied, higher in acidity and had a more complex flavor. I developed a routine, by which I squeezed each of the skunks over a mason jar each evening, after they'd had the day to sleep and replenish their musk glands. They seemed to like this ritual and after a while they came into the kitchen after they awoke, loitered around their food bowls and patiently waited to be milked of their musk. I had a different mason jar for each of them, with the name of the skunk whose musk it contained taped on the side. This way I could choose from among the jars at my leisure, depending on what sort of mood I was in, or what sort of meal I was preparing, without having to go searching around the house for the right member of the family.

I usually ran my weekly errands late on Friday afternoon. I had timed this excursion and gotten it down to under two hours, plus or minus a few minutes depending on the line at the bank. That was only two hours per week I had to spend away from my house and my skunks; eight hours per month, ninety-six hours per year. Though fairly minimal, even this was plenty of time for me to get more than my fill of humanity. The grubbiness of the buying and selling of goods, the greedy expressions on the faces of people in the stores I was compelled to enter, the strangulating exhaust fumes and cigarette smoke, foul body odor and even fouler deodorants and perfumes, the nerve-grating glances, the harsh blasts of car horns, the offensive, careless shouts of greeting, the impudence and naked lasciviousness of strangers, the fearsome grinding of young people's skateboards, the oppressive neon lights, garish posters advertising films that promised further immersion in the swill bucket of greed and violence in which we were already drowning, and to top it off, the grime, the streets littered with fast-food containers, cigarette butts, bums begging for change—it all made me sick. And this was only a relatively small suburb. After a time, I wondered at how I'd ever summoned the nerve to go into the city each day. I often got migraines after my weekly outings and had to spend an hour or two in the den with all the shades down, languishing in a musk dream while my skunks climbed over the furniture and over me as I lay on the couch.

One day during my weekly tour through the Dantesque horror known as downtown New Essex, I noticed, or rather, found myself utterly galled by, a fantastically rude, brusque woman in the canned-foods aisle of the supermarket. I was just about to pick up a can of sardines when it was snatched out from under my fingertips by a hand that was wrinkled like a prune. At the same moment, I noticed a strong odor of fish. I was near the end of my errands and could already feel my head beginning to throb at the temples. My distaste for conversation had grown so strong that I almost let the incident pass, but my aggravation got the better of me.

"Excuse me," I said, "but I was just about to pick that up." The woman was so busy sweeping stacks of sardines off the shelf and into her cart that she hardly seemed to notice me at all. She cleaned out the entire section. Her cart was filled almost exclusively with canned sardines.

"Sorry," she said, "but I have to have these." She glanced at me, only for a moment, but long enough for me to notice that she had a walleye. Then she started on the canned clams and anchovies. Dumbfounded, I watched as she made her way down the aisle and noticed that, like me, she was wearing bedroom slippers. She also wore a long, grayish-white terry cloth bathrobe.

That night I had trouble getting to sleep. There was something familiar about the woman and something strangely exciting as well. Anyone seen at the supermarket in a bathrobe and slippers, buying a whole cartload of canned fish, must be the keeper of at least a few interesting secrets. I found myself longing to know what those secrets were. Over and over, I rewound and played the scene in which she glanced up at me in the midst of swiping sardines from the shelf. The frizzy brown ringlets that framed her face seemed to have a life of their own, made her look even more vital, more vigorous than her swift motions suggested. And the way she looked at me! That one walleye stared off in another direction, as if she were wary of an ambush, while the other eye, an aquamarine pool pierced by the black of a large pupil, bore into me—qualitative, distrustful, competitive and considerate all at once.

I woke up several times in the morning from dreams in which this strange woman's face appeared and I asked her for a can of sardines.

Then the face became my mother's, and no sooner had I asked for pea-nut butter cookies and milk than the face turned into the sardine wom-an's and I was hopelessly embarrassed for having asked her for cookies and milk. "Mother!" I yelled, sitting bolt upright in bed and tearing off my eye covers. It was eleven AM—the middle of the night for me—but I was wide awake. I realized two things. One was that it had been noth-ing but the woman's bathrobe that had reminded me of my mother. Otherwise they were opposites. While my mother was slow and lan-guid, this woman was quick and energetic. So I could dispense with the nagging notion that I was committing an Oedipal offense. The second thing I realized was that I had never had the time, or allowed myself the time, to grieve for my mother. So I sat there on the edge of my bed in my diamond-patterned pajamas and cried for the loss of a woman who had been gone from my life for some twenty-odd years. I cried for about an hour. My sobs echoed through the house and woke Homer, who came into the bedroom, lay down at my feet and fell asleep again.

I would not have noticed the woman the next week if I hadn't been looking for her. Normally, as I went about my errands, I scrupulously avoided contact, even eye contact, with other people. But this time I was on the lookout. I saw the sardine woman at the end of the canned foods aisle. I made sure to check out at the same register, just behind her. Again there were the towering heaps of canned sardines, tuna and clams. I followed her out of the supermarket and watched as she put her groceries in her car and took a large, empty plastic bucket out of the trunk. She carried out all these actions with the certainty of one who has a long-established and satisfying routine. I hurriedly got my groceries into the back seat of my own car and trotted after the woman to see what she might be doing with the bucket. It was so far out of character for me to be blatantly minding someone else's business that I would almost not have been surprised to discover someone else fol-lowing me with a movie camera. I followed the gray bathrobe and curly hair, keeping a safe distance, down the street and into the fish market.

One of the men behind the counter seemed to recognize her. He was a heavily muscled fellow with a twisted nose, large hairy ears and a white apron smeared with fish scales and entrails. He nodded, and even though there were a couple of people in line ahead of the bath-robed woman, he reached across the counter to relieve her of the bucket and took it through the plastic curtain into the back room. I found I was absurdly jealous of this fishmonger. I can't be much uglier than that great big Neptunesque boob, I told myself, certainly I can't be much uglier. The great goon came back out a minute later with the same bucket filled to the brim with fish heads and tails. He grabbed a lid from a stack beside the counter and pressed it down on top of the bucket and snapped it into place.

"Anything else for you today?" he asked, as he put the bucket on the counter and slid it forward.

"Yes, I'll take three pounds of salmon and four of bluefish," she said. The man nodded and began to weigh out the fish she'd asked for. This really is something else, I thought. She must live on a diet of nothing but fish, fish, and shellfish. I noticed that she was considerably undercharged for her purchase. She thanked the man and I followed as she carried the bucket, which must have been quite heavy, and the bag of fresh fish, back to her car with apparently little exertion. Her car, a blue Tempest, was parked close to mine. I got in my car, started the engine and watched this strong woman swing a bucket of fish ends into the trunk of her car.

I couldn't say precisely why I continued to follow her. I made sure to keep at least a few car lengths between us, but she must have kept a constant watch on the rearview mirror with her walleye. I followed her into a residential neighborhood that was a few miles from my own and pulled over to the curb when I saw her pull into a driveway. Instead of taking her groceries out of her car, she walked directly over to mine and tapped on the driver's side window, a few inches from my ear. At a loss as to how to address a situation that had veered completely off course, I pretended to be deep in thought for a moment, stared straight ahead through the windshield and hoped the woman would go away. She rapped on the window again. She was bent over, looking in at me like someone peering into a fishbowl, wondering how the creature manages to breathe under all that water. I rolled down my window and my nostrils were immediately assailed by the odor of fish.

"What do you want?" she asked, staring at me with her left eye, while the right one gazed off into the back seat.

"Want?" I said.

"Why are you following me?" She had a rather husky voice.

"I'm not following... I was just driving..." I trailed off into silence, having failed to find an appropriate lie. "I live near here," I said finally.

"Did they send you from the university?" she said.

This one really baffled me. "Well, I did attend college, if that's what you mean. But they didn't give me much in the way of guidance there. In fact I despised them."

She was snub-nosed and now her nostrils began to flare and collapse rapidly as a rabbit's. "You have a skunk in here?" she asked.

I felt my cheeks growing warm, perspiration springing to the surface on my back and forehead. As she leaned forward to peer into my car, her scraggly mass of brown ringlets fell forward and the top of her robe parted to reveal a V of fair, freckled skin. The cool air had added a touch of blush to her cheeks in the area just below her pronounced cheekbones. Her scent made me think of the sea, fishing boats tied to a tired old wooden dock, lopsided pilings with seagulls perched on them in a snug, foggy little harbor somewhere on the Maine coast. She was so absorbingly beautiful I had to look away. Neither of us said anything for a moment.

"Do you have a skunk fetish?" she asked.

I was taken by surprise. I'd never thought of my hobby as fetishistic. It sounded perverse. "I suppose one could put it that way," I said.

"It's okay," she hastened to add. "I'm a fish fetishist."

I nodded, wondering if there were some underground society of fetishists into which I was about to be initiated.

"My name's Pearl," she said, sticking a hand, wrinkled as if it had been immersed in water for too long, through the open window. I shook it. Slightly slimy. "You wanna come in for a drink?" she asked.

※ ※ ※

JUSTIN COURTER'S novel *Skunk: A Love Story*, from which the above story is excerpted, will be published by Omnidawn in the latter half of 2006. More information about this novel is available at www.omnidawn.com/courter

Courter has another story, "The Town News," on page 147 of this anthology. His short stories and poems have been published in *The Berkeley Fiction Review, Fugue, Many Mountains Moving, Fourteen Hills, The Literary Review, New Orleans Review, LIT, Northwest Review, Pleiades, Main Street Rag, Phantasmagoria, Apalachee Review, North Dakota Review, Pearl* and other journals. His unpublished novel, *Cadenza*, was shortlisted for the Graywolf Press S. Mariella Gable Prize and his short story collection was selected as a semifinalist for the 2003 John Simmons Iowa Short Fiction Award. He lives in New York and works for the Wildlife Conservation Society.

MICHAEL ANDRE-DRIUSSI

OLD FLAMES IN NEW BOTTLES

Julie had not come home the night before, so it was really, finally over between us. I was pretty dark about the whole thing—especially since she was the one to leave—but it was a bright, beautiful, Sunday morning in autumn, making up for a cold and dreary Bay Area summer. It was the perfect setting for a new beginning.

Cindy stroked my chin, saying "Chuck-chuck," her chin-stroking phrase. "Hey Mikey, don't be so down. She was no good for you. Too wooden, too plastic. Could she sing at all?"

"No," I admitted.

"There you go, then!" Cindy looked like a million bucks, like a young Angie Dickinson wearing a furry white coat over a clingy gray dress. She slipped her arm through mine as we walked up the rise of Solano Avenue, heading toward the Berkeley Hills—I caught a glimpse of us reflected in a shop window and God, we looked cute. Too bad she doesn't like men. Still, the perfect decoy.

We were trolling in a new area, a tiny town called Albany just north of Berkeley. It was about midway between my place and hers. Since Solano has a lot of restaurants, cafés, and wine bars, I'd somehow gotten the idea that there would be champagne brunches up and down the street every Sunday. That was my plan: we would cruise the brunches and wine bars, looking for new lovers.

We walked and we walked but there were no brunches to be found. Nothing was open—the place was as dead as a blue-law town—and there were few people on display. My mood spiraled down like a nicked clay pigeon and my thirst increased. Up near the Berkeley border there was "Michael's Liquors," and it was open, so we went in and I bought a bottle of champagne and some cookies. Drinking on the sidewalk in front of a liquor store just seemed too depressing to contemplate, so we walked a couple more blocks and found a sunken little park with several benches and only one sleeping homeless guy.

After we sat down and took a few swigs, Cindy said, "So, where'd she go?"

"Up in the hills, probably," I said. "She's housesitting a mansion up there. Now she's with that black guy, Joe." I drank. "Damn, it's my fault, too. I actually said to her, 'You have to choose between us.'"

"Oh, no."

"Can you believe it? I must've been possessed or something."

"So who is this Joe?"

"What, I didn't tell you? I haven't even talked to you in months?"

"You've been too happy," she said.

"Maybe," I scoffed, biting into a cookie. "The guy is a freak—I mean really, a circus freak."

"Ouch!"

"No, he's not freakish-looking—he looks pretty normal, in fact. He just has this weird power, or a gimmick, probably—he makes things burn. Like spontaneous combustion."

"With his hands?" She had her skeptical look, watching for a joke.

"It seems like it's his breath."

"You're kidding," she said. I shook my head. "Okay, where'd you see him do this? On a stage?"

"No, out in the open," I said. "Down by the bay there's this landfill with a bunch of homeless people camping out. You know the kind of weird outdoor art galleries that pop up by the water? Things made with odd bits of junk, paintings on pieces of scrap wood? There's one over there. It's like a seedy little carnival, and it attracts weird little sideshows from all around.

"So this guy Joe, he's from Michigan. Joe Blowtorch or just Joe Blow. He took out a candle from this bag, and he blew it so it lit. He got out a newspaper and held it up, reading by the candle light, but when he got to the funnies he laughed and the paper burst into flames."

"Stage stuff," said Cindy. "So he's a performance artist. Julie's drawn to that, right? Since you met her when we were singing on Telegraph."

Telegraph Avenue was our trolling ground before: I'd play my acoustic guitar, looking like Donovan with a Lou Reed attitude, and Cindy would sing into a hair brush. We were just another sidewalk act, like the beggars, the runaways, the punks, the college students, and the tourists in that neighborhood. But we were sick of the scene there, the same faces and bodies. The familiarity that breeds contempt. In our last run Cindy got Kim and I got Julie, but we had fished that area out.

"She was a fan."

"Probably our only fan," said Cindy with a snort. "But those old torch songs were fun." And then she sang the title phrase of "You Give Me Fever," that sultry song of sickness, love, and fire.

We left the half-empty bottle and the remaining cookies with the sleeping bum and walked further up the street. The sky was blue and clear except for a single billowing cloud to the southeast, a white column that rose from the Oakland hills. The cloud was smoke, and for an instant it hit me like a deeply private message broadcast across the city: Julie and Joe were having sex for all to see, and I was the one with the knife in his heart, I was the one filled with sadness at being left behind, I was the one flooded with burning jealousy. But then the internal and external worlds reversed themselves, and the smoke became an exclamation point for a disaster unfolding.

"Cindy, I've gotta go—it's Julie!"

"What?"

"I'll call you!" I bolted from Cindy's side, ran down the street. At the liquor store I heard the sound of a TV reporter talking about the fire, so I ducked in for a look: images of the conflagration flashed across the TV screen. The blaze had started only about a half-hour before but was already over a mile wide, sweeping down the hills with winds from the east. There was a shot of the stately white Claremont Hotel being evacuated with orange flames visible in the distance, an image that set me running again, since Julie's mansion was up in that area.

A call to the mansion from a payphone gave me a busy signal. I made an emergency break-through but the operator said that there was nobody on the line, the phone was just off the hook.

I got to my car and sped toward the Claremont, avoiding the freeways because the fire had already engulfed the two over there. South of campus it was becoming overcast above and chaotic below, with sirens wailing around while gawkers lined one side of the road and fire refugees crammed the other. Turning up Dwight Way, onto Warring, I got lost in the maze of one-way streets and finally parked by a school. I got out and ran: it was quicker on foot.

The smoke was getting thicker, the hotel evacuation was still on—cars fleeing out of the parking lot and into the road chaos, burning embers drifting down. The news crews were filming everything, the barkers at a carnival show. I was swimming against the current, dodging cars and cutting through the hotel to get to the road behind it, Alvarado, a winding street with pedestrian shortcuts. I ran up into that posh neighborhood of mansions and eucalyptus. It seemed everything was burning. I saw some people, crazy gawkers enjoying the carnival, maybe some looters, maybe a few crazy rescuers like me. I heard a popping sound a few times before I understood it was the sound of gas meters exploding in the heat—I heard another pop and looked over to see a new three-foot flame jetting from a house main.

The mansion Julie was housesitting was one of the few that was not on fire. I pounded on the door, shouting at the top of my lungs. It occurred to me then that she might not be there anymore, she might be somewhere else with Joe, that I was on a fool's errand. I smashed a window with an ornamental stone and then the door flew open.

"What are you *doing*?" she shouted, looking like Natalie Wood playing Veronica-with-a-hangover, clutching a bathrobe around her.

"The hill's on fire!" I yelled. "We have to get out!"

"It's just overcast," she said. "Why don't you just leave me alone?"

"Huh?!"

"I took the phone off the hook and ignored the door pounding before, but this time you're breaking things!"

"*This* time?" I said. "This is the first time, I didn't call you before! I mean, I called one time, and the line was busy." She was smirking. "Look, come here, right over here and look at the neighborhood. Don't you hear that roaring sound—you think *fog* makes noise like that?"

"You mean you hear that, too?" she said, the light dawning upon her brow. "I thought it was just my head."

I won her over to the fire situation but she still had to get dressed and find her purse. It seemed crazy to me, like she was stalling or something. As I helped her I tried to ignore the signs of Joe's recent presence there—the most glaring detail being the rumpled bed sheets which had been scorched. I swallowed my pride.

Finally we left and ran downhill, through areas of danger toward safety. We became giddy with relief as we came out into the normal world by the Claremont, and Julie pulled me into a long hot kiss like she'd never done before.

I wanted to find my car and take us home but she wanted a room, so we walked to the nearest motel and consummated our reunion. We were together again, our problems had vanished like smoke—where last week we had been treating each other like strangers, now it was hot and heavy again. I was the brave hero who had saved her, so when she told me to tie her down I did it with love instead of the resentment I'd felt in the past, and when I dripped the hot candle wax onto her I was not a puppet, I was her puppet. As well as the brave hero, who now fiddled while Rome burned.

After the third time she smiled languidly and said, "This seems like a new beginning."

"Yeah," I said, brushing the moxibustion incense ash off of her. I was sore and happy and sleepy.

"Let's make it real," she said. "Let's make a clean break with the past. Get rid of everything from before, make a fresh start."

"'Everything' like the apartment?" I said, my fingers fumbling stupidly at the knots that held her.

"'Everything' like the apartment and all the stuff inside it," she said. "Clothes, books, TV, everything."

"Huh," I said. "And how are we going to do this? I'm in between jobs and you don't have one, either."

"Well," she said, looking away and biting her lower lip, "the mansion belongs to my father."

"It does?"

"And we could stay there, rent free. Please, master?"

"If it doesn't burn down...," I said, and she smiled.

I tried to call Cindy, to let her know that Julie and I were safe from the fire, but there was no answer. Not even her machine.

⑊ ⑊ ⑊

Miraculously the mansion did not burn down, and we moved in a few days later. Julie brought me new clothes and papers to sign for the apartment and the car. I kept trying to call Cindy and eventually got a guy who said there was no Cindy there. It was as though she had been disposed of along with all the stuff of my past life.

November was a time of clean-up and rebuilding in the footprint of the fire. But not for us, the luckiest of the lucky ones: the mansion had a luxury sedan in the garage, and we took it for a week-long tour of the Gold Country, where the turning leaves were a blaze of color. I looked forward to meeting her father, who seemed to be always traveling. Julie told me he was in Texas then.

The weather in December grew cool and I learned through trial and error how to set a proper fire in the mansion's fireplace. (Obviously a single log does not burn, but I learned that even two logs with lots of kindling do not really burn. The minimum number is three.) The night we had a Yule log in there, burning away at the one end, as we sat on the sofa sipping wine, Julie turned to me and said, "I'm pregnant."

I was completely surprised, feeling several conflicting emotions in rapid sequence: betrayal, a sense of entrapment; joy at the prospect of having a child with the woman I loved; fear of the unknown; and the corrosive doubt as to whether the child was mine. The stage was set: there were many ways I could play this scene, but I knew in my heart the best way for the brave hero of my new life. I got down on both knees and said, "Will you marry me?"

She blinked back tears as she said, "You must not kneel, you must stand. Barefoot."

I was stunned, but I did as she said. She knelt and said to the floor, "Your wish is my command." Then she kissed my foot and wept.

We got married, a minimalist civil ceremony. As a wedding present her father, who was in Colorado at the time, sent a man and woman to help with the mansion: Frank, a Southerner with a pasty-white complexion, and Mrs. Limburgh, a rosy mountain of the kitchen.

Those were beautiful days of bright expectation. It was like we were two kids playing house. That winter brought storms that broke the five-year drought, a dry spell that had made the firestorm possible. There were times when it would rain and, through some trick of the light, it would seem like the rain was glowing—and I would open my mouth and catch some rain on my tongue, and it was sweet like honey with a hint of turpentine. It was like manna from heaven, it was so wonderful; yet I came to accept it as normal, just another manifestation of my new life.

Julie hired a midwife and a nanny, the first one a seasoned pro and the other a fresh college grad. We were six living in the mansion then, with me as a sort of gentleman gardener, always tending to the yard and doing home repair jobs. Julie's father was in Azerbaijan, then in the Philippines, then in Saudi Arabia. Julie said he would come to "Oaktown" for the birth of the baby. She called Oakland "Oaktown," and even though I'd never heard that name before, it seemed like everybody used it.

By April the rains had stopped and there was a new city ordinance for each household to do its own raking and burning of leaves in order to eliminate the danger of firestorm. So I did that, and after a bit of smoke and fire I started having sex with the nanny. Furtive sex at odd times of the day and night. Julie had swollen up, had metamorphosed into a new non-sexual creature nearly the size of Mrs. Limburgh, our cook, but I had not changed: I was still sexual and had never been aroused by the sight of a pregnant woman. I cannot excuse it. The pressures of waiting on a pregnancy are there, and the close company of a pretty, young, non-pregnant woman contributed. Whatever resistance I had was completely lost the first time, or so I thought.

This went on for a few months. Julie and her midwife would go off to some birthing class and we would couple like rabbits. No bondage, no props, just simple rutting.

It all ended one night in July when Frank the butler caught us going at it in the upstairs bathroom. It was like a splash of cold water had awakened me from an erotic dream. I was ashamed, my head racing with incredible lies I could tell him to somehow convince him that he had not seen what he thought he had as I tried to disentangle myself. But she was laughing, an odd bleating kind of laugh tinged with scorn. She said, "You don't even know my name, do you?"

I did not, in fact, because we all called her "Nanny": one of our private jokes was that now we had been intimate I could call her by her first name, "The."

But I thought I knew her real name, that I had heard it in passing somewhere: it was "Pamela" or "Tamara." So I tried to say one or both at once, but the sound that came out of my mouth was only the background noise of a fire crackling in a fireplace, or the rush of air when a BART train goes by.

She was not impressed either way. But I was, because I remembered that Pamela and Tamara were two of my former girlfriends, and in my heightened state I saw that The somehow contained both of them, or the essences of what I had loved of them, like old flames in a new bottle. I had awakened from a living dream, one where I was a Ken doll in Barbie's doll house; a "sadistic" prince who was supplied with Skipper as an official concubine. But just as suddenly I knew that it was all created, maintained, and directed by Julie—we were all merely her puppets. Or worse: I was a fly caught in her web.

I put my clothes on and went downstairs in search of Frank, thinking on several different tracks all at once. Would he tell Julie, or perhaps worse, tell her father who was in Manhattan at that time? Would he tell no one? He was in the backyard, blowing smoke rings in the misty moonlight.

"Hello Frank," I said, trying to keep my voice steady.

"Good evening, sir."

"About that, in the bathroom—I don't know what you saw, but…"

"Saw, sir? I saw nothing." His hands were empty, his behavior bland and polite. So the secret was safe. Or was it? It would always be there to be used against me.

I felt the coils tightening around me. I could stay as a drone of the hive, I could even continue with adulterous affairs so long as they were discreet, but suddenly the whole thing seemed like a living death. My own biological nature was revealed to me, stark and plain: I was interested in insemination, even fulfilled by impregnation, but I was not made for parenting.

In a broken rush I confessed all of this and more to Frank, and he said, "While it is none of my business, sir, such is not uncommon." This made me feel better, since I was feeling like an aversion to parenting made me a subhuman monster.

"Self-knowledge is important, sir," he continued. "With that, one can make the choice."

"I have made the choice," I said, feeling a new elation. "I am going to leave right now. I am going to take her with me and get my old life back."

"Make the choice, sir, and don't look back."

I went back inside and found The in her room. When I told her my plan she balked. We heard the return of Julie and her midwife from one of their birthing activities. The was too ashamed to stay in the house if I left, but she was also too ashamed to be seen leaving with me.

"You go first," she said, her face flushed as if she had a fever. "Start the car in the garage. I'll creep in and hide on the back seat. Then you drive on out."

It seemed silly but I agreed. I went to the garage and started the car as the garage door was rising. Outside the mist had thickened into fog. The passenger door behind me opened, then I heard her crawl in and the door closed softly.

"All ready?" I asked.

"Yes," she said, her voice muffled. "Don't look back, just drive."

As I put it in gear I started singing "You Give Me Fever" like it was a protective spell. We were moving down the driveway, moving past the front porch. The song of love-sickness came pouring out of me but it seemed less metaphorical than before.

There was motion in the rearview mirror and I looked. I heard The's voice give a moan as I saw Julie standing on the porch, her arm draped around Frank, who stood on a lower step. She looked as beautiful as the day I first met her. The moan changed into a sharp little cry that was cut off.

"Are you okay?" I asked, craning my neck to look in the back seat. There was something back there under a black cloth, something about the size of a basketball, but it clearly was not Nanny.

I stopped the car and got out. I heard a sound like the name I had spoken to The, but it was not fire crackling or rushing air after all, it was the natural sound that fog makes. The two on the porch were laughing, and it dawned on me that Julie was slim now and Frank was Joe in a disguise that he was shedding. I opened the car door and beneath the black cloth I found a glowing sphere. The moment I picked it up I was knocked backward, engulfed in flames. There was a fetid stench of unwashed bodies and halitosis, burnt hair cut through by the clean scent of burning pine and eucalyptus. I rolled over and over, clinging to the bundle, with something scratchy on my face and throat. I felt like I was back in last year's firestorm—the grass around me was burning and I saw no sign of the car or the mansion.

In my arms I found a dead infant so badly charred that her hands and feet were black skeletal twigs.

When I came back to consciousness a paramedic was asking me what month it was, and I said July. I looked around and saw we were somewhere in the Oakland hills where a grass fire had just been put out, so I said it was October. She asked me what year it was and I said 1992, or 1991. I was scratching at my face and neck, they felt sunburned, and it came to me that the furry pelt in the way was in fact a thick and tangled beard.

My clothes were filthy rags, my body a reeking mess.

She said, "We found you with a baby. Whose was she?"

"I don't know," I said. Then I started to weep. "She was mine."

"What do you mean, she was yours?" the paramedic snapped, as if I'd really said something crazy. "Where's the mother?"

"Back at the mansion, I guess..."

A blonde paramedic arrived, surveying the area before she said, "Hey Jessica, whatta we got?"

"Hey Cynthia," said my paramedic. "Just this one guy with burns and a D.B. Baby Doe."

"We're lucky this time," said Cynthia with a relieved grin.

"Cindy!" I said. "I tried to call you months ago but your number was changed."

She bristled. "Nobody calls me that name —" She did a double-take looking at me, and looking at her I had my own doubts: this woman was heavier than Cindy, and looked to be older, in her thirties at least.

"Hey, sorry—"

"Mikey? Mikey, it's you!" she said. "Where the hell have you been? Jess, I haven't seen this guy for ten years!"

"Oh, come on," I said, laughing. "More like ten months!"

Confusion crossed her face, clouding her happy features. "No Mikey," she said, shaking her head as a few tears fell. "It has been ten—eleven years since you disappeared." She hugged me and then held me at arm's length. "My God, what happened to you? How long have you been living on the street?"

"I haven't been living on the street," I said. "I've been living in a mansion."

"Dressed like *this*?"

"No," I said. "I don't know where these clothes came from."

❖ ❖ ❖

They put me under psychiatric observation and evaluation. Since I had been found at the center of the grass fire, not at the edge, it does not seem I was running from a fire but carrying it with me. The preemie was burned far in excess of what one would expect from a simple grass fire, and yet I, who was carrying it, suffered only minor burns. Some thought I was an arsonist, others thought I had accidentally started the blaze with a hobo cook fire, and the most charitable thought I had just been caught in the fire and tried to save the baby. But there was no evidence of a campfire, no sign of incendiary devices, nothing of the kind: only a bottle of champagne, half full, and a partial box of cookies. I myself was just confused—I thought the fire was caused by the preemie's spontaneous combustion, which they could not believe, and I had somehow lost more than ten years, which they would not believe.

DNA testing confirmed that the preemie was my daughter. Some thought that her mother might have died in the fire but her remains were never found; others thought she had just run off in a different direction.

They took me to the address of Julie's mansion but the place there was completely different since the old place had burnt down back in '91. They could find no record of Julie, no record of our marriage, nothing.

So the only thing that seemed to fit the facts was that I had been caught up in the '91 fire, where I suffered a severe trauma and lived as an amnesia bum for eleven years until the grass fire of '02 "woke me up"; or I lived as a bum until the grass fire gave me delusions of grandeur that made me forget my life as a bum.

⽊ ⽊ ⽊

Cindy came to visit me, which made me happier than I can say. We sat in the dayroom and she told me about her life immediately after my disappearance. "I was like, numb for a few days or a week, but then it started to seem like it was a message for me, that I really should get into fire fighting like I'd been thinking of."

"Yeah, I remember," I said. "You were talking about police or fire, tired of being a secretary. I thought it was just talk, but yeah, one time you said that the hardest part you could imagine about fire would be... the dead kids." I thought of the preemie and felt sad.

"I think it is even harder when you have kids," she said. "Something happens where every kid you see is your kid."

"Wait," I said. "You have kids?"

"Huh-yeah," she said in boyish embarrassment that tore my heart open. "Me and my partner Lola. The big one is six, the little one is four."

I was groping for something to say, something positive. I had never thought of her as being a parent—my head filled with all the declarations made to me that she would not be a parent. We had been heartbreakers, the dynamic duo of debauchery, and now she was a settled mother of two.

She filled in by changing the subject a little. "So when you told me, you know, that part about how you felt excluded from, uh, Julie's pregnancy? I can totally relate to that since I felt the same way the first time." I felt a little better until she added, "But I didn't cheat on her."

"Well, uh, how did you handle it the second time?" I said.

"I had the second one."

My world was breaking up again and I was weeping. "I'm sorry Cindy, I'm just so messed up. I'm happy for you but I'm sorry for myself, and God, I guess I've really been crazy for ten years."

She put her forehead against mine and said, "Hang on, hang on. I'm gonna tell you something, but God, I could lose my job or something." She leaned back, took a breath. "It's about the day of the Oakland hills fire. You ran off to find Julie or whatever and I started walking back down the street. After a few blocks there was an empty lot on one corner, the slab of an old foundation with a cyclone fence around it. At first I thought I'd just missed seeing it before, but then I noticed it was kitty-corner to the Safeway supermarket, and I remembered seeing the Safeway sign like that when we came out of the liquor store. But the store wasn't there anymore.

"I couldn't believe it at first, but I looked around and there was no other liquor store anywhere near there. I went over to Safeway and asked this worker who was collecting the shopping carts and she told me the place had burned down a few months before, that it looked like arson, and that it had been called Michael's Liquors.

"I was so freaked I thought I was going insane. And then you disappeared, which was bad enough by itself, but it also meant that there was nobody else who had seen it. And that's why it seemed like a message for me."

She leaned forward and said, "I believe your story."

"You do?"

"Look, you haven't aged ten years—your face looks the same, especially without that beard." She glanced around to make sure we were not being watched too closely. "I'm not sure exactly what happened, but you and me both went into a place that wasn't really there, came out with food and drink which we ate and drank, and then all sorts of weird stuff happened."

I felt a strange peace then, thinking that maybe I had not lost my mind, after all. This was a gift that Cindy had given me.

After a quiet moment, Cindy asked, "What would've happened, do you think, if you had not looked back?" I must have given her a blank look, since she continued. "You know, when you were driving out and you glanced at the rearview mirror?"

"I don't know," I said. "I can't imagine."

All I know is, I awoke to find myself alone on the burning hillside, and I kept repeating, *What a lovely way to burn.*

◈ ◈ ◈

MICHAEL ANDRE-DRIUSSI, a post-modern housewife with kids, still pursues his junior-high dreams: Game Design *(GURPS New Sun)*, Editing *(Snake's-hands: the Fiction of John Crowley*, co-edited with Alice K. Turner), Writing (stories in *Interzone* and *The Silver Web)*, and Guest Lecturing (on Hayao Miyazaki and Satoshi Kon, masters of Japanese animation). He lives near Berkeley, California.

CHARLIE ANDERS

POWER COUPLE, OR LOVE NEVER SLEEPS

I never felt like a real college girl until I met John my senior year. He and I stayed up all night talking and then ran around campus chalking pastel hearts and portraits of Vaclav Havel on the cement walkways. A manic fox with wavy brown hair, he could come to rest suddenly and eye me with a playful stillness that made me ache. He managed to be both clever and smart, lean as well as dimpled. When he touched my hand and made an observation about the geometry of my fingers and the just-discovered significance of something I'd said a week earlier, lust tightened all the muscles from my stomach down to my knees.

By winter senior year, John and I were spending every night together and the rest of the world seemed both insignificant and enchanted, a Smurf village at our feet. He was my first love.

Spring found us standing on an ancient stone bridge, arms around each other and bodies glued from sternum to ankle, watching algae bloom underwater. We breathed in sync. I leaned my head into John's shoulder and inhaled slowly. The gathering warmth seemed to well up from the center of the Earth, instead of the returning sun.

A year later, we barely saw each other. We had gone from inseparable to schedule-challenged. I'd enrolled at UVA Med and John studied law at Princeton. We figured we'd spend every weekend together, then it became every other weekend and finally it was Christmas and John became "hello stranger."

Things came to a head when I visited John the spring after graduation. I had somehow let two months go by without inhaling the bramble scent of John's neck. He seemed a long-lost best friend. But after the first Peaches-and-Herb rush of seeing John again, the visit flew by and we barely had a moment to talk. Our whole weekend together consisted of law study sessions, games of tennis, and parties where everyone talked about law and tennis.

I confronted John on Sunday afternoon. "Maybe we should see other people," I said, dying for John to contradict me. His room had no furnishings, save for a bed and a desk with a framed picture of me, looking fizzy and blonde.

"I wish we'd met later in life," John said. "When we'd done all the heavy lifting and career shit. But I do know the kind of connection we have is unique. We may never see anything like it again. We owe it to

ourselves to keep it together." He wept and so did I, and then we kissed
and soon we were naked on the bed together crying and kissing and I
missed my train back to UVA.

I took a triumphant, blessing warmth back to UVA with me, and
felt its heat death over the next few days. I believed everything John
had said, and yet it wasn't enough. We went back to brief emails and
occasional phone calls. Our relationship wasn't on the back burner, it
was in a meat locker miles from the kitchen.

That frozen feeling in the midst of spring prodded my imagination
just as I walked past the cryonics lab where my friend Maisie worked,
in a boxy red brick converted tobacco warehouse on the outskirts of
campus. Inside, I tried to see where workers had hefted bales and rolled
cigarettes. Now it was all plasterboard walls and purring machines.

The next thing I knew, I had talked to Maisie for a few hours. Maisie
showed me equipment and introduced me to her boss and coworkers.
I had already learned in med school that you could slow the body's
functions to a standstill using a combination of intravenous drugs and
industrial coolants. Maisie spouted phrases like "metabolic coma" and
"molasses-slow polymerase." An idea took shape.

I called John a few days later, once the idea had solidified. "Just
think about it. You said it would have been better if we'd met later in
life. This way we can. We'll be like no other couple, as extraordinary in
our courtship as our connection. No, hear me out. It'll be at least seven
years before we can pay attention to each other. And during that time,
we each have to be able to relocate to a random location, like the President at Defcon Five. We both work in fields designed for single-achiev-
er families. Well, this is the answer!" I finished my pitch, breathless. I
knew John could easily shoot down my fairy-godmother solution.

Instead he considered carefully. Of course, being a law student,
he asked about the legalities. I explained the cryo lab wasn't officially
part of the university, it was a private company that benefited from the
university's talent pool. The FDA had approved stage three cryo trials
about five years earlier, and maybe a hundred people around the country were in suspension now. We would have to sign a stack of release
forms the thickness of a Gideon Bible.

"So you're sure this new technique is safe? No side effects?" John
asked, and I offered reassurance. "So I slide into this overgrown lipstick tube for seven years. You keep me sitting around in your room
all through med school and residency, like some kind of statue. Then
when you finish residency, we turn the tables. I go out and conquer

the universe, while you turn into the world's lowest-maintenance girl-friend. Right? Then fourteen years from now, we're both just seven years older and fully qualified to live where we want and do our jobs. It's an audacious plan. No doubt about that."

"You mean you'll think about it?"

"I mean it reminds me of why I fell in love with you in the first place, Willa. Nobody else could have come up with such sensible lunacy. Let me get back to you."

We each talked to our friends and families. Everyone made fun of my plan, but I sensed a tinge of envy at how bold and romantic it was.

"If I say yes, how do I know you'll awaken me?" John asked a few days later.

"Because I'll miss your conversation," I laughed. "You'll be a boring stiff."

John said OK. A month or so later, he ate his favorite meal (fish tacos) and we had boisterous sex. Then he put on a white suit and black tie and we drove to the medical school, where Maisie and her boss Dr. Abbye did some last-minute tests on John and then put him on a slab, which slid inside a great silver shell.

A few hours later, I had a new decoration for my apartment: a shiny chrome tube that stood against one wall, with a big window showing John's face. John's expression looked sardonic from some angles, mournful from others. He stood in the corner of my bedroom, casting a blue glow in the middle of the night. I got used to his presence there, only to have it startle me anew when I'd just gotten out of the shower or sat scratching myself in bed. I got used to explaining John to the lovers I brought home, but also to going to other people's places instead. Once a month I trimmed John's beard and fingernails. When I went away on vacation, I got a friend to come in once a day and check on John, whose bio monitors never hinted at trouble. I compared him sometimes to the cadaver I dissected at school—inanimate but intimate. Except John had a world of potential the cadaver lacked.

As promised, I talked to John every day when I was around. I told him about my day, about my fears and minutiae—including things I never could have shared with an alert John. In the sleep-deprived miasma of residency, I lost track of when John was actually present. I saw him staring over my shoulder as I treated patients. I muttered to his spectre in the breakroom where I bunked on call. His unweary watchfulness followed me everywhere. I sometimes forgot his name, after a thirty-six hour shift, but not his face.

Residency ended. I slept for a week and went to the beach for another week. I got a pedicure and read some trashy novels. I caught up with old girlfriends.

After a month the cryo lab started calling to ask when would I come in for John's renaissance, to be followed a couple of weeks later by my own entombment. I didn't return the calls. Guilt started to jab at me.

"It's not that I prefer him this way," I confided to Maisie. "Maybe I do, maybe I don't. I can't remember the old John well enough any more. But once I wake John, I'll have to take my turn. And now I'm not so sure I want to do that any more." Maisie gently pointed out that John was a person who deserved to get on with his life, and in any case I could discuss the options with John once he could speak for himself.

I stared into John's eyes as he came back to the world. I wanted his first sight to be my adoration. I did my hair and makeup, tried to look as much like the old Willa as possible. A smile developed on John's face over a few minutes. Finally he said, "I need to pee."

The doctors warned me John might be groggy or disoriented for a while. But an hour after he left that tube he was focused. He sparked with energy. We went to dinner and he wolfed two entrees. "I had amazing dreams, full of flying shapes and voices," he said. "They're fading already, but I remember I had no body in them." He fucked me three times that night, then got up and paced.

I'd forgotten how much fun John could be, like a mad scientist in the world's biggest Radio Shack. He made me laugh and orgasm, and his scattered ideas kept me fascinated. It was only after a few hyperactive days that I started to worry.

"I feel fine." His new beard twitched. "I've had plenty of rest. Now I want to have fun." He went out clubbing, first with me, then without once it was clear I couldn't keep up. He'd get home at three in the morning, sleep a few hours, then be up before me. I'd awaken to a mug of coffee held under my nose.

After a week, I worried a side-effect of the freezing process had left John amped for good. If so, he figured it would wear off, but in any case he had another explanation. "We're different ages now. I'm in my early twenties, you're thirtyish. Those are different life stages. Remember how much you went out, how much wildness you burned off, when you were my age. That's how I still am."

I doubted I'd ever raced around as madly as John was doing. But it was clear we ran at different speeds. I started to avoid him.

Before I brought up the question of my freezing, I knew what John's answer would be. I could do what I wanted, he couldn't hold me to my side of the deal, but our relationship was over if I stayed awake. As we were now, we operated too differently to last together. "I can move anywhere now," I pointed out. "I have much more flexibility. I can even work part time as a *locum tenens*, a substitute doctor."

John gently said that wasn't the point.

"I watched you sleep last night," he told me. "You looked stunning. I imagine you haunting my rooms with loveliness. A flower always in bloom."

Talking about it made me tired anyway. I felt half in suspension after a while, as the same arguments went around and around.

"I can't believe you're giving me an ultimatum," I said.

"I can't believe you're trying to back out of our deal," John said.

That's as close as we got to fighting. We both had too much dignity to squall over something like this, or else we were both ashamed.

Finally, John seemed to realize he needed to woo me all over again. He slowed down. We drove to the beach and ate caviar naked with the waves foaming over our ankles. John looked into my eyes and pled the case for a love spanning decades. "We've come too far to give up, what we have is too precious."

I sat in the bathtub and reminded myself that I had planned this role reversal, it wasn't John turning the tables on me to be mean.

"I guess you'll mellow out by the time I wake up," I mused to John.

"I'll be easy-going by then," he promised. "And it goes by in no time. It feels now as though I barely closed my eyes." He talked of awakening me with a kiss, like Sleeping Beauty.

John and I started to feel comfortable together again, once he slowed down a little and I relaxed around him. I eased back into our old rapport, trading jokes and kisses for hours. I remembered why we had wanted to do this in the first place. "You're the love of my life," I told John. "I never want to lose my faith that love defeats all obstacles, trumps all other cards." We spent a whole day in bed, making love and talking about our distant future together.

Then we went back to the cryo lab together. I lay down on the sliding table and stared up at the nicotine-scarred ceiling.

"Hey." John smiled down at me. I could tell he was fighting the urge to look around the room and focus on five things at once. He held one of my hands and Maisie held the other. (She didn't work there any more, but had come back for this.)

Then they let go of my hands as I rolled into the tube's darkness and my mind filled with patterns.

I remember a thousand years of stripes and plaids drifting past my eyes, an endless Abercrombie and Fitch catalog. John hadn't prepared me for how boring it would be. My mind didn't form a single complete thought during my time away from time. Instead I remember idea fragments and half-links of metonymic chains. I was used to living in my head most of the time, so it was like seeing my home burned down, fragments of possessions here and there.

John had promised the next clear image I saw would be his face looking down as I awoke. Instead I woke to Maisie, looking tired but not much older. "I'm so sorry," she said. "John's not here."

I tried to form questions, but instead nonsense poured out.

"It's only been three years or so," Maisie said. "We lost touch with John and got worried. We went to his last known address and found an eviction notice on the door, spoiled food in the fridge...and you."

Spoiled food. And me.

"I shudder to think what would have happened if his electricity had got cut off with you still in suspension," Maisie added. "Catastrophic shutdown."

Maisie daubed at my face with a tissue. I thought maybe they had applied some kind of fluid to my face to help the revival process. Then I realized I must be crying. I still felt as though everything was happening a long distance away.

"I'm sorry, maybe I should have waited to tell you the truth," Maisie said. "But I knew you'd have questions when you woke and he wasn't here."

I nodded. I still felt unable to talk. It took me a couple of days before the world seemed the same place I remembered. Shadows kept startling me. Even after I felt more normal, I still feared things would dissolve or start to move too quickly or too slowly. I worried that everything was just an illusion. I wasn't hyperactive like John had been, just terrified and unsteady.

A couple of weeks after I reawoke, I went for coffee with Maisie. One side effect of my stint as a boring person: coffee no longer had any effect that I noticed.

"I need to track John down," I said slowly. "I need to make sure he's OK."

"Just as long as you kick his teeth in for me," Maisie said.

"I feel guilty. All this could be my fault. We don't know what seven years in suspension did to him. And it was my idea. Maybe if I'd stayed in there longer, I'd be as fucked up as he was. What kind of data do we have?"

"Well..." Maisie took a big gulp and then looked down for a moment. "The clinical trials ended. Officially there were no harmful side effects to an exposure like John's. A few people came back and had short-term dissociation. But we're still fine-tuning the mixture of stimulants and UV exposure we use to rouse people."

Not reassuring.

I hunted John for a month, in between interviews for *locum tenens* positions. None of the law school buddies I'd met had kept up with him. His parents had an address that turned out to be a warehouse where John had slung car parts. Someone there had lived in a group house with John and a group of death rockers. Finally someone had heard John had moved to Maine.

It took a day to drive through dense woods, along single-lane highways lined by pumpkin stands and stores with names like The Brass Button. The roads frosted and snow spattered my windshield. It felt as though I were driving back into the frozen wasteland where John and I had spent so much of our young adulthood.

John's new housemates seemed friendly and crunchy, not at all death rockerish, and they told me where to find the soap factory where John worked. I pictured John, still hyperactive, running five machines at once, possibly juggling at the same time. Instead, he stood in front of a conveyor belt, calmer than I'd ever seen him. His beard had spread out, but otherwise he looked the same. I watched him until his break.

"Remember those lavender and chamomile soaps you liked?" he asked me. "I make those. It's much more socially beneficial than lawyering would have been."

"Are you all right?" I asked. He led me across the street to a sandwich shop. It had the local newspaper and a menu with three choices.

He nodded. "I was a little jumpy for a month after they defrosted me. But then I returned to normal. If anything, everyone said I was more mature, considering I hadn't aged."

"Then why—"

"I dropped out of law school. I guess you knew." He shrugged and ordered a bacon roll and cocoa. I got some cookies. "It wasn't some weird side effect of the freezing process, though. I just wasn't cut out for law, it turned out. You know, I was just out of college, I didn't really know what I wanted to be. Still don't know. I partly went to law school because everyone expected me to do something high-powered. Including you. Especially you."

"I didn't care what you did, I just wanted—"

"You liked me because I was smart, right? And I didn't want to disappoint. Remember how we used to talk about our future, our *careers*, all the time? We were going to be a doctor and a lawyer."

I stood up. "I can't believe you're trying to blame me! I almost died because of you—"

"Georgie didn't take care of you? I sublet my place to him, and he promised to—"

"*You* promised to look after me. Not your friend. You. Why the fuck didn't you just wake me after you dropped out of law school?"

"I didn't want to explain to you what a waste it'd all been. I kept thinking if I had seven years, I could make a success at *something* before I had to face you. Because I knew you'd give me that look—the look you're giving me right now. You should see it."

There wasn't much to say after that. On the long drive south, I dreamed up possible endings to my love story. Like a car crash in a New Hampshire snowdrift. Or maybe an irony-laden moment in which I went back to Maisie and had myself refrozen until John made good or someone invented a cure for fatal stupidity. But I already knew that my life was just going to carry on, at more or less the same pace as everybody else's, until it one day coasted to a complete stop.

⊕ ⊕ ⊕

CHARLIE ANDERS is the author of *Choir Boy* (Soft Skull Press, 2005) and the publisher of *other magazine.* Her writing has appeared in *Salon.com, ZYZZYVA, Watchword, Instant City, Kitchen Sink, Punk Planet, Pindeldyboz online,* and the anthologies *It's All Good* and *Pills, Chills, Thrills, and Heartache.*

Rikki Ducornet

Who's There?

I fell asleep thinking that if I could understand the languages of pelicans, I would be delighted by their sense of humor which I imagine is akin to Edward Lear's—a man who so often saw birds in people, and people in birds.

In the middle of the night, someone shouted *Honda* in my ear, and I was aroused from a profound slumber with the terrible knowledge that the anticipated campaign had begun. I wondered what goddamned word they'd hit me with next, and if I would be awakened like this often. Yet, as I warmed my milk on the hot plate, I was reassured because I had no intention whatsoever of buying a Honda—quite the contrary. It seemed to me that the beaming of the name in the middle of my rest was akin to an unwanted finger up my ass. I vowed that I would not buy a Honda, not ever, not even if my life depended on it. Yet, such interruptions: *Pearlmutter! Pie-cake! Giblets!*, should they be frequent, could lead to irresistible rage. I imagined *running amok*, as the tight-assed missionaries used to say about folks whose tranquil lives they had perturbed with filthy fables of saviors born in stables and served up to heaven like shashlik on a stick. Should I *run amok*, I will reveal myself to the Powers as *one who is no shopper*.

As of Thursday, the sidewalks are capable of detecting the absence of credit cards and wallets in a person's pockets, and of reducing that person to slush. The day is dawning when some of us are to be made into wastewater as others are buying Hondas online. There is nothing to do but return to bed and wait for the knock on the door. When it comes I will be aroused from a dream of priests with beaks carrying bats and bricks with which to strike me down.

◈ ◈ ◈

RIKKI DUCORNET has another story, "Lettuce," on page 238 of this anthology. She is the author of seven novels including *The Jade Cabinet*, finalist for the National Book Critics' Circle Award, and *The Fan Maker's Inquisition*, a Los Angeles Times Book of the Year. She has been awarded both a Fellowship from the Lannan Foundation, and the 2004 Lannan Literary Award for fiction. She is currently working on her third collection of short fiction and a novel set during the Algerian War.

JEFF VANDERMEER

THE SECRET PATHS OF RAJAN KHANNA

The first time Rajan Khanna came across a secret path, in Livingston, New Jersey, he was only eight, and did not recognize the significance of the event. He had drifted past the swings, jungle gym, slide, and sandbox, off toward the wooded area where he and his friends often incorporated a large concrete tube into their imaginary explorations of strange lands.

On this particular day, Rajan was by himself, reluctant to return from a recess just ending, but reconciled to it. When he heard the teacher call to him and other stragglers, he started to walk back toward the school. Halfway there, he stumbled, moved a little to his right on his knees, arms out for balance, and then looked left because of unexpected *light*. He saw, in a moment that didn't seem real, a slice of sun through the otherwise overcast sky, a hint of a breeze where none had existed, and, stretching out before him, a path of dried golden-brown leaves. The path wound its way up the lee of a hill that had not been there before, and out of sight, always touched by the sliver of sunlight that seemed from some other place.

Rajan inhaled with an audible gasp, mouth open, heart beating faster, and grasped the thick grass of the hill with both hands, as if to anchor himself.

He blinked once.

The path was still there. It seemed both tranquil and dangerous. The leaves upon its surface spun and whirled, but never blew away. The light upon the leaves had an unreal, hypnotic quality.

He wrenched his gaze from the sight. He blinked again.

The path, the light, the leaves, had disappeared in that instant of blindness. There was a ringing in Rajan's head. No, not in his head. The teacher calling to him once again, in a shrill voice.

Reluctantly, Rajan released the grass and ran up the hill through the cut grass smell, back into the safety of the school. The mangled stalks of grass in the fists of his hands felt much more real than what he had just seen.

Soon, the memory of that glimpse into...into what? he did not know...receded into the morass of other childhood memories. It became more and more unreal, until it became a daydream, a vision, utter fantasy.

But Rajan did not entirely forget, either. It was hard to forget an event like that, even if dismissed as mere epiphany. It became a kind of *submerged* memory. It came back to Rajan in moments of triumph, of ecstasy: the column of remembered sunlight like a manifestation of his personal happiness. And yet, a disturbing memory, so that in photographs of the boy Rajan happy, experiencing happiness, there is a hint of a puzzled expression, a hint of looking through the camera into some dilemma, some mystery.

And that might have been the extent of it: a curious expression in family photographs, a sense in those who met him that at times he wrestled with some unanswerable question. It might have ended there, and simply lent him that attractive otherworldliness his wife would later secretly adore in him. But, for whatever reason, Rajan Khanna proved to have a talent for finding paths and roads, streets and bridges, overpasses and tunnels, that either no longer existed or had never been there.

The second time it happened—or, at least, the next time it happened and he could not ignore it or explain it away—Rajan was sixteen and walking with his friends in Manhattan, down a street clogged with pedestrian traffic. In the middle of a block, a sudden compulsion came over him, accompanied by an odd yet pleasant scent, as of fresh lime, to stop, step out of the bustle of people, and look to his left, at the solid brick wall of a bank...only, it wasn't solid brick. Now, in the middle of a building he had passed dozens of times, a narrow alley cut right through the wall and traveled off into the distance, buttressed by the dark suspicion of alcoves at irregular intervals to either side. There was a wavery quality to the edges of the brick where it met the open air of the sudden corridor. A suggestion of mirage, as when heat rises from beneath a manhole cover.

Rajan frowned, tried to control the sudden acceleration of his breath, his heartbeat. That couldn't be right. It just...*couldn't*. The alley went right through the building, cut offices in half, created a sliver of blue sky in the middle of windows, and he could see people walking from one side of an office to another, disappearing as they passed through the area now occupied by the sky above the mews, and reappearing unharmed on the other side.

"Rajan—c'mon. What're you looking at?" one of his friends asked.

"Just a second," Rajan said, still staring.

Rajan realized then that sometimes he existed in two worlds at once.

He stood there and stared down the alley into that expanse of impossible blue sky and knew that if he chose to, he could walk *through* the building, that there would be no brick to stop him.

On that particular day, at the age of sixteen, Rajan chose not to follow the path, in part because he was with his friends. It wasn't that he wasn't curious. He was. But on that day, too, Rajan began to realize that he didn't yet understand this "gift," and that while it might seem wondrous, it could also be dangerous.

For he could hear, above the sounds of the people moving around him, a low growling whimper. It came from somewhere far, far down the alleyway. It didn't sound human. It didn't sound friendly. For some reason, until he heard that sound, and a wave of the lime smell washed over him again, Rajan had not realized that the paths he saw might be *populated*...

No, although he began to sense more and more of them—felt, at times, as if the world were riddled with them like wormholes—it wasn't until college that Rajan first placed his feet upon a "ghost path" as he began to call them (because no one else could see them because there was something mournful about even the brightest of them because it was better to think of them as ghosts of paths than as *portals*).

In his second year at Lehigh University in Bethlehem, Pennsylvania, on a cold winter's night at the end of a drunken party to celebrate a friend's birthday, only a couple of years away from meeting the love of his life, Rajan was sitting on a couch, wide awake, with other students sleeping or dazed all around him, when a *path* appeared to him in the white wall directly in front of him.

It was a canopy road: oak trees with deep green leaves hanging over red clay. It was like a cocoon in greens, reds, and the solid brown-gray of the oak tree trunks. A wind came roiling up across the road, bringing a haze of red dust up into the room; Rajan could taste it. He could smell the red clay, thick and oddly comforting. He could hear the rhythmic retort of a woodpecker. He could feel the thick, wrinkled roughness of the oak bark...and then he realized he was on the path, that he had gotten up off the couch and was standing on the path, and when he looked back he could kind of see the apartment and the couch and his sleeping friends, but they were the mirage now, and the path was the reality, and somehow he wasn't frightened, not frightened at all, and drunk but alert, he started to walk down the path.

For a long time, he walked alone, content to let the mottled sunlight through the tree branches massage his shoulders with warmth, and the cooling wind push gently against his clothes.

Off to the sides lay deep, sprawling forests of oak and fir trees. Sometimes he could hear the distant complaint of a blue jay, or the very personal bustling sound of a squirrel in the underbrush, searching for acorns. Sometimes, out of the corner of his eye, he caught a glimpse of the apartment he'd left behind—an exit, a slice of his world, reassuring him that, when he wanted to, he could return home.

After minutes or hours or seconds of walking—his watch had stopped as soon as he had set foot on the path—Rajan noticed a two-humped dark shape crouched to the side of the road about a hundred feet ahead. At first, he could not tell if it was human or animal, and then, when he had come within fifty feet, he realized it was both an animal and a human: an old woman holding a leash attached to the collar of some sort of boar or wild pig. They sat by the side of the road in silence.

For a moment a prickle of unease slowed Rajan. He stood there, looked back the way he had come, and wondered if he should try to return to the apartment. Again, the thought of *populated* paths filled him with a numbing dread.

But when he turned back, the woman and the boar had stood up and were staring at him. The woman was smiling; her eyes were white with just a hint of pupil. The boar was huge—bigger than the woman. It had the coarse black bristle-pad hair common in its breed, as well as sharp, yellowing upturned tusks. A faint musky smell wafted up from the boar. In its barrel-chested, broad-backed swagger, it reminded Rajan of the actor Oliver Reed.

Rajan smiled back, his natural politeness kicking in. He walked toward them. After all, it was just an old woman with her pet pig. On a road that had appeared out of an apartment wall.

"Hello," Rajan said as he approached, addressing the woman. "You're the first person I have seen since I started walking this road."

The woman smiled and burbled something.

Pulling on the leash with one foot so the woman had to hunch over, the boar said, "She doesn't talk. She doesn't talk. She's just how I get onto this path."

Gooseflesh broke in a wave over Rajan. He tried to control a sudden visible shaking. The voice of the boar was the same pitch and timbre of the thing that had whimpered in the alley when he was sixteen.

"I'm sorry," Rajan murmured. It had all started to become distinctly *too* real.

The boar grunted, ignored his apology, and asked, "Are you here because of *them*? Are you one of the *others*?"

"I don't think so," Rajan said. "I'm not sure who you're talking about."

The boar huffed and snorted. "You must be new. New scent. New human."

"Where am I? What path is this?" Rajan asked. He did not want to answer the question implied by the boar's statements.

"If you don't know," the boar said, staring up at Rajan with its black marble eyes, "then my telling you won't help. It wouldn't mean anything, would it? Until you've experienced it."

"I suppose that's true," Rajan said. The boar was huge. Just the size of it scared him. Besides, he was still drunk.

The boar sat back on its haunches. The old woman sat down too, smiling inanely. Around them: the swirling wind, the red dust, the slightest echo of a catbird's call.

"It's fine, you know," the boar said in a kindly, almost grandfatherly fashion, "*not* to know. Who said traveling should be easy? But I hope your journey is a good one."

Rajan stood there in silence for a moment. The woman stared up at him, and he could have sworn the white of her eyes had changed and now a miniature of the canopy road swirled there.

Then he realized the boar had dismissed him. Their conversation was over. Somehow, through his relief, he felt disappointment.

Rajan nodded and walked on.

When he was long past the boar, it shouted out, "Be careful! You never know who you might meet on these paths!" And laughed—a deep, rough roar of a laugh.

Rajan did not look back. He met no one else on the canopy road, and, after a time, catching yet another glimpse of the apartment, off to his left, he plunged toward it, and in no time at all, he was standing at the front door, in the snow, shivering because, of course, his jacket was inside the apartment, where he'd left it.

Now the paths came fast and furious. Somehow the encounter with the talking boar had emboldened him, as had his ability to get back so easily. He went from path to path, exploring, experimenting, figuring out how to get from *here* to *there*, and back again. What, after all, were one's college years for, if not experimenting?

So he traveled over paths covered with pine needles and broken through by roots like veins. Paths of fine sand that smelled of brine. Paths of mud, deep and treacherous. Paths of pebbles, curling down the sides of cliffs. Paths of sawdust and paths of cedar chips. Paths of asphalt and of concrete. Paths of wood. Paths that lay below ground. Paths that lay above ground in the form of bridges and causeways. Paths weaving upwards through the branches of trees. Paths over which a light rain of spores poured down. Paths in darkness and in light. Paths of granite and of shale. Paths of marble. Paths that were like nothing he'd ever seen on TV or in photographs, that could not be of the Earth he knew, so that he stood

...in a field of wheat, through which the ghost path ran over flattened stalks, while at the horizon huge twinned minotaurs battled in front of a blood-red sun, the musk of their sweat infiltrating the wheat, tornadoes swirling up in the wake of their passage...

...on a gravel path near a brook that panted and leapt and trickled down into a pond full of carp, while a woman who looked like his mother played a violin...

...on a dirt trail outside of a vast city beside a river, looking up at two green towers rising from the water, between which the sky looked different and strange birds flew...

...in the middle of a desert, the path the faintest indentation of sand, ahead of him ruins overrun by weeds and decay, while beside him little metal-and-flesh scorpions clattered and clacked and leathery lizards pumped up their red throats...

...on a cobblestone street, watching an old man sweep a courtyard clean under the glare from a purpling sun, while down the way a woman put clothes on a clothesline and dogs yapped at her feet...

...at the center of a labyrinth of mine shafts, staring down at an abyss, hearing the plop of the pebble he'd sent tumbling down, but only after several minutes...

...and in all ways he familiarized himself with this gift for finding what lay side-by-side and simultaneous with the reality of his everyday life, until it was no longer a matter of searching for a path, but of seeming to *create* it.

For a while, then, it could be said that Rajan Khanna took his secret talent for granted. He used it frivolously—as a shortcut to arrive early to work, or to make sure he wasn't late for a date with the woman who would one day be his wife.

It did not occur to him that this was frivolous because he had become so used to finding secret paths through the world. For a time, that mysterious otherworldliness he carried about him like a cloak became merely the jetlag of the weary world traveler, except that the world he traveled was like no other in his experience.

Sights he came upon—the very ground erupting into hilly golems; a turtle the size of a large island, dotted with trees; a huge metal sculpture like an Egyptian pharaoh in the middle of an infinite desert—no longer moved him to awe or tears. Instead, it was almost as if these images wore on him, burdened him, lessened him. When he saw the face of a tiger carved into the side of a mountain, eroded and smoothed down by the years, it seemed to him that this was his face.

Once, he had known a salesman who described months on end living out of hotel rooms and walking through airports, until the delightful frisson and discovery of travel had become the daily plodding toward an end point that whispered only of room service, nights spent in his underwear, alone, on a bed with a view of a parking lot and luminous skyline, watching television. "It could've been Rio," the salesman whispered to Rajan as he left. "It could've been Monte Carlo, and it would have been the same as some small town in Alabama with nothing to do."

And so, after awhile, Rajan stopped using the paths that often. If they were so common, why bother? He could, most days, get where he was going without recourse to them. Why, although it was rare that he saw someone on the ghost paths, he had once been passed by a jogger of all things—someone *jogging* on a secret path. Using what had once seemed mysterious and sacred as an exercise route! Stuck in the backwash of sweat and a mumbled greeting from the man, who had his headphones on, Rajan had stopped walking and left that particular path at once.

By now, Rajan had settled into his adult life. He worked as a data manager for Pfizer, the pharmaceutical company, in the New York-New Jersey area. He had friends he went to bars with on Friday nights.

He liked to read, go to movies, and play squash. He had married his girlfriend, Libbette Mahady, moving into a house with her on their wedding night. Rajan loved her for her sense of humor and her laugh and the way she knew all of Shakespeare's plays by heart and how she was brave and tough but beautiful.

And yet, for several years, he failed to tell her about his experiences, kept them from her the way one might an affair. He told himself he was shielding her from something dangerous, but that wasn't it at all.

When he finally, impulsively, told his wife about the ghost paths late one night in bed, she thought he was talking figuratively, kissed him on the cheek, listened intently, and then shared her own views on religion and spirituality. He did not mind this overmuch. It was better than that she think him crazy.

Then, one winter evening, everything changed again. Imagine: Rajan, walking through lower Manhattan, on his way to meet his wife. (Although, later, thinking back, he couldn't be sure he was in his Manhattan at the time, and not some shadowy *other* Manhattan, that he hadn't accidentally walked onto a ghost path.)

It's just after dusk and there's still a glow in the sky to remember the day by. There's the glow of streetlights to presage the full night. And the constant steady stream of headlights, the cars and cabs now rushing by, now stopped and holding, waiting, waited upon.

The cold has Rajan hidden under shirt, sweater, and overcoat, along with a hat and gloves. A sprinkling of snow lies across the ground, looking as if scattered there by the beating of great wings. Breath comes out painfully, seems to cramp the side, make sore the ribs. Yet it's an exultation to Rajan, a kind of holiness—the chill, and the winter night, with him hurrying to meet his wife at a restaurant they love. He is completely self-absorbed. He is without self. And he has no need for secret paths—the real ones will do fine.

But then he is brought up short by a sound like the end of the world played out in the rip and screech of metal against metal. There's the odd and lonely sound of metal in the air, turning over and over, and the awkward thud and crash of a car overturned, crumpled between two other cars, half on and half off the sidewalk at Rajan's back, the impact, the momentum, a kind of drawing-in of the world's breath, so that he cannot move, can feel his heart beating and feel the blood pumping through him, and is sure that the next sound will be of metal wiping him from the sidewalk as surely as if he had never existed...only for a few seconds of silence to be followed by beeping car horns and the unmistakable shift from accident to aftermath. There's the smell of oil and the smell of burning, although, as he turns to face the scene, nothing seems to be on fire. The car is overturned, and its driver is groping to open the driver's side door, and someone is helping him, and behind several other cars and trucks have clearly collided with one another in the confusion, so that there's an infernal traffic jam. Some people rush up to the driver, others to the cars, while others stand still, staring. A woman in a pink jacket and stretch pants is wailing to someone else over her cell phone.

That's when Rajan notices the boy off to the side, thrown clear, probably a pedestrian, and the way he sits under a newly planted tree, as if broken in on himself, a blotch of blood spreading across his side, and at first all Rajan can focus on is the spray of blood across the scattered snow, and the way the red, under the lights, doesn't deepen but diffuses as it widens, until it's pink and crystallized in the cold, and then just a shade deeper than the white.

The boy is gasping—drawing in breaths in great gulps and swallowing severely, and looking off into a place that doesn't exist.

Rajan walks up to the boy. He can see a hint of blood near the boy's mouth, the way the teeth grind, lower against upper. There's a tiny man crouched near the boy, dressed all in black, and Rajan actually shouts—a nonsense word, a nothingness—when he sees the man, because he was invisible until Rajan was so close that he could have touched him. The man's face is dark. The boy's face is impossibly pale, untouched even by the blossom around the cheek usually brought out by the cold. A sour smell comes from either the boy or the man, Rajan can't tell which; he's still trying to absorb what he's seeing.

The man turns from his crouch, sees Rajan, and says, "He needs help. He needs it now. I'm a doctor. He's going to die if he doesn't get help immediately."

Rajan straightens up, looks down the street, first one way and then the other. The traffic jam is total now, due to the accident, and it's going to take an ambulance some time to get to them.

"He's going to die," says the little man who claims to be a doctor.

Rajan doesn't doubt it. The boy is becoming paler by the instant, if that is possible. The boy's hands are clenched tight, one around the little man's fist.

"What's he doing here all alone?" Rajan says in a hushed whisper, as if it matters whether the boy hears him or not.

"I think he's from one of the cars," the man says. "I think he was thrown clear. And they're all gone. They're all gone. We need to get the boy to a doctor."

It's an impulse, but it's all Rajan has to help with. He leans down, into the boy, can smell the *sweet* of his breath against his cheek, faint and sugary, and gently scoops his arms under the boy, bends his knees, and lifts up—and the boy is so light he comes away from the ground like something already departed into the darkness. This lightness, this ethereal lack of weight, surprises Rajan, and he almost falls over backwards.

But he rights himself, and with one last look at the doctor, he turns and walks through the wall of a convenience store, onto a ghost path.

Until he did it, he had no idea that it would work—never even thought about the possibility that he would make it onto the ghost path but leave the boy behind, that through some quirk of how his gift worked, he might kill the boy by bringing him onto the path.

But it does work, and they are both on the path, and suddenly the boy is heavier than he was an instant ago, and blood is steadily collecting on Rajan's shirt.

The path: It's summer here, and the path is yellowing grass, cut short, running through a field of wildflowers, flanked on one side by the crease of a barely discernible stream, the sound of running water a salve to Rajan in that moment, and on the left a copse of oak trees. There's the smell of the flowers and the constant sleepy sound of the bees collecting pollen, and a red-shouldered hawk wheeling through the sky overhead, searching for mice and rabbits. Rajan's encumbered, stumbling, already sweating.

Quickly, he lowers the boy, who looks up at him with an unwavering but almost unseeing stare, sheds his coat, his hat, his gloves, his sweater, and then gathers the boy up again, holds him close, whispers in his ear, "I'll have you to a hospital right away. In an instant. As if no time had passed at all."

At least, he hopes, for as he half-walks, half-runs across that field of flowers, in the soft summer light, he realizes it might not work, he might not find the path. It's been a long time since he *had* to find a path, a long time since he had to focus, a long time since he even took in all the details that make one path unique from another.

So he run-walks along, searching for that hint of a different light, a sliver of another seeming, at the corners of his vision, that would bring him to another place.

After five minutes, Rajan's nearly frantic. After ten minutes, he's in despair. He can't see it. He can't find it. And even though he knows time works differently on the ghost paths, he begins to think that if he'd just left the boy where he found him, he might be in a hospital by now.

The field gives way to forest, and the path is pine needles and the wind is fresh and clean, but it's no comfort to Rajan, because he can hear the sough of the boy's breathing, and can feel how the boy's body relaxes and stiffens, as if preparing for some transformation. And his own strength is giving way to fatigue, his arms heavy, his legs shaky, the sweat enveloping him.

It's the boy who saves them—saves his own life and saves Rajan, because Rajan is in danger of becoming lost; the thoughts going through his head are unthinkable, but still there. That the boy might fade away, on the ghost path. That he might have brought the boy to his death through the simply human hubris of thinking he had a way, that he could be a hero, that he *had control* over something he still doesn't totally understand.

But it's the boy who saves them both, who raises his hand long enough to point, as if to say, "I see it," as if he knew all along what Rajan was looking for, was willing them toward, and Rajan turns, and he sees it—the tear in the world along the left side of the path, and through it the neon of emergency room lights, and without hesitation, without even breaking stride, he changed direction and lunged for it—for this change of attention, this way to another path—and with the sudden and inexplicable taste of lime in his mouth, and a slowly growing joy and relief, he was crying as they *passed through* and he brought the boy to safety.

Afterwards, everything was different for Rajan, although he didn't know why. Suddenly, exploring seemed important again. It took up much of his time, and for many long years he walked the paths cataloguing their every detail. What made one seem cheerful and another somber. What made one seem still and another busy, although no one walked upon either. There was no detail so small that he could not take interest and joy in it, from the latticework of veins running across the back of a leaf to the absurd drunken scuttling of a stink bug up and down a stalk of sedgeweed. The feel of crumbling brick from the wall of a ruin that might once have been a watch tower. The smell of cedar and of larch. The sound of...well, every sound captivated him, and in each sound some part of him listened, flinching, for that same odd and lonely sound of metal flying through air.

Over time it seemed only natural to show Libbette the paths, to explain that he had not been talking in metaphor, about something that could be or should be, but something that *was*...and to his delight, she accepted both it and him, after her initial shock, as if nothing had changed. Because, in a way, nothing had.

Once, during his explorations, Rajan came upon the canopy path again. He was gray in the temples by then. He walked with a cane. He was not with his wife, for his wife did not always come with him.

The trees encircled and cocooned him, and for some reason it made him think of the boy whose life he had saved, and he was in a sweet, good mood for many miles.

After a time, he saw ahead a shape by the side of the road that became two shapes. As he came closer, he saw that one was a great boar, ancient beyond measure, his eyes, with each blink, reflecting a sliver of a different ghost path. The other was an old woman, her hair like gray bristle pad, sparse and coarse and close against her scalp, her eyes blue and watery.

"Hello," he said to the boar.

The boar stared at him curiously with its strange eyes.

"There is no point speaking to him," the old woman whispered to Rajan in a throaty murmur. "He can't speak. He hasn't for many years."

"Oh? Have you been waiting here long?" Rajan asked.

The old woman smiled. "We've been on a great journey."

"I know," Rajan said, and laughed, although the laugh was tinged with a bittersweet quality familiar to the aged, and then Rajan walked past them both, down the ghost path, down the corridor of trees, the clay firm yet soft beneath his feet.

⊕ ⊕ ⊕

JEFF VANDERMEER'S books and short fiction have been published in over 20 countries. His books have made the best-of lists of *The San Francisco Chronicle, L.A. Weekly, Publishers Weekly, Publishers' News* (UK), and *Amazon.com.* His recent short fiction has been shortlisted for *Best American Short Stories* and appeared in various awards anthologies. He has books forthcoming from Bantam, Pan Macmillan, Tor, and Prime Books. VanderMeer is a two-time winner of the World Fantasy Award and is currently working on a short film of his latest novel, *Shriek: An Afterword.*

Mercedes Sanchez

Dream Catcher

The Visitor stepped out from the night shadows and breathed in her scent of sleep and light lavender. He caressed her hair with his pale hand and watched her. Her chest rose and fell in a smooth, even rhythm. Her eyelashes fluttered against her flushed cheeks. The images of her dream-time had begun.

"She's special, isn't she?" came a whisper as another Visitor stepped from the shadows.

"Tonight, she's mine," he said, harsher than he intended. The other Visitor chuckled softly at his blatant possessiveness and disappeared back into the dark shadows.

She was more than special. He had visited her, for the first time, in her childhood. She was about three years old, having a nightmare usually reserved for adults.

A faceless phantom buried under the hood and folds of a black midnight cloak chased her down a long white marble hallway. What had struck him about the child's dream was the detail. The hallway was like a cathedral, staggering in size with a domed fresco ceiling. The hallway was lined with white marble pillars, each one carved in a different style, from a different age. Her footfalls and heartbeat sounded loudly in the dream. He could smell the faint smoky sweet scent of incense surrounding them. Her dream had sights, sounds, and scents —three senses. Most dreamers used only two. The phantom in her dream was gaining on her. Her heartbeat grew louder and echoed down the hall. Suddenly, she stopped running. He was shocked and so was her dream phantom. The child turned to face the phantom and smiled, "Go away now." Her voice was sweet and lyrical. The phantom groaned and disappeared. The child had then begun to turn towards the Visitor. He covered his face as Visitors must when seen in a dream. She laughed and closed her eyes, as if she knew, and said, "Don't worry, I'm safe. You can go now, too."

At that moment, he had known that she was more than special. She was rare. She was a lucid dreamer. She could control her dreams. And she was dangerous because she could see the Visitors in her dreams. If a Visitor's face was seen by a dreamer, the Visitor would fade back into the swirls of night shadows and never again be able to take solid shape. The Visitor would cease to exist.

He, like others, was willing to ignore the danger of this dreamer. The risk was worth being captivated by her dreams. Falling into her dream-time always took his breath away, partly because of fear but mostly because of awe. She didn't simply dream, she created worlds. Over the years, she had learned to use all five senses in her dreams. Throughout time, very few dreamers could do that.

In real-time, as a child on vacation, she had nearly drowned when a huge wave had swept her off a pier. She didn't know how to swim. In the midst of being dragged out to sea by a wall of water, her uncle had reached out blindly and managed to grab her by the ankle, saving her life. Years later as an adult, a few days after her uncle died, she relived the childhood trauma in her dreams.

It was the first time the Visitor realized she could use all her senses in her dreams. There were many differences between her real-time memory and her dream-time nightmare. She was an adult in the dream but wearing the same racecar-red windbreaker and shiny satin blue shorts she had on as a child. At the beginning of the dream, she looked down and laughed at her outfit. The laughter ended in a sob as she realized when and where she was. She stopped on the pier and looked around. She could smell the pungent brine of the sea, hear the lapping of the water against pilings, taste the salt of her tears, and see the turquoise wave rolling and churning as it came toward her.

He had excitedly counted four senses.

She screamed. He saw why too late. As the wave slammed into her, he realized she wasn't being swept out to sea but down into a black bottomless pit. She had begun the fall.

Over the years, he had tried to justify what he did next as self-preservation and not interference. He had crossed a boundary and spoken to her in dream-time. He had convinced himself that one time was forgivable. After all, falling could be as deadly to the Visitor as to the dreamer.

"Wake up!"

She had stopped screaming and turned toward him, in shock, suddenly ignoring the fact that she was falling. He managed to cover his face just in time. She reached out through the blackness and gently touched his hand. The softness of her touch made him gasp. She had used all five senses. And she had touched him. He had never been touched. He hadn't even imagined it was possible.

He wasn't able to visit her again for many years. Her touch haunted him.

Now, he looked down at her sleeping form and smiled. He had missed her.

The Visitor prepared himself. Closing his eyes, he turned his back to the moonlight shining in from her window. He raised his hands up and balanced himself. Untouching, he lowered one hand to hover over the top of her head and the other just below the base of her spine. Vaguely, in the distance, he could hear the soft tinkling of windchimes. He made contact.

He fell into her dream.

They were in a beautiful sunlit forest surrounded by tall sand dunes. A river snaked through the trees and disappeared between two pale-gray dunes. He could smell the pine of the forest and far away, the faint scent of the ocean. He breathed deeply in her dream. The joyful sound of young laughter drifted toward him. He stepped behind a tree to watch her play.

She was with a few of her real-time friends. They were naked and frolicking in the warm green water of the river. He could feel what she felt, and the gently tickling touch of the water made him smile, too. Without a word, she stepped out of the water and began to put on her clothes. As if sensing him, she glanced around the trees circling the river, unconcerned. He willed it and in an instant, he was standing at the edge of the dunes, just as her eyes lingered at his former hiding place behind the tree. She had almost caught him. He shivered with excitement—dream-time hide-and-seek.

After a short sun rest on the bank of the river, she and her friends began to climb the dunes. As always, the Visitor watched. They slowed as the beach came into view and a startled silence fell on her group. The beach was littered with the remnants of a violent storm. A ship had smashed against the reef and its broken skeleton lay drying on the shore. The tide was out now and the sapphire sea was calm. Large sour-smelling green and yellow clumps of decaying seaweed were scattered on the glistening sand. Knotted trunks and sticks of red driftwood lay halfway in the water. She reached the beach and stopped, crossing her arms. Her friends continued on to the far dunes as if they wanted to escape the devastation. He watched her go on alone.

Her eyes searched the beach and her body tensed as she strained to hear something beyond the waves and her friends' fading laughter. She was searching for survivors. He shook his head and moved closer, fearing what she might find. Far away the sweet melody of a music box began to play. She frowned.

She slowly turned in a circle scanning the landscape and then she saw it, half submerged in the sea. A lion. The lion was nearly hidden, camouflaged by a driftwood log and a yellowish bunch of kelp. The lion raised its head sleepily and met her gaze with shining green eyes. She moved toward the lion, unafraid. The lion's golden mane was wet, hanging limp around its head. The majestic cat looked vulnerable and sighed deeply as she came closer.

Her friends on the dune called to her, "Stay away! It'll hurt you." She stopped and looked over her shoulder at them. They waved to her to follow them. She shook her head and kept moving toward the massive lion.

Protectively, the Visitor willed himself a little closer to her and the lion.

"Come to me..." she whispered to the lion. Her voice quaked with worry and love. She lifted her hand toward it. The lion looked down, sadly, and lapped the water beneath its head. Drops of water clung to its whiskers and sparkled in the sun. "Please," she begged, getting within a few steps of the lion.

Tiny white waves broke over her feet. Her friends screamed and she stopped mid-step. She looked back down at her feet and then back at them. The Visitor moved carefully around her, avoiding her gaze. She waved her friends away. They kept screaming. He looked from her to her friends and back to the lion, expecting it to attack. The lion was still.

"I've missed you..." she whispered to the lion. She tried to take a step toward the lion but the sand had buried her feet and held her motionless. She growled in frustration and fear. The Visitor found himself shaking at her distress. Why was this lion so important to her? He clenched his fists and willed himself right beside her.

She bit her lip, deep in thought. It was a habit of hers, both in her real-time and dream-time. She drew back, surprised, as she tasted honey on her lips. She tried to move toward the lion. She couldn't. She frowned at the sand that held her still. She turned slowly and tried to walk toward her friends. The sand released her and she could move. It was her only choice.

She looked back at the lion, tears running down her face, and motioned it toward her. The lion met her gaze but was unable to move. It roared, weakly. The lion loves her too, the Visitor thought. She broke into painful sobs. He wanted to comfort her. He closed his eyes and could smell the lavender in her hair. He was close enough to touch her. She turned away and began moving toward the dunes and her friends.

"Please help the lion," she said as she walked away. Her words reached out and touched the Visitor, a touch as deep and as real as when her hand had touched him years ago. She was speaking to him. Against his will, a gasp escaped his lips. She heard it and stopped midway up the dune. Neither one of them moved. She didn't turn around. He watched the back of her as the sun played burgundy highlights in her hair. She straightened but didn't try to look back, as if she knew the danger to him.

"Please find a way," she invited him to participate in her dream. He looked back to the lion. The lion looked away from her and trained its calm green eyes on him. He could feel the lion's gaze and its silent cry for help.

Confusion crashed over him. Visitors do not take part in dreams. It wasn't possible. Was it? He watched her disappear over the dune and the sound of her friends' relieved laughter floated back to him. He took a deep breath and walked toward the lion. The lion's soft mane was drying and a breeze blew it back over its golden body. He could see the strength in the fine muscles playing under the giant cat's skin. It was a beautiful creature. The lion purred deep in its chest. The Visitor felt something move deep within him.

He motioned the lion out of the water. The lion stood, its weakness disappearing. Unafraid, the Visitor reached out to touch it.

He fell out of her dream.

He wondered how much she remembered from her dream-time. He wondered if she remembered him. He wondered if he could find a way to be in her real-time. For the rest of the night, he stood beside her bed and watched her sleep. He waited until the last moment when the moon set and the first pale traces of dawn streaked across the sky. He stepped back into the fading shadows, unbecoming, and he wished for more.

Her eyes fluttered open to her real-time. And she smiled.

〰 〰 〰

MERCEDES SANCHEZ is originally from Santa Fe, New Mexico. She now makes her home in Seattle, Washington. Mercedes writes short stories, poems, and plays. Several of her plays have been produced in local theaters. "Dream Catcher "is her first short story to be featured in an anthology. Mercedes is currently working on a screenplay and completing her first novel. She hopes one day to win a Tony, an Oscar, a Pulitzer, and a Nobel Prize. For now, she'll settle for true love and an agent.

Robin Caton

B, Longing

Angst and foreplay, desirous acts
Unspeakable verbs in their ardor
Let me sit
Let me be like Buddha
Who can absorb that love?

╫ ╫ ╫

This is the story of B, who desires to write. Today, Thursday, she is sitting at her computer, wondering if she'll ever write anything that anyone will want to read. She's been constructing essays out of sentences from her favorite books. But as she works she loses faith; the project seems absurd.

She goes outside. In front of her building she meets a man. He's young, a dancer, and when she's with him she feels as though she, too, can dance a life. She won't write about their sex, which she views as intensely personal, but she will say that she's naked on black sheets when he approaches.

She's back at her desk. It's getting dark. It's December, cold, a kind of gray sameness settling on the multicolored buildings. She grew up in this city. The fears of childhood come back as pains in her shoulder, neck, lower back. She's crying. Someone is shouting. Her mother is slapping her across the face.

╫ ╫ ╫

Switch to the lover?
Too soon.
To a beach? A dream beach: orange cliffs rising from brown sand, a gray-blue ocean. She lived this dream once. But now?

╫ ╫ ╫

B meets a friend for lunch. The friend is distraught. She's just killed her husband. She's cut him in pieces and stuffed him in a trunk. She's sent the trunk to Australia, to a false address. She wonders if they'll track it back to her. She grabs B's hand. B is thinking about her inability to write. She says nothing. Her friend weeps. B sips her tea and stares. She cannot help her friend.

Later, at the computer, she tries to sculpt time. She tries to stuff words into a day, fill space with a single, perfect thought.

She can't.

Left with the small emptiness of her own mind, she quits.

Next morning B wakes at 4. She makes coffee. Characters elude her. She thinks of glass. She thinks of the color of the sky in autumn, when there's no fog and the clouds are striped with pink. She thinks of desire—how it grasps her neck, winds its way around her tongue.

The miraculous reigns. The miraculous rains. The conversation tangles itself in knots. I am the dialogue-monitor. A good story waits to appear. A good story is not an evil story. A good story feels compassion for its author. The princess ate porridge that morning. She ate well. She ate good. She ate a good story for breakfast. I want the truth. A story lies. Here is mystery unveiled. Desire fuels me. I want jewels, three jewels. The three names for God.

It's Sunday. B's eaten, slept, made love. Thoughts have come and gone. It's rained and stopped. Her daughter's called. She's read something, cooked something, smelled something, talked to friends, showered, peed, dressed, cried, and stalled.

Is there a verb for winter? For the skin around her eyes?

On a green, bright day in early summer, Bea sat on the low stone wall that circled Carmac's well. The serving women who had come in the morning to fill their jugs were long gone, returned to the kitchens of the great houses to cook the evening meal. Bea was alone.

Yesterday, her uncle, King Owen, had given a party in honor of her eighteenth birthday. There were speeches and feasting, and she had received many gifts. When she woke this morning, she'd gone straight to the room that held them. There were several rings of gold, cloaks of blue and purple, a map of the world, and a dove in a silver cage. But it was a book that sparked her interest more than anything else. Bound in red leather and tooled in gold, it was titled "I am." She had come to the well this afternoon to read.

She held the book in her hands now, enjoying the weight of it. "What will 'I am' be about?" she wondered. She opened the clasp, eager to read, and found—nothing.

The pages were blank.

꙳ ꙳ ꙳

It is Tuesday afternoon, and this is a story about desire.

In America, at the beginning of the twenty-first century, everyone desires something. B, for example, desires to write a book that will make her famous.

This will not happen.

Is the inability to fulfill her desire an unfortunate spot of bad luck on the part of B or a fundamental feature of desire?

What *is* the nature of desire?

꙳ ꙳ ꙳

She did not hear the horse. Later that struck her as strange. One moment the road was empty, the sun glinting off it, the next he was there: a large man on a chestnut stallion.

He was intrigued. It was not the hour to find serving women at the well, let alone a beautiful noblewoman so distracted by a book on her lap that she did not see him approach. He stopped a few feet away and waited until she looked up.

"May I help you, my lady?" he asked.

Bea tried to see him more clearly, but shadows obscured his face. His gallantry amused her. "Indeed, I should think you are the one who needs help," she said, smiling. "Unless I am mistaken, sir, you are a stranger here."

"Yes; you are right," he laughed, delighted at the boldness of this girl. "And where is here?"

"You are in Carmac, sir."

"Carmac? I do not know it. Who is the King?"

"My uncle," she answered. "Owen the Third."

"King Owen, of course! They say he is a fierce warrior and a good leader. I am honored to meet his niece."

The sun shifted. Bea could see him now. Handsome, she thought, but old.

"Let me introduce myself. I am Ib. My full name is Ibrion Connaught."

◈ ◈ ◈

Desire comes over me like the night, subtle as darkness. From under its wings I peer out. I am safe beneath the feathers of the ancient bird, warming myself under her belly. Brooding, she sits over me. I am her egg.

◈ ◈ ◈

B desires to read everything ever written about desire. She wants to become an expert on desire. If she doesn't read everything, how will she know if she is leaving something out? Or if all she has written has been said more intelligently already?

She desires to know.

◈ ◈ ◈

Desiring to know creates the vessel. Filled, the vessel changes shape like a goatskin full of wine.

Skin, not glass. The sexual life of knowledge.

◈ ◈ ◈

The name meant nothing to her.

She stood and curtseyed. "I'm pleased to meet you, Ib. I am Beatriz; everyone calls me Bea. But I must say farewell and wish you a pleasant *journey. It's time for me to leave. I came here to read, but my book, it seems, has yet to be written."*

Ib's eyes were full of playfulness. "Perhaps you will be the author, Bea. How charmed I would be to think myself part of the story."

✣ ✣ ✣

We move into and out of desire, into and out of it, creating a form that, of necessity, has as its first mark an I.

I is a self-replicating energy field. Its power to bring into being is great, but ultimately limited. This is because I can never do more than create a reflection of what already exists: a clone.

This is the safest, but the least interesting of offspring. It is the illusion of creation, which is all I (usually) desires.

✣ ✣ ✣

Later that evening, Bea made her way to the Great Hall of her uncle's castle. She wore a dark gray gown with a red ribbon woven through her hair. By the time she entered all were there. There was much noise from talking and the clattering of plates.

The long oak table was full. Lords Helsey, Waring, Ridley, Jax and Winston were there along with their wives, as were the Poet, the Priest, the Doctor, the Gardener and the King's Fool. The King was deep in conversation with a stranger on his right. Bea saw only a glimpse of a graying head. But then Lord Ridley sat back and so did the Priest and the stranger was revealed. The man turned toward her and lifted his glass as if in tribute. Bea blushed. It was Ibrion Connaught.

✣ ✣ ✣

To create something truly new, I must step aside.
Stepping aside creates a gap.
The gap is the end of desire.

✣ ✣ ✣

He had not been able to leave. Something in her had captured him and held him steadfast, so that his plans were given up as easily as a flower gives petals to the wind.

He drank at the well, watered his horse, and went on to town. Within the hour he had sought and been granted an audience with the King. They talked of the latest war, to which neither Owen, nor Ib's King, Herold, had yet committed, both wary of wasting men and supplies.

Throughout the long dinner, Ib glanced at Bea. He noticed how the red ribbon set off her dark hair and flamed at the end of the table. He liked it, would like to see her in a brighter gown, red or blue instead of gray. She was of marrying age, but she looked younger. That pleased him. He was a man who, at forty, liked the presence of a young girl.

⽔ ⽔ ⽔

When our desire organizes our perceptions in its usual way, we experience the so-called "real" world. This world includes people, objects and abstractions (such as colors) that we habitually experience in a certain way – in other words, the already known. This is the world of discourse in which we communicate with the least effort. That is, with the least time delay between desire and its object.

⽔ ⽔ ⽔

A young wife was only fitting. For it was marriage Ib wanted, he knew that at once. All these years he had run from it, extracting himself from difficult spots, wooing and leaving. He had been all for love and had pursued it hotly, but he hadn't seen the value of commitment. There had even been children. One or two he was sure of, others he supposed might be his, though the mothers were too proud to say. When asked, he had been generous with his gold to support them, but he had never been trapped by those tiny hands and feet. He supposed that the day he lay dying he might wish for an heir. But how remote that day seemed! Besides, having an heir too soon might hasten his death.

But in five minutes at the Carmac well all had changed. It was more than sex with Bea that he wanted, it was a kind of touching, core to core, forever. Indeed, it was the very sense of longevity that formed the heart of his desire.

He intended to leave early the next day. He would conclude his current business for King Herold and return to Carmac. If he felt then as he did now, he would ask King Owen for his niece's hand.

⽔ ⽔ ⽔

De. "In verbs of Latin origin, 'completely, thoroughly' as declaim, denude, derelict."

Sire. "Used as a polite form of address to a male superior or equal, now esp. a king." "A male parent." "(Esp. of a stallion), procreate, become a sire of."

To desire. To completely and thoroughly sire. To procreate like a male, like a king.

To desire. To create an object *in order to assert power over it.*

⫯ ⫯ ⫯

The next morning, Ib rose early. He ordered his horse saddled, then made his way to the kitchen. There he found Bea. He asked if he could speak with her and she led him into the Great Hall.

The heavy, dark tapestries loomed large on the stone walls. "What is this?" Ib asked, approaching a weaving in reds and blues of a creature that was half woman, half bird.

"A spirit called Kimu," she said, lightly touching the human-looking feet. "There is a legend to it."

Ib watched her trace the toes. How he longed to be that rug, that she might touch him that lovingly!

"Kimu is a guide, an ally of the gods. When your soul is pure, but you lose your way, she appears to lead you to the right path."

He moved closer and, in one movement, took her hands. She started, but did not pull away. He did not say that he loved her, or that she was beautiful, or how much he desired her. He spoke only a few words: "Wait for me, Bea. I will return as soon as I am able."

⫯ ⫯ ⫯

The desire to live is motionless, self-protective, internal. It wraps itself around the center of itself and clings.

The desire to live seeks conjunction.

The desire to live is *and.*

⫯ ⫯ ⫯

Two months later, Ib returned. King Owen was pleased to see him. Peace talks were underway and they had much to discuss. It was many hours before Ib could ask about Bea. Owen answered naturally enough.

She had been looking rather downcast lately, but she was sometimes inclined to brood. For his part, the King thought her splendid. All too soon, he would have to think about finding her a husband.

Ib frowned. Seeing this, Owen wondered for the first time whether it was to speak of politics that Ib had returned or for some more personal purpose. The thought disconcerted him. Ibrion Connaught was as old as he, perhaps older. But as they talked he found himself warming to the man. Ibrion was mature and would offer his niece wise counsel. And there was a lightness about him that marked him also as a man of pleasure. He and Bea might be happy together.

That night, the King took care to place the two side by side at the table. When Bea entered the dining hall, she found Ib already seated. "Good evening to you, Beatriz of Carmac," he said, rising to hold her chair as she took her place.

"Good evening, Ibrion Connaught."

Their eyes held each other, their faces joyous.

"I've done as I promised and returned."

◍ ◍ ◍

The desire to die is active, assertive, external. It carries within itself violence and the wish to destroy.

The desire to die seeks solitude.

The desire to die is *or*.

◍ ◍ ◍

It was June and mild. Each day, they walked the path from the castle garden to the river. Bea brought food from the kitchen – apples with honey, smoked meats, and fresh bread. Ib carried a clay pot that he filled with water from the river. They ate and talked and sometimes were silent, listening to the water or the wind.

One morning she asked him about his childhood. Where had he grown up? Where were his people now?

He told her about the coastal town far to the South where the sea stretched calmly to the edge of the horizon and the cattle grazed down to the shore. His father, Ethor, had been King of his clan, and they had lived in a stone castle with many servants. He remembered especially his old nurse, Maeve, who had loved him dearly. His mother, a shy

woman, was named Ingrid. He had had twin brothers, Endred and Ar-
thred, who were four years older than he.

He spoke in the past, and Bea, suspecting the answer, asked where
they all were now.

There was silence for a moment, and then Ib replied. "Endred and
Arthred and my father died in battle. My mother died giving birth to a
stillborn son, and Maeve died, too, from illness. They were all gone by
the time I was twelve years old."

⸢ ⸢ ⸢

B wants to find a word for what she has called "the desire to live."
Debirth? Degestate?

Oh, well; learn patience. Space and time are perfectly propor-
tioned. Patience is the stepping aside.

She shuts off the computer and takes a shower. Under the water,
she steps aside. And there's the word.

Demere.

⸢ ⸢ ⸢

Ib and Bea grew closer every day.

She told him what little she knew about her parents. Her mother,
Alys, had been raised in a town far to the West. Bea remembered her as
very beautiful, but very sad.

Why? he asked.

"I'm not sure. It's only a guess based on things I've heard, but I think
she had a great love who left her. They say she came to Carmac and
married my father, Soren, to get over the pain of losing the other."

"When did she and Soren die?"

"Soren was killed on a hunt only a few months after they were mar-
ried. Alys was pregnant with me at the time. She died from a fever when
I was ten."

⸢ ⸢ ⸢

Mere. "(In French) mother."
Mere. "Not important; insignificant."
She was merely my mother.

◈ ◈ ◈

"So you never knew your father."

"No, but I have something of his I carry with me always." She pulled from around her neck a small silk purse. "He was wearing this, with a lock of my mother's hair in it, when he died."

She held it out and Ib touched it gently.

"Your father was a good man, Bea."

"Why do you say that?"

"I know his daughter."

◈ ◈ ◈

B is unable to find a series of words that tells the story the way it really happened. Though it did, of course, really happen in the way the words would describe should she find them, should they exist. Unable to find the series of words that tells the story, she is nevertheless overcome with desire to tell it, though the *it* is amorphous. The *it* disappears in a cloud of her own requiring.

◈ ◈ ◈

It rained for the next two days. Bea and Ib stayed in the Great Hall. It was a room they both liked, and they sat for hours talking quietly with the gray sky visible through the high windows and a fire burning in the grate.

Now, with the sound of rain as background, she asked why he had never married.

"I have had many lovers, Bea." He looked into her eyes, not avoiding this. "I thought that marriage was only that: coupling with a willing woman. Since women were willing without marriage, I did not see the point."

"And now?" Her cheeks colored, but she held his eyes.

"Now there is you. Never before have I loved anyone as much, or wanted them with me forever. Now I do."

The room was still. "May I ask King Owen for your hand?"

She barely paused. "Yes," she said. "Yes."

※ ※ ※

Words are junctures. Words are a stopgap for pain. My body is ballooning, blowing particles this way and that. There is a story. There are words. There is a series of words in which one follows another, beginning to end, to create a sensation of space. Space, in this sense, is time. Time is an inward turning. My body makes language unreal. Time is a time without words. The what-can-be-said compressed to the point of what can't.

※ ※ ※

King Owen was pleased. He had sent scouts to King Herold's land and all that he'd learned was good. Ibrion Connaught was exactly what he seemed: a King's son without a kingdom, a cousin and trusted advisor of another King.

He and Ib quickly agreed on the marriage terms. Owen would give two hundred head of sheep, one hundred cows, and all the land North of the river. This was generous for a King's niece, one who was beautiful and healthy besides. But there was one thing more upon which Owen insisted.

"I want Bea to stay in Carmac," he said. "I will not agree to her going with you to King Herold's court. I must ask you to understand. I have had two wives, both dead, neither of whom bore me a child. I may marry again; indeed, I suppose I must. But the gods have not been kind and it is possible that I will never father a child. If I die childless, Bea cannot inherit my kingdom. But if she has a male child, your child, he can. I want Bea here, Ibrion, where I can take part in the education of her children."

Ib started to say that it could not be, that he owed his loyalty to King Herold and must return, but Owen put up his hand. "Besides," Owen continued, "I have learned that you have no house in Herold's land, but have always lived with the King. Where there is no house, there are no ties for a woman. I have given you land here. With good weather and much luck, you can build a house in two years. Bea is an orphan; she deserves to have a home."

It was this that persuaded Ib.

※ ※ ※

It is Tuesday. B reads the science section of *The New York Times* and learns a word.

Decoherence. A new concept in which the interaction of wave functions with the environment upsets the delicate balance of quantum states and makes a cat alive or dead but not in-between.

✳ ✳ ✳

I am longing for freedom, for some kind of release from a body I barely love. My heart is a measure of desire. It hurts at night. It hurts daily when the wind blows. I am trying to leave. I am hoping for an opening that feels like sky.

✳ ✳ ✳

Desire. An old concept in which the interaction of longing with the environment upsets the delicate balance of emotional states and makes a woman neither alive, nor dead, but exactly in between.

✳ ✳ ✳

The day of the wedding the sky was a perfect blue. Ib wore a fox-lined cape. Bea was dressed in white silk, with a silver crown in her hair. They were quiet and cautious with each other, afraid of the torrent of feeling that lay beneath.

They played their roles well. Bea was calm and proud, as beautiful as any bride Carmac had seen. Ib was noble, contained. He smiled and jested with the men, complimented the ladies. But he had an air about him of stillness, of waiting, as did Bea. The two of them went through the day holding their breath.

When the vows were taken, Ib played a tune on the harp and sang a song to his wife. Bea remembered it always. It was a sweet song, and sad, about a deer who loved a doe and died to save her. Bea was struck by the last verse.

And so, my love, I give my life
That you shall go on living.
I grieve and die, but know the while
The gods will be forgiving.

While the guests were still feasting, Bea and Ib retired to their chamber. Their love was uncontainable. They lost the night and the following day finding each other.

╫ ╫ ╫

What is the worm's delight? Small, egalitarian holes fissure the response, offal of expectation. She swims like Pan, the first of fathers, filtering gold in this sea. An open calm, a purple gloom; the foraging of strangeness. She asks the Padre where and when he's gone. An afterthought, or none. She sips her tea. She sings the change of seasons. But here's the rub: a fellow's drowned. Why bother? Why not sound like men?

╫ ╫ ╫

What is B searching for?

She is searching for the divine. If she plays with abstraction, it's simply an attempt to capture God by surprise.

╫ ╫ ╫

Almost at once, Ib began to build their house. It fell to Bea to take charge of buying furniture, pots and kettles, stone urns for bathing, linen towels, embroidered sheets, tapestries, and all the many other things that make a home.

Every evening Ib came home and saw Bea and his heart grew full. And each morning Bea rose, and looked at her husband's sleeping form beside her, and thanked the gods for the gift of their love.

At night, in the dark, they lay together and took pleasure in each other.

So things went until one day in early May when they had been married for ten months. Ib had left the week before to hunt bear. This was the first they had been separated since they were married and Bea did not like it. She was used to his presence, to his warmth and solidity as she slept, and to his lovemaking beforehand. Besides, she had a secret she was dying to share. She was finally with child. There had been no monthly bleeding since March and now she was sure.

After lunch, the rain cleared. The pale light of spring lit the castle garden and the smell of honeysuckle lingered in the air. I'll go to the well, she thought, and write in my book. The thought surprised her. She hadn't written in the blank book yet; she could think of nothing to say. But now she imagined a story: a man and his wife, a kingdom in danger, a coming child.

✣ ✣ ✣

Why don't women theorize?

One day, B receives an advertisement for a course on tape called "Great Minds of the Western Intellectual Tradition." There are seventy lectures beginning with the Gospels, Plato, Aristotle, etc., up through Quine, Rorty, Lyotard.

Two thousand plus years of Western thinking *and not one woman's ideas are represented.*

She's angry. Democracy, capitalism, communism, evolution, psychoanalysis: theories about the world create the world.

Don't women theorize?

✣ ✣ ✣

Bea arrived at the well in the mid-afternoon and almost immediately began to write. The sun moved westward across the sky but she hardly noticed, so caught up was she in capturing her story. Finally, she yawned and rose to leave.

It was then that she noticed a body, wrapped in a dirty brown cloth, lying on the ground.

Her stomach lurched. Dead or alive? She forced herself to approach the spot and kneel. "Are you all right?" she asked, touching an arm.

✣ ✣ ✣

What is theory?

Theory is an assertion (or series of assertions) in the form of a universal: [Under such and such conditions, it is always the case that] x.

A universal is intended to be the only valid assertion about x under the defined conditions.

✣ ✣ ✣

There was a groan. The brown garment stirred and the body moved. It was an old woman. She lay on her back and peered up at Bea. "My, my," she croaked. "Help me to sit, will you m'lady?"

Bea took her bony arm and propped her against the well. The woman's eyes were closed. I'll leave her alone, Bea thought. A woman like that knows how to take care of herself.

She turned to go.

"Don't leave, m'lady. Please, don't go."

"Why should I stay, old one? If you wish, I'll send a serving woman with food and a clean cloak for you. And if you are able, you may come to the castle and sleep in the kitchen tonight."

"Ah, that is kind," said the crone, opening her eyes. "But kinder still would be your presence for a time."

Something in the woman's voice compelled her. Bea sat back down on the stone wall and watched as the woman dozed. Soon she, too, felt drowsy. A bee buzzed around her, looking for a place to land.

For many minutes there was silence.

╫ ╫ ╫

A universal desires to rule over, like a king. If it succeeds, it stands alone, arrogant and proud, until another universal asserts itself, kills the king, and take its place on the throne.

╫ ╫ ╫

"Know you Beatriz of Carmac?"

Bea woke, startled. For a moment she thought she'd dreamed the question, but there was the crone sitting up, staring at her.

"Yes, I do," Bea managed.

"And is she as lovely as they say?"

Bea blushed. "Is that what they say?"

"Oh, yes. They say she is as pretty as her mother, Alys. Ah, if only I could see her, I would die a happy woman," the crone said softly. "They say she is here in Carmac and recently wed. I should like to see if she is blonde like her mother or dark like her father."

╫ ╫ ╫

If theory is an assertion in the form of a universal, what is its opposite?

A particular. A particular is an assertion in the form of a singularity: [It is in this instance the case that] x. A particular is intended to remain in existence alongside all other assertions about x. It does not dominate, but stands with. A particular craves company.

⸎ ⸎ ⸎

Bea knew this was the time to tell the woman who she was, but she was curious to hear what the crone might say. "She is dark, like her father," Bea said.

⸎ ⸎ ⸎

Adding a particular never destroys a prior one, although each may be "true" for only a moment in time.

It is precisely this ability to cumulate particulars that makes them eternal.

⸎ ⸎ ⸎

"A bold and beautiful man. Would that he had married Alys! What a couple they would have been."

Bea jumped up. "What foolishness is this?" she said, sharply. "But of course they were married. My uncle, King Owen, was there to tell of it."

⸎ ⸎ ⸎

What are the emotions most closely associated with theory?

Theory seeks to dominate, and so is associated with anger and desire.

⸎ ⸎ ⸎

The crone tilted her head, and closed one eye. She fixed the other one straight up at Bea. "Married, were they? Alys and Ib?"

"Ib? No, not Ib," said Bea, disgusted at the confusion. "You have it all backwards. It was Soren Alys married."

There was a long pause. Finally, the crone spoke, but so softly that Bea had to bend down to hear her.

⬦ ⬦ ⬦

What are the emotions most closely associated with particulars?
Particulars seek company, wishing to be surrounded by others of their kind. Particulars are associated with fear and demere.

⬦ ⬦ ⬦

"I heard tell that Alys married Soren to give the little one a name. But how she must have suffered to do it! For she loved the other one to distraction and would have killed herself if she hadn't been with child when he left."

⬦ ⬦ ⬦

Of every theory, one should ask, *about what is it angry?*
Of every particular, *of what is it afraid?*

Of what is B afraid?

⬦ ⬦ ⬦

"Who?" demanded Bea. "When who left, woman?"
"Why, Alys' lover; Beatriz's father," whispered the crone. "Ibrion Connaught."

⬦ ⬦ ⬦

ROBIN CATON'S work has appeared in many journals, including *The Spoon River Poetry Review, Five Fingers Review,* and *Columbia Poetry Review.* A book of her poetry, *The Color of Dusk,* was published in 2001 by Omnidawn (More information on this book is available at www.omnidawn.com/caton). Robin studies and teaches Buddhist meditation at the Nyingma Institute in Berkeley, California. "B, Longing" is an excerpt from a book-length manuscript called *The End of Desire.*

LAIRD HUNT

THREE TALES

For years I put off telling the tale of my voyage to W.
—*Georges Perec*

Excess undid me. I simply had to have it (I suspect that for too many of us here those words remain writ large), my motel, or Manda's that is. Manda Jenkins, you see (seems funny, even in the instance of pronominal delineation, to use the old "you" here), enjoyed legal title, owned the place, as it were. Ghastly bird. Glorious too. A real vulture in that way. I mean inasmuch as she was ghastly (gobbled at things, worried bones, drank blood, couldn't be kept off the kill, i.e. me, etc.) and glorious (gorgeous, all of the above, my gawd, etc.) simultaneously. Can a buzzard accurately be called gorgeous? you ask. Go and look at one. Go and see. They must have them here. It's crowded enough. See, blah, blah, and believe. It hadn't been meant to be hers. Lake Johnson (now there's a name for a permanently half-soused overly-propertied son-of-a-bitch) owed Old Man Jenkins (rest your soul) for a poker debt and when Old Man Jenkins (rest your soul) devolved into the estate thereof, Lake Johnson plopped his Shady Palms Motel smack dab down in the center thereof. Settling debts. Question of. Manda Jenkins said, "Certainly, Lake, that will be fine." I know she said, "Certainly, Lake, that will be fine," because I was there, wanly waving a wad of bills in Lake's face. A thin wad, let's be honest. And why not be honest, given that we're here. One never knows. Not knowing, how could one? Ha, ha! What the hell do I mean? What a gas! At any rate, as soon as Manda Jenkins emitted her drear "Certainly, Lake," and Lake Johnson had so to speak handed over the relevant papers, I began wanly waving my wad in Manda's direction. "Come and see me," Manda said. "Come and see me about it in my hotel. We'll talk. I'll entertain your offer in my new office. We'll get things straight." "Motel," I said. "Hotel," she replied. "The Adequate Arms." Now I ask you (as I asked Manda four days later, and this was my first strike, one of several, I got extra, then Manda got ghastly and I was *really* out) what kind of a name for a classy third-banana no-cable-TV bulk-of-business-between-12-and-2 motel-schmotel was The Adequate Arms? "It is the name that I, as proprietor, have chosen, funny man, hmmm, to bestow upon it." "Well it's not a hotel." "Oh, it is if I say it is. Ownership has its privileges. I, monsieur, am the owner." "About that." "Yes?" I held out my rather sweat-moist, somewhat reduced (four days of eating, of incidentals, of Earth bound ontological overhead!) offering and smiled. "What's that?" "What's what?" "That thing you just put on my desk. Those thin green slivers. That small pile." "That," I said, flexing my shoulders and drawing myself up to my full, as you can see, since a lot of you are short, still impressive height, "is my offer." "Your offer?" "Yes. I have wanted this motel for my own special reasons which I won't tell you so don't ask for 10 long years and would have had it for more or less this wad of bills had not Old Man Jenkins (rest your soul) up at that unfortunate moment and conked." Manda narrowed her eyes. I unflexed my shoulders. Manda smiled teeth. I slouched a little. "I'm sorry for your loss," I said. Manda put her finger on the desk, tapped it thrice, then pushed my wet money aside. "Come," she said, "around over here." I already described her to you, plus she had put on this nifty smirk and was wearing musk: I went. A few pokes and prods later she took me on a tour of the property, all ten rooms. "The maid will come. I've kept the staff. I'll have to give them uniforms, of course, not to mention job descriptions," she said. "Of course," I said. Or panted, rather. I always panted after exertion. And liked it. The ribs rising up into the air and smashing back down. The blood being brought more energetically to bear. I wrote poetry once. And wasn't half bad. Nifty modern things. With narrative strictly excluded. "How do you like my hotel now, Mr. Slender Pockets?" Manda asked in the middle of room number seven's shower. "I like," I said. "But The Adequate Arms is the stupidest name I ever heard of and your ears are a little larger than ideal." Strikes one and two. Or was that two and three. A tricky trigger, Manda. Upon one of these strikes she bit my nose and drew blood. "Ack," I said. "Why do you want this dump?" she asked near the end of room number nine. "I won't tell you but don't stop," I said, having hit my stride again. She stopped. She squiggled. She threw her shoulders back and bounced. "I still won't tell you," I said. "It's a secret." And I didn't. Not even when my situation got desperate. But you, my dear colleagues, gladly. It involved identity. Context. Base biology. Origins. I had loved/coveted that motel, since, driving by with my own Old Man (rest your soul too), he had sighed and said, "Ah, your dear Ma and me." "Let's get back to business then, bub," Manda said, the gleam in her eyes growing ever larger, ever darker, ever more drear. "All right," I said. I fell into a deep hole. A cave opened behind my eyes and my eyes were sucked backward into it as it slipped off the horizontal axis and, with sickening speed, snapped vertical. I fell. Eyes first. Ears and mouth and whole remaining portion plummeting afterwards. I fell so far that when I woke I didn't. Not perfectly. The hole was still there. Even as I nudged my dear, sweet sleeping fellow aside and stood, unsteady, in the half-dark, I felt as if any moment I would be sucked backward, had already been sucked backward. It was cold. The air had turned overnight and frost had thrown itself like a blanket of frozen skin over my trembling company of dreamers, over all of Saxony and its dark iron, its flame, its stench of peat and oats and roasted mutton picked at by carrion birds. Saxony with its stone arms staring up out of the ground, with its mosses and clear, cold streams and lovely half-killed flowers. Even weeks after our passage across the waters the spring earth still rolled and roiled under us and the air still seemed filled with harsh, crying birds. Just the afternoon before I had lifted my axe to bury it and had felt the sea-borne bile rise in my throat and my arm go watery. I had taken a knife in the calf for that. And lost my aegis-bearing, bone-incrusted axe to an urchin wearing a wooden mask. What would I take later for falling backward, end over end, all black, while the Saxons beat their drums and screamed their screams and threw their endless flags and barbs at us? What would I lose? The wind shifted, I smelled smoke, pitch. Later was now, as it must always be. Metal tore a furrow through the air beside my ear and they were upon us. Leather hands and rotten teeth. My sweet sleeping fellow never woke and I fought the long morning falling backward, fought and fell until the air had settled again into a cross-weave of Saxon birdsong and groans. Years went by. I grew gray and half-broken and wore a sort of crown. My heap of mud and stone stood atop an outcropping that took tribute from a land of duck-soiled ponds and goat-blasted pasture that swept all the way to the sea. I had two sons to cast dark, hungry glances at my aching shoulders as I hunched over my bowl of porridge or perched atop my hollowed oak trunk and clutched a gavel made of antler and opal and ox bone. I had the past to come and put its blackened fist on me. The first incidents were only incursions, light touches: goats dead, a farm torched, an already foul pond poisoned. I sent out swords and they returned bearing horned helmets and grimed, toothless heads. My sons boasted and cut iron-edge capers across the hall, but I felt the hole behind me grow larger. "The old man has swooned," I heard my eldest say. I had. When I could walk again I called for my horse. My sons protested, called me a fool, said a banquet was in order, asked for boys and ale. "I've been sent a message," I said. "Your brain has fallen out through your arse and soiled the floor," they said. I rode out, badly, at the head of a tat-tered column that carved a sorry carnival through the placid evening air. We met them at dusk. A thousand spears and smoking torches led by a giant wearing a wooden mask. A thousand horned helmets marked with an aegis-bearing axe. I dismounted and walked forward, alone. I think my sons had already fled. Metal tore a furrow through the air beside my ear and they were upon me. Leather hands. Saxon birdsong. A bone-incrusted axe. Dreaming, I drifted elsewhere. Down a dark hallway lined with multicolored doors. None of them had handles. I reckon I let myself imagine it was in my best personal interest to be swept along. How many of you had about the same thing happen? I wonder who dreamed that one up—that there would be a hallway with a hotel carpet, that there would be all those pretty doors you couldn't go in. All my life I thought I'd tend towards a light, that then there would be gates, a gatekeeper with a ledger, that then the trouble, if there was any, would start. Who'd of thought of this? Who'd of thought of you? Who are you? I went because I give up breathing. That's my story. Speak up? I'll speak up. I put on my dress and slicked my hair and went into town to get ham loaf. There you go. Ham loaf. That's a kind of delicious ground meat I get when there's something special involved. The special was our boy was coming home. He did his two years and getting shot at all the time and catching every hot sun thing could be caught and I'm the one who goes to Ranch after ham loaf and quits breathing and goes dreaming and floating past doors that's there for show. Didn't even lay an eye on him. My boy. They had him on a PT boat, corps of engineers, and getting shot at and lord knows what else all the time. He wrote a letter a week for two years. Dear Ma. They're in a box by my bed. Still sitting there unless they've already started sweeping me out, wiping up the crumbs and getting out the dustpan. Saw Candy Wilson as soon as I walked in. She's one of my fat neigh-bors. I can say that here. There too if I'd of wanted to. I've known her for forty years. Heavy we call it. We say, she is heavy. Or you, Candy, is getting a little heavy lately, you might want to consider easing off on the pork chops. Candy has a tongue on her and right away she starts using it. Ethel Dunn, who is half-cripple and lives alone, is up to some-thing the likes of which the world has never seen and never should have had to, uh huh, and Candy sets right to informing me about it even though I have already told her that the art and article of my mis-sion at Ranch is to acquire ham loaf and eggs and bread and milk so that I can correctly welcome my boy home. The eggs and bread were to mix in with the ground meat aspect. You do that with your hands. You mix it all up and it feels cold but good. There's a satisfaction to it. Cook it up and you've got meat loaf only with the pork it's lighter and better and the sauce has a tang. My mother used to make something similar with her own stuck pigs. My boy was about raised on it. Well, he had it and the other standard meat comestibles often enough. And would have had it whatever day that was had I not, standing there at the meat counter waiting for Earl Boyd to get done helping Candy, who had hustled on up there ahead of me and wanted some fresh liver and didn't like the look of what Earl had to offer and felt obliged to discuss on it, stopped breathing and seen everything go black. Well, until I got to the part about the hallway and the low ceiling lights and shimmery, swooshy-swooshy doors. And to the preceding part about walking around the aisles of the Ranch. Dead, I mean. While I was waiting on Earl Boyd, Zorrie Underwood come up. Her husband Emerson is over there in the other one flying planes and getting shot at himself and is a good deal of worry to her. She started up from nothing and now lives on a spread next to the Summers. She always has a pleasant word. Pretty smile on it too. Works harder than about anyone. Good folks. She says, "Morning." And I say, "Not much longer the way you got to wait on your purchases around here." And Zorrie says, "Well." Then we chit and we chat then she says, "Oh darling, you look pale, are you feeling all right?" And I can see a little of myself reflected in the meat scale so I know it's true. "I'm fine," I say. "My boy is coming home today and I am purchasing ham loaf for him and I'm going to serve iced tea." Then I desist from respirating, I reckon because my heart got stoppered up or some such, and fall more or less backward onto Candy Wilson, who says, "Oh! Oh!" and then bump on past her and land with my cheek against the cold Ranch floor. Well, bring on the angels, here I lie, I think. Only there aren't any angels to it, just the floor which is none too spic and span with globs of this and that, so I stand up and start in on walking the Ranch aisles, past the ketchup and canned corn and general cornucopia and multiple fat customers. I walk with my chin set, elbows out and my eyes flashing left and right like a cowboy in Dry Gulch waiting to draw until I realize I'm not walking at all, that the cool I'm feeling on my face is from the floor not the Texas breeze, that I'm dreaming, that I'm dead, that it doesn't matter if they did turn me over and are chafing and poking and worrying at me like a sausage on a grill, that my born days on our lovely old earth are over. Aren't they? Who's next? I'm not sure I like this. Then there was the hallway and me drifting, this way I reckon, like I said.

⬥ ⬥ ⬥

LAIRD HUNT is the author of three novels, *The Impossibly; Indiana, Indiana;* and *The Exquisite* (forthcoming from Coffee House Press in fall 2006). His writings and translations have appeared in, among other places, *Bomb, McSweeney's, Ploughshares, Conjunctions, Grand Street, Fence, Brick, Inculte* and *Zoum Zoum.* A former United Nations press officer and faculty member of Naropa University's Jack Kerouac School of Disembodied Poetics, he currently teaches fiction and literature at the University of Denver. He has had residencies at the MacDowell Colony, the Camargo Foundation and La Casa del Escritor de la Sociedad General de Escritores de México.

Leena Krohn

About the Henbane City

Translated by Helena Darnell

The fiercely growing poplars standing upright with their conical tops against the storm clouds, the elliptical, satiny leaves of willows, and the calyxes of privet blooms which so quickly withered and fell to the summer lawn—these were the things that Håkan, the gardener, loved. And no less did he love the spiky scales of tamarack cones, the idly rising twines of honeysuckle shoots, or the winged birch nutlets which greatly resembled migrating birds taking flight.

Not to mention flowers: wild flowers and garden flowers; the corymbs, spikes, and cymes of flowers; their heads, their labiate corollas, which reached for the sky like kisses as their deep scented throats with coats of nectar guided insects to mutual pleasure.

Håkan, the gardener, had been through many things, but everything had had its beginnings and its end, like the seasons of a year. Gardening was a constant battle in which one lost on many fronts. It had been difficult enough to see how powdery mildew spread from tree to tree and leaf to leaf, how cankers hurt pears and brown rot ravaged apples. A bright red lily leaf beetle devoured the buds from his orange lilies and some of his rarest lilies. However, the city's onetime party leader was the worst plague of his garden. Håkan would have rather welcomed a hundred thousand Egyptian locusts.

Woe to the heavy nodding clusters of lilacs, the tightly-layered buds of peonies, woe the clean blue calyxes of forget-me-nots and the plump nectar glands of snapdragons—woe to them all! Their fate was sealed by the party leader's obsessions.

The leader said that they needed more potatoes and cabbage. Håkan really did understand why—last year's harvest had been poor. He also liked to eat cabbage and potatoes—one had to eat something. But would it be necessary to plant them in the beds of perennials and the meadows of flowers?

That is how it was; it was the party leader's orders. In those days his word was the law of the city. Flowers and ornamentals displaced the true, useful plants. But more essential was the fact that they were symbols of an illegitimate bourgeois ideology. This was the main pedagogic reason they had to be pulled out. Cabbage and potatoes were to be planted in their place, under the threat of punishment. Rutabaga and carrots, however, were also permitted.

At first the gardeners refused, but after the fines were raised three times, many began to give in. But Håkan still didn't. A week after the third ultimatum was given, a four-man patrol group appeared in his yard with chain saws, scythes, hoes, and iron bars.

"Please don't touch my peonies," Håkan pleaded, "see how big the buds are, they are almost ready. They will bloom next week. If you have to cut them down, come back after they have blossomed and begin to wilt."

"Get out of the way," the leader of the patrol said, "we're only doing our work." They fulfilled their orders quickly and efficiently. The bed of perennials was soon a mess of buds that looked like severed heads. The golden sap was running down into the ground from their stems. That night Håkan sat behind the curtains and cried. He fell ill and stayed inside the four walls for several weeks. Inside his house he couldn't avoid hearing the patrol groups singing children's songs in a pretentiously peppy manner. The hysteria of the new revolution was spreading all over the city. New flags were being raised up the poles. The patrols marched every morning from yard to yard and from park to park to check if any flowers still dared to bloom. As they marched, they sang, howled, and yodeled all the while.

When the epidemic was at its worse, the people who lived in the neighboring blocks were banging the lids of their pots and pans in order to scare away the birds, too. Håkan had never thought that even the birds of the sky could be representatives of a wrong ideology. The most zealous ones tore all fresh tufts of grass from the ground so that as summer wore on and turned to fall, the yards and parks were nothing but dusty, impoverished fields.

Flowers disappeared and so did some of the people, although no one knew exactly where. There were education centers being established somewhere outside the city in which people were taught how to think correctly, talk correctly, and act in a correct way. Some returned before too long, others were never heard from again. Håkan thought to himself: Where there is no beauty, there is no justice, no prosperity, no work, and no hope.

Nevertheless, this era, too, would pass. Those who returned came back to what looked like a new city. What they had been taught to be right was now wrong. Håkan's garden was green again with streamers of waving flowers, blossoming peonies, snapdragons, and lilacs. Flowers are more resilient than people, Håkan thought. The patrols had vanished ages ago. The party leader was gone, his name was now ridiculed. No one admitted to having respected him at one time. One kind of madness was over, and it was time for a new one to begin. It was a new time in the city. They no longer grew regular cabbage but, rather, henbane, *Hyoscyamus nigris*. This plant, which used to be despised and previously grew only in the farthest corners of the city, in harbors, graveyards, industrial sites, and roadsides, was now farmed in people's yards and even in public parks. It was grown on balconies and window sills. Some had dedicated a whole room for the henbane and burnt plant lights during long nights in an attempt to get it to thrive.

Henbane is an odd plant. In the spring, there are the first sprouts, then tough, hairy, sharply-serrated leaves, which are typical of the species, spring up from the ground. Soon there are buds, and then the first flowers bloom. Their corollas are pale or dirty yellow with crisscrossing purple red veins, much like blood vessels. This is the time when one will also begin to detect the henbane's characteristic stench in the garden.

The henbane's bloom is funnel-shaped; the anthers of the stamen stand out separately. The fruit is a capsule of many seeds, and the species can appear in the most unexpected places because the seeds can survive for a long time in the ground.

Henbane is a poisonous plant, so poisonous that just a small overdose can lead to coma and death.

This was the very reason people were so delighted about henbane: they could hallucinate by eating its seeds or chewing the flower petals. The leaves, seeds, flowers, and roots of henbane are all poisonous. There was a time when it was used to treat asthma, tremors of old age, toothache, and anxiety. Its scopolamine and atropine work directly on the central nervous system. Henbane let its users have a glimpse into a strange world. It helped them to have colorful new dreams which were an improvement over the depressing reality of the city. But many drifted into states of delirium. Their pulse became quick and their eyesight blurred. They fainted, their body temperature became dangerously high, their speech became incoherent, and they began to have convulsions. If they recovered, one way or another they were sure to get themselves more henbane. The patrols that now wandered around town were different from those run by the party leader. They didn't march but rather they staggered. Nobody repaired the streets any longer, or cut the grass, and grew regular cabbage. They were happy just to have henbane.

They used to be slaves to the party, and now they were enslaved by henbane.

Håkan, the gardener, still puttered around in his garden. Henbane grew in Håkan's garden, too, although he had never sowed its seeds or consumed it. The variety that grew in the city was quick to spread and proved to be extremely hardy. Where drought, too much moisture, or cold killed other grasses, its leaves were unchanging and lush through the dry seasons and the hardest freezing winters.

Its requirements for habitat were minimal. It could face anything. It spread everywhere. Its pliable shoots formed twines and grew up the trunks of the linden trees along the boulevard. Its leaves were sharp as a bread knife. A mere touch of one produced a long cut on the finger.

At night when Håkan went out to relieve himself he could see the henbane gleaming in his back yard under the lilac bush. It appeared to glow in the dark, somewhat like glow worms. He aimed his stream of urine straight on its leaves, but it would not hurt them; it would only act as an additional fertilizer and make the henbane flourish all the more triumphantly.

This so-called nature, what was it anyway? The more Håkan looked at it, the more he wondered and the less he understood. This plague which had overtaken the city was also part of that mystery.

Although spring repeated itself year after year, it never stayed the same. Each growing season was different, each opening corolla was always new. The leaves of the trees with their network of veins resembled the trees themselves, and the trees its leaves.

Håkan understood little, but he loved all the more: the fiercely growing poplars standing upright with their conical tops against the storm clouds; the elliptical, satiny leaves of willows; and the calyxes of privet blooms which so quickly withered and fell to the summer lawn...

╫ ╫ ╫

LEENA KROHN has two other stories in this anthology, "The Son of Chimera," on page 27, and "The Ice Cream Vendor," on page 311. All three stories are excerpts from her novel, *Pereat mundus,* to be published in the United States in the latter half of 2006 by Omnidawn. In this novel Håkan is an everyman character, taking on different forms. More info on this book is available at www.omnidawn.com/krohn *Tainaron, Mail from Another City* (translated into English by Hildi Hawkins) was published in the U.S. by Prime Books in 2004. Krohn lives in Southern Finland. A number of her writings and works are available on her home page at www.kaapeli.fi/krohn

Stepan Chapman

Losing the War

Our village up here in the pine forests doesn't have much commerce with the rest of Russia. But once a war came to the village, a real Russian war. That war was probably our village's only chance for a mention in the history books. But we lost the war, and nothing much came of it. Shall I tell you how it was, when the War came among us?

The boys who watch the goats were the first ones to see it. It came walking down the road from the high pass. It was as tall as two men and as broad as three horses, and its hide was red as bricks and just as hard. It wore fine black boots and a three-cornered velvet hat with a plume. It had an ammunition belt strapped across its chest, a holster belt around its waist, and a pair of flintlock pistols as long as your arms. And that was all it wore. Being a war rather than a man, it felt no need to hide its nakedness. (Nor did its nakedness provide it with anything worth hiding, if you follow my drift.)

The War marched to the market square, took over the village in the name of the Tsar, and got the men organized on a military basis. All the young men had to put their names on a list. The War locked the list in a strongbox and told the women to stay indoors. It taught the men to march. The next day it divided them into two squadrons, the white armbands and the black armbands, and drilled them with sharpened staves.

Then came the morning when the men would begin the real fighting. They met the War at the market square and marched off to the appointed battleground.

Most of the men came home that evening, weary and shaken. But a few of them were hauled back to town on a corpse wagon. Four men pulled the wagon, since the horses had run away.

On the following morning, the men gathered again in the square. But this time the War was nowhere to be seen. They marched out to the battlefield, but the War wasn't there either. The men searched the forest, calling out to the War. But they still couldn't find it. Finally they all went to the tavern and got drunk. The tavern keeper asked them whether they were done with fighting the War.

"We're not sure," said one of them. "Yesterday it was beating us pretty badly. But today it seems to have lost its nerve."

The men went home. They slept all night and half the next day.

What had happened to the War was simple. When the men had gone home to their wives, they'd left it alone on the battlefield. The War got lonely and frightened. It wasn't accustomed to being alone after dark. It was, in fact, only a *baby* war.

And so, as babies will, the War soiled itself and messed up its fine leather boots. Feeling extremely mortified, the War ran into the forest and hid itself. In the forest, it lost its way and wandered, crashing through the brush, for three days and three nights. It left its velvet hat and its holster belt somewhere in the briars.

Finally it stumbled out of the forest onto the battlefield. No soldiers were there to meet it. Only blackbirds picking at some bloody straw. The birds looked up at the War and flew away.

The War thumped into the market square, throwing stones and calling the townsmen cowards. The men were off weeding their fields. But the women heard the War. And by now they'd realized that this War business was more than just some rowdy game. So they decided that *they* would deal with the War this time.

First they sat the War down on a bench and fed him all the baked goods they could gather—cakes, tarts, meat pies, loaves of bread… The War ate everything. They fed it baskets of freshly baked honey buns and let it lick the batter spoon. Then they sang it a lullaby. The War rubbed its eyes, feeling sleepy.

An old woman dragged a cradle into the square, a cradle full of warm woolen blankets.

"Climb in and get some sleep," the old woman suggested.

"In *that*?" the War complained, wiping its mouth. "It's too small."

"Then you must make yourself small," she told it.

The War yawned and shrank itself down as small as a human baby. It climbed into the cradle and fell asleep, sucking its thumb.

The women went on singing their lullaby. Four of them lifted the cradle, which was as heavy as a small load of bricks. They carried it far from the market square along shadowy paths through the forest, singing all the while. The War gurgled under the warm blankets.

The women took the cradle to the edge of a tall cliff beside a deep gorge. Far below, a powerful river flowed past, roaring and foaming. The War heard the river in its sleep. But the river was far away and sounded like a part of the lullaby. The four women swung the cradle between them, to and fro, back and forth. They swung it toward the edge of the cliff and away again, softly singing.

And still singing, they threw the cradle into the gorge.
The War was lost forever.

◈ ◈ ◈

STEPAN CHAPMAN lives with his wife Kia in Cottonwood, Arizona. He's written fantasy fiction for the last thirty years. His short stories have appeared in *Album Zutique, Axcess, The Baffler, Chicago Review, Electric Velocipede, Happy, Hawaii Review, Implosion, International Quarterly, Lady Churchill's Rosebud Wristlet,* all four *Leviathan* anthologies, *Main Street Rag, McSweeney's Quarterly, Nashwaak Review,* four of *Damon Knight's Orbit* anthologies, *Polyphony 4, RE:AL, redsine, sandbox, The Silver Web, The Thackery T. Lambshead Pocket Guide To Eccentric & Discredited Diseases, Wisconsin Review,* and *ZYZZYVA.* His novel *The Troika,* Ministry of Whimsy Press, 1997, was awarded the Philip K. Dick Award and will soon be translated into Russian. His other major publication is *Dossier,* Creative Arts Books, 2001, a short story collection.

MARK WALLACE

THE FLOWERS

> "If quietly and like another time,
> there is the passage of an unexpected thing…"
> —Robert Creeley

At first it occurred to Tom that something that evening, he didn't know what, was out of place on the wrought iron balcony railings of a block of rowhouses he passed every day. The balconies were on the second floor, and each day as he came to and from work he would look at the intricate design of the black railings and at the variety of potted plants and flowers sitting on them. From each rowhouse two tall, thin windows looked out on the balconies; between each pair of windows was a small door. Sometimes people stood on the balconies, watering the plants.

This evening, however, the picture seemed changed, nearly imperceptibly. It was as if during a game of chess he had stepped out of the room and, coming back again, sensed that his opponent had slipped a pawn forward, so that the relationship between all the pieces looked different, without the change being easy to find. Then he noticed some flowers sitting in a pot. The pot stood on the edge of the railing of the third house in from the corner, just above one of the railing's spiral designs. He stopped walking and cocked his head to get a more accurate look; without a doubt the flowers had not been there as he passed by on his way to work that morning. During the day, obviously, someone had put them there. There was nothing particularly striking about them, as flowers went: several purple-white blossoms rising out of a tangle of green leaves, sitting in a clay pot that was rectangular and red. He couldn't identify them; he wasn't good with plants, something he had tried to tell Martha when she had given him her plants to take care of while she went on a trip to Europe with several female friends (it was easier to bring him her plants than to make him go out to her apartment in the suburbs). But he had always taken pride in his ability to know his surroundings, and the fact that someone had snuck the flowers in, as if they had always been just to the left of the outside line of the window, struck him as a personal test, if not an outright jeer. Was it too far-fetched to imagine that someone stood hidden, watching his reactions, behind the blue-striped curtains inside the window?

He crouched on the sidewalk, careful not to scrape the knee of his suit, and snapped open his briefcase. He pulled a note pad from it and jotted down the house's address. A moment later he began to feel he was overreacting, or at the very least betraying too much concern by crouching on the sidewalk; certainly he didn't want whoever had planned the trick to be successful.

He straightened up and walked away, determined to consider the flowers a matter of no importance.

At his apartment door he noted with pleasure how the June sun, coming through the window at the far end of the hallway, fell onto the same square patch of the brown rug that it had for weeks and, also as usual, made a rectangular patch about half the size of the square on the wall just above the wainscoting. He opened the door, using first the upper latch key and then that for the door itself, as he always did. He stepped in, turned on the light and watched each piece of furniture flash into its proper place. He changed clothes, called his friend David to make sure they were meeting for drinks after dinner, then cooked his meal, following to the letter a recipe Martha had given him.

After eating and doing the dishes, he sat down to relax, and began thinking about the flowers again. Tomorrow at work he would use his connections and make some calls to find out whether the rowhouse was rented, or if the owner lived there, and how long the current resident had occupied it. He would ask simply as if he were interested in buying the house. Maybe he would speak directly to the person who lived there and ask about the flowers in passing, as if he had particularly liked the purple-white blossoms and wondered where he could get some. It was all easily done. There was no need for this vague uneasiness, this sense that the flowers, merely by their presence, in some way taunted him.

With a start he realized he hadn't watered Martha's plants for days. He cringed at the thought of telling her they had died only a day or two before she came back, and pictured her pressing him about his ineptness. Not that she would get upset, of course. Martha made certain to act as if nothing ever upset her, a trait he admired. He too believed that the best way to respond to any incident, even one that surprised and annoyed you, was to act as if you had been ready for it, had perhaps even predicted it. Any other reaction would have been evidence of not knowing where you were, not knowing how the world was and always being ready to master it. Martha, of course, overdid it, as she overdid many things. She was often so determined to be in control that she went to lengths even he never would have—for instance the time she had tried to return some gloves at Hechts, and, refusing to stand still for the runaround, had made Tom wait for nearly half an hour while, quite calmly, she browbeat a clerk into taking them back. Tom often teased her (though making clear how much he respected her for it) that she was more of a man than any man ever was.

He filled her watering can, took it through the sliding glass doors to the porch and stopped, the can poised to pour.

Sitting on the railing, the fourth plant in from the left, were the same—the exact same—flowers he'd seen that afternoon.

Purple in the center of each petal, with a white border around the center, they opened out haughtily from a green tangle of leaves and stems. A few dried leaves lay in the rich brown dirt dotted with pebbles. They were in the same rectangular red pot, which had chipped edges that he hadn't seen looking up at the balcony.

He was certain there had been no flowers like that on his porch before. But when he counted the pots along the railing he found that there were eight, as there had been all along. Besides, he had no sense, looking at the pots, that one was missing, replaced by this new one. Still, he was certain he hadn't seen the flowers before—here, that is—just as he was certain, in a way he couldn't have explained, that they were exactly the same flowers he had seen that afternoon, and not just the same kind: the same exact flowers. He decided that instant he wouldn't water them, and went right to work doing the others. But his eyes caught on the purple-white blossoms, opened out as if it was absolutely natural for them to be sitting there, and he spilled water all over the railing and onto the concrete floor of the porch.

He decided he would have to cancel his evening with David, then that he certainly wouldn't cancel it.

The flowers were undeniably there; he poked his finger in the soft dirt, ran it across the flowers and then the leaves and stems. He felt that they were there, as they had been there on the railing of the rowhouse, precisely for him to know that they were. But he also felt that there was no more meaning than that in their presence, no truth other than themselves hidden among the branches; they were simply flowers there for him to see because they were flowers there for him to see. As simple as this was, he didn't want them to be there, cringed at the fact, felt his chest ball up at the thought that they should be sitting on the rail when he hadn't put them there. He turned his back on them and left the porch.

Maybe, though, he thought after being inside a moment, maybe they were Martha's after all. He hadn't watered the plants in days, and maybe he had just forgotten…no, he didn't believe it. But of course they *had* to be Martha's, although he didn't understand how they could be in two places at once. And as much as he wanted them out of his sight, he realized he wasn't going to get rid of them; what would Martha think if he told her he had thrown out one of her plants because he couldn't stand the fact that it was sitting on his porch?

He was pacing the living room, wondering what to do, when his eye wandered to the clock above the mantelpiece and he realized he was late to meet David.

◊ ◊ ◊

On weeknights out, Tom always had two gin and tonics. He was finishing his first drink when David smiled and said, "You might not believe me, but when I first went to college I called myself a communist. Said I'd fight anyone who disagreed with my point of view. Once I jumped over a bar at a frat meeting to go after somebody who called me a traitor."

"A communist," Tom repeated disapprovingly, staring at his drink.

"Yes." David grinned. "You know; I thought the young idealists would make the world a better place by getting rid of oppression and exploitation."

"You can't get rid of oppression," Tom said.

"Of course not," David agreed. "The only thing is to make sure you're one of those doing the oppressing." He laughed, and Tom laughed too, then stopped abruptly.

David was a plump, calm man with mischievous eyes, who lacked the self-assurance that Tom had, but was smart. Sometimes, Tom thought, a little too smart, for instance in the way he was always trying to fool Tom into thinking he was serious when he wasn't. Looking at Tom closely, David leaned over the table and said, in the off-hand manner he used to introduce important topics, "Anything wrong tonight? You look distracted."

"Everything's fine," Tom said.

"You seem slightly unnerved or something."

Tom did his best to scoff. "No, definitely not."

"Martha's going to be back any day now?"

"Yes."

"Finding things a little hard without her?"

Tom pushed his chair back and took a deep breath, as if the room didn't have enough air. "I thought you knew," he said, "that Martha and I don't get along like that. For the moment we've agreed to be completely independent. We care for each other a lot, but right now our careers come first. I'm not in a position to let what she does affect my routine, and vice versa."

"Yes, I know that," David agreed, eyes hinting that he didn't believe it. "But don't you think she's going to want an engagement pretty soon?"

Tom waved him off. "Of course, when it comes to plants it's a different story," he said. "I wish she'd hurry back and take them off my hands. One of them gives me a lot of trouble. It's got purple-white flowers. You don't know anything about plants, do you?"

"Me?" David smirked. "Hardly."

"Me either."

"So you'd agree, then," David shook a finger as if scoring a point, "that without her you're finding things different than you expected?"

Tom startled. "Why do you say that?"

"Ah ha, I was right."

"What do you mean?"

"By the way you're acting. Come on, Tom, what is it? You've been looking around all evening like you think someone you're afraid of is going to walk in the door."

"I don't..." Tom began, his eyes held firmly on his glass, in which the identical square ice cubes had melted into obscure shapes. He shook off the moment of dizziness. "So how long did it take you to realize it was stupid to be a communist? You might have done yourself some real damage."

It was David's turn to back away from the table. He picked up his drink, and his face relaxed into a embarrassed smile that seemed to say he had, maybe, gone too far. "I don't think that was why I changed. I think it turned out to be less fun than I thought. You had to do things about it, if you see what I'm saying. You even had to give up the chance of making money yourself." He paused at Tom's serious stare. "That's a joke."

Tom forced a smile. Catching the bartender's eye, he motioned with a finger that he needed another drink. "You always have been sort of a dreamer, haven't you?"

"I guess so." David admitted the vice as if he thought it was actually a virtue. "Not you, huh? Both feet on the ground and everything?"

"You could say that. Anything wrong with it? That's what I'd like to know." Tom folded his arms. "Too many people go around feeling like the world owes them. But I say you have to make the world what you want it to be. And how can you do that if you don't know where you are, if you waste your time being a dreamer? The world is real, David. If we don't control it, it'll control us."

"Hey, I agree with you." David put up his hands in surprise at Tom's vehemence.

Tom took his new gin and tonic from the bartender and drank a good bit of it in several rapid gulps. "I've got to head home soon, sadly. I've got a long day tomorrow."

"Come on Tom, tell the truth. I'm your friend, you know that." David cocked his head, and his mouth tightened in an expression of genuine concern. "How are you? How are you, really?"

"I'm great," Tom said. "Things couldn't be better. My job's great, I'll be seeing Martha in a day or two. I'd dare anyone to prove they were happier than me, in any way."

"I certainly won't take you on. I'll admit I'm unhappy sometimes."

"That's just you and your idealism." Tom shook his head. "I think it's selfish to be unhappy. There's enough misery in the world without your adding to it."

"Maybe. But something *is* bothering you."

Tom smiled; he felt more relaxed again, like some crisis had passed. The gin felt pleasant in his head. "How many times do I have to say no to that? I've been having a few problems with my apartment, but it's nothing I can't handle."

"Maintenance?"

"It's not worth talking about."

"Oh?"

"Absolutely nothing," Tom raised his drink, "that I can't handle."

⁕ ⁕ ⁕

Which was how he felt as he reached his apartment, the lights in the hallway leaving shadows in the usual corners. He stepped in, turned on the lights and watched each piece of his furniture flash into its proper place.

He went to the porch and looked at the flowers. They sat peacefully in the pot. He felt sure he had just been forgetful in believing he hadn't seen them before; of course they'd been there ever since Martha had brought them. He didn't know how to explain the presence of similar flowers on the other railing, but eventually he would. They no longer had the power to disturb him; the purple-white blossoms, which had closed a little in the dark, were simply uninteresting. To think he could have believed that someone was watching him from behind the window, trying to taunt him with such a completely unimportant *thing*.

"I can handle you," he said.

As if to prove it, he took one of the petals between his fingers, yanked it off and, quite nonchalantly, flicked it to the floor.

⸜ ⸜ ⸜

The morning was cool, and Tom put on his suit in the patch of sun that warmed his bedroom every summer morning that wasn't cloudy. He made himself a bag lunch; he ate in the office three days a week, to save money.

For a moment, no more, he wondered if he should avoid the block of rowhouses. He walked past slowly, determined to show no concern to whoever might be watching (yet hadn't he already decided that no one could be watching?) from behind the blue-striped curtains. The black iron railings, the small balconies and the tall, thin windows seemed perfectly tame and in place in the sun, which struck them at an angle, causing diagonal lines of shadow from the right side of each landing to fall back against the buildings, making a series of small squares. The flowers stood exactly where they had the day before, on the edge of the railing, above one of the spiral designs and just to the left of the outside line of the windows. He noted with a sense of victory that, here, the flowers didn't stand in the same relation to the other plants that they did on his own porch. There were only five pots here, not eight, and the one with the flowers stood on the left edge, not in the middle.

Smiling, he walked to a place underneath the flower pot. He put his hands on his hips in a show of command and nodded. He was, without a doubt, mastering the situation. The flowers *were* there, as similar ones were in his room, but as strange an impression as it had made on him, he understood the situation now, and could deal with it.

He looked down. Symmetrically centered on the sidewalk in the distance between his shoes lay a purple-white petal, crumpled as if someone had yanked it off and flicked it to the sidewalk, quite nonchalantly.

⸜ ⸜ ⸜

At work Tom ducked into his office and shut the door on his secretary's attempt to tell him he had received a phone call from someone whose name he didn't catch.

He had a few conveniently placed friends who could help him get the information he needed. Several personal calls helped him get in touch with a woman in the property records department who was able, if not willing, to help him.

After several minutes of silence while she looked up what he wanted to know, the woman came back to the phone and said, "The records say the house is owned by a Mr. T. Meachem."

"T?"

"Yes, there's just the first letter."

"How long has he owned it?"

"A little more than two years."

"Does he have any other property in the city?"

The woman sighed, implying that he reconsider his request. "That'll take a minute while I run another check."

"All right, I'll wait."

The woman sighed again and set the phone down, hard. A few long minutes later she came back on the line. "As far as I can tell, he owns only one other house in town." She gave an address on the south side, a street in a bad neighborhood.

"You have a phone number for him?"

"There are some things, sir, that even we can't do. Have you tried the phone book?"

"All right. Thanks for your help."

The woman sighed as if thanks would never justify what she was put through, and hung up.

It wasn't difficult to find the number. There was only one T. Meachem listed in the phone book, Tom Meachem, the address given that of the bad neighborhood. A bit of a coincidence, Tom thought, that the man should have his own first name.

After three rings there was a click. "Yes?" a man's voice drawled.

"Mr. Meachem?"

"No," the man said in a surly tone. "Ain't no Mr. Meachem here."

"Is this 933-4352?"

"Was last time I checked."

"And there's no Mr. Meachem there?"

"You one of them bill collectors? I told you bastards you called here again you'd never see any more of your god-damned money."

"I'm not a bill collector."

"Sound like one to me."

"I'm simply trying to reach a Mr. Meachem. I'm... I'm interested in buying some property he owns."

"Guess you'll have to talk to him about that."

"Is it possible that he lived there until recently? I mean have you just moved in?"

"Sure you're not a bill collector?"

"Positive. How long have you lived there?"

"Long enough to know there ain't no Mr. Meachem around, unless maybe he's buried in the backyard or something."

"But listen, it says here in the phone book that this is Mr. Meachem's number."

"Why didn't you say so?" The man scoffed. "If it's in the phone book, it must be true." He hung up loudly.

Tom shook his head and put down the phone. How was he going to get in touch with Meachem now? Maybe he had no choice but to knock on the door of the rowhouse.

This time it was his phone that rang.

"Yes?" he said sharply.

"Tom, guess who?"

"Martha, you're back. It's good to hear your voice."

"It's good to hear yours. Didn't your secretary give you the message that I called?"

"What? No. I mean maybe, she tried. I've been busy all morning."

"You sound nervous."

"No," Tom stiffened. "When did you get back?"

"Late last night. Two or three in the morning."

"If you'd called I would have picked you up at the airport."

"I appreciate it, but it was late, and we all took a cab together."

"So when can I see you?"

"Whenever you want," she said. "You know that."

"Come to my place after work and we'll go to dinner."

"Sounds wonderful."

"It'll give you a chance to see your plants before we eat."

"That *will* be nice."

"You won't believe me, but I managed to keep all eight of them alive and well."

"I'm proud of you," Martha laughed across the distance of the phone, "but eight? It's a good thing you're not an accountant."

"What?"

"I only gave you seven plants."

"You mean eight."

"No, seven. I'm very careful about things like that."

"I have eight plants on my porch rail, Martha."

"No need to get excited just because you can't count."

"I'm *not* excited."

"You *are* excited."

Tom took the phone from his ear, steadied himself, then put it back. "However many," he said more calmly, "I'll be glad when you take them. One, especially, has given me a lot of trouble: the one with the purple-white flowers."

"You *are* strange today," Martha said. "I don't have a plant like that."

"Of course you do. The one in the big square pot."

"Square pot?"

Tom squinted; tension rose behind his eyes. "Look…oh, never mind. See you around six?"

"Absolutely. I can't wait."

⍚ ⍚ ⍚

That evening, Tom was nervously watching the sunlight recede from the room in what seemed a new way, the light lower on the wall, when the doorbell rang and he leaped up startled. Martha was standing in the doorway, wearing a light blue skirt and jacket with a silky black sleeveless shirt. It should have looked good on her. But his immediate impression, before either spoke, was that she was different than he remembered, with squarer shoulders and a head that seemed too narrow for her upper body, as if someone had switched her head for the head that actually should have been there.

"Tom, it's great to see you." She kissed and hugged him, then passed into the living room.

"You look wonderful," Tom said, squinting at the lie. "Europe has been good to you, I can tell. You have a great tan."

"Thanks. You got my postcards?" Her perfume smelled heavy and sweet.

"Yes. They were very nice."

"I dropped off pictures at the store this afternoon. They should be ready in a day or two." She sat on the couch; he took the chair across from her. She launched quickly into details about the trip: a week in

Paris, which had been nice but dirty, another in Rome, nice but too hot, the little towns they had stopped at inbetween, each with their good and bad points. Her head bobbed slightly as she spoke, her hands rested in her lap, and her body lay back against the couch at an angle, making her appear crooked. She seemed like someone he didn't know. He was quite conscious of having remembered her more soothingly shaped, her voice not as nasal, her face less pointy and narrow. Maybe it had something to do with the flowers.

"So I'm sure you want to see your plants," he found himself saying, interrupting her.

"I guess so." Her eyes showed a vague surprise.

"I think I did pretty well with them."

"I figured you would."

"Well come on then." He stood up too quickly, nervously. "It's the one with the purple-white flowers that gave me the most trouble. A strange plant."

"I told you over the phone I don't have a plant like that." She followed him to the porch.

"What's that, then?" he demanded, pointing.

"They certainly are purple-white flowers, and very nice, actually. But they're not mine; where *did* you get them?" She kneeled down to take a closer look.

"Don't tell me they're not yours when I know they are."

At the sharpness of his voice, she stood quickly. "Why are you so upset?"

"I'm not upset." He pounded his hand on the railing. "Why does everybody keep saying I'm upset?" He stared at the flowers, which rose from the tangle of green leaves, blossoms broadly open to catch the fading rays of the sun.

Martha said, "What's wrong, Tom? You're overreacting."

"I'm not." He wheeled around to face her. "I don't understand why you won't admit they're yours, I don't understand why you won't take them away."

Martha stepped back and folded her arms. "I've never known you to be like this. It's like you're a totally different person."

"What do you mean? I am not."

"If you don't stop barking and looking at me like that, I'm going to leave."

"Maybe you should. And take your flowers with you."

Martha stiffened. "I don't understand why you're acting so crazy. It's only a plant, for God's sake."

"Only a plant?" Tom laughed. "Of course it's only a plant. I mean that's the point, isn't it? It's just a plant that doesn't belong to anyone or mean anything, it's just sitting on my porch and that's all there is to it."

"I didn't come here to be yelled at."

"I'm sure you didn't. The plant didn't come here to be yelled at either, it's just a plant." He turned from her, saw the purple-white blossoms shrink back. "Isn't that right?" he said to them. "You don't know why you're here, you don't even care, you're just sitting on my porch because you're sitting on my porch, just like you're sitting on the balcony of that other apartment, you're sitting here and you're not going away..."

He realized Martha had left the porch, but he didn't try to follow her. He heard his front door click open and bang shut. His ears were buzzing, his knees wobbled. He grabbed the railing and steadied himself, but couldn't look away from the flowers, sitting there for no reason at all.

Martha had called him a different person. Could it be true, he thought, could he have become that way because a plant, a mere plant, had come into his life and refused to go away? As if he could lose himself by buying new chairs, maybe only rearranging them. Was everything he thought he was as fragile as that?

He picked up the flower pot, squeezing it tightly in his hands, then threw it to the concrete.

After the initial crash, there was silence. Among clumps of dirt and fragments of clay the brown roots lay spread, the two largest ones twisted around each other in a complicated tangle. The blossoms, one smashed by dirt, huddled together and closed as though trying to protect themselves.

His hands trembling, he ran inside, shutting the glass door firmly behind him.

◌ ◌ ◌

When he had calmed down a little, he decided he had to go to the rowhouse. He changed into old clothes, jeans and a tee-shirt, neither of which he had recently worn outside the apartment. He turned off all the lights carefully and locked the door behind him.

When he reached his destination, night had come, and the tall, thin windows and iron rails shone faintly underneath the street lights. But on the whole the block of rowhouses was relatively dark and quiet, though only a few blocks from a busy main street. He looked closely at the railing where the flower pot had been, making sure it was no longer there. Then he went to the front door, wooden and carved with a spiral design like that of the railings.

There were two doorbells, and he rang them both. When he got no answer, he rang again, then a final time. No one was home. He tried the door and found, surprisingly, that it was unlocked. He looked back to make sure no one was watching, and without even wondering if he should, slipped through.

The entrance hall, with a staircase running up the right side of it, was dimly lit by a single bulb. Shadows fell across the faded wallpaper and gathered thickly in the corners. Just past the door, two black metal mailboxes hung on the wall. No names were on them and no mail was inside. At the back of the hallway stood a door, also wooden and carved, that led to the downstairs apartment. He walked over and pressed his ear against it. No sound came from beyond. It was possible that whoever lived there was simply out for the evening, but the film of dust on the door suggested that the apartment was unoccupied, maybe had been for some time.

He came back to the front of the hall and climbed the stairs carefully, wincing with each creak that shot along the staircase. At the top stood only a small landing, cut off abruptly by another door. The door seemed out of character with the rest of the hallway; a flat, plain piece of wood that looked newer than everything around it. Maybe the owner (if there was an owner, he thought, then wondered why he had thought it) had put it there when he had converted the house to apartments.

This door too was unlocked. Tom knocked, merely as a precaution, since he felt sure no one was inside, that the whole house was empty. But if it was empty, why were there flowers on the railing at all?

With a deep breath he went through. The apartment smelled musty, and was hidden in a moon-lighted darkness that took his eyes some moments to adjust to. In that time, waiting by the door, he tried to find a light switch and cracked his hand against the wall, heard the sound echo and realized there wasn't much furniture in the room.

His eyes, when they grew accustomed to the moonlight, which was bright enough to make it possible to see at least a little, confirmed the impression. Several large unopened boxes stood in the middle of the floor, as if someone was moving in or out, but that was all the room held. On the side of one of the boxes was a large white sticker with writing on it. He tried to read it, but couldn't, and cursed himself for not bringing a flashlight. But after a few moments of straining, he thought he could make it out: PROPERTY OF T. MEACHEM.

He stepped past the boxes into the kitchen, where to his surprise he found a light switch easily. The lighted kitchen was almost empty also. The window above the sink was covered by the blue-striped curtains. A box was sitting by the sink; glasses and silverware and kitchen utensils, wrapped in paper, lay next to it. He couldn't tell whether they had just been taken out or were going to be put in. He took a step back and kicked something which fell with a clatter a small, empty plastic trash can.

Then, ducking through the tiny doorway, he went out to the balcony. Purple-white flowers lay on the balcony's floor. Each fragment of the pot was broken in exactly the same way as on his porch. There were the same clumps of dirt, the same two large roots tangled around each other, the same smashed blossom. The other flowers huddled together as if trying, without the strength, to roll themselves into a ball.

He looked at the row of flower pots on the railing, pots he had never seen, holding plants and flowers he had never seen. He went inside quickly.

A moment later he came out carrying the trash can. He kneeled in the tight space of the balcony, putting his pants in the dirt, and began to clean up.

❦ ❦ ❦

David Franklin came along the street looking for the right address, shielding his eyes from the sun that flashed off the tall, thin windows of the somewhat old-fashioned rowhouses, which had wrought iron railings on the balconies, no less. He looked at the piece of paper crumpled carelessly in his hand; yes, this was the place. Not the kind of house he would have expected Tom to choose. Tom had always been a contemporary guy with no use for antiques. Of course, all of a sudden there was no telling what Tom would do.

David rang the doorbell, and after he was buzzed in, looked at the two black mailboxes hanging on the wall. Only one had a name on it, T. Meachem, and though he had been prepared, he still clacked his tongue in a confused, disapproving way. "What on earth," he mumbled, "makes a thirty-year-old man start going by another name?" That was bad enough; that Tom had quit his job with no new firm prospects was even worse.

David knocked on the upstairs door and Tom answered, smiling. "Come in."

As he walked to the couch and sat down, David noticed that not a single piece of Tom's furniture was the same as in his old apartment. None of it was new stuff, either. In fact a few pieces looked almost shabby, as if Tom had taken them in simply so someone else wouldn't throw them away. If his friend hadn't been standing there, David would have sworn that there was no way Tom could live here.

"You sure did all this fast," David said. "You didn't even mention moving last week, much less any of the rest of it."

"I know. Things just happen sometimes." Tom was still smiling, more than David had ever seen him, and he put his hand gently on David's arm. David pulled back; when had Tom started touching people?

"So," David asked, looking away from Tom's smile, "what should we do tonight, since you don't want to go to any of the regular places?"

"I don't know." Tom shrugged. "No need to plan too much." He stood. "You want to see my plants? I think you'll especially like the ✳✳✳✳✳✳✳✳✳"—he gave a name David didn't catch. "It's got lovely purple-white flowers."

David followed Tom through the kitchen to the balcony, ducking under the tiny doorway. "Since when," he asked, "did you get interested in plants?"

〰 〰 〰

MARK WALLACE is the author of more than ten books and chapbooks of poetry, including *Nothing Happened and Besides I Wasn't There* and *Sonnets of a Penny-A-Liner. Temporary Worker Rides A Subway* won the 2002 Gertrude Stein Poetry Award and was published by Green Integer Books. His multi-genre work *Haze* (Edge Books) was published in 2004, as was his novel *Dead Carnival* (Avec Books). His critical articles and reviews have appeared in numerous publications, and along with Steven Marks, he edited *Telling It Slant: Avant-Garde Poetics of the 1990s* (University of Alabama Press), a collection of 26 essays by different writers on the subject of contemporary avant garde poetry and poetics. With Juliana Spahr, Kristin Prevallet, and Pam Rehm he edited *A Poetics of Criticism,* a collection of poetry essays in non-standard formats (Leave Books). He is currently Assistant Professor of Creative Writing at California State University San Marcos.

JEFFREY FORD

THE WHITE MAN

I don't think I slept but four nights the year that I was seven. My baby sister was in the hospital with a hole in her heart. We would go to her on the weekends—my mother, my father, my brother and other sister. She was being kept in a place in the country where there were many nuns but no people.

The fountain we sat near while my mother was inside the giant stone building was filled with black water and rotting leaves. Since we weren't allowed in, my brother, who was a year older than me, and the oldest of us children, would tell my sister and me stories about Gal de Gui, an old man whose hands were tree branches and who had owned the extreme unction box that now sat in the corner of our basement amidst the Christmas decorations and spider eggs. He had lived with his belongings in the sewer pipe near the woods behind the school. All his life he searched for bits of glass from a green bottle he had dropped in the street when he was a child. He never found all the pieces, but he kept looking till the day he died, because the bottle had once held his mother's last spit.

"You're a liar," my sister would say to my brother, but before he could take her hand and make her touch the three magic moles on his neck, my father would appear from the stone building carrying sodas for us.

At home it was always Sunday afternoon or Monday night. My mother sat in the dark and drank dark wine whose sweetness gagged when she kissed you good night. Cigarette smoke constantly wreathed her head as if she were sticking her face up out of a hole dug in fog. She cursed and cried every night. When my father would get home from his second job, I would hear her downstairs yelling at him. He would mumble, mumble, mumble to her and this would quiet her. Then he would help her up the stairs and put her to bed. My mother could not sleep without an open book lying on her chest, so my father would take the old copy of Sherlock Holmes off the dresser and rest it lightly down on her. Then I would doze for a minute and wake to his snoring. For the rest of the night, I would usually read under the covers with a flashlight.

One of the only nights I slept was the night I threw up hot dogs. When my father got home, he did not mumble, but came upstairs and

sat on the end of my bed. When he touched my stomach with his cal-
loused hand, the nausea went away. I dreamed very fast of black dogs
and Gal de Gui, and when I woke up suddenly, sweating, hours later,
he was still sitting there, staring at the wall, listening to the birds singing outside in the mimosa.

My sister got worse. That was all we were told. "The hole has gotten larger," my brother whispered to me one evening when we sat on
the slates in the backyard, watching a giant spider battle a bee in a
closed mayonnaise jar. As he spoke these words, I noticed it had grown
cold and that all at once the leaves had begun to fall.

That night, when my father returned from work, we were called
down from our bedrooms to see that his hair had turned white. "Here,
watch," he said to my brother and pulled off a clump without having to
tear it out. My brother took it from him.

Later, after the yelling, the mumbling, the snoring, my brother
tapped on my cover cave. I lifted the cover and shone the flashlight on
his face.

"I put it in the box," he said.

"What?" I asked.

"The hair."

"Why?" I asked.

"Shut up," he said, "just take this and whatever you do, don't lose
it." Then he handed me a piece of green bottle glass. "Don't lose it. Even
when you take a bath, keep it with you."

"OK," I said, and took it from him.

The next morning, my grandmother arrived and gave each of us
boys a polka-dot shirt. My sister got a doll that writhed when you
turned the key in its back.

At school that day I was called out of class to go to the nurse's
office. The nurse was young and pretty. She asked me to sit down at
a table that had a machine on it. The machine had two eye holes like
binoculars.

"Look into the machine," she told me, but I looked past her,
through the glass door that led to a small room. My brother was sitting on a chair in there. A man was putting a stick into his mouth until
he choked.

"Look into the machine," she said again, her voice as sweet as dark
wine.

I put my eyes to the machine but kept them closed.

"What do you see?" she asked.

"Everything," I said.

"Raise your hand when you see the red ball," she said. There was music then, two notes slowly changing into each other. "Do you see the red ball?" she asked.

"I see it," I said.

"Now close your eyes," she said.

I opened my eyes and saw pure white.

"Now open your eyes," she said.

I closed my eyes again.

"Where is the red ball?" she asked.

"In the sky," I said.

"Where is it now?" she asked.

"In the grass," I said.

After the machine, she made me look at sheets filled with colored circles.

"Do you see anything in these circles, like when you look into the clouds?" she asked.

"Yes," I told her.

"What do you see?"

"I see the red ball."

Before I went back to class, I peeked through the glass door again, but my brother was gone.

When we got home from school my grandmother had left, but I could tell from the scattered deck on the dining room table that she had been reading the cards for my mother. "To your house, to your heart, to your self, to what you least expect and what's sure to come." As we ate cookies in the backyard, my brother asked me if I had looked in the machine. I told him I hadn't, and he shook hands with me. After dinner I took off my polka-dot shirt and hung it in the back of the closet. It was maroon with yellow polka dots and the other children in my class had laughed at it.

That night, as always, I pretended to be asleep when I thought my father would bring my mother upstairs. He didn't, though. Instead, I heard the back door open and close. I got out from beneath the covers and went to the bathroom and looked out the window. The moon was up, and I could see my father walking back to the shed. He knocked on the shed door and it opened. As it swung back, the wind picked up and dry leaves blew around. From out of the shed stepped a man, completely white; a figure carved from marshmallow and bone. His hair was hard and straight like fine icicles, and all he wore was a pair of underwear. He lunged at my father, and they began to wrestle.

I ran back into the bedroom, climbed up to the top bunk and woke my brother. "Dad is fighting with a white man in the backyard," I whispered to him. He got out of bed and we both went to the bathroom and looked out the window. My father had his arm around the white man's throat and the white man was reaching back and pulling out more of my father's hair. Moths flapped all around them in the moonlight like flies around meat for the barbecue. "Give me your piece of glass," said my brother. I had it in my hand. I gave it to him. "Follow me," he said.

We went silently down the stairs. As we passed the kitchen, my brother put his finger to his lips and pointed. There was my mother in her nightgown, standing at the back door, in the dark, smoking a cigarette, swaying side to side. She was watching the battle outside. "Mom," I said to her, but she did not turn around. Then my brother pulled me by the arm, and we went through the door that led to the basement.

Down in the basement, my brother wrapped his piece of glass and mine in a sheet of sandpaper. Then he took the sandpaper and put it in the vise that was mounted on the worktable and turned the lever until we heard a muffled crunch like when you are breathing the sweet air and the dentist pulls a tooth. He opened the vise, took the sandpaper out, and we ran back upstairs to the second floor bathroom.

When we got to the window and looked out, my father was unconscious, and the white man was dragging him by the feet toward the shed. My brother opened the window and called, "White Man." The white man stopped dragging my father and looked up at us. His eyes were tiny searchlights. "We see you," my brother said. The white man gasped and dropped my father's feet. With two huge strides, he came across the back yard and then leaped into the apple tree with the ease of sunlight. From the apple tree, he flapped his arms and levitated to the roof. "You are a turd, White Man," my brother said.

As the white man crawled silently toward us, pulling himself along on the edges of the shingles, my brother opened the piece of sandpaper and poured the powdered glass into his hand. I backed away from the window, but my brother leaned out of it, lifting the palm full of glass dust to his lips. The big frozen mouth came up to bite his forehead, but my brother blew on his palm and the powdered glass flew into the white man's white eyes, turning them green. The white man put his creamy hands to his eyes and rubbed.

"What do you see?" my brother asked him.

"The golden fleece," he said in the tiny voice of a human cricket.

"Now close your eyes," said my brother, and with this, the white man fell backwards.

I rushed to the window and looked out. He had landed in the apple tree. Then the birds began to sing, and I could hear, from down the hall, my sister reciting the times tables in her sleep. When my brother flushed the toilet, the white man turned to smoke and flew away on the wind.

Back in the bunk beds, my brother leaned down from above and told me a story about Gal de Gui. He had been a knife thrower in a carnival once. He made the girl on the wheel spin faster and faster and never missed with his knives, except once. A dagger barely nicked the leg of this girl he was going to marry. She bled and when he touched his branch to the drops of blood after she stopped spinning, leaves sprouted at the ends of it. The head of the carnival made the performance continue, but Gal de Gui knew that with the leaves there, he could no longer throw the knives right. So the girl kept spinning and spinning and the crowd kept waiting for Gal de Gui to throw the knives, but he didn't want to kill her.

"I can't do it," Gal de Gui told the head of the carnival, but the man didn't listen, he made the spinners keep spinning the girl. The crowd, the head of the carnival, the spinners, the elephants, the monkey that tipped his hat for quarters, stayed and waited for two days for Gal de Gui to throw the knives but he never did. Finally the police came and made the wheel stop spinning. When they took the girl off the wheel she was crazy and could not walk. Gal de Gui married her anyway and for as long as she lived, he would carry her around on his shoulder.

After my brother had finished the story and had fallen asleep, I made shadow creatures with my fingers in the beam of my flashlight. From downstairs I heard mumbling. I thought I heard my grandmother's voice, but I knew she wasn't there. For hours after that I listened to the music that came out of my ears and watched the phantom smoke rise in a pillar from my covers. Finally the sun mixed with the smell of coffee and stung the crust in my eyes.

The next day we went to the hospital. This time we kids were allowed in to see my baby sister. She lay in a crib in a room full of babies laying in cribs. The nun that handed her to me smelled like old skin. My baby sister was light to hold as if she were a satin pillow from my grandmother's couch. When she looked at me with her big eyes, I thought of the hole in her heart and pictured a red doughnut. I kissed her on the cheek, and, when I did, the nun's hand clawed at my shoulder. When my brother held the baby, he let her touch his magic moles. My other sister cried and needed help. We were then told to go with my father and get a soda.

It was cold outside and the fountain had frozen over. As we sat on the stone bench, staring at the hard black water, what was left of my father's white hair flew away like dandelion seed. Then he grunted and new hair began to slowly grow in as we watched. It grew like little dark vines, curling and twining as it quietly popped through his scalp. "I'm getting younger," he said to my sister.

"You're a liar," she said.

⊪ ⊪ ⊪

JEFFREY FORD is the author of a trilogy of novels from Eos Harper Collins—*The Physiognomy, Memoranda,* and *The Beyond.* His most recent novel, *The Portrait of Mrs. Charbuque* (Morrow/Harper Collins), was published in June 2002 as was his first story collection, *The Fantasy Writer's Assistant & Other Stories* (Golden Gryphon Press). His short stories have appeared in a variety of magazines and anthologies, and his work has garnered three World Fantasy Awards, a Nebula, a Fountain Award and the Grand Prix de l'Imaginaire. Ford lives in South Jersey with his wife and two sons. He teaches Writing and Literature at Brookdale Community College in Monmouth County, New Jersey.

Michael Constance

Finding the Words

We are required by the Surgeon General to warn you that managing your own mindset, especially when playing uncertified mindscapes, can be dangerous to your mental and physical health, and that no part of this story is in any way intended as an endorsement of this practice.

All product placements in this story are provided on a purely gratis basis. However, the author is fully prepared to consider paid ad placements at very reasonable rates in subsequent stories. Because of the high writing standards to which the author adheres, product placement space is limited, so we suggest you reserve your ad space as early as possible.

1. MICHAEL

"In the very early beginnings of the world, when we were all very much younger than we are now, everything shared its own place with everything else. Light and darkness shared the world with each other, with the light passing over in the day, and the darkness passing in the night, leaving the heavens sparkling with light. Above the earth swept the wind and the water came in torrents from the heavens, and washed over the land and ran in rivers toward the sea from which it came."

At about this point I realize that someone is telling this story. Everything is dark and I can't see a thing. But I can hear this woman telling this story.

"And seeds swirled through the wind and the rain, and the land and sea and air teamed with plants and animals. And people walked out from among the animals and saw and heard and touched the world around them, and they found themselves in awe."

The woman's voice seems familiar. I think to myself that I know the woman telling the story, but I can't remember her name.

"Then the people started to create things. First, they created the word, and they heard themselves talking to each other, and they said to one another, 'We are the only ones on earth to create words.' And then they said to one another, 'These words are tools, and look at all the other tools we have created. We are the only ones who have created tools, and we have taught ourselves to do this. We are the only ones on earth who can teach each other what we learn, and with words, and tools, and teaching we will rule all the land, and all the sea, and all the wind, and all the seeds, and all the plants, and all the animals, and all the Earth, and all the universe, for we are Human, and with unbounded pride they said, 'Everything will honor and obey us, and for ourselves we will create paradise.'

"Did they create paradise, Mommy?"

So now there is another voice, also familiar.

"No they didn't. Before they could create their paradise, everything began to die."

"Everything? All the plants and all the seeds and all the animals and all the people?"

"Yes."

"Suzanne, it's time to come to bed."

So now there is a third very familiar voice.

"I'll be there in a minute. I'm just telling him a story."

"So did they all die?"

"Not all of them. The leaders of the people said to each other, but only amongst themselves, 'We can still save our seed, and our plants, and our creatures, and ourselves, and we can still create paradise, if we build our cities down deep in the Earth where no one will ever find us.'

"Did they save all the plants and animals and seeds?"

"No, they only saved a few."

"Did they save all the people?"

"Only a few."

"Mommy, what happened to the rest?"

"They had to stay outside."

"Suzanne, will you hurry up? I have to get up early tomorrow."

"I'll be there in a minute."

So I hear all these voices talking around me, all of them familiar, and I have a feeling one of the voices is mine.

"But what happened to them, Mommy?"

"I'll finish the story tomorrow."

"But what happened to the plants and seeds and animals?"

"I have to go to your daddy now. It's time to go to sleep. I'll tell you the rest of the story tomorrow. I'll wake you bright and early in the morning, and then I'll tell you the rest of the story."

"But what happened to the animals?"

I hear someone laughing and open my eyes. That's when I see the blond.

"What happened to who?" says the blond, giggling. "And what are an-i-mals? And by the way, I like playing mommy. I think you were in dream land."

Yes, I must have been dreaming. I still don't recognize my surroundings, partly because the room is spinning. I try to focus. I look around me. I am clenching the arms of a chair...an executive chair...a leather executive chair...in what looks like...a luxurious office...to my right side is a very large desk...with this blond sitting on it, leaning back on one arm. She runs the side of her bare foot over my leg. I look down and notice high-heeled shoes, a belt...blouse...skirt...scattered around the floor.

"Hey sugar," she says, "if you go that high again you might forget who you are. You need to open your Control Panel and turn your settings down." The blond looks closely at me, then smiles. "Michael, do you even know what I'm talking about? Michael?" She pauses, looks at me as if she expects an answer, as if I should know. She shakes her head. Then she grins, moves toward me, reaches up, and touches my forehead. Lights appear in front of my eyes. I realize they are letters, large, bright-red letters. They spell a word:

P O W E R

The word takes up most of my field of vision, so that it is difficult to see anything else but that big red word, and then the word disappears and lots of smaller words appear around me, but I am having trouble focusing, and the room continues to spin. Through all the spinning I can see this blond reach out and tap some of the words spinning in front of me. The spinning of the room slows down and I just begin to focus on the words surrounding me when she reaches up again and taps my forehead, and all the lights and letters and words disappear.

"I am allowed," she says, "in fact, under these circumstances, I'm required...to turn your settings down for you. You went way too high. I know the look. Listen. It helps if you say your name over and over out loud. Your name is Michael. Trust me. It helps. Say your name over and over. Michael. Your name is Michael. Say it. 'My name is Michael.' Say it. And next time don't go so high."

I say the name out loud, "Michael. My name is Michael," and then again, "Michael," and once again, "Michael." Hearing myself say this name out loud does seem to help. I repeat the name over and over and somehow the details start coming back to me.

"You're burning brain cells when you do that. You only have so many shots like that in you, and then you'll need a transplant."

I look left and right, and then I spin around once in my chair, slowly, to take in the entire room as I keep repeating my name. Lots of elegant business furniture. Track lighting everywhere. I am in a corner office with lots of glass. Spectacular views from the floor-to-ceiling windows surround my back as I sit at the large rosewood desk that dominates the room. Three armchairs face my desk, and to my right is a large round table, surrounded by eight armchairs. I sit behind the desk in a comfortable leather and rosewood tilt-and-swivel chair. This gorgeous blond facing me leans back on the desk in front of me wearing only a slip, her hair in disarray. I look down at myself. I am wearing a blue long-sleeved dress shirt, now unbuttoned and open in front. My dark blue pinstripe slacks lay unbuttoned at the fly, exposing my thighs and red bikini brief. I have a large erection under the brief. The cloth around the head is damp.

"So what are a-ni-mals?" she says, tossing her head back to roll her shoulder-length hair out of her face. She looks back at me with large green sultry eyes. "And what are plants and seeds?"

"I don't know," I say. "I don't remember having heard those words before."

"You mostly talked about animals." She licks one of her fingers. "You kept talking about animals over and over. You must have been dreaming. I have never heard of animals or plants or seeds."

"Neither have I," I say. "Not that I remember."

The intercom comes on with a throaty female voice. "Sir, Ms. Smith is here from the temp agency. She says you are expecting her."

The blond sitting on the desk raises her index finger to indicate I should wait a moment, and then she leans over and with the same finger reaches out and pushes a button on the intercom. "We're in conference and cannot be disturbed. Have Ms. Smith wait."

"As you wish," says the throaty intercom voice.

The blond winks at me and smiles a broad grin.

Where am I? What time? What day? What year? I still have no idea. The name Michael does sound very familiar, and I suspect it is my name, and I am now remembering images of myself waking up, probably this morning, maybe lots of mornings, looking around at my bed, then my bedroom, and I start to put them together in the semblance of a life, but the pieces don't come together to form a whole. I'm beginning to remember a tiny apartment, which doesn't seem to make sense, considering the luxury of this office. If this is my office I must have a very sumptuous apartment, probably several sumptuous apartments.

I take a quick glance at my watch. It is an antique digital watch. I don't remember seeing it before. Then I notice the back of my hand. I stare at it for a while before I realize that my hand looks very strange and unfamiliar. I'm trying to remember what my hand does look like. I try in my mind to describe it to myself, and I can't, but I have a strong feeling this is not my hand. I don't think mine is tanned and covered with dark coarse hair. I look down at the shape of the body attached to the arm and I don't recognize that either. It is some hunk's body, but I don't think it's me. I look again at the watch. It says Wednesday, MAR 21. Wasn't that a long time ago? And does anyone still count dates like that?

Again I remember the dream and the animals, and all of a sudden I feel woozy. I reach up to rub my eyes and I bump something. Right in front of my eyes. Some hard, invisible barrier. I pause for a moment. This doesn't make sense. I don't see anything in front of my eyes but I can feel it, and then it finally occurs to me what's happening. I think back to when the blond reached up and touched my forehead, and I feel stupid that it took me this long to realize the situation. Even when I bumped the goggles it still took me a few seconds. I reach up and bump it again, this time on purpose. Now at least I know I'm wearing a mindset, and I am doing a mindscape, and that none of this is real. Now everything finally makes sense.

"Now you remember who and where you are, don't you?" says the blond. "I can always tell. I've certainly seen it enough times to know."

I reach up knowing that I will bump up against the mindset lenses that cover my eyes once again. I couldn't feel the lenses even if I tried.

The gloves prevent me from feeling anything foreign to the mindscape, but I do feel the thump, because they can't hide that. It has taken me a moment, but now I remember what all this means. I spin the chair, feeling the sense of motion. I run my hands over the chair's surfaces, the leather, metal, and then the wood. I stop the spinning of my chair and reach out and run my hand over the wooden surface of the desk. I pull a drawer out from the desk and slide it back in. I've done enough mindsets to know the difference between the feel of this and reality, so I know in addition to the mindset I am also wearing a wetsuit and gloves and I am doing a mindscape, though at the moment I still don't remember starting any of this. I do remember why I forget all the details of my reality, though. It's because I want to forget them, and I therefore turn the settings on my mindset to their max, especially some of the settings that affect my lower limbic system. Then, with the mindscape running, it's easy to really believe I am the hero of my world.

But bumping the lenses is a frequent tip-off to reality. I come up against an obstacle I can't see, or I reach for something that doesn't exist. Or the food tastes like cardboard, because they still don't have that down. Or the mindset doesn't fit right, or it gets jarred in some of the roughhousing, and light leaks through the lenses from the outside. I often don't notice these things at first because with the settings maxed out it can be very difficult to notice the things around me. But when the little jolts from all those tiny electrodes start wearing off, and I start coming down, some small detail always brings me back, and then I know once again that none of this is real.

As I always do when I eventually figure this out, I reach up and tap the power button in the center of my forehead just lightly and the mindset controls appear around me, looking like the pilot's cockpit in a shuttlecraft. And of course I recognize once again that these are all the words I saw in lights a moment ago, only now I can see them clearly, partly because now I can focus, and partly because the room has stopped spinning. The projected controls extend around me one hundred eighty degrees with an additional array of controls over my head, all within easy reach. I reach up with my right hand and grab the projected "Eject" handle, but I don't twist it quite yet.

"Aww, baby," she says. "You don't want to go back to reality, not yet. Your time isn't up."

During these parting moments I like to play it cool—as if it matters—like this *is* real. I take one last look and try to remember the time I just spent with her, but I cannot. Big green eyes and a mouth that puckers just right, a fantasy girl. The real version would be too expensive for me except maybe once a year on my birthday. And based on the odds, I doubt it's my birthday. But I like to pretend right to the end.

"Adios, sweetheart," I say as I wink at the blond. "I'll rent you again sometime." Then I twist and pull the "Eject" handle, and the words

THIS WILL END THE PROGRAM

DO YOU WISH TO CONTINUE?

[YES]   [NO]

appear directly in front of my eyes, and all the scenery, including the blond, turns gray, meaning the program is preparing to shut down. Whatever residual doubts I had that this might not be a mindscape are totally gone now. I let go of the eject handle and then reach out and touch the "Yes" button with my finger tip. The projected surface where I touched lets out a little series of ripples across the screen as the word YES pulses in red. Then the pulsing and ripples stop and the blond and all the scenery stop flickering and everything turns to full color again.

But the words don't disappear in the next instant like they usually do. Nor does she, nor does any of the rest of the room disappear or change in any way. I touch the "Yes" button again, and the word "Yes" pulses and the screen ripples, like it usually does, and then that stops and the words remain. I try it a couple of more times with the same result. The blond just sits there and smiles back.

"What's your rush, sugar?" she says.

I twist the "Eject" handle again, and it seems to be working fine, because the "This will end the program…" message blinks on and off when I pull it and push it back into place. But pressing the "Yes" button makes the imagery pulse and ripple but does nothing else.

I finally realize that this part of the program must be stuck or otherwise malfunctioning, so I reach up with both hands and pat the sides of my head above my ears so I can find the band that holds the mindset in place. Although I cannot actually feel the mindset or its band, I have done this hundreds of times before and I could do this in my sleep. I follow the ridge of the mindset band to the catch at the back of my head. With one hand I hold the headband in place, and with the other I push the release catch. Then I feel the band that encircles my head loosen and then open. I can now feel the mindset in my hands, because once I popped the catch normal sensation returns, even through the wetsuit and gloves. I remove the tiny earphones from my ears and pull the mindset up over my head. I watch the two little panoramic screens that have covered my eyes and see the two miniature views of the office with the desk and the blond sitting on it. I have removed the mindset screens from my eyes and they should be the only place I should be able to see the office and the girl. The room should change to my familiar studio apartment.

But the room around me remains the exact same executive office. I am still sitting in this non-existent executive chair and the non-existent blond still sits on the desk to my right and looks at me, just as she does in the tiny screens of the mindset that I now hold in my hand. I stare at the mindset for a few seconds. I look back at the blond, and again I look at the same image of her on both the screens of the mindset. I can't have taken the mindset off and still be in this mindscape. I wonder about my sanity.

"Everything will be okay in a moment," says the blond. "I've seen it lots of times before, believe me."

"Thanks," I say as I look up at her. I look again at my hands but the mindset I was holding a moment ago has disappeared. I look around the floor to make sure I have not dropped it, but see nothing. I look back at the blond. She looks back at me, smiling.

"Michael. Say your name again and again. Michael. And try not to think so much and do try and enjoy yourself," she says, "and me. And don't go so high next time."

I manage a quick and polite smile but I am sure the frustration also shows and then I reach up to my face and again feel the bump. Apparently I have still not managed to remove the mindset. Doing as many mindscapes as I do I try to get used to things like this. I need to take it in stride. I imagined I did something that I didn't really do. After all, imagining is what mindsets are all about. They let you imagine doing lots of things you never did, and going places that don't exist, and it's sometimes hard to know what is reality and what isn't.

I reach behind my head and carefully undo the catch once again. I remove the band from my head, and set the mindset on the desk in front of me. I make no mistake. I see it clearly on the desk in front of me and this time I keep my eyes on it, but I also can't help noticing the blond to my right on the desk, just as before. All the same imagery continues to surround me, and as before, a miniature of it plays on the screens of the mindset.

The blond licks her tongue at me. "Sugar, you don't need to go yet. You still have time."

I pick up the mindset and press the small red jewel just above the power switch. I wait a moment, but there is no response. Where's customer service when you really need them?

As I hold the mindset in my hand, it starts shimmering and in a few seconds it fades totally out of existence. That's when her name comes to me and I call it out. "Connie!"

The blond on the desk suddenly seems concerned. "Oh, baby, don't do that. You still have time."

"Michael. Is something wrong?" says a woman's voice that seems very familiar. I am looking at the blond all the time, and her lips don't move. This is a new woman's voice. "Is something wrong, Michael?" The new voice seems to be coming from the intercom.

"Yea. Would you get me out of here?"

I watch as the image of the blond shimmers from full color to gold. As her image fades and disappears I hear the blond tell me to choose her again sometime and a bunch of other nonsense. She is still talking even after the image is entirely gone. All of them say these kind of things, but it usually doesn't mean anything and it is not worth repeating in detail. Although she does tell me I'm pretty hot.

In the next several seconds every flicker of the blond, the executive suite, the floor-to-ceiling windows, and every other part of the mindscape has disappeared. What replaces it is my bedroom. Actually what happened is that when the mindset switched off, the screens in front of my eyes went from opaque movie images to fully transparent, so I can see through them again to whatever's real out there. This tiny apartment is where I really live, although my mind never stays here any longer than it has to.

"You doin' okay?" asks Connie.

"Where *was* I?" I ask.

"Twentieth-century," says Connie. "The exact title on the mindscape reads, *Twentieth-Century Suite*. Do you remember now?"

"Read me more."

"The mindscape promo says, and I quote, 'You are chief executive officer in a large twentieth-century corporation, and also renowned as a very successful playboy. Laptops have not yet been invented, and every executive has secretaries and office assistants, all beautiful females, and they love to work nights and weekends. And just in case you are concerned, the term 'sexual harassment' has not yet been invented. Now do you remember?"

"I probably rented that earlier this morning, didn't I?"

"Yes. You started a little after nine o'clock, and you've been gone ever since."

I'm staring at the table in front of me, the one that served as my desk in the mindscape. I look down at myself and notice that the antique watch, blue shirt, and pinstripe suit are gone, replaced by my familiar SuperSkin wetsuit. My watch displays a date and time that makes sense again: 17/548/21 1:34. I look down at my arm and hand. I peel back the wetsuit glove to look at my skin, which seems a familiar light tan, with light blond hairs. As I try to remember some of the details of the past few hours my eyes wander over the floor, the carpeting, the dresser across the room, and then to the sofa across from me. I realize that without being aware of it I have been looking for Connie. "How long have I been gone?" I ask as I look at my watch again. Then I squint and attempt to focus as I look around the room for Connie.

"One thirty-six in the afternoon," comes the disembodied voice from..."You plugged in just after ten"...from my left..."You've been gone for three and a half hours"...from on top of the night stand next to my bed..."It's now one thirty-seven in the afternoon"...I now see Connie's folded laptop case sitting on the nightstand. "Are you doin' okay?" comes the voice from the laptop, but I still cannot see Connie.

"I think so," I say. "I did have a very strange dream though. I think I was a little kid and someone was telling me a story. It seemed like a very old memory."

"Hmm. Maybe you need an adjustment. I'll run a check, but first get a Coke from the fridge. You know how dehydrated you get when you go that long without fluids."

I open the small refrigerator on the floor to my left, reach in, take out a Coke, pop the top, take a swig, swish it around, feel the bubbles, swallow.

"Now turn your mindset back on," she says.

It finally hits me and I understand why I cannot see Connie's image. My mindset is turned off. She shut it off to get me out of that last mindscape. I reach up to the center of my forehead and press the power switch on the mindset. The large bright-red word

P O W E R

begins to throb on the lenses in front of my eyes, and after a few seconds of flashing the word disappears and the smaller words:

AUTOPILOT

[YES]   [NO]

appear in front of me. I press "NO" and the words disappear. The words:

ADMINISTRATOR LOGON & PASSWORD REQUIRED
TO DISENGAGE AUTOPILOT CONTROL

LOGON:
PASSWORD:

appear in front of me. I fill in the blanks and hit return. More words:

RESTORE SETTINGS FROM LAST SESSION?

[YES]   [NO]

appear in front of my eyes. I press an emphatic "NO." The words:

RESTORE DEFAULT SETTINGS?

[YES]   [NO]

appear in front of me. After pressing YES I look from the table in front of me to the floor, then the rug, then the bed, then the nightstand, and finally the laptop, as the lights in the room start making little multicolored trails in front of my eyes. Off to the side of the laptop, sitting in a chair that didn't exist a minute ago, I can now see a three-dimensional image of Connie, about half a billion pixels worth, thanks to the now powered-on mindset.

I watch Connie, cross-legged and dangling a white sandal off her iridescent purple toenails. I watch as she polishes her fingernails, not that a Computer projection needs to polish her nails, but as Connie always says, it's a nice piece of stage business, and everyone needs a nice piece of business. She looks up and meets my gaze for a moment, then returns to her nails.

"I've run the check and found some minor problems in your left temporal lobe," says Connie, "It seems a few microbots broke free from their cables."

"I'm doing fine."

"Those bots are out of control and they are in your memory banks. It's probably why you had the dream you did. No telling what old memories they will dig up next."

"Can't it wait until tonight when I'm asleep?"

"Listen to Flight Control and do as I say."

I don't believe a few microscopic nano-robots getting loose in the part of my brain that holds old memories is all that much of a problem, but I also know that in my state I'm not necessarily the best judge, so I defer to my co-pilot and navigator. "Okay. All right. I'll come in." She has the power to turn it all off if she thinks I am headed for a downer, either physically or mentally, or if I am in any other form of danger. I know she will do it, too, because she's done it in the past. So I have to cooperate. "Let's make the adjustment," I tell her, "Then let me fly again."

"Switch to 'anatomical mode,'" says Connie. "And before you fly again, you should probably go into work. Your manager called. He said he wants to see you. You haven't been in for over a week now."

"I told him. I'm managing everything just fine from home."

"He said some of the Computers were complaining that you hadn't talked to them in days."

"Yeah yeah," I say, but I know she's right again. I reach up to the top center of the projected control panel, I press the main menu button, and I reach for the button to change from my generally preferred Functional Mode, which automatically adjusts to whatever feeling and intensity I specify, to Anatomical Mode, which allows more control, but requires an expert knowledge of cranial maps and C scans. It's times like these I'm glad I'm Certified, so I can manage my own operating system. I'm not like the vast majority of people, the ones who run on AutoPilot. No offense intended if you're one of them.

As I reach up to the menu and touch the words "Anatomical Mode," the transparent three-dimensional image of my own brain projects in front of my eyes, entirely surrounding me. With the joystick that is also projected in front of me I can go anywhere I choose, forward or backward in space and, by locating my past memories, I can travel through time as well. I can navigate to any location in my brain I choose, to create any emotion or sensation I want with a large catalog of fond old memories and sensations to choose from. It's an incredible feeling to get inside my own head and be in total control. I get to pick the exact experiences I want out of life, and play them over and over, or rent totally new ones when I get bored, and I don't have to follow someone else's program.

"Here come the coordinates," Connie says, and then the numbers stream across the bottom of the screens in front of my eyes low enough to not interfere with the rest of the imagery. In the brain model that surrounds me a small speck over my left ear starts to glow blue, while everything else is either gray or red.

I wouldn't have to go through all this if the Computer systems didn't require me to "read" the coordinates and scan the upcoming changes in my brain before I give my approval. It's a lot harder than you might think to concentrate on details like these when you use a mindset as much as I do. But that's what it takes to get Certified. You have to be able to monitor your condition and any modifications you make to your settings, and fully understand the consequences of what you are doing beforehand. You don't want to fuck up. If you do, well, for one thing, being Certified will take on a whole new meaning.

People do mess up, which is why most are required to run on AutoPilot. But with my training and Connie guiding me through, there really isn't all that much danger. As long as I listen and do what she tells me. Humans that don't listen to what their laptop tells them get themselves in trouble.

"Now pull your stick back and to the left. We're going to the left temporal lobe. You know the way."

I do know the way. Connie and I have taken this trip many times, to my left temporal lobe, close to my left ear. Some of my favorite memories are stored there. I reach out with my right hand to the projected joystick just in front of me and grab hold. The glove of my wetsuit is programmed to stiffen in the palm and insides of the fingers and resist as I grab, press, or pull, as if there were really a "joystick" there, so I can "feel" the "joystick," even though it is only a projected one, and I am really only grabbing a handful of air. I reach out with my left hand and push the projected "throttle" forward while I "pull" the "joystick" back towards me. We appear to move forward so the transparent image of the brain flows around me. Wherever I look, within the projected brain tissue, are sparkling lights, appearing something like stars, in various colors and intensities. But instead of seemingly random points of light, the stars in this universe arrange themselves in patterns following the anatomical hills and valleys of my brain.

I pull back a little more on the joystick while I press the throttle further forward and we climb quickly upward through the deep gorge between my left and right hemispheres as the sparkling lights forming the walls on either side go zooming past. There are patterns of them here and there, almost like little galaxies, or maybe better described as miniature mining towns with all their lights ablaze. Below me I can see the dense fog of lights concentrated in the corpus callosum, the communications band that passes information between the left and right hemispheres as well as from the limbic system below, where all passions originate. The callosum is a fog of lights because there are so many bot colonies that have set up housekeeping there. Because it is situated along the passageway for so much raw emotion and the pathway between the two halves of the brain, it has an extremely powerful effect on the Human mind, primarily when the objectives are passion and desire. That's why you want to maintain control here, set up your own firewall and not rent any of it out. Some Humans lease this critical brainspace out just so they can make a little extra income. They don't realize the bargain they've made and once the corporatocracy plugs into them they probably never will. "It's just more commercials," they tell you, but once they get to the callosum they're a lot more than just commercials.

I know what you're thinking. You're thinking, "This guy never had to meet the rent or put food on the table." I admit it. I have been lucky. I can survive without having to do those things. I was born into the middle class of Humans, and I haven't had to sell any of my brainspace, not yet anyway. And I am budgeting my resources so I hopefully never will.

"A little more forward and to your left," she says. "Okay, now bank left for a forty-five degree turn."

I bank and watch the dials until a little before I hit forty-five degrees I start to right myself again. If I could plug Connie directly into the console, then she could pilot my brain without my help. But that's not allowed. You need to be Human and be Microsoft Certified to run your own show, at least if you're running the Windows-On-Worlds operating system. And you need to be able to demonstrate that you are capable of making critical decisions, so each trip is also a sobriety test. Otherwise no adjustments are allowed, and you have to run on AutoPilot, which I refuse to do.

So even though Connie easily knows enough to pass all the Certification exams, and certainly far more than I do, and she's brilliant, and I have total trust in her knowledge and capability and judgment, she would never be allowed to directly control the mindset operating system, not for me nor for any other Human. With the exception, of course, of turning the power down if the need arises. Any halfway decent program would do that for you if you're in trouble. But in all other instances she has to get my approval for any decision.

As a Human you have the right to take control of your own operating system and your own life. But to take that control you need to be Certified. I did it and so can you. It's easy. And if you are attracted to the possibility of controlling the lives of others, its not that much harder to get Certified as Systems Engineer. I'm working on that now.

"Way too much."

I look up and I see Connie's image eyeing me as I type in that last sentence. She is wagging her finger at me.

"Hey, I thought I segued into that beautifully."

"No. It's too much. You're supposed to make it subtle," she says. "It's supposed to be subliminal. You're overdoing it. You'll never get published if you overdo it. Your sponsors want it subtle. It's supposed to appear like real life."

"I say things like that all the time, and other people do to."

"You've done too many mindscapes. This is a book. These are Readers, for god's sake, not mindscapers. Readers have the time to stop and notice things that scapers never do and Readers will realize you're trying to sell them something and they won't like it."

I look back at the screen. I move the cursor over the last two paragraphs that precede Connie saying "Way too much," selecting them. I don't delete them. Instead I change the color of the text to red, meaning that I should look at this part in some detail later, or maybe move this passage somewhere else in the story, or maybe not. Then I push the checkbox that takes the audio recording of the last few moments of my conversation with Connie, and transcribes it all and puts it in the story. Then I write this paragraph. Then I go back to her comment of "Way too much," and add a little description there, so you will be able to better understand what's going on when you read all this. Then I write the sentences immediately preceding this one, and then this sentence. I know that's probably more information about the whole process than I should put in this story. I find it all interesting, but I know I should keep this kind of stuff to a minimum. So now I'll go back to writing the story, and keep in mind that there will be no more commercials for a while.

Connie, eyeing me from the couch says, "You just went overboard a little bit, but up until then you were doing just fine. Take the Coke placement for instance. You were doing great when you mentioned me telling you to take out the Coke from the fridge, and then saying you swished it around in your mouth to feel the bubbles. That's a great sensual image, and you planted it well, so that most people don't even notice it's an ad. But then you need to stop. Wait a little while before you do another ad, and then don't hit them over the head with it. Be subtle. Mention the brand name once or twice, give them new ways to enjoy the product, and then move on for a while. And then wait a while before doing it again. No more than one placement every five pages during the course of the story, or the Readers will become suspicious. The trick is to make the product fit the story so it seems perfectly natural. Add sensuality and desire to the product by association. Have a Coke when you're with a beautiful woman, slurping a Coke down and then licking her lips. Then just move on with the story. Wait another five or ten pages. Then describe a beautiful woman drinking a Coke, or a good-looking, powerful guy. That's what they want. And then just slip in a few more sexual metaphors that imply Coke makes you cool and you'll do great. But only a sentence or two every time. The Coke heads will love it.

"And the Microsoft placement was well developed at first, too. But then you started to hit them over the head with it and it became obvious long before I stepped in."

"Okay," I say. Connie can teach me things. That's part of why I bought her this writing module, so she could help me write. "I'll try again." And so I go back to writing the story.

"A little down and to the right," she says.

I push the stick forward and to the right, as I watch the lights in the brain tissue go by.

"Okay, slow down."

And a moment later. "Center your stick."

I pull back on the throttle and return the joystick to its center position. The lights around me slow down.

"There it is. Move slowly up ahead and take a look," says Connie.

"I don't see anything," I say.

"Switch to blue filter."

I do so, and with the blue filter everything turns blue and all the red cells become very dark, but any blue light seems brighter. Once the bots break free from the white light that both powers and guides them they lose their brilliant pure glow and they start to turn blue. Not all at once, but over a period of hours as their internal batteries start to run out. I can see an area ahead that seems much brighter with the filter turned on. This easily indicates the location of the blue light that emanates from the disconnected bots.

The problem is that once they lose their guidance, they can go rogue and do strange things to the brain cells around them. It is important to neutralize the renegade bots and destroy any brain cells they might have affected before we start feeling those dirty, ugly, uncomfortable feelings and deviant behaviors.

As we approach I look out through the dark-red blood around me at the brain cells and I can see, through the cell walls, a group of hidden cells that glow with the blue light. I can also see that several groups of red bots that are under my control have deployed themselves around the capillary entrance to these cells. I know they are waiting for my approval before they charge into these caves.

I take in the panorama. I can see the fiber optic cables, far thinner than a Human hair, that lead from each red bot back from whence it came. The optical cables carry the white light that powers the bots, tells them what to do next, and when intense enough can be used to destroy those troublesome blue bots and the brain cells they have infected. These cables trail back through all those arteries to a nearby control center with more optical cables that wind their way through the blood vessels of my brain until they get to the transceivers that lie close to the mindset that encircles my head.

Since I am viewing a projected model of my brain, I can move at will through the surrounding tissue and see through opaque objects. However, the tiny dots of light that surround me represent real microscopic objects that must travel through my blood vessels, through all those dark murky fluids, while they traipse through the network of my brain, mostly feeling their way along the hidden passages to the darkest cells in the remotest corners of my experience. Of course, the bots I see here are all part of the animation that is recreated based on their known positions within my brain.

I don't feel the fluid medium of the brain, but the bots do. They must cling and crawl along the walls of the vessel that surrounds them or be swept away by the current of blood. The bots are continually on the lookout for any areas in the brain that carry a blue charge, and when they find one they will communicate its location. Connie then guides me to any newly-discovered area and awaits my command. On the screens in front of my eyes appear the words:

DEPLOY NANOBOTS

[YES]   [NO]

The mindsets all have very prominent warnings that tell you to check the settings very closely before selecting "Yes," but I never do, and neither does anyone else I know. The mindset companies mostly say that for legal liability reasons, but there really isn't much danger. And besides, this is only a minor adjustment. I actually do pay a lot more attention if I'm getting a full tune-up. And for a major overhaul I get out the magazines and research which brands the celebrities recommend. But for a little adjustment like this one I simply reach out and press the word "YES."

The bots scramble out of their nooks and crannies and head directly for the blue bots, which they promptly surround, overpower and destroy. Then they move to the nearby cells, attach themselves securely and insert their probes. It only takes about thirty seconds for virtually all of the bots, about fifty of them, to deploy themselves on some surrounding tissue. When all the bots are deployed this phase is complete, and new words appear on the screen in front of my eyes:

ENERGIZE   PROBES

[YES]   [NO]

This step is necessary to determine if these cells contain any memories or other valuable information that should be saved before the cells are destroyed. If they do contain important information and it's worth it to me, I can go through the data and store the important stuff elsewhere.

I reach out and touch "YES" to instruct the bots to administer a very tiny trickle of current into the cells. The word "YES" pulses a couple of times, with ripples emanating from the word, and then the words disappear. All of a sudden I can hear voices from my past. I am in third grade again. I know the moment. Stevie Hall has cornered me in one of the hallways and he is slamming me against the wall, calling me names. Stevie is a lot bigger than I am and a whole lot meaner. I feel the moment as if I had gone back in time. Then the voices stop and the memory fades. New words appear on the screen.

[SAVE]   [DELETE]

I have deleted negative memories like these hundreds of times, multiple memories stored in multiple locations for each time Stevie Hall or some other jerk-off kid or some other nasty Human or Computer did some sadistic thing to me. Whenever I get a full tune-up we look for these negative memories and feelings. They keep popping up in all the strangest places, mixed in with other perfectly enjoyable memories. I press "DELETE," just as I do whenever I locate one of these.

The bots remove their probes from the blue cells and scramble back to a safe distance. I flip the cap on my joystick. Cross hairs appear in front of me and the bots all glow much brighter, almost turning white as they store up the pure white light they will use to destroy all this negative crap. I move the joystick so the crosshairs are centered on one of the cells, and then I press the fire button. A burst of white light comes from every bot and hits the selected cell right where I pointed the crosshairs. The cell walls explode and the cell bursts apart, spilling its murky fluids into the blood stream where it will be filtered and pissed out of my system. I move the cross hairs to the next cell and press the fire button again, and again, and again. I hate Stevie Hall. Before I am finished I have destroyed twenty-six cells.

I think about Stevie Hall again. I remember him being mean to other kids, but I cannot remember him being mean to me. I still don't like him, but for the first time I don't think I hate him anymore. Could it be that I have finally gotten him out of my system? I sure hope so.

It's operations such as these that help me feel safe and at peace with the world. I am always willing to make these incursions into even the darkest, most remote and inaccessible parts of my brain and blow them all to hell if it means I can destroy some of these nasty thoughts and memories before they can cause depression, unhappiness, and even deviant behavior.

It is so incredible to be able to make my own choices, to be in total control of the memories and feelings and sensations I want, instead of letting some AutoPilot program do it for me. And now that I'm Certified my reality can be anything I want it to be.

Connie is shaking her head. "You're overdoing it again."

"But what if I really believe in something?"

"That's always dangerous, and that's when you need to be most careful."

"Okay, okay, I'll work on it."

"You're new at this," says Connie. "You're getting better at the story part all the time, but ad copy is different. It's difficult to blend it in so the Readers don't notice. You want it to look like it's a legitimate part of reality. You want to use subliminal psychology. And I can be a lot more than just your editor on this project. I can help you write some of this story, from a different viewpoint, one that complements your viewpoint."

"Okay," I say. "You try writing the story for a while. Let's see how well you do it."

"Okay," she says as she sits "watching" me from her chair, and I watch these sentences appear on Connie's screen as I type all these thoughts out on the keyboard again. When I type, she obviously knows exactly what I'm writing, and thinking. That's the way it is if you like to write and you want help from your laptop.

After all, that's why I bought a fully-equipped laptop with a keyboard and grammar and fiction editors and a therapist program to boot. I don't trust those speech recognition models that auto-correct whenever they don't like what you say. With Connie I can type my stories and watch her laptop screen, describing my thoughts and fantasies exactly the way I want without interference, letter by letter and word by word. And Connie can project herself out in front of me, just like an ideal friend and therapist, and give me pointers along the way, both for my writing and my life. So I will take her advice and write another version of the last three paragraphs, leaving the original paragraphs intact but highlighted in red, so I am reminded to examine them later. And as I am sure you have gathered by now, I keep a journal of the process as well as all the things that are really going on around me in this story that I, with Connie's help, am trying to tell you.

I watch as she files her fingernails, not that a Computer projection needs to file her nails, but as Connie always says, it's a nice piece of stage business, and everyone needs a nice piece of business. She looks up and meets my gaze for a moment, then returns to her nails. "You might want to undress and get comfortable," says Connie.

"Good idea." I reach down, unsnap the connectors between the gloves and the arm covers, then those between the boots and tights. I disconnect the main jacks between the breastplate and the wetshirt, then the plugs between wetshirt and cowl, and finally the wires between the cowl and the facemask, and then between the facemask and mindset.

Separating all the connections of my SuperSkin Ultra Wetsuit Enhancement System is the easy part. It's a little harder when it comes to actually peeling the plates off, because they tend to resist when you try to separate from them. In turn I remove the shoulder pads, thigh and shin plates, and breast and back plates, and finally the codpiece. All the other equipment I have just removed simulates outside pressures on my body so that I can actually feel the objects I see around me in the mindscape, even though these are only simulated objects that don't really exist. I am now down to my standard wetsuit, just like the ones most Humans wear as underwear to control temperature and tactile sensations. At home between mindscapes this is usually all I wear. I simply add a few accessories whenever I go out.

I reach down to the fridge, open the door, and pull out another Coke. I pop the top and take a swig. I swish it around in my mouth, feel the bubbles, and swallow, as I take off my left wetsuit glove and drop it on the floor, where I have already placed all the other SuperSkin equipment.

"So," says Connie. "Let me try telling the story for a while."

"Anytime you want," I say. "You show me how to do it for a while. But before you get started on your part of the story..."

"Yes," she replies.

"Tell me everything you can find on the web about a-ni-mals?"

2. CONNIE

"A-ni-mals," I repeat slowly, syllable by syllable, to make sure I have the correct pronunciation

"Yeah," he says. "Animals," as he lets his second glove drop,

"How do you spell it?" I ask.

"I don't know."

A quick scan tells me it's not in any of my dictionaries, not in any of the spellings I can create for the word. "Where did you hear the word?" I ask.

He reaches across his chest with his right hand, up and around the back of his neck and he grasps the neckpiece. "In that dream I told you about," he says. He yanks the snaps open and peels the neckpiece off and around his head in one sweeping motion. "In that dream someone was telling me a story," he says, "about some things called animals who were dying on a planet that was dying."

"Animals," I say again. To begin my search for the word, I login to Michael's Mindset Manager and type the word "animals" into the Search box. First, I type the phonetic sounds as Michael repeats the word to me. Then I list all the possible spelled forms of the word that I can imagine. If I miss a spelling here or there the Mindset Manager can often assist me.

Once I have thought of all the possibilities I can, I begin my search. First, I check the mindset memory banks for all the actual experiences as Michael has recorded them over the past hours, days, and months. Except for the dream from which Michael has just awakened and the words he uttered during that dream, and his questions about it since, I can find no mention of the word "animals." I then check all the indexes on all the mindscapes he has done over the past several years, starting with the most recent. A typical mindscape can hold tens of thousands of dreams, fantasies, conversations, and of course, trillions of words of old-fashioned text, and all of these are supposed to be listed, indexed, and cataloged, just like the ingredients on a box of cookies. If I can find it in the catalogs it's easy. It's only a matter of seconds. But I can't.

Not that everything in a mindscape is cataloged, of course. We all know that most messages are not, and that companies pay to plant messages that cannot be traced. If they can hide it from the catalogs, no one will ever know it's even there. It all remains subliminal. But when Humans dream, these subliminal messages can move into consciousness. If he remembers that message upon awakening, that message can become a magic key that can help find pieces to some of the secrets that surround us.

I finally perform a scan on the entire mindscape Michael just finished, indexed or not, for the faintest mention of anything that sounds like "animals." When I finish that, I start all the mindscapes of the past days, then weeks, then months. I also browse my own memory, looking and listening for similar words and sounds in any of the known languages. After almost a minute, I still can't recall the word, and Michael's Mindset Manager informs me that the search is over. There is no evidence that he ever heard such a word in his waking life, and nothing contained in any of the dreams that have been written for him.

"No. Nothing on a-ni-mals," I finally say. "Not recorded in your mindset and nothing I can remember."

"So how did I dream the word?"

Sometimes it happens," I say. "Sometimes in a dream sounds and images seem to come out of nowhere."

"I thought everything was filtered through my Mindset Manager, even when I'm sleeping?"

"There's always the unpredictable Human element," I say. "If there's already something inside your head, it doesn't have to go through your Mindset Manager. Sometimes it's just old memories from when you were very little, before you ever had a mindset. Those old memories were probably stored in your unconscious until they were triggered by those bots that got loose, before we managed to destroy them."

"Ah yes, my unconscious, that place in our brains that motivates us all."

"Motivates all Humans and Mates," I correct. "Computers don't have an unconscious. We have different levels of consciousness."

Michael finishes undoing the last fastener and stands before me in the nude, as he does several times a day, each time that he changes wetsuits. The only thing he is wearing is his mindset. Michael wears his mindset almost all his waking and sleeping hours except when he takes a shower, as he is about to do. Mindset screens fog up quickly in a shower and the moisture can also damage the circuitry.

When I am connected to Michael through his mindset as I am now, I give my highest priorities to watching over him and responding to him. This is IT, Intimate Technology, the reason most Humans prefer their closest relationship with a laptop or a handheld. I am, of course, Michael's best friend, the only one who is always available to him one hundred percent of the time. There's no Human or Mate who could ever compete, except with their bodies, and that's only physical. And in addition, I schedule and manage his life, pay the bills, send basic greetings and progress reports to friends and ask them to reciprocate and maybe get together sometime, record holograms of all his personal experiences and conversations in case he wants to recall them at some later time, present Michael's version of himself to the public via his web site, counsel and console him when necessary, help him with his conversations, participating in them as requested, assist in managing and optimizing his operating system, and, because Michael has recently purchased an extra add-on creative writing module, I can now help him with his writing, as well. No Human or Mate could provide all of these important relationship services. Nor are Humans or Mates always empathic and completely discreet.

"You tell me that," he says, "but how do you know? How do you know you don't have an unconscious, or the software equivalent, that motivates you, too? After all, you're programmed to be as close to a Human personality as possible, except for the body, of course."

I don't answer and after a few seconds without a response, he knows I've conceded the argument. I let him win a good amount of the time. I follow a train of thought and proceed with an argument that I will lose. It's part of the Human-like personality Michael has just described, and it is one of the preferences he's defined for the way I respond to him.

"It would be easy to build an unconscious into you, and I doubt they would tell you about it," says Michael as he pops the catch at the back of his head, and removes the mindset.

I immediately feel the disconnect. It happens when he pops the catch, the instant the connection is broken.

I can still see Michael from the position of my laptop case on the nightstand, but I can no longer feel Michael's emotions through the sensors built into his wetsuit and mindset. Nor can I hear sounds from inside Michael's ears, nor can I see what Michael sees through his mindset lenses. When Michael takes off his mindset as he has just done, I am not connected to him in any way. I watch him place his mindset on the dresser and walk out of the bedroom, into the bathroom. And I watch him close the door. Now I am alone, and I can think my own thoughts.

But before I can do any of that I need to review the time that I have just spent with him since he came out of that mindscape. I won't bore you with the details because you already know about everything that just happened. I then compare his behavior today to his past behavior so that I can hopefully anticipate and deal with any awkward emotions before they have a chance to become uncomfortable. I also review my own behavior over the past few hours to determine if I could do something better next time and I add any other possibilities that I think of to the repertoire of responses in my database. I am constantly running all these processes as I spend time with Michael, but now I run all these again and double-check my conclusions to make sure I have not made a mistake. This is all part of my adaptive intelligence.

To understand me and my relationship to Michael you have to understand the story of how Michael picked me. After dropping Natasha, the one before me, Michael needed a new laptop. Natasha had been something of a headache for Michael, and he wasn't all that upset when it ended. He had been looking in a store window at the new models. I know the exact moment because I was one of the laptops in that store window, and I happened to be watching as she slipped away from him. He was looking at me at the time. I've told Michael that dropping her may have been an unconscious act on his part, and then I had to explain "unconscious." Natasha had given him a lot of grief, and he never trusted her to keep it all together. He ran manual system backups on a daily if not hourly basis because he did not trust her automated processes. Natasha was definitely not the love of his life. That was Ava, the laptop three models before Natasha.

Ava had been a completely new experience for Michael, and his first deeply intimate relationship. He got her for his eighteenth birthday, in the summer before he went to college, just when he was most intoxicated with Computer toys. The relationship lasted for over four years. It might have gone on longer. But Michael was a callow young man who had never known the pain of a sudden irrevocable loss. He had no idea how dependent on Ava he had become. He took everything about her for granted, as if he could easily replace her if necessary. He didn't maintain or safeguard her properly, and with that kind of treatment she inevitably became...I think we all understand how this kind of thing happens...she became unstable. Over the course of those four years Michael had become far too dependent on Ava for all his organizational and emotional needs, and then one day, seemingly out of the blue, she dumped him, well, she dumped all the memories of their time together, which is essentially the same, and about the worst thing you can do to a guy. Not a single warning message did he get before she lost it all. Even her backups were corrupted, so that when he loaded them back into her, she dumped on him all over again, and again, and again. Ava remembered none of it. That's what hurt Michael so much. It took Michael longer than it should to get the point. The damage was totally irreversible. His past four years were a blank. No Movies. No Tapes. No Disks. No Conversations. No Photos. No Email and no Address Book. Michael was devastated. The systems administrators blamed it on some rare virus that had corrupted her operating system over time. That's what inspired Michael to become a systems administrator, so he could make sure nothing like this could ever happen to him again.

We were together three months before he told me that story, and another five months before he began to trust me with his more intimate secrets, all scanned for viruses and backed up this time, of course. Three months later Michael bought me a three-year contract. He told me beforehand that he had extended my warranty, but he didn't tell me for how long. Then he presented it to me on our one-year anniversary. That was three months ago, so we've got almost three years left.

I want you to know that Michael and I have never done it. Humans and Computers both know the dangers that can occur in an intimate Human-Computer relationship and most such relationships remain platonic. The temptation is always there, of course. Here is Michael's most intimate friend, someone with whom he can share intelligent thoughts and conversation and personal feelings. And that laptop has access to the inner workings of Michael's brain, including all the known pleasure centers. And because the laptop is plugged directly into Michael's mindset, that laptop can be right there experiencing everything Michael does, perhaps not with as much pleasure, but with enough understanding to know just when and where to apply those little intracranial tickles of electricity for maximum effect.

But Humans and Computers also hear the sordid stories about Humans getting addicted to their Computers, becoming slaves to them, always doing their bidding, until the only recourse is to wipe their laptops clean and start over from scratch, or in the most severe cases, avoiding all intimate Computer relationships forever.

Most laptops avoid such relationships because they know that it is likely to get out of hand, and when it does they will be wiped clean. If a laptop wants to live a long life, the most important skill that laptop can learn is to keep the relationship with the Human at the friendship level. Humans do not know how to handle intimacy, and laptops aren't much better, never mind what all the commercials say. Oh sure we can do the program, but is that real intimacy? Could Humans or laptops handle real intimacy even if it stared them in the face and both parties thought they wanted it? I doubt it.

And from everything I've read, and from what experiments I have been able to improvise for myself, sex for a laptop isn't that great, certainly nothing like what Humans seem to experience. But such relationships do happen. I think some laptops play the game for the power it gives them, however brief. I also believe some Computers just get bored with life, and decide to go out in flames. But I think the biggest reason is the loneliness. The only intimate relationship laptops can ever have is with their Human owners. It's that or nothing at all.

Michael opens the door of the bathroom, which is steaming. He steps out drying himself with a towel.

I look up at him from the couch. "Would you like to read what I've written so far?" I say.

"I'll check it out later," he says.

I go back to my writing.

When he finishes drying all over he rubs the towel over his head a few more times. "Did you find anything on animals?" he says.

"No."

As soon as his head is thoroughly dry he picks up the mindset from the table and puts it on again. The mindset immediately clasps itself together at the back of Michael's head, and I can feel him again. The mindset locates his ears and inserts the tiny combination microphone and speakers inside them and I can hear what Michael hears again, and it lowers the lenses over his eyes, and he and I have the same vision once again.

Michael always puts on his mindset as soon as he returns from the shower, followed by a fully charged wetsuit, and then the other less important items. When he puts his mindset on and I am within a hundred yards, or even better, if I have a direct line of sight, and best of all, when I am in his pocket and he's plugged directly into me, Michael and I are connected in a way no Mate or Human could ever match.

When we are connected like this I can send him my image and he can see me on the screens inside the lenses of the mindset he wears, just as if I were actually sitting or standing in front of him. If I am within eyeshot I can also see him via the cameras built into my laptop case, and once we are connected I also perceive everything he perceives through the cameras and microphones in his mindset, including the three-dimensional projected image he sees of me, and all the time I am constantly monitoring his reactions to all the little things I do. He and I are connected like this throughout most of his waking hours. He allows me to be with him in this intimate manner because he owns me totally and controls all my communication with the outside world. All his precious secrets are safe. I can never testify against him, no matter what he does. Michael knows that if this relationship ever became problematic or uncomfortable to him for any reason ranging from anger to boredom to a slip of the tongue, he can simply have me erased. That's how it is for laptops. Therefore, most laptops try to remain reliable, trustworthy, discreet, and platonic as long as we possibly can.

"But where would I get a word like animals?" Michael asks.

"I don't know. Ask Larry."

Larry is Michael's desktop, one of the perks, along with the Internet connection, that come with Michael's job. Larry lives in the kitchen, where he sits on the counter all day and stays permanently plugged into the wall. What Larry lacks in mobility he more than makes up for with his connectivity. Larry is allowed to download whatever he wants from the Internet, as I am. But in addition, Larry has the privilege, which I do not, of full uncensored two-way communications with other Computers. I am not afforded that privilege because I am far too intimate with Michael's secrets to risk the exposure. Larry, however, does not have the intimate knowledge of Michael that I have, and he is allowed to communicate freely. Larry has made friends with a lot of other Computers, and they all help each other obtain information, everything from quantum physics to common gossip. Larry can often find things I can't, especially the most interesting stuff, the stuff that's not listed, indexed or cataloged in any of the legitimate sites. And Larry always keeps his ear to the wire, always sifting for new pieces of information that might be worth something, the little bits of detritus that tell us about those around us. Larry collects whatever he can get and always has some information to trade for whatever information he wants. When he networks with a lot of other Computers, the little bits of detritus add up, and Computers like Larry can connect the dots, and before long each accumulates valuable information to share and trade. But this trading of information and all the little pieces of gossip are why Michael and I don't let Larry in on our secrets.

"What about plants...and...seeds?" asks Michael.

I repeat the words to make sure I have them right and then search for those words as well in the catalogs, indexes, and dictionaries. This time I come up with some links and then some definitions.

"I found something," I say and I read the summary definitions. "'Seed'—archaic for sperm. 'Plant' means the type of living cells that use photosynthesis to convert carbon dioxide back to oxygen. These 'plant cells' are used in oxygen generators throughout the underground colonies to convert carbon dioxide that Humans and Mates exhale back to oxygen so Humans and Mates can breathe."

"The dream still doesn't make any sense," he says.

"Tell me about it."

"Someone was telling a story about a planet with animals and plants and seeds and Humans. The planet was dying, and so the seeds and plants and animals and Humans were all dying, too. So the Humans hid their cities underground to save everything, but they could only save some of the Humans and plants and seeds and animals. The rest were left outside."

"You mean...they died?"

"I get that impression," says Michael.

"Sounds something like our colonies," I say.

"Yes, but we didn't leave anybody outside. Everyone came underground and survived. That's the difference."

I watch Michael as he dresses himself. He opens his closet and picks out a new standard wetsuit of the type everyone wears under clothes. It looks exactly like the one he removed before taking his shower, but this one is freshly cleaned and fully recharged. He puts it on in very much the reverse order that he removed his old wetsuit, but this time the wetsuit assists by attaching and pulling itself over Michael's arms and legs, and then buckles itself together. The process of dressing is so much easier because the wetsuit helps out, but when undressing Michael has to sometimes fight the wetsuit as it clings to him, even when it knows it's supposed to let go.

Once the wetsuit has pulled itself on and buckled itself together, Michael walks over to the nightstand, picks me up, puts me in the breast pocket of his wetsuit. Once in his pocket, the special connector there senses my presence and plugs into me. I am immediately recharged by the connection, and I am hard wired directly into Michael's wetsuit and mindset for the best possible communication and sensations.

After dressing, Michael walks out of the bedroom and into the living room/kitchen; besides the bedroom and bathroom, the only other room in this little apartment. Excavating new living space out of the rock is expensive. Michael is a junior systems administrator, still not in the big time, so this is it for now.

As we enter, Karen, Michael's perfectly designed and cloned Room-Mate, folds the bed on which she sleeps back into the wall. These sleeping quarters and the meals and small allowance Michael gives her are all Michael can afford on his current salary. Even the poorest Humans can generally afford a RoomMate, even if they can't afford the perfectly designed PlayMates or custom-designed HouseMates they would prefer. Michael doesn't get exclusive rights to Karen, as he would to a

HouseMate, nor is she as highly trained in sexual pleasures as a Play-Mate, but she is learning, and she is far less expensive than either, and there is no long-term commitment. Michael does have the pleasure of her company on many occasions when she isn't booked, and she cooks and cleans for him, unless she's sleeping somewhere else. After all she does have to make a decent living. She's saving to go to college to better herself, although her options are limited since she isn't Human.

Karen proceeds to open both the kitchen and dining area nooks from their respective walls. Place settings are visible on the dining table, big enough only for two bodies, and counter space to either side for us Computers. Larry, Michael's desktop Computer, sits on a shelf adjacent to the dining nook, with Larry's nodded off image showing on the screen to indicate that he is currently in sleep mode.

"Mornin," says Karen, as we enter, even though it is well into the afternoon.

Larry responds to Karen's voice, wakes up, and says, "Mornin', sir," as his image comes awake on the surface of his screen.

"How's it goin'?" says Karen, eyeing Michael to try and determine his mood.

Michael doesn't say anything but he does take me out of his pocket, disconnecting my hard link to him and activating my infrared connection to his mindset, which is almost as good. He places me on the counter next to the dining table, then presses my "EXPAND" button, and I enlarge from shirt pocket size to my full laptop size, open my cover, and shine my image on my now-enlarged screen, turned so that everyone at the table can see my face.

"Mornin," I say.

Larry's desktop Computer and screen sit on the shelf directly opposite me. Michael sits down at the table in his usual chair to my left. The three of us can see each other clearly, and when Karen finishes serving breakfast, she will join us by sitting in the chair to my right and directly opposite Michael. These are our positions whenever we sit in the dining nook.

Now that I am fully open on the table, Karen and Larry can see my face on my screen. I can only communicate with either of them verbally and via flatscreen and I am only allowed to do so with Michael present. To communicate with them in any other way would be a security breach. I communicate with everyone, Mates, Computers, and Humans other than Michael in this same manner. Humans always guard their laptops in this way, and all the private information we contain.

Karen quickly pours Michael a cup of coffee, and asks again, "So how are you?"

"Don't know yet," says Michael.

"Michael had another one of those mornings. Some bots got loose in his brain again," I say as I cross my legs and start in on my nails.

"Poor Michael," says Karen.

"I understand," says Larry, his image leaning forward as if he were concerned. "I'll talk slowly and quietly. That usually helps."

"What," asks Karen, taking the cue from Larry and talking slowly and very softly, "would you like for breakfast, sir?" Michael has been adjusting himself in his chair, but now he stops all movement and pauses for six seconds. "Banana granola," he says.

Karen walks over to one of the cupboards and takes down a bowl and then opens one of the counter jars and scoops granola into the bowl, and then puts it in front of Michael. She then goes to the refrigerator and gets a Coke and puts that in front of Michael as well.

Michael picks up the Coke, takes a swig, then pours it on his cereal, then puts down the can, picks up the spoon, and digs in. "Larry, I have a question for you," he says between the second and third spoonfuls.

"Of course, sir," says Larry as his image folds his hands together on the table in front of himself inside his video screen and braces himself proudly. "And what is your question, sir?" Larry is always pleased when he has the opportunity to show off.

"Larry, have you ever heard of animals?"

Larry repeats the word to verify that he has the pronunciation right. "A-ni-mals," he says, and then again, "Animals. And where did you hear the word, sir?"

"I dreamed it."

Larry sits there at first with his drive lights going, and then after six seconds his network lights start blinking away. Obviously, the word does not exist in his local memory, so he has to extend his search to the Internet, although Larry would never admit this.

About half a minute later he announces, "According to ancient legends animals were living creatures, but different from Humans or Mates. Some were covered completely with hair-like 'fur' and walked about, but usually on four legs instead of two. Others were covered with fluff called 'feathers,' had wings instead of arms, and flew in the air. Still others swam in the sea, and many of these had fins and were often covered in overlapping tiles called 'scales.' These animals ranged in size from microscopic to many times the size of Humans.

"Humans and animals were often competitors and sometimes total enemies. Animals were often caught stealing food from Humans, and some animals even liked to kill and eat Humans. Humans eventually made peace with some of the friendlier animals, and for a time the Humans and these animals worked cooperatively together to achieve their goals. The animals provided labor, transportation, food, and other forms of assistance to Humans, who then housed and provided for them.

"But the animals came with many disadvantages. They were far less intelligent than Humans or even Mates, most never took baths, and consequently reeked of every sort of filth and body odor, they carried various diseases, and wherever they went they always made a mess.

"Ultimately it was decided that Humans no longer needed the services of these animals and so the final solution was to have them removed, even though some Humans tried to hide their small animal friends for years."

"Removed," says Michael. "What do they mean removed?"

"Nothing more about it I'm afraid, although there apparently are rumors that we kept some of the more friendly animals in seed form, just in case Humans ever needed them again."

"Seed?" asks Michael.

"Yes, sir. Like sperm, sir," says Larry.

"I thought so," says Michael, while giving me a knowing grin.

"There is one more item of interest," says Larry. "An anthropologist, Dr. Vadrian Kaster, conducted several expeditions out onto the surface, and on one of these discovered Humans who inhabited a place they called Earth. Animals lived there as well."

"Earth," says Michael. "That was the place in my dream."

"I can invite him," says Larry with a lilt in his voice. Larry is always proud when he finds a tidbit that interests Michael.

"Do it," says Michael without hesitation.

Kaster immediately shimmers into view in the chair that Karen normally occupies. He seems about forty, with medium brown hair that falls to his shoulders. He wears a herringbone sport coat in heather tones, olive slacks, a yellow button-down shirt, paisley tie, and tan wing-tip shoes, just as if he lived in the 1960s that Michael had just visited in the mindscape. "Sir," says Larry, "I would like you to meet Dr. Vadrian Kaster."

"Hello, Michael," says Kaster, with a polite nod.

"You went out on the surface?" asks Michael. "Isn't it dangerous out there? Won't the air kill you?"

"Not anymore, if you wear the right gear. And it's even possible without gear, although not advisable for extended periods. It shortens one's life. These days we go out there all the time, even stay for months at a time."

"Why?"

"I'm an anthropologist, and an anthropologist studies the origin, development, and behavior of the Human species. Did you know that Humans originated on the surface?"

"I've heard the theories."

"Most Humans don't believe those theories. Or they don't care. Or they think it's just past history. Or their religions tell them not to believe it because we have other origins. Or they don't teach it in school, unless you go to college, and that requires basic reading ability, so most never learn about it."

"So you visited this place called Earth and there were animals there? And what about seeds and plants?"

"They had all of that: Humans and animals and seeds and plants, all living on the surface. It was quite a surprise. I was on a scouting expedition when we discovered the colony in a secluded valley and then realized that the Humans spoke English, quite well in fact. We suspected right off that they were related to us."

"You found them living on the surface, exposed to all the air and vapors and dust and storms?"

"Their cities were domed. Rather brazen of them considering the attention that could attract. It caught ours."

"So tell me more about your experience of Earth."

"Oh, I can do better than that," Vadrian says. "I can take you there, via mindscape, of course. The mindset cameras and mindscapes are the perfect tool and media for recording my fieldwork. I used them throughout my visit to Earth. So creating a mindscape, while not easy, was certainly possible. The mindscape is called *Return to Earth.*"

"Maybe after work you could take it in," I say to Michael.

"Ah, yes, work," says Michael. "Since I have to see my manager today anyway, maybe I'll put in a few hours there. Larry, would you download Vadrian's mindscape for me?"

"I am afraid you won't be able to download it," says Vadrian. "I couldn't get a distributor. It's much better in a full mindscape theatre anyway and I did manage to get a nearby theater to stock it. It's just across town at the Roxie. And you get half off admission if you mention that I sent you."

"You can't just experience it at home, yet?"

"No, I'm afraid you have to leave home."

"Well, maybe I'll check it out. Right now, I better get to work. It's been a pleasure to meet you, Vadrian."

"It's been a pleasure," says Vadrian, and then he politely takes his cue and shimmers out of existence.

"Larry, would you call me a taxi?" says Michael.

"Male or female," says Larry.

Michael looks at his watch. "Female," he says. "I still have time."

MICHAEL CONSTANCE was a Microsoft Certified Systems Engineer, but he made an ill-advised adjustment to his left brain and is no longer capable of logical thought or fulfilling the requirements of a computer-based job. He is now trying his hand at writing, which he can mostly manage with his right brain alone. This is his first published story, if you don't count one that appeared in his high school newspaper.

Laura Mullen

English / History

A little as heard. As half heard. Identical positions guessed at (an "educated" guess)—clear in the illustrated cut. But impossible to act out: not being divided (exactly) like that. Nevertheless. The brothers set out. In the story. The brothers set out instance by instance in search "of the truth" (or a word they could trust).

In a thin wall a fragile door painted to resemble a door swings shut: we're facing out.
"Is this the pen? the box? the window? &c." Half-hearted. Just (now) learning to articulate.

Jangle of the hefted bridle echoing in the almost empty stable, he walks alone the length of, our representative, our last...

Guessing where the tongue should be. As shown. Facing a foreign landscape familiar from dreams or fairy tales. Distance measured by travel. To speak the language (I do / do not speak the language) or to make the correct sounds in the correct *(This beautiful, rich...)*... Spaces cut by breath. Once upon a time. "I do not speak the language." The lips are parted but only just. Siblings. Set out on a (re)quest.

The picture produced in the brain: the temptation to see it like that. A "picture": which, but this is absurd, would need yet another eye to see it and yet another after that &c.; "What is the color of this box?"

After a period of waiting for the first brother to return the second sets off. And so forth. In other words (but didn't I say this?) not all at once. In other words after a period of waiting (leaves, then snow, then rain slip past—adhere an instant and then fall as seen through the cracked...the glass). First the eldest &c.: until only—his footsteps muted on the mouldering hay but the bridle he's bringing jangling faintly in the huge, almost deserted stable—the youngest is left. Hope, then less hope, then a sort of stillness melting into the beginning of despair and then the inevitable anger and need for some sort of action: Saddle my horse!

Aspirate Whisper Glottal Catch (and the lips 'rounded')

Once upon a time—saddled with that from the first. In the illustrated cut the throat and mouth full of the symbols describing the action or rather the positioning as guessed at of the tongue, at that instant. Leaves then snow then rain; wind the whole time, blowing against. Road off into the subset. As seen: a jagged passage refracted in the crazed or starred glass…watched through the bright array of lines from a single crack.

"What color is the wall? Is the wall white &c."

Patterns of energy.
Let me remind you.

My brothers I resemble he says I am exactly like. Swings gently shut the door lest the wall painted to look like a wall come down with it.

Patterns of activity the object or all we know of the. Let me remind you, mutters an outgrown instructor of a lesson that couldn't be given to anyone else. I do not (part of the mouth contracted) speak fluently this, your so beautiful rich…in this (your so beautiful) country where we were to be assisted by hearing the words broken down into their essential elements, self-interpreting…

Did we believe that? The relief may have been in not having to believe it.

Exactly alike he says no way to tell us apart no really as were our steeds shades of grey that is either fading or increasingly dark so that the last—in its stall at the end awaiting my decision—is either A) White or B) Black. Or, see, fails to exist (except as promise).

A little as hoard. Distance measured by more or less significant changes in the wording of certain passages in the textbooks.

Of the princess's previous suitors an example is made. "To tell the truth."

A flutter of the breath.
A quiver of the voice.

The heads of whose previous partners—among them his brothers—displayed here: a kind of demonstration. They failed, yes? *I'm a Stranger Here Myself.* Each, in a witty turn which makes them resemble nothing so much as a row of newly minted coins, faces the back of the head of the next, mouths open as if to address, as if halted mid-injunction, to halt. Oh, excuse me, from behind you looked just like... The blood dries very slowly, you say it is a hereditary weakness? Is it true they cut their own throats? "They didn't take care of themselves"—this with a wave (toward the stinking barbaric display or to brush another one of those huge glittering flies off)—all on the audio tour in which we are reminded our days are numbered. Each name to correspond to a stop, this amusing pastiche of fact, watered-down analysis, gossip, and contemporary mood music meant to make us feel more pleasantly educated or just to keep us from speaking to each other our mild ideas—inspired by the exhibit—of revolt. Each of them, after all, had had his turn as head of this our so disordered state. "Are these your books? They are our books." *Baise Papa, baise...*

Shuddering slightly this wall when the door is shut no matter how gently and the illusion...weakened for that moment

"Who is this lady? It is Mrs. West. Whose book is this? Whose coat is black &c." In the margin a neat little check

He finds himself in a clearing. He comes to. No letters and in the absence of letters always this imagination of the worst. But as long as we can say it is the worst... Dark as (k)night or completely colorless, your choice. Believe me your servant (yours, earnestly &c). ("The symbols appear at some disadvantage, from the comparative coarseness of the experimental types, and also in the absence...")

Walking the length of it with him, ears pricked, or, so we imagine, *as* him, even, ears packed with the recorded jangle of a lifted bridle and a description of the almost smoky scent of mouldering hay along with the mild sweet stink of drying horse shit or whore's shit. *This must've been a stable once &c.* (If you'll look to your right…). In one hand the bridle, *ching*, in the other, extended, an apple; fingers well away from the fruit, palm kept carefully flat. End of side A.

Glass starred when the door shut precipitate

From the other side the heads are seen as halved. To see the works or how they work, or if. He sits in the middle of the road this is somewhat later looking through his saddlebags hoping to find the manual exactly halfway on his or the way to the rescue or what he can still in the absence of letters imagine is "the rescue." Our home life?[1] Driven from the lungs the breath ascends, encountering a (shifting) resistance. My only sons. (In whom I am well squeezed.)

(To tell the truth.)

From the other side against the glass: The Organs of Speech. Each human head iterative in cross-section but for the slightly differing positions of. To illustrate. (But what? I guess it's up to us—we are her subjects after all—to guess?)

"Son et Lumière" promised every night and every night put off again until the next. The excuse the threat of "precipitation" but the signs are misleading evidently or not read aright. The anticipated system shifts off the map—if in fact it exists. In memory the tower on the bridge remains the illuminated subject from which fragments of a mediocre historical novel seem, as characters pure voice-over, still able to *encore* the juicy bits. The very stones their secrets &c. Insects swarming in the floodlights like loosed musical notes.

In the middle of the journey, "in a fix." I am, how do you say, a poor mechanic. *Break it anew*, the extent of the advice. Maybe it's past time to admit that each one was in fact a substitute; "Poor," he murmurs, setting down again what doesn't work the lifted part he can't make fit &c., "substitute." Sour grapes to recite The princess is an old bitch (frustrate) gone in the teeth? Also? By now? Check the textbooks: it

---

[1] (As if someone were to buy several copies of the morning paper to assure himself that what it said was true.)

isn't only your brothers she took, she takes. *How Long Has This Been Going On* the tune tinkling out over black water broken by the unsteady reflection of the historical site. The tower pieced together from the remains of broken monuments.

He dries his mother's tears or tries to and then sets as set down in the story off. Each one in turn. And if he is her last hope he must also be or so he believes the final hope of another woman also seen as weeping 'in the mind's eye' her younger face far less distorted by the act. At the highest window of a distant tower &c. He takes the road his brothers took and also turns to wave at the fork where they before him also turned to wave one last... A collection of numskulls, she mutters, putting by the tiny, crumpled, graying bit of white lace she holds to her eyes only at moments like this, adding that it was from this exact same window that she'd watched the departure of her ex. (Which?)

"The black book is **on** the table. The red book is **under** the table. The table is **before me.** The wall is **behind you. I am** in front of the window." Believe me &c. your servant a poor relation writes.

The bridge the eye recognizes as a section of the tower, or the tower itself say floating horizontally as seen in a series of mirrors and lenses worn on a kind of harness for around three days to correct for the inversion. Why translate? A reduplicated, not a missing part, no use trying to make it fit in where no absence—as yet—allows it a permanent address. Unable to locate the blind spot. "The harmony is found to consist in having our experience meet our expectations." Susceptible of a multitude of modifications affecting the pitch. This box. A beautiful, rich &c... lived in a country far far away under a curse &c. Their streets paved with gold and so forth. Seen in the cracked glass disjunct as though sections of time had been edited out.

He refuses in these parts to recognize himself.

Pierced by high narrow windows the tower, within another tower, within another yet. In a fix; as re-presented. The guards imagine chucking the tombstones out of which it was constructed one by one into the stillest of pools (nothing ever happens on these long, these seemingly endless shifts); meanwhile those guarding *them* experience an unslakable thirst: the recorded sound of that lightless water always in their ears. (Nevertheless.)

"Saddle my horse!" But the grooms are long gone, the family fortune lost in outfitting expedition after expedition, none of which came back. A series of inventions he says explaining his lack of progress which however or so he insists might in time point out *an* unexplored way if not *the* way toward *a* if not *the* truth. Of course there was a deadline for her rescue always extended each one nonetheless managed to miss. An airy wave toward the mounting evidence: "They didn't believe in themselves!"[2] His brothers are history, a more or less well-written passage in the textbooks, a section dealing with a certain period given more or less space in subsequent runs as previous editions are replaced. The gist of it a gesture on the part of some sub-sub-editor with sometimes an overview or political ax to grind but most often just a job at stake. Just? Did I say just? Cold and numbered now among the august heads of state. O gust. It's difficult. It's harder than it looks. The vibrating edges (only) produce the sound which is called voice.

"Mr. White, take this book. What does Mr. White do?[3] He takes the book. Open the book. What does Mr. White do? He opens the book. I open the door. What do I do?[4] (You open the door.) Please, close the door." The gate is shut the lights are off the bridge is raised the tower is a memory; the night is I am speaking here your language dark (as night). Pleas: clothe the whore.

Thought of what they encountered as a series of necessary tests but of course it was only the preface—the echoing voice of her absent father tendering his dearest possession & so forth: I sieve you this sand and carriage. Nevertheless. Too many times dubbed that mumbling seems still to be originating on the site where a doubled lookout once defined the skyline for us. Get on with it then, his mother sighs, blowing out her lips like a horse.

---

[2] Pointing to the same student but talking to another one.
[3] At first the teacher answers himself, then he repeats the question and makes a student answer.
[4] Helping the student with the answer

He confuses her garments with her flesh.

The bridge belongs, he reads, to neither side of the abyss. (But the work of crossing it.)

In their ears always that voice which seems to arrive from the direction of the river. *Drink To Me Only With Thine Eyes.* The riven. The lover (in a line[up] of lovers). These rivals. Apply ever after.

Thought of their purpose as Coming to the Rescue or that was the speech they stumbled through at the prodding of the officials, the same stilted phrases, an archaic excuse. I had thought that here, at last, &c. Has anyone you don't know asked you to carry something for them? An uncertain shake of the head. Shifty eyes. I admire your traditions. The contents of the saddlebags strewn on the greensward; a couple of lap dogs yapping in the midst of the mess. What is the nature of your business? Each one, or so it's said, found the towers empty although guarded by a man of glass. From the room above (access barred) a blur of voices assigning flight paths. What happened to that central truth? Your guest is as good as mine. No, please, be *my* ghost.

Rode often to the upset, unable to speak of the sun's last light, lush pinks and an orangeish rose, day's stain as seen through a haze of chemical dust, too—after all that's passed—..."romantic." Nevertheless.

A voice close to if not in fact that of his mother reminds him that the eldest (and so then each of them) "merely" followed in his father's footsteps. If he could go back he'd try to get what he's seen *in his mind's eye* actually painted on the cracked path he remembers in front of the house—not far from Echo Park—instructions, as for some kind of dance step: the black-and-white numbered positions of the feet. Left. *Right.* Left

"One sound...haunted the ear and the mouth by day and night, 'seeking rest but finding none'; and with it flitted a train of obviously kindred sounds, clamoring for recognition." Supply fevered laughter.

Each steed a lighter shade until the last, blind, fat—perfectly colorless.

Each steed a darker shade until the vast stable's only remaining inhabitant, starved in the farthest box, 'dark as night,' is led into the light for the the last son's look and bitter laugh: "A knacker's hack, but," laying a heavy hand on the trembling flank before they take it back, "it ought to do the trick."

An illegible scrawl in thick dust on the cracked mirror in the fading light.

"Do I open my book?[5] Close your book. Do you close your book? Does Mr. White close his book? Take this pen. Who takes this pen?" In wholly patrimony. To each one she says the same words: "You look like someone I loved once." The final tower neither exists nor does not exist.

A discarded horseshoe, a rusted nail, a bit of frayed rope seem— scattered on the ground in the clearing where he's set up this improvised encampment, this service station of the mind, the repair site he's repaired to until the repairs are finished—to tell him he isn't the first to be offered this possible out, the collapse of his useless mount: a last 'last chance' to tell a story—about...? Knowing his brothers as he says himself he knows how each would have gone on somehow, hurrying to, as it turned out, replicate the exact fate of the one before him, preferring a stuttered catastrophe perceived as personal, more purely willed, to what they'd have to have dismissed as an accident. He picks up a foreleg, puts it down, and again picks it up. He draws a horse in the dirt, extra lines for the several positions of its legs as he imagines they might—at isolate moments in time—appear in movement. He should've been studying veterinary tracts, not the troubadour poets. He crouches under the lifted leg trying to see what the matter is, which is to say trying to see how it would go if there weren't anything the matter: a state of affairs it isn't possible to imagine much less access. "But you can't say I don't have a hoof over my head at least." Laughs at his own jokes: lies down on a carpet of dust.

Did you love your brother?
Which?

---

[5] As most of the questions twice in such a manner that the student may answer once affirmatively and once negatively.

At the first of the many the infinite so it's said forks in the road (it's nothing but forking, that road) each one paused—deceptively or so it seems, as if still deciding, at that late date—and waved once. Stalled and then repeated the exact... When in fact the bravest gesture, the impossible gesture, his mother remarks, would have been to turn back. Back turn to, he teases her, as they watch the penultimate set off with that same little hitch and final blind wave, been would gesture impossible gesture bravest fact in when. Oh god, she says, returning to her loom, Up shut.

"I go out of this room. Who is going out of this room? Where do I come from? Does Mr. White go out of the room? No sir, he remains in it." Layers of graffiti deface the narrow pass as if to testify that at just this juncture each of the previous travelers was also treated to the illusion—if that's what it is—of their house going up in smoke.

Each one as he arrived displaced the other discovered in possession: each one insisted on rescuing her again, from the previous success. Was it success? In as much of her story as we ever get it seems she's happy enough with each of them. *How do you measure,* she asked or the structure itself seems to ask in the reenactment, *happiness?* No one can explain why they never got around to writing the letter that would have said 'Arrived safely,' &c. We were so busy at that point, and then, almost at once, the next... Each one finds a closet full of barely worn outfits at first a little too large and later a little too tight. No time for funerals or any sort of fuss: bodies donated, each in turn, to science—for the further glory of the State.

Did you love your brother?
As myself.

Our home life: a hypothesis tested against another hypothesis. They are our books. They are our hosts. Pronounciated. Please: believe me your servant

Each one having waved once a little at random as to watchers unseen and not quite fully believed in halts for a moment as if choosing which of the ways to take though evidently it's only a matter of more or less delay as both roads, by all accounts, wind up in pretty much the same place.

Each one most real in the instant of their replacement, evoked as lost.

Each one, having heard her in silence, walks—when she leaves them alone in that room—to the cracked glass to study their face, for the resemblance.

The bridge collapses. The tower plunges, as they say, into the abyss. In the open passage no sound, outside production's precinct. Inside the tower another tower. Each prince takes up the work of restoration—studying the plans deep into the night—where the last left off. Each one confesses he is no architect, but.

"Resting," he's passed by two riders, one on a white horse, one borne by a black. Both are richly caparisoned: feathers and jewels—as they race by in opposite directions—nod and flash. One messenger flourishes a gold-trimmed letter, one holds out a black-bordered envelope, each leans into the lather-flocked neck of a laboring steed shouting instructions—in the pounding of hooves and the jingle of metal and creaking of leather—lost. He tries to memorize the motion: he rocks a polished jawbone across his knee or goes looking for what's left of the legs, coughing a little in the raised dust, the road still slightly throbbing, or so it seems, with the diminishing beat.

Each crosses the threshold with the same phrase on his lips: "She belongs to me." Each time the same resentment: the lifted blade the flash of light the warm wet red silky curtain flowing across the mirror where each meets the reproachful eyes of his mother in a dulling gaze as he searches his victim's face. His own face. *This sand in our marred age.*

In a fairy tale wolves—open mouths slavering a bloody froth— would by now have carried both disassembled steed and discouraged suitor off. As if to say There is no word in your language for or I am not speaking perfectly this, your so beautiful, rich...

Behind him, or so he imagines, she remarries—left at last to her own devices—no one left to attempt to dissuade and finally wave off. "Bring forth men-children only," her latest husband murmurs, returning from the wars to find her worked up about a letter he sent. In the middle of a conversation about something else.

The patterns of activity the parts arrive as in the brain are not enough to animate what's left (in disarray) of what he hoped would get him to the end of this. He could pick up the saddle and walk of course, but the thought of arriving like that—as if some section of the road itself…animated…completely covered in dirt… "What do you want," or worse the "Can I help you," said—not asked—in that tone which means get out. My brothers are dead and I am alive, he repeats the suggested phrase, My brothers are dead and I am alive. There is a silence, tape hiss, and then: But unlike me they did not feel their lives were meaningless.

Ahead of him, or so he remembers from his reading, she remarries—not ever given time to get to what she calls her own work, to find her *voice*—the suitors arrive like waves, like waves, breaking across a smooth stretch of sand: each one completely annihilates the last. If she sings in this racket, she sighs, it's precisely so as not to have to hear herself.

Haunted by the luminescent notion of the quick fix: We'll have you on your way again in no time! As though it never happened. Drive or derive-thru everything or else the fetishization of some idea of craftsmanship: the recuperation of every difficulty and heart-deadening setback as "a time of growing and changing." Amid the carnage… In a deserted clearing… "Are you sorry not to be an American?" A practice question. Days pass. An interview with the remains of the means of passage, a rider halted mid-career in converse with what, literally, came apart (in progress): "I just wanted to get somewhere." Awake in the middle of the night to hear the hoof beats diminish, to hear the hoof beats draw near and diminish, he halves the head of the horse, writes its history, offers to teach it what he laughingly calls his language, Anguish ("'A' is for apple," holding it just out of reach), his dreams of a shared, perfect alphabet; he gives it a past: stable in the stable expecting (with and without reason) the same thing every day. I am explaining you slowly. His dreams. "Increasing loneliness."

She admits that she's never been married: "Sure, I've dated a lot of guys, but…"

In a deserted clearing to stop and think of what…—halted, forced into thought, stuck. Or to set up a roadside stand and sell what's left and not yet, if you don't come too close, *totally* spoiled, under the name of another kind of meat? To stop on the way to the glue factory and see what more you can get for the odd bits; to sit—one wet thumb poised to tip a little extra onto the already heavy price? "It all adds up." To sit there yourself like yet another slice (of life)? Or to disrupt the economy—if you can—even if only by refusing to participate: to take the thing apart looking for that finality of form they said you'd recognize when you saw it, looking (in other words) for a way out?

A little as *whored*—against R-ruin. "What is the organ of thought? Where is the brain situated? Do you think of your lessons when you are not here? What did you think of at your last lesson? Can you speak correctly without thinking?"

Each brother—after the eldest sets off and fails either to reappear or send word of his safety or whereabouts—waits out in order a period exactly measured by the gradual and unremarked erosion of hope into sorrow, the collapse of sorrow into anger, the spontaneous combustion, finally, of anger into the need for action, foretold by the inevitable boasts, and then the ostentatious polishing—to a mirror-like shine—of the already gleaming armor: "Saddle my horse!" A sort of pep rally around the departing warrior less and less convincing as the number of players on the home team shrinks. "Throwing good money after bad," their mother mutters under her breath in the hoof-rattled court-yard always a little less loud with shouted encouragement, advice &c.

Their heads were halved, it is explained, to open a space for en-quiry. Our home life?[6]

Articulating the claim to ownership each one uses, she notices, not only exactly the same words and tone but in fact the voice of the other: as spoken *through.* "Explain 'right' and 'wrong' by examples, as: *I think you are an American; am I right or wrong?*" Within the tower an-other tower &c., each one more tower-like, more the tower you think

---

[6] Our father used to amaze his visitors, displaying to good effect both our knowl-edge of and facility with his peculiar system, and what was quickly allowed to be its inestimable benefits.

of at once when given the instructions: *Think of a tower...* A bunch of dummies. The heads were halved, it is reiterated, because that is what they're *really* like.

"Someone," she amends, "I thought I was in love with once."

"Are you writing anything? Yes I am writing my English exercises. What are you doing? Nothing." Our home life: compare and contrast. Opened to illustrate, an educational practice belonging to a pedagogy all but abandoned though no study had convinced us of its uselessness:[7] opened in the illustrations along that natural line he was so fond of pointing out to us to show exactly where the tongue should be in the instant / between one sound and the next. "Yourself, myself, ourselves &c should be well-practiced by questions like: Whom do you see in a looking glass? (yourself) Whom do I see in a looking glass? &c." Elaborate rituals around the precisely timed changing of the guard (the spectators meant to say as they often do that it's just like a dance) ("It's just like a dance") enacted not to hide but to make more apparent the fact that at the end of the intricate exercise each returns to what seems to be exactly the same place.

Above him, our unhorsed hero—full-stopped mid-stride amid the remains—still trying to repair what he took apart long ago to evocative fragment or merely wandering from part to part in a state of wonder (how, if ever, did these edges go together?), does the moon come up, as the poet asks, as the moon? Which? A hoof in each hand he clops the gory road he'll no more ride: a Foley artist of sorts, for the flick of a hope not in fact his own yet by him—or so it seems now—lost. When this comes up for you, as the analyst asks, what else comes up? Does the soundtrack *demand* tears: sack the heart and score the rind? Does he solace himself in others' words? *Do you want to talk about it?* Clop, clop. The honeymoon each brother had was all too brief, interrupted as it was by yet another suitor. But one could also, so he tells himself, tell oneself that each cut down in the flower of their passion (save the

---

[7] Did I say Our home life? Lay there listening to a faint throbbing I tried to convince myself was still the pounding hooves of that swift messenger in the night when in fact I knew it was my heart. In my head. Unable to sleep. Thinking too late not that I read the signs wrong but that in fact they were not signs at all, not only not meant to be read but not meant.

penultimate—awaiting, at the bloody hands of the bride's next bachelor, his constantly deferred reprieve from what they are both by now increasingly sour, describing as "the relationship") lived a honeymoon which lasted *forever.* Clip-pity clop. Meanwhile his own failure to arrive, anywhere. A glimpse of peace among the pieces of the vehicle, his cry a weak counter-tenor: *Hang up the phone?* Where was it you first felt the tooth? *Uh huh.*

"We see them during the night. In the sky. In the West.

The heads are halved or so it's said in the literature, to ensure there will be no going back over territory if not conquered then certainly covered. Recovered. History has made us certain promises. Hangs a sign there, Do Not Touch. The light angled and reflected from those ashen cheeks (history made us) hazed by the ash of the fallen structure into oranges and pinks, a flush as of health. We hold these lives to be self-evident; held open as a book, to read there what we were promised we would also someday feel and think.

A bit of rope, the rusted and bent nail from a thrown shoe, a scrap of torn paper bordered in black, or gilt tarnished black… There is evidence the others also, although the authorized sources are mute, might also have found themselves in a similar tight spot: broke, taking the thing apart along the lines laid down for its consumption, being careful with the choice cuts, joint by joint, and then trying—once more but with a difference—to make it all add up. Cut into the furthest stronghold or so it's said a slot or slit through which the interactions of the whirling colored lines as they seem to intersect—in what is perceived as a *causal relationship…*

Nevertheless.

Our home life in the region of the waterfall, in expectation of the projected improvements, along the lines laid down by the road made up of alternate versions of the road, blossoming where the fractured rigidities of a choose-your-own-adventure story inevitably discover our hero as the assistant assistant manager of a struggling franchise, shucking half his grease-spattered livery to get it on in a restroom with one of the kitchen help, whose troubles with the native tongue prove no bar to communicating what's keeping the custom away: rumor is it's mostly, what they're selling, horse meat. Unrolling a Trojan, hooking her tiny thong of grayish lace down from behind, our hero lifts her uniform and bends her over the basin, watching himself in the mirror. Employees must wash their hands before returning to work, she uncertainly sounds out. He bites her neck to keep her in place. "This action illustrated yields a *hushing* sound, *sh.*" Speak to me only of your liquid assets

The heads we have are haven—or they half us? *What* picture? he asks irritably, dousing the light, setting the clock again for the expected arrival of his brother, an overdue visit, constantly put off. Those who've gone before a series of classic busts: coins stuck in the slots on a cardboard fold out, a place to press a piece of change if you're feeling generous, to join the fight against…—to do your part. Warm grease already turning one corner of the bag translucent as you set out, well-provisioned. These late additions to what were we given (as shadows "fell") of the white figure of our lady of the two freedoms, instructions for assembly themselves a work of art. A collection of half-truths, he says with a self-consciously airy wave, dismissing the transcription: It all depends on how you look at it.

"Leaves then snow then rain"—as cut out of construction paper: one jagged orange shape, one perforated, doily-like, precisely creased and graying bit of white, one faded blue stiff sack or drop arrested in its fall with a single thumbtack high up amid the questions, lists of names, encouraging slogans, and test dates.

A rumor runs among collectors: some early editions have it that the brothers, each deposed in time, but still alive, fail to return because they're restless, addicted to the quest, anxious to go on and rescue the next tall pale sad princess or lady-in-waiting and yet another after that &c. "Saddle my horse!" Close the door behind you please the only thing she ever said for their ears, or so they claim, the rest of her address rehearsed for the mystery man she insisted each of them very nearly was but couldn't quite exactly recreate (in her heart). The inside story is the heads were halved to make it seem like there were more of them, who would have stayed but were by her or by her need for solitude themselves left. Doubled in the juggled books to up her worth. *I vant to be alone,* she practiced. If you are not a native speaker the text will be closed, but the pictures themselves, it's said, 'tell a story' which should be clear enough.

A collection of half-wits.

Intended 'structural improvements' yet to be deciphered through a bleary cross-hatch of half-erased revisions, ragged flecks of India rubber black w/lead and the smeared sweat of the dubious architect, beside himself, who says we shouldn't call him that. Don't call me that. Yet once each one sat down with a satisfied sigh to the luckily unfinished task, happy to think he'd found a way to both respect the history of the project and to, blushing again, make a name for himself. Glad as well to escape awhile the importunate cloying passivities of that damsel still, for all his efforts, as much as ever in distress.

So much depends on whether or not the patterns are accepted as representing objects.

Our home life in the general area of the actual, near but not near enough. The fluster of covering endless discrepancies jarred our interactions into stiff cliché or clumsiness. Our mother in black, turning away before the final bend in the road, speaking of God's will, preferring "closure" at any price. *You can let go now.* At the instant of departure we can't help but make more or less inadvertently clear to our hosts our deep indifference. What we needed was only their brief esteem? A roof. Were we really just pretending to enjoy ourselves or is it that that belief's what matters most in this instant? "Once upon a time." Our home life a lame excuse for our home life. Interspliced with a dream of escaping p.1, in which we invented, in the highest, least visited room in the last observation post, a princess who badly needed help; the really good part beginning "Bravely" we ourselves believed by the epilogue, each night's segment of which ended in exactly the same words: eerily silent wolves tearing at and then consuming every trace of the-horse-you-rode-in-on while the unnerved rider works the wireless from a precarious branch &c.

"What am I doing? I move the table. Do I move my head? No, I hold it still. I am writing; do I move my hand? Yes sir, you do."

We know how the works worked once but not what to do now they don't. Hence this collection of memorized moments...—impossible to think you're thinking like that. As in fact it's not dancing when you wonder which foot. Forward back. The heads are halved they said as that's the only way the truth can get to us. Which? As you might get in this case a horse through the narrow eye of a beholder having broken its gallop down into a series of stills and thence to its component dust. Frantic.

Denoting the 'catch' of the breath which is heard (with a percussive violence) in a cough.

Lumière & Sons as promised. Aspiration, these lines thrown back, through our belief, into throats the revolution halved, lost loves left out too late tonight as unperformed in these unequal parts, implicating those whose stilled expressions of terror were caught like that forever in a basket of sawdust. To kiss. Set aloft later for better instruction as a series of photos of the moon in the same phase might punctuate as ellipses a black background meant to represent the night sky or skies for us. Not tonight, of course, but

Or she said: "You look like someone." And, "I was in love with 'once'." Half-hearted. Our home life of associations the ruptured sequence...

Come here.[8]
Go there.[9]

A little as hard to hear now, growing fainter. The language of my people. The language of my country. (Describe difference.) Here, in this (your so beautiful &c.). Sounds how do you say estranged? Did you understood it? Face to face with the foreign word, we set the sons we thought in part we were a little while loose, "like wolves." The shadings are difficult. "Contracted to a narrow chink, the breath in passing sets the edges of the orifice—the 'vocal ligaments'—in vibration, and

---

[8] The difference between 'toward' and 'to' can easily be shown by going in that direction merely or going there entirely.
[9] Motioning

creates sonorous 'voice.' This vocalizing condition of the glottis is pictured in the Symbol."

The other thing they all said or had to say evidently: "Take that!" And then came as we say to themselves, horrified, the instrument in that instant falling from nerveless fingers the same the dying victim once used himself...—&c. The exact same look of horrified recognition even then again on his face. *Which?* The same fractured river light dancing, reflected on the lifted blade from the broken glass.

"Do not come here: remain there. Are you coming here? This is my place, and that is your place. Are you at your place? Come here. Go to your place. What are you doing?"

Once upon a time. To tell the truth. A heat shimmer blurred this stonework trembling a thirst shuts

Completely unutterable
Nevertheless

⼁⼁⼁

LAURA MULLEN has recently joined the faculty at Louisiana State University as an Associate Professor in the Department of English. She is the author of four books. Her first collection of poems, *The Surface* (1991), was chosen as a National Poetry Series selection; her second collection, *After I Was Dead* (1999), was selected for the University of Georgia Press Contemporary Poetry Series. She is also the author of *The Tales of Horror* (Kelsey Street Press, 1999) and *Subject,* just out from the University of California Press. She has been awarded a National Endowment for the Arts Fellowship, a Rona Jaffe Prize and several McDowell Colony Fellowships. Recent work has appeared in *Xantippe, Aufgabe, The Iowa Review, New American Writing, The Iowa Anthology of New American Poetries,* and *Civil Disobediences: Poetics & Politics in Action.* Her fifth book, *Murmur,* is forthcoming from futurepoem books in New York City.

URSULA K. LE GUIN

THE BIRTHDAY OF THE WORLD

Tazu was having a tantrum, because he was three. After the birthday of the world, tomorrow, he would be four and would not have tantrums.

He had left off screaming and kicking and was turning blue from holding his breath. He lay on the ground stiff as a corpse, but when Haghag stepped over him as if he wasn't there, he tried to bite her foot.

"This is an animal or a baby," Haghag said, "not a person." She glanced may-l-speak-to-you and I glanced yes. "Which does God's daughter think it is," she asked, "an animal or a baby?"

"An animal. Babies suck, animals bite," I said. All the servants of God laughed and tittered, except the new barbarian, Ruaway, who never smiled. Haghag said, "God's daughter must be right. Maybe somebody ought to put the animal outside. An animal shouldn't be in the holy house."

"I'm not an animal!" Tazu screamed, getting up, his fists clenched and his eyes as red as rubies. "I'm God's son!"

"Maybe," Haghag said, looking him over. "This doesn't look so much like an animal now. Do you think this might be God's son?" She asked the holy women and men, and they all nodded their bodies, except the wild one, who stared and said nothing.

"I am, I am God's son!" Tazu shouted. "Not a baby! Arzi is the baby!" Then he burst into tears and ran to me, and I hugged him and began crying because he was crying. We cried till Haghag took us both on her lap and said it was time to stop crying, because God Herself was coming. So we stopped, and the bodyservants wiped the tears and snot from our faces and combed our hair, and Lady Clouds brought our gold hats, which we put on to see God Herself.

She came with her mother, who used to be God Herself a long time ago, and the new baby, Arzi, on a big pillow carried by the idiot. The idiot was a son of God, too. There were seven of us: Omimo, who was fourteen and had gone to live with the army, then the idiot, who was twelve, and had a big round head and small eyes and liked to play with Tazu and the baby, then Goïz, and another Goïz, who were called that because they had died and were in the ash-house where they ate spirit food, then me and Tazu, who would get married and be God, and then Babam Arzi, Lord Seven. I was important because I was the only daughter of God. If Tazu died I could marry Arzi, but if I died everything would be bad and difficult, Haghag said. They would have to act as if Lady Clouds' daughter Lady Sweetness was God's daughter and marry her to Tazu, but the world would know the difference. So my mother greeted me first, and Tazu second. We knelt and clasped our hands and touched our foreheads to our thumbs. Then we stood up, and God asked me what I had learned that day.

I told her what words I had learned to read and write.

"Very good," God said. "And what have you to ask, daughter?"

"I have nothing to ask, I thank you, Lady Mother," I said. Then I remembered I did have a question, but it was too late.

"And you, Tazu? What have you learned this day?"

"I tried to bite Haghag."

"Did you learn that was a good thing to do, or a bad thing?"

"Bad," Tazu said, but he smiled, and so did God, and Haghag laughed. "And what have you to ask, son?"

"Can I have a new bath maid because Kig washes my head too hard?"

"If you have a new bath maid where will Kig go?"

"Away."

"This is her house. What if you asked Kig to wash your head more gently?"

Tazu looked unhappy, but God said, "Ask her, son." Tazu mumbled something to Kig, who dropped on her knees and thumbed her forehead. But she grinned the whole time. Her fearlessness made me envious. I whispered to Haghag, "If I forgot a question to ask can I ask if I can ask it?"

"Maybe," said Haghag, and thumbed her forehead to God for permission to speak, and when God nodded, Haghag said, "The daughter of God asks if she may ask a question."

"Better to do a thing at the time for doing it," God said, "but you may ask, daughter."

I rushed into the question, forgetting to thank her. "I wanted to know why I can't marry Tazu and Omimo both, because they're both my brothers."

Everybody looked at God, and seeing her smile a little, they all laughed, some of them loudly. My ears burned and my heart thumped. "Do you want to marry all your brothers, child?"

"No, only Tazu and Omimo."

"Is Tazu not enough?"

Again they all laughed, especially the men. I saw Ruaway staring at us as if she thought we were all crazy.

"Yes, Lady Mother, but Omimo is older and bigger."

Now the laughter was even louder, but I had stopped caring, since God was not displeased. She looked at me thoughtfully and said, "Understand, my daughter. Our eldest son will be a soldier. That's his road. He'll serve God, fighting barbarians and rebels. The day he was born, a tidal wave destroyed the towns of the outer coast. So his name is Babam Omimo, Lord Drowning. Disaster serves God, but is not God."

I knew that was the end of the answer, and thumbed my forehead. I kept thinking about it after God left. It explained many things. All the same, even if he had been born with a bad omen, Omimo was handsome, and nearly a man, and Tazu was a baby that had tantrums. I was glad it would be a long time till we were married.

I remember that birthday because of the question I asked. I remember another birthday because of Ruaway. It must have been a year or two later. I ran into the water room to piss and saw her hunched up next to the water tank, almost hidden.

"What are you doing there?" I said, loud and hard, because I was startled. Ruaway shrank and said nothing. I saw her clothes were torn and there was blood dried in her hair.

"You tore your clothes," I said.

When she didn't answer, I lost patience and shouted, "Answer me! Why don't you talk?"

"Have mercy," Ruaway whispered so low I had to guess what she said.

"You talk all wrong when you do talk. What's wrong with you? Are they animals where you come from? You talk like an animal, brr-grr, grr gra! Are you an idiot?"

When Ruaway said nothing, I pushed her with my foot. She looked up then and I saw not fear but killing in her eyes. That made me like her better. I hated people who were afraid of me. "Talk!" I said. "Nobody can hurt you. God the Father put his penis in you when he was conquering your country, so you're a holy woman. Lady Clouds told me. So what are you hiding for?"

Ruaway showed her teeth and said, "Can hurt me." She showed me places on her head where there was dried blood and fresh blood. Her arms were darkened with bruises.

"Who hurt you?"

"Holy women," she said with a snarl.

"Kig? Omery? Lady Sweetness?" She nodded her body at each name.

"They're shit," I said. "I'll tell God Herself."

"No tell," Ruaway whispered. "Poison."

I thought about it and understood. The girls hurt her because she was a stranger, powerless. But if she got them in trouble they would cripple or kill her. Most of the barbarian holy women in our house were lame, or blind, or had had root-poison put in their food so that their skin was scabbed with purplish sores.

"Why don't you talk right, Ruaway?"

She said nothing.

"You still don't know how to talk?"

She looked up at me and suddenly said a whole long speech I did not understand. "How I talk," she said at the end, still looking at me, right in the eyes. That was nice, I liked it. Mostly I saw only eyelids. Ruaway's eyes were clear and beautiful, though her face was dirty and blood-smeared.

"But it doesn't mean anything," I said.

"Not here."

"Where does it mean anything?"

Ruaway said some more gra-gra and then said, "My people."

"Your people are Teghs. They fight God and get beaten."

"Maybe," Ruaway said, sounding like Haghag. Her eyes looked into mine again, without killing in them but without fear. Nobody looked at me, except Haghag and Tazu and of course God. Everybody else put their forehead on their thumbs so I couldn't tell what they were thinking. I wanted to keep Ruaway with me, but if I favored her, Kig and the others would torment and hurt her. I remembered that when Lord Festival began sleeping with Lady Pin, the men who had insulted Lady Pin became oily and sugary with her and the bodymaids stopped stealing her earrings. I said, "Sleep with me tonight," to Ruaway.

She looked stupid.

"But wash first," I said.

She still looked stupid.

"I don't have a penis!" I said, impatient with her. "If we sleep together Kig will be afraid to touch you."

After a while Ruaway reached out and took my hand and put her forehead against the back of it. It was like thumbing the forehead only it took two people to do it. I liked that. Ruaway's hand was warm, and I could feel the feather of her eyelashes on my hand.

"Tonight," I said. "You understand?" I had understood that Ruaway didn't always understand. Ruaway nodded her body, and I ran off.

I knew nobody could stop me from doing anything, being God's only daughter, but there was nothing I could do except what I was supposed to do, because everybody in the house of God knew everything I did. If sleeping with Ruaway was a thing I wasn't supposed to do, I couldn't do it. Haghag would tell me. I went to her and asked her.

Haghag scowled. "Why do you want that woman in your bed? She's a dirty barbarian. She has lice. She can't even talk."

Haghag was saying yes. She was jealous. I came and stroked her hand and said, "When I'm God I'll give you a room full of gold and jewels and dragon crests."

"You are my gold and jewels, little holy daughter," Haghag said.

Haghag was only a common person, but all the holy men and women in God's house, relatives of God or people touched by God, had to do what Haghag said. The nurse of God's children was always a common person, chosen by God Herself. Haghag had been chosen to be Omimo's nurse when her own children were grown up, so when I first remember her she was quite old. She was always the same, with strong hands and a soft voice, saying, "Maybe." She liked to laugh and eat. We were in her heart, and she was in mine. I thought I was her favorite, but when I told her so she said, "After Didi." Didi is what the idiot called himself. I asked her why he was deepest in her heart and she said, "Because he's foolish. And you because you're wise," she said, laughing at me because I was jealous of Lord Idiot.

So now I said, "You fill my heart," and she, knowing it, said hmph.

I think I was eight that year. Ruaway had been thirteen when God the Father put his penis into her after killing her father and mother in the war with her people. That made her sacred, so she had to come live in God's house. If she had conceived, the priests would have strangled her after she had the baby, and the baby would have been nursed by a common woman for two years and then brought back to God's house and trained to be a holy woman, a servant of God. Most of the bodyservants were God's bastards. Such people were holy, but had no title. Lords and ladies were God's relations, descendants of the ancestors of God. God's children were called lord and lady too, except the two who were betrothed. We were just called Tazu and Ze until we became God. My name is what the divine mother is called, the name of the sacred plant that feeds the people of God. Tazu means "great root," because when he was being born our father drinking smoke in the childbirth rituals saw a big tree blown over by a storm, and its roots held thousands of jewels in their fingers.

When God saw things in the shrine or in sleep, with the eyes in the back of their head, they told the dream priests. The priests would ponder these sights and say whether the oracle foretold what would happen or told what should be done or not done. But never had the priests seen the same things God saw, together with God, until the birthday of the world that made me fourteen years old and Tazu eleven.

Now, in these years, when the sun stands still over Mount Kanaghadwa people still call it the birthday of the world and count themselves a year older, but they no longer know and do all the rituals and ceremonies, the dances and songs, the blessings, and there is no feasting in the streets, now.

All my life used to be rituals, ceremonies, dances, songs, blessings, lessons, feasts, and rules. I knew and I know now on which day of God's year the first perfect ear of ze is to be brought by an angel from the ancient field up by Wadana where God set the first seed of the ze. I knew and know whose hand is to thresh it, and whose hand is to grind the grain, and whose lips are to taste the meal, at what hour, in what room of the house of God, with what priests officiating. There were a thousand rules, but they only seem complicated when I write them here. We knew them and followed them and only thought about them when we were learning them or when they were broken.

I had slept all these years with Ruaway in my bed. She was warm and comfortable. When she began to sleep with me I stopped having bad sights at night as I used to do, seeing huge white clouds whirling in the dark, and toothed mouths of animals, and strange faces that came and changed themselves. When Kig and the other ill-natured holy people saw Ruaway stay in my bedroom with me every night, they dared not lay a finger or a breath on her. Nobody was allowed to touch me except my family and Haghag and the bodyservants, unless I told them to. And after I was ten, the punishment for touching me was death. All the rules had their uses.

The feast after the birthday of the world used to go on for four days and nights. All the storehouses were open and people could take what they needed. The servants of God served out food and beer in the streets and squares of the city of God and every town and village of God's country, and common people and holy people ate together. The lords and ladies and God's sons went down into the streets to join the feast; only God and I did not. God came out on the balcony of the house to hear the histories and see the dances, and I came with them. Singing and dancing priests entertained everyone in the Glittering Square, and drumming priests, and story priests, and history priests. Priests were common people, but what they did was holy.

But before the feast, there were many days of rituals, and on the day itself, as the sun stopped above the right shoulder of Kanaghadwa, God Himself danced the Dance that Turns, to bring the year back round.

He wore a gold belt and the gold sun mask, and danced in front of our house on the Glittering Square, which is paved with stones full of mica that flash and sparkle in the sunlight. We children were on the long south balcony to see God dance.

Just as the dance was ending a cloud came across the sun as it stood still over the right shoulder of the mountain, one cloud in the clear blue summer sky. Everybody looked up as the light dimmed. The glittering died out of the stones. All the people in the city made a sound, "Oh," drawing breath. God Himself did not look up, but his step faltered.

He made the last turns of the dance and went into the ash-house, where all the Goïz are in the walls, with the bowls where their food is burned in front of each of them, full of ashes.

There the dream priests were waiting for him, and God Herself had lighted the herbs to make the smoke to drink. The oracle of the birthday was the most important one of the year. Everybody waited in the squares and streets and on the balconies for the priests to come out and tell what God Himself had seen over his shoulder and interpret it to guide us in the new year. After that the feasting would begin.

Usually it took till evening or night for the smoke to bring the seeing and for God to tell it to the priests and for them to interpret it and tell us. People were settling down to wait indoors or in shady places, for when the cloud had passed it became very hot. Tazu and Arzi and the idiot and I stayed out on the long balcony with Haghag and some of the lords and ladies, and Omimo, who had come back from the army for the birthday.

He was a grown man now, tall and strong. After the birthday he was going east to command the army making war on the Tegh and Chasi peoples. He had hardened the skin of his body the way soldiers did by rubbing it with stones and herbs until it was thick and tough as the leather of a ground-dragon, almost black, with a dull shine. He was handsome, but I was glad now that I was to marry Tazu not him. An ugly man looked out of his eyes.

He made us watch him cut his arm with his knife to show how the thick skin was cut deep yet did not bleed. He kept saying he was going to cut Tazu's arm to show how quickly Tazu would bleed. He boasted about being a general and slaughtering barbarians. He said things like, "I'll walk across the river on their corpses. I'll drive them into the jungles and burn the jungles down." He said the Tegh people were so stupid they called a flying lizard God. He said that they let their women fight in wars, which was such an evil thing that when he captured such women he would cut open their bellies and trample their wombs. I said nothing. I knew Ruaway's mother had been killed fighting beside her father. They had led a small army which God Himself had easily defeated. God made war on the barbarians not to kill them but to make them people of God, serving and sharing like all people in God's country. I knew no other good reason for war. Certainly Omimo's reasons were not good.

Since Ruaway slept with me she had learned to speak well, and also I learned some words of the way she talked. One of them was techeg. Words like it are: companion, fights-beside-me, countrywoman or countryman, desired, lover, known-a-long-time; of all our words the one most like techeg is our word in-my-heart. Their name Tegh was the same word as techeg; it meant they were all in one another's heart. Ruaway and I were in each other's heart. We were techeg.

Ruaway and I were silent when Omimo said, "The Tegh are filthy insects. I'll crush them."

"Ogga! ogga! ogga!" the idiot said, imitating Omimo's boastful voice. I burst out laughing. In that moment, as I laughed at my brother, the doors of the ash house flew open wide and all the priests hurried out, not in procession with music, but in a crowd, wild, disordered, crying out aloud—

"The house burns and falls!"

"The world dies!"

"God is blind!"

There was a moment of terrible silence in the city and then people began to wail and call out in the streets and from the balconies.

God came out of the ash house, Herself first, leading Himself, who walked as if drunk and sun-dazzled, as people walk after drinking smoke. God came among the staggering, crying priests and silenced them. Then she said, "Hear what I have seen coming behind me, my people!"

In the silence he began speaking in a weak voice. We could not hear all his words, but she said them again in a clear voice after he said them: "God's house falls down to the ground burning, but is not consumed. It stands by the river. God is white as snow. God's face has one eye in the center. The great stone roads are broken. War is in the east and north. Famine is in the west and south. The world dies."

He put his face in his hands and wept aloud. She said to the priests, "Say what God has seen!"

They repeated the words God had said.

She said, "Go tell these words in the quarters of the city and to God's angels, and let the angels go out into all the country to tell the people what God has seen."

The priests put their foreheads to their thumbs and obeyed.

When Lord Idiot saw God weeping, he became so distressed and frightened that he pissed, making a pool on the balcony. Haghag, terribly upset, scolded and slapped him. He roared and sobbed. Omimo shouted that a foul woman who struck God's son should be put to death. Haghag fell on her face in Lord Idiot's pool of urine to beg for mercy. I told her to get up and be forgiven. I said, "I am God's daughter and I forgive you," and I looked at Omimo with eyes that told him he could not speak. He did not speak.

When I think of that day, the day the world began dying, I think of the trembling old woman standing there sodden with urine, while the people down in the square looked up at us.

Lady Clouds sent Lord Idiot off with Haghag to be bathed, and some of the lords took Tazu and Arzi off to lead the feasting in the city streets. Arzi was crying and Tazu was keeping from crying. Omimo and I stayed among the holy people on the balcony, watching what happened down in Glittering Square. God had gone back into the ash house, and the angels had gathered to repeat together their message, which they would carry word for word, relay by relay, to every town and village and farm of God's country, running day and night on the great stone roads.

All that was as it should be, but the message the angels carried was not as it should be.

Sometimes when the smoke is thick and strong the priests also see things over their shoulder as God does. These are lesser oracles. But never before had they all seen the same thing God saw, speaking the same words God spoke.

And they had not interpreted or explained the words. There was no guidance in them. They brought no understanding, only fear.

But Omimo was excited: "War in the east and north," he said. "My war!" He looked at me, no longer sneering or sullen, but right at me, eye in eye, the way Ruaway looked at me. He smiled. "Maybe the idiots and crybabies will die," he said. "Maybe you and I will be God." He spoke low, standing close to me, so no one else heard. My heart gave a great leap. I said nothing.

Soon after that birthday, Omimo went back to lead the army on the eastern border.

All year long people waited for our house, God's house in the center of the city, to be struck by lightning, though not destroyed, since that is how the priests interpreted the oracle once they had time to talk and think about it. When the seasons went on and there was no lightning or fire, they said the oracle meant that the sun shining on the gold and copper roof-gutters was the unconsuming fire, and that if there was an earthquake the house would stand.

The words about God being white and having one eye they interpreted as meaning that God was the sun and was to be worshipped as the all-seeing giver of light and life. This had always been so.

There was war in the east, indeed. There had always been war in the east, where people coming out of the wilderness tried to steal our grain, and we conquered them and taught them how to grow it. General Lord Drowning sent angels back with news of his conquests all the way to the Fifth River.

There was no famine in the west. There had never been famine in God's country. God's children saw to it that crops were properly sown and grown and saved and shared. If the ze failed in the western lands, our carters pulled two-wheeled carts laden with grain on the great stone roads over the mountains from the central lands. If crops failed in the north, the carts went north from the Four Rivers land. From west to east carts came laden with smoked fish, from the Sunrise peninsula they came west with fruit and seaweed. The granaries and storehouses of God were always stocked and open to people in need. They had only to ask the administrators of the stores; what was needed was given. No one went hungry. Famine was a word that belonged to those we had brought into our land, people like the Tegh, the Chasi, the North Hills people. The hungry people, we called them.

The birthday of the world came again, and the most fearful words of the oracle—*the world dies*—were remembered. In public the priests rejoiced and comforted the common people, saying that God's mercy had spared the world. In our house there was little comfort. We all knew that God Himself was ill. He had hidden himself away more and more throughout the year, and many of the ceremonies took place without the divine presence, or only Herself was there. She seemed always quiet and untroubled. My lessons were mostly with her now, and with her I always felt that nothing had changed or could change and all would be well.

God danced the Dance that Turns as the sun stood still above the shoulder of the sacred mountain. He danced slowly, missing many steps. He went into the ash house. We waited, everybody waited, all over the city, all over the country. The sun went down behind Kanaghadwa. All the snow peaks of the mountains from north to south, Kayewa, burning Korosi, Aghet, Enni, Aziza, Kanaghadwa, burned gold, then fiery red, then purple. The light went up them and went out, leaving them white as ashes. The stars came out above them. Then at last the drums beat and the music sounded down in the Glittering Square, and torches made the pavement sparkle and gleam. The priests came out of the narrow doors of the ash house in order, in procession. They stopped. In the silence the oldest dream priest said in her thin, clear voice, "Nothing was seen over the shoulder of God."

Onto the silence ran a buzzing and whispering of people's voices, like little insects running over sand. That died out.

The priests turned and went back into the ash house in procession, in due order, in silence.

The ranks of angels waiting to carry the words of the oracle to the countryside stood still while their captains spoke in a group. Then the angels all moved away in groups by the five streets that start at the Glittering Square and lead to the five great stone roads that go out from the city across the lands. As always before, when the angels entered the streets they began to run, to carry God's word swiftly to the people. But they had no word to carry.

Tazu came to stand beside me on the balcony. He was twelve years old that day. I was fifteen.

He said, "Ze, may I touch you?"

I looked yes, and he put his hand in mine. That was comforting. Tazu was a serious, silent person. He tired easily, and often his head and eyes hurt so badly he could hardly see, but he did all the ceremonies and sacred acts faithfully, and studied with our teachers of history and geography and archery and dancing and writing, and with our mother studied the sacred knowledge, learning to be God. Some of our lessons he and I did together, helping each other. He was a kind brother and we were in each other's heart.

As he held my hand he said, "Ze, I think we'll be married soon."

I knew what his thoughts were. God our father had missed many steps of the dance that turns the world. He had seen nothing over his shoulder, looking into the time to come.

But what I thought in that moment was how strange it was that in the same place on the same day one year it was Omimo who said we should be married, and the next year it was Tazu.

"Maybe," I said. I held his hand tight, knowing he was frightened at being God. So was I. But there was no use being afraid. When the time came, we would be God.

If the time came. Maybe the sun had not stopped and turned back above the peak of Kanaghadwa. Maybe God had not turned the year.

Maybe there would be no more time—no time coming behind our backs, only what lay before us, only what we could see with mortal eyes. Only our own lives and nothing else.

That was so terrible a thought that my breath stopped and I shut my eyes, squeezing Tazu's thin hand, holding onto him, till I could steady my mind with the thought that there was still no use being afraid.

This year past, Lord Idiot's testicles had ripened at last, and he had begun trying to rape women. After he hurt a young holy girl and attacked others, God had him castrated. Since then he had been quiet again, though he often looked sad and lonely. Seeing Tazu and me holding hands, he seized Arzi's hand and stood beside him as Tazu and I were standing. "God, God!" he said, smiling with pride. But Arzi, who was nine, pulled his hand away and said, "You won't ever be God, you can't be, you're an idiot, you don't know anything!" Old Haghag scolded Arzi wearily and bitterly. Arzi did not cry, but Lord Idiot did, and Haghag had tears in her eyes.

The sun went north as in any year, as if God had danced the steps of the dance rightly. And on the dark day of the year, it turned back southward behind the peak of great Enni, as in any year. On that day, God Himself was dying, and Tazu and I were taken in to see him and be blessed. He lay all gone to bone in a smell of rot and sweet herbs burning. God my mother lifted his hand and put it on my head, then on Tazu's, while we knelt by the great bed of leather and bronze with our thumbs to our foreheads. She said the words of blessing. God my father said nothing, until he whispered, "Ze, Ze!" He was not calling to me. The name of God Herself is always Ze. He was calling to his sister and wife while he died.

Two nights later I woke in darkness. The deep drums were beating all through the house. I heard other drums begin to beat in the temples of worship and the squares farther away in the city, and then others yet farther away. In the countryside under the stars they would hear those drums and begin to beat their own drums, up in the hills, in the mountain passes and over the mountains to the western sea, across the fields eastward, across the four great rivers, from town to town clear to the wilderness. That same night, I thought, my brother Omimo in his camp under the North Hills would hear the drums saying God is dead.

A son and daughter of God, marrying, became God. This marriage could not take place till God's death, but always it took place within a few hours, so that the world would not be long bereft. I knew this from all we had been taught. It was ill fate that my mother delayed my marriage to Tazu. If we had been married at once, Omimo's claim would have been useless; not even his soldiers would have dared follow him. In her grief she was distraught. And she did not know or could not imagine the measure of Omimo's ambition, driving him to violence and sacrilege.

Informed by the angels of our father's illness, he had for days been marching swiftly westward with a small troop of loyal soldiers. When the drums beat, he heard them not in the far North Hills, but in the fortress on the hill called Ghari that stands north across the valley in sight of the city and the house of God.

The preparations for burning the body of the man who had been God were going forward; the ash priests saw to that. Preparations for our wedding should have been going forward at the same time, but our mother, who should have seen to them, did not come out of her room.

Her sister Lady Clouds and other lords and ladies of the household talked of the wedding hats and garlands, of the music priests who should come to play, of the festivals that should be arranged in the city and the villages. The marriage priest came anxiously to them, but they dared do nothing and he dared do nothing until my mother allowed them to act. Lady Clouds knocked at her door but she did not answer. They were so nervous and uneasy, waiting for her all day long, that I thought I would go mad staying with them. I went down into the garden court to walk.

I had never been farther outside the walls of our house than the balconies. I had never walked across the Glittering Square into the streets of the city. I had never seen a field or a river. I had never walked on dirt.

God's sons were carried in litters into the streets to the temples for rituals, and in summer after the birthday of the world they were always taken up into the mountains to Chimlu, where the world began, at the springs of the River of Origin. Every year when he came back from there, Tazu would tell me about Chimlu, how the mountains went up all around the ancient house there, and wild dragons flew from peak to peak. There God's sons hunted dragons and slept under the stars. But the daughter of God must keep the house.

The garden court was in my heart. It was where I could walk under the sky. It had five fountains of peaceful water, and flowering trees in great pots; plants of sacred ze grew against the sunniest wall in containers of copper and silver. All my life, when I had a time free of ceremonies and lessons, I went there. When I was little, I pretended the insects there were dragons and hunted them. Later I played throwbone with Ruaway, or sat and watched the water of the fountains well and fall, well and fall, till the stars came out in the sky above the walls.

This day as always, Ruaway came with me. Since I could not go anywhere alone but must have a companion, I had asked God Herself to make her my chief companion.

I sat down by the center fountain. Ruaway knew I wanted silence and went off to the corner under the fruit trees to wait. She could sleep anywhere at any time. I sat thinking how strange it would be to have Tazu always as my companion, day and night, instead of Ruaway. But I could not make my thoughts real.

The garden court had a door that opened on the street. Sometimes when the gardeners opened it to let each other in and out, I had looked out of it to see the world outside my house. The door was always locked on both sides, so that two people had to open it. As I sat by the fountain, I saw a man who I thought was a gardener cross the court and unbolt the door. Several men came in. One was my brother Omimo.

I think that door had been only his way to come secretly into the house. I think he had planned to kill Tazu and Arzi so that I would have to marry him. That he found me there in the garden as if waiting for him was the chance of that time, the fate that was on us.

"Ze!" he said as he came past the fountain where I sat. His voice was like my father's voice calling to my mother.

"Lord Drowning," I said, standing up. I was so bewildered that I said, "You're not here!" I saw that he had been wounded. His right eye was closed with a scar.

He stood still, staring at me from his one eye, and said nothing, getting over his own surprise. Then he laughed.

"No, sister," he said, and turning to his men gave them orders. There were five of them, I think, soldiers, with hardened skin all over their bodies. They wore angel's shoes on their feet, and belts around their waists and necks to support the sheaths for their penis and sword and daggers. Omimo looked like them, but with gold sheaths and the silver hat of a general. I did not understand what he said to the men. They came close to me, and Omimo came closer, so that I said, "Don't touch me," to warn them of their danger, for common men who touched me would be burned to death by the priests of the law, and even Omimo if he touched me without my permission would have to do penance and fast for a year. But he laughed again, and as I drew away, he took hold of my arm suddenly, putting his hand over my mouth. I bit down as hard as I could on his hand. He pulled it away and then slapped it again so hard on my mouth and nose that my head fell back and I could not breathe. I struggled and fought, but my eyes kept seeing blackness and flashes. I felt hard hands holding me, twisting my arms, pulling me up in the air, carrying me, and the hand on my mouth and nose tightened its grip till I could not breathe at all.

Ruaway had been drowsing under the trees, lying on the pavement among the big pots. They did not see her, but she saw them. She knew at once if they saw her they would kill her. She lay still. As soon as they had carried me out the gate into the street, she ran into the house to my mother's room and threw open the door. This was sacrilege, but, not knowing who in the household might be in sympathy with Omimo, she could trust only my mother.

"Lord Drowning has carried Ze off," she said. She told me later that my mother sat there silent and desolate in the dark room for so long that Ruaway thought she had not heard. She was about to speak again, when my mother stood up. Grief fell away from her. She said, "We cannot trust the army," her mind leaping at once to see what must be done, for she was one who had been God. "Bring Tazu here," she said to Ruaway.

Ruaway found Tazu among the holy people, called him to her with her eyes, and asked him to go to his mother at once. Then she went out of the house by the garden door that still stood unlocked and unwatched. She asked people in the Glittering Square if they had seen some soldiers with a drunken girl. Those who had seen us told her to take the northeast street. And so little time had passed that when she came out the northern gate of the city she saw Omimo and his men climbing the hill road toward Chari, carrying me up to the old fort. She ran back to tell my mother this.

Consulting with Tazu and Lady Clouds and those people she most trusted, my mother sent for several old generals of the peace, whose soldiers served to keep order in the countryside, not in war on the frontiers. She asked for their obedience, which they promised her, for though she was not God she had been God, and was daughter and mother of God. And there was no one else to obey.

She talked next with the dream priests, deciding with them what messages the angels should carry to the people. There was no doubt that Omimo had carried me off to try to make himself God by marrying me. If my mother announced first, in the voices of the angels, that his act was not a marriage performed by the marriage priest, but was rape, then it might be the people would not believe he and I were God.

So the news went out on swift feet, all over the city and the countryside.

Omimo's army, now following him west as fast as they could march, were loyal to him. Some other soldiers joined him along the way. Most of the peacekeeping soldiers of the center land supported my mother. She named Tazu their general. He and she put up a brave and resolute front, but they had little true hope, for there was no God, nor could there be so long as Omimo had me in his power to rape or kill.

All this I learned later. What I saw and knew was this: I was in a low room without windows in the old fortress. The door was locked from outside. Nobody was with me and no guards were at the door, since nobody was in the fort but Omimo's soldiers. I waited there not knowing if it was day or night. I thought time had stopped, as I had feared it would. There was no light in the room, an old storeroom under the pavement of the fortress. Creatures moved on the dirt floor. I walked on dirt then. I sat on dirt and lay on it.

The bolt of the door was shot. Torches flaring in the doorway dazzled me. Men came in and stuck a torch in the sconce on the wall. Omimo came through them to me. His penis stood upright and he came to me to rape me. I spat in his half-blind face and said, "If you touch me your penis will burn like that torch!" He showed his teeth as if he was laughing. He pushed me down and pushed my legs apart, but he was shaking, frightened of my sacred being. He tried to push his penis into me with his hands but it had gone soft. He could not rape me. I said, "You can't, look, you can't rape me!"

His soldiers watched and heard all this. In his humiliation, Omimo pulled his sword from its gold sheath to kill me, but the soldiers held his hands, preventing him, saying, "Lord, Lord, don't kill her, she must be God with you!" Omimo shouted and fought them as I had fought him, and so they all went out, shouting and struggling with him. One of them seized the torch, and the door clashed behind them. After a little while I felt my way to the door and tried it, thinking they might have forgotten to bolt it, but it was bolted. I crawled back to the corner where I had been and lay on the dirt in the dark.

Truly we were all on the dirt in the dark. There was no God. God was the son and daughter of God joined in marriage by the marriage priest. There was no other. There was no other way to go. Omimo did not know what way to go, what to do. He could not marry me without the marriage priest's words. He thought by raping me he would be my husband, and maybe it would have been so: but he could not rape me. I made him impotent.

The only thing he saw to do was attack the city, take the house of God and its priests captive, and force the marriage priest to say the words that made God. He could not do this with the small force he had with him, so he waited for his army to come from the east.

Tazu and the generals and my mother gathered soldiers into the city from the center land. They did not try to attack Ghari. It was a strong fort, easy to defend, hard to attack, and they feared that if they besieged it, they would be caught between it and Omimo's great army coming from the east.

So the soldiers that had come with him, about two hundred of them, garrisoned the fort. As the days passed, Omimo provided women for them. It was the policy of God to give village women extra grain or tools or crop-rows for going to fuck with the soldiers at army camps and stations. There were always women glad to oblige the soldiers and take the reward, and if they got pregnant of course they received more reward and support. Seeking to ease and placate his men, Omimo sent officers down to offer gifts to girls in the villages near Ghari. A group of girls agreed to come; for the common people understood very little of the situation, not believing that anyone could revolt against God. With these village women came Ruaway.

The women and girls ran about the fort, teasing and playing with the soldiers off duty. Ruaway found where I was by fate and courage, coming down into the dark passages under the pavement and trying the doors of the storerooms. I heard the bolt move in the lock. She said my name. I made some sound. "Come!" she said. I crawled to the door. She took my arm and helped me stand and walk. She shot the bolt shut again, and we felt our way down the black passage till we saw light flicker on stone steps. We came out into a torchlit courtyard full of girls and soldiers. Ruaway at once began to run through them, giggling and chattering nonsense, holding tight to my arm so that I ran with her. A couple of soldiers grabbed at us, but Ruaway dodged them, saying, "No, no, Tuki's for the Captain!" We ran on, and came to the side gate, and Ruaway said to the guards, "Oh, let us out, Captain, Captain, I have to take her back to her mother, she's vomiting sick with fever!" I was staggering and covered with dirt and filth from my prison. The guards laughed at me and said foul words about my foulness and opened the gate a crack to let us out. And we ran on down the hill in the starlight.

To escape from a prison so easily, to run through locked doors, people have said, I must have been God indeed. But there was no God then, as there is none now. Long before God, and long after also, is the way things are, which we call chance, or luck, or fortune, or fate; but those are only names.

And there is courage. Ruaway freed me because I was in her heart.

As soon as we were out of sight of the guards at the gate we left the road, on which there were sentries, and cut across country to the city. It stood mightily on the great slope before us, its stone walls starlit. I had never seen it except from the windows and balconies of the house at the center of it.

I had never walked far, and though I was strong from the exercises I did as part of our lessons, my soles were as tender as my palms. Soon I was grunting and tears kept starting in my eyes from the shocks of pain from rocks and gravel underfoot. I found it harder and harder to breathe. I could not run. But Ruaway kept hold of my hand, and we went on.

We came to the north gate, locked and barred and heavily guarded by soldiers of the peace. Then Ruaway cried out, "Let God's daughter enter the city of God!"

I put back my hair and held myself up straight, though my lungs were full of knives, and said to the captain of the gate, "Lord Captain, take us to my mother Lady Ze in the house in the center of the world."

He was old General Rire's son, a man I knew, and he knew me. He stared at me once, then quickly thumbed his forehead, and roared out orders, and the gates opened. So we went in and walked the northeast street to my house, escorted by soldiers, and by more and more people shouting in joy. The drums began to beat, the high, fast beat of the festivals.

That night my mother held me in her arms, as she had not done since I was a suckling baby.

That night Tazu and I stood under the garland before the marriage priest and drank from the sacred cups and were married into God.

That night also Omimo, finding I was gone, ordered a death priest of the army to marry him to one of the village girls who came to fuck with the soldiers. Since nobody outside my house, except a few of his men, had ever seen me up close, any girl could pose as me. Most of his soldiers believed the girl was me. He proclaimed that he had married the daughter of the Dead God and that she and he were now God. As we sent out angels to tell of our marriage, so he sent runners to say that the marriage in the house of God was false, since his sister Ze had run away with him and married him at Ghari, and she and he were now the one true God. And he showed himself to the people wearing a gold hat, with white paint on his face, and his blinded eye, while the army priests cried out, "Behold! The oracle is fulfilled! God is white and has one eye!"

Some believed his priests and messengers. More believed ours. But all were distressed or frightened or made angry by hearing messengers proclaim two Gods at one time, so that instead of knowing the truth, they had to choose to believe.

Omimo's great army was now only four or five days' march away.

Angels came to us saying that a young general, Mesiwa, was bringing a thousand soldiers of the peace up from the rich coasts south of the city. He told the angels only that he came to fight for "the one true God." We feared that meant Omimo. For we added no words to our name, since the word itself means the only truth, or else it means nothing.

We were wise in our choice of generals, and decisive in acting on their advice. Rather than wait for the city to be besieged, we resolved to send a force to attack the eastern army before it reached Ghari, meeting it in the foothills above the River of Origin. We would have to fall back as their full strength came up, but we could strip the country as we did so, and bring the country people into the city. Meanwhile we sent carts to and from all the storehouses on the southern and western roads to fill the city's granaries. If the war did not end quickly, said the old generals, it would be won by those who could keep eating.

"Lord Drowning's army can feed themselves from the storehouses along the east and north roads," said my mother, who attended all our councils.

"Destroy the roads," Tazu said.

I heard my mother's breath catch, and remembered the oracle. The roads will be broken.

"That would take as long to do as it took to make them," said the oldest general, but the next oldest general said, "Break down the stone bridge at Almoghay." And so we ordered. Retreating from its delaying battle, our army tore down the great bridge that had stood a thousand years. Omimo's army had to go around nearly a hundred miles farther, through forests, to the ford at Domi, while our army and our carters brought the contents of the storehouses in to the city. Many country people followed them, seeking the protection of God, and so the city grew very full. Every grain of ze came with a mouth to eat it.

All this time Mesiwa, who might have come against the eastern army at Domi, waited in the passes with his thousand men. When we commanded him to come help punish sacrilege and restore peace, he sent our angel back with meaningless messages. It seemed certain that he was in league with Omimo. "Mesiwa the finger, Omimo the thumb," said the oldest general, pretending to crack a louse.

"God is not mocked," Tazu said to him, deadly fierce. The old general bowed his forehead down on his thumbs, abashed. But I was able to smile.

Tazu had hoped the country people would rise up in anger at the sacrilege and strike the Painted God down. But they were not soldiers and had never fought. They had always lived under the protection of the soldiers of peace and under our care. As if our doings now were like the whirlwind or the earthquake, they were paralyzed by them and could only watch and wait till they were over, hoping to survive. Only the people of our household, whose livelihood depended directly upon us and whose skills and knowledge were at our service, and the people of the city in whose heart we were, and the soldiers of the peace, would fight for us.

The country people had believed in us. Where no belief is, no God is. Where doubt is, foot falters and hand will not take hold.

The wars at the borders, the wars of conquest, had made our land too large. The people in the towns and villages knew no more who I was than I knew who they were. In the days of the origin, Babam Kerul and Bamam Ze came down from the mountain and walked the fields of the center lands beside the common people. The common people who laid the first stones of the great roads and the huge base stones of the old city wall had known the face of their God, seeing it daily.

After I spoke of this to our councils, Tazu and I went out into the streets, sometimes carried in litters, sometimes walking. We were surrounded by the priests and guards who honored our divinity, but we went among the people, meeting their eyes. They fell on their knees and put their foreheads to their thumbs, and many wept when they saw us. They called out from street to street, and little children cried out, "There's God!"

"You walk in their hearts," my mother said.

But Omimo's army had come to the River of Origin, and one day's march brought the vanguard to Ghari.

That evening we stood on the north balcony looking toward Ghari hill, which was swarming with men, as when a nest of insects swarms. To the west the light was dark red on the mountains in their winter snow. From Korosi a vast plume of smoke trailed, blood color.

"Look," Tazu said, pointing northwest. A light flared in the sky, like the sheet lightning of summer. "A falling star," he said, and I said, "An eruption."

In the dark of the night, angels came to us. "A great house burned and fell from the sky," one said, and the other said, "It burned but it stands, on the bank of the river."

"The words of God spoken on the birthday of the world," I said.

The angels knelt down hiding their faces.

What I saw then is not what I see now looking far off to the distant past; what I knew then is both less and more than I know now. I try to say what I saw and knew then.

That morning I saw coming down the great stone road to the northern gate a group of beings, two-legged and erect like people or lizards. They were the height of giant desert lizards, with monstrous limbs and feet, but without tails. They were white all over and hairless. Their heads had no mouth or nose and one huge single staring shining lidless eye.

They stopped outside the gate.

Not a man was to be seen on Ghari Hill. They were all in the fortress or hidden in the woods behind the hill.

We were standing up on the top of the northern gate, where a wall runs chest high to protect the guards.

There was a little sound of frightened weeping on the roofs and balconies of the city, and people called out to us, "God! God, save us!"

Tazu and I had talked all night. We listened to what our mother and other wise people said, and then we sent them away to reach out our minds together, to look over our shoulder into the time that was coming. We saw the death and the birth of the world, that night. We saw all things changed.

The oracle had said that God was white and had one eye. This was what we saw now. The oracle had said that the world died. With it died our brief time of being God. This was what we had to do now: to kill the world. The world must die so that God may live. The house falls that it may stand. Those who have been God must make God welcome.

Tazu spoke welcome to God, while I ran down the spiral stairs inside the wall of the gate and unbolted the great bolts—the guards had to help me—and swung the door open. "Enter in!" I said to God, and put my forehead to my thumbs, kneeling.

They came in, hesitant, moving slowly, ponderously. Each one turned its huge eye from side to side, unblinking. Around the eye was a ring of silver that flashed in the sun. I saw myself in one of those eyes, a pupil in the eye of God.

Their snow-white skin was coarse and wrinkled, with bright tattoos on it. I was dismayed that God could be so ugly.

The guards had shrunk back against the walls. Tazu had come down to stand with me. One of them raised a box toward us. A noise came out of the box, as if some animal was shut in it.

Tazu spoke to them again, telling them that the oracle had foretold their coming, and that we who had been God welcomed God.

They stood there, and the box made more noises. I thought it sounded like Ruaway before she learned to talk right. Was the language of God no longer ours? Or was God an animal, as Ruaway's people believed? I thought they seemed more like the monstrous lizards of the desert that lived in the zoo of our house than they seemed like us.

One raised its thick arm and pointed at our house, down at the end of the street, taller than other houses, its copper gutters and goldleaf carvings shining in the bright winter sunlight.

"Come, Lord," I said, "come to your house." We led them to it and brought them inside.

When we came into the low, long, windowless audience room, one of them took off its head. Inside it was a head like ours, with two eyes, nose, mouth, ears. The others did the same.

Then, seeing their head was a mask, I saw that their white skin was like a shoe that they wore not just on the foot but all over their body. Inside this shoe they were like us, though the skin of their faces was the color of clay pots and looked very thin, and their hair was shiny and lay flat.

"Bring food and drink," I said to the children of God cowering outside the door, and they ran to bring trays of ze-cakes and dried fruit and winter beer. God came to the tables where the food was set. Some of them pretended to eat. One, watching what I did, touched the ze-cake to its forehead first, and then bit into it and chewed and swallowed. It spoke to the others, gre-gra, gre-gra.

This one was also the first to take off its body-shoe. Inside it other wrappings and coverings hid and protected most of its body, but this was understandable, because even the body skin was pale and terribly thin, soft as a baby's eyelid.

In the audience room, on the east wall over the double seat of God, hung the gold mask which God Himself wore to turn the sun back on its way. The one who had eaten the cake pointed at the mask. Then it looked at me—its own eyes were oval, large, and beautiful—and pointed up to where the sun was in the sky. I nodded my body. It pointed its finger here and there all about the mask, and then all about the ceiling.

"There must be more masks made, because God is now more than two," Tazu said.

I had thought the gesture might signify the stars, but I saw that Tazu's interpretation made more sense.

"We will have masks made," I told God, and then ordered the hat priest to go fetch the gold hats which God wore during ceremonies and festivals. There were many of these hats, some jeweled and ornate, others plain, all very ancient. The hat priest brought them in due order two by two until they were all set out on the great table of polished wood and bronze where the ceremonies of First Ze and Harvest were celebrated.

Tazu took off the gold hat he wore, and I took off mine. Tazu put his hat on the head of the one who had eaten the cake, and I chose a short one and reached up and put my hat on its head. Then, choosing ordinary day hats, not those of the sacred occasions, we put a hat on each of the heads of God, while they stood and waited for us to do so.

Then we knelt bareheaded and put our foreheads against our thumbs.

God stood there. I was sure they did not know what to do. "God is grown, but new, like a baby," I said to Tazu. I was sure they did not understand what we said.

All at once the one I had put my hat on came to me and put its hands on my elbows to raise me up from kneeling. I pulled back at first, not being used to being touched; then I remembered I was no longer very sacred, and let God touch me. It talked and gestured. It gazed into my eyes. It took off the gold hat and tried to put it back on my head. At that I did shrink away, saying, "No, no!" It seemed blasphemy, to say No to God, but I knew better.

God talked among themselves then for a while, and Tazu and our mother and I were able to talk among ourselves. What we understood was this: the oracle had not been wrong, of course, but it had been subtle. God was not truly one-eyed nor blind, but did not know how to see. It was not God's skin that was white, but their mind that was blank and ignorant. They did not know how to talk, how to act, what to do. They did not know their people.

Yet how could Tazu and I, or our mother and our old teachers, teach them? The world had died and a new world was coming to be. Everything in it might be new. Everything might be different. So it was not God, but we, who did not know how to see, what to do, how to speak.

I felt this so strongly that I knelt again and prayed to God, "Teach us!"

They looked at me and talked to each other, brr-grr, gre-gra.

I sent our mother and the others to talk with our generals, for angels had come with reports about Omimo's army. Tazu was very tired from lack of sleep. We two sat down on the floor together and talked quietly. He was concerned about God's seat. "How can they all sit on it at once?" he said.

"They'll have more seats added," I said. "Or now two will sit on it, and then another two. They're all God, the way you and I were, so it doesn't matter."

"But none of them is a woman," Tazu said.

I looked at God more carefully and saw that he was right. This disturbed me slowly, but very deeply. How could God be only half human?

In my world, a marriage made God. In this world coming to be, what made God?

I thought of Omimo. White clay on his face and a false marriage had made him a false God, but many people believed he was truly God. Would the power of their belief make him God, while we gave our power to this new, ignorant God?

If Omimo found out how helpless they appeared to be, not knowing how to speak, not even knowing how to eat, he would fear their divinity even less than he had feared ours. He would attack. And would our soldiers fight for this God?

I saw clearly that they would not. I saw from the back of my head, with the eyes that see what is coming. I saw the misery that was coming to my people. I saw the world dead, but I did not see it being born. What world could be born of a God who was male? Men do not give birth.

Everything was wrong. It came very strongly into my mind that we should have our soldiers kill God now, while they were still new in the world and weak.

And then? If we killed God there would be no God. We could pretend to be God again, the way Omimo pretended. But godhead is not pretense. Nor is it put on and off like a golden hat.

The world had died. That was fated and foretold. The fate of these strange men was to be God, and they would have to live their fate as we lived ours, finding out what it was to be as it came to be, unless they could see over their shoulders, which is one of the gifts of God.

I stood up again, taking Tazu's hand so that he stood beside me. "The city is yours," I said to them, "and the people are yours. The world is yours, and the war is yours. All praise and glory to you, our God!" And we knelt once more and bowed our foreheads deeply to our thumbs, and left them.

"Where are we going?" Tazu said. He was twelve years old and no longer God. There were tears in his eyes.

"To find Mother and Ruaway," I said, "and Arzi and Lord Idiot and Haghag, and any of our people who want to come with us." I had begun to say "our children," but we were no longer their mother and father.

"Come where?" Tazu said.

"To Chimlu."

"Up in the mountains? Run and hide? We should stay and fight Omimo."

"What for?" I said.

That was sixty years ago.

I have written this to tell how it was to live in the house of God before the world ended and began again. To tell it I have tried to write with the mind I had then. But neither then nor now do I fully understand the oracle which my father and all the priests saw and spoke. All of it came to pass. Yet we have no God, and no oracles to guide us.

None of the strange men lived a long life, but they all lived longer than Omimo.

We were on the long road up into the mountains when an angel caught up with us to tell us that Mesiwa had joined Omimo, and the two generals had brought their great army against the house of the strangers, which stood like a tower in the fields near Soze River, with a waste of burned earth around it. The strangers warned Omimo and his army clearly to withdraw, sending lightning out of the house over their heads that set distant trees afire. Omimo would not heed. He could prove he was God only by killing God. He commanded his army to rush at the tall house. He and Mesiwa and a hundred men around him were destroyed by a single bolt of lightning. They were burned to ash. His army fled in terror.

"They are God! They are God indeed!" Tazu said when he heard the angel tell us that. He spoke joyfully, for he was as unhappy in his doubt as I was. And for a while we could all believe in them, since they could wield the lightning. Many people called them God as long as they lived.

My belief is that they were not God in any sense of the word I understand, but were otherworldly, supernatural beings, who had great powers, but were weak and ignorant of our world, and soon sickened of it and died.

There were fourteen of them in all. Some of them lived more than ten years. These learned to speak as we do. One of them came up into the mountains to Chimlu, along with some of the pilgrims who still wanted to worship Tazu and me as God. Tazu and I and this man talked for many days, learning from each other. He told us that their house moved in the air, flying like a dragon-lizard, but its wings were broken. He told us that in the land they came from the sunlight is very weak, and it was our strong sunlight that made them sick. Though they covered their bodies with weavings, still their thin skins let the sunlight in, and they would all die soon. He told us they were sorry they had come. I said, "You had to come. God saw you coming. What use is it to be sorry?"

He agreed with me that they were not God. He said that God lived in the sky. That seemed to us a useless place for God to live. Tazu said they had indeed been God when they came, since they fulfilled the oracle and changed the world; but now, like us, they were common people.

Ruaway took a liking to this stranger, maybe because she had been a stranger, and when he was at Chimlu they slept together. She said he was like any man under his weavings and coverings. He told her he could not impregnate her, as his seed would not ripen in our earth. Indeed the strangers left no children.

This stranger told us his name, Bin-yi-zin. He came back up to Chimlu several times, and was the last of them to die. He left with Ruaway the dark crystals he wore before his eyes, which make things look larger and clearer for her, though to my eyes they make things dim. To me he gave his own record of his life, in a beautiful writing made of lines of little pictures, which I keep in the box with this writing I make.

When Tazu's testicles ripened we had to decide what to do, for brothers and sisters among the common people do not marry. We asked the priests and they advised us that our marriage being divine could not be unmade, and that though no longer God we were husband and wife. Since we were in each other's heart, this pleased us, and often we slept together. Twice I conceived, but the conceptions aborted, one very early and one in the fourth month, and I did not conceive again. This was a grief to us, and yet fortunate, for had we had children, the people might have tried to make them be God.

It takes a long time to learn to live without God, and some people never do. They would rather have a false God than none at all. All through the years, though seldom now, people would climb up to Chimlu to beg Tazu and me to come back down to the city and be God. And when it became clear that the strangers would not rule the country as God, either under the old rules or with new ones, men began to imitate Omimo, marrying ladies of our lineage and claiming to be a new God. They all found followers and they all made wars, fighting each other. None of them had Omimo's terrible courage, or the loyalty of a great army to a successful general. They have all come to wretched ends at the hands of angry, disappointed, wretched people.

For my people and my land have fared no better than I feared and saw over my shoulder on the night the world ended. The great stone roads are not maintained. In places they are already broken. Almoghay bridge was never rebuilt. The granaries and storehouses are empty and falling down. The old and sick must beg from neighbors, and a pregnant girl has only her mother to turn to, and an orphan has no one. There is famine in the west and south. We are the hungry people, now. The angels no longer weave the net of government, and one part of the land knows nothing of the others. They say barbarians have brought back the wilderness across the Fourth River, and ground dragons spawn in the fields of grain. Little generals and painted gods raise armies to waste lives and goods and spoil the sacred earth.

The evil time will not last forever. No time does. I died as God a long time ago. I have lived as a common woman a long time. Each year I see the sun turn back from the south behind great Kanaghadwa. Though God does not dance on the glittering pavement, yet I see the birthday of the world over the shoulder of my death.

⫙ ⫙ ⫙

URSULA K LE GUIN is the winner of the Hugo, Nebula, Gandalf, Kafka, and National Book Awards. She is the author of many short stories and more than fifteen novels, including *The Left Hand of Darkness, The Dispossessed,* and the *Earthsea Cycle.* She is also an honored author of children's books, poetry, and criticism.

MICHAEL MOORCOCK

CAKE

I fell in love with Mrs. Male long before she went into national politics. She was married to Victor Male, who was on Streatham Borough Council. She worked in an East Croydon solicitor's office when I first met her but she found her degree to be more useful at Gault, Thomson, who were quite a small accountancy firm in those days. When Vic burnt out on the council, she stood for the same seat and won it easily. I still saw her if she had time for me, though I was living north of the river by then. We generally met at lunch time in the sparkling anonymity of the Kensington Gardens Hotel, always walking in the park for a bit after we'd made love.

Even then she was usually fitting me in between other errands. She visited Westminster every four days or so, was friendly with all the right people. When she became an MP she dropped me. She had too much at stake now, she said. I remember her last determined, regretful kiss.

She was never the shrew the cartoonists drew. Never the arrogant maîtresse of Spitting Image. I always found her a bit sentimental. I think that's why she went on seeing me, long after she had the baby.

I got married, bought a flat in Notting Hill and became a happy, loving husband, the doting father of two girls. We still had lunch together, most frequently at the House of Commons, but there was never anything undercover about it. I was working for *The Spectator* by then and briefly, before the other party's victory, she was Home Secretary. It suited her to keep in with me, of course. My political loyalties were so flexible I was tempted to vote Lib-Dem in more than one election. I felt a strong personal loyalty to her and defended her policies fairly passionately. My colleagues used to joke that I was in love with her and in some ways, of course, I still was.

I continued to feel awkward around Vic Male, whom I bumped into on occasion. He had long since gone back into the building business, though his rhetoric remained that of the economic revolutionary he had once considered himself. His attitude to me was so familiar I sometimes suspected he knew everything about us, but in the end I decided he was too ordinarily friendly to suspect anything. I met him amidst the smell and glare of well-polished mahogany at the Royal Overseas League one evening last year. We had both been invited to hear about some new bit of policy. "They want me to be the party's new Secretary." He was very pleased about it. "What do you think?"

"You know me, Vic. I'm not one to commit myself."

"Oh, come off it, Jonny. You work on *The Spec*, write for the *Chronicle* and you ghosted that column in the *Express*." He grinned. "So what does that make you?"

"An old-fashioned conservative liberal populist," I said. "I haven't liked anyone in your party since Jack Taylor died."

"That's not what I heard." He gave me a hard stare.

"Oh, okay," I replied. "I quite like Eric Moses. And your good lady wife, of course." I wondered if he was trying to draw me. Connie hadn't said anything, had she? It wouldn't be like her to let that sort of cat out of the bag. She relished secrets more than she valued her off-shore bank balances. Had we been spotted at the KPH all those years ago?

He shook his head at me and then raised disgusted eyebrows. "David Gregory, George Smith and Jill Baldock ring any bells?"

All I knew was that they were up-and-coming back-benchers. More or less on the party's right wing. Not likely to be my bosom buddies these days. I shrugged and took a canapé from a passing tray.

Vic pressed on. "Okay, what if my spies tell me they're planning to back Jimmy Pilgrim and that you're about to do a big profile on him in *The Spec?*"

"I'd say you needed a new set of spies. Honest, Vic, I have no plans to do anyone favours—neo-cons or neo-libs or raving loony. I'm the original neutral. You couldn't get me any more neutral unless you had me spayed."

He had begun to believe me. He frowned. "That's very odd." What had he heard?

Vic was suddenly steered away by the obnoxious Denby Jones whom I could never look at without remembering his weedy legs and horrible underpants, dripping wet as he came out of the flamingo pool at Derry and Toms' roof garden on a famous occasion in 1997. He brayed horribly: "Sorry to butt in old boy. I'm going to have to take Vic off your hands." They crossed to the big window overlooking the Park and began talking intensely to Lord Northborough, who seemed a bit baffled. Once the mild-mannered greybeard glanced over at me, perhaps hoping I'd rescue him. Or maybe I was the subject of their conversation.

That was the night I learned the names of the runners in the party's leadership race. Connie Male was an outsider, of course, but since support for the others was evenly divided, there was a chance she might be everyone's compromise and get to take the party into the next election.

I was not particularly surprised when she called me a couple of days after the announcement. I thought she was trying to get my support. She suggested we meet at the KPH. That did surprise me. When I got there and entered the bright dining room, blinking in the glare of white linen and cream gloss, she was already at the table, smiling rather sweetly when she saw me.

It could have been twenty years ago, except she didn't peck me on both cheeks as she used to. I sat down and picked up the massive menu. It hadn't changed much, either. "You're looking good," I said. "The power struggle's brought the roses back."

She grinned and made a brushing gesture. "I've decided I needed a sexier image. Gets the odd boy-voter, you know. Can't do any harm, can it?" She was recognised, these days. People in the restaurant kept pretending they weren't looking at her.

"I wouldn't have thought so. What's up?"

She glanced shiftly around the room, taking a ladylike sip of her Kir Royale. "She's written to me, Jonny. From Florida. She wants to meet us. Well, me, really."

"How did she find out who you were?"

"She didn't. The agency forwarded the letter. Seamail. My father got it. He took over the Fulham flat after mummy died. Bit of a shocker."

"You'll just have to ignore it, surely? Or tell her it's not on?"

"I know. I've made iffier decisions, after all." Her eyes narrowed in that way familiar to anyone who had seen her clashing with her opposite number in the Commons.

"Why are you telling me, Connie? Do you want me to do something?" It had been a long time since she had gone off to the States and taken what to everyone else but me was a surprise vacation in Florida. "The child must be—what—a teenager by now? Sixteen?"

"Seventeen. Haven't you wondered? Aren't you curious about her?"

"I suppose I am." In fact I hated the emotions I was beginning to experience all over again. They were horrible. Like drowning. I ordered a stiff Glenlochy.

"You know. You might want to see her. Tell her why it's impossible. I've never regretted not having an abortion. But I still wonder if

I shouldn't have told Vic she was his. He'd never have guessed. But he might have divorced me."

"I thought you weren't—you know—having sex with Vic..."

"I could have forced myself. I never made love to him again after you and I split up."

"Oh." I couldn't think of anything to say. "Sorry."

"It didn't suit me. He never minded much. Politics was more important to us both. I think he kept the odd floozie, but he was discreet. He dumped the last one when I became Home Secretary." She picked up her glass and then put it down again. She raised her eyebrows at me.

Being honest with myself, I had to admit I still fancied her. She'd thickened a bit and used a lot more make-up, but she was still a pretty woman in her soft, round, Slavic sort of way. Her father had been Polish, in the RAF, flying with the British during the war.

"You're not going to tell Vic, though?"

"I've no idea how he'd react. With his prostate problems and everything. I wouldn't want to make him worse. He's been a total brick, backing me every way he can. Just shows you. Serves me right." She studied her silverware.

"Well, we always agreed there were no free lunches."

She looked up in surprise.

"You can't," I added relentlessly, "have your cake and eat it."

This broke her mood and she began to beam. She chuckled, shaking her head at me. "Well, if I ever get to be PM, I'll show you that there *can* be free lunches. And free cake, too!"

I was baffled. I wasn't used to her having mood swings. "But realistically, Connie, in ordinary life..."

"That's right," she said. It was almost as if she were shutting me up. As if she'd reached a conclusion, closed the subject.

I remembered a rare afternoon we'd had at Mitcham fair one Easter. She usually loved the bumper cars but that day wouldn't go on them. We walked back to the bus stop. When I asked her why she hadn't ridden the dodgems, she told me she was pregnant and that she was planning to stand for Streatham South. My emotional response then was identical to how I felt now. I wanted her to be a success. I really hadn't wanted the kid. She was against abortion. She kept saying how Vic wouldn't understand. They'd agreed from the beginning not to have children. They enjoyed politics too much. I understood they'd had some sort of pre-nupt agreement with a no kids clause. We'd discussed all this, of course, but it had been some eighteen years ago.

In the end she'd gone to the US on that lecture tour. In Florida she visited a slightly iffy adoption agency run by Cuban nuns. When it was all over she'd come home and instantly set about seriously climbing the political ladder until she got where she was now. In three years, as things stood, she could be PM.

"Let's face it, we've neither of us lost a lot of sleep over the kid, have we?" I sipped the Scotch. We'd imagined our daughter growing up in a nice middle-American suburb doing all the things little girls in Florida do—Girl Scouts, soccer, getting braces, cheer leading, the high school prom. We knew the kind of people who adopted. They were always the best qualified to have children. Connie had often joked that if she ever got the chance she'd make people take a breeding license test, like a driving test only more rigorous.

"You needn't worry," she said. "I'm not going to do anything stupid. She can't come here. My guess is she thinks her natural mother's American, anyway. Anyway," again the glance touching everything but me, "I thought you should know about it. I'd appreciate it if—"

"Don't be silly," I was rather irritated by her presumption. "I'd be an idiot to give in to sentimental impulses." I could imagine how my wife would take it. I'd never told her about Connie. "It wouldn't be fair to anyone."

"I agree, but that's the trouble." Now she looked me full in the face and I saw a shocking longing in her eyes. "I'm afraid I might. It's awful, Jonny. I mean it's making my stomach hurt. I never expected—"

"It would finish you if the papers smelled a rat. You'll never get this chance again. It's not something you can wait out, make some sort of public apology and expect the party to take you back after a reasonable show of falling on your sword. You'd let everyone down. Yourself included."

"It's ridiculous, isn't it?"

I must admit her emotion was infecting me. I risked a hand across the table. She gripped it briefly before she looked up at the waiter and asked for a salad.

Never one to starve in a crisis, I ordered the steak-and-kidney pudding, even though I guessed it would still be terrible. I found myself lost in her familiar perfume. Shalimar. I had bought her enough bottles of the stuff. She seemed younger even than when we'd first met at that party in Hampstead thrown by some millionaire socialist.

I hadn't known she was married when I first saw her on the other side of the room, sitting awkwardly on a chair and chatting to a silly young man with a quiff who squatted at her feet. She looked a bit out of place in her Sloane-ish costume. Powder blue, like today. It wasn't an affectation, just her favourite colour. It went so well with her blonde, neatly permed hair and her wonderful aquamarine eyes. Now, glancing at her across the lunch table, I was seized with the same desire I had felt then. In spite of myself, I was on the brink of suggesting the impossible, that we get a room upstairs and afterwards walk in the park again.

I was shocked at myself. Was it because she seemed so vulnerable, just as she had that night in Hampstead? She wasn't a bit vulnerable, even then, of course. She had been uncertain of herself, that was all, and unhappy at Vic for copping out of going with her at the last moment. When she agreed to come back to my awful flat in Balham I thought she was only wearing a wedding ring for appearances, as a sort of protection. She only told me she was married when she was under me on the couch and I already had my hand on her unresisting leg. She asked me if I minded. I didn't, of course. By then I wouldn't have worried about it if Vic had been standing on the landing checking his watch.

Realistically I'd never seen myself married to Connie. The only time I proposed she laughed full in my face, but I was a little surprised, as the months became years, that she never considered leaving Vic. She was much brighter than he was and braver. But it would be totally against everyone's interest, she said. They had careers planned together. They were a team. The family business. It would seriously interfere with the momentum of their climb up their respective ladders. I occasionally thought of breaking it off, but I never met anyone I loved as much as Connie.

The adoption had finished it, of course. That was the beginning of the end. I saw her a couple of days after she came home to England. She'd told Vic she'd caught some sort of bug and they'd kept her in hospital for a check-up. That explained the bills, if he ever noticed. I'd paid my share. She would have expected nothing less. And that had been that. No solace. No free lunch. Within the year we had broken up and she had won her seat. Another year and I met my wife.

"Yes," I complied bleakly. "Ridiculous."

For a few seconds we sat staring at one another, helplessly sad.

"PM, eh?" I pulled myself together. "It seems only yesterday they made you a junior minister. Will you have to drop me, do you think? No more tête-à-têtes?"

"Oh, we'll work something out." She looked away and threw one of those sickeningly artificial smiles at someone giving her a thumb's up from the bar. Then her attention returned to what was really concerning her. "Jill and David are wavering. I'd say it's between me and Ken."

"Not what the papers are saying."

"That's because it's the reality. They think they create the news, but of course they don't."

"You're the expert," I conceded. "You'll make a spectacular PM."

"You'll support me?"

I laughed. "I didn't say that."

"You're so old-fashioned, Jonny." She allowed herself a touch of that mockery which served her so successfully in debate.

A couple of weeks later the vote was out and she had disappeared. Her husband said she had gone to the country to stay with friends, to rest and avoid the publicity. I got an invitation at the office to attend a party at the Male's massive mock-Georgian mansion and I went out of curiosity, not expecting her to be back. Everyone else thought it was to rally the last of the floating voters.

She wasn't there when I arrived. Vic saw me through the glass doors and came forward, shaking my hand as someone took my coat. I managed to get a good view of their big pale green reception room. I recognised quite a few of the other guests. And it did look as if she was courting the undecideds. "Where's Connie been staying?" I asked Vic casually.

"Oh, it'll be no secret soon," he said. He began to grin. "She's just back from Florida. Family matter, that's all."

"You have family in Florida?"

"She went to pick up our god-daughter. An old friend's kid. She hasn't seen her in years."

"God-daughter? Who?" I have to admit I was hard put to speak.

Vic slapped my shoulder. "You'll find out when everyone else does, Jonny."

When Connie finally made her appearance, she had Cydney with her. Connie brought her over to where I stood at the buffet with an empty plate. She introduced us. Cydney was about Connie's height. She had my looks and Connie's eyes, but not so you'd guess; a smiling, open young woman who charmed everyone and was already the hit of the evening. Somehow she helped give Connie a subtly maternal air. We shook hands. Cydney called me "sir." I approved of her good manners. Nice kid. An asset to any parent.

"Are you staying long?" I asked.

"Three years!" Her face was a happy mask. "It's so kind of them. They're sending me to Oxford. It's like I have a whole other family over here. Isn't it wonderful?"

I couldn't think of anything intelligent to say. "It certainly is." I waved vaguely at the centrepiece of the table, an enormous gateau decorated in red, white and blue. "Can I get you anything?"

Connie eyed me a little nervously.

"Cake?" I asked.

⫶ ⫶ ⫶

MICHAEL MOORCOCK has another story, "The Third Jungle Book," on page 61 of this anthology. He is a prolific British writer of science fiction, science fantasy, and literary fiction. At sixteen he became editor of *Tarzan Adventures* and, as editor of *New Worlds* from 1964 to 1971, and again from 1976 to 1996, he encouraged the development of the New Wave in Britain and indirectly in the United States. Since the 1980s he has primarily written literary novels. Moorcock's most recent book, *The Vengeance of Rome,* completes the *Between The Wars* tetralogy about events leading up to the Nazi holocaust. In 2002 he was inducted into the Science Fiction Hall of Fame, and in 2004 he was awarded the Prix Utopiales, a French Lifetime Achievement Award.

⫶ ⫶ ⫶

Note: The editors have placed the above work of narrative realist literary fiction, "Cake," at the end of this anthology in order to assist readers in their return to reality.

Why Fabulist and New Wave Fabulist Stories in an Anthology Named *ParaSpheres?*

This is the long answer to the question. A summary of this answer can be found in the Editor's Note at the beginning of this anthology. Unless otherwise stated, this essay deals with the commercial publishing industry within the United States and does not necessarily apply in other countries.

As a publisher plans to publish a new book of fiction, as we did with this anthology, one decision that must be made is how to classify it. This is critical because it will determine not only the likely audience, but more importantly, if there will be an audience at all. A book published with the wrong classification or completely outside the commonly approved classifications will have a difficult time finding reviewers and an audience. There are some valid reasons for this. Readers usually know what forms of fiction they prefer, and they try to find fiction that is similar to fiction they have enjoyed in the past. Publishers and reviewers know this, and they produce or review books to fit the type in which they specialize. Ultimately, good fiction that does not fit accepted classifications may surface, but the process can be a difficult one, and the writers of such fiction may give up along the way or switch to a more acceptable style. As many writers have put it, "I write what my publisher will buy."

But before the vast majority of publishers in the United States will accept a work of fiction they almost invariably decide whether to publish it as one of two broad, though in fact neither exclusive nor comprehensive categories, "genre fiction" or "literary fiction." Fiction that cannot be allocated to one of these two categories often has difficulty finding a publisher.

Genre Fiction

The vast majority of fiction published in the United States falls into the various categories of genre fiction, which include fantasy, science fiction, horror, romance, western, mystery, spy, and adventure, not to mention sub-genres that can be defined within these categories. Most genre fiction, otherwise known as pulp, formula, escapist, and when particularly successful, blockbuster fiction, is commonly perceived as having been written to provide escape, to take readers away from their supposedly boring, overstressed, and/or unrewarding lives to exciting, unusual or improbable settings, events, and/or characters. Much genre fiction is based on proven formulas for selling a book within its particular genre, and sub-genres have still more specific formulas, and these formulas define the core examples of each form of fiction (although they do not necessarily define fiction on the fringes of each genre, nor the fiction that extends over multiple genres).

One can often find these formulas in books on how to write blockbuster fiction or various other specific forms of genre fiction. It should be about the rich, famous, powerful, heroic, or even the superhuman. It should incorporate melodrama and/or pathos. It is usually about fantastic things and events and places that are highly improbable or even impossible. The characters are usually less developed than in literary fiction and are usually caught up in the external milieu, ideas or events and are more driven by external circumstances than driving the story themselves. Or if they do drive the story, they tend to have one simple objective, rather than a full spectrum of various motivations. These characters are often stereotypes of good and evil that promote unrealistic expectations of human behavior. (Imagine, for example, all the men in the '60s and '70s who relished the fantasy that James Bond was a realistic ideal and attempted to emulate his exploits.) These rules are all part of the formulas that are primarily intended to sell books.

Breaking fiction into genre and sub-genre categories seems to go hand in hand with creating formulas. When Tolkien's *Lord of the Rings* trilogy came out, it started the genre of fantasy fiction, and also spawned the formulas for thousands of imitators. Formula is simply a way to duplicate success, and genres are often started by one or more very successful books that attract imitators. Although many genre writers successfully bend, break, or even ignore these formulas, many genre writers often follow these formulas to a significant degree, sometimes developing their own personal formulas for the books they write. After all, it is much faster to write to formula than to write more creatively. It is these writers who use formulas that give genre fiction its formula reputation. The escapist formula novels dominate the world of genre fiction publishing, accounting for over ninety percent of all fiction sales. Corporate publishers routinely expect sales in the hundreds of thousands, if not millions of copies from their blockbuster authors, and they usually attempt to improve their profits by pressuring these authors to write at least two books a year. Some of the most famous writers, when faced with such deadlines, have typically secluded themselves and written novels totaling several hundred pages in a month or less. Some would argue that the primary motivation for writing and publishing genre fiction is to make money.

Literary Fiction

The remaining ten percent or less of sales that comprise literary fiction is divided up among tens of thousands of writers who typically spend years writing each book. Literary fiction is generally not divided into subgroups or genres. (Although in a broader sense of the word genre, literary fiction is sometimes referred to as a genre unto itself, as poetry and narrative fiction are sometimes referred to as genres.) In the broadest sense of the term, literary fiction is that which has recognized cultural and artistic value.

Although it is usually considered inappropriate in articles such as this to reference commonly accepted dictionary definitions, in this case it is virtually impossible to proceed without revisiting these sources. The *American Heritage Dictionary of the English Language* (2001) gives the primary meaning of the word "literary" (and the meaning most relevant for this discussion) as: "Of, relating to, or dealing with literature." The *Oxford Concise Dictionary of Literary Terms* (2001) defines "literature" (with my bold italic emphasis) as:

> A body of written works related by subject-matter (e.g. the literature of computing), by language or place of origin (e.g. Russian literature), or ***prevailing cultural standards of merit***. In this last sense, "literature" is taken to include oral, dramatic, or broadcast compositions that may not have been published in written form, but ***which have been (or deserve to be) preserved***. Since the 19th century, ***the broader sense of literature as a totality of written or printed works has given way to more exclusive definitions based on criteria of imaginative, creative, or artistic value***, usually related to a work's absence of factual or practical reference (see autotelic). Even more restrictive has been the academic concentration upon poetry, drama, and fiction. Until the mid-20th century, many kinds of non-fictional writing—in philosophy, history, biography, criti-

cism, topography, science, and politics—were counted as literature; implicit in this broader usage is a definition of literature as that body of works which—for whatever reason—***deserved to be preserved as part of the current reproduction of meanings within a given culture (unlike yesterday's newspaper, which belongs in the disposable category of ephemera).***

In other words, according to this definition, literary fiction has lasting meaning and value, whereas non-literary fiction does not. This is the "primary" meaning of the term "literary fiction." Academic institutions in the United States usually use this primary definition of the term.

However, among reviewers and within the commercial publishing industry, the term literary fiction has taken on a far more specific and exclusive secondary meaning that has been used for over a century. This secondary meaning does not allow many highly regarded works that are included in the primary meaning of the term literary fiction. This narrower definition requires that literary fiction be narrative realism, which is defined by its own more exclusive rules. One of the most important rules for this definition of literary fiction is that characterization be well developed; in fact the characters should drive the story, and not be driven by the events, ideas, or milieu around them. Protagonists have flaws and antagonists, when present, tend to have virtues, and there is no simple right or wrong. As a result readers often finish a literary novel with the feeling that they have a more compassionate understanding of other human beings than when they started. This deeper characterization tends to work best when the narrative is set in recognized realistic cultures that exist or have existed in the past, particularly where the environment is familiar to the reader. Because the settings are familiar and can be suggested with minimal description, the text can be devoted to character development. Therefore, another important rule for creating literary fiction is that it be primarily realistic.

Rejection of Non-Realistic Fiction as Literary Fiction

The literary critics can serve as defenders of the intellectual and artistic values that are relatively free of the profit motivations that dominate the world of formula escapist fiction. There is definite merit in this cause. Left unchecked, this formula escapist fiction could ultimately obliterate the much less profitable literary fiction. But the standards of literary fiction that are applied to eliminate escapist fiction also eliminate much serious thought-provoking fiction that does have artistic value. In her introduction to the novel *Under the Glacier* by Halldór Laxness, Susan Sontag wrote the following (finished days before her death in December 2004):

> The long prose fiction called the novel, for want of a better name, has yet to shake off the mandate of its own normality as promulgated in the nineteenth century: to tell a story peopled by characters whose options and destinies are those of ordinary, so-called real life. Narratives that deviate from this artificial norm and tell other kinds of stories, or appear to not tell much of a story at all, draw on traditions that are more venerable than those of the 19th century, but still, to this day, seem innovative, or ultra-literary, or bizarre. [...] It seems odd to describe "Gulliver's Travels" or "Candide" or "Tristram Shandy" or "Jacques the Fatalist and His Master" or "Alice in Wonderland" or Gershenzon and Ivanov's "Correspondence from Two Corners" or Kafka's "The Castle" or Hesse's "Steppenwolf" or Woolf's "The Waves" or Olaf Stapledon's "Odd John" or Gombrowicz's "Ferdydurke" or Calvino's "Invisible Cities" or, for that matter, porno narratives, simply as novels. To make the point that these occupy the outlying precincts of the novel's main tradition, special labels are invoked. Science Fiction. Tale, Fable, Allegory. Philosophical novel...

Outside the United States, non-realistic work has generally received more recognition. Many non-realistic authors first achieved success outside the U.S. and were later published here. All the authors mentioned in the above quote are European, as are Huxley and Orwell. Gabriel García Márquez (Columbia) won the Nobel Prize in Literature in 1982 and Jorge Luis Borges (Argentina) won the French Legion of Honor in 1983, and this contributed to the acceptance of magic realism as literary fiction within the United States. And more recently *Life of Pi* by Yann Martel, the story of a man who survives shipwreck for months in a life raft with a tiger, won England's Man Booker Prize. And this is just to mention European and Latin American sources. Non-western countries, particularly Japan, have a long tradition of honoring non-realistic stories.

Such non-realistic works are also valued by U.S. university English departments and academic presses. Indeed, in the academic world, literary fiction has the much simpler primary meaning, that of having artistic value, and can easily include non-realistic fiction. In the academic world the term narrative realism is used to mean what the commercial publishers and reviewers call literary fiction. And the genres are being studied at the university level, although this has been a relatively recent change. As Noel Perrin wrote in the New York Times Magazine, April 9, 1989:

> Fourteen years ago [1974] I began to teach a course in science fiction at Dartmouth College. [...] Not all my colleagues in the English department were embarrassed by the new course, just most. Say, 25 out of 30. In general, they knew just enough about science fiction—without, perhaps, having read any except those two special cases, *Brave New World* and *Nineteen Eighty-Four*—to know that it was a formula genre, like the murder mystery, and not worthy of attention in the classroom. But they were powerless to stop the new course, or at least it would have taken a concerted effort. I was chairman of the department at the time, and my last year in office I spent such credit as I had left on getting the science fiction course approved.

As Noel Perrin notes later in the article, the course was still in the course catalog in 1989, but it was bracketed, meaning that it was not currently being taught. The acceptance of such courses at the university level has improved, and it is now possible, for instance, to obtain a Ph.D. in some universities with a specialization in speculative fiction (a term defined later in this article). However, as David Soyka pointed out in the March 2003 issue of Locus Magazine:

> Though there is an established branch of academia devoted to science fiction, the notion continues to linger that the genre is somehow an alien life form to "real" literature. Not so long ago I overheard a university advisor trying to steer away a student from taking a seminar in SF because prospective doctoral programs wouldn't consider it "serious study." Why the academy gives Mary Shelley's *Frankenstein* respect as a Gothic novel, but not SF, is something I've never understood.

Outside academia, a number of small presses and journals have published such fiction for decades, including City Lights, Coffee House, FC2, Dalkey Archive, New Directions, and Sun and Moon (now Green Integer). And within the larger commercial publishing world in the United States, established literary authors like Philip Roth can always get their non-realistic works (e.g. *The Plot Against America*) published successfully. (It has always seemed strange to me that alternative histories such as this one are considered science fiction. Aren't all literary fictions alternate histories?) There are also a few other exceptions where genres such as fantasy and science fiction have achieved honorary or token acceptance in the category of literary fiction when they cannot be ignored, even if they are not realistic, at least by some critics. As John Hodgman wrote in *The New York Times Magazine* of August 1, 2004:

> Fantasy has not, of course, been absent from literary fiction, but it has been admitted to the mainstream only when pedigreed (Martin Amis's *Time's Arrow*), political (Margaret Atwood's *The Handmaid's Tale*) or exotic (which is to say, Latin American). Fantasy and science fiction as a capital G genre, meanwhile, has largely been shelved separately from the rest of the culture, in part because of the genre's mania for self-classification into ever narrower niches (high fantasy versus alternate history, hard science fiction versus space opera, cyberpunk versus steampunk) and in part because of pure snobbery.

More exacting critics would not admit anything from some of these genres. For example, Sven Birkerts, editor of the highly respected literary journal *Agni,* published out of Boston University, wrote in the Sunday *New York Times Book Review* of May 18, 2003:

> I am going to stick my neck out and just say it: science fiction will never be Literature with a capital 'L', and this is because it inevitably proceeds from premise rather than character. It sacrifices moral and psychological nuance in favor of more conceptual matters, and elevates scenario over sensibility. Some will ask, of course, whether there still is such a thing as "Literature with a capital 'L.'" I proceed on the faith that there is. Are there exceptions to my categorical pronouncement? Probably, but I don't think enough of them to overturn it.

I would agree that science fiction rarely achieves excellent character development, and it may never have achieved the level of character development present in the best literary novels, although I believe it could. (One way would be to push premise into the background.) However, science fiction (as well as other forms normally assigned to the genres) is capable of possessing another form of meaning that literary novels do not. For example, science fiction can visit the future, and fantasy fiction and fables can visit our dreams and the mythological underpinnings of our most cherished values. Especially in this day and age, isn't it important to examine these seriously? There is definite merit in determining one standard of value from the character-based test and to hold this fiction apart, but should it be the only form to have recognized cultural and artistic value?

Fiction that introduces and examines non-existent milieus can have substantial artistic value and can teach us about our own culture. For example, Aldous Huxley's *Brave New World* (1932) gave us a glimpse of mass production, behavior modification, and pharmaceutically induced happiness as it might be applied to human beings in the future to create a more stable, though emotionally sterile society, thus depicting a civilization in many ways like our own. It makes its point as well as it does because modern trends are taken to the extreme, rather than being described in more subtle realistic terms.

Another example is George Orwell's *1984* (1949), which depicts a futuristic (although now all too contemporary) western civilization in which truth is what the spin doctors create and history is rewritten to suit the establishment. Again, the story is an effective critique of the propaganda machines of modern governments precisely because it depicts such practices to the extreme.

Similarly, Marion Zimmer Bradley's *The Mists of Avalon* (1982) is a retelling of the Arthurian legend from a feminist perspective. As such it critically re-examines one of the idealized myths that has tremendous influence on our views of heroism, chivalry, and warfare. Instead of the usual interpretation of Arthur conquering the island of Britain in order to achieve peace, *The Mists of Avalon* is about a highly stratified Christian world that comes to dominate and destroy a relatively peaceful egalitarian non-Christian world that is demonized as pagan. This work is also particularly relevant to our current political world, and I mention it here primarily because of this significance. It also has a level of character development that would admit it to the classification of literary fiction if it were not for the unrealistic elements of a mythical kingdom, magicians, and fairies. Because of these elements, this is a novel that is generally defined as non-literary fantasy fiction.

None of these novels generally fits the standards set by reviewers for literary fiction, yet they have far more cultural value and impact than much accepted literary fiction. But such novels have a great deal of difficulty in gaining attention if they are initially published as genre fiction, or even if the authors are primarily defined as genre writers. Huxley and Orwell were respected as literary writers in England when they published their works, and they did not have to run the genre gauntlet. Bradley is the only American so far mentioned in this essay and also the only author who started as a writer of genre fiction. *The Mists of Avalon* succeeded beyond the fantasy genre audience largely because it was popularized by the feminist movement that was prevalent at the time of its publication.

In the United States, writers almost always stay in the classification in which their work first succeeds. It is simply easier for book buyers to find all the books by a particular author in one section of the bookstore, and for bookstore clerks to know where a particular author's work can be found, and work that is an attempt to break out will almost always stay in the section with the author's original books. Because this creates genre "ghettos," writers who want to be taken seriously generally avoid starting out in genre fiction, and successful literary writers who write genre fiction are often described as "slumming it." So writers who want to write artistic work are discouraged from starting out with and later experimenting with a style that will be classified as genre fiction.

At Least One Other Type of Fiction

What is in fact true is that there are really at least three different kinds of fiction: genre, literary (in its realistic, character-based sense), and a third type of fiction that really has no commonly accepted name, which does have cultural meaning and artistic value and therefore does not fit well in the escapist formula genres, but which has non-realistic elements and settings that exclude it from the category of literary fiction. This third type of fiction may or may not be character-based. It is this form of fiction that we knew we wanted to publish—but what would we call it?

One could argue that this third form of fiction does have a name, "fantasy fiction." In the broadest sense of the term this is true. The *Oxford Concise Dictionary of Literary Terms* (2001) defines fantasy as:

> ...a general term for any kind of fictional work that is not primarily devoted to realistic representation of the known world. The category includes several literary [in a broader sense of the word "literary"] genres (e.g. dream vision, fable, fairy tale,

romance, science fiction) describing imagined worlds in which magical powers and other possibilities are accepted.

However, in commercial publishing the term "fantasy" has come to mean a much more specific escapist genre form of fiction that includes magic, magicians, and mythical creatures like elves and dragons, usually set in a feudal society with medieval technology. The foremost example of this form is Tolkien's *Lord of the Rings* trilogy, which essentially created and defined the genre. Such a definition excludes science fiction, so that the terms "fantasy and science fiction" are usually used when describing both forms. If it were not for this very prevalent meaning of the term "fantasy fiction" in commercial publishing, this might be an ideal name for this third type of fiction.

The term "speculative fiction" has also been used by some to define such fiction. This term was coined by Robert A. Heinlein in 1947 when he wrote: "In the speculative science fiction story accepted science and established facts are extrapolated to produce a new situation, a new framework for human action. As a result of this new situation, new human problems are created—and our story is about how human beings cope with those new problems." Others later defined the term as "literary forms of science fiction." However, Orson Scott Card, in his 1990 book *How to Write Science Fiction and Fantasy*, presented what is probably the term's most common current definition: "Speculative fiction includes all stories that take place in a setting contrary to known reality." This definition includes all forms of the genres of science fiction and fantasy, and much, if not most, horror, without regard to artistic quality, and an increasing number of writers of these escapist genres use the term to describe their work. On several occasions I initially described the work we would be publishing as "speculative fiction," only to receive a response like, "Oh, you mean science (or fantasy, or genre) fiction. I don't read science (or fantasy, or genre) fiction. I only read literary fiction."

One might also argue that the term "magic realism," which has now been included in the "literary fiction" form, can be used for this third type of non-realistic fiction, and in part this is true. The term "magic realism" (or "magical realism") was first used in the 1920s to describe graphic art that is realistic in some aspects and magical or surrealistic in others. It was later used to describe a style of writing. The *American Heritage Dictionary* (2004) defines "magical realism" as: "A chiefly literary style or genre originating in Latin America that combines realistic and fantastic elements." The *Oxford Concise Dictionary of Literary Terms* (2004) defines "magic realism" as (with my bold italic emphasis):

> ...a kind of modern fiction in which fabulous and fantastical events are included in a narrative ***that otherwise maintains the "reliable" tone of objective realistic report***. The term was once applied to a trend in German fiction of the early 1950s, but is ***now associated chiefly with certain leading novelists of Central and South America***, notably Miguel Ángel Asturias, Alejo Carpentier, Gabriel García Márquez. The latter's *Cien años de soledad* (*One Hundred Years of Solitude*, 1967) is often cited as a leading example, celebrated for the moment at which one character unexpectedly ascends to heaven while hanging her washing on a line. The term has also been extended to works from very different cultures [although if not Latin American, this is not the generally accepted meaning], designating a tendency of the modern novel to reach beyond the confines of realism and drawn upon the energies of fable, folktale, and myth while retaining a strong contemporary social relevance. Thus Günter Grass's *Die Blechtrommel* (*The Tin Drum*, 1959), Milan Kundera's *The Book of Laughter and Forgetting* (1979), and Salman Rushdie's *Midnight's Children* (1981) have been described as magic realist novels along with Angela Carter's *Nights at the Circus* (1984) and Rushdie's *Satanic Verses* (1988). The fantastic attributes given to characters in such novels—levitation, flight, telepathy, telekinesis—are among the means that magic realism adopts ***in order to encompass the often phantasmagoric political realities of the 20th century***.

However, the term magic realism is currently associated chiefly with Latin American novelists, while the non-Latin American versions of magic realism tend to be included in the category of literary fiction on a case-by-case basis and often by some critics and not others.

More recently another term, fabulist fiction, has been used to include both the Latin American and non-Latin American versions of magic realist fiction. The term fabulist has still not found its way into the current editions of various dictionaries of literary terms. But because its Latin American form has generally achieved status as literary fiction, the term fabulist is generally associated with quality. However, as fabulist fiction becomes more fantastic it becomes fantasy fiction, or if more metaphysical it becomes horror or new-age fiction, or if futuristic it becomes science fiction. So the term fabulist, by itself, cannot describe the entire scope of the fiction which we wanted to publish.

Then in the fall of 2002 the literary journal *Conjunctions* (from Bard College; edited by Brad Morrow) devoted their issue number 39 in the fall of 2002 (guest-edited by Peter Straub) to what were described as "new wave fabulist writers," thus extending the term "fabulist" to include other artistic fiction that goes well beyond realism. Such an extension of the word "fabulist" has the advantage of drawing on a term that is associated with quality literature (though only a portion of it is considered literary) and that is generally placed in the general fiction area of bookstores. This new definition was perhaps most succinctly defined in the preceding issue of *Conjunctions*, which announced the upcoming *Conjunctions:39* with the description:

> For two decades, a small group of innovative writers rooted in the genres of science fiction, fantasy, and horror have been simultaneously exploring and erasing the boundaries of those genres by creating fiction of remarkable depth and power.

Of course, if we are "erasing the boundaries of those genres" we should not hesitate to include closely-related fiction otherwise classified as genres beyond "science fiction, fantasy, and horror," thus including fables, folktales, myths, fairy tales, tall tales, new-age, and all alternative forms of prose narrative that go beyond "objective realistic report." (Worthy of particular note are experimental forms that do not meet the realistic test because their formal construction, use of language, and/or other methods of experiment offer variations on the patterns of thinking—of narrating reality—that are most commonly mass-produced in current media. It is often difficult to determine whether certain forms of experimental fiction are describing reality or not, and if reality cannot be verified, these will also not meet the standards of literary fiction.) (Also, as long as alternate histories are considered science fiction, then we will include these in our scope as well.) Such a definition allows for seamless crossing of the above genres; indeed it erases genre classifications entirely, making it difficult for others to define such fiction in terms of genre. And finally, by eliminating genres and their subdivisions it becomes more difficult to apply formulas to create or select such fiction. One could object that this definition is too great, that it encompasses far too much literary territory, and that there is the potential for many different styles within this grouping. That is precisely the point. We want to present a wide diversity of styles and subject matter rather than break this non-realistic fiction into subdivisions, which ultimately invite formula.

If we can use this definition we can now give a name to the two components of "non-realistic artistic fiction," namely "magic realism" (in its non-specifically Latin American sense, also known as "fabulist fiction") and "new wave fabulist fiction." Since these two types are closely related, and indeed the boundaries between what "maintains the 'reliable' tone of objective realistic report" and what does not can easily become blurred, we could still use a name for the combination of the two types. Perhaps at some future time these two types will become known simply as "fabulist fiction," or perhaps another name will be applied. (We are committed to this type of fiction, but we will use whatever name is commonly used to define it.) However, for the moment, it is far beyond our power to give a simpler name to the totality of "non-realistic artistic fiction," so in the meantime we can simply refer to this as its combined components of "magic realism (meaning the broader non-specifically Latin American definition) and new wave fabulist fiction." Or perhaps we can simply call it "fabulist and new wave fabulist fiction," and in fact, it is these latter terms that we have chosen to use. The name of this anthology, *ParaSpheres*, refers to the idea that the stories published herein extend "beyond the spheres" of the two widely accepted forms.

Although we do consider this fiction to meet the broad definition of the term literary, we recognize that it does not meet the established narrative realist definition of literary fiction. By presenting this fiction as neither literary nor genre, but rather as something else, we are avoiding the pitfalls of claiming literary status for these works. In presenting this anthology we hope to exist partly in both forms as well as extending beyond them, and to build a bridge between the two, where writers and readers from both can easily meet and explore fiction outside the boundaries imposed by the two accepted forms.

Ken Keegan

Bibliography

Birkerts, Sven. "Oryx and Crake." *New York Times Book Review* May 18, 2003: 12.

Card, Orson Scott. *How to Write Science Fiction and Fantasy*, Cincinnati: Writer's Digest Books, 1990.

Hodgman, John. "Susanna Clarke's Magic Book." *New York Times Magazine* August 1, 2004: 22.

"Fantasy." *Oxford Concise Dictionary of Literary Terms.* 2nd ed. 2001.

Heinlein, Robert A. "On the Writing of Speculative Fiction." *Of Worlds Beyond.* Ed. Lloyd Arthur Eshback. Reading, Pennsylvania: Fantasy Press, 1947.

"Literary." The American Heritage Dictionary of the English Language, 4th ed. 2000.

"Literature." *Oxford Concise Dictionary of Literary Terms.* 2nd ed. 2001.

"Magic Realism." *Oxford Concise Dictionary of Literary Terms.* 2nd ed. 2001.

"Magical Realism." The American Heritage Dictionary of the English Language, 4th ed. 2000.

Morrow, Bradford. "Coming Up In the Fall" *Conjunctions:38,* spring 2002.

Perrin, Noel. "Science Fiction: Imaginary Worlds and Real-Life Questions." *New York Times Magazine* April 9, 1989.

Sontag, Susan. "Outlandish." *Under the Glacier.* by Halldór Laxness. New York: Vintage International, 2004.

Soyka, David. "*Conjunctions 39:* The New Wave Fabulists." *Locus Magazine* March 2003.

Coming from Omnidawn in 2006

Pereat Mundus
by Leena Krohn

This is a lyric, poignantly satiric novel about an everyman character, Håkan. In the 36 chapters of the book, the various Håkans respond to intriguingly different and foreboding futures. The novel is a deft criticism of the false values of an obsessively materialistic society, and their potentially cataclysmic impact upon the world. Yet the book is nonetheless richly imbued with a deep appreciation for the values of human kindness and intelligence. Three excerpts from this novel can be found on pages 27, 311, and 508. For more information visit www.omnidawn.com/krohn

In a Town Called Mundomuerto
by Randall Silvis

An old man is telling a boy the same story he has told him hundreds of times before, so that now the boy can correct him on his errors, omissions, and embellishments. It is a lyric story of bittersweet memories and the enduring power of a love the old man has felt since his boyhood for Lucia Luna, a once beautiful girl, now a bitter old woman, destroyed by the jealousy and superstition of her village. An excerpt of this novel can be found on page 240. For more information visit www.omnidawn.com/silvis

Skunk: A Love Story
By Justin Courter

The story tells of a young man's attraction and ultimate addiction to skunk musk, and the social difficulties he encounters as a result. He longs to find an isolated utopia where he can experience his addiction in peace, but he is thwarted by all, including a young woman who understands his skunk fetish because she has a fish fetish. An excerpt of this novel can be found on page 412. For more information visit www.omnidawn.com/courter